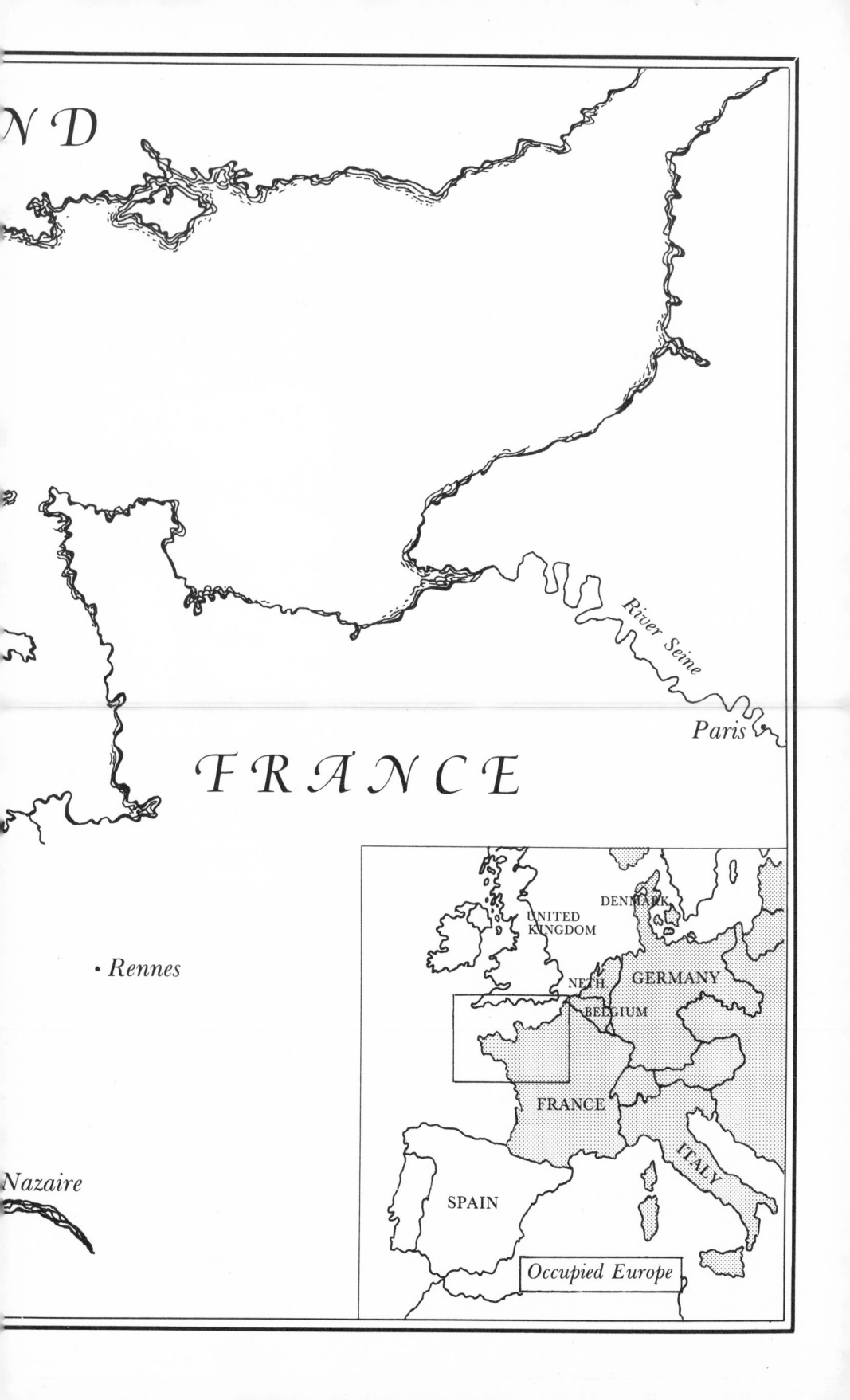

ND

River Seine

Paris

F R A N C E

• *Rennes*

Nazaire

DENMARK

UNITED
KINGDOM

NETH GERMANY
BELGIUM

FRANCE

ITALY

SPAIN

Occupied Europe

NIGHT
SKY

NIGHT SKY

Clare Francis

William Morrow and Company, Inc.   New York   1984

Originally published in 1983 in Great Britain by William Heinemann Ltd

Library of Congress Cataloging in Publication Data

Francis, Clare.
Night sky.

1. World War, 1939-1945—Fiction.   I. Title.
PR6056.R268N5   1984   823'.914   83-17351
ISBN 0-688-02633-8

Printed in the United States of America

First U.S. Edition

1 2 3 4 5 6 7 8 9 10

BOOK DESIGN BY LINEY LI

For my son, Thomas

ACKNOWLEDGMENTS

My thanks to David Birkin, who navigated motor gunboats on clandestine missions during the war, and who let me study his collection of original charts and log books; to David Beaty and Tony Spooner, who flew Wellingtons and Liberators on U-boat hunting operations and were kind enough to provide me with much useful information; to Patrick Beesly for his help on the U-boat tracking techniques used by the Admiralty during the war; and to Robin Coventry and Sir Brooks Richards for their long and informative letters.

CONTENTS

NIGHT SKY

PART ONE

✦

1935–1939

1 He was in a tiny dark cupboard, the door locked, the air foul and hot. Outside he could hear voices, sometimes loud and coarse, sometimes low and secretive. He tried to call out but he could make no sound. His body would not move, though nothing held it down. At some point he must have wet the bed, for the sheet underneath him was damp. His stomach heaved and without warning a thick trail of vomit streamed out, covering the pillow, clogging his hair. He was desperate to clean up the mess, but there was no water, no cloth, so he tried to mop it up with a corner of the sheet, wretched with the knowledge that this too was a mistake.

He lay back on the bed, shivering despite the heat. Tears of misery rolled down his cheeks and he cried a single "Maman!" Then he remembered that he was not allowed to call out, that he must stay silent. The loneliness enveloped him; he wanted to close his eyes and sleep forever.

There were voices again now: his mother's, steady and light, and a man's, low and furtive. The voices droned on, then rose to a higher pitch. There was a scream, then silence. Suddenly he was in a room and he saw his mother lying motionless on a bed. She was held down by the man, her arms twisted behind her, unable to move. She was looking up at the man, her lips open, her teeth bared. She did not cry out; instead she smiled. His mother and the man moved in a strange way he did not understand. Then the picture faded.

He was in the cupboard again, unable to breathe, suffocating with the heat. He could hear voices still, but they were more distant now. The despair pressed in on him, crushing and hopeless. But this time he did not cry: he was learning how not to cry. He felt as if he had been alone all his life.

* * *

Paul Vasson woke with a start. For an instant he couldn't remember where he was. Then he recognized the familiar outlines of the shabby room and, exhaling slowly, sank back onto the pillow. The voices from the dream murmured on. He listened and realized that they were floating up from the street outside. One, with a thick *provençal* accent, he recognized as that of the old concierge next door. He tried to sleep again, but it was no use. He had been dozing fitfully for less than half an hour and now he was wide awake.

He sat up and swung his legs to the floor. His mouth felt dry, his stomach unsteady. It was the fear. And worse than he'd imagined: stabbing, cold, dragging him down. The nightmare hadn't helped either. The dream was always the same: the small room, the locked door, the suffocating heat. And such detail—so vivid. He remembered the shame of discovery and how, when his mother opened the door, he had wept even before she struck him. Later she had washed and dressed him in clean clothes and then —then she had given him a brief kiss on top of the head.

Or had that one startling kiss happened some other time?

He got up suddenly and, groping for the shutters, let in a small shaft of warm afternoon sunlight. He never let in too much light: it showed up the shabby furniture and the peeling paintwork.

He wondered what the time was—probably about four. Still too early to go out. He picked up *La Dépêche du Midi* from the floor and flopped back onto the bed. The headlines didn't interest him: half a million unemployed; France protesting against something called the Anglo-German Naval Treaty; increasing numbers of Jewish refugees arriving in France from Germany.

He skipped to the sports page but couldn't concentrate and threw the newspaper back onto the floor.

God, he was nervous.

He stood up abruptly and walked naked across the room. Taking a clean towel from the dresser, he wrapped it around his waist and poured some water into a tin bowl that stood on the only table. He splashed his face and looked into the small mirror above. Usually he avoided mirrors, they made him uneasy, but today he wanted to be sure he looked normal, *ordinary*. The thin face stared back at him, the eyes small and dark. And frightened. Mustn't show the fear. Dear Lord.

Picking up a razor, he scraped at the soft stubble that sprouted unevenly on his chin. After a while he dropped his hand and, staring into the mirror, swore quietly. His skin, always sallow, had developed a yellow-gray tinge. He shivered and felt his stomach twist with griping pain. He realized with disgust that he must get to the toilet and quickly.

He hurried out of the room and made for a door at the far side of the landing. He went in and almost retched. A foul stench rose from the pan and he saw that it was blocked. There was another toilet two floors down, but there wasn't enough time. He crouched miserably on the seat, muttering, "Dear Mother of God!"

The spasms faded at last and, his bowels empty, Vasson got to his feet and stepped quickly onto the landing, gasping for fresh air. The house was quiet. Faint street sounds drifted up the stairwell and the murmur of snores floated across the landing. Most of the women were asleep or out, though some might have customers. No one had seen him.

He went back into his room and was sure of one thing—he would go ahead with what had to be done. There was no going back, no giving up, not if he was to get out of this terrible place. And he had to get out.

It wasn't just the filth and the disgusting women, it was the humiliation. The *Patron* had put him in charge of this house on purpose, just to humiliate him, he was certain of that. Any cheap *mac* in the *quartier* could have done the job. The women were old, worn out and pathetic, their only customers drunks or perverts. He loathed the sight of them. The job was an insult.

At first Vasson had thought that the job was a testing ground, that after a short time the *Patron* would ask him into the Business himself. But after six months he realized the move would never come. The *Patron* was purposely excluding him from the real action, purposely keeping him here in this hole. Treating him like rubbish. A very stupid man.

He dressed carefully, choosing old but freshly ironed cotton trousers and a cool white shirt. He hesitated over the choice of shoes: his old ones were badly worn, the new ones hidden in their box tantalizingly smart. They were two-tone black and white in softest Moroccan leather and very expensive. But too risky, he finally decided. The most junior of house-minders did not have the money for things like that.

He leaned down and unlocked the bottom drawer of the old *commode*. He went through the contents carefully: new suit in pale blue linen, white silk shirt, tie, cotton socks, and a wallet, including identity card, driving license and seven thousand francs in large notes. He was particularly pleased with the suit: it had been a real bargain. At first Goldrich, the tailor, had pressed him for the full price but Vasson had soon worn him down. Belonging to an organization did have one advantage: people didn't argue with you. Anyway, Goldrich was a Jew and Jews could always afford to reduce their prices.

The identity papers had taken a lot of finding. But, as Vasson kept reminding himself, they were almost untraceable and therefore worth every bit of the effort. He had gone to Lyons, a tedious two-hour train journey. But the farther from Marseilles the better. Even if worse came to the worst and they thought of checking up, Lyons was an unlikely place to go for documents. Anyway, they wouldn't find anything: Vasson had avoided going to the local dealer—even if one existed, which he doubted. Instead he had watched outside the Collège des Sciences Physiques in the Rue de la Trinité until, after two long days, he had finally seen a student who bore a resemblance to himself. The youth's height and coloring were right and Vasson judged his age to be about twenty-one or twenty-two. Vasson himself was twenty-three, but he never thought of himself as young. He had never felt young, even when he was a child.

He had followed the youth back to a tall ugly house on the edge of town and seen a light come on in a top left-hand window. Vasson had been sick at the thought of what he might have to do next: he loathed the idea of physical violence. But there was little possibility of the student leaving his wallet and identity card lying around in the daytime. Vasson would have to take them while the boy slept, although the risk of discovery—and of having to defend himself—was appalling.

As it was, the whole thing had been ridiculously easy. The side door of the house had been open and, astonishingly, the student's door too. Vasson's heart had hammered so loudly that the *tête de con* must surely hear, but no, he slept on and it had taken only minutes for Vasson to find the wallet lying casually on a side table. He had crept out, sick with excitement, and vomited in the alleyway beside the house.

The wallet contained an identity card in the name of Jean-Marie Biolet, aged twenty-two, resident of 17, Rue Madeleine in the town of St.-Etienne. Vasson had been disappointed in the photograph: the likeness was not as good as he'd hoped. But a change of hairstyle and some glasses would hide the differences. The driving license was a real bonus, though, and more than made up for the photograph.

Vasson was immensely pleased with the result of his three-day excursion. He could easily have bought an identity card on the Marseilles market, but that would have been stupid: once the pressure was on, someone, somewhere, would have talked. As it was, the card in the name of Jean-Marie Biolet could never be linked to Vasson. The knowledge gave him deep satisfaction. The identity would mean a complete break with the past. After today Paul Vasson, born in the Old Quarter of Marseilles, would cease to exist. The thought gave him a curious thrill.

Vasson examined the last item in the drawer: a leather money belt. The remaining two hundred thousand francs should fit into the neat pouches, but he couldn't be sure until he actually got hold of the money. He'd asked for large notes, as large as possible, but they would still take up a lot of space. He would have to worry about that when the time came.

Vasson locked the drawer again, picked up his toilet kit and put it into a valise with his raincoat and felt hat. He would leave the rest of his possessions; they would be no loss, no loss at all.

His eye caught a magazine cutting pinned to the wall above the bed and he took it down. It was an advertisement showing a stylized drawing of a car. Vasson examined it closely as he had a hundred times before. It was a D8SS Delage. The most beautiful, *perfect* thing in the world.

He had often imagined what it must be like to drive such a thing, to feel it around his body: the leather seats, the throb of the 4-liter engine accelerating to over 160 kilometers an hour, and the shiny newness of the long, smooth body, as sleek as a cat's.

He folded the cutting and put it in his wallet. Soon—by tonight —he would have enough money to buy a D8SS. The thought made him sick with excitement and he almost giggled.

The air was very still, the cooling wind that sometimes wafted up from the harbor had died away and the atmosphere in the

room was stifling. It was still a bit early to meet Jojo, but Vasson had to leave, to get going before he started thinking too much. Thinking was all right when he was making plans: he liked planning. But it was no good now—he kept thinking about what might go wrong.

Anyway, it was too late.

And then he remembered with a jolt that it really *was* too late.

He ran quickly down the stairs and out into the cobbled street, blinking at the harsh afternoon light. The Old Quarter was crowded and he had to push his way through knots of people meandering along the hot narrow alleys. A couple of Arabs walked toward him, their arms around each other, and Vasson cursed as he was forced to step around them. One of the Arabs laughed and brushed his lips across the other's bearded cheek. Barefooted children were playing in the doorways while their mothers hung washing between the tall crumbling houses and leaned over the latticed balconies, shouting at one another.

Vasson regarded the scene with distaste: it had not changed since he had been a child here twenty years before. The people lived like pigs, squashed together. They had no will to change, no drive to escape. They were happy to exist like this all their wretched lives.

A child came pelting out of a doorway, shouting with laughter, and ran straight at Vasson so that he almost tripped. He swore loudly. The child swerved quickly away, scampering down an alleyway, its feet flying. Vasson watched it angrily, half-determined to chase it. Suddenly the small figure lurched and fell forward onto the cobblestones, its limbs sprawled.

Vasson was glad; it served the little devil right. The child did not move. Vasson wandered up the alley and looked down at it. He prodded its ribs with his foot. The child slowly lifted its head and turned toward him, its bleeding face crumpled with misery. Vasson stood and watched. The child lowered its head and began to cry noisily.

There was something despairing about the sobbing shoulders. Tentatively Vasson reached down and touched the child. The child seemed not to notice. He grasped the small body and lifted it to its feet, holding it at arm's length. It was a strange sensation, to be holding a child. He patted the child's cheek. "All right?"

The child did not answer but continued to cry. Vasson went on one knee and, very slowly, pulled the child toward him, putting an arm round the narrow shoulders. He felt the child stiffen. "Don't you touch me, you bastard!" The small face, so close to his, was ugly with contempt. Vasson got hastily to his feet and choked back his anger. The child ran off, screaming obscenities.

Vasson strode furiously back into the street. The stupid child had tricked him, made a fool of him. Children were no different from anyone else; they were out to get you, like the rest.

He turned onto the quay and hurried along the harbor, but went past the street where Jojo lived. Only when he felt calmer did he go back and walk up to Jojo's. He was still half an hour early. He paused, wondering whether to wait or go straight up to the apartment.

It was the thought of Jojo's woman that made him hesitate.

She was a bitch, first class. She made Vasson feel uneasy. She was crafty, clever, like a cat, and when she wanted to she could make people feel small—especially men who didn't go for her. Not that there were many of those. She was beautiful in a flashy, grotesquely physical sort of way and men made fools of themselves over her. Vasson always went out of his way to avoid her.

Also, she was a whore.

For several minutes Vasson waited, full of indecision, angry that he should be nervous with the wretched woman.

But he made up his mind and strode into the building, thinking: Christ, what the hell am I worrying about?

Today Jojo's woman was going to be the very least of his problems.

Solange lay on the bed and drew heavily on her cigarette. Her hands were shaking. She wasn't surprised: she'd never been so angry in her life. Her temper was, she knew, appalling. But it wasn't her fault, it was just the way she was made. It was the mixed blood or something. She liked to think she had some of the gentle qualities of her Cambodian mother, but her father seemed to come out in her every time. He had been half-French, half-Martinican, and his favorite sport was fighting. He'd died in a bar brawl.

Jojo had finally gone too far. She loved him most of the time

but at other times she could kill him. This afternoon was one of the times when she could positively strangle him. Why, oh why couldn't he get going and actually *do* something? All he did was talk—and even then he backtracked.

There were sounds from the tiny kitchen and she guessed that Jojo was making some of his beloved black treacly coffee. She considered whether to go in and have it out with him again but she knew it would end the same way as before, with her throwing something. Just half an hour ago it had been an ashtray—the shards were still lying on the floor—but as usual Jojo had ignored her.

The row had been about the same old subject: their future.

They had discussed their plans more times than she could count. At first Solange had loved going over the details, it would cheer her up. The idea was simple: as soon as they had saved enough money they were going to take an apartment off La Canebière. Something really smart with large rooms and a beautiful bathroom, and live there together, just the two of them. During the day Solange would see her high-class johns, but strictly by appointment; she would have a maid-*cum*-secretary, dressed in elegant black, to answer the door and the telephone. Then Jojo and she would have the evenings all to themselves, to go walking down La Canebière and look at all the smart shops and visit the top restaurants, like that La Babayette place where the waiters wore stiff collars and the crepes were flambéed at the table.

It was all going to be wonderful. She just *knew* their new life would be a success.

Solange had saved nearly all the money, even though it had meant taking on tricks she would normally have turned over to someone else.

Then Jojo had got cold feet. He had started to mutter about the problems, always the problems. Solange had the unpleasant feeling he was just frightened, nervous of the *Patron* and how the old man would feel about it. To hell with it—girls had left the *Patron*'s establishments before and nothing had happened. Jojo was just a goddam coward.

It was more than she could bear to think of staying on at the Red House. It was a dead-end job: the decent customers didn't dare be seen around the place too often because of its reputation, though they all said they would love to visit her more frequently.

And those who *did* come regularly were rubbish: no finesse, no style at all. Solange admired style.

She deserved better, everyone said so. But she couldn't get out on her own, she had no illusions about that. She needed Jojo to protect her, and she needed him *now,* damn it.

Jojo appeared in the kitchen doorway and she could see that he was still sore with her. He was avoiding her eyes and shuffling his feet like a spoiled child. She didn't have the energy to yell at him anymore. Her frustration and rage began to evaporate. She went toward him and hugged his back. "I'm sorry."

Jojo pulled a face. He enjoyed being a martyr and Solange knew she would have to cajole him into forgiving her, a process which could take two days or more. She thought: The bastard, how he's putting it on. But at the same time she knew she would play the role of repentant sinner to the full, as she always did.

She sighed. "Am I forgiven?"

Jojo stared out of the window and shrugged, but she could see he was softening.

"Let's go out for a drink. Come on. I'll buy!"

He moved away, a sheepish look in his eye. She thought: He's feeling guilty about something, he's got something to hide.

He murmured, "I've got to go out. Vasson's arriving in a while and we're . . . going on a job."

Solange froze. She knew exactly what that meant. It meant they were going to deliver a consignment for the *Patron.* The anger came surging back. "You're mad! You . . . you realize that you could go down for *years* if you're caught. And it'll be *you* who gets caught, not the *Patron*! He should do his own dirty work." Jojo started to move hurriedly around the small apartment, collecting clothing. She followed him, shouting, "How do you think he gets so rich, eh? I'll tell you—by getting fools like you to move all the stuff around for him. And I suppose it's the hard stuff, *noire*! . . . eh? Jesus—"

He turned on her. "Shut up! Do you want everyone to hear?"

In the fraction of silence that followed, she heard a shuffling sound at the apartment door and stared at Jojo, horrified. He had heard it too and reached the door in two strides. He flung it open and she saw him relax. "Oh, it's you. Come in, for Christ's sake."

Vasson came through the door and Solange glanced at him furiously. She turned to Jojo, catching his arm. She heard herself

shouting again. "You have no brains, none of you. You think you're so clever!" She threw her hands up in a gesture of despair.

Jojo turned slowly to face her. He spoke deliberately, his eyes cold. "Shut up, you nagging cow. You talk crap. Stick to what you're good at."

Solange stared, aghast. He had never talked to her like that before. He'd always treated her with respect. But she realized why he'd said it: to impress Vasson.

She glanced at Vasson with distaste. She didn't like him at the best of times. He was a real little creep, always trying to muscle in. Some people were fooled by his polished airs and his educated accent—the Jesuits had schooled him, so they said—but not she. She had his measure: she recognized him for the shifty little rat he was.

There was something else about him too, though she couldn't quite put her finger on it; something not quite right, something that made her hackles rise.

Vasson was looking at her uncomfortably. She thought: Good.

She pulled her mind back to the problem: something had to be done to persuade Jojo to drop this idea. She hated pleading with him in front of Vasson, but there was no other way. She whispered gently to him, "*Please*, Jojo. Don't go, don't get mixed up in that side of the business. The *Patron*'s just using you, don't you see that?"

"Look, I do as I'm told and then I have a quiet life, okay? Anyway, it's extra money." To Vasson he said, "I'll be with you in a minute." He pulled off his shirt and, taking a towel, disappeared into the kitchen.

Solange yelled, "You're crazy!" at the closed door, then groaned with exasperation. There was no getting through to the stupid idiot. He would end up in prison for years and she would be stuck in this tomb forever. She thought: God, what a mess.

Vasson was sitting on a small chair in the corner, lighting a cigarette and pretending not to listen, but hearing everything.

Solange hesitated. She hated the idea of asking him anything, far less a favor. But—it might just work. She pulled up another chair and sat beside him. "Look, what do you think about this? I mean, you must agree that it's mad. If you're caught you'll take the time, not the *Patron*."

He looked down at the floor and for a moment she thought he

wouldn't answer. Then his dark eyes darted up to her face, and she was surprised by the intensity of his stare. He said, "I just do as I'm told, like Jojo." He smiled, but Solange noticed that his eyes were cold. "You see, I'm a new boy around here, and I've got to stay on the right side of the *Patron,* otherwise I'm out."

His eyes held hers, still smiling. So he was trying some charm on her, was he? Right, if that was the game, she could play it too.

She put her hand on his leg. "You're an intelligent man. You can see it's far too risky." She gave him a long intense look from under her lashes. It was her favorite weapon and it usually did the trick. But almost immediately she saw that she had made a mistake. A look of alarm had come into his eyes, a look almost of . . . for a moment she was puzzled, then she had it: it was *revulsion.* She thought: Ah, so that's it, that's what I couldn't pin down: you're a woman-hater.

She withdrew her hand and stared at him. His smile had vanished and he was watching her coldly. Eventually he said, "Nothing's risky if you're careful enough. Jojo was right, you should keep to your work and mind your own business." He had put a small but unmistakable tone of insolence into the word work.

Solange gritted her teeth. He had humiliated her and she thought: One round to you, but not the last!

Jojo came into the room and Solange moved away. One glance at Jojo and she knew he wasn't going to listen to any more arguments. She sat down on her favorite piece of furniture, a little pink chaise longue, and thought: To hell with him.

Jojo planted a kiss on her cheek, and said, "See you later. Don't know when."

Solange did not reply, but sat stiffly on the chaise staring out of the window. She felt the dull ache of anxiety in her heart and she knew she wouldn't stop worrying until Jojo was safely back.

Vasson watched Jojo striding ahead of him and wondered why he was in such a hurry. God forbid that the pickup was going to be early. That would ruin everything. He had told the Algerian that it would be at ten, and everything had been arranged accordingly. Damn, he would have to make sure.

He put in a couple of loping strides and came up beside Jojo. "What's the hurry? We've got hours yet. It's only six, you know."

"Eh?" Jojo slowed up and looked around him, as if realizing for

the first time where he was. "Oh. Sorry. I was . . . still thinking
. . . you know."

Vasson was relieved. It was the woman who was on Jojo's mind,
not the pickup. He shivered at the memory of the woman, with
her roving hands and her large open mouth. She had no idea of
how disgusting she was: the foreign brownish skin was somehow
greasy and unclean.

But at least she'd got Jojo in a state and not thinking straight,
which should make things easier. He wondered what to ask first.
Best to make sure about the time. He said casually, "It is still on
for ten, isn't it?"

"What? . . . Oh, yes, yes. There's no change."

Vasson gave the other man a sidelong glance. Jojo was frowning, his eyes on the paving in front of his feet. Vasson decided that
some sympathy, some intimate conversation, was needed before
it was safe to go on. He touched Jojo's arm. "Look, I'm sure it'll
all be all right when you get back. She'll have forgotten why she
was angry."

Gratitude flashed across Jojo's face and Vasson saw that he had
been right to bring up the subject. Jojo shook his head. "Honestly
. . . I don't know why she has it in for me sometimes. It's a mystery
to me. Trouble is . . ." He looked across with an expression that
Vasson couldn't fathom. "I like having her around."

They turned a corner and Vasson had to drop behind Jojo to
pass two black-scarved women talking in the middle of the street.
He considered whether to ask the big question now or wait until
later. Jojo might refuse to answer in such a public place. It might
be better to wait until they'd had a couple of pastis and Jojo was
more relaxed. On the other hand time would be getting short by
then and the right moment might not come up again. Vasson
prided himself on judging the right moment.

He decided that this was the best moment he would get. It was
only fear, he realized, that had held him back.

He swallowed and said, "Look, I've got a bit of a woman problem too. I want to see this girl tonight. She's really hot stuff.
. . . But, well, she can't get off work until nine and . . . it would
mean a lot to see her for just half an hour or so. Is there any
chance that I can meet you *there*?"

Jojo looked at him sharply. Vasson put on a rueful, sheepish

expression and laughed. "I know it's stupid, but I'm really mad about her and there's this other guy hanging about. If I don't get to see her tonight, he'll be there like a shot." He sighed. "He's got the lot: money, a car, flashy clothes. My only hope is to see her and tell her . . ." He trailed off and tried to look lovelorn.

They turned onto the quay and up a small road beside the fish warehouse where the car was kept. Jojo still hadn't answered and Vasson glanced across at him, trying to read his face.

Jojo paused to unlock the garage door. He was frowning. "I'd have to tell you where the pickup was and you know the *Patron*'s rules about that."

Vasson stroked his chin. "Yes, of course. I hadn't thought of that."

Jojo backed the car out. Vasson closed the garage door and got into the passenger seat. The Citroën set off toward the quay, bumping gently over the cobbles.

Jojo lit a cigarette one-handedly and said brightly, "Well, where's it to be? Hamid's? Or shall we go to that new bar just off the Rue Caisserie? There's a place next door that does a really good couscous."

Vasson thought: Shit! He's not going to buy it. That meant that Vasson would have to contact the Algerian to arrange a tail and then stay with Jojo all evening, right up until the end. He didn't like that idea at all: it would mean slipping away at the very last moment, which would be horribly risky. He felt angry. Christ, he didn't ask much. Just a little confidence, and Jojo, who was meant to be his friend, wasn't even going to give him that!

Jojo was waiting for an answer. Vasson shrugged and said in a tight voice, "I don't care where the hell we go."

"Oh, for God's sake, it's that bad, is it? This girl, I mean."

"Yes, it is."

Jojo sighed deeply. Eventually he said, "Okay, okay, you win. But if it ever gets back to the *Patron* that I told you *where* to go, I'll kill you. He's really nervous at the moment. There's a lot of pressure, as you know."

"Oh?"

"The Algerian. He's trying to move in again. You must have heard."

"Ah. No, I hadn't." Vasson enjoyed lying, mainly because he

found it so easy. The best thing in the world was to carry a lie through all the way, to build on it, to refine it. It gave him a lot of satisfaction.

Vasson appeared to consider, then said, "Well, of course, there's no way the *Patron* is going to find out, but . . . if you really think there's a problem?"

"No, go on. See her. Just don't let me down, that's all. *Be* there, and on time."

They stopped at a junction. Jojo turned and said softly, "Okay, the place is a small store off the Quai de la Rive Neuve. Behind the big warehouse, L'Entrepôt du Midi. It's got Laborde et Fils over the main door. It's on the same street as that nightclub, La Ronde."

"Thanks. Thanks a lot. I'll remember the favor." Vasson smiled warmly. He really *was* pleased. Jojo had done him the biggest favor of his life.

"Where to, then?"

"Hamid's. I don't like that new place." Vasson didn't like the new place because there was only one telephone and it was on the bar itself.

Hamid's was already crowded and the air was thick with smoke and the smell of herbal tobacco. The two men squeezed in at the far end of the counter and ordered Pernod. Vasson didn't attempt to keep the look of triumph off his face. After all, he had every reason to be happy: he was in love, wasn't he?

There was only the phone call left now, and that would be easy. He waited for Jojo to order another round, then made a show of looking at his watch. "Look, I can get her on the telephone at work now. It'll save me having to go round to meet her."

Jojo stirred the water into his Pernod. "Where does she work?"

"La Belle Époque. It's a dress shop off La Canebière. Very classy."

"What's her name?"

"Marie-Hélène. Hey, why all the questions? You're not thinking of pinching her, are you?" He gave Jojo a friendly dig in the ribs and leered at him, thinking: This inquisition has got to stop.

Jojo laughed. "No, I've got enough trouble with Solange. She doesn't give me enough time for other women. Anyway, I'm not an educated type like you. I'm not into classy pieces who work in dress shops."

Vasson took out his wallet and put some money on the bar. "Here. Have another while I'm phoning." A drink would keep Jojo busy.

Jojo caught his arm. "What's that you have there?" He was peering at Vasson's still-open wallet.

Vasson's heart missed a beat and he thought: God, what the hell's he spotted?

Jojo, taking the wallet, pulled out the newspaper cutting of the Delage. "That car again, eh? What with girls from La Canebière and cars like this . . ." He shook his head and flicked the picture with his finger. "You have expensive tastes. Very expensive."

Vasson shrugged. "No harm in dreaming, is there?"

"None at all." Jojo replaced the cutting and handed the wallet back to Vasson. "No harm at all. Just as long as you don't try to get it the easy way." He grinned broadly to soften the words, but Vasson thought: Goddam you, you're treating me like a child too.

He said lightly, "I know there's no easy way."

He pocketed the wallet and, moving quickly down the bar, went through a door into the back. Hamid was there. Vasson asked, "Mind if I use the telephone?"

Hamid looked up. He was a Tunisian Arab who, after twenty years in Marseilles, still wore a jellaba. He indicated the telephone on the desk. "Salām, my friend. Please, please."

"It's a private call. Do you mind?"

"Of course, of course." The old man disappeared into the bar and closed the connecting door.

Vasson thought carefully. There was a second extension in the bar itself, but he would know immediately if anyone listened in because of the noise. It was possible there was another extension upstairs, but doubtful. Hamid was a careful businessman. He wouldn't spend money on luxuries like that.

He raised the receiver and asked for the number he'd been given. There was a long silence and for a moment Vasson was worried in case he'd memorized the wrong number. But then there was a voice on the line. "Yes?"

"It's me."

"Have you any news?"

"Ten tonight, a store named Laborde et Fils, behind L'Entrepôt du Midi, on the other side of the harbor."

"Got it."

"And the other address?"

"When you deliver what you owe·me."

There was a silence. "All right. A briefcase will be delivered to you at the corner of Rue Caisserie and Rue Roger at exactly ten-thirty. Make sure you have that address written on a piece of paper ready to hand to the driver. Good-bye."

Vasson replaced the receiver and found a pencil and a piece of clean paper under the piles of till receipts. In block capitals he carefully wrote the address of the heroin-processing laboratory that the *Patron* maintained in a quiet suburb on the south side of the city, beyond the hill of Notre-Dame de la Garde. He had delivered some stuff there once. They had told him it was only a safe house, but he had checked on it. He had gone back and watched the place: two men arrived at eight and left at four on the first day. And the second day. And the third. Regular little workers, they were.

He had followed one home. A garrulous neighbor had informed him that the worker was a chemist who used to work for a big pharmaceutical company somewhere. No one was sure where he worked now. Vasson hadn't bothered to check on the second worker: he knew he'd found the laboratory.

He put the piece of paper in his back pocket and went through into the bar. Realizing what was expected, he smacked his hand in the crook of his elbow in the age-old obscene gesture.

Jojo laughed and shouted, "Lucky devil!"

Yes, thought Vasson, how right you are.

Vasson peered up and down both streets again. Occasionally the headlights of a car swept the Rue Caisserie, but none of them slowed down. He felt sure it must be after ten-thirty, but without a watch he couldn't be positive. He had left Hamid's just before nine and gone to a strange bar to the north of the quarter until just before then. Since then he'd been walking the streets for at least half an hour. He decided a watch was one of the first things he was going to buy with the money. He liked the new metal Rolexes: smart yet practical.

He'd never had real money before, but he knew exactly what he was going to do with it. There would be a small rented apartment in the 18th Arrondissement, a D8SS Delage—though he probably wouldn't be able to afford a new one—and a nice little

business. A club probably, with high-class girls and some expensive decor. But whatever the business, he would work hard at it and it would be a success. He couldn't understand people who spent wildly instead of investing for the future. There was no way he was going to be caught in *that* trap. Apart from the Delage, which would have to be bought for cash, he was going to invest every penny.

There was still no sign of a car. Vasson began to feel nervous. They must come soon; they needed that address.

A terrible thought came to him. Suppose . . . suppose they had got the address out of Jojo . . .

Of course. Why hadn't he thought of it before? If Jojo had talked . . . then they wouldn't turn up in a million years. *And they wouldn't bring the money.*

Oh God, please don't let it be true, please.

He leaned back against the wall and stared through the darkness at the building opposite. The thought of not having the money was so appalling that he couldn't imagine it. The money was everything . . .

He stood immobile against the wall, as if by freezing his body he could postpone the moment of truth.

The time must be at least a quarter to eleven.

There was a sudden flash of light. A long low car was sliding into the curb. He stared at it uncomprehendingly.

A car . . . *the car* . . .

Oh dear God, thank you, *thank you.* He stepped forward, half chuckling, half crying.

The rear door opened and a voice called, "Get in."

Vasson stood by the open door. "No, I'd rather not." Through his elation he thought: I'm not going to be caught by that old trick.

The voice said, "I thought you'd want to count the money."

Vasson considered. They were right, of course. But it was still too risky to get in; he would take a quick look at the cash and he'd soon know if there was a lot missing. "No, just hand it over."

"You have the address ready?"

An old attaché case appeared from inside the car and Vasson crouched on the pavement to open it. In the dim light of the streetlamp he saw piles of clean new bank notes. "They're new! I asked for old!"

"They're straight out of the bank. Clean as a whistle."

"But how do I know they're not hot?"

"They're not pinched, if that's what you mean."

Vasson cursed, but he knew he was beaten. He'd have to accept the new notes and like it. He thrust the piece of paper into the car and a hand reached out to close the door. Vasson leaped for the door and held it open. "Stop! You promised! You promised to tell me what happened." He clung onto the door. No one was going to close it until he had an answer.

There was a pause, then the voice said, "Okay, okay. We gave the news of the pickup to our friends at the police station."

"Why? Why *them*?"

"We owe them a favor. Anyway we want them to get the odd conviction; it keeps everyone happy."

So, it was prison for Jojo. He'd got off lightly then. Vasson was glad: he'd quite liked the guy.

The voice had fallen silent. Vasson prompted, "Well? What about the *Patron*?"

"We've already dealt with him. He had . . . a little accident, about half an hour ago. And the laboratory, the technicians—we'll be taking them over ourselves." There was a pause, then the voice said mockingly, "Does all this meet with your satisfaction?"

The car revved up. "You won't be staying around, will you? The Algerian doesn't think it'll be very healthy for you."

"Don't worry, I'm going on a long trip. To Algeria."

As the car drove off, Vasson laughed. To Algeria. He liked that. Very neat.

He walked rapidly, the attaché case swinging in his hand. God, what a coup! What a strike! Perfect—the whole thing had gone perfectly.

He had only one regret: that he hadn't been able to see the *Patron*'s expression when he realized he'd been outmaneuvered. The bastard, that would teach him.

Vasson paused near the house. The place seemed quiet. If possible he wanted to get to his room without meeting any of the girls.

He crept up to the doorway and into the hall. No one. He ran lightly up the stairs to the landing outside his room. He put his ear to the door and listened carefully.

There was no sound; nothing to worry about. Everything was going to be all right.

He put the key into the lock and in that instant he knew that it had all gone dreadfully wrong.

The door was already unlocked.

As it swung open he saw the bottom drawer gaping at him. The lock had been broken, and there was someone in the room.

It was Jojo's woman.

She was staring at him, her eyes wide and angry.

For a moment neither of them moved. The woman was panting heavily. Slowly Vasson looked around the room and understood why. The bitch had been through the place. Magazines spilled off the shelves; his new suit lay in a crumpled ball on the floor. The beautiful white silk shirt hung off the side of the bed, a smear of dirt showing gray on its sleeve.

He thought: God, why did she have to *spoil* everything? Why couldn't she have left me *alone*?

Then he saw the money. The thirty thousand francs advance payment lay neatly stacked on top of the chest. Next to it were some papers.

Oh God. The papers.

He closed the door slowly behind him and faced her. "Why? Why did you come here?"

"You bastard! You shopped Jojo! You bastard!"

Vasson thought: Damn, damn. He had to think clearly but it was impossible while she was still yelling. "Shut up!" he shouted.

Her mouth closed in surprise.

Quickly he said, "What gave you that idea? That I shopped Jojo?"

"I *know* you did! My friend told me, my *Inspector* friend."

"Impossible."

"Oh, he didn't *say* it was you." She was beginning to scream again. "But as soon as he told me someone had, I knew it *had* to be you. And what do I find, eh? *All this!*" She picked up the money and shook it at him.

He thought: Perhaps she hasn't seen the papers, perhaps it's all right after all. But then he realized she *must* have, when she had taken them out of the drawer.

She knew his new name.

He took a step forward and said quietly, "Give me the money."
She started to move to one side and he saw her glance at the door.
God, she was stupid. He took a step sideways and cut her off.

She stared at him defiantly. "You bastard, take your bloody
money!" She threw the notes at him and they fluttered down to
the floor.

She's done it again, he thought. Dirtied everything unneces-
sarily, spoiled it all.

He reached for her and saw the fear leap into her eyes. He
would have to be quick, otherwise she'd scream. He grabbed at
her but she pulled free and ran for the door. Even before she got
to it, he knew he would be able to catch her. She was grappling
with the handle. He came up behind her and got a hand around
first one arm then the other. Then he thought: God, what do I
do next?

She was kicking backward at him and he pulled her closer so
that her legs would lose their momentum. As she started to yell,
he realized what he would have to do. He put an arm around her
throat and when her hand shot up to pull it away, he raised his
other arm. After that it was a simple matter to slide his hands onto
her neck.

He squeezed and the yelling stopped. Her breathing changed
to a series of loud agonizing rasps. It was too noisy: he would have
to squeeze harder. The noise changed to a gurgle and he thought:
That's better. Then she started to fight, twisting her body from
side to side and kicking her legs again. It occurred to him that it
would be much easier on the floor.

He turned her around and started to push her down. At the
sight of his face she went for his eyes, her nails digging into his
skin. Panicking, he squeezed harder and she grasped desperately
at his hands again. Her eyes began to pop, and he was amazed
at the enormous size of the human eye.

He wondered how much longer it would take. He was running
out of strength. It was much more difficult than he'd thought: she
was so strong. She was purple now and her tongue was protruding from her mouth. The sight was disgusting and he closed his
eyes.

At last he looked again. Her eyes were staring blankly and the
obscene tongue was hanging swollen from the mouth. Tentatively he let go. The head lolled sideways. The body lay still.

He backed away on hands and knees, crying quietly. What a stupid bitch! Why couldn't she leave well enough alone?

His stomach heaved and he lurched to the basin to throw up. Afterward he dipped a cloth in the water jug and washed his face for a long time.

Eventually he realized it was late. The last night train left in half an hour. He picked up his crumpled clothes from the floor and began to change. By facing toward the basin, he could avoid looking at the body. When he had finished he picked the money up from the floor, leaving one note protruding from under the woman's head. He packed the money into the money belt along with the notes from the attaché case. The new identity papers went into his jacket pocket.

At last he was ready. The clothes didn't look too bad, though the shirt was badly creased. He would have it dry-cleaned when he got to Paris.

He looked in the mirror. He looked just the same but he didn't feel it. He would never *feel* the same again. That woman had tainted him with her dirt. It must never happen again. He would make sure of that.

Thank God at least for the money, the sweet, beautiful money. That made him feel clean again.

2 It was a clear, cloudless September day. In Plymouth Sound anchored warships were silhouetted black against the sparkling sea and twelve miles away, on the horizon, the tall Eddystone Lighthouse was clearly visible, a dark needle against the pale blue sky. A fresh southwesterly breeze was blowing in from the sea and on the exposed height of Plymouth Hoe it was cold. Only a handful of people were braving a stroll along the historic pathways where, according to popular legend, Drake had played his game of bowls.

Julie Lescaux sat on a bench and stared out beyond the break-water to the wide English Channel. She thought: I could always kill myself.

But she knew she wouldn't. She hadn't the nerve to do something like that. Even at school she'd never done anything daring or risky. When some of the other girls had dressed up to look eighteen and gone dancing in the city, she'd ducked out. They'd called her a goody-goody. And they were right: she had always been anxious to do the right thing.

Julie thought: If only they knew the truth.

It was strange how life changed—and so quickly, without warning. She'd always thought of herself as an ordinary sort of person who would always have an ordinary life. Well, perhaps ordinary sounded a bit dull. Average was better.

Yes, she thought, that's what I am—average.

·And yet it was she who was going to be different from all the others. She, the goody-goody. Bad things were half expected of girls like Maggie Phillips, who had penciled her eyebrows and worn high heels at sixteen; Maggie, who had lots of boyfriends and was considered "flighty."

But it hadn't happened to Maggie; it had happened to Julie.

Julie could imagine what people would say. They would use all the stock phrases, all the old clichés.

But there was no way around it.

She was just nineteen and pregnant.

She had got into trouble.

She had been "easy."

She had ruined her life.

She tried to imagine what it was like, to have people whispering and sniggering about you, talking behind your back and pointing you out. It would be terrible, she knew, not just for her, but for Mother. Her mother believed in respect and being able to hold your head up. She set great store by what people thought.

It would be like stabbing her in the back.

Unless Julie got married. But she knew there was no chance of that, none at all.

Her mother . . . Julie had no idea how she was going to tell her. Whichever way she did it, her mother would die of shame and anger and bitterness. She would accuse Julie of ingratitude and

34

disloyalty and selfishness and say she had ruined both their lives. Julie could hear her very words.

The only thing worse would be another interview with Dr. Hargreaves. Julie shrank at the memory. Her visit to him had been deeply humiliating, much worse than she'd ever imagined. He had called her shameless and ungrateful. He'd asked her why she'd gone and thrown herself at the first man who'd asked.

She hadn't replied. She'd thought: Perhaps he's right. Perhaps I am shameless, ungrateful.

In the end he had told her he would keep her as a patient, but only out of loyalty to her mother. Then he said—and the words had taken Julie by surprise—that the baby would need to be adopted and that he would arrange it.

She hadn't thought about what would happen to the baby. How strange! The whole fuss was about having a baby, and she hadn't thought about the actual baby, the object of it all. She knew nothing about babies, she'd never even held one. Did she want a baby? Would she love it? She had no idea.

A gust of wind blew across the Hoe and lifted the hem of her frock. She pushed the skirt down and pulled her coat around her knees. When she looked up she was aware that someone was staring at her. It was a sailor. Julie looked quickly away and waited nervously for him to pass.

For an awful moment she thought he was going to try to pick her up. But, after pausing for a moment, he quickened his step and walked away.

Julie relaxed and sat back on the bench. It would have been surprising if he had tried to pick her up. She rarely had trouble of that kind. She supposed it was because she didn't look the type. She was wearing the white gloves her mother insisted on, and a frock at least two inches longer than the current calf-length fashion; not exactly the outfit for a scarlet woman. She didn't *look* easy, *even if she was.*

She stood up and began to walk slowly along the Hoe.

Easy . . . But she hadn't been "easy," far from it. It had only happened twice, and then after days of argument and fierce persuasion. Even when she'd agreed to it, she'd had terrible doubts. She had realized that there should be much more love and tenderness and caring. But Bill had been very clever. He had swept

away all her arguments and told her she was being too romantic and that life wasn't like that. He had made her feel very gauche and silly. His favorite word for her was "immature." He told her that all the other officers slept with their girl friends and no one thought anything of it. He had made her feel like the odd one out.

She had held out for a long time, then he had threatened to take another girl to the Summer Ball. It was Mother who had been horrified at the thought of Julie not going. The Summer Ball was the social event of the season. She had forced Julie to write to Bill and make up.

So she had gone to the ball and drunk gin, which she had only tried once before, and then wine, which she wasn't used to either. Afterward Bill had driven her up onto the moors and it had happened for the first time.

It was brief and painful and Julie had wept. He had promised her it would be better the next time. But if anything it had been worse. On the second occasion they had driven onto a remote headland. This time he didn't say a word, he didn't even kiss her, he just grabbed her and pulled at her clothing. Then he lay on her and hurt her again, except that it lasted much longer and she hated it even more than the first time.

Afterward she had felt miserable and unclean. If that was love then she didn't want anything more to do with it. One thing she knew straightaway: she would never let Bill do it again.

She had felt wretched for weeks. Her mother had put her unhappiness down to being in love. Poor Mother! She still thought that Bill was marvelous: well-spoken, dashing and a gentleman. Mother had never let Julie go out with anyone she considered common, certainly not to the Golden Dance Hall to meet the noncommissioned ranks like the rest of her school friends did.

The idea of Bill being a gentleman made Julie smile grimly. She had used the risk of pregnancy as a reason for not giving in to him, but he had swept that aside as he swept everything else aside. Nothing, he had assured her, would happen; he would take care of that.

A small sailing craft had appeared by Drake's Island and was heading out into the wide expanse of the sound. She thought how pretty it looked, with its white sails and gay red hull. It was skimming over the waves, fast as the wind.

36

She rose from the bench and for no particular reason thought of her father. Perhaps it was the boat that reminded her.

She remembered his dear gruff voice. His death when she was twelve had broken her heart. She still missed him dreadfully.

Her father would have understood about this. He would have listened and sighed and looked at her with love in his eyes and taken her in his arms and said, Juliette, my Juliette. He would have found a way for her to survive it all.

Perhaps he would have taken her away . . . Julie stopped abruptly.

She hadn't thought of that. That would be an answer. To go away. But where? She had only a few pounds saved. As a junior secretary she earned just fifteen shillings a week and it was hard to save on that. Anyway, she couldn't stay in her present job: she'd have to leave Plymouth and go to a new area and find a new job, and that wouldn't be easy. And then what? She had few relatives to go to. There was only Aunt Beryl at Ramsgate, and she—well, she was like her mother.

She had never met her father's family in Brittany; her mother had always discouraged any contact with them.

Julie walked down the long flight of steps into Grand Parade and wondered if it was five o'clock yet. She usually went out on Saturday afternoons, either to meet some of the girls for tea at the teahouse, or, in the old days, to go out for a drive with Bill. She always promised to be back by five-thirty.

Today she had told her mother she was going into town, but nothing more. Her mother had been suspicious and as soon as Julie got back to the house there would be questions. Then the truth would have to come out, and nothing would ever be the same again.

Julie turned into West Street and walked down the hill toward Radley Terrace and her home at Number 34.

As she drew near the bottom of the hill two women came around the corner, walking arm-in-arm. One of them was Maggie Phillips. Julie's first thought was to get away, but she realized that Maggie had seen her and was waving. It was too late. She made herself walk on.

"Hello, Julie! A long time since we saw you round these parts." Maggie gave her a dazzling smile between vermilion lips. She

modeled herself on Joan Crawford, down to the padded shoulders and the peep-toe shoes. "We thought you'd got too grand for us."

Julie felt herself blushing. "No, I—I haven't been doing anything special."

Maggie looked at her inquiringly and said, not unkindly, "It's like that, is it? No more boyfriend, eh? Oh well, there'll be others. What about coming to the Golden tonight then? Joan and I are going, and maybe Phyllis. It'll be fun—they've got a really good American-style band."

"Thanks . . . it's kind of you but I can't. I . . ."

"Oh, come on. We'll get a table and sit all demure and ladylike on the side." She giggled.

"Really, my mother's not keen . . ."

"Your mother doesn't own you, does she? Break loose, my girl, that's what I say! What about next Friday then? Joan and I are going to the Rialto with two nice Navy lads. They can bring along one of their mates. It's the new Gable-Crawford movie!"

Julie felt worn down and heard herself say, "Oh, all right."

"We'll meet you outside for the early house then. Byeee!"

Julie walked quickly away. She could have kicked herself. Why had she agreed to go to the pictures? She didn't want to go anywhere with anyone, let alone a group of strangers. Why did she always agree to things she later regretted?

She paused at the corner of the street and thought: Yes, that's the problem. I agree to things I don't really want to do. Why? Why *had* she agreed to Maggie's suggestion? To avoid unpleasantness perhaps. But no, there was more to it than that. She had wanted to *please* Maggie. That was the key: she had been anxious to please. Just as she always tried to please her mother. And her employer. *And* Bill. She hated to remember it now, but she had tried to please *him* too.

Julie thought: What a revelation. I live to please other people. And look where it's got me! Into the oldest trap in the world.

She quickened her pace. It would be time for tea at Number 34, and she mustn't be late.

Julie wondered how much longer it would be before she could get to bed. She was desperately tired. The emotion and tears of the

last few hours had left her feeling drained and now a small ache at the back of her neck was threatening to become a full-blown headache.

Anyway there was nothing new to say, nothing that hadn't been said already.

The road outside was lit by the soft glow of the streetlamps which cast a pale light into the small front room. Normally Mother would have the curtains drawn and the lamps lit by now. But the ritual had been forgotten and the room seemed eerie and unreal in the gloomy darkness.

There was a loud sniffle from her mother. Mrs. Lescaux was sitting on a low stool, rocking back and forth. Now and then her body shook with a great sob and her breath came in long shuddering gasps. At other times she moaned and shook her head and put a large wet handkerchief to her eyes.

Julie wondered what she could say that would help. But there was nothing. . . .

Mrs. Lescaux blew her nose loudly and raised her head. "How can you be *sure* he doesn't love you, that's what I want to know."

"I just know, Mum." They had been over that one half a dozen times already.

"Well, *how* do you know?"

"I told you, he's been avoiding me. And . . ."

Mother said impatiently, "Yes?"

"Well, I saw him with another girl. She seemed much more his sort."

Mrs. Lescaux got wearily to her feet and moved to a chair nearer the window. Her eyes were red-rimmed and bloated, and her face mottled with angry red patches. Julie had never seen her mother look anything but neat and composed before, and it made her feel terrible.

Mother said, "What do you mean by that? More his sort?"

"I mean . . . she was more his class, Mother."

"I don't see what that's got to do with it! You're as good as anyone else. As good as *anyone.* No!" She shook her head vehemently. "That can't have anything to do with it!"

Julie thought that class probably had a lot to do with it, but it was best not to say so. Instead she nodded and said, "Maybe I'm

wrong, maybe that didn't make any difference. But the fact is he doesn't love me, Mother."

"But you can't be sure of that! Perhaps he just never *told* you. . . . Anyway, love can grow. Take it from me."

Julie thought: Oh God, how do I make her understand? She said gently, "Mother, please believe me when I tell you this. He doesn't love me."

He had come to the house for tea a couple of times and Mother had gone to a lot of trouble, making cakes and sandwiches and laying everything out properly. But though he had been polite enough, she had sensed a mocking edge to his comments when he thanked her for the tea or admired the china or inquired about her mother's health. Now Julie could see that he must have thought it all very quaint, the tea parties with the lace doilies, and Mother's refined manner, and the polite conversation.

If I'm right, Julie thought, then I'd rather die than let him know I'm in trouble.

Mrs. Lescaux cleared her throat. "You must try once more, try to *tell* him at least. He might well ask you to marry him. How can you be certain he won't?"

"I'm certain, please believe me."

"I've a good mind to tell him myself. Or his commanding officer. He'll probably be *ordered* to marry you."

Julie felt a surge of anger. "Mother, if you so much as *think* about doing such a thing I shall never speak to you again!"

"Well! That's a fine way to speak to your own mother! There's a daughter's loyalty for you! And after the way you've treated *me*! Bringing such shame on me!"

"Please don't start that all over again. I told you, I'll go away. No one will ever know."

"Go away! On what! Where will you go?"

It was a good question. "I'm not sure yet. But it would be the best thing, Mum. At least that way no one will know. You can make up some story about me getting a job somewhere else. . . ."

Mrs. Lescaux dabbed at her eyes. "Well, if there's no other way . . . but . . ." She threw her head back, looked up at the ceiling and closed her eyes in a gesture of suffering. "But . . . goodness knows where the money's to come from. It'll cost, mark my

words. I can't send you to Aunt Beryl's, I couldn't face that. That means a boardinghouse—dreadfully expensive. And you wouldn't be able to find work, not in your condition!"

"I could go to Brittany."

"What—?"

"It's out of the way, isn't it? And Dad's people would probably take me in. For a while at least."

Mrs. Lescaux looked horrified. "You've never met them. You don't understand. They're not like us. They're . . . they're . . . farmworkers . . . fishermen, that sort of thing. . . ."

Julie remembered her loving kindly father and thought that, surely, his family couldn't be so different from him. He'd come to Plymouth on a French frigate before the Great War and met Mother at a tea dance in the town. Later he had returned and they had married. He'd worked at the fish market, eventually rising to foreman and wearing a suit that always looked uncomfortable on him. To please Mother, he'd never spoken French or talked about his family—at least within earshot.

With Julie it was different. At bedtime he spoke to her in French, telling her stories about the mythical sea creatures of Breton legend; talking about his family, his childhood and Brittany itself. Sometimes he even spoke Breton, the strange harsh language which was his native tongue.

He had been a good father and she had loved him with all her heart.

"No," her mother said decisively, "you can't go there. You must go somewhere else. You could be back four or five weeks after the—event. They might even give you your job back."

Julie frowned. "Mother, I don't think I could come back. You see—there'd be the baby."

"What are you talking about? You won't even see it. It'll be taken away from you straight *after*."

"But I'm not sure. . . ." A vivid picture came into Julie's mind, of a tiny baby lying in her arms looking uncertain and frightened. It was crying and reaching out for her, for *her*. She hated the thought of someone taking it away and sending it to a strange, anonymous place that she'd never be allowed to see or to know about, a place where—God forbid—it might not be loved. She said, "Suppose I wanted to keep the baby . . ."

41

Mrs. Lescaux snorted. "Don't be so silly! It's out of the question! All the girls who—who have this problem have their babies adopted. It's quite normal."

"But I think I might want to keep the baby very much. I'd never forgive myself if I gave it away."

"Now I've heard everything! How selfish can you get! First you get yourself into trouble, then you want to ruin *my* life as well as your own! Really! You young people just don't *care*!"

"Please don't shout."

"I'm not shouting!" Mrs. Lescaux blew her nose again. Then she said, more quietly, "The only way to keep the baby is to marry, don't you understand that!"

Julie felt sick. They were going in circles.

"At least *try* to see him once more. Do just that for me, just that one thing. Is that too much to ask?"

"But I won't tell him. I won't ever tell him."

Mrs. Lescaux shook her head in exasperation. "All right, all right. But at least see if he still cares for you. Please, I'm asking you this one thing. *Please.*"

Julie stared angrily at her hands. She hated the thought of trying to see him again. It would be humiliating and shaming and she knew it wouldn't help. Anyway, what excuse could she find for visiting him? She would rather die than just turn up and ask to see him; he would think that she still liked him, that she was still prepared to go off in the car with him. . . . The thought made her shudder. "Mother, I can't just go and see him, not like that, he'll think I have no pride."

"Well, you didn't, did you—" Mrs. Lescaux bit her lip.

Julie had cried so much she didn't think she could manage any more. But the tears came nevertheless, rolling effortlessly down her cheeks. She thought: I can't face any more.

She was tired of crying, tired of arguing. Her head throbbed and her throat ached. All she wanted to do was sleep. She would do anything for that, and for the privacy of her own room.

Wearily she said, "All right, Mother, you win. I'll try to see him tomorrow."

The bus lurched into bottom gear and began to climb slowly up the hill behind Millbay Docks. It was only a mile or two to the

Naval Dockyard, a journey which would take fifteen minutes at the most. Julie fought back a rising panic. She had found only the flimsiest of excuses for going to see Bill and she had the unpleasant feeling that he would see straight through it.

But it was the only pretext she had and it would have to do.

Back in the early summer Bill had taken her to a party aboard a small sailing boat moored in a creek near the dockyard. Late in the evening a few people started to sing sea ballads and everyone stopped to listen. Some of the ballads were mournful, about the cruelty of the sea and the separation of lovers. Julie had been taken by them. The evening had been still and utterly peaceful and, though the lights of Plymouth were brightly reflected in the calm water, the city seemed very far away. Julie had looked out beyond Drake's Island, to where the water was dark and cold, and she'd thought how romantic it all was. The sea, so vast and cruel, which asked so much of the noble men who sailed on it . . . and the songs, they were so lovely, so sad, with their tales of brave sailors who withstood so much only to drown in the icy water.

Afterward she told Bill how much she'd loved the songs. Two days later he thrust a book in her hand. It was a pocket edition of *Naval Songs and Ballads,* the only present he'd ever given her.

And now she was taking it back on the pretense that it had been a loan. He wouldn't be fooled for a moment, of course—he had told her it was a gift at the time—but it was the best she could do. And when they met it would at least give her something to talk about.

If they met. He might not be there at all. With a bit of luck he would be out for the day, driving up onto the moors with his new girl friend for a quiet Sunday lunch.

One thing at least, she hadn't dressed up for him. If he *was* there she didn't want him to think she had spent a lot of time over her appearance. There were no white gloves today, nor a hat. She was wearing a plain blue summer frock with an off-white linen coat. Her long dark hair was drawn back from her face by two combs, but otherwise it was loose and unpinned, as if she were going out on an errand. That was exactly the impression she wanted to make.

The bus trundled past the main gates of the dockyard and came to a noisy halt in the next street. Julie got out and walked toward

the gates of HMS Drake, the shore establishment attached to the dockyard. She was dreading the next part. She would have to ask for him at the gate and admit that no, she wasn't expected, and the men on the gate would look at her knowingly, and smile at each other. She thought: Still more humiliation. It never ends.

She approached the gatehouse and saw that there were three sentries on duty. As she came toward them, two of them exchanged glances. She thought: Oh God, this is going to be even worse than I thought.

Suddenly there was a burst of noise.

Julie jumped with fright and spun around. It was the roar of a car engine. The car itself, a vivid blue Austin 7, rattled past and ground to a half beside the sentries. A young man was leaning out of the window waving a pass in his hand.

Julie stood stock still and tried to regain her breath. She was shaking with fright.

The young man was looking back at her with a rueful expression. Then his head disappeared into the car and the door was flung open. He leaped out and said, "I'm terribly sorry, I didn't mean to startle you. I came round the corner rather fast, I'm afraid." He grinned at her, then looked serious again. "I say, you're really shaken. I'm so sorry. What an idiot I am."

"I'm fine. It was rather a shock, that's all."

"You're sure you're all right then?" He peered at her solicitously and put a hand on her elbow.

"Yes, really."

"Well . . . if you're sure." He glanced at the sentries. "Are you being looked after? I mean, can I find anyone for you?"

"No, no, I . . ." Julie paused. The young man looked vaguely familiar and she realized she must have met him before. He was dressed in a large shapeless sweater and baggy rust-colored trousers, and on his head was an old black cap speckled with paint. He looked rather roguish, like a pirate.

He was smiling at her; there was no doubt he was very charming, but Julie wondered if it wasn't laid on. Bill had been charming too, but that had meant nothing, nothing at all.

He was waiting for an answer and she said, "I was hoping to see a friend, but I think I've missed him. . . ." It sounded weak and she trailed off.

"It's impossible to find anyone on a Sunday. But if you want me to ask . . . ?" He was regarding her intently, waiting for her reply, his eyes friendly and inquiring. Maybe she'd been wrong: maybe he was everything he seemed, and wasn't the sort to make fun of her. She decided to trust him after all: it would be a lot less embarrassing if he, rather than the sentries, asked about Bill.

She said, "Well, perhaps you could ask if Bill Crozier is around." She looked down, a little flustered, then remembered the book and fumbled in her handbag. "I wanted to return something he lent me." She held the book up as if it were a trophy.

"No problem." He smiled and she noticed the eyes again. "Why don't you hop in the car and we'll go and ask in the wardroom. Someone there might know."

Once they were inside the establishment, he laughed. "We're not allowed to drive fast in here, so you're safe!" He negotiated the car around a sharp corner and she could feel him looking at her. He said, "Didn't you come to that party on my boat? The one where we had the singsong?"

"Oh, was it your boat? I didn't know."

"Yes, *Dancer*'s her name." He laughed again. "Oh, and my name's Richard Ashley. We were probably introduced, but there were so many people there . . ."

"I'm Juliette Lescaux."

"Of course!" He lifted both hands off the wheel in an expansive gesture. "I remember the French name now. *Are* you French in fact?"

Julie thought: God, he knows my name. Perhaps I'm infamous already. Perhaps Bill has been talking about me. . . . She glanced across at the young man but his expression hadn't changed, it was still interested and amused. No, she thought, I'm being stupid: he really did remember my name because it's French.

She said, "Half. I'm half-French. My father came from Brittany."

"What a fantastic place to come from. I sailed over there last year and had the most wonderful time. The locals were so amazed to see old *Dancer* and me all alone that they couldn't do enough for us."

"You sailed the boat alone?"

"Oh yes, always do if I can. Nothing to compare with it."

Julie didn't reply immediately: she was thinking of what would happen if Bill was in the wardroom. She dragged her mind back to what Richard Ashley had said. "Isn't it risky? I mean what happens in a storm?" They drew up outside the wardroom. Julie regarded it with horror.

"In a storm?" Ashley was considering her question. "Oh, I just shorten sail and go below for a sleep." Leaving the engine running, he got out of the car and stuck his head back through the window. "Unless I'm about to bump into the land. Then I sail like hell!" He grinned. "Won't be a minute." She watched him walk to the door and disappear into the building.

Julie sat still, thankful for the safety of the little blue car. She began to pray that Bill wouldn't be there. The last time they'd met, Bill had made it plain that he didn't want to see her again. Well, he hadn't actually *said* so, not in so many words, but she'd known by the long silences and the way he'd avoided her eyes.

The door to the wardroom opened and Julie's heart went into her mouth. Richard Ashley came out and shut the door behind him. He was alone.

Richard slid back into the driver's seat. "Sorry, no luck, no one seems to know where he is. But he *is* expected back fairly early this evening."

Julie wondered what to do next. She didn't want to go home, not yet.

"I say . . ." Richard's face was alight with enthusiasm. "What about coming down to *Dancer*. I'm doing a bit of work on her today. I could use someone to help . . . I mean with the sandwich-making and all that. Everything's on board: cheese, bread, you name it. It would be much more fun than working on my own. Then I could bring you back here later."

"Oh—" The invitation took Julie by surprise. She didn't know this man, and she wasn't sure she wanted to spend an afternoon with him. Anyway she wasn't dressed for a boat. She looked down at her flimsy dress and stockinged legs. Climbing about in boats would ruin her stockings and probably dirty her dress too.

Richard followed her look. "Don't worry about your clothes. As long as you don't mind taking your shoes off, then the heels won't damage the deck."

At first she wondered how a boat's deck could be so important, then she saw the funny side of it and smiled a little. He looked at her, puzzled, then understanding flashed into his eyes. He said, "You'll have to forgive me. You see, *Dancer*'s the love of my life and, like all good women, she has to be pampered!" Laughing, he let in the clutch and the car moved off.

They stopped for a moment outside another building, and after he collected some things from his quarters, they were through the gates and heading toward the Tamar River. Julie realized they were on their way to the boat, though she hadn't actually said she would go. But she was glad. Why not? She had nothing better to do.

They left the main road and started slowly down a rough lane. As the car bumped and swayed along, Julie asked, "How did you manage to find this amazing color?"

"Sorry?"

The little car was noisy and Julie raised her voice. "The car, why is it such a bright blue?"

"Ah! What color is every *other* Austin Seven in the world?"

"Black. Or sometimes gray. Or a sort of beige."

"Exactly! Very dreary. That's why I decided to paint this one blue!" He laughed again. He seemed to laugh most of the time, and Julie found herself smiling too.

She decided she was glad she had come.

The afternoon was warm and Julie lay on the foredeck with her face toward the sun. She had taken her stockings and shoes off in the car and left them on the back seat with her coat. Richard had lent her a waterproof jacket to put around her shoulders in the small rowing boat and then, when they arrived on board *Dancer,* he had found her an enormous sweater. She probably looked extraordinary in it, but she didn't mind. Somehow it didn't seem very important.

She had done very little all day and it had been wonderful. She had made the sandwiches and boiled up the kettle for a cup of tea. Then she had lain down here and let herself be lulled by the lapping of the water and the gentle movements of the boat.

Eventually she drifted off into a pleasant dreamless sleep, very different from the long, troubled nights of the previous week.

Only the occasional noise of hammering or loud humming from the inside of the boat interrupted the stillness of the day.

When she awoke she guessed it was late afternoon, about four or five o'clock. Richard was sitting on top of the cabin roof with a mug of tea in his hand, watching her with amusement. He grinned. "Have a nice sleep?"

"Oh, I'm sorry. I didn't mean to sleep so long. I just seemed to nod off."

"Yes, it does that to you, the sea." He put down the mug and said, "Look, I've finished my carpentry. Well . . . I wouldn't say my carpentry was ever exactly *finished,* but it's as *done* as it ever will be—and it's still standing. So why don't we go for a short sail? Just into the sound and back. Won't take long." He stood up and made a sweeping gesture with his arm. "It'll blow the cobwebs away!"

Julie had never been sailing before and the idea didn't appeal to her at all. Yachts always seemed to be on the point of tipping over. She also suspected that she was prone to seasickness. Once she and Mother had gone on a steamer trip to Fowey and Julie had felt very peculiar on the way back. Anyway, she knew absolutely nothing about sailing.

He was waiting expectantly and she said, "Thank you. It's awfully kind of you to offer but . . . well, I've never sailed before."

"Then it's high time you did!"

"No, really, I . . . I get seasick."

"Don't worry! Most people do—*especially* me. I'm always sick as a dog for the first day or two. But that's out at sea. It'll be fine in the sound, there's not a ripple, not a wave. Honestly, trust me!" He leaned down and offered her his hand.

She stared up at him and thought: Yes, I do trust you, it's impossible not to. She took his hand and let him pull her up.

He pushed her gently in the direction of the cockpit and went forward to untie a rope.

She called, "Where shall I sit? On the seat in the back here?"

He laughed. "It's called the cockpit, and it's situated in something called the stern! This sharp end up here, this is called the bow. Yes, just sit there, next to the companionway."

Julie sat down and gripped the piece of wood that ran around the cockpit. She watched him pull up the sails and arrange the

ropes. Then he threw a chain off the front of the boat and she realized they were off. For a moment everything flapped and there was the most terrible din. He ran back to the cockpit and pulled some more ropes. The sails stopped flapping and *Dancer* leaped forward.

For a while the yacht skimmed along quite steadily and Julie relaxed a little. Then the little boat shuddered and the next moment it was tipping over. Julie gripped the side and felt a touch of fear. It seemed to her that there was nothing to stop the boat from going all the way over and turning upside down, yet, on looking back, she saw that Richard was steering the boat quite happily.

He said, "Isn't this wonderful! There's nothing like a good sail! It's a wonderful day for it, too. A really nice breeze."

Julie looked toward the bow again. It seemed to her that there was altogether too much wind. The boat was still leaning over at a sharp angle and showed no signs of coming upright again. Julie found it impossible to believe that everything was all right. She could not rid herself of the feeling that something unexpected and frightening would happen at any moment.

Dancer sped past Drake's Island and into the open sound. Small wavelets rushed at the boat and *Dancer*'s bow pushed a curtain of fine spray up into the air and back into the cockpit. Julie shivered slightly and wondered how much farther they would go. Then Richard leaned forward and loosened some ropes. The boat changed direction and gradually came upright again. Immediately the motion was easier and the waves, instead of rushing at the boat, seemed to be traveling with it.

"That's better, eh? No point in getting wet." He looked at her with a funny mock frown, and she realized he had changed course for her, to make the sail more enjoyable.

"Thanks. It's better like this."

"It's always better going with the wind. I only wish the wind always blew from behind. But it never does. Quite the opposite, in fact." He cast his eyes skyward. "Sometimes I think there's a heavenly conspiracy to make sure it always comes from ahead."

"Do you really get seasick?"

"Most certainly. There are two stages to seasickness, so they say, one when you want to die, and the second when you're

frightened you're not going to. I go through both! The only remedy is to keep busy, stay on deck as much as possible—and remember it can't last forever."

"And do you often go far? To places like Brittany?"

"Whenever I have the time I do. This summer I went to the Scillies. Now the Scillies! They're the most wonderful islands in the world. I spent a whole fortnight there and, you wouldn't believe it, but I anchored at a different place every night. Most of the islands are uninhabited. You can walk all day and see nothing but birds. At one point I didn't see another living soul for four whole days."

Julie thought: What a strange one you are. All that laughter and charm and you like being on your own.

He went on, "The Scillies are covered in wrecks, literally hundreds of them. Not surprising really, when you consider where they are, stuck miles out into the sea in the entrance to the English Channel. And they're low, of course; ships can't see them until they're almost on top of them. Not a good place to find yourself in bad weather." He laughed as if such danger were a great joke and Julie suspected that he would like nothing better than to be sailing off the Isles of Scilly in a storm.

He started to tell her some stories about the Scillies; about the famous wrecks and the people who lived there and the beautiful scenery. As he talked Julie found herself watching him. He was attractive, there was no doubt about that, but not in an obvious way. He wasn't as good-looking as Bill had been, and he would probably put on weight when he was older. But those eyes did light up his face. He reminded her of a teddy bear, kind and safe and—yes, cuddly.

She decided that her first impression had been wrong. His charm was not laid on, it was perfectly natural; it stemmed from his enormous enthusiasm for everything he did.

She thought: I could have liked you a lot. *Could have*—she had used the past tense automatically. There would be no boyfriends now: that was all over.

Anyway, he probably wasn't interested. Why should he be? There was nothing special about her; Bill had made that quite plain at their last meeting. Besides—how stupid of her not to think of it—he probably had a girl friend already.

Dancer was sailing quietly into the Cattewater, the creek that

leads to the Barbican—the oldest part of the city—and to the fishing harbor. Julie was quite enjoying herself now that there were no waves and hardly any wind.

Richard said, "Best not get into the harbor itself. We'll probably meet a fishing boat coming out. I'll jibe her round and we'll head back to the mooring."

Julie nodded, not having the slightest idea of what jibing involved. The next moment he shouted, "Mind your head," and there was a great crash.

For a second Julie thought the mast had come down, but then she realized that it was the noise of the sail changing sides. She laughed and put her hand to her chest. "You might have warned me!"

"Sorry, I forgot you didn't know about sailing. Listen. I'll explain a few of the basics. It's really quite simple. There are just three things to remember. First, always know where the wind's coming from. Second, pull the sail in just enough to stop it flapping. And three, always try to avoid jibing!"

Julie found herself laughing with him. "Then how do you turn round?"

"Ah, you turn *into* the wind. That's called tacking."

She shook her head. "I'm afraid it's all beyond me. In future I'll leave the sailing to you."

He didn't say anything but stared at her, searching her eyes. She glanced quickly away, angry with herself. He had taken her remark as an indication of interest; he had thought she was staking a claim. She'd have to make it quite clear that she hadn't meant anything of the sort. What a pity. The day had been going so well.

He was talking again and she saw that he was serious now. "Sailing is a wonderful freedom, you know. You can just set off for who-knows-where whenever you please. I always keep *Dancer* stocked up with food and water so I can just up and go whenever I have the time."

"Isn't it enough to be in the Navy?"

"Oh no, it's not the same at all. Being at sea with three hundred other people in a tin ship is . . . well, it's my job. I enjoy it, but it doesn't compare with setting off on your own. There's nothing like it."

"But why on your own?"

He thought for a moment. "I don't always go on my own. I often sail with my father—*Dancer*'s really his boat, not mine. But half the trouble is I haven't met a crew who wants to do the same kind of sailing as I do. So, there's no other solution. You see, I believe you've got to go out and do what you want to do."

Julie stared at him. It must be wonderful to be so sure of what you wanted and to have such confidence in your ability to succeed. She admired him for his ability to make his own decisions. She thought: Why can't I be like that? Why am I so bad at deciding? It was easier when you were a man, of course; somehow men had fewer people to consider. But all the same, she should be able to do it, to decide things for the best.

As they sailed back across the open sound the wind increased, and *Dancer* pulled away, cleaving a straight path through the waves. Julie tried to enjoy herself but felt the unhappiness closing in on her again. The day was almost over. Soon she would have to decide whether to return to the wardroom and risk the dreadful humiliation of seeing Bill, or give up and go home to face her mother. What a choice!

Dancer drifted slowly into the creek and Richard Ashley sprinted forward to lower the sails. As soon as he'd finished he ran back and pushed the tiller hard over so that *Dancer* turned in a neat semicircle. Then he picked up a boathook and, running forward again, used it to fish a bright red buoy out of the water. He was breathing hard. He called back, "You see, nothing to it! You could learn in no time!"

She smiled. Sailing was as much a mystery to her as it had been at the beginning of the day. The only thing she *could* say was that the experience had been less unpleasant than she'd thought. But the sea still terrified her. She decided she had no desire to try it again.

By the time they returned to the bright blue car it was six o'clock. On the journey back to the officers' quarters, he asked, "Well, what do you want to do? Shall we see if Bill's there? Or do you want to give me the book to pass on?"

"I . . . I don't know."

"Shall we see if he's there then?"

Julie was frozen with indecision. Whatever she did would be wrong. And now there was the added complication of this man

—he must have guessed what the situation with Bill was: boy gives girl brush-off, girl can't take hint. He must think she was cheap, to be chasing after a man like this.

Suddenly she made up her mind. "No, I'll go straight home, thanks. The book really isn't important. I can catch a bus outside the dockyard."

"No. I won't hear of it. The least I can do is to drive you home. Where do you live?"

She told him and leaned her head back on the seat, happier than she had been for days. It was lovely to have made a decision, and now she had taken it she knew it was the right one. It would have been dreadful to go cap in hand to a man she didn't love and certainly didn't respect. Bill had made it plain that the affair was over. It was up to her now, to make the best of a bad situation.

She would go away and make a fresh start.

She glanced across at Richard Ashley. His face was set in lines of concentration as he negotiated the narrow streets of Plymouth. She was thankful to him. He was right about reaching out for things and leading your own life. If you didn't, it seemed to her that everyone else used you to lead theirs. Her mother meant well, but she had always pushed Julie into doing things *she* wanted her to do. And Bill, he had used her too.

Yes, she would definitely go away.

But not to anywhere in England: here there was nowhere to go and no one to help her. It would have to be France then. The thought was frightening. She had never met any of her father's immediate family. All she knew was that her grandparents must be very old by now—perhaps dead even—and that she had an uncle and an aunt. And possibly some cousins, though she wasn't sure about that either.

She would have to tell them she had been married, of course, and that it hadn't worked out. They probably wouldn't believe her, but it wouldn't matter as long as appearances were kept up. She would go out and buy a wedding ring. The thought gave her a curious thrill. She would call herself Mrs. something—but not Crozier, that was for sure. She would have to think up a good name.

She would need a passport, she hadn't thought of that before. She seemed to remember that when you were under twenty-one

you had to have parental permission. That would lead to problems with Mother. Julie sighed at the thought of yet more battles ahead.

"Anything the matter?" Richard was looking at her, concern on his face.

Julie realized she must have sighed out loud. "Oh no, nothing. I was just thinking, that's all."

The little car drew up outside Number 34 Radley Terrace. Julie had no doubt her mother would be peering through the curtains, but she didn't care. She turned to him. "Thanks so much. It's been a lovely day. I can't tell you how much I enjoyed it."

"It was *my* pleasure entirely!" He glanced down at his hands, then said, "Look, it would be super if you could come again sometime. Would you like that? I could do with a first mate."

"Oh, I . . . I'm very honored to be asked. But, well . . . I'm going away soon, very soon."

"Ah!"

He was taken by surprise, she could see that, and she tried to smooth the moment over. "I'm going to live with my relatives in France for a while, to work there and learn the language. I've always wanted to go."

"To Brittany?"

She nodded.

"Well, I hope you have a good time there. I'm sure you will. The Bretons are wonderful people." He sounded disappointed and a little puzzled. He must think her devious for not having mentioned the trip before.

Julie wished she could explain, but there was no point in starting explanations she couldn't finish. It was best as it was.

She opened the door and said, "Good-bye, and thank you again."

He smiled at her and the kindness was back in his eyes. "Bye. I hope it all goes well!"

What a nice man you are, she thought.

She closed the door and walked up the path. The sound of the noisy little engine faded down the road. She turned to wave, but the bright blue car was already out of sight around the corner.

She paused at the front door, the key in her hand, and thought: Brittany. Yes, I'll definitely go to Brittany.

It was easy to say now, surprisingly easy . . . but would she ever be able to go through with it?

She thought: I'm going to *have* to.

And she opened the door and went quickly into the house before she changed her mind.

3   The Bay of Lübeck is wide and open. On its southern shore lies the busy port of Travemünde and beyond that, some miles up the broad Trave River, is the city of Lübeck. On the northwestern shore of the bay, some twenty miles from Travemünde and well away from prying eyes, is the small harbor of Pelzerhaken. Here the German Navy had built one of its principal research establishments, a group of low, ugly buildings surrounded by barbed wire.

On this September day a blustery northeaster was blowing in from the Arctic, bringing a cool foretaste of the winter ahead. Out in the wide bay short steep seas bowled in from the open Baltic, throwing angry white surf on the holiday beaches lining the shore. At the single wharf in Pelzerhaken Harbor the trials ship *Welle* tugged uneasily at her lines as the strong wind pulled at the mass of aerials and strange dish-shaped objects sprouting from her superstructure.

David Freymann shivered and pulled his jacket tighter around his neck. He felt the ship move slightly and hoped that, once they got under way, he wouldn't be seasick. He usually was, even in a rowing boat.

Ellen said he was stupid to go on this trip because he was bound to disgrace himself. She also said that the only reason he got seasick was that he was overweight and didn't take any exercise. Ellen had a way of implying that everything was somehow David's fault, but he didn't mind. In most ways she was a good

wife and she wasn't having an easy time at the moment. She complained about being neglected and she was absolutely right. His work was taking up more and more of his hours. He had tried to explain to her how important it was and how much it meant to him, but she didn't understand. That, he thought fondly, was women for you.

He realized with a shock that, come October, they would have been married fifteen years. On their anniversary it would be a good idea to spoil her a bit; he would take her out for a meal in Berlin, to a good restaurant on the Unter den Linden. Fifteen years: he could hardly believe it. Little Cecile was almost eight. It was strange how the time flew so quickly, yet one remained young inside. He'd be forty-five this year, almost middle-aged.

Still, as long as you achieved something lasting, age didn't really matter. He looked up at one of the dish-shaped objects above the *Welle*'s bridge. Now *there* was something lasting, something that really mattered. An achievement that any man would be proud of.

David walked across the deck to where Hans Rathenow was standing. Hans had been David's colleague for a year, ever since they had joined the new Gema Company together. Hans was a good sort: hardworking, straightforward and kind. David liked him a lot. There was a bond of fellowship and camaraderie between them which came from working on the same project. Together they had solved the problem of range measurement. It had been a hard one to crack but David had known they would do it.

Hans inclined his head in the direction of the land. "The brass are late."

David laughed. "That's their privilege."

"How many are there going to be? Do you know? I hope there aren't too many, otherwise we'll never be able to deal with all their questions." Hans liked to have plenty of time to consider questions, so that his answers could be as precise and complete as possible.

The two men watched a truck bump along the wharf and stop in front of a warehouse. Hans turned and said, "By the way, have you heard the rumor about Telefunken? Evidently, they're to be given a government contract like ours, but to develop a device for aircraft."

"Oh." David tried to hide his surprise. "I thought *we* were to do the work on small devices. I . . . I've been working on the program scheduling."

"Yes." Hans gave David a sympathetic glance. "I know. And I know you are right in your approach. But I fear that Schmidt does not see it your way."

David stared into the distance and sighed. Schmidt, head of the research program and recently appointed Chief Scientist of the Third Reich, had long been a thorn in his side.

David touched the other man's arm. "I tell you something, my friend—not only am I sure that it is possible to develop small devices for aircraft, but I am certain those devices could be made incredibly powerful. Can you imagine what definition and detail could be achieved by using exceptionally short waves?"

"Yes, but, David, no valve exists which is remotely capable of such a thing. Where is your power to come from?"

"I have an idea; I believe it could work. It would take less than six months to prove either way. All I need is two people, a bit of space and some resources." He ran a hand through his hair. "But this new contract . . . now Schmidt will have the perfect excuse to refuse me permission. And I've no doubt he *will* refuse."

The wind gusted across the deck and David stamped his feet to ward off the cold. He said, "I could offer my services to Telefunken, I suppose. Perhaps they might be prepared to follow my idea in spite of Schmidt."

"I doubt it very much." Hans paused, deep in thought. When he finally spoke, it was very quietly and David had to turn his head to hear. "You must think very carefully about your position, David. I worry about you."

"What do you mean? Schmidt cannot eat me. He is stupid and arrogant, certainly, but he knows my worth."

"It is not Schmidt himself I worry about. It is the . . . the official policy."

David began to understand. "You mean I will be pushed out because I am Jewish?" He shook his head. "First, I don't believe this silly campaign will go on. Second, they will never interfere with work like mine; it's too important."

"I hope you're right, but I think you're being too generous. I fear it will get worse, not better."

David shrugged. The events of the last year had been . . . unfortunate, even—yes—deplorable. The Nuremberg decrees had been a shock. Most Jews had been deprived of their citizenship and intermarriage with Aryans was forbidden.

Too late for Ellen and me, David thought. They can't *unmarry* us after all these years.

There were other things, of course. A number of Jews had been arrested and never seen again. But then the same was happening to others: leftists, intellectuals, troublemakers. It wasn't *only* the Jews. It was just a question of keeping your nose clean. Staying out of trouble.

"No, Hans. I honestly don't think it'll get any worse." He thought of adding: anyway, not for me. But it sounded too selfish and uncaring.

A fleet of cars appeared at the end of the wharf and there was a flurry of activity around the ship as sailors stood to attention. The two men began to walk slowly along the deck toward the group already waiting at the top of the gangway. Hans was still frowning and David said softly, "So the Jews are excluded from the professions, but that is nothing new. It was the same before the Great War. Anyway, I am more German than Jewish. I'm only half-Jewish, in fact. I haven't been inside a synagogue for years, my wife is gentile, my daughter goes to a nice Christian school. I am no threat!"

"That's not the point," Hans persisted. "You are officially Jewish. You have your scientific status—*at present*—but you are not safe where you are. Why don't you think about working in this place?" He indicated the complex of stone buildings that made up the research establishment.

David stood still, astonished. "Here? Why?"

"Haven't you heard? The Navy is refusing to throw Jews out of the service. Old Raeder is defying Hitler. As a naval scientist you would be safe. Hitler will never take on the whole Navy: he's too frightened of it."

David walked on slowly, shaking his head. Hans meant well, there was no doubt about that, but come and work here? No, it was impossible. Very little original work was done in the establishment. He would die of frustration.

The two men joined the rest of the scientific and naval personnel standing silently in a knot by the rail.

David stroked down his windswept hair and watched the new arrivals make their way up the gangway. He recognized the well-known figure of Grand Admiral Raeder, Commander-in-Chief of the German Navy, but he was not certain about the others. He was no expert on rank or uniforms, but he guessed there were at least five other admirals in the group. Behind the Grand Admiral was Schmidt, looking as officious and self-satisfied as ever. David sighed inwardly. How simple life would be if the Schmidts of this world were not allowed to poke their noses into the *real* work. The problem with Schmidt was that he was not overblessed with brains. He had never been a good scientist, let alone a great one. Perhaps that was why he had grabbed an administrative job: it was the only thing he could do.

David stood back as Schmidt started to introduce the managers of the Gema Company to the naval officers. David thought how strange official protocol was, when the organizers came before the people who actually did the work. Still, as long as he was allowed to get on with his project, he didn't mind who took the glory.

When it was David's turn to come forward he tried to concentrate on the name and rank of each man as he shook hands with him, but apart from Raeder, he managed to memorize only about half of them. After the introductions, one name—Doenitz—stood out in his mind and he tried to think why. Then he remembered: it had just been announced that Doenitz was to command the new submarine arm of the Kriegsmarine.

U-boats: now there were vessels in need of a really small high-definition apparatus. If the opportunity arose it would be interesting to talk to Doenitz. David looked at the rings on Doenitz's sleeve to make sure that his rank was indeed no higher than that of captain. There was a chance, then, that David would be allowed to talk to him without Schmidt interrupting. Schmidt did not like anybody talking to really senior officers without his being present. He said it was a matter of protecting his scientists from outside interference, but David knew better. Schmidt just hated anything going on without his knowledge, particularly when a scientist had views that differed from his own.

The main group had moved off toward the bridge. Schmidt was pointing to the bowl apparatus and explaining the reason for its shape which differed considerably from that of the earlier

prototypes. As Schmidt's voice droned on, the deck vibrated beneath David's feet and the *Welle* moved gently away from the wharf. The wind was coming in great gusts now; the sea outside must be very rough.

David began to wish he hadn't come. He'd always disliked physical discomfort—as a child he'd been hopeless at sports and rough games—and he had no doubt the *Welle* would toss and roll like a pig.

Schmidt's voice had ceased and everyone moved into the large chart room behind the wheelhouse. David followed and looked for a quiet corner to stand in, but Schmidt impatiently beckoned him forward and directed him to join some junior officers. A group had formed a circle around a large metal cabinet bolted to the chart room floor. On the top of the cabinet was a circular screen which the senior officers were watching expectantly.

Schmidt cleared his throat and announced, "It will take us a few moments to get to the open sea, where the device can best be demonstrated. We beg your indulgence, but we assure you that the wait will not be in vain. You will not be disappointed!"

David felt faintly embarrassed at Schmidt's manner. He was turning the demonstration into a circus performance. The brass were intelligent men; they didn't go in for dramatics.

Suddenly there was a quiet voice at David's elbow. A young officer stood with his hand outstretched. "We have not met. My name is Fischer, Karl Fischer."

"Ah, I'm Freymann, David Freymann." He shook the hand, then said by way of explanation, "I work on this project. My field is radio ranging."

"It will be most interesting to see this device working. I had no idea anything like this was being developed. It is really most extraordinary."

"And yourself, are you on the naval staff?"

"No, no." As Fischer spoke, David noticed how even and finely drawn were the younger man's features. The hair was blond, the eyes pale blue: he supposed this was what the Nazis meant by Aryan. Then he thought: Why on earth did I think that? I'm getting as bad as Hans.

Fischer was saying, "I have come here with Captain Doenitz. I'm with the First U-boat Flotilla at Kiel, in command of *U-13*."

"Ah." David did not know much about the new submarine arm.

"It is the first operational flotilla, and it is a great honor to serve in it."

"Indeed, indeed. It is wonderful that Germany has submarines again, after all these years."

Fischer pointed to the device humming quietly in the center of the chart room. "And that, will it be useful for submarines?"

"Well, at present—in this form—no. As you see the whole thing is too large. Really it is only suitable for use on ships—or on land, of course. It would never fit into submarines or, for that matter, aircraft."

"I see, I see. And what about being *detected* by such a thing? Could an enemy detect *us* easily? I am thinking particularly of when we are on the surface at night."

David looked at Fischer with new respect. Here at least was someone who recognized the possibility of an enemy possessing this device, which was more than Schmidt did. He said, "Well, yes, a surfaced submarine *could* be picked up. But it would be difficult. A submarine is so low in the water—and so much smaller than a ship, of course—that the conditions would have to be perfect for an enemy to see you. I mean, a calm sea and the range between three and five miles. But even if a ship did manage to detect you I imagine there would be plenty of time to dive and get away. A plane . . . now a plane would be a bit more tricky. If a plane managed to detect you it could be on top of you very quickly."

"I thought you said it was impossible to construct a device small enough to fit in a plane."

"Ah, no. What I said was, *this* device is not suitable for planes. I did not say it was impossible to develop small devices. Quite the opposite."

Fischer nodded slowly. "After the demonstration, could we talk again? I know that Captain Doenitz would be most interested in what you have to say."

"Of course." David was pleased. It would be an honor to talk to Doenitz.

The *Welle* was pitching gently and David realized they must have reached the open sea. Through one of the chart room's large ports he could see rolling, white-topped waves. He tried to

concentrate on the horizon: someone had told him it stopped you from feeling sick.

Schmidt was speaking again. "As you know we have been working hard on the development of the DT device. Incidentally, I shall continue to call it by its cover name, the DT Apparatus, because secrecy is so important. Originally you may have heard it called the revolving turret device, but more properly it should be called a radio detection and ranging device, or radar for short." He cleared his throat and paused. Ever theatrical, David thought. Well, perhaps he was right. It was, after all, a special occasion.

"When we last demonstrated the device, we could not give you great range accuracy. And of course it is not much good if you don't know how far away your opponent is. But now . . ." Schmidt put a hand on the metal cabinet. "I am glad to say that, by means of a revolutionary new concept, we can give you the range of your enemy to within about a quarter of a nautical mile."

Schmidt's audience was silent and expectant. For a moment there was no sound except the hum of the device and the vibration of the ship's engines. Then the chief scientist continued, "We have developed a *pulse* system which sends out a short but powerful radio signal in a single burst. It then waits for the signal to return before sending another. By measuring the time it takes for the signal to get to its target and return, we can measure range with a good degree of accuracy."

Schmidt raised his voice. "Furthermore, gentlemen, that range is now improved. You will be able to see land approximately ten miles away, other ships eight miles away, and aircraft as much as fifteen miles away."

He stepped to one side. "And now I invite you to look at the screen, to see for yourselves." Schmidt pointed to a piece of coast visible on the port side and put his finger onto the screen. Comparisons were made and there was a great deal of nodding; the brass were obviously impressed. David felt pleased. Schmidt then ordered the aerial to be rotated and the group examined the echo of a ship which was just visible on the horizon. Raeder summoned more of his colleagues and Schmidt began his explanations afresh.

David was feeling sick. The trick of staring at the horizon had

not worked at all. The *Welle* seemed to be rolling and pitching in every direction and each new movement took his stomach by surprise. He edged toward the door in case he had to make a sudden dash for the rail. He realized he should try to be unobtrusive, but he was fast getting to the stage where he didn't care.

Suddenly the sickness welled up. David pulled open the door and heaved over the rail. As soon as his stomach was empty he felt better. The fresh wind helped too; it blew the cobwebs out of his head. But he decided against going back into the chart room; he wouldn't last five minutes in there.

After a while he became mesmerized by the rise and fall of the waves. At one point he looked down to where they growled along the ship's side. But that was a mistake—it brought the nausea back—and he quickly looked up again. Then he tried closing his eyes and found that, despite the sharp wind, he was able to doze where he stood. The sensation was quite pleasant: he felt as if he were floating, gently suspended in water.

"Ahem." Someone was clearing his throat. For a moment David hoped the sound might go away, but it was repeated. Reluctantly he opened his eyes and turned round.

It was Fischer. Beside him stood the tall, erect figure of Captain Doenitz.

Fischer said, "Herr Freymann, may I introduce Captain Doenitz. The Captain would be most grateful if you would answer a few of his queries."

David tried to wake himself up. He smiled thinly and said, "Of course."

The captain had a sharp face with thin lips and protruding ears. But most of all David noticed his eyes, which were small and penetrating, like those of a small animal.

Doenitz spoke slowly, choosing his words carefully. "I have grasped the principles of the DT device. I understand how it can be used against aircraft and surface vessels *by* surface vessels. But I gather this device will never be suitable for submarines. Is that correct?"

"In its present form, no. It is too large and cumbersome."

"Can it be made smaller?"

"It is possible, but it means using much shorter wavelengths."

"And this can be done?"

"Work on slightly shorter wavelengths is to start soon, I believe."

"Slightly—?"

David looked down. What was he to do? Tell the truth and suffer Schmidt's wrath, or toe the official line?

He brought his eyes back to Doenitz's face. The captain's expression was inquiring but anxious. The answer was obviously important to him.

David thought: Why not? This man deserves to know.

He said, "Yes, only *slightly* shorter. Investigation into really short wavelengths is not being considered at present. There is a belief that such short wavelengths are impossible to generate— and that they would be *less* efficient rather than *more* efficient. But," David said firmly, "this is only a belief. It is by no means proved."

Doenitz was absorbing the information. "But if it *was* possible," he said slowly, "it would be useful for us?"

"Not just useful, it would be *revolutionary!*" David talked rapidly, his sickness forgotten. "First, short waves would make the device very small indeed. It would be no more than the size of— of, say, a large suitcase standing on its end. Obviously it would fit easily inside a plane or a submarine. That would mean—well, you can imagine! For the Luftwaffe, it would mean they would be able to see enemy planes coming from miles away, even at night. For you, it would mean you could find your enemy and make your attack in the blackest of conditions!"

David always liked to understand the practical applications of his work. So few scientists did, and that, he believed, was a great mistake. It meant you were much slower to appreciate the shortcomings of your inventions—and slower, too, to *foresee* problems.

David paused before going on. So far he had stated facts that were generally accepted—although Schmidt would have a seizure if he knew David had mentioned them. But it was the next part —the most *important* part—that was really David's personal theory. And not only was the theory unproved, but Schmidt was bitterly opposed to it.

He hesitated, then said quickly, "It would also be revolutionary for a second reason—though I must tell you immediately that I am almost alone in this belief. I believe that a valve could be

developed to give enormous power on short waves. This would mean that the device would be small *and* immensely powerful. It would give the most incredible definition . . ."

He was not explaining it properly. These men wanted to know what it meant in practical terms. He searched for the right words. "It would *pick out* each individual object in a group of objects, almost like a photograph. This device here"—he indicated the cabinet in the chart room—"is useful only for seeing objects against the *sky,* so to speak—for things standing out against a blank background, like an aircraft in the sky or a ship on the horizon. Even then it would be of limited use in a plane because when it is angled down to the land or the sea it cannot pick out individual targets. It gets too many echoes back from the sea or the land for the user to distinguish individual towns or buildings or ships out of the blur."

David paused to make sure he had been understood. The two men nodded and he went on. "Now a shortwave device could see like a pair of eyes. From the air it could look *downward* and read the land like a map. It could pick out individual towns, rivers, lakes and roads; it could identify individual bombing targets; it could see small objects floating on the surface of the sea; it could see a submarine sitting on the water. *Nothing* would be hidden from it."

Doenitz stared at David in alarm. "If this is true, it is very important. But you say that there is doubt about this, that some people believe such a device would be *less* efficient?"

David spoke carefully. "There is a school of thought which believes it is impossible to develop the power. But personally I believe the necessary valve *can* be developed."

"If there is the slightest chance of it, then—" Doenitz pursed his lips and looked out to sea.

"Of course I would have to do a lot of work on it. And I would need official support . . ."

Doenitz looked at him sharply. "I have no say in scientific policy. However . . . I shall do what I can."

David nodded and found himself wondering how much longer he could survive without being sick again. He gave himself a minute, certainly no more. It had been all right while he'd been talking.

Doenitz fixed his dark penetrating stare on David and said, "So a submarine would be particularly vulnerable to a shortwave device?"

"Yes."

"Do we know if anybody else is working on it? The British, for instance?"

"I'm not sure. I can only say that, as a scientist, I have read nothing—I have heard nothing—to indicate that they have the secret."

"If they did . . ."

David thought quickly. "If they did then we could produce a warning device, a detector, to tell a vessel that radar was being operated against them."

Doenitz's eyes lit up. "Ah, so there *is* a defense."

"Yes, but we can only develop a detector when we have developed our own technology. No technology, no detector." David was forced to be brief; he had only a few seconds left.

"I understand. Thank you." Doenitz inclined his head and for a moment David thought he would continue. But he turned and walked away.

David threw himself across the rail and heaved miserably. Though his stomach was empty, the convulsions went on for several minutes. When he finally looked around the two naval officers had gone.

David laid his head on his arm. He no longer cared what he looked like; nor did he mind if people were laughing at him. He just wanted to die. There was no sign of land, and it seemed to him that they were still heading out to sea.

Hilf mir Gott! It was an expression his father often used. His father—dead, and thank God for that. He had been Jewish and proud of it.

"Freymann! Freymann!"

Without bothering to look up David knew it was Schmidt.

"Freymann, I am appalled!" The voice was angry, hissing like a snake. David waved a hand of acknowledgment. Nothing would make him raise his head again.

"I absolutely forbid you to speak to anyone else during this trip. You are absolutely not to be trusted. How dare you give people the idea that we don't know what we're doing!" The voice

spluttered for a moment. "Your lunatic ideas! They are dangerous and stupid and . . . I will speak to you later. In the meantime
keep away, just *keep away*!"

David waved a hand again. Schmidt's order suited him perfectly: no more talking and no more questions to answer. If no
one was going to believe him, there was no point anyway.

He was beginning to think Ellen was right: he should never
have come.

Doenitz excused himself from a discussion on the use of radar in
surface warfare and left the chart room. He chose to go out onto
the starboard side of the ship so as to avoid the scientist, Freymann, who was still wedged firmly against the port rail.

Doenitz walked slowly toward the afterdeck and wondered if
there had been any truth in what the odd little man had said. The
fellow had been so enthusiastic, so *sure*, that Doenitz had almost
been convinced. But then he had talked to Schmidt and Schmidt
had been adamant that Freymann was talking nonsense. In fact
he had been so vehement Doenitz suspected that there was a
great deal of animosity between the two men. Personal differences should not be allowed to interfere with people's judgment.
Doenitz never allowed such things to happen among his men.
One's duty was to serve, and to serve to the utmost of one's
ability.

But these scientists were different. They seemed incapable of
working as a team. Still, Doenitz thought, one has to learn to live
with them, irksome though they may be, if one is to benefit from
their extraordinary inventions.

He considered whether to bring up the subject of Freymann's
theory with the Grand Admiral. But he decided it would not be
necessary. Schmidt had promised Doenitz that the theory would
be investigated and finally and conclusively proved or disproved
either way.

Besides, Doenitz had more important things to worry about.
For years Germany's strength had been severely curtailed by the
humiliating Versailles Treaty, but at last the Anglo-German Naval
Treaty had been signed and Germany was allowed to build a navy
again.

It was a race against time.

German U-boat development had never really stopped—it had been carried out secretly in Holland since 1922—but it would be years, perhaps as many as ten, before the Kriegsmarine—and particularly the U-boat arm—would be powerful enough to take on the Royal Navy.

There was a tremendous amount of work to do. It wasn't only a question of building vessels but of development and training . . .

Doenitz turned and started to pace back along the deck. Ahead of him was the figure of Fischer, waiting patiently a few yards away. The U-boat arm needed more men like Fischer, men who served with skill, optimism and enthusiasm.

He beckoned the younger man over and the two of them fell into step. Doenitz said, "It has been an interesting day, hasn't it?"

"Yes, sir. Most fascinating. This device will obviously be very useful to us."

"We will see. I don't always believe everything that these things are meant to do. When we've had a chance to try it *on exercise,* then I will believe it!"

"Will we have a fleet exercise soon?"

"In the spring, I expect. And then we will be able to display our tactics for the first time. It is very important that we show the High Command the effectiveness of the wolf pack. They must understand that our success depends on numbers."

Fischer looked at his new commanding officer with gratitude. "Thank you for telling me. It makes me realize how important our training program will be this winter."

Doenitz's policy was always to tell his junior officers as much as possible. Above all else he valued trust and loyalty, and he believed that they grew not from aloofness, but from mutual openness and understanding of each other's problems. He intended to be involved fully in the day-to-day activities of his men. Whenever possible he would meet boats when they returned from exercise, he would attend debriefings, he would hear about operational problems firsthand. He did not intend to lose touch with his men, ever.

There were certain things they could not be told, of course. It would be wrong to talk about the power struggles between the Navy and the Luftwaffe, which Goering, as Hitler's favorite, was already winning; it would be wrong too to say how worrying

Hitler's ideas about warfare were. Hitler had made a friendly gesture to Britain, it was true, and that was the wisest thing to have done, but Doenitz wondered if Hitler appreciated that a war, if it came, would inevitably be fought against Britain. And the only way to beat Britain was to choke off her supplies, to sink all her merchant shipping, to make her slowly but surely starve.

For that they needed U-boats and lots of them.

Doenitz said, "Yes, we have much to do this winter. As soon as the flotilla is up to strength, we will work up our tactics. The wolf pack will revolutionize warfare at sea. Think of the number of ships that can be sunk by a group of U-boats hunting together; it will be three to four times the total that all U-boats could achieve on their own. Also, I believe that such tactics will take our enemies by surprise."

Fischer frowned. He was wholeheartedly behind his new captain and just as anxious to prove that these new tactics would work. But he, like everyone else, had heard about the new British invention, asdic, which used sound waves to detect submarines underwater. The British seemed to think their invention would mean the end of the submarine as an offensive weapon. Tentatively he asked, "What about asdic? The British are boasting about it. They seem very confident in it."

Doenitz stopped. "But it's only effective against *submerged* boats. When we attack, it will be at night on the *surface.* They will have no defense against that. Of course, after an attack they will come after us and then, once we have dived, they will use it against us. But even so, we only have their word for its effectiveness. It's like this radar here; I will believe it when I see it!"

The captain started pacing the deck again and Fischer had to stride to keep up with him. Doenitz said with emphasis, "In fact, asdic has done us a good turn. It has made the British complacent. You know they have fewer submarines than the French? They think submarines will not be important. Well, if war comes, we will prove them wrong."

"What about the small DT device the scientist was talking about? Will we be getting some for our boats?"

Doenitz shook his head. "Apparently the little man suffers from overoptimism. He was talking about a really small device, but it seems this will not be possible. If we are lucky we will get

something that might just fit into a U-boat. Even then I will want its effectiveness proved."

Doenitz clasped his hands behind his back and wished the *Welle* would hurry back to her berth. He wanted to return to Kiel as soon as possible. There was so much to do and so little time to do it in.

Fischer went on, "And the British—they don't have the DT device?"

"No, they don't." Doenitz almost added: at least that's what we're told. Schmidt had better be right about that, otherwise the consequences hardly bore thinking about.

"That's the main thing anyway," Fischer said. "At least we'll be free to make surprise attacks on the surface."

"Yes." And if we don't have that, thought Doenitz, we don't have anything. If, by any dreadful chance, the little scientist was right, if a device could be made to pick out a submarine on the surface in any weather, on the thickest of nights, then his wolf-pack strategy would be in ruins.

His boats and his men would be desperately vulnerable.

Like sitting ducks.

The Hamburg–Berlin express lumbered slowly into Lehrter Bahnhof. The squeal of brakes and the hiss of escaping steam woke David up. He stretched his arms and nudged Hans, still snoring in the seat beside him. "We're here."

It was late, almost ten o'clock. David couldn't remember when the last train to Hennigsdorf left, probably about eleven. He should have plenty of time to get to Stettiner Bahnhof and catch it.

Hans was looking at his watch and cursing. "I must rush. My train goes in half an hour!"

David followed him onto the platform and said, "You go ahead. I'm going to see if I can get something to eat."

Hans laughed. "What, more?" Then he waved and strode off.

David went into the station buffet and ordered bratwurst, sauerkraut, black bread and beer. He was amazed at how hungry he was, even after the substantial dinner he had eaten on the train. One good thing about seasickness—the *only* good thing—was that you felt marvelous afterward.

Ellen said he ate too much, and she was right. But there would be nothing hot waiting for him when he got home; Ellen liked to dine early and have the kitchen tidied by the time she went to bed at ten.

She was a good wife, Ellen, but she did like her sleep. David had long since realized that she couldn't function without at least nine hours a night. He never disturbed her when he came in late and he always woke her in the mornings with a cup of lemon tea. On Sundays he did not wake her at all, and she often slept until ten or eleven. Then he would take Cecile for a walk, and they would have long talks about how trees grew, and why steam drove trains and what made lightning strike church steeples. She was a bright child and David was immensely proud of her. Her science reports were very good and David secretly hoped she might be a physicist or perhaps a biologist. He never said as much to Ellen, who thought science not only dull but extremely unsuitable for a girl.

It was ten-twenty and David hurriedly finished his meal. The last train might well leave before eleven and it would be stupid to miss it.

Outside the station he waited for a bus to Stettiner Bahnhof. But when none had appeared after five minutes he decided to walk. It would do him good. Anyway the station wasn't far, just ten minutes away along Invalidenstrasse. There was plenty of time. He needn't have worried.

Ellen said he didn't worry enough, and there was some truth in it. Yet he did worry about things that mattered, like Cecile and her education and her happiness. What he couldn't see any point in fretting about was money or the cost of living or politics or any of those things.

When David arrived at Stettiner Bahnhof he discovered he had ten minutes to spare. The last train for Hennigsdorf was due to leave at ten-fifty-five.

He sat on a bench to wait. Somehow he had known he would have plenty of time. He often got a feeling about things. He had a feeling about his shortwave research project. He just knew that somehow, somewhere, it would go ahead. It was just a question of waiting and putting his case before the right people. Whether his talk with Doenitz had helped or not he didn't know, but it had certainly stirred things up a bit. Schmidt had

been purple with anger. David smiled and thought: Well, it can't do any harm.

The Hennigsdorf train arrived and he got into an empty compartment. Eventually the train pulled out and began its slow journey into the suburbs.

David watched the bright lights of the city pass by and considered his project. The more he thought about it, the more determined he was to get the thing off the ground. They all said the idea was impossible, that no valve could ever produce the sort of power he needed. True, nothing existed at the moment—but it *could*. It *would*. He would make one.

The train drew into Hennigsdorf and he got out, turning the matter of the valve over in his mind. Once outside the station, he automatically turned left, toward home, his head down, deep in thought. At present there were two kinds of valve, the klystron and the magnetron. If he could take the best qualities of both and combine them . . . keep the magnetron but use a closed resonator . . .

He was passing a shop when something in the window caught his eye. It was a large notice pasted across the window. It said, simply, JUDE!

David realized it was old Finstein's shoe shop. He stood staring at the window for a long time. He knew this happened in the center of the city, but here, in Hennigsdorf? This place was so quiet, so safe. Everyone knew each other. Damn it, everyone knew old Finstein.

He walked slowly on, thinking of what Hans had said. He couldn't believe there was really a risk of losing his job. For others, well, he had to admit that it was not a good time to be in business or one of the professions. But the Jews had been through periods like this before. As he'd said to Hans, there had been some unpleasantness before the Great War, but it had passed as these things always did. The new laws would make marriages like his and Ellen's illegal. Well, he repeated to himself, they couldn't *unmarry* two people who had been married fifteen years. As for Cecile, nothing would happen to her. She was a second-generation *Mischlinge*, or mixed-blood. She counted as German. And as for making him leave—they were doing that to the poor and to the business people but they would never do that

72

to him. They *needed* him; they knew it and he knew it. There was no more to be said.

He turned into the street where he lived and felt the familiar warmth of anticipation. Whenever he walked up the slight hill under the row of linden trees, he looked forward to the first sight of his small house, so neat and pretty. It gave him a peculiar thrill to think that this was his own small patch.

The house was dark, as he knew it would be, and he opened the door very quietly so as not to wake anybody. He checked that all the doors were locked and then climbed the stairs. He paused on the landing and crept toward the open door of the back bedroom. He looked in and saw Cecile's dark hair spread across the pillow.

He knelt beside the bed and caressed her hair.

He whispered the words he had always whispered, ever since she was a baby. "I love you, *meine kleine Rosenknospe,* I love you."

He thought: What a lucky man I am, to have so much—my work, my house, my family. And you, my *Liebling,* most of all, to have you.

And then he whispered out loud, "I will love you and protect you always. Always."

4 The tolling of a single bell echoed faintly over the city. Vasson thought: Is it really Sunday? He'd quite forgotten.

Mea culpa! Mea culpa! Lord forgive me, for I have sinned . . .

To hell with it. He hated Sundays.

It was a perfect August day, clear, sunny and not too hot. The sunlight was bright yellow, transforming the drab streets of the *dix-huitième* into brilliant ribbons of light. Vasson screwed up his eyes and walked slowly across the Place du Tertre. A couple of artists sat doggedly at their easels, painting yet more bad pictures

73

of the Sacré-Coeur. They were probably English or American like most of the so-called artists in this quarter. Vasson had heard that many were packing their bags and disappearing back to their own countries. Apparently the wealthy American tourists had already left their expensive hotels and crowded aboard the transatlantic liners in Cherbourg.

Let them go, Vasson thought. They're no loss to anyone. Life in Montmartre would be just the same without them.

He walked gently toward Pigalle—gently because his head ached and his eyes hurt and he had a stinking hangover. He should have stayed in bed.

On the street corners and in the cafés the news-vendors were doing a roaring trade. It seemed that all the residents of Montmartre wanted a newspaper today and when Vasson tried to buy *Turf,* the only paper he ever bought nowadays, he found it had sold out like all the rest. It was annoying. He was planning to bet on a big race at Longchamps and now he wouldn't be able to study the form.

The world had gone mad; everyone was behaving like a lot of frightened rabbits. So the Germans were going to swallow up the Poles. So what? Vasson couldn't see how that affected France. Poland had nothing to do with France. At least it damned well *shouldn't.*

He emerged on to the Boulevard Rochechouart and walked the last few yards into Place Pigalle. The club was situated in a tiny street leading off the circle. In the harsh light of day the facade looked drab and slightly seedy, but in darkness, when the name was illuminated in scarlet and the doorway open to reveal the softly lit staircase, the effect was inviting and seductive.

Vasson went down the stairs into the darkness of the club, grateful to rest his eyes from the painful sunlight. The floor had been washed and the chairs were upturned on the tables. He walked around the edge of the room to the bar. Without a word the barman poured him a coffee and pushed it across the counter.

Vasson pulled a chair off the nearest table and sat down wearily. He cast a critical eye around the room. He had the feeling that the previous night's takings must have been high. The club had been crowded from ten onward and most of the customers

were big spenders. But . . . He sighed. There was so much room for improvement. The takings could be so much better, maybe even *double,* if only—

If only—

He knew exactly what made a successful club. He had analyzed the ingredients countless times during the last four years.

There was the music. Now that was the one thing this club could boast about. Its music was much classier than you generally heard in the small intimate clubs. Instead of an accordion or solitary piano, there was a three-piece band, with piano, bass and drums. And the band was good. They played a few of the new-style swing numbers for those who wanted a wild dance, but for the rest of the time they stuck to slow romantic stuff. Perfect for getting the customers close to the girls and keen to spend their money.

The decor: now that could be much better. It was very out-of-date, all red plush and gilt. From the look of it nothing had been changed since 1910. Vasson would have liked to see mirrored walls, chromium furniture and a black linoleum floor, the kind of simple sophistication which was all the rage.

But the main problem was the girls. Some of them were distinctly rough-looking even in the near-total darkness of the club. Only the drunkest or blindest customers managed to find them attractive. They should be replaced, and straightaway. It was stupid to economize on the girls' wages. Much better to pay more and get top-class women who would not only attract the money but be highly skilled at extracting it.

He downed his coffee and took the cup back to the bar. The barman was washing glasses. Vasson called, "Hey, how *were* the takings last night? They must have been good."

The barman eyed Vasson impassively. "Good enough, I should think."

"But, I mean, a record or what?"

The barman stared and there was a hint of insolence in his expression. Vasson was irritated; the man was being less than cooperative. He said impatiently, "Look, I need the information if I'm to run this place properly. That *is* what I'm meant to be doing, you know, running the place!" He knew he sounded peevish but he couldn't help himself.

The barman smirked and shrugged his shoulders. Vasson wanted to hit him.

Suddenly there was a voice at Vasson's shoulder, so close that it made him jump. "Yes, you run the club—but it's me that runs the money. And don't you forget it."

Vasson flushed and turned around. It was Birelli. Birelli was small, fat and bad-tempered. He was wearing a flashy suit and expensive gold cufflinks, every inch the proprietor of a small club.

Which was precisely what he was.

Birelli owned three clubs, and this was one of them.

Vasson said nothing. Birelli wanted a reaction and he sure as hell wasn't going to get one.

Birelli took out a cigar and slowly lit it. Finally he said, "While I'm the owner of this place, I will worry about the takings, and no one else." The little man exhaled and the stench of garlic hit Vasson's nostrils. Instinctively Vasson pulled back, but Birelli moved closer and said with emphasis, "You would do better to mind your own business and stick to your job, such as it is. If you go on poking your nose into things that do not concern you, you'll be amazed at how quickly you'll be out in the street."

Vasson shivered. He had the urge to crush the man's head against the wall. He wanted to yell obscenities at the pompous self-satisfied little pig, then beat him into pulp. And to think he had actually put up with this cheap little crook for more than six months. It was obscene!

Birelli was watching Vasson's reaction with satisfaction, and Vasson realized the little man knew exactly what was going through his mind.

Birelli drew breath and said, "Furthermore, while we're on the subject of you and your incompetence, I'm tired of hearing about your grandiose ideas. They are idiotic rubbish; they're not worth anything. You have no idea what makes a club go. You can *spend* money, oh yes! But you have no idea what *makes* money. You think your ideas are so much better than anyone else's. Well, if you're so brilliant why aren't you a tycoon, eh? Why don't you own all the clubs in the area? Eh?"

Vasson gripped the side of the bar. He wanted the heat to go out of his anger so that he could think clearly. He needed to be calm when he decided what to do next.

The coolness came over his body and then he knew.

Very slowly he reached forward. At first Birelli looked bemused, then realization dawned and he turned white. As Vasson's hands closed around his neck, he screamed and tried to step backward.

Vasson began to shake the man, slowly at first, then rapidly so that the head snapped back and forth like a puppet's. He lifted him by the neck, thrust him against a wall and started to smash his head against the hard surface of the red flock wallpaper.

Birelli had been screaming but now, as his head thudded dully into the wall, his breath came in long gasps. Blood began to smear the red flock and his eyes were round and staring like little white eggs.

Vasson found the movement of the head hypnotic as it snapped backward and forward; he wondered what it would take to make the head snap right off. He had got into a rhythm and it was strangely satisfying. He wanted the rhythm and the feeling of satisfaction to continue.

From behind an arm encircled Vasson's neck and forced him to let go. Vasson felt an overwhelming disappointment and then, almost immediately, relief. He was sorry that the disgusting little man was going to escape lightly. On the other hand, he was glad he had been stopped. He had forgotten himself, and he didn't like doing that.

The armhold was viselike and Vasson felt a moment of panic. He should have remembered about the barman. The man was large and powerful: he could hurt people.

Vasson tried to think. It would be a mistake to struggle; better to play dead. He made himself go limp and heard the barman grunt as his arm took the additional weight.

For a second Vasson thought nothing would happen, then there was a sickening blow to his kidney and he screamed.

After what seemed a long time the barman finally loosened his grip and let Vasson slide to the floor.

Vasson lay still for a moment before sidling quickly under a table, out of reach. God, the pain was terrible, a great stabbing ache in his side. He felt sick.

He heard a sound and saw the barman's feet advancing toward the table.

Vasson crouched lower and shouted, "I've no argument with you, friend. How about laying off, eh?"

There was silence. Vasson crawled out on the other side of the table and got cautiously to his feet.

The barman was hovering, fists clenched. Vasson panted desperately. "Look, lay off. You've hurt my back and I'm in agony. You've done your bit, *for Christ's sake.*"

For a moment the barman stared at him, then he hissed, "Coward!"

Vasson didn't care what the man thought, just as long as there was no more fighting.

The barman advanced again. Vasson retreated quickly toward a wall.

Suddenly there was a loud groan. The proprietor was slumped untidily on the floor, blood pouring from his head, his face sheet white. Vasson thought with satisfaction: Perhaps I really hurt him after all.

The barman murmured angrily, "You've half killed him!"

"No!" Vasson said hastily. "He'll be all right. It's only superficial. Looks worse than it is. Really—" He let out a great moan of pain and clutched his back. "God, my back! The *pain*!" The barman was impressed, just as Vasson had intended him to be.

The barman lowered his arms. He was still unhappy but it was obvious the fight was over. Vasson almost smiled with relief.

Birelli was groaning again and the barman shuffled over to take a look at him. Quickly Vasson straightened his jacket and tie and smoothed down his hair. He moved rapidly away from the barman, around the room to the stairway.

The barman spotted him and said, "Hey! Hold on!"

Vasson poised himself on the bottom step and snapped, "Just tell the ugly bastard that if he has any silly ideas about getting his own back, I'll tell the cops about the extra activities upstairs! Okay?"

As the barman started toward him, Vasson sprinted up the stairs, three steps at a time, and ran into the street. He didn't stop until he was across Pigalle and into Montmartre.

"Bastard! Bastard!" He kicked a wall angrily. He wished he'd finished Birelli off, squeezed his neck *tight* until he'd choked! At the same time he hated himself for having lost control.

"God damn it!" He roared on up the street, bumping into people and forcing a woman off the pavement.

At a pavement café, he threw himself disgustedly onto a chair, still shaking with rage and humiliation.

Later, when the rage had subsided, he walked on, more slowly this time, wondering what the hell he'd done to deserve his luck.

It had been four years now. Four years since the disaster.

Even now he could hardly bear to think about it. He could hardly bear to remember the smell of that lovely, sweet money.

Paris was just as he imagined it would be, except better.

For the first few days he had stayed at a good hotel and strolled around, eating at different restaurants and watching the smart ice-cool Parisians as they ate and talked and went about their business. He was cautious: he wanted to get a feel for the latest fashions before buying any clothes; and he wanted to be sure that he had found the right neighborhood in which to rent an apartment. For the moment he was happy to watch and listen and relax; to savor the freedom that money brought. The money: it was like the feeling of hot sunshine on your skin, warm, sensuous, intoxicating.

When he felt ready he slowly began to acquire the trappings of a successful man. First he bought a few really good clothes and some gold cufflinks. Then he looked for an apartment. It had to be fairly near Pigalle, where the club would be, but not too near. Montmartre was impossibly vulgar, so it would have to be the *neuvième*.

It took several days to find what he wanted. The apartment was in a quiet street off the Rue de Clichy. It was in need of decoration, but it would do until he was properly established, and then he would go to an even better place in the *huitième*, somewhere off the Champs-Élysées.

The only luxury he would allow himself at this stage was the car. He had wanted it so long that he couldn't bear the idea of waiting any longer. He decided, rashly, to have a new one after all. There was a showroom on the Champs-Élysées which had Delages and Bugattis in the window. It gave him a curious thrill to walk in and ask for a D8SS, for immediate delivery. The manager himself came out of his office and showed him a car with

Falaschi bodywork in green. He liked the body—very much. It was open, with sleek wings which flowed into the running boards and a long, long hood.

Perfect—except for the color. He wanted red, ruby red, with black leather upholstery. The manager was downcast. That could take weeks, maybe months.

Vasson said he would wait for it.

The manager went to the telephone and returned smiling. It would be only two weeks, after all.

Two weeks. Vasson enjoyed the idea of waiting. It would be a sort of sweet agony. It appealed to his sense of Christian guilt. Yes, he would wait for the red one.

He paid a deposit, in cash as usual.

The money was lasting well; the hotel, the month's advance rent for the apartment, the new clothes and the cufflinks had hardly made a dent in it. But the car would, of course. For the deposit he had to dip into the crisp new notes for the first time.

The two weeks passed surprisingly quickly. He busied himself looking at premises around Pigalle. It would take quite a while to set up the club: there were difficulties—permits, licenses, access and so on. And he had to be careful; his new identity wouldn't bear detailed examination by the police. Everything must be in order; none of the paper work must be forgotten. If anything the difficulties made him more determined.

Then at last the two weeks were up and he telephoned the showroom. Yes, the car was there, ready.

It was like Christmas, or a birthday, except he'd never known what it was like to get presents before. His heart hammered with excitement as he walked along the Champs-Élysées. He approached from the opposite side of the avenue, under the trees, and stopped at an intersection to cross the wide boulevard. He looked across at the showroom and frowned. He couldn't see a ruby red car anywhere, either in the window or on the wide pavement outside. He thought: Damn, it hasn't arrived after all.

He was just about to cross when he saw something that made him freeze. A man was leaning against a tree pretending to read a newspaper, but actually watching the showroom.

There was another farther up the avenue, standing in a shop doorway, smoking a cigarette.

Oh God.

They were waiting for him.

Sweat started from his forehead and he went quite cold. For several moments he stood absolutely still.

The man in the doorway threw his cigarette away and looked up and down the avenue. Vasson turned quickly away and walked rapidly toward the Étoile. At one of the large pavement cafés, he went into the bar and asked to use the phone. He called the showroom and said he was delayed. Were they certain the car was absolutely ready? There was a slight hesitation, then they had assured him it was ready, there and waiting. He told them he wanted to drive it straight off and did they have it parked right outside? There was a moment's silence, then they told him yes, it was just outside, ready to go.

Vasson watched the showroom for ten minutes. No red Delage was visible and none arrived while he waited. Instead there was plenty of activity among the men staked outside. A man came out of the showroom and spoke first to the man under the tree and then to the one in the doorway. There was a third Vasson hadn't spotted before, in another doorway on the other side of the showroom. After their discussions they looked more relaxed, as if they had been told that the action was off for the moment.

Vasson turned away, sick at heart.

It must have been the money, it could only have been the *money*. The money must stink to high heaven.

He walked a long way, then went into a café and had a drink. It made him light-headed and slightly hysterical. He had the dreadful desire to cry.

Later he sat in a daze, thinking hard. At last, late in the evening, he left the café and walked slowly toward the apartment.

He stayed in the apartment for three days, lying on the bed smoking or sometimes pacing up and down, trying to figure out a way to utilize the money.

There was no solution. He had known that immediately, but it took him three days to face it. Then he wept.

He had been so naive it was incredible. How the Algerian must have laughed! How they all must have laughed! They'd probably been wondering how to get rid of that rotten money for years. The Algerian wouldn't have printed it himself, it wasn't his style,

but he'd probably bought it cheap for an occasion like this. . . .

At one point he thought of revenge, of nailing the Algerian with the money, of doing a deal for perhaps half the two hundred thousand francs.

But he was frightened. If he went to Marseilles he knew the Algerian would kill him. He wouldn't get within a mile.

He tried to remember how lucky he was not to have been caught. And there was still some money from the down payment: clean money. But it didn't help. He had been robbed and cheated, and it hurt like hell.

A week later he tried to shift some of the bad money with a bullion dealer. The dealer got the scent of the money even as it came out of the briefcase: Vasson saw it in his face. He made a quick exit before the dealer reached for a telephone. It was no better at a small pawnbroker's: the old Jew handed the money back and yelled, "Get this rubbish out of here!"

Vasson realized the money was well known. It must have been around for years.

Eventually, in desperation, Vasson sold the lot for three thousand francs to a *pied-noir* who hoped to pass it in Tangier.

The good money lasted a year, spent carefully. There was no club, no car, no security.

He was back where he'd started.

Vasson strode up the steps and steeply climbing streets that led into the heart of Montmartre, sweat soaking his back. He walked faster again, pushing his body harder and harder to ease the pain in his kidney and the bitterness in his mouth.

Finally he turned into a small dark café and sat near the window. The group of men at the counter glanced at him and resumed their conversation. They knew he never said hello. The waiter brought him a coffee.

He considered ordering a pastis; it might just revive him. He'd drunk enough the night before. He couldn't remember exactly how much. The memory sickened him, not only because of the hangover but because the evening had cost at least a hundred francs.

Raoul had talked him into going. Well, Raoul could damn well buy him a pastis.

He tried to remember what it was like to feel well; there had

been too much drink and too many cigarettes. And now the kidney, which was still aching viciously.

Someone sat down at the table. It was Raoul. Vasson said, "Buy me a drink, you *tête de con.*"

"Have you read the news? Have you read the news?" Raoul unfolded his newspaper and started to read avidly.

Vasson waited for a moment, then leaned forward and took Raoul's wrist. "Look, after last night you owe me a goddam drink!"

"Oh for Christ's sake shut up, will you? I'm reading this." He flicked his hand across the newspaper. "This Polish thing . . . it means war, do you realize? We will be at war by the end of the week!"

Vasson controlled his annoyance. Raoul thought he knew so much about world affairs, but he couldn't even run a couple of girls at a profit. "War? So maybe there'll be a war. But it's not going to affect us."

Raoul slowly lowered the newspaper. "Listen, big-time operator, this is the end of it, as far as I'm concerned. If France is going to war, then I will be there fighting, and you can rot here, hatching your grand plans. Alone."

Vasson regarded him with contempt. "Then I'm sorry for you, because I'll be the richer."

"That's what you've been saying for the last three years—and I'm still counting my *sous.*" Raoul stabbed a finger across the table. "And so, for that matter, are you!"

Vasson flushed. They'd had an idea to open a club, but it had failed for the usual reason: lack of money. They'd tried to borrow some, even tried to extort some, but it all came to nothing.

Vasson retorted, "At least I try, which is more than you do." Raoul was a lazy swine who'd be quite happy to sit around forever, earning nothing and drinking himself stupid. Vasson added, "None of your ideas are worth a sou."

Raoul shrugged; he'd heard it all before. "There's nothing wrong with my ideas. It's you! You just find problems that aren't there."

Vasson gave a short laugh. He knew Raoul's ideas all right: bank robbery. The quickest way to go to jail, short of stabbing a *flic* and waiting to be arrested. God!

Raoul bought two pastis and plonked them on the table. "Look,

the idea of setting up your stupid club would never have worked anyway. We're small fry. We could never have set up a big place like that. Hundreds of women indeed! High-class decor!" He shook his head. "For a start our police contacts just weren't good enough. And then do you think the existing businesses would have made room for you without a fuss? I tell you it would never have worked."

Vasson watched him coldly and decided he was a very stupid man.

Raoul said tolerantly, "You know, you should use that learning of yours, and get a good job with prospects. You *do* have an education, don't you, eh? I mean you read books and all that. It's obvious that someone stuffed the knowledge in somewhere."

Vasson stiffened. He loathed people referring to his past.

Raoul went on, "Was it the priests? That gave you the learning, I mean? I knew a lad once who'd started life with nothing—on the scrap heap at five years old, he was—and the priests took him in and stuffed his head full of books and Latin and he ended up a professor, a *professor*! The nephew of my mum's best friend, he was. Very proud, his family, very proud." He turned to Vasson. "Was it the priests, then?"

"Shut up," Vasson snapped.

He downed his pastis and stood up. Raoul looked at him in surprise. "Where are you off to?"

"Away. Somewhere. So I'll say good-bye. I hope you enjoy the army and getting killed. Should be fun."

"Don't be like that."

Vasson leaned over the table. "We'll see who's the clever one, and I tell you, it isn't going to be you!"

The room was at the back of a tall, dingy house in the Rue St. Vincent. It cost him a few francs a week, so that, after meals and clothes, he could save about one hundred a week. When he had a job.

The idea was to save enough for a lease on a club premises. By any calculations it should take twenty years to buy even the most modest property. Even assuming he had a job. He grimaced: it was pathetic, laughable.

Wearily he climbed the dirty narrow stairs and opened the door of the room. It was dark inside. He felt his way across to the win-

dow and opened the shutters. Even then there wasn't much light: the window gave onto a narrow opening between tall buildings.

The room was a mess. High-heeled shoes lay scattered on the floor and piles of skirts and dresses were draped over the two chairs. I'll have to get rid of her, Vasson thought. She was a brainless little country girl named Yvette, and she was cluttering up his life. It had been her idea to move in, not his. He should have kicked her out straightaway.

He threw some cheap magazines off the bed and lay down. His head ached and his kidney was still hurting badly. He wondered if the damage was serious. Perhaps he should go and see a doctor, except that doctors cost money and he begrudged paying them.

He lit a cigarette and began to think.

No job. No prospects. He'd been through it before. There'd been four, maybe five jobs in the last four years. The story was always the same: they wanted him to work like hell, but they offered him nothing in return. No real share of the action. No opportunity to change or improve things. And then—then came the disagreements. They always blamed him—*him!*—though the problems were their own stupid faults.

He felt cheated. Frustrated. Bitter. Especially now. Because he hadn't managed to control himself and he'd half killed a man and that frightened him.

But it was the fault of the system. It was the system that was killing him. The fat kings ran the system and they had it sewn up. You didn't have a chance without weight and influence—and that meant money. And you couldn't get the money without the influence. The system stank.

Christ, he thought, I just go round in circles. And the circle always comes back to money.

Suddenly he was tired. He stubbed out his cigarette and closed his eyes. He liked sleep. He liked the blackness and the peace of it and the way it passed so much of the time.

The dream, when it came, was vivid. He was back in Marseilles, in the Algerian's car. His arms were bound and he was lying on the floor. The Algerian was discussing how he would kill him. But Vasson didn't care because he had the money on the floor next to him. *He had the money.* He knew he'd be all right.

But then he was slipping, across the floor of the car, onto the road. Someone had opened the door. It was his mother. As he fell

he called to her, but she looked past him at the Algerian and smiled.

There was darkness. He was in the cupboard again. He shouted and yelled, but the door was made of steel and so thick that no one could hear. Finally, after time which seemed to have lasted forever, the door was opened. He did not want to come out. But it was one of the priests and refusal was not allowed.

He asked for his mother.

"Your mother is a long way away, Paul."

"But I want her."

"Paul, your mother has not yet found the way to the true God. She is—searching for Him. While she searches, she cannot come to you."

No, she was near, he knew she was near. Why did they lie to him? Why did they keep her away?

Maman, Maman—

He awoke. Someone was in the room.

It was Yvette.

"You all right?" She teetered across to the bed on her high heels and put her heavily made-up face close to his. He closed his eyes in disgust.

"You were muttering away. I thought you were awake, talking to yourself! Sorry, did I actually wake you up?" She was using the little-girl-lost voice she usually kept for fat rich men. It annoyed him.

He said irritably, "Get out. I want to sleep."

"Oh, well, don't mind me. I'll stay quiet as a mouse. You won't even know I'm here." She began to stroke his forehead.

He brushed her hand away and reached for a cigarette.

"Let me get you a cold drink, eh?" she persisted.

"No. And I've something to tell you. I'm going away."

She stared at him and then nodded. She wasn't surprised. "Can I come too?" She knew it was risky to ask, he might fly off the handle like he sometimes did. But she wanted to go with him, to look after him.

He said, "No."

She kicked off her shoes and lay on the bed beside him. She knew exactly how far she could go before he got angry. She put an arm across his waist and moved her head against his.

"I'll miss you terribly."

"Like hell."

"I know I don't suit you . . . I mean I'm not attractive to you, and all that. But I'd take care of you, you know that."

Vasson sighed. The sex thing again. It was her only level of understanding. Everything began and ended with sex. She couldn't understand how repulsive she was to him, how he couldn't bear her to touch him.

He sat up suddenly and, pushing past her, stood up. "I'm off tomorrow, so you'd better find somewhere else."

"Where are you going?"

"I don't know."

"What about this war then?"

"What about it?"

"Well, *that* might offer some opportunities, I mean for the two of us." She was always trying to think of moneymaking ideas. They were always pathetic, just like her.

He didn't answer, but began to pack his suitcase.

She fluttered valiantly on, "There'll be shortages, right? And a black market. Bound to be. And that's where the money'll be. In buying things up cheap. You've got enough saved to make a start. It'll be a real money-maker, you'll see!"

Vasson paused. "And what do you think people will be short of?"

She thought for a moment, her penciled eyebrows puckered in concentration. At last she said, "Oh, stockings, makeup, clothes, things like that . . . and food I suppose. And I could think of lots more, I'm sure I could—"

Vasson stared out of the window. The silly girl might actually have something. Perhaps there *would* be a war, perhaps it would go on for some time, perhaps there would be plenty of money to be made.

Pushing the last few things into his suitcase, he said abruptly, "I'm off then."

"Oh, please . . . !" She started toward him, a pleading expression on her face.

He glanced at her, thinking again how repulsive she was, and turned away to open the door.

She yelled, "You shit!" But he walked quickly down the stairs

and by the time he reached the street he couldn't hear her anymore.

He walked rapidly, needing to get away. He thought: It's good
to be free again. He would get another room, alone. He would
start over.

He stopped for a coffee and a cigarette in a place he hadn't
been to before and thought about the girl's idea. There definitely
might be something in it. Luxuries, food, what else had she said?
Stockings. Yes, and cigarettes would be short too.

A war might be a good thing after all.

5 The coast is wild and rugged and utterly beautiful.
From its border with Normandy to the point where
the land turns to face the open Atlantic the north Brittany coast
measures little more than a hundred miles as the crow flies. But
this means nothing. It is so indented with bays and deep estuaries
that its true length is at least twice that distance. Most of this
length is impenetrable to anything but the smallest craft—and
then only in good weather—for the land is defended by a great
barrier of natural hazards.

A thousand storms have shaped the jagged cliffs and eaten
into the soft rock, leaving a dense fabric of reefs, islands and
islets to seaward. Some of the dangers stand proud and high in
the water: great stacks of rock rising like dragon's teeth, or
larger islands which lie cowed and barren before the wind. But
most of the perils are near the surface: sharp reefs marked only
by breaking water, or islets so low that they are almost invisible.
These dangers reach out four, five, sometimes twelve miles
from the land.

Then there are the tidal streams. They run very strong along
these shores, ripping across rocks and reefs, tearing through the

deep channels, and swinging into bays and inlets, making accurate landfall difficult even for the most careful of navigators.

The strongest winds come in winter, blowing storm force from the Atlantic. They send before them armies of waves which curve in toward the shore, gathering speed until they break on the myriad of rocks and islets in a caldron of white foaming surf, then advance, still snapping and roaring, onto the fragile mainland itself.

This coast is no friend to the sailor. Only those familiar with its dangers dare approach it with impunity; strangers must rely on good charts and blind faith. At night the dangers are marked by the powerful beams of tall lighthouses; with the help of leading lights and channel buoys it is even possible for small fishing craft to navigate one or two of the estuaries in darkness. But for the most part this coast does not invite visitors; the great lighthouses serve to warn rather than welcome.

The wind blows the fine salt mist several miles inland, so that only the hardiest vegetation can grow there—gorse and heather and thin coarse grass—and the pastures, such as they are, support only a small number of cattle. Farther inland there are market gardens and fields of wheat and richer pastures, but even here the land gives grudgingly and there is none of the lush abundance of Normandy or Picardy.

Like all wild, windswept places the land is rich with romantic legend. Except that in Brittany fact and fable are closely intertwined. The people who have inhabited this land for centuries are quite alien to their neighbors in the rest of France. Brittany is French by nationality, but not by race, language or culture. The proud, tough Bretons are not Gauls but Celts, and their closest links are with Cornwall, Wales and Ireland, from whence they came centuries ago. The Breton language sounds harsh to the French ear and the names of the rocks and headlands are more easily spoken by a Cornishman than by a Frenchman: Beg an Fry, Mean Nevez, L'Aberwrac'h, Lizen Ven, Pen Ven. You would even be forgiven for thinking you were in Scotland when you hear their music, for they play not the accordion, but the plaintive, mournful bagpipes.

To the great nation of France, Brittany is something of a backwater, not sufficiently fertile or industrially developed to demand

a great deal of attention. For the Bretons, proudly nationalistic and stubbornly independent, their subjugation to the mother country is tolerated with equanimity, and the benefits, if any, absorbed. The idea of freedom has long been forgotten—the land has been fought over often enough as it is—but the people remain independent in spirit.

The land is poor and in places infertile, but the Bretons find it sufficient for their needs; the way of life is simple and austere and not to the taste of the sophisticated French, but for the Bretons this is the only life they know. Many of them live off the sea, and the sea is the harshest life there is.

It was a pleasant day in August and the coast looked almost benign.

The sun had penetrated the morning mist at midday and now in the late afternoon the ragged headlands and narrow estuaries were lit in firm bold colors. The greeny purple of the sparse vegetation showed clearly against the gray and terra-cotta of the jagged rock formations. The sea itself was a pale gray-blue and unusually calm. There had been no gales for some days and only a slight swell washed around the walls of rock and onto the narrow pebble beaches.

Julie lifted her head and let the soft salt wind caress her face. For a few moments she stood quite still, listening to the gentle murmur of the surf far below, watching the waves ripple across the wideness of the sea. The cries of seabirds echoed faintly on the wind; occasionally one would fly high into the air and she followed it as it glided motionless on the breeze.

Julie closed her eyes, thinking: It's so beautiful and I love it all.

She loved it partly because it *was* beautiful and partly because she was happy here. She loved the peace and the loneliness; on a day like this you could walk for hours and never see a living soul. At first the remoteness had been strange and unsettling after the close warmth of the city. But slowly she began to appreciate the austerity and rugged beauty of the landscape. Now it was so familiar that she might have lived here all her life.

Standing on the headland it was difficult to believe that Plymouth and England lay just a hundred miles across the Channel. It seemed like a thousand. The small house in Radley Terrace

belonged to another life, another *person*. That's what she had been then—another person.

Suddenly she remembered she should have counted to twenty by now. Peter must have been hiding for ages. She yelled, "Twenty! I'm coming!"

She knew exactly where he would be. There were few places to hide on the windswept headland. The heather and gorse grew low and sparse, clinging to the stony soil around the rocky outcrops, and there were no trees. The only object capable of concealing a small boy was a large boulder which stood round and gray against the skyline. There was also a slight dip in the ground where someone could lie still and remain unseen, but Peter preferred a really solid hiding place, so it had to be the boulder.

But it was important to make a proper show of searching. She said in a loud voice, "My, my! Where *can* he be?" then called, "Peter, Peter, where are you?" At this point he often gave the game away by calling, "Whooo-hoooo!" a funny cry that always made her laugh. But he had become much cannier recently and had finally realized that keeping quiet was the smart thing to do.

Julie approached the boulder and waited. Sometimes Peter couldn't bear the suspense any longer and jumped out with a loud "Boo!" but he was being patient today.

For a moment she thought she was mistaken and he wasn't there after all, but then she heard a small giggle. She crept silently up to the boulder and, running quickly around it, pounced on the small person crouching behind. With a shriek he tried to run away but her arms went around the little body and the two of them rolled onto the ground, yelling and giggling.

They wrestled and tickled each other until Julie cried, "Enough, enough!" She rolled onto her back, panting hard. Peter plonked himself on her stomach and grinned triumphantly.

"I give up. You win, you horrible child!"

Peter bounced with delight, then chanted, "Again, again. Please let's play it again!"

"In a minute. Give your poor old mum a chance to recover."

He nodded gravely as he always did and, getting up, wandered off to examine some tiny blue flowers peeping up through the heather. He was always fascinated by tiny things.

He called, "Mummy."

"Yes, darling."

"Shall I pick you some flowers?"

"That would be lovely."

She watched as he carefully bent down to search for the stems of the flowers. When he was younger he had yanked the flowers off at the top but she had explained to him why it was better to pick them at the bottom and he had listened with his little head on one side. Now he set about doing the job properly, a frown of concentration on his forehead.

She smiled as she watched him. He was almost three and a half years old, but there remained a lot of the baby in him. Most of the rounded chubbiness had gone and every one of the baby-ish creases, but he still had lovely velvety skin, and when his little arms went around her neck and he hugged her tight she loved to feel its softness against her. He still needed plenty of hugs, thank goodness. She couldn't bear to think of him growing up and not wanting them anymore. The two of them spent at least two hours a day just talking and reading. Julie looked forward to those hours: to the little body that wriggled into bed in the mornings and snuggled close; to the small fellow who demanded a hug when he'd grazed his knee; and to the sleepy bedtime boy who wanted just one more story before falling asleep in her arms.

Her only regret—and it was a big one—was that she had to spend so many hours away from him, working. But that couldn't be helped: they couldn't survive without money.

Sometimes she wanted him to stay just the way he was, not to grow up and drift away from her. At the same time she was fascinated by his development, the way he picked up new words and slotted them into one of his two vocabularies, French or English, and the way he thought things out for himself. The other night, when he'd been up late, he'd announced that, since the moon was nowhere to be seen, it must have forgotten to put its light on. She had been careful not to laugh—the logic was, after all, irrefutable.

Peter was striding toward her, lifting his feet high in the air to get across the carpet of springy heather. In his preoccupation he forgot to hold the bunch of flowers upright and a few of the tiny blooms were torn away by the ragged branches.

When he arrived breathless beside her he looked at the flowers in surprise, puzzled that some should have so mysteriously disappeared. But apparently the loss was not too serious: he thrust his arm out and proudly announced, "Here's a present, just for you!"

Julie thanked him and got to her feet. "They're quite lovely. I'll put them in water when we get back." She placed the flowers in a pocket of her cardigan and glanced at her watch.

It was nearly four-thirty, time they went back for tea. They walked up to the path which led inland toward the village.

"Mummy, hide and seek again? You promised."

Little demon. He never forgot.

They played two more games, first Julie hiding, then Peter, and then it really was time to head for home.

They climbed the narrow path which led upward around the side of a rocky bluff and along the top of a steep cliff. Although the cliff was fenced at this point and the drop a safe distance away, Julie gripped Peter's hand more tightly. At a corner where the path led away from the cliff, they paused.

Peter said, "Look, a fishing boat!"

Julie followed his gaze. A small boat was drifting gently a short distance from the shore, its tan sails hardly filling in the windless lee of the headland. Several rocks were plainly visible just above the surface on the seaward side of the vessel. Julie shook her head. The Bretons were known for their knowledge of this coast, but all the same . . .

At night she could see the flash of a light from her bedroom window. Now, squinting her eyes against the sun, she could make out the form of the lighthouse itself. A tall gray and red structure standing stark and solitary in the middle of the sea, it marked a plateau of rocks lying just beneath the surface some miles offshore. She shivered slightly; the tower seemed lonely and somehow sad.

She turned away. "Come on, darling."

They climbed up to the top of the ridge and walked slowly toward the village, just visible through a dip in the land. Although the path was fairly level now, Peter was puffing and panting as he strived to match her step. Julie wasn't surprised when he said, "Mummy, please carry me."

She lifted him over her head and onto her shoulders.

She said, "I don't promise to take you all the way. You're too heavy, young man!"

It was true: in five minutes or so her shoulders would ache and she would have to put him down. A man could have done it easily. But there wasn't a man.

She hardly ever thought about Peter's father. It was as if he belonged to another world that had existed a long, long time ago. Her memory of him was completely neutral; she neither hated him nor cared about him. It was almost as if she had never known him. The only thing she felt, possibly, was gratitude: he had, after all, given her Peter. But at the same time she never thought of Peter as belonging to him. Peter was hers and hers alone.

She adored her son from the start, and it surprised her. In the months before the birth she didn't have much time to think about how she'd feel; she was too busy sorting things out—difficulties mainly. It was only in the last few weeks that she had realized she was about to give birth to a *person,* somebody who would rely on her for everything. It frightened her, but she was determined to do the right thing, to do her *best.*

Settling in Brittany had been far from easy. Looking back, she wondered how she'd stuck it out. In fact, at one point just after she arrived, she'd nearly given up and gone home to England.

The village was in full view now, a group of gray stone cottages standing out against the pastel gray-greens of the fields. Julie regarded it fondly. She was glad she hadn't given up and run away.

As soon as she'd decided on Brittany Julie had written to her uncle and aunt. She didn't know their full address, only the name of the village: Trégasnou. She asked if she could stay with them while she found somewhere to live.

The reply came in two weeks, short, stiff and impersonal: they would be expecting her and they had a spare room for her.

The journey lasted three days. She took a ferry from Dover to Calais and then a train to Morlaix. She had to change three times and wait two hours for a bus from Morlaix to Trégasnou. By the time she reached the long hill to the small gray house, a heavy suitcase in each hand, she was exhausted.

94

The farmhouse was typically Breton; it was built of gray stone with a high, pitched roof and low eaves which came almost to the ground-floor windows. There were two small dormer windows in the roof where the upper rooms must be. Various outbuildings extended from the back of the house and, as she approached, Julie heard the sounds of animals stamping and shuffling in a barn somewhere.

The house was silent and, though it was almost dark, no light was showing in the window.

Julie knocked on the door. There was no reply. She knocked again, louder. After a minute there was the flicker of a light as an inner door was opened. Finally the front door swung open and a large, rather fierce woman stood in the doorway.

Julie smiled and said in French, "I'm Julie."

The woman called something over her shoulder, then beckoned Julie in.

A small, squat man appeared from the back room and with a shy smile shook her hand. "You are welcome, welcome. Please come in."

She was shown to a chair by the kitchen range and offered coffee. Her uncle and aunt sat opposite, watching her politely. Julie realized they were nervous. They were sitting upright in their seats, their hands clasped in their laps, looking strangely uncomfortable. For several moments no one could think of anything to say.

"It's kind of you to have me to stay," Julie said at last.

Her uncle smiled. "Not at all, not at all."

Her aunt took a decisive breath and said, "Well, let's make sure you're comfortable. First, have you had something to eat?"

"I had a sandwich on the train."

"Perhaps you would like some soup?"

"Oh, thank you."

Her aunt got up and put a pan on the stove. She started speaking again, more rapidly this time. Julie concentrated on what was being said, but to her chagrin, missed several key words. Before she could ask her aunt to repeat them her uncle was speaking and Julie realized with bitter disappointment that she could not understand all he was saying either. It was the accent, perhaps, or maybe her French was rustier than she thought.

At one point her relatives started to speak in Breton until, remembering Julie was there, they returned apologetically to French.

Julie felt depressed. She'd assumed that because her father came from this village she would have some bond with these people, some feeling of belonging. Instead she felt a complete stranger, a foreigner who knew and understood nothing.

And it was clear that her uncle and aunt found her equally strange. They'd probably never met an English person before— or, for that matter, any kind of foreigner. She was beginning to realize just how remote the village was.

It was clear too that the farmer and his wife were not used to having guests. Julie had the feeling that she was upsetting the routine of the small household, and that they didn't really know what to do with her. When finally she said she was tired and they showed her to a tiny upstairs room, she knew they were relieved.

The next day started well. Julie tried hard to make conversation and offered to help her aunt with the chores. But soon she was depressed again. Her aunt was obviously uneasy about something and refused to let Julie help her with even the simplest tasks, while her uncle treated her with rigid politeness and exaggerated respect. The effect was chilling.

That evening it came to a head. They had finished supper and Tante Marie started to clear away the dishes. Julie got quickly to her feet and carried the cheese and butter toward the larder.

"No, no!" Tante Marie made her put the plates down. "We can't have you doing these things."

"But I must help, otherwise . . ." Julie struggled to find the right word. ". . . I will be a burden."

Tante Marie looked crosser than ever. "But you are a guest. You must not work."

"But please . . . I feel I am imposing on you."

"It is no imposition." Tante Marie looked quite shocked.

"You are kind. But you must let me pay you, for my food and my bed, at least until I can find a room to rent. I will look for one tomorrow."

"A room? But—why?"

Julie wondered what they had understood from her letter. "Well, I can't stay with you forever."

Her uncle and aunt exchanged glances. Her aunt sat down slowly. "You mean, you're staying a long time?"

"I want to." She laughed nervously.

Gently Tante Marie took her hand and patted it. Then Julie found it easy to explain everything they hadn't understood from the letter: how she wanted to stay in the village, how she was going to find a room, then a job . . .

It was more difficult to talk about the baby, of course, particularly when she had to explain about the husband who was meant to have deserted her. But she did it, because they'd have to know sometime and it might as well be now.

After she'd told them, she felt much better. At least everything was out in the open.

It was different then. In some strange way, her aunt and uncle were pleased. They insisted she stay with them. Terms for board and lodging were soon agreed. Everything was settled.

They went out of their way to make her feel at home. Her uncle prepared a room for her at the back of the house in the lower of two rooms which had once been used for storage; her aunt allowed her to help with the chores; and the formality of the evenings was replaced by their well-established routine of occasional conversation interspersed with long silences.

But it was a long time before she did feel at home, partly because the way of life *was* so different and partly because she was lonely. The villagers did not take easily to strangers, let alone foreigners. And she had the unpleasant sensation that they did not believe her story about the disappearing husband. Doubtless one or two of them were aware that she was entered on the Aliens Registration at Morlaix as Juliette Lescaux, not Juliette Howard, the name she had called herself when she arrived in France. She had chosen it after Leslie Howard, her favorite movie star, and then laughed at her stupidity: *h* was the one letter the French could not pronounce.

Finding a job was the hardest part. There weren't many around, even for those who spoke good French and weren't pregnant. But she persevered. At last, when her money was beginning to run low, she was taken on as a secretary to a vegetable

wholesaler in Morlaix. She suspected that the manager was tickled by her English accent, but whatever the reason, she wasn't going to turn the job down.

She was still there, three years and a baby later.

Peter was like a lead weight on her shoulders. She said, "You're breaking my back. I'm going to chase you home!"

Peter giggled. "I'll win! I'll win!"

She lowered Peter to the ground and the two of them ran down into the village and along the main street. Trégasnou was small, no more than a scattering of cottages built around a crossroads. There was one shop and a café. The shop sold bread brought in daily from the larger village of Plougat, as well as butter, cheese, simple provisions and a rough local wine. For everything else you had to go into Plougat itself, or, for really special shopping expeditions, to Morlaix.

Because Julie worked in Morlaix she often delivered or collected items for her neighbors. She was pleased to do it because it helped her to get to know them. Not an easy thing by any means. At one stage she despaired of being accepted by them. But then she realized it was a mistake to be too interested in their customs or too curious about their lives. They distrusted that. It was better to show polite interest and then offer information about England and how things were done there. They respected national pride and liked to hear about foreign customs, if only to reassure themselves that, all things considered, their way of doing things was the best.

Julie thought some of their ways quaint, others just out-of-date —it wasn't done for women to go into the café, for instance—but she never commented on anything. That was the way things had always been done around here, and she wasn't about to change them.

Now, on Sunday afternoons when almost everyone in the village took a stroll, it was impossible for her to get down the street without stopping for a chat. Most people made a pretense of talking to Peter and she realized it was shyness which had held them back. Some were intractable—the old people mainly, who distrusted French-speaking people, let alone foreigners—but most treated her with kindness and warmth.

Peter was running ahead, his small legs flying in a funny wheeling motion peculiarly his own. Because it was a Sunday people were in their best clothes, black for the older women, simple printed cotton frocks for the younger. The men wore ill-fitting suits and shirts too tight at the neck so that they ran their fingers inside their collars. Julie smiled. The women loved dressing up, but how the men hated it!

Peter disappeared into the lane that formed one arm of the crossroads. When Julie turned the corner, the small figure had slowed down and was waiting for her. She caught up with him and bent to kiss him, then together they climbed slowly toward the small house which stood alone on the brow of the hill.

After a while Peter began to drag his feet. His breath came in short pants, like a small steam engine. Julie reached down and, taking his hand, squeezed it tightly.

She said, "Not far now." He gripped her hand tightly and looked up, "Mummy, it *is* a tall hill, isn't it?"

She nodded and smiled. She thought: Why can't it always be like this? Why did Monday ever have to come?

When they reached the house, Julie pulled the latch and they entered the darkness of the front parlor. The room was simply furnished with a large dark-wood table, six straight-backed chairs and a dresser. The walls were covered with a traditional Breton wallpaper, a pattern of flowers on trelliswork, and were bare of pictures except for a cheap religious print framed in gilt. The ceiling was low and supported by heavy beams.

As they took their coats off there was a call from the kitchen and Tante Marie appeared. As soon as she saw Peter her round face broke into a smile.

She leaned down to pinch Peter's cheek. "And how did you enjoy your walk, my hero?"

"Oh, we saw a boat, and I picked Mummy some flowers. . . ."

Peter chattered on in his broken French, and Tante Marie listened studiously, exclaiming loudly at the amazing things that had happened, and sighing deeply at the list of creatures that had not, on this occasion, presented themselves for Peter's inspection. There had been no ant's nest this time, or a nesting plover.

Julie sank gratefully into a chair by the old stove and watched Tante Marie's face as it went through all the necessary reactions

from astonishment to amazed delight. Julie decided, not for the first time, that it had all turned out pretty well. Not only did the old woman love Peter, but she took trouble with him. During the day, while Julie was away, she taught him things, about why plants and flowers grew, and how things worked; and they drew pictures and built paper castles together.

The old woman straightened up and, going to the larder door, emerged with bread, cold meat and a dish of late strawberries. "Here, a surprise!" She put them on the table and Peter wriggled up onto a chair, his little face glowing with delight.

Tante Marie sat down on the other side of the kitchen range and smiled as she watched Peter. "I picked the strawberries this afternoon. We'll have a few more bowlfuls yet."

When the old woman smiled her face was transformed. She was only about fifty, but she looked ten years older. Like many of the women in the village she made no effort with her appearance beyond neatness and cleanliness. Her gray-black hair was parted in the center and scraped back into a bun at the nape of her neck. Her figure was full and round and it was a long time since she had made any attempt to lose weight. Now she thought it unimportant. Her clothes were simple to the point where she had two working dresses, which she wore alternate weeks, and one best dress. She hardly ever felt the cold and made no concession to the weather, except when there was snow on the ground, and then she wore a cardigan.

Her face was round and plain and red-cheeked. To her, life was a serious business. When her husband read from the newspaper she always tutted and shook her head: she thought the world mad and she viewed people's motives with distrust. The only important things, she believed, were the family, honest work and fear of God.

But with Peter she was different. With Peter she smiled a lot. She had never had children of her own.

Peter pushed the cold meat to one side and got down to the strawberries. Tante Marie turned to Julie and sighed. "Your uncle is very worried. He thinks war will really come."

Julie frowned. She hadn't been following the news very carefully. Occasionally she glanced at her uncle's newspaper, or listened to a neighbor's wireless—there was none in her uncle's

house—but her real passion was for books. In England reading hadn't interested her. But in Brittany she'd turned to books to fill the long evenings and improve her French. Now they were a great pleasure and she was rarely without a book in her hand.

"Do you think there'll be a war?" Julie asked.

"I think people are selfish and cruel enough to do anything. Particularly the Germans." Tante Marie had firm opinions about almost everything.

"But why? Why do the Germans want war?"

Tante Marie shrugged. "You ask me? I wish I could tell you. The usual things, I suppose. Power and hate and jealousy."

There was the sound of a door opening. Tante Marie inclined her head toward the front parlor. "Here's your uncle. Ask him. He's been down in the village talking about it most of the afternoon."

The parlor door opened and Jean Cornou came in. He pulled up a chair and sat down, breathing heavily after his climb up the hill.

"The news is bad, bad."

Jean Cornou was short and square, with wide shoulders and muscular arms. He farmed the land around the house the only way he knew, and that was the old way, with little machinery and a lot of hard work and the help of a single farmhand. His face was uneven, open and kind. In his best clothes, which he wore now, his rough hands and face and muscular body looked oddly out of keeping with the dark three-piece suit and white shirt. The waistcoat was too tight for him and his stomach bulged against the buttons.

He leaned forward to take off his jacket, then unbuttoned his waistcoat and sighed deeply. "The Germans look as though they are going to attack Poland. If they do there'll be a war. A war!" He snorted with disgust.

Julie frowned. "But who . . . which countries will fight?"

"Oh, Britain and France will fight Germany. Now that those filthy Russians have signed up with Germany, there'll be no stopping Hitler. Communists! They're not to be trusted. They've sold us down the river, just as I always said they would. Nothing but trouble, trouble. The great hope of France, they were meant to be. And what happens? They sell out at the first opportunity."

Tante Marie tutted quietly.

Peter had dropped a book on the floor and Julie automatically went to pick it up. Peter said, "Mummy, read me a story!"

"Later, darling, I'm talking. Here, look at the pictures in this one. When you've finished I'll tell you a story. Promise." Julie stroked his head and returned to her chair.

She looked at Jean. "So what will happen? Will it last long? I mean, surely it will be settled quickly?"

"Who knows? With every country in Europe jostling for position, anything can happen. How can anyone say who will get involved and how far the fighting will spread? All I know is that, thanks to those spineless Communists backing Hitler, the cause of socialism has been set back fifty years. Everyone's anti-Communist now—*and* anti-Socialist. They put the two together, Communist-Socialist, Socialist-Communist! Everything that the workingman has won in the last five years will be lost forever! We think of Hitler as a Fascist, but this Daladier government of ours is not far behind. And speaking of Communists, Michel was down at the café."

Tante Marie glanced up from her knitting and they both looked at Julie. She blushed, mainly because they were expecting her to. Michel Le Goff was Tante Marie's nephew by marriage. He came to the house quite often. Julie enjoyed his visits; he was clever, well informed and politically argumentative. He was probably quite attractive too, if you cared to think about him that way. But she did not, not at the moment anyway. She hadn't closed her mind to the possibility of liking him, but she wasn't ready to encourage him yet. Perhaps she never would be. Until her mind was made up, she did wish people wouldn't pair them off.

Peter was fidgeting at the table. "Mummy, I've finished. Read me a story now. Please. You promised!"

"Yes, of course, darling. And it's almost bedtime, too."

She picked him up and carried him through the back door of the kitchen into the extension. There were two rooms, one on the ground floor and, at the top of some steep, narrow stairs, a small attic bedroom. Julie used the main room as a bed-sitting room, though she nearly always sat in the kitchen during the evenings. The room was simply furnished with a bed, a chest of drawers and

a chair. Soon after her arrival she had whitewashed the walls and hung a couple of colorful pictures to brighten the room up. Though she didn't like needlework, she had even made some curtains for the window.

On the chest of drawers were several framed photographs of Peter, and one of her mother. When Julie thought of her mother, she sighed. She wrote to her mother regularly, every month or so, but she rarely got a reply. The few letters she did get were bitter and full of reproach, begging her to come back to England and live in Plymouth again. Her mother never missed an opportunity to make it clear that she felt abandoned and betrayed. Disloyal and ungrateful were her favorite words.

It was clear to Julie that her mother could not have paid attention to any of her replies, otherwise she would have understood. Julie had explained that she was happy here, that she enjoyed her work and she loved the people. But now, after so much time, Julie suspected that Mother did not want to understand. Mother hated the idea of Julie liking Father's people and living the kind of life Father had lived and which Mother had tried so hard to drag him away from. The suspicion made her sad but all the more determined not to go back. Life at the little house in Plymouth would suffocate her. Here at least she was free.

She undressed Peter and gave him a quick bath. As she dried him he wriggled away from her and dashed around the room, attempting as usual to evade capture, pajamas and bed. Julie chased him, roaring like a lion. At last she caught a flying arm and threw him giggling onto the bed.

Peter cried, "Again!"

Julie put her head on one side and listened; there was the sound of a new voice from the kitchen. It was Michel's. She said firmly to Peter, "No."

"If you don't, I'll cry."

"And if you don't let me put these pajamas on, there'll be big trouble." She gave him a mock glare.

Peter's lower lip wobbled and he began to cry, though rather halfheartedly. He often cried when he was tired. She kissed him and felt the soft, cool arms encircle her neck. She put her arms around his small body and, taking him on her knee, rocked him gently back and forth as she had when he was a baby.

After a while she felt a kiss on her ear and a small voice said, "Story now?"

"Yes, we'll have *two* stories tonight."

She read him three stories because he'd been a good boy and because she always read him one more than she said she would. Then she carried him up the narrow stairs to the attic bedroom. It was small, with one bed and a tiny window, but it was snug and Peter loved it because when he woke up in the night he could call down to her and, in the morning when he crawled into her bed, it wasn't far for him to come.

She gave him a last kiss and went down the stairs to the chest of drawers. She opened the top drawer and, taking out a small mirror, examined herself critically. She didn't like her face much. Its shape was all right—oval—and her skin was as clear as a bell, but the face struck her as incredibly ordinary. Her best feature, she supposed, was her eyes, which were large and dark and fairly pretty—but she'd never dared pluck her eyebrows as the fashionable women did and so her eyes probably made little impression. Nose—all right but definitely nothing special; there was nothing very special about any of her.

Except her hair. That *was* something she was proud of. It was dark—*auburn,* they called it—and naturally curly where it met her shoulders. She never did much to it, usually parting it in the middle and holding it back with a comb at either side. She'd tried a fancy rolled style once or twice, but the hairdo detracted from the hair itself and she'd let it down again.

She brushed it now until it shone, added a touch of lipstick, and stood back.

No, nothing special about her tonight. Anyway, it was only Michel.

But at least he was a man, and unmarried at that. And she didn't meet very many of those. She was beginning to think it would be a good idea for her to have a husband. She took a last look in the mirror and thought: I'm nearly twenty-four, I mustn't wait too long. She smiled ruefully; some people would say she was already over the hill.

She straightened her dress and walked into the kitchen.

Michel was saying, "But you have to understand, it's only political expediency—political *survival*—that's all!" Julie's heart sank a

little as it always did when Michel and Jean started on politics.

Michel spotted her and got quickly to his feet, his gaze hard and penetrating. Julie decided, not for the first time, that there was something altogether too earnest about Michel. After a moment he stooped to kiss her on both cheeks.

He said apologetically, "I'm defending myself as usual, Jean thinks my politics stink." He half smiled. But Julie knew that, behind the casual manner, he was deadly serious about his opinions.

Michel sat down to face Jean again, saying, "Look, it's not something the Soviet Union wanted to do, but they had no choice, don't you see? We and the British offered them nothing, no guarantees, no treaties, just hot air . . ."

Julie listened quietly, trying to follow the arguments. Something about the intensity of Michel's opinions was unnerving. He spoke with an earnest fury that tolerated no opposition. It was a pity, she decided, because in most other ways he had a lot to recommend him.

He was dark, like many of the French: his hair was almost black and his eyes deep brown. He was pleasant-looking, though he had a way of frowning which made him look severe. He dressed well, and Julie guessed his clothes cost a lot. She smiled to herself: only in France could you find a Communist who dressed like a capitalist. But then half the population were Communist when it suited them. The rest of the time they were Socialists, or Republicans, depending on their mood.

Michel worked in Morlaix, in an insurance office. She sometimes bumped into him when she was out shopping on her lunch hour and occasionally he would buy her a coffee. Then—when he was off the subject of politics—she enjoyed his company much more. He had a dry wit and an interesting way of describing everyday things. But she'd avoided seeing him in the evenings; that would imply there was more to their relationship than family friendship, and she didn't want that.

Now Michel was speaking forcefully, his fists clenched.

"The Soviet Union does not want war. So what's wrong with her maneuvering to avoid it? If we had any sense that's what we'd be doing too instead of pledging support to Poland, which can't be defended anyway!"

Jean Cornou picked up a poker, flipped open the door of the stove and stabbed thoughtfully at the fire. "But someone has to protect countries that need protecting. Your precious Russia, she doesn't care about anyone else at all. She may be avoiding war for herself, but not for everyone else!"

"Nonsense, war should be avoided at all costs. Who wants to fight? You? Me? Of course not! The end justifies the means!"

Julie said suddenly, "There's nothing wrong with avoiding war —so long as it achieves real peace. If it just gives the bullies time to move into a stronger position, then it's no good, is it? That's what it's all about, it seems to me—bullying." She added almost to herself, "They should let the women run things, then we might have a bit of sensible government and people would be left to live in peace."

Everyone was looking at her in surprise. She'd never spoken during a political argument before. There was a long silence and Julie dropped her eyes. She'd gone too far.

She added nervously, "Anyway, why don't we talk about something else for a change. This subject is very depressing."

Tante Marie put down her knitting. "A good idea. I'll put some supper on the table. Michel, will you stay for a bite?"

There was no reply and Julie looked up. Michel was staring at her.

"A fine speech!"

There was a mocking note in his voice and she wasn't sure if he was laughing at her or not. She got up and helped Tante Marie to lay the table. As she passed Michel's chair he said, "Really, it was a fine speech."

He sounded as though he meant it and she thought that maybe she'd misjudged him. She put her hand on his arm and smiled.

They sat down at the table and talked about the harvest and the fishing industry, the weather and the fruit crop.

Eventually Michel said, "And what about your job, Julie? Are you happy there?"

"Happy enough. It's quite interesting really. I've become something of an expert on vegetable prices." She didn't add that she was often bored. But it was a job and it brought the money in. That was all that mattered.

"I only wish—" She paused. "I only wish I had more spare time."

"You should ask for shorter hours!" The subject of long hours was one of Michel's favorite subjects. He considered anything over a forty-hour week to be slave labor. "The other way is to give up work altogether."

Julie gave a short laugh. "And how would I live then?"

He shot her a glance. "You could find someone to support you."

She felt herself blushing and looked furiously at the table. I walked straight into that one, she thought.

Michel was looking at her with a smug, self-satisfied expression. Suddenly she wanted to wipe the smirk right off his face.

She said crossly, "I'm not interested in marrying just to find someone to support me. Women who do that are fools and the men who marry them are even more stupid. When I find a man I want to marry, *then* I'll be happy to let him pay the bills!"

"But marriage is a practical arrangement. If you think it's made in heaven, then you are not as clever as I thought you were."

He was warming up for an argument, Julie could see that. He would call it a discussion, but it would really be a sparring match. Michel always won those kinds of arguments. He had a way of twisting words and turning logic until his opponent's opinions appeared ridiculous.

Suddenly Julie wanted to be on her own. She made an elaborate pantomime of looking at the clock over the mantelpiece. "Goodness! Is that the time? I really must get to bed."

She stood up and made herself smile. "It was nice to see you, Michel. Good night." They kissed each other on both cheeks, and she saw that he was looking pleased with himself again. Damn him, she thought, why does he have to be so self-satisfied?

Later, when she lay in bed, she went over the conversation in her mind. Until now she'd thought Michel kind and thoughtful under his facade of cleverness and indifference. But she was having second thoughts. He wasn't kind at all; he was conceited and intolerant. There was no question of letting their friendship develop; it would never work. She'd never be happy with a man who had to score off everyone as if the whole of life were a political debate. And she hated the way he was amused by almost everything she said, like a patronizing father listening to a child.

No, whatever happened, she could never love Michel.

She thought of the alternatives—none—and wondered if she

was being too fussy. A lot of women grabbed the first man who came their way and lived happily ever after. Or did they? One never knew.

All she wanted was someone kind, thoughtful and reasonably attractive. She smiled to herself. Not much! Just what everyone else was after too.

She turned over and tried to sleep. She remembered rather guiltily that she hadn't given another thought to this war. It was difficult to be worried about an event that everyone must be working so hard to prevent. If it *did* happen it would, of course, be dreadful. But she couldn't help thinking how lucky it was that Peter and she lived so far from the German border, and that her uncle was too old to fight. The war, if it came, would hardly touch them at all. It was awful to think so selfishly, but one couldn't help it.

No: whatever happened, her little family would be safe.

It was a comforting thought and almost immediately she fell into a dreamless sleep.

6 David looked at the note on his desk. It read: "Please report to the Director at your earliest convenience." The message was innocent enough, but it gave David a twinge of uneasiness. In the past few days the laboratories had been rife with rumor. It was said that several projects were to be canceled and that many more of the clerical and administrative staff would be liable for conscription. Already some seventy of the nonscientific personnel had been called up.

David took off his white coat and pulled on his jacket. Absent-mindedly he pushed his hair out of his eyes and looked at the note again. Best to get it over with, whatever it was. Automatically he checked his desk to make sure there were no confidential files

lying around. He always did that; you could never be too careful.

The Director's office was on the third floor and David decided to walk up the stairs rather than use the elevator: it would be good for him. He only wished he could find more time for exercise.

He arrived in the outer office breathing heavily and, when the secretary asked him to wait, he was glad of the chance to sit down for a moment. They'd never asked him to wait before. The Director usually made a point of not keeping the senior scientists waiting, and on minor matters he liked to come down to the laboratories rather than call them away from their work. Still, one shouldn't attach any undue importance to that. It probably meant nothing.

There had been other incidents, of course, and David was well aware that they *did* mean something. When a new steering committee had been set up within the Gema Company he and another scientist had been excluded from it. Both of them were Jewish. Shortly afterward, for no apparent reason, he had been told that he would not be attending a demonstration of the new Wassermann early-warning radar system.

And then there were the small things: the way people avoided him, the way he seemed to be left off circulation lists of important documents. David knew that it all meant something and it left him apprehensive. But at the same time David trusted the Director. They had worked well together for a long time. The man had gone behind Schmidt's back and provided David with facilities and a decent budget for the Valve Development Project. The man knew the importance of science. And, David thought without vanity, he knows the value of a top-rate scientist.

Ten minutes later the secretary showed him into the Director's office. The Director was sitting behind his desk, busily reading some papers.

"Do be seated, please." He didn't look up.

Eventually the Director shuffled the papers into an untidy pile. "Herr Freymann—" He looked out of the window, then down at the desk. "I regret to tell you that due to a major policy decision all long-term research is to be canceled. This has come from the highest level, you understand. It is out of my hands. In fact"— he met David's eyes—"the order came from the Führer himself."

"So the Valve Project is to go?"

"Yes."

David wasn't entirely surprised. The project was, after all, a shot in the dark as far as Gema were concerned. Back in 1936 Schmidt had produced a document which "proved" that short-wave radar was not only impossible to develop but not worth developing anyway. By supporting David for the last two years—albeit secretly—the Director had gone out on a limb. He couldn't be blamed for backing out now.

The Director cleared his throat. "It's not as if you had achieved concrete results. I mean, the valve does not produce the required power, does it?"

David looked him straight in the eye and said, "No, I'm afraid it appears not to."

"Well, there we are then." The Director picked up a paper-weight and moved it nervously from hand to hand. "There is also another problem and that is—this special scientific status. It appears that this special status is to go and . . . there is to be no widespread immunity from the draft." He pursed his lips. "Only those involved in work vital to our present needs are to be kept on."

"You mean—" David didn't understand.

The Director spoke rapidly. "I mean that only those essential to the development of existing systems like the Freya and the Wassermann are to stay. All others are to go. Your work on the development of new systems is too futuristic and . . . and your contract is not to be renewed."

"But it has two years to run. I can continue to work on *some-thing.*"

The Director looked uncomfortable. "No, it has been decided to let you go. Immediately."

David felt a tremor of fear. "I am to go?"

"Yes, I am sorry, but these are my instructions. It is out of my hands. I have been *told,* you understand."

David's throat was dry and he swallowed repeatedly. He was trying to understand, he wanted to understand. . . . But all he could see was a great hole opening up in front of him. Without his scientific status, without protection, he would be completely vulnerable, open to dispossession and God only knew what else. He felt as if his feet were being knocked from under him.

The Director was examining the paperweight and looking unhappy. David said, "Herr Director, we have known each other for a long time. You realize what this means for me? You know that without special status I am—I have no protection?"

"I am sorry. There is nothing I can do. I myself am most upset about this treatment we are getting. Science is obviously not very highly rated by those in authority. It is most unfair! Most unfair! Really—there is nothing I can do. I am sorry."

The man was avoiding David's eyes. The decision itself was bad enough but this—this could impersonal expression of regret was terrible. This man had been his colleague, his co-worker . . .

"Herr Director, I realize that perhaps you cannot help me directly—to work here—but you can help me in other ways—"

David thought rapidly. Without protection he and Ellen and Cecile would have to leave. There was no other choice, not if one wanted to work and live freely. What would he need? His passport was in order, thank God, complete with its red *J;* Cecile was on Ellen's passport, so that was all right; but they would need emigration papers. Or what did they call them now? Deportation papers, that was it, deportation papers . . . David asked, "Could you help me get deportation papers? If I can't continue with my work it would be best to leave. I hear that one needs help to get these papers. Would you? Help, I mean?"

"I'm sorry, I really don't think I can help. If I could, believe me, I would. Now, if you'll excuse me . . ."

David sat frozen in the chair. He could hardly believe his ears. Perhaps the Director had not understood. It would only take a word from him, a telephone call, that was all.

"Please, all I ask is your backing. Just to leave. That's all I want to do. Really, it won't be much trouble."

"Herr Freymann, I cannot help. It would not be *right* of me to interfere. It would not be appropriate. I try to keep out of politics —and such matters." He stood up. "I am sorry."

David got unsteadily to his feet.

"Oh, and—" There was a note of embarrassment in the Director's voice. "I will need all your confidential papers. I will send my secretary to collect them shortly."

David made his way back to his office. He walked again, but this time because he needed to be alone. He was stunned; he felt like

a child who was being punished for something he hadn't done. Not only had he done nothing to be ashamed of, he had worked hard and with brilliant results. He couldn't believe that such achievements could be overlooked and ignored. He thought: How can they do this?

But even as he thought, he knew they could—they *had*!

He felt tremendous anger, but not at them: at himself for being so ostrichlike. He had hidden behind his scientific status; he had believed he was important enough to escape this persecution. What a fool he had been, what a fool. He had made the mistake of thinking he was *different.* The sin of pride!

He closed the door of his office and sat heavily in his chair. Almost immediately there was a knock on the door and Hans came in.

"David, David. What can I say?"

"Nothing."

"What will you do?"

"Try to get out, I suppose. Except that it's probably too late for that." He laughed bitterly.

"And your special research?"

"Ended. I go, it goes. All for nothing."

"But it was going well?"

There was a pause. David looked into Hans's eyes. "Don't ask me, just don't ask me. It's better that way."

There was a sound from the door and David jumped slightly. It was the Director's secretary. She was already in the room. He thought: Now they're not even knocking before they come in. Without a word, he got up and unlocked his filing cabinet. He took out the batch of files marked with a red star and handed them to her. She accepted them and left the room.

Hans asked, "Your results?"

"Yes, everything."

Hans sat down and put his head in his hands. "Is there no end to their stupidity? Have you heard? Singers and entertainers are to escape conscription—apparently they are indispensable—but not scientists. Hitler has no idea, no idea! No."

Hans asked quietly, "What will you do?"

"There's nothing I *can* do. I imagine they will confiscate my identity card and issue me with a new one—with the name Israel,

just like everyone else. I mean"—he smiled ruefully—"just like other *Jews.*"

And there'd be more, David knew: there'd be the star on his clothes, the declaration of his wealth and, shortly afterward, the confiscation of all his belongings.

"Haven't you protected yourself?"

"The house is in Ellen's name, and some of our savings. But I couldn't transfer everything. They stopped all that."

"But Ellen—? Your marriage is privileged, isn't it? I mean she's not Jewish, is she?"

"The special status of mixed marriages ended sometime ago."

"Oh, I didn't realize."

"Nothing can save me, Hans. I have been a fool, a fool." Near to tears, he turned his head away.

Hans said anxiously, "I wish I could help."

David shook his head. "No, my friend, I don't think you can. My only hope is to buy some deportation papers. I hear they're very expensive, but . . . I might have enough money."

"If there's anything I can do . . ."

For a moment David felt a glimmer of hope. "Not unless you know an official? Someone with influence?"

"No, I'm sorry."

Everyone seemed to be saying they were sorry today. Sorry but unable to help. At least Hans meant what he said; he was a good man. But David made him leave: he couldn't bear to be pitied anymore. Besides he wanted to be alone. Hans said he would look in again before the end of the day. But he didn't: they both knew there wasn't any point.

David sat in the chair for a long time. No one came to see him and eventually people began leaving for home. Finally everything was quiet. At seven he heard the night watchman closing doors and checking windows. He put on his reading light and spread some papers on his desk. When the watchman put his head around the door David was engrossed in his work.

The watchman wanted to know how long David expected to stay in the building. David replied that he would be gone by ten.

As soon as the watchman had gone, David got up and went to the door. He listened and, satisfied that the building was empty, walked quietly down the corridor to the first laboratory. He went

straight to a small cabinet and tried the door. It was locked. He crossed to a desk and, feeling behind a drawer, found the spare set of keys the technicians kept there.

The key which fitted the cabinet was smaller than the rest and David found it immediately. He opened the door of the cabinet and took out the camera and rolls of film which he knew he would find there.

David went back to his office and opened the filing cabinet. His mouth was dry with excitement. The file he wanted was marked "Corporate Structure." The papers it normally contained were unclassified and uninteresting; it was a file people hardly ever bothered to look at, which was why David had chosen it.

He took out the file and laid the papers on the desk. He loaded the camera, checked the exposure and, putting the first page under the light, pressed the shutter.

At first he couldn't keep the camera still, his hands were shaking so. He sat for a moment and tried to calm down. It was vital to get good pictures; it was the only hope.

He stood up again and this time he could see the page clearly through the viewfinder. The job took over an hour, because he took two pictures of each of the ten pages and checked the exposure every time.

He wound the film onto the take-up spool and removed it from the camera. He replaced the camera in the laboratory cabinet and then returned to his office. He picked up all the papers that he had photographed and, putting them in the wastepaper basket, set fire to them.

It gave him a curious feeling to watch the beautiful drawings and the results of the last two years' work crinkled and blackened in front of his eyes. So much work! So much love!

He felt a stab of uncertainty. It was such a final act, this burning. It meant there was no going back. But then there had been no going back the moment he had lied to the Director about the Valve Project. The Director had asked him if the valve was producing the necessary power and David had said it wasn't. There had been no point in telling the truth. The decision to cancel long-term research had been taken at the highest level. The truth wouldn't have saved his project—or himself.

Why had he concealed the truth all this time? He still wasn't

sure. It was partly caution—he wanted to announce his results only when they were fully proved so that Schmidt couldn't tear them to ribbons. And it was partly—what? Foreboding, an uneasy feeling that he might after all be vulnerable to the Nazi campaign? Yes, that too. But also—and he was ashamed to admit it—also pride. He wanted to keep the glory for himself, to show them that they were wrong and that he had been right, and show them in a dramatic way, by demonstrating a shortwave radar itself. That was still a good way off yet, and he would have needed more resources and at least ten assistants. It would have been difficult to keep it quiet much longer. . . .

Over the last few months he'd been falsifying the test results, only a little—but enough to make the Director think the valve was not going to be a success. His assistant had seen the results, but he was young and easily persuaded that there were still immense problems to be solved.

But there were no immense problems. Once he had discovered the best way of combining the two types of valve, he was there. Within a few months he'd produced a valve which generated 500 watts on the very high frequency of 3,000 megacycles. Despite its immense power the valve could be made very small, just as he had predicted. The radar that could be developed from the valve would be very small too. And he had predicted that also.

He felt a glow of pride. He had been *right* and Schmidt *wrong*.

It was a pity Schmidt would never know.

He tucked the spool into an inside pocket of his jacket and, wiping the sweat from his forehead, took a last look around the office.

This had been his second home, the place where he had come to do the work he loved, the place he associated with contentment and security and achievement. And he would never see it again.

Oh dear Lord. He wiped the tears from his cheeks and, closing the door behind him, walked down the passage.

As he approached the main entrance, a stab of pain shot through his stomach. Heartburn, probably. He always got it when he was late for a meal. Then, as he emerged into the darkness, it occurred to him that it was not heartburn at all, but fear.

He looked over his shoulder and, pulling his hat down over his face, walked rapidly into the night.

The room was hot and stuffy and David was having difficulty staying awake. At about four he nodded off. A loud voice announced "Next!" and David woke with a start. There were three people ahead of him and about fifty behind—there would be many more, perhaps a hundred, in the street. With a bit of luck he might get in today. Otherwise he would have to wait outside in the street all night until they reopened the office in the morning. He'd already been waiting three days.

He looked at the man ahead of him. He was well dressed and prosperous-looking; he'd probably been a jeweler or a clothing manufacturer before the crackdown. But they would have confiscated his business by now. David guessed he'd been clever and hidden plenty of money and valuables. Otherwise he wouldn't have bothered to come here. Yes, he looked the clever sort. Not like me, David thought, with no money and no influence.

It was stupid of him to have come. But he was doing it out of duty to Ellen and Cecile. He had to *try* to get the papers, he owed them that much at least.

It was five when he finally got into the Gauleiter's office; David was the last before they closed for the day. A young man looked at his papers and asked, "What are your means?"

David thought rapidly. Did they want to know what he was supposed to have or what he *actually* had? After confiscation you weren't meant to have much left.

He answered, "Enough."

"Are you sure?"

"Yes."

The young man gave him a hard stare and waved him through to the next room. It was a long palatial office at the end of which was a large desk. Behind it sat a gross figure smoking a Bavarian pipe, and beside him a male assistant with a red ledger in front of him.

The large man was reading a newspaper. He took no notice of David.

Without looking up the assistant said, "Deportation papers will cost you two hundred and fifty thousand marks. How do you intend to pay?"

David gulped. When he'd last heard they had been priced at

150,000 marks, which he might have been able to borrow from Ellen's father. But this!

"Well?" The assistant was impatient. It had been a long day and he wanted to get home.

David thought: I must say something—anything—just in case. He said, "I'll pay in cash—but it'll take a week."

The assistant looked at the fat man. "Herr Deputy Gauleiter, he wants a week to pay."

"What?" The fat man seemed irritated at being disturbed. "No, no, no! Get him out! No money, no papers."

It was all happening so fast. David tried to think. He said, "Tomorrow then! Tomorrow!"

The assistant stared at him, then nodded brusquely. He scribbled on a card and handed it across the desk. "This will get you straight in here tomorrow. But if you do not have the money you will be arrested for wasting the Deputy Gauleiter's time."

David went out into the street and leaned against the wall. He was tired, so tired. He looked at the long line of waiting people, each wearing a star, each with a look of resignation on his face. Probably one in fifty could raise 250,000 marks. For some people it amounted to a lifetime's pay. For David it was about ten years' salary.

There was only one source he could get the money from: Ellen's father. But it would represent a vast amount of money to him, more than his life savings. David began to walk. How much was he worth to his father-in-law? Not that much, never that much.

Why then had he bothered to go through that playacting back there? It was a waste of time: he'd known it was no use the moment he'd heard the amount they wanted.

Suddenly David made up his mind. He'd given them their chance; he'd tried to do things their way. Now they left him no choice.

He took a tram to the Tiergarten. On the south side of the park were some of the principal embassies in Berlin. He hadn't thought which embassy he would try first: perhaps the British, then the French. If he had no luck there he would try the Americans or one of the Scandinavian countries.

He got off at the end of Tiergartenstrasse. In the park he could

see a group of *Jungvolk* training for their initiation into the Hitler Youth. Some were running the compulsory 60 meters, others jumping the 2.75-meter long jump. Another group were sitting in a circle chanting the *Schwertworte,* the short version of the Nazi dogma which had to be learned by heart. The children looked so sweet, sitting there in the sun in their neat uniforms, that David stopped to watch them for a moment.

As he neared the embassies he pulled his raincoat on. It wasn't raining but he wanted to hide the star stitched onto his jacket. They might stop him otherwise; they might prevent him from going in.

The first embassy was just visible through a thick screen of trees, an imposing white mansion set back from the road behind metal railings. David was fairly sure it was the United States Embassy. Perhaps he should try there: in the last ten years the country had taken a lot of Jews in. Yet at the same time it was neutral—perhaps they wouldn't be interested in trading his information.

Outside a group of people was gathered on the pavement, standing quietly, waiting. Between them and the gates of the mansion were stormtroopers, weapons held ready across their chests.

David walked slowly up. It was definitely the United States Embassy. The waiting people were Jewish. No one was being allowed in. He asked one of the waiting men: no one had been allowed in for weeks.

It was the same outside the French Embassy, and the British. Except that there were fewer people waiting.

He thought: I'm so stupid; of course they're not going to let people in. Of course!

The telephone, he should have used the telephone. He walked rapidly through the streets until he found a post office. He went up to the counter and asked for a booth. The girl behind the counter was young and quite pretty. She glanced up and then stared at him hard. David thought: She's going to make trouble. The girl blinked, then asked, loudly and deliberately, for his identity papers. The other counter staff fell silent; people looked. David reached in his jacket pocket and passed over his papers. Quickly, he pulled open his raincoat: it was a serious offense to

hide the star on his jacket. The girl looked at him triumphantly and said, "Non-Aryans are not permitted to use the telephone here."

It was a new restriction David had never heard of. In fact he was certain that no such restriction existed. But there could be no argument: that was one thing he'd learned during the last week.

They watched him as he turned away. He heard the girl laughing as he closed the door, and the heat of humiliation burned his cheeks. He shrank into the porch and leaned against the cold stone. The tiredness hit him like a hammer. He hadn't slept properly for three days and he felt sick with fatigue.

He looked at the time: it was nearly six. The embassy staff would have shut their offices by now anyway. It was too late to do anything more today. Another day gone and nothing achieved.

He thought: I'm tired, just tired.

He went to the station and took the train home. As he walked toward his house he passed the little shoe shop. The posters marked JEW! had long since disappeared from the window. Now there was one small notice discreetly placed among the shoes on display. It read: UNDER NEW MANAGEMENT. David wondered what had happened to Finstein. No one bothered to ask about their neighbors anymore; it was better not to know.

When he came around the bend in the road the sight of the small cozy house no longer thrilled David. Instead it reminded him of his family and his responsibilities. He wanted to protect his family, to provide and care for them. If a man couldn't do that then he wasn't worth much.

He wondered if Ellen would be crying again. She had been crying almost continuously since he had lost his job. He couldn't blame her, of course; she had every reason to cry.

He called a hello and waited for Cecile to come bounding into the hall and give him a hug as she always did.

There was silence and he called again.

The kitchen door opened and Cecile came out. She was sobbing into a handkerchief. She didn't run up to him but hovered miserably by the door, shaking her head from side to side. "Oh Daddy, Daddy!"

David stepped forward, his arms outstretched. "My little rab-

bit, whatever is the matter?" Cecile had never cried before, not like this. She was usually so brave, so fearless.

Ellen appeared in the doorway behind her. "It was no good, I suppose? You haven't got the papers?"

"They wanted . . . too much."

Ellen said firmly, "Go upstairs, Cecile. I want to talk to your father."

Cecile gave a sob and ran past him up the stairs. David looked at Ellen in bewilderment. She beckoned him into the living room.

"David, I have something to tell you." She paused and started fiddling with a china dog on the mantelpiece. Eventually she said, "Cecile and I are going away. I've been talking to my father and we've agreed that it's the only way."

"What do you mean?"

Ellen took a breath and turned to face him. "We want the best for Cecile, don't we? Well, there's only one way to be sure she doesn't suffer. And that's for us to leave. I'm sorry, David, but I think it will be better if we . . ." She licked her lips nervously. ". . . If we live apart."

"Live apart?"

"Yes, Cecile and I are going away, to a new place."

"A new place? But . . . it'll be so difficult for Cecile . . . settling into a new school. And . . . at least everyone knows us here, accepts us . . ."

"Accepts us? Are you mad? Don't you realize what it's been like for me? And for *Cecile*? You have no idea what she's been through at school. They all *know* about you, they know that Cecile is partly Jewish. They taunt her, do you hear me, they *taunt her*!" Ellen was spitting at him, her eyes blazing.

David sank into a chair and murmured, "Oh God, oh God."

"I told you it was happening, but as usual you had your head in the clouds, where it always is. I told you last November, when . . . when . . . those awful things happened, but you wouldn't listen!"

She was referring to Crystal Night, a major attack against the Jews; many synagogues, shops and flats had been destroyed.

David shook his head. "But wherever you move to they'll still *know*. You'll still be my wife and you can't hide that."

Ellen drew a deep breath. "I am going to divorce you, David.

I'm going to take a new name and make a fresh start. For Cecile, it's for Cecile. You must see . . . how important it is, for her sake."

David was dumbfounded.

She couldn't be doing this to him. The idea of losing his little rabbit was almost more than he could bear. Then a terrible thought came into his mind. He trembled as he asked, "When? When are you going?"

"Tonight. My father's coming to collect us in the car."

A vise tightened around David's heart. He gasped, "Oh no, oh no. Not yet, please not yet." Then he remembered the telephone call and how he would sell his invention. "You *mustn't* go, not yet. I forgot to tell you. I've got to make a telephone call in the morning. There's a really good chance we'll get papers. Really! The best chance yet! I'll go to the post office first thing."

Ellen moved impatiently toward the door. "David, these schemes of yours . . ." She shook her head. "Anyway, I don't want to live abroad. I want to stay here with my family."

David cried bitterly, "I'm your family too, remember!"

But she had gone.

He tried to think, but it was no good, he was just too tired. Hopelessness and despair overwhelmed him.

After a while he climbed the stairs to Cecile's room. He found her lying on the bed, crying silently. He went to her and touched her arm. She reached out and together they sat on the edge of the bed, their arms around each other, rocking gently.

David thought: Everything I want is here, my family, my daughter. Is it so very much to ask? What did I do that they should take it away from me?

Finally, after a long time, he said, "My little rabbit, it's for the best, you know. Your mother is right. You will be safer with a new name and a new place to live." Cecile started crying again and he said, "I want you to be very brave. I want you to go away and to make a success of your life. And to forget about me."

"I couldn't, Daddy, I couldn't."

"But you must. I'm going to go abroad. I can't be a proper father to you when I'm away."

"But you'll always be my Daddy."

"Yes, I'll always be your Daddy." David hugged her tightly and wept quietly.

Then there were sounds from below and without a word Ellen came and took Cecile downstairs. David couldn't bring himself to watch them go. Instead he sat on Cecile's bed and put his head in his hands.

The silence pressed in on him and, when he couldn't bear it any longer, he lay down and put his arms over his head. Finally he fell asleep and dreamed that Cecile was dead.

When David woke it was dawn and he was very cold. For a while he lay on the bed watching the thin gray light illuminate the toys and gay pictures that decorated the neat, feminine room. The room looked cold and unused, as if Cecile had been gone a long time.

His head ached viciously. Lack of sleep and food.

Mechanically, he went into the bathroom to wash. In the main bedroom he found a clean shirt and his best suit, and put them on.

He went downstairs. The house was deathly quiet. Normally Cecile would be chattering away in the kitchen while Ellen made the breakfast. He decided to turn the radio on as soon as he got into the kitchen.

But first he went into the dining room and, reaching up to the top of the dresser, felt for the black canister. As his fingers closed over it, he experienced a thrill of excitement. So much in such a small container!

But small though the canister was, it was still too large. It would be impossible to hide on his body. Any good search would soon discover it under his arm, or strapped to his leg. He opened the canister and took out the roll of film. It was only half an inch high and an eighth of an inch in diameter.

In the kitchen, he found a piece of greaseproof paper. He cut an oblong strip and rolled it around the film, then tied the ends with cotton.

David was pleased. It was small enough now to be hidden in his mouth. Or even in other places where people wouldn't look. Well, hopefully not.

Getting the film developed had been the most difficult part. The local photographic shop had been out of the question; they would have reported him straightaway. There was a man at Gema

whose hobby was developing and printing his own photographs, but it would have been far too dangerous to contact him. Then David had remembered the processing laboratory which the Gema Company used for all its photographic work. He went there straightaway, before the laboratory knew he had been dismissed and while he was still angry and had the nerve to ask them to process the film and transfer it onto the smallest possible negative. He said it was top secret, and they mustn't talk about it. His own daring had amazed him.

It was the strangeness of the request which made the laboratory carry out the work without question. The technicians were called in from the processing lab and everyone was so engrossed in deciding how the reduction could be done they didn't stop to query it. They didn't even notice the sweat on David's brow or the way his hands shook as he passed over the film.

Now David held the tiny packet in his hand and wondered where he should hide it for the moment. Best to be on the safe side. He took some surgical tape from the first aid box in the bathroom and stuck the roll onto the underside of his upper arm. It was not very satisfactory—if they were actually looking for a roll of film they would find it—but it would have to do.

He found some bratwurst and black bread in the kitchen. There was a spoonful of coffee in a jar; he put it in a strainer and poured hot water over it. It tasted foul. He sat at the kitchen table and looked out at the small, neat garden. In the summer they always spent Sunday afternoons there, just the three of them. David turned on the radio. The set was a new Volksempfanger People's Receiver; he had bought it as a present for Ellen's birthday.

David listened halfheartedly, thinking of Cecile. The announcements were always the same nowadays. People were exhorted to greater service and sacrifice for the Fatherland; they must unite against the enemies of Germany; the young men must be ready to serve in the cause. Today the enemy seemed to be Poland, who was even at this moment threatening the very security of the beloved Homeland. Poland? It had been Czechoslovakia for so long that David couldn't get used to all this talk about Poland. But perhaps Poland had been the enemy for some time; he hadn't been paying attention.

The announcer turned to home news: today another great step

had been taken in the eradication of the common enemy! The filthy Jews would no longer be permitted radios. No longer would they be permitted to enjoy the fruits of their thieving and usury! Millions of honest Germans would now be free to listen in peace, in the knowledge that not a single conniving Jew was defiling their beloved programs!

David froze with a piece of bread halfway to his mouth and felt vaguely sick. He should have realized that this campaign was much, much worse than the ones before. And now it was almost too late. But not quite.

He washed up the breakfast things and went into the hall. It was eight-thirty. The telephone stood on a small table beside the stairs. The embassy offices would be staffed by now; he should call as soon as possible. And yet—not from here. The operator might have instructions to report all calls made to embassies; she might listen in; *they* might listen in. No, he would go to a post office, a different post office from the one last night, and hope he wouldn't be questioned. That would be safer.

At the post office there was a line for the telephones. David waited quietly. The important thing was not to attract attention or get in anyone's way. At one point a large woman came bustling in and, seeing the line of people, sighed loudly. Without a word David stood back and let her take his place. She started to say something but, seeing the star on his jacket, tightened her lips and turned away.

Eventually only one person was ahead of him and no one behind. David eyed the girl at the desk nervously. When his turn came she glanced up quickly and, without comment, directed him to a booth.

So far, so good.

He gave the operator the number of the British Embassy and waited, swallowing nervously. He hadn't really thought of what he would say. It was so difficult to know when you didn't even know who you'd be speaking to.

There were several loud clicks on the line and a woman's voice said in German, "British Embassy."

"Hello. I wish to speak to . . ." He thought: *Who?* ". . . To the attaché who deals with scientific matters."

There was another click. A man's voice said, "Yes?"

"I am a scientist," David began lamely. "I wish to emigrate. I—"

The voice interrupted, "The immigration section of this embassy has closed. We are not dealing with any new applications."

"But you don't understand, I . . . I have special information." David hated to say such a thing over the telephone but he had the feeling the man would soon hang up.

"Who are you?"

David paused unhappily. "I'd rather not say . . . it's too risky. Can't I meet someone? Or come to the embassy?"

"One moment, please."

David waited uneasily. He hadn't thought about the problems of making contact. It was horribly dangerous . . .

The voice said, "It is regretted, but we cannot be of assistance."

David's heart lurched. "What do you mean? I have vital information, of great value!"

"We regret but, in view of the gravity of the international situation, it is impossible for us to become involved."

David stared at the wall of the booth, the receiver forgotten in his hand.

The voice spoke again. "Hello?"

"Yes."

There was a pause as if the owner of the voice was considering what to say. "We are not alone. Do you understand what I mean?"

"Yes." David understood. The conversation was being listened to.

Confused, he replaced the receiver. The certain knowledge that the embassy phone was tapped had been a shock. He hadn't been ready for that. He must think again.

Perhaps the Swedes? Yes, the good neutral Swedes. He found the number in the directory and gave it to the operator.

After a few seconds there was a reply. David was about to speak when there were two loud clicks. He froze, then slowly replaced the receiver.

He paid for the calls and left the post office.

He had to think: *he had to think.*

He walked into the street, his head down, his mind working. One thing was clear, absolutely clear: to try to contact an embassy would be suicide. He would never get near them. If he arranged

a meeting the Gestapo would be there first. If he tried to deliver a message they would intercept it.

It was awful to give up the idea—but there was no choice. What else could he do? He thought desperately, but there wasn't much. Only escape. Escape without papers, without help . . .

The black jackboots were right in front of him before he saw them. He tried to step sideways but a second pair of boots blocked his way. David looked up and felt a stab of fear. Two young SS men were facing him; they were both smiling. David stepped quickly against the wall and tried to slide along it. The young men laughed and shouted. He felt a sharp blow on his head. He knew he had to run. They were coming for him again. He gathered his strength and made for a gap between a uniformed body and the wall. He pushed through, felt a blow on his shoulder, pushed again and ran.

He ran as he used to do at school: fast, his chest out, his arms pumping. His lungs were bursting, they wouldn't draw enough air. His legs were heavy as lead. He rounded a corner and staggered against a wall, his chest heaving, his head pounding.

He looked behind. There was no one.

Thank God. Thank God.

He thought: How stupid! How stupid! Must be more careful, must be more careful.

He walked slowly toward home, his heart hammering, his breath rasping in his throat. So unfit! So pathetically unfit!

Finally he neared the house. The windows were dark, the front door closed as he had left it.

The front door yielded easily to the key. The living room looked untouched, as neat and ordered as usual. He peered out of the window into the street. Nothing.

But there wasn't much time, he knew that now.

He waited for his hands to stop shaking and thought: I'm too old for all this, too old and too tired.

Then he looked through the bookcase until he found Cecile's world atlas. He knelt on the carpet and studied the map of Europe. He would go west, that was certain; the east was trouble. That meant Switzerland or France or Belgium or Holland. Switzerland was out; they were too uncharitable and, even if you got over the border, it was rumored that they sent you back again.

Belgium or Holland; he wasn't sure about them. But France
. . . France had taken lots of Jews, he knew that. And even if he
couldn't stay there they would send him on somewhere else.

France . . . He turned to a map that showed the Franco-German
border more clearly and wondered where it would be best to
cross. The border would all be heavily militarized, of course, but
it shouldn't be too difficult to get through, not if he was patient.

A long section of the border ran along the Rhine, so that was
no good; the bridges would be heavily guarded and he couldn't
swim. Where the border turned west then, toward Luxembourg.
He put his finger on the Saar region. What was wrong with the
map there? Of course. He sighed; the atlas was pre-1935 and
didn't show the new border. In 1935 the Saar had become German again. He didn't dare cross there; it would be hopeless if he
didn't even know where the border was. That left the stretch to
the east of Saarbrücken.

He looked at the railway lines. How far could he get without
risking being picked up? Mannheim perhaps. Then what? It was
sixty kilometers from Mannheim to the border. He made up his
mind: although he was unfit, he would walk. He would *make*
himself walk. He'd been quite a walker in his day. When he was
a student he used to go hiking in the Bavarian Alps, covering
twenty kilometers a day sometimes.

He would need food, money and equipment. He tore the page
out of the atlas and put the book away. Money: he had enough
to buy his train ticket and a few meals, no more; but it should be
sufficient. Anyway he would be taking as much food as possible.
He went into the kitchen and looked in the cupboards. There
were cans of sauerkraut, beef and fruit. He decided to take them
all. But he would need something to carry them in. Not a briefcase; people associated them with wealth and money, and he
might be robbed. A shopping bag? Even that wasn't very safe
nowadays. He looked around the kitchen. There was nothing
else: the shopping bag would have to do. It was made of woven
straw and should be fairly strong. He would make straps for it,
to carry it on his back. He thought of the lovely rucksack he had
in his bedroom, but that was out of the question; it was far too
obvious.

He took a sharp knife from the kitchen drawer and wedged it

into the bottom of the bag. What else? A small flashlight, some string, a can opener . . . But he mustn't take too much. He had a long way to walk.

Shoes, he would need good shoes, and some warm clothing. A raincoat, a warm sweater . . .

Finally it was done. He tried to think of what he might have forgotten, but everything else of use was too heavy and bulky to be carried.

When should he go? It was a long journey to Mannheim—at least a day, even by express. It would be best to start first thing in the morning so that he could avoid arriving at Mannheim in the middle of the night, when they would spot him easily. In the meantime he would rest and go over all the details.

He went to his room and lay on the bed. Occasionally he took out the map and had another look at it. Toward evening he made himself a hot meal of eggs and sausage and then went upstairs for a bath. He removed the package from under his arm and put it in the pocket of his jacket. He would tape it back on in the morning. After his bath he went straight to bed, his clothes already folded beside him.

He didn't sleep immediately but stared out of the window and watched the clouds darkening in the gathering dusk. He was really quite pleased with his preparations. Ellen had always accused him of never getting on with things. Well, she couldn't say that now. He had planned it all and he was going to go through with it. And when he got to France he would sell his secret and buy himself a new life. One day he would send for them, Ellen and Cecile, and they would be proud of him. Yes, proud.

He fell asleep surprisingly easily and awoke only when a dog barked in the next-door garden. He flicked on the light and looked at the time. It was five to twelve.

He went straight back to sleep and dreamed that Cecile was in the kitchen, laughing in the sunlight.

When the crash came he thought it was part of the dream, a plate dropped on the floor.

Then he was wide awake.

There was a moment of ear-splitting silence. Then there was another crash and a loud drumming noise. The noise got louder. It was the sound of people running up the stairs.

David sat up and started to get out of bed.

The door burst open and David knew it was too late, too late for everything. In that instant he knew he would never see his little rabbit again.

There were two of them. They grabbed him and dragged him onto the landing. He heard a dull thud and realized his head had crashed against the doorframe. At the top of the stairs he was pushed. He fell forward, putting his arms out to break his fall. He came to a stop halfway down. He got slowly to his knees, holding onto the banisters while he caught his breath.

When the kick came it took him entirely by surprise. He couldn't understand why the hall was rushing up toward him. He put his arms out in front of him, but he was going too fast, too fast. There was a sickening crunch, his head snapped around and he thought: They've killed me!

Then he was being pulled to his feet, a terrible pain in his shoulder. He cried out. But they were dragging him again, pulling on his shoulder. He nearly fainted with the pain. He could hear them talking, but the voices seemed a long, long way away.

They threw him down and, after a while, he opened his eyes. He was in the living room. All the lights in the house were blazing; they hurt his eyes. He could hear movements above and dull thuds and crashes, they were going from room to room. He thought: They're searching, they're searching for the film. It was sitting in his jacket pocket. They would find it. *God, how could I have been so stupid?* He sat up gently and leaned against an armchair. The pain in his shoulder was agonizing.

Boots drummed down the stairs and David felt his stomach turn. The footsteps went into the kitchen, where there was a deafening sound of breaking china and glass.

Finally the men came in. David was surprised to see that they were quite young, only about twenty. There were three of them, not two. They had some of Ellen's jewelry and the nice piece of Meissen china from her dressing table. David felt relief: perhaps that was all they'd been after.

"Up, Jew! Now!"

David struggled to his feet. Although he had pajamas on he felt naked and bare. Why hadn't he slept in his clothes? That would have been the sensible thing to do.

Two of them came up to him and David's bowels turned to water. One said, "Where's the gold, Jew?"

"I have no gold." David saw this would not please them and added quickly, "Only money. Upstairs in my wallet."

"Where's the gold, Jew?"

"I have none."

They punched him in the stomach first, then around the head. When he was down, they kicked him.

Then they pulled him to his feet and told him they were going to break his fingers.

Through his swollen face David said, "There's no gold, I promise."

One of them grabbed his hand and David closed his eyes. He felt himself dirtying his trousers. Then he fainted.

They slapped his face until he came round.

One of them said, "Put him in the truck."

David knew he had to do or say something now, or it would be too late. "Please, can I put my clothes on?"

There was no reply.

"Please, I've dirtied myself."

The leader pulled a face of disgust and indicated he could go upstairs.

David clambered up the stairs to his room and went to his jacket.

The film was still there. *Thank God.*

He started to pull his pajamas off. He fumbled with the buttons, then tore at them. He was taking too long: they would come for him. He tried to hurry but his hands wouldn't stop shaking and the pain in his shoulder was agony.

He pulled on his shirt, some underpants, and started to climb into his trousers.

He heard clattering on the stairs and pulled desperately at the trousers. As he fumbled with the buttons a young corporal came in and pulled him by his arm.

David yelled, "My jacket! My jacket!"

The corporal stopped while David picked it up.

David thought: God, nearly lost it again. *God.*

He ran quickly down the stairs. He was learning, learning: if you didn't run you got pushed.

They were taking a last look around. David waited by the door, leaning against the wall. When they weren't looking he took the packet out of his pocket and slipped it into his mouth.

When they had taken all they wanted, they took him out of the house and pushed him into the back of a truck. It drove off so fast that David had only a moment to gaze back at the house. It seemed so strange, its lights still blazing, its front door open. David almost shouted for them to stop so that he could go back and lock up. It was wrong to leave it like that, so vulnerable, so open.

But then he realized it didn't matter. What hadn't been smashed or stolen tonight would be taken the next morning anyway.

PART TWO

1940-1941

7 The waiting was the worst.

Vasson lay on his bed and listened to the approaching rumble of cannon and the occasional blast of a distant explosion. The cannon was German, he decided, and the explosions were French. The gallant French Army was presumably pausing long enough in its rapid retreat to destroy fuel dumps. About all they had managed to do, Vasson thought with contempt.

By afternoon he knew he was right about the fuel dumps. The sky over the city had turned black with the smoke of burning oil. It was as dark as night. Paris looked like a lost city: there were no lights, hardly any people and total blackness.

Then the rain came. It was a steady downpour and it fell in thick black droplets, streaking houses, pavements and the odd passerby with oily grime.

Vasson was annoyed. He had planned to go out for a pastis at about five—assuming somewhere would be open—but now he'd have to stay in or risk having his clothes ruined.

Several times during the afternoon he went downstairs to the front door and looked out. The streets were almost deserted, except for the occasional refugee making a last attempt at flight.

Vasson couldn't see any point in leaving the city. For days people had been packing their belongings and setting out with nothing more than a few pathetic bundles tied onto bicycles or handcarts. They had no idea where they were going, or where they would get food and shelter. It was madness. They would starve—or get shot. It was much better to stay. The Germans wouldn't eat everybody. Life would continue, one way or another.

The war had been going on for nine months now. In that time Vasson had been busy. As soon as war was declared he spent all

his savings on stockings, gasoline and car tires. It was an enormous risk to spend every penny, yet it was hard to see how he could go wrong. He bought himself a cheap secondhand car and stored the stuff in a rented garage out in the suburbs at Clichy. As soon as things started to get short, he began to sell.

He sold slowly, carefully, realizing only enough cash to buy new stock, when he could find it. He traveled to small towns, to the suburbs of northern cities and the outskirts of Paris. When the price was right he bought more stockings as well as perfume and lingerie. He also bought more food: coffee and sugar mainly. The prices were high, but not half as high as the selling prices in central Paris.

It took him five months to double his stock; now he looked forward to the real payoff. It wouldn't come for a while, of course. He'd have to be patient. But when rationing and severe shortages came, he'd be ready to clean up.

The war was going to be a little gold mine, no doubt about it.

But the waiting was the worst.

It was a short night. The sounds of explosions and cannon fire continued until two in the morning. Then there was silence. For a long time Vasson did not sleep, but lay awake smoking and thinking about money. Finally, at about three, he dozed off. As the early summer dawn broke, the motorcycles came. They were far away, probably on one of the main boulevards, but the sound carried on the still June air. Vasson was instantly awake. So they were here at last.

At about six the streets were still deserted. The Germans wouldn't bother with Montmartre yet, he reasoned: they would tie up the city center and the military posts first. He went back to bed and sank into a dreamless sleep.

He woke at midday. He got up straightaway, washed thoroughly and dressed. He chose his best clothes, such as they were. It was silly to bother really, but he wanted to look good.

He left the rooming house and headed toward the Étoile and the Champs-Élysées. If anything was happening, it would be happening there.

He saw his first Germans at Pigalle. There were six of them in an armored car, looking relaxed and at ease. They know they've won, Vasson thought, they know there won't be any trouble. He

watched them for five minutes. They laughed and joked and pointed at things that interested them. They watched the Parisians politely, but did not attempt to talk to them. It was just as Vasson had thought: they didn't want to stir up trouble, they just wanted life to go on as usual.

Most of the cafés were closed, some boarded up, but Vasson found one which was open and stopped for some breakfast. He had no trouble buying a coffee but there was no bread, so he ate biscuits instead. The proprietor and his wife were talking loudly as they served their customers. Death to the Germans! They would rather die than serve the filthy Boches! They would make the scum realize they weren't welcome here! Vasson thought: A month and they'll be serving the Germans happily at double their normal prices.

He walked on toward the Champs-Élysées. When he arrived he found a large crowd already lining the long boulevard. Everyone was waiting, but no one knew what for. There was no information, but that was nothing new: there had been no information for weeks. Vasson leaned against a tree and lit a cigarette. People should welcome the Germans: they couldn't be any worse than the French Government. Not only had the Government deserted Paris without telling anyone, but they had left everything totally disorganized. There had been no call for resistance, no advice on what people should do, no preparations for evacuation. All they had done was put up posters telling people to "keep calm." The newspapers had been censored for weeks. It was laughable!

The Germans could only be an improvement.

When they came, they came in style. In triumph. There were tanks, armored cars, mounted troops, and ranks of field-gray infantry marching in precise formation. It was an incredible sight. Most of the people stared in silence, their faces angry or disbelieving; some shouted bitter comments. Vasson watched, his face impassive, and wondered how long it would be before the Germans emptied all the shops and set him up for life.

The first month was all brass bands, martial songs and jackboots. The Germans seemed to be everywhere, their music blaring out day and night in every part of the city. Posters appeared saying: TRUST THE GERMAN SOLDIERS. Strange new newspapers came

onto the newstands: *Aujourd'hui, La France du Travail,* their pages full of German propaganda. Even the long-established *Le Matin* and *Paris-Soir* soon came out with glowing pro-Nazi headlines. The swastika appeared over hundreds of buildings.

The first week was good for the retail trade—or so people believed. The Germans made straight for the shops and swept up all the lingerie, perfumes and stockings they could find. And paid for them. Motor coaches brought hundreds of soldiers into Montmartre to see the sights—ostensibly the Sacré-Coeur, but really the nightclubs and the girls. The Parisians were pleasantly surprised.

By the end of the month there was chaos. The Germans had paid for everything in occupation money which was found to be worthless; the food disappeared from the markets to feed the German Army; gasoline suddenly vanished from the filling stations; and, overnight, prices shot up.

Vasson began trading. He started by selling coffee and gasoline to the French. He dealt only in francs, in cash. As soon as he had money he spent it again, increasing his stock.

A few weeks later it was time to start dealing with the Germans. They had an almost insatiable desire for luxuries. Now that they'd emptied the shops they were happy to buy on the black market. But Vasson needed a contact: someone in supplies, who would buy his lingerie and perfume in exchange for food or tires or gasoline—he wasn't prepared to deal in worthless German money.

It didn't take long to find his man, a quartermaster sergeant called Seiger. Vasson would have preferred an officer, to make the operation more permanent and aboveboard, but right from the start Seiger and he understood each other perfectly. It was too good an opportunity to miss. By September Vasson had doubled his stock, rented a decent apartment and bought himself two new suits.

This time Vasson was determined not to fall into any traps. He would go carefully, always consolidating, always spreading the risks. The best way to spread the risks was, he realized, to branch out into other businesses. He started looking for opportunities. The girls racket was no good: everyone was onto that one and anyway half the girls had developed a bad case of patriotism and

wouldn't go with Germans. The clubs were no good either; they were still wrapped up too tight.

For a while he settled for dealing in a wider range of goods—more foods, more imported goods—but he still wasn't happy: if for some reason he was closed down he would have nothing to fall back on.

Then he stumbled on the answer, accidentally.

He'd been tipped off about a large quantity of lingerie in a warehouse in the southern suburbs. He'd never been to the place before and didn't know who ran it, but that didn't matter. He'd discovered that, when offered cash on the spot, people were quite happy to do business with him. This one would be no exception.

But he was wrong. The warehouse was run by an old Jew called Goldberg, and Goldberg did not want to do business with him. Not on any terms, not at any price. He would not say why; instead he was belligerent and rude. He called Vasson a leech and a verminous parasite and shut the door in his face.

Vasson went to Seiger; Seiger arranged a meeting with a smart young man in the black uniform of the SS; the smart young man took him to see a man in civilian clothes, someone by the name of Kloffer. They met in an apartment in the Rue Lalo behind the elegant Avenue Foch.

Kloffer was different from the Germans Vasson had met before. He was quiet, cool and slim, like a snake. He hardly spoke while Vasson told him about the Jew with the warehouse full of lingerie. He merely nodded slightly and, when Vasson had finished, gave a small bow and left. There was no time to ask questions. Vasson felt slightly cheated. Would they do anything? He wasn't sure. And, if they did, would they tell him?

After a few days Vasson could bear the uncertainty no longer. He drove to the Jew's warehouse to see if anything had happened. As he neared the place he was filled with a delicious sense of anticipation, as if he was about to be given a treat. He was not disappointed. The doors of the warehouse were open, the interior gaping and empty. The glass in the windows had exploded from the force of a fire which, from the scorch marks on the walls, must have raged for hours. Vasson was pleased; the Germans must have been impressed by what he told them. As for Goldberg, he'd deserved it. He hadn't listened.

Vasson expected to see Kloffer again, but he heard nothing. He wanted to talk about the raid, to go over the details and to remind Kloffer that it was he, Vasson, who had provided the information. He wanted his contribution to be recognized; yes, damn it, and properly acknowledged. But there was nothing.

During the rest of September and October the Germans dropped their softly-softly approach to the population: the honeymoon was over. There were arrests of Communists, trade unionists and leftist-intellectuals; the bread ration was low, unemployment was high.

In November there was more trouble: a mass demonstration by students in the Champs-Élysées on Armistice Day. The Germans arrested the ringleaders for left-wing activities.

Every week Vasson went to meet Seiger in a small bar near the Porte de Clichy. The place had two advantages for Vasson: no one knew him there and it was near the rented garage where he kept his stock.

Early in December Vasson bought a batch of high-quality stockings off a little shopkeeper in the *vingtième*. He decided to offer them straight to Seiger. He would ask for cigarettes in return; cigarettes always sold well and at the moment they were fetching particularly high prices.

He walked into the bar feeling excited, as he always did. He enjoyed doing business. It was lovely and clean and *definite*. He liked thrashing out the terms with Seiger, playing the game they always played: hedging and evading, stating and overstating, until finally the bargain was struck. There was nothing like it.

But today there was no Seiger. He searched the small bar, but the familiar uniform was missing. How irritating! Vasson did not like arrangements to go wrong.

No, there was no Seiger. Instead—Vasson's heart gave a small thud—instead there was Kloffer. He was sitting alone at a table. He gave no sign that he recognized Vasson. Vasson wondered what to do. Should he go up to Kloffer and admit he knew him? Or should he ignore him? He decided it would be safer to ignore him. He went to the bar and sat down. The proprietor sniffed at him. "Your friend not here today then?"

"No."

The man sneered. "Well, that's a loss, isn't it?"

Vasson ignored him. Another cheap patriot. He ordered a coffee, then changed his mind and asked for a pastis. He glanced at Kloffer. The German was sitting staring out of the window. Vasson downed his drink and, as he put the empty glass on the counter, he saw Kloffer get up and leave the bar. Vasson paid and followed the German out.

When Vasson reached the street, Kloffer was disappearing around a corner to the left. Vasson followed quickly. There was a black Citroën beside the curb. Kloffer was waiting at the open rear door. Two men in raincoats and fedora hats were sitting in the front. They might as well have a sign on the side saying GESTAPO. Kloffer said, "Get in."

Vasson got in, the car sped south, toward the Étoile. Vasson asked nervously, "May I ask where we're going?"

For a moment Vasson thought Kloffer wouldn't answer, then he said, "To my office."

Vasson wondered where that would be. But he didn't ask. Something about Kloffer's manner discouraged questions.

The car rounded the Étoile and turned into the Avenue Foch. When Vasson realized where they must be going, his mouth went dry. The Gestapo and the SS lived down here: the street was fast getting the pseudonym Avenue Boches. But why were they bringing him here? A nasty suspicion flashed through his mind and for a moment he thought: They're busting me, they're going to close me down. Then he decided not. If they were busting him they would have got him at the garage and taken his stock and ransacked his apartment.

The car drove under the archway of Number 82 and stopped. This was the lion's mouth: Gestapo headquarters. Its two neighbors, Numbers 84 and 86, were occupied by the SS.

Vasson followed Kloffer up the stairs to the third floor. When they finally entered a large room with deep carpets and a large empire-style desk, he felt calmer. It was difficult to believe anything terrible could happen in these surroundings. Vasson looked at the luxurious decor and realized that Kloffer was important.

When they were both seated Kloffer stared straight at Vasson and asked, "What is your name?"

Vasson almost let the surprise show on his face, but he covered

it quickly and said, "You know my name: it's Jean-Marie Biolet."

"No, your real name."

"That *is* my real name."

A flicker of impatience crossed Kloffer's face. "Come now, I know it is not."

Vasson thought quickly: How? How did he know? It *must* be a guess. Vasson had *never* been taken in by the police, not once; no one had checked his identity since he arrived in Paris.

It had to be a bluff.

"It's my real name," Vasson repeated.

"We could get the prefecture to check it. Somehow I don't think your thumbprint would match that on your identity card."

Vasson shrugged. "So check them. You'd be wasting your time. I am Jean-Marie Biolet and I come from St.-Étienne." He added, "Anyway, what does it matter? Either I can help you or I can't."

Kloffer's sharp ratlike eyes looked at the pad on the desk in front of him. Vasson realized he wasn't going to press the matter. *Thank God.*

"Very well," Kloffer said, "I want someone. I think you can find him for me."

Relief flooded over Vasson. So that was all they wanted—a person. It was to be a job like the one he'd done on Goldberg. Find and identify. Simple. But he was puzzled. Who could it be? He didn't know anyone these people might want.

Kloffer continued, "The person we want is a Communist agitator by the name of Cohen. He is a professor at the Sorbonne but has recently . . . gone to ground."

"But I've never heard of Cohen, I don't know Cohen . . ."

"Exactly. You will be perfect for the job."

Vasson began to understand. This was no Goldberg job. This wasn't a simple matter of pointing out an insignificant Jewish wholesaler, it was more, much more.

Vasson said stiffly, "But why me?"

"Oh, come now. You will be excellent for the job. You have all the qualifications. You have already proved that."

"But supposing I fail . . . ?"

"Oh, you won't do that. I have a feeling about you." He stabbed a finger at Vasson. "A feeling that you will be very good at the little tasks I ask you to do."

"But . . . where would I start? How will I find him?"

"We have some information. Cohen is a history professor at the Sorbonne. He is also the leader of a Communist cell. We have detained most of them. Now I want Cohen himself. We picked up his girl friend the other day, her name's Marie Boulevont. We released her"—Kloffer cleared his throat and looked unhappy—"but we lost her. She was living at Fifty-six, Rue Brezin. Now she too has disappeared."

In other words, Vasson thought, they've made a mess of it.

"We will give you a new name and student's papers and anything else that might be useful. Normally we would wait for someone to tell us where Cohen is, but in this case we want him in a hurry. As soon as possible. You understand?"

Vasson had expected all kinds of things. But this . . . It would be difficult, and very dangerous. Political activists would kill him without a second thought.

The money would have to be good, very good. Vasson looked up sharply: the German hadn't mentioned that.

Vasson said, "I'd want money for the job, in francs or gold, on delivery. What are you offering?"

Kloffer looked amused. "Oh, a great deal. Freedom from arrest. Your little black market operation is, after all, totally illegal. It could get you into a lot of trouble. Also freedom from investigation into your background and your—what shall we say?—dubious identity."

Vasson waited. Kloffer said, "That is all."

God! Kloffer was nothing but a cheap blackmailer. He might have known. The humiliation burned Vasson's cheeks. He thought: No, you're damn well not going to get away with it.

Vasson looked calmly down at his hands and said casually, "No."

"What do you mean?"

"I mean that I don't accept your terms. I have nothing to hide. You can close me down if you like." There was silence. Vasson glanced out of the window. "Now if we were to come to a sensible arrangement I could do a first-class job . . ."

"Go on."

"I mean that you could get any rat to do a mediocre job on those terms. But me? If I am paid a decent rate for the job, I will

do it well. And *quickly.* If not . . . if not, it would take you a lot longer to find your man, wouldn't it? Bust me if you wish—it really makes no difference." Vasson stared him straight in the eye and thought how it would, of course, make a hell of a difference: it would put him right back in shit street without any money.

Kloffer put his fingertips together and touched his lips thoughtfully. "How much would you require, Monsieur Biolet?"

"Fifty thousand francs."

"Out of the question."

"How much are you offering?"

"Ten."

They settled on ten. Vasson didn't want to argue. He didn't want Kloffer to lose too much face, otherwise he'd bear a grudge. Anyway, Vasson thought, it would be silly to push my luck.

He could always ask for more next time.

He knew there *would* be a next time. The job was right up his street. He liked everything about it except the idea of getting caught: *that* terrified him. But the rest? Yes, very nice.

He was intrigued by the idea of a new identity, a new personality which, after the job, would disappear without trace. It was neat. A clean *out,* with no comeback. It was a challenge too. It would give him a chance to show what he could do. He liked that.

And then there was the money, the lovely money.

The next day Vasson went back to the Avenue Foch, to an anonymous office on the ground floor, and collected a complete set of cards covering identity, student status, food ration, tobacco ration and military service, all of them in the name of Legrand. When Vasson saw the cards he went white with anger: the cards were hard, clean and unscuffed. They looked brand new, which was exactly what they were. He wondered if Kloffer was trying to nail him, or just being stupid. It was probably stupidity fueled by the German passion for efficiency.

Another thing: there was no student enrollment card, which was necessary for the Sorbonne. Furthermore the card would be inspected frequently, so it would have to be genuine.

He went up to the third floor and told Kloffer what he wanted.

Kloffer was not pleased. "What you ask is very difficult as well as unnecessary."

"It's essential."

Kloffer nodded curtly. It was agreed.

Vasson returned to the ground floor and settled down to wait because he didn't want to be seen going in and out of the building too often. Eventually, late in the afternoon, a sergeant called him into the ground floor office and passed him a new set of cards. The name was now Philippe Roche, and the student enrollment card was obviously genuine. Vasson guessed the other cards were genuine too: they were soiled and scuffed. He was uneasy again: suppose this Philippe Roche had been at the Sorbonne? Suppose Vasson bumped into someone who knew him?

"Is this person known at the university?"

The sergeant shook his head. "No."

"Did he ever go there?"

The sergeant eyed him lazily. "No, he never went there. He never started his course."

Vasson nodded. He didn't want to know any more.

On the way back to Montmartre Vasson bought some slacks, two casual shirts, two sweaters and a jacket from a cheap shop. Back in his room he crumpled and dirtied them a little, then changed, leaving all his own clothes behind. He packed a small bag containing his toilet kit and some pajamas, then left. He went straight to the Left Bank and wandered around the bookstalls beside the river until he found some old textbooks on French history. At a stationery shop nearby he bought a couple of blank pads, some pencils and a pen. Finally he wandered into Montparnasse and rented a room.

Then he was ready.

He would start with the girl who was meant to be a special friend of Cohen's.

But first he spent a morning just walking around the Sorbonne and the Left Bank cafés, watching the students, listening to their conversation. It was fairly easy to gauge their mood: most of them were angry, either about the Armistice Parade arrests, or the disappearance of university staff, or the curbs on student activities. Some even spoke of countermeasures, or demonstrations and open defiance.

They were incredibly naive, Vasson decided. They talked in public places, without realizing the need for discretion. Beyond

lowering their voices they had no sense of secrecy, no idea that informers might be listening. Vasson thought: This could be easier than I imagined.

In the afternoon he went to 56, Rue Brezin, the last known address of the girl friend, Marie Boulevont. Now that Kloffer's watchers had gone, she might have returned. But she hadn't. The concierge hadn't seen her for weeks and didn't know where she'd moved to. Vasson wasn't surprised. The girl would have been stupid to return.

He would have to start from scratch then. In a strange way he didn't mind. It was more of a challenge that way.

The next morning he examined the mass of notice boards in the history department at the Sorbonne and decided to go to the lecture on enlightened despotism in the eighteenth century. It was well attended, but the lecture was long and tedious. Vasson spent his time looking at the hundreds of faces around the hall. They all looked the same: like Communists. Finally, when the lecture was over and everyone was crowding through the exits, he chose a group of five students who were talking heatedly, as if they might be political types. He followed them to a café on the Boulevard St. Germain.

He sat at an adjoining table and listened. They were still talking heatedly—about lectures clashing because of the appalling new timetable. Vasson waited impatiently. This group was a dead end, he could sense it. Damn. He would have to think of a surer way.

Then Vasson realized that their voices had dropped and only the occasional word was reaching him. One of them was saying how terrible something was and the others were agreeing. Vasson strained to hear.

". . . he was arrested . . . that is certain . . ."

The voices dropped again and Vasson lost the reply. Then a third voice said, "But it's terrible to sit and do nothing!"

How right you are, Vasson thought.

Impulsively he got up and stepped over to the students' table. "I . . ." He hovered nervously. "I saw you in the lecture . . . I'm a new student. May I . . . ?" He indicated his chair and looked suitably uncertain.

One of the students nodded. Vasson stuttered, "Thanks," and drew up his chair. They made room for him, and he laughed nervously. "It's hard to find your way around!"

One, a boy with thick pebble glasses, said, "We've been here a year and we still can't find our way around!"

"Is there—" Vasson searched for the words, "—is there a lot of trouble in the university? I mean, what should one *know* about?" He peered round the table earnestly.

"Just don't get involved in—well, anything political."

There was a silence. Vasson bit his lip. "And . . . have there been many arrests?"

The boy with the pebble glasses answered. "Yes, students and staff. Efforts are made to discover what has happened to them but . . ." He trailed off.

Vasson looked grave. "I was assigned to Professor Cohen, but now I am to be in another group. Did he— Was he . . . taken?"

Pebble Glasses shrugged. "Nobody's sure what happened to him. It's thought he's in hiding, but I wouldn't know."

Vasson realized with disappointment that he was telling the truth.

It was worth one more shot. He said, "Also I was given the name of a friend of his, by a friend of my family. But—well, it's very upsetting, because she too has been taken or disappeared. And I don't know what to tell this friend. It's all very tragic, very tragic."

"Who's Cohen's friend?"

"Ah!" Vasson made a show of looking through his pockets as if for a scrap of paper which he couldn't find. By an effort of concentration he suddenly remembered the name. "Er. Oh yes. Yes, it was Marie, Marie Boulevont. That was it!"

One asked, "Marie Boulevont?"

They were shaking their heads. Vasson stood up, still saying, "Very sad, very sad." He added brightly, "Well, thank you for filling me in. See you again soon!"

Damn.

He would have to find a better way. There was only one problem: he couldn't think of one.

Damn. The next day he inspected the lecture room more carefully and chose a serious-looking student of about twenty-seven. He seemed much more the type: thoughtful and politically committed. But the student went back to his room and stayed there all day. Another dead end.

On the following day, Friday, there was no major history

lecture but a series of small seminars on specialist subjects. Vasson thought: What would a Communist be studying? He decided on European history from 1860 to 1930, the period covering the Russian Revolution.

There were only thirty students in the seminar. One, he noticed, was staring at him. He was about twenty-two, with short curly hair and glasses. His gaze was intense and hard; he was summing Vasson up. When their eyes met the student looked away and a few seconds later Vasson saw him exchange an almost imperceptible glance with another student across the room. Vasson's pulse quickened. This one was clever and sophisticated enough, that was certain.

The seminar, about the decline of nineteenth-century liberalism, was interminable. At one point the professor asked each student for a definition of liberalism. Vasson felt a moment of panic. He hadn't reckoned on that. But in the end it was easy, he just gave a garbled version of two earlier replies, defining it as freedom of the individual from excessive central control. As he spoke he was aware that Curly Head was watching him. When it came to Curly Head's turn his reply was clipped and informed; he was obviously a thinker. There was also a hint of intolerance and dogma in his speech. He even dared to differ with the professor on a point concerning "old" liberalism versus "new."

At the end of the seminar, when they all got up, Vasson stood aside to let Curly Head pass. The student went by with his head averted. But Vasson thought: He knows I'm here, he knows it very well.

Vasson let Curly Head disappear down the corridor, then asked the student next to him, "Who was the one going on about new liberalism?

The student was in a hurry. He was irritated at being detained but answered, "Eh? Oh, Laval."

Vasson picked up Laval-Curly Head as he left the building. It was four, almost dusk. The student was heading south down the broad pavement of the Boulevard St. Michel, his thick woolen coat flapping behind him, his head thrust forward. Vasson followed at a safe distance, his pace settling into a steady rhythm.

Quite suddenly Curly Head glanced over his shoulder and looked straight at Vasson. Vasson thought: He's onto me.

Curly Head hurried on. Vasson slowed his pace, walking more casually, and made a point of keeping his head down and his eyes on the pavement.

At the next corner he turned down a side street, away from the main boulevard. When he guessed he was out of Curly Head's view he crossed the street and doubled back at a run. At the corner he stopped and searched the length of the boulevard. Curly Head was some way ahead, still walking fast. Vasson pulled his coat up around his ears and followed. After a few moments Curly Head looked back again, but Vasson stepped quickly behind another pedestrian. This time he was not seen.

Curly Head walked across the south side of the Jardin du Luxembourg and into the streets of Montparnasse. He turned around only once more, just before entering a small rooming house. Again, Vasson was certain he hadn't been seen. He took up a station near the house, but on the same side of the street so that he couldn't be spotted from the windows. It was bitterly cold and after an hour it began to rain.

Vasson huddled in a doorway and thought of going back to his own room. But he decided not: the wait wouldn't do him any harm.

By seven the feeling had left his feet. All he could think about was drinking hot soup and red wine in a warm bistro.

At almost eight Curly Head came out. It was so dark Vasson almost missed him. He seemed more relaxed than before and strolled along quite casually. He didn't go far; just to a café in the next street. Vasson peered through the window. The blackout curtains were too effective and he couldn't see anything. He went to the door. Here there was a slight crack between the frame and the black cardboard stuck to the inside of the window. Vasson put his eye to the crack and saw that Laval had joined a group of people at a table. Vasson recognized two of them: one was the student who had exchanged the glance at the seminar; and the other, a girl, had been there too, sitting at the back.

Vasson walked away and looked for another café where he might get something to eat and warm up. But there was nowhere. In disgust he settled down to wait in a doorway opposite.

It was a quarter to ten and very cold when they drifted out. It

was too risky to follow Curly Head again and anyway there wasn't much point: he was probably going straight back to his rooms. Vasson decided on the girl instead; she might be an easier nut to crack. She went straight to a cheap rooming house, rather like the one Curly Head lived in. Nothing was likely to happen that night, Vasson decided. He noted the address and went back to his room to sleep.

He returned to the girl's place early, at seven. The girl wouldn't have gone out yet. He was right: she didn't emerge until midday. He followed her to the Boulevard St.-Germain. She went shopping. Just as Vasson began to worry that this was going to be another dead end, she went into a glass-enclosed pavement café and sat at a table by herself. She started to read a book, looking up only to ask for a coffee. She did not watch the street. She obviously wasn't expecting anyone.

He went into the café and walked past her table, then doubled back and stooped down to look at her. "Hello, aren't you—? Haven't we met—?"

She was plain, with thick black eyebrows, dark lanky hair and unattractive glasses. Definitely the intellectual type. Brainy but not clever, Vasson decided. She said, "Sorry. I don't remember . . ."

Vasson introduced himself. "No, why should you remember? We only met briefly, ages ago. And then I saw you in the seminar yesterday. I've just switched courses, from geography."

She squinted at him through her spectacles. "Where did we meet first then?"

"Ah, well . . ." He looked carefully round the café. "Perhaps it's best to say at mutual friends and leave it at that."

She said nothing but licked her lips uncertainly.

Vasson dropped his voice. "One can't be too careful. I saw Laval in the seminar too, but I didn't contact him. Too dangerous. Anyway he may not remember me. Did he mention seeing me yesterday?"

"No . . . he said nothing."

"Just as well."

"Shall I mention seeing you? To Jean, I mean."

Jean must be Laval. "Best not to. I—" Vasson tried to appear hunted. "I have to be very careful . . ."

She said in a low voice, "One cannot be too careful, that's for sure."

"If only more precautions had been taken in the beginning."

"Yes."

A waiter came up and Vasson ordered coffee. He smiled brightly at the girl. "I don't even know your name!"

For a moment she looked startled, then said quietly, "Sophie."

"What a beautiful name!" He thought: For such an ugly girl. She was pleased. "Oh. Thank you!"

Vasson looked at the parcels beside her. "Been shopping?"

"Yes. My allowance came through—I needed some clothes. There isn't much in the shops but . . . ." She laughed and pushed some strands of greasy hair back from her forehead. "I found a couple of things."

God, she's plain, Vasson thought, plain and boring. But he wanted the conversation to continue in the same vein. He bought her another coffee and they talked about her life, her family and the poor opportunities for women in publishing, where she hoped to get a job.

He listened attentively for twenty minutes, then decided the moment had come. He leaned toward her and, looking deep into her eyes, said, "I can't tell you how good it's been talking to you. I'd love to see you again. Can we meet later, for a bit of food? It would be fun." He touched her hand.

"Oh. Yes. I—er—yes." There was a blush on her cheeks.

Vasson hoped he wouldn't have to keep this up much longer.

The girl, flustered and confused, was making a mess of gathering her belongings. Vasson picked a package off the floor and smiled at her. "I can see I'm going to have to look after you." Her face went scarlet and she looked down at the floor.

He suddenly became serious. "By the way, perhaps you can tell me—?" He put his hand on her arm. "I've been a bit out of touch. On purpose, of course. But"—he lowered his voice to a whisper —"I've been dying to know . . . is Cohen all right, have you heard?"

Her eyes came straight up to his. She said immediately, "He's all right. He's safe."

Vasson made a show of beating his hand on his forehead. "Thank God for that!"

She started to pull on her coat while still in her seat and was soon struggling with a sleeve. Vasson jumped up to help her. When the coat was on he let his arm brush across her shoulders. Then he sat down again and put his face close to hers.

"We'll win in the end, you know. We *will* because we *must!*"

She nodded emphatically, her eyes shining back at him.

They stood up. Then he pulled her down into her chair again.

"One thing—" He wrinkled his brow. "I have reason to believe Marie may be in danger."

She gasped. "Marie . . . ? Why?"

"The word is that they're looking for her again. I don't know how to warn her."

The girl said, "Oh God. She was in a safe house, but now . . ." She trailed off unhappily.

"Now—?"

"I'm not sure . . ."

"I tried to find her at the Rue Brezin, but of course she hasn't been back there."

"Oh no, she wouldn't. The Boches have been watching it. She's —well, I *think* she may be at Su's place." She used the expression *chez Su.*

"Su's."

The girl nodded. "Yes, Su's." Obviously this Su was well known. Suzanne perhaps?

"Ah . . . where do I find Su nowadays?"

The girl regarded him sharply. A shiver ran up Vasson's spine. Something was wrong: he'd made a mistake.

She said, "Surely . . . you must know . . ."

He tried again. "I just haven't seen Su for some time . . . you know how it is . . ."

She said slowly, "But you are acquainted with her?"

Vasson smiled. "Of course."

The girl's face went sheet white. She got up from the table and, grabbing her possessions, stumbled out. Vasson followed, cursing softly.

Su? Who the hell was Su?

When he got out of the café he spotted the girl, half running, half walking down the street. From time to time she looked back. She didn't see Vasson. He guessed she was nearsighted.

152

She crossed the boulevard and hurried toward the Sorbonne. She passed the main university building and turned down a narrow back street. Vasson got to the corner and edged slowly along the last few inches of wall before peering cautiously around.

The girl was two yards away, coming straight toward him.

He yanked his head back and sprinted away. He dived into a recessed doorway, and pressed his body against it, panting hard.

The girl came into his field of vision. She searched anxiously up and down the street, then turned on her heel and disappeared.

He waited five seconds and looked out. No one. He approached the corner again and peered around. She was walking away from him. She began to turn her head. He pulled back.

He looked again. She had gone.

He walked toward the spot where she had disappeared.

There were three doorways in the vicinity. One belonged to a dingy restaurant. He glanced at the name over the door.

Chez Le Maréchal Suchet.

Chez Su.

Vasson groaned inwardly. No wonder she was onto him. Every student must know this place. Su was no lady; Su was a bloody *maréchal.*

He wondered what to do next. The girl friend, Marie Boulevont, might be here. If she was, she'd have to come out sometime. But most likely she'd go straight to ground. Damn! He'd really blown it.

He decided to wait. There was nothing else to do.

Half an hour later the girl poked her nose out of the door. Even from several yards away Vasson could see that her face was bright red. She'd probably been crying. She took a careful look up the street and disappeared into the doorway. When she came out again, another girl was with her, someone older, prettier, more self-assured. She was carrying a small case. Marie Boulevont?

Yes, Vasson decided, Marie Boulevont.

At the end of the street the women stopped, spoke excitedly for a moment and split up. Vasson followed Marie.

She was clever. He almost lost her twice. At the Boulevard St.-Germain she took the Métro to the Étoile, then hopped on a bus just as it was leaving. Vasson was lucky to jump on another bus going in the same direction. She got off at Montparnasse,

almost back where they'd started. Then she walked again, constantly glancing over her shoulder. At one point she dived into a shop. Vasson took a guess and sprinted around the block to the back of the building. There was a tradesman's entrance. Just as he got there, the door opened and Marie came out.

Got you! Vasson thought.

Then she walked again, quickly. She doubled back once more, glanced over her shoulder one last time and disappeared into a doorway beside an *épicerie*.

Vasson waited uncertainly. He had no idea what this place was. It might be a safe house she was going to use. It might just be a friend's place. There was no certainty Cohen was there.

After an hour she reemerged. She nervously searched the street, then walked quickly off. She was empty-handed. That meant she had left her case inside. That meant she would be coming back.

Vasson came to a decision. He walked in the opposite direction until he found a telephone. He called Kloffer.

He said, "Just two men—and not with Gestapo written all over them."

"What do you mean?" Kloffer replied.

"I mean choose fellows without leather coats and felt hats—people with *French* clothes for Christ's sake."

Then he went back and waited. God, Kloffer's men were taking forever. The girl would be back soon. Shit!

After ten minutes Vasson swore again, louder.

Finally he saw Kloffer's men. They still looked like Krauts.

"Come on!"

Vasson led the way angrily along the street and into the door Marie had come out of. The house was on five floors. Off each of the two landings there were three doors.

Vasson guessed at a front room. They knocked on the first door. There was no reply and one of the Germans opened it with his shoulder. Nothing. A door at the back of the house flew open and an old woman thrust her head out. Nothing there either. The old woman said the third room wasn't occupied.

They went to the next floor.

Cohen was in the front room.

Vasson knew it was Cohen the moment the pale, narrow face

appeared at the door. He was small and dark, and came out quietly, with resignation. Vasson was vaguely disappointed. The man hadn't even tried to escape.

Kloffer's men searched Cohen, then the room.

Vasson was impatient to go. "Come on!"

The Germans went first, Cohen between them. Vasson hung back and followed them at a distance. In the next street was the inevitable black Citroën. Vasson sat uneasily in the front. He didn't like being seen with Kloffer's heavies. On the other hand he wanted to be there when Cohen was brought in. He wanted to watch Kloffer's face.

There was no sound from Cohen in the back. Vasson half turned his head. "You should always choose a room with another way out, you know. That was silly of you. The girl was stupid as well—she led me straight to you." He shook his head. "It was all too easy."

There was silence. Vasson craned his head around until he could see the man's face. "You weren't very clever, Professor."

Cohen was staring out of the window, his face white and expressionless.

Vasson turned back, uneasy and vaguely angry. The sight of the man was disturbing. His silence was accusing. Vasson decided it had been a mistake to travel in the same car. The next time he would take care not to.

The driver glanced across at Vasson and said, "Don't worry. He won't be so quiet when we've started talking to him."

Vasson shuddered and wished the journey would end quickly.

When the car finally arrived at 82, Avenue Foch, Vasson ran into the building without looking back. He didn't feel comfortable until he was shown into Kloffer's office.

The German had a faint smile on his face. "Very good. Very good."

Vasson relaxed. Kloffer was obviously more than satisfied. Immediately he considered doubling his price next time—perhaps even tripling it.

There was only one loose end. The plain girl with glasses. She could identify him. That had been a silly slip, about Su's. He would have to be more careful in future.

He gave Kloffer her name and the address of her room, then

pushed her out of his mind. He didn't want to know what Kloffer would do with her.

That night he returned to his apartment, burned the student clothes, carefully hid the bundle of student identity papers, and assumed the name of Biolet again.

He went to bed content. All things considered it had gone pretty well really, even if there had been a slip or two. He must be careful not to let that happen again, it might not be so easy to cover himself next time.

8   Julie took a last look around the small whitewashed room, picked up her bag and went through the kitchen into the front parlor. Tante Marie and Peter were already outside, standing by the waiting fish truck. As she closed the front door behind her, she thought: I might never see this place again. It seemed all wrong, to be going. This was her home, her life, and she was abandoning it like a rat leaving a sinking ship.

Peter was in Tante Marie's arms, his eyes fixed intently on the tears running down the old woman's cheeks. He still didn't understand why they were going. But then why should he? He was four years old: Germans and conquerors meant nothing to him.

Nor, for that matter, did the problems of having a British passport in a country occupied by an enemy power.

During the last few days Julie had tried to imagine what that might mean. At best the two of them might be deported to England. But Uncle Jean thought that unlikely; the Germans weren't that considerate, he said. So what *would* happen? Perhaps they would be interned or sent away; perhaps they'd be forced to work in camps; or worst of all, separated. Julie couldn't bear the idea of Peter being taken away from her and ill treated or half starved. It was unthinkable. It was her duty to get him away. That was what she was doing. Her duty.

Uncle Jean came around the front of the truck and, taking Julie's bag, threw it into the back. He turned to her and put his hands on her shoulders.

"Now Georges here will drive you to Morlaix. The boat you're going on is called *Fleur*. Make sure Georges takes you all the way to the boat and gets your bags on board for you. There's chaos everywhere, they say, so be sure to stick with him, eh?"

He went on, "It's a good boat, *Fleur*, one of the newest and biggest in Morlaix. It'll get you safely to England." Then he embraced her with a ferocious loving hug which left Julie breathless and a little tearful.

Jean took Peter and handed him into the cab. Julie and Tante Marie embraced and the old woman said, "It's for the best, you know that. We'll be happy because we'll know you're safe."

Julie nodded and got into the truck. The engine coughed into life and they were off, bumping down the road, away from the little house. Peter bounced up and down, waving wildly, as if it were a day outing. Julie waved more slowly and, when the house and the two figures standing in front of it had disappeared, she blew her nose.

Peter craned his head to stare at her face. "What's the matter?"

"Oh, I'm just thinking." She smiled briefly.

"When will we be coming home again?"

"As soon as the Germans have gone, darling."

Peter put his head on one side. "When will that be?"

Julie sighed, as much from the relentless questioning as from the problem of finding an answer. "I honestly don't know. It depends on lots of things. . . . Perhaps it'll be a very long time."

"They won't kill Uncle Jean and Tante Marie, will they?"

"Of course not! Only soldiers get killed."

"They'll be all right then?"

"Yes." She gave him a reassuring hug, and wondered if the old couple *would* be all right. She knew she'd worry herself sick about them. There were bound to be shortages and severe hardships. Already meat was on sale only three days a week; the *pâtisseries* were closed two days a week; gasoline was rationed. And that was *before* the defeat. Under the Germans, it would be worse, much worse.

Still, Julie remembered, this was an independent, self-sufficient community. They should be able to manage. Tante Marie had

told her about terrible droughts and unusually cold winters in the past when people had almost starved. Those hardest hit were helped by the others. Then later, when things were better, the debts were repaid in kind and with interest.

This time there was one major difference, though. The shortages might go on for years.

As the truck bumped gently through the soft greens and bright yellows of the lovely June countryside, Julie tried to imagine the Germans here, with their trucks, their tanks, their hard gray efficiency. They would take over everything, bully anyone they chose.

They'd arrive in just two days, so it was said. That was the incredible part. Julie didn't understand how Paris could have fallen so easily, almost without a murmur; how the Germans could sweep across the country in so short a time. But then she knew nothing about fighting.

Even so, it was strange that no one else had guessed what was happening either. There had been no warnings until the Germans were almost in Paris. Why hadn't the Government said something? Why had they avoided telling anyone? It seemed extraordinary.

The driver, Georges, said, "There might be a delay when we get near the town. Evidently some of the roads are almost impassable in places."

Julie looked at him questioningly.

"The people. Thousands of them. All on their way to Brest, to get on ships and get the hell out of here. Can't blame them either!"

They saw the first of the refugees just before reaching the main Lannion–Morlaix road. There were people sitting beside the highway, resting and sleeping, while others foraged in the fields, pulling up vegetables and chewing on them, raw. Some waved to the fish truck and shouted, "Any food?"

When they got to the junction itself there were many, many more people: women pushing prams piled high with bags and children; men striding along with heavy bundles on their backs; one family with a cage full of rabbits tied to a bicycle. Again, there were cries of "Food? Some food? Anything to spare, friend?" Every family, every child that Julie saw wrung her heart.

158

She murmured, "I wish I could give them something."

The driver shook his head. "No. It's each man for himself. If you have some food with you, my advice is, keep it! And guard it well. We'll all have to look after our possessions from now on!"

The truck slowed to a crawl as they came up behind a knot of people who stayed obstinately in the center of the road. Julie guessed they were just too tired to step aside. Where had they come from? Paris? Even farther? It must have taken them days to get here. And where had they slept? Had they eaten?

It took half an hour to cover the last three kilometers. The road leading to the quay was thronged with people. Most were standing in lines outside food shops, waiting silently, their faces resigned. At one corner several men were pushing and shouting at each other. Two of them were trying to tear down a poster. Julie recognized it as one that had been pasted up all over the town. It read: WE WILL WIN BECAUSE WE'RE THE STRONGEST. As the fish truck passed, the two men started to fight, their arms flailing the air. Julie shuddered. "Why are they fighting?"

Georges shrugged. "Disgust at the Government, I should think. After all, we're not the strongest and we've lost, haven't we!"

At last the truck reached the quay and Georges said, "This is it. The boat's just down there." Julie gasped. The port was a mass of fishing boats. She had never seen so many in harbor, not even when a storm was blowing. Groups of refugees were standing on the quay, looking hopefully at one or two of the boats, but most of the people were walking dispiritedly away.

Georges indicated the boats. "They can't handle all this lot, so they're only taking servicemen and special cases." He opened the door and added with contempt, "That is, those boats which are going at all."

Julie asked, "Are you going?"

"Of course. I'll fight with the British, or anyone else for that matter. I'm not going to stay here and say good day to the Germans, am I?"

Georges shouted at a man on a nearby boat, then led Julie and Peter along the quay. They had to cross the decks and climb the bulwarks of four boats before Georges finally said, "Here we are."

Julie passed Peter over the last bulwark and climbed aboard

herself. Carefully she checked that the two cases were all right and that she hadn't forgotten the small basket of food that Tante Marie had given her. The luggage and the food made her feel secure.

Georges was leaving and Julie thanked him. Someone—Julie supposed it was one of the crew—took her cases and told her to find a place on deck. She sat on a hatch cover with Peter on her knee, watching the people on the quay, some waiting in line for bread outside a *boulangerie,* others gazing longingly at the boats. They're wishing they were here in my place, she thought. It made her feel guilty, mainly because she was so glad it *was* her and not them.

She wondered how long it would be before the boat left. She knew that the fishermen always sailed on the tide. Morlaix was quite a distance from the sea, up a winding river. At low tide the upper reaches of the river were too shallow, but at Morlaix a lock kept a good depth of water in the basin. The lock opened only for a few hours around high water.

Fleur was a large boat, about 80 feet long, and would need the full height of the tide to get down the river, Julie guessed. Jean had arranged for Julie to come on this boat because she was large enough to be safe for a Channel crossing, and because he knew the men who had built her.

A truck pulled up on the quay. Some soldiers, apparently wounded, were helped out. A group of fishermen were mustered and the wounded were carried or helped across the boats to *Fleur.*

The soldiers were taken below to where Julie guessed there must be a small cabin. Now there were more people arriving. Like Julie, they were civilians. Most were carrying heavy luggage and wearing thick coats and jackets. More than twenty passengers were on the deck now; there was nowhere else for them to go. The soldiers had the cabin and the small wheelhouse was clearly the crew's domain. Those on deck would have to stay on deck. If the weather turned bad, they would freeze. . . .

Julie looked anxiously at Peter's coat. It was warm, but not waterproof. If it rained he would get soaked to the skin. And her own coat . . . she grimaced: such vanity! She had worn her best coat—a lightweight linen one—with a raincoat over it. She was cold already.

One of the crew was passing. Julie touched his arm. "Do I have time to get something from my luggage? Some warmer clothes?"

"Ah!" he shrugged. "The bags are piled up in the hold. It'll be a job to get yours out. We're just leaving. If you're cold I'll find you something later. All right?"

Julie hesitated. She wanted to press the matter, but then it was too late, he was gone. The boat's engine throbbed into life and they were moving, first into the lock, and then down the long, narrow river by fields and tree-covered slopes toward the sea. A young man shouted, *"Vive la France Libre!"* And everyone laughed and cheered.

A man sitting next to Julie grinned. "We live to fight another day. Eh?"

Julie suddenly felt happy; the laughter and cheerfulness were infectious. And he was right; by going to England they could at least *do* something to fight back.

After a while the river widened into the flat expanse of the estuary. The sky was overcast but the sun was making a brave attempt to shine through a patch of thinner cloud. Suddenly it succeeded, and the land turned from a dark somber gray to a paler shade of green. Over to the right, beyond the low hills, was Trégasnou. Already it seemed distant and remote.

But I'll be back, Julie thought. She hugged Peter and said, "Everything's going to be all right. Wait and see!"

As the boat emerged into the open sea a stiff wind began to blow across the deck and Julie pulled her coat more tightly about her. The deck was long and exposed. The only place that might offer some shelter was the side, next to the deep bulwarks. Julie was just about to move Peter across when the boat rolled and water splashed up through some sort of drain holes. Soon the part of the deck where she had planned to sit was drenched with water.

It would have to be somewhere else. The bow, high and flared, with a tiny triangle of decking, might offer a bit of protection. Anyway it was better than nothing. Holding tightly to Peter's hand, Julie made her way unsteadily forward. The boat rolled again and she grabbed for the rail. Her hand missed and she staggered sideways, falling over someone's leg and almost sitting on a man's lap. A voice said, "Hey! Watch where you're going!"

Peter cried, "Mummy, Mummy! I've bumped my knee."

Julie gasped, "Sorry," and got to her feet. With Peter firmly in one hand, she held tightly to the rail with the other and started forward again. Holding on made the trip much easier and they got to the bow without further trouble.

In the bow there was a large winch, which, Julie guessed, was for pulling up the anchor. Around it were several coils of wide oily rope. Julie sat on the largest and pulled Peter down beside her.

Almost immediately he said, "I'm cold, Mummy."

"Come onto my lap then." She undid her coat and raincoat and stretched them around Peter's body, hugging him to her.

It was definitely less windy up here. On the other hand the motion of the boat seemed worse—or maybe it was her imagination. The roll was the same, but now the deck was going up and down as well. Then the boat lurched and seemed to plunge into thin air. Julie felt her stomach take off and she reached down as if to hold it.

Peter said, "Mummy, I feel funny."

Oh God, Julie thought. She said calmly, "Well, lie down, darling, then you'll feel better." She stretched him across the coil of rope and laid his head on her lap. His face was sheet white and he burped slightly. He'll be sick in a second, Julie thought. She searched for the nearest place to take him. The sides of the boat were too high here; she would have to take him several yards down the deck before the sides were low enough for her to hold his head over the water. Perhaps it wasn't so clever to have come up here after all.

She looked down at Peter again. His eyes were shut and his mouth slightly open: he was sound asleep. She relaxed and leaned against the rope. Thank goodness for that. It would be nice if she could sleep too. . . .

The boat leaped again and Julie's stomach twisted. She shivered and thought: Why didn't I get those clothes? She felt Peter's cheek and hands: he was cold too. What a fool she'd been! But it wasn't too late; she could fetch the extra clothes now.

It meant a trip to the wheelhouse to ask one of the crew. She looked down the deck: it suddenly seemed a long way off and the deck was treacherous with running water. It wouldn't be so bad if she didn't feel so tired. . . .

The other passengers were lying across the top of the hold or draped over the rail being sick. One woman raised her head and vomited on the deck. The sight made Julie retch and she knew she couldn't make it down the deck, at least not quite yet. If only she could get her head down . . .

She lifted Peter's head and shifted her body until she was more or less lying on her side, then moved him until he was sheltered in the curve of her body. She felt much better, and the cold didn't seem to matter so much like this. She closed her eyes and thought: I'll definitely get the clothes in a minute.

A cry woke her and she looked up to see some of the passengers brushing spray off their clothes. The motion was worse than before and now and again the bow came down with a terrible shudder, as if the boat had hit something. The wind was reaching into the bow, whistling around, icy and chill against Julie's skin. The longer she waited to get the clothes, the worse it would be. And yet she knew she would be sick if she got up, and she daren't leave Peter . . .

She thought: I'm just making excuses.

She forced herself to sit up. She tucked Peter into the coil of rope and, getting to her feet, started gingerly down the deck. The wind blew her hair into her eyes and something cold and solid hit the back of her head. She gasped with the shock. Cold water seeped down her neck.

She got halfway to the wheelhouse and leaned over the rail. A vague memory came to her, something someone had said about being seasick: first you want to die but then you're afraid you're not going to. Who'd said that? She couldn't remember. Whoever it was, he was right.

But afterward, when her stomach was empty, she was surprised to find she felt much better, and she continued down the deck with new determination. The crew member she had spoken to before was standing outside the wheelhouse. As she reached him he held out a helping hand and she accepted it gratefully.

"Thank you so much. It's a bit rough for me, I'm afraid." She looked up at him, a smile on her face. He began to smile back, then his expression froze and he stared past her at a point over her head, his mouth open.

Suddenly he was shouting, so loudly that Julie stared at him in

amazement. Everyone was yelling and pointing, and Julie turned to see what they were looking at.

It was a plane. It was coming straight for them, low over the sea.

The yelling stopped and there was silence. Everyone was watching the plane. It was coming closer and closer, its gray outline getting darker, more solid. Julie felt her heart beating against her chest. It couldn't be, surely . . .

The plane tipped its wings and went off at an angle, then tipped the other way, circling round them. A voice yelled, "It's German! It's a German!"

There was a crash; the wheelhouse door opened, and a large, red-faced man came roaring out, shaking his fist at the plane. "Swine! Dirty swine!" Julie guessed it was the skipper.

"What should we do? What should we do?" someone said.

The skipper shouted, "Nothing, that's what. Absolutely nothing!"

The plane straightened up and flew in the direction of Morlaix, waggling its wings. Then it turned back toward them. But it didn't circle again. Instead it came straight for the boat, passing so low over the masts that Julie thought it would hit them.

A passenger cried, "Turn back! He's trying to tell us to turn back. Quick, otherwise he'll shoot us!"

People started arguing and shouting. One man—a fairly well-dressed man in his fifties—got to his feet, lurched up to the skipper and ordered him to turn around. The skipper told him to do something unpleasant to himself and, when he'd finished, to mind his own business. The passenger yelled back, his voice shrieking above the sound of the wind and the waves. A couple of women screamed as the plane made another pass close over the masts.

Julie thought: They've all gone mad. It's a nightmare.

The plane turned and headed toward the boat again. The noise, when it came, was staccato but very faint, as if it didn't come from the plane at all. At first Julie didn't understand what the noise meant and she was puzzled to see the passengers throwing themselves onto the deck. For a second she stood against the rail, frozen with surprise. Then at last she realized: bullets. She dropped like a stone and crawled against the raised side of the hold.

She thought: Peter! and looked up along the deck to the bow. There was someone in her way and she craned her head up farther.

He was sitting up, bemused. He was swinging his feet over the rope coil and putting them on the deck.

He was going to stand!

Julie screamed, "Peter! *Get down! Get down!*"

He was looking around, searching for her.

Then he stood.

The plane swooped over in a roar of noise.

Julie got up and started to run.

She started well, keeping her balance as she ran up the deck. Then the boat rolled and she swerved sideways. There was a sharp blow to her ankle, and then pain. She got a grip on the rail and ran on. The bow sank into a wave with a thunderous roar and a sheet of spray came swooping across the boat. She considered ducking, but then it had slapped into her and she gasped at the coldness of the water: it had gone straight through her clothes.

Another two strides and she reached Peter. She rolled into the coil of rope, pulling him down with her, and sobbed with relief.

Peter pushed away from her and said crossly, "Mummy, you're all wet! You're all wet!"

She caught her breath and tried to gauge what was happening. They must be turning: the wind was blowing differently, and the boat was not bumping so ferociously into the waves. Turning . . .

She listened for the plane, but there was nothing. She stood up quickly. Yes, they were definitely turning: the land was almost ahead of the boat now. They were going back toward Morlaix.

Julie knew she should be disappointed, but her only response was an overwhelming sense of relief; nothing ashore could possibly be worse than staying out here on this awful boat. All she wanted was to be warm, dry and safe again.

The sound of the plane's engine came softly over the water, a faint buzz gathering into a deep drone as it approached once more. Julie crouched beside Peter. This time the plane did not fire, but swooped straight over the boat. Everyone froze, listening and watching, but it flew straight on, heading into the distance until, no more than a small black speck near the horizon, it was lost in the low gray cloud.

"And good riddance!" It was the skipper. He was smiling broadly and talking excitedly. As he spoke, a few people cheered and someone cried again, *"Vive la France Libre."* Some of the passengers still looked unhappy and a few were arguing. But then, Julie thought, there were bound to be some people who didn't like turning back. It was inevitable. At least they weren't about to die out here, shot like rabbits or drowned.

The skipper strode into the wheelhouse and Julie sank back onto the rope coil, her teeth chattering so loudly she had to clench her jaws to stop the noise. She remembered the clothes again. She really should make the effort to get them, but her mind was numb. It was nice, the numbness, like a dream. Nothing seemed very important anymore, nothing except sleeping and lying here. . . .

The bow hit a wave and water splattered and sloshed over the deck. People complained again. There was another wave and, as the bow fell fast, down into the void, Julie and Peter were almost lifted off the deck.

Suddenly Julie was awake. Why were they hitting waves again? What had happened? Julie staggered to her feet and looked for the land. It was *behind* them. They had turned again. They were heading back toward England.

No. It was the wrong thing to do. Wrong.

Angry and frightened, she swayed down the deck and opened the wheelhouse door. The skipper was at the wheel, a cigarette clamped between his teeth.

Julie asked, "Why? Why have we turned back?"

The skipper barely noticed her. "Because, dear lady, we are going to England. And no stupid Boches are going to make me change my mind! That's why."

"But what if they come back? They'll shoot us."

"Don't worry your head about that."

"But I do—we must. People could get hurt."

The skipper drew hard on his cigarette. "Look, we go on. And that's final. Now go back on deck."

"But what does everyone else want? Aren't they worried too?"

"Look, lady, you wanted to go to England, didn't you? Well, it's a bit late to change your mind. I can see the problem—you're wet, you're sick, and it all seems a bad idea. You ladies are never happy

166

at sea, but I'm afraid you're just going to have to put up with it."
He shook his head knowingly. "That plane won't come back
again. I'm sure of it!"

For a moment Julie didn't trust herself to speak. His attitude
was exasperating. How did he know the plane wouldn't return?
It seemed highly likely to Julie that it would—and soon.

She made an effort to pull herself together. "But suppose the
plane *does* come back . . . what then?"

The skipper shouted down into the small cabin below, "Someone! Show this lady back onto the deck!"

Shaking with anger and tiredness, Julie tried to calm herself.
"Don't worry, I'm going. But please, my son and I, we're wet and
cold . . . do you have anything warm . . . ?"

"Here." He passed her a jacket from a peg on the side of the
wheelhouse and added, "If it gets much worse we'll see if we can
find your child a place in the cabin."

Julie's anger melted away. "Thank you."

She wiped a hand over her face, put the jacket on and started
the long awkward journey back. Halfway along the deck she
waited a moment while spray flew across the boat, then, when the
coast was clear, she set out on the last few yards. But before she
reached the protection of the bow she felt the thud of the boat
meeting a wave and a curtain of spray rose into the air in front
of her. The water looked insubstantial but when it hit her it was
like something solid, as if a powerful man had slapped her in the
face. The force took her breath away and for a moment she almost
lost her footing.

She gripped the rail more firmly and hurried into the shelter
of the bow. The jacket had kept some of the water off her clothes
but an ice-cold river of seawater was streaming down her back.
She said, "Oh God!" and gritted her teeth as she lay down beside
Peter and pulled him inside the jacket.

Despite the jacket, she was shivering violently. Peter was still
cold too; his skin was cool against her cheek. She prayed: Dear
Lord, please let this end soon, please get us there *quickly.* But she
knew it was hopeless; the journey had only just begun. They must
be only ten or fifteen miles from the coast, and the English Channel was at least eighty—or was it a hundred miles wide? She
couldn't remember. However far, it would take hours, all night

and most of the next day at least. She couldn't even imagine that amount of time.

The plane came back half an hour later.

This time it did not bother to circle. It started firing straightaway. The noise was much louder this time; the staccato *rat-at-at* of the bullets filled the boat. There were loud *ping*s too and the sound of tearing wood. Someone screamed, a piercing and dreadful scream. It was a man; he was clutching his stomach, a look of horror on his face. Julie found herself staring: she had never heard a man screaming before.

Peter was sobbing, "Mummy, Mummy! What's happening?"

Julie hugged him tightly, then something caught the corner of her eye. It was the plane, banking behind the boat, then leveling up. It was coming in for another run, heading straight for her. Straight for Peter.

She looked around desperately. There was nowhere to hide, nothing . . . just the winch.

It might be enough. She pulled Peter to his feet and yanked him across the deck. He tripped, the deadweight of his body pulling at her shoulder. He was crying now. She grabbed him under the arms and swung him in behind the winch. She crouched in front of him and put her arms around him. She tried to make herself as narrow as possible. The winch base was about two feet wide: her shoulders must be sticking out . . .

As she put her head down the din started. This time it was deafening: the clanging of metal, the whistle and thud of the bullets. There was another scream and several shouts.

The seconds stretched out endlessly. She heard each bullet as it hissed and thudded around her. She waited for the one that would tear into her body.

It never came.

In a roar of engines the plane was overhead and gone again. And they were both alive. Julie whispered into Peter's hair, "Oh my darling, my little darling. It's all right, it's all right."

She looked at his big round frightened eyes, and said, "Now, stay here. Right here, do you understand? I'll be back in a moment."

Peter screamed, "No, Mummy! Don't go! Don't go!"

But Julie was already on her feet. *"Stay there!"*

She ran down the deck and straight into the wheelhouse. When she opened the door she was almost sick. Two men were lying on the floor: one had a terrible red oozing mass of brains and bloody flesh instead of a face. The other was the skipper. His eyes were staring straight at her, sightless and also dead.

She gulped and forced her eyes up to the man at the wheel. He was staring blankly, his mouth gaping and his eyes dazed.

Julie said firmly, "Turn round! Towards the land!"

His mouth moved noiselessly.

Julie said again, "Turn now or we'll all be dead!"

The buzz of the plane was getting louder. Julie reached over and started to turn the wheel. The man's eyes suddenly focused and his hands fumbled at the wheel too.

The boat began to turn, but slowly, so slowly. The noise of the engines was getting much louder again.

Julie sobbed: "Oh *please, please.*"

At last the boat was turning more quickly.

The plane roared over. There were no bullets this time.

They were going to be all right.

Julie waited to see that the helmsman was keeping the boat on course, then closed the wheelhouse door and walked quickly back to Peter.

They were going home.

Perhaps, Julie thought, we were never meant to go away at all.

The boat couldn't get up the river; it was low tide. Instead they picked up a mooring off a small fishing village at the top of the estuary, where it narrows into the Morlaix River. The dead were covered with canvas and left on board, the living were ferried ashore in a small rowboat.

As they waited their turn for the boat Julie stood at the rail with Peter in her arms, looking at the quiet, golden land and thinking it was like a dream. In the shelter of the river the air was warm and languid; a perfect summer day. The afternoon sun burned hot on her back, warming her slowly, deliciously. It was hard to imagine that the appalling boat trip belonged to the same day.

At last it was Julie and Peter's turn to go ashore. They squeezed in the back of the dinghy next to a young man whom Julie recognized as the one who had cried *"Vive la France Libre!"* when they

set out. Now there was no laughter in his face; he was silent, staring into the distance ahead.

They landed at a stone dock. When Julie felt the solid stone beneath her feet she sighed with relief. The young man passed Peter across and Julie hugged him tightly to her. "It's all over, darling. It's all over."

The young man carried their baggage as far as the main road, then left. Julie sat Peter down on a grassy bank and stretched out beside him. For a moment she closed her eyes and let the sun warm her face. The relief of being on dry land was almost as great as the comfort of knowing they were safe. She reached for Peter's hand and said, "I love you, darling."

Peter rubbed his eyes. "Mummy, I'm hungry and I want to go home."

"Of course, sweetheart. We'll start with some food!"

Julie unpacked the food basket and they ate. She was surprised to find she was ravenous. The two of them consumed a whole section of sausage, a large slice of hard cheese, four chunks of bread and two apples. It was wonderful to eat in peace and quiet, the land steady beneath one's feet, the wind no more than a slight breeze rustling in the trees.

While they ate Julie began to think. This village was on the opposite side of the river from Trégasnou. To get home they would have to go all the way inland to Morlaix and then double back. It was a long way. The alternative was to find someone to ferry them across the river. But the river was still very wide at this point. And the country on the other side was pretty remote; she wasn't sure if they'd be able to find any transport once they got there.

The thought of home was wonderful. More than anything she wanted to return to the safety of the small gray house. Yet the problem of having a British passport remained. Peter would still be in danger. For his sake perhaps she should make another attempt to get away. To Brest: that was where the ships were.

It was so difficult to decide. In her heart she wanted to stay, yet her main responsibility was to Peter.

She would think about what to do on the way to Morlaix, she suddenly decided. Morlaix was the way home *and* the way to Brest. Yes, she would make up her mind there.

One thing was soon clear: if they wanted to get into the town they would have to walk. While they had been eating only one car had come out of the village and, though Julie had stood up and waved, it hadn't stopped. There was a bus stop, but the next bus wasn't due for another two hours. If it came at all.

As soon as they finished eating Julie stood up. It was six in the evening; they must get to town before dark. The bags were a problem: she hadn't packed very much, but there was still too much to carry. She took the essential clothes and crammed them into one suitcase, leaving the other by the roadside. She wrapped the remaining food in some paper and put it in her raincoat pocket. Now she had one case, her handbag—and Peter.

How far could a four-year-old walk before he got tired? One thing was sure: it wouldn't be as far as Morlaix.

He was very good to begin with, marching well, his little arms swinging back and forth. But after twenty minutes, he began to flag. Their pace slowed. After another fifteen minutes Peter said, "Mummy, please can we stop? I'm so tired."

"Of course, darling. We'll stop for a minute." They sat at the roadside. When they started off again, Julie tried to make a game of it, pretending they were soldiers marching to save Morlaix from ferocious bandits. It worked for a while, then Peter flagged again.

At first, Julie half carried, half pulled him along. Later she put him on her shoulders, though the extra weight made her arms and back shoot with pain and she often had to stop and catch her breath. Her feet were agony and she cursed herself for wearing unsuitable shoes. But hiking hadn't been part of the plan.

In the end it took three hours to walk the twelve kilometers. The bus never came; Julie'd had a feeling it wouldn't.

When finally they arrived in Morlaix it was strangely quiet, the streets empty of people, the shops and restaurants shut and boarded. Only a few bars were open, their customers peering furtively out as if they were expecting the Germans at any second. Perhaps they are, thought Julie. She didn't honestly care. She sat on a bench near the port, her head back and her legs outstretched and Peter cuddled against her side. She decided that whatever happened they would walk no farther tonight.

She thought of going to her employer's house. He lived on the

edge of town, ten minutes away. Or there was a girl from her office who had an apartment nearby. Or there was Michel.

Michel would know the best thing to do; she would go to Michel.

The building he lived in was five minutes away. She looked at Peter; he was asleep. She left him on the bench and searched for a place to hide the case. In the end she put it under a parked van. If anyone drove the van off, it was too bad.

She took Peter in her arms and walked. The rest on the bench had been a mistake: it had given her feet a chance to swell up and the blisters to weep. She stopped, kicked off her shoes and tucked them into the top of her handbag. It was a great improvement.

When she reached Michel's apartment building the door was locked and a ring on the concierge's bell produced no answer. There were individual bells for each apartment. Beside each bell was a number but no name. She didn't know which apartment was Michel's, so she pressed them all. At last a man opened the door. It wasn't Michel, but he let her in and told her which apartment she wanted.

When she reached Michel's door there was no answer to her knock so, with Peter fast asleep in her arms, she sat outside in the hall and waited.

He returned at eleven.

When she saw him she smiled stupidly and said, "Thank you for coming back."

When she first woke up she couldn't remember where she was. The room was dark and shuttered and she couldn't make out its features. Then she remembered and, hugging Peter's warm body closer to her, shut her eyes and slept again.

Later she was awoken by someone opening the shutters. Brilliant sunshine streamed in and she screwed up her eyes against the light. She was lying on the sofa where she'd sat on her arrival the night before. She hadn't had the energy to move, though Michel had offered to take the sofa and give her his bed.

Now he was beside her, holding out a cup of coffee. "I found your case all right."

Julie exclaimed, "Oh! I'd forgotten about it!" Then added hurriedly, "Thank you."

"Now, there isn't much time, so we've got to hurry."

"What do you mean?"

"I mean that the Germans are almost here. They'll arrive some-time today. At least that's my interpretation of the complete blackout on news. There's nothing on the radio except people telling us to keep calm. That *must* mean we're in for it!"

Peter was waking up, rubbing his eyes.

Julie said, "Then—should we go to Brest? Get on a ship?"

Michel laughed. "Hah! There is nothing but good French chaos there. A friend has just come back. He told me all about it. Evidently there are thousands of people at the port trying to get on ships that do not exist. The military got away all right, then they started to let civilians on the few remaining ships. Some made it, but one large ship had a collision with a naval boat and sank. Right there, just outside Brest." He lit a cigarette. "Now? Well, there are no ships left apparently, just people trying to hide, running round in circles because there's nowhere to go. They also say that it's as black as night all day long. The fuel dumps at Maison Blanche were set on fire. It sounds like Dante's Inferno!"

Julie shivered. Thank God she hadn't gone there. She was frightened by crowds and disorder. That's what she'd hated most on the boat, the hysteria, the loss of control when the plane had fired on them.

She said calmly, "Then I shall go home."

"Yes. But first we have work to do—" He indicated that she should get to her feet. "Comb your hair, change your dress. We're going out."

He was so firm, so definite, that it never occurred to her to question him. Instead she looked at herself. She *did* look dread-ful. Quickly she washed, tidied her hair and put on a clean dress. She changed Peter's shirt and trousers, gave him a *tartine* of bread and jam to chew on and came back into the living room. "We're ready."

Michel stuffed his wallet into the back pocket of his trousers and led the way out. Michel walked fast and Julie had to pick Peter up and half run to keep pace with him. She was too breathless to ask where they were going.

They turned a corner, then another, until they came to some

173

double doors set in a high stone wall. Michel took out a key and, unlocking the padlock, swung open one of the doors and brought out a motorized bicycle: a *vélo*.

He locked the door again and said, "Hop on."

The little motor coughed into life and they were off, Michel bicycling furiously to get up speed and Peter giggling with delight on Julie's lap.

In contrast to the night before, the streets were busy this morning, people hurrying everywhere with baskets and bags in their hands. There were long lines outside the *boulangeries* and the *charcuteries*. After a few minutes they came into a square and stopped. Michel got off. He jerked his head in the direction of a large building and said briefly, "We're going in there." Julie recognized it immediately: it was the Sous-Préfecture.

Inside people were milling around, rushing from office to office, shouting, looking harassed. All the doors were open, showing empty desks and stacks of papers. Two women were going toward the main door carrying boxes. One said to Julie in amazement, "These are all to be burnt! I ask you—burnt!"

Michel lifted Peter into his arms and took Julie's hand. He led her up the stairs and along a corridor with numerous doors. He looked at the names on the doors and finally said, "Ah, here we are!"

The office was empty. Michel gave Peter to Julie, went straight in and started searching the drawers and filing cabinets.

"Michel!" Julie exclaimed. "What are you *doing*? Someone might come!"

There was an old safe sitting on the floor in the corner. Michel tried the handle. It was locked. He told Julie to wait and left the room. Julie sat down and tried to understand what was happening. Why had Michel brought her here? In a moment Michel was back. With him was a woman who went to the safe and opened it with a key from a large ring hanging on her belt. She nodded at Michel, said, "It's a pleasure," and left. She didn't even look at Julie.

Whatever was going on, the woman was in on it too. Julie lifted Peter off her knee and stood up. "Michel, please tell me what's happening!"

Michel grunted, "Here we are!" He took two cards from the

top of the pile and passed them to Julie. "Start to fill one in, will you? The second's just a spare. I must go and make sure your name vanishes from the Aliens Registration and appears on all the voting lists."

The cards he had handed her were identity cards. They were blank.

Michel was disappearing down the passage. Julie ran and called after him, "Michel, I may be down under the name of Howard as well as Lescaux!"

He waved an acknowledgment and vanished into another doorway.

Shaking her head, Julie went back and sat at the desk. Suddenly she smiled. Peter looked up at her and asked: "Happy Mummy?"

She grinned down at him. "Yes, very happy Mummy!"

She looked at the blank card and thought carefully. After a moment she began to write in some of the details. She kept her name, Lescaux, and entered her father's name correctly. But instead of her mother's name she put "Jeannette Lescaux." For her mother's maiden name she put "Leforge" because it was the first name that came into her head. Under the heading "Name Before Marriage" she put nothing. To pretend to be married would complicate matters. She slipped the second identity card into her handbag.

Then her eye caught the safe. It was still open, the pile of blank identity cards visible at the front of the shelf. On an impulse Julie reached in and took a batch off the top.

She stuffed them into her bag, her heart beating furiously. It was risky. But why *not* take them? They might be useful. She had never stolen anything in her life before.

Michel came back and rummaged through the rubber stamps on the desk. He found the one he wanted, picked it up, inked it and stamped her new card. He then inked her thumb and pressed it on the space left for thumbprints. "And again. Here." He pressed her thumb on an official form. It was an application for an identity card.

Julie whispered, "You're a magician!" She could see he was pleased.

"How on earth did you *do* it though? I mean, why did that woman open the safe for us?"

"Oh. I told her the Germans would torture and kill you if we couldn't find you a proper identity."

"You're amazing!" And I mean that, she thought. "I owe you a debt of gratitude. I hope I can repay you one day."

"It's nothing. Anyway"—he gazed into her eyes—"it is an honor to do it for you."

Julie blushed. Perhaps she'd been wrong. Perhaps she had misjudged him and he was rather nice after all.

Her eye caught the rubber stamp. "Are there two of those?"

"Why?"

"I want one, that's all."

"Good God, what for?"

"I don't know . . . just in case, I suppose."

He handed her the stamp. "Don't get caught with it, that's all."

They walked quickly down the passage and out of the building. By the *vélo* Michel asked, "Can you drive one of these things?"

"I think so, but—what about you?"

"I have things to do. You drive back to Trégasnou. I'll deliver your suitcase and pick the machine up another time." He glanced nervously around the square and Julie thought: He's going to stir up trouble somewhere.

She said, "Do be careful. You're not going to do anything silly, are you?"

"My friends and I have got to make our plans, that's all."

Julie regarded Michel with admiration: already he was making plans against the Germans, arranging meetings, doing something positive. She said, "I won't ask what you're planning. But whatever you do, don't risk your neck! And good luck!"

"What?" He was mildly surprised.

"I mean, the Germans . . . they might catch you . . ." She trailed off, uncertain.

"Ha! I won't be going in for cheap heroics, if that's what you mean. Quite the opposite. I think the Germans and I might get on very well."

Julie blinked. "What do you mean?"

Michel leaned over the bike until his face was close to hers. "My dear, I'm with whoever rids us of the scum corrupting this country—the right-wing dictators who've robbed the working people

176

of their rightful inheritance for more than a hundred years. I'm for whoever's against them!"

"But you're not going to work *with* the Germans?"

He shrugged. "Who knows? It depends what there is to be gained."

"But they're overrunning our country. They're—enemies!"

"Yes, but they won't stay forever. And after the war—*after*—there'll be a chance to build a new state, a people's state. In fact, it's the best chance we've ever had to sweep the system clean!"

Julie got silently onto the *vélo,* lifting Peter up in front of her. Michel untied a piece of cord attached to the small luggage rack and gave it to Julie. "Here, you'll need this to keep Peter on." He added, "You shouldn't meet any Germans yet. But do watch out for planes. If you hear one, make for the ditch, and fast." He took her face in his hands and without warning kissed her firmly on the lips.

Julie didn't move or respond. While he kissed her she stared at the side of his head and thought: Why did I ever think I might like this man?

Michel stood back and said, "Juliette, keep yourself safe for me, won't you?"

"No!" she exclaimed. "Look, I owe you a big favor which I will try to repay one day. But while you . . . play your dirty games, forget anything else. Especially friendship! How you can consider dealing with the Germans is beyond me!"

He was annoyed. "You don't understand."

"That's right, I don't. Good-bye, Michel." She moved slowly away, wobbling slightly as she got her balance.

He was shouting, "I'll send your suitcase over when I can."

She didn't turn around but pedaled rapidly until the motor fired.

Peter squealed with excitement. "Mummy, we're going so fast!"

Julie didn't answer. She was thinking about Michel. How could Michel? How *could* he? Whatever one believed it must be wrong to actually *help* the enemy. As the bike accelerated, she muttered in disbelief. God only knew what Tante Marie would say when she heard.

The thought of Tante Marie and the small gray-stone house cheered her. She bent slightly and briefly kissed Peter's head.

Peter's small voice came floating up. "Mummy, are we going home?"

Julie said firmly, "Yes, we're going home."

9   At last a tender came into sight, nosing its way around the end of the distant pier and heading toward the warship anchored in the middle of the large natural harbor. Although the harbor was well protected from the rolling Channel seas and long Atlantic swells, a blustery west wind was funneling between the hills, creating an unpleasant little chop which made the tender roll slightly as it progressed steadily across the water.

Richard Ashley watched it approach and thought longingly of sleep. He'd snatched only a couple of catnaps in the last thirty-six hours and now he was dog-tired. It would be sensible to go back to his bunk and turn in. But he couldn't bring himself to do it. An evening's run ashore was not something to be given up lightly, not when you'd gone without leave for three weeks. And particularly when the leave was here in Falmouth.

The place had happy memories for him—of sailing in *Dancer*, first, in the early days, with his father, then later with friends from Dartmouth. Once, though, he had come here alone. He'd been on passage to the Scillies, and Falmouth, being the most westerly port on the English mainland, had been the last stopping place before setting out on the final sixty miles of open sea. He remembered that holiday among the beautiful, bleak Scillies with special fondness.

A group of sailors clustered at the rail, waiting impatiently for the tender. For them, Falmouth was just another port with another lot of pubs.

Not that pubs weren't a consideration for Ashley too. He enjoyed drinking. Just as he enjoyed the other opportunities ashore. In his wallet he had the telephone number of a girl he vaguely knew who lived not far away. He would take her out to dinner if she was free. It had been well over a month since he'd spent an evening with a girl.

A night out would cheer him up. Like everyone else in the ship he needed it. They'd had a rotten couple of months. After Dunkirk they'd started convoy work, escorting ships along the south coast and through the Dover Strait, fighting off increasingly heavy air attacks. By the end of July they were losing ships at an alarming rate and, when three destroyers were sunk in the space of a few days, the Admiralty was forced to abandon daytime passages through the eastern half of the Channel. Now even the western Channel was difficult. On this last convoy, which had been westward bound, they had been attacked by Stukas south of the Isle of Wight and had lost five ships before the attack had been driven off.

The tender was closer now, turning in a long slow arc which would bring it neatly alongside the destroyer. Ashley put his face up to the blustery west wind and breathed deeply, willing himself to wake up.

"God, they're not letting you loose too, are they, Ashley?"

He turned and saw Blythe, the gunnery officer, also in best shoregoing uniform.

"Of course. Begged me to go actually." He thought how trite and out of place the old jokes sounded now, yet one trotted them out as a matter of course, to maintain a feeling of normality.

"Want to join forces? I thought of sampling the ale in a few of the local establishments."

Ashley considered the offer. An evening with Blythe would be ruinous. The two of them had been out drinking together once before and ended up drunk as skunks on the floor of a hotel ballroom in Weymouth. His hangover had lasted two days.

He chuckled at the memory. "Just a quick one then. But I won't be able to stay long."

"Aha!" Blythe gave him a steely glare. "A woman, is it?"

Ashley grinned enigmatically and started down the gangway to where the tender was waiting, already crowded with the sailors who, anxious to start their precious leave, had swarmed aboard the moment it came alongside.

As the two men took their seats the boat drew away and Ashley got a good view of the forward bulwarks, where a damage repair party was working on a series of dented, hole-peppered plates. A gunner had died up there during the last air attack. Although England had been at war for a year, it was the first time Ashley had seen a man die at close quarters. The scene was still vivid in his mind.

He muttered to Blythe in an undertone, "You feel so damned ineffectual." Blythe knew exactly what Ashley meant. In company with another destroyer they had been trying to protect fourteen ships against a dozen or more enemy aircraft: an unpleasantly one-sided fight.

Ashley added, "Let's hope the RAF have more luck soon." The Battle of Britain had been raging for a couple of months and still the enemy bombers came, against convoys, against ports and military establishments and, increasingly now, against cities and civilian targets.

The tender buffeted its way upwind toward the town nestling comfortably in the lee of a hill, its buildings rising haphazardly from the water's edge. Eventually they came to the small-boat moorings, where coastal patrol boats, oyster smacks and the occasional yacht lay swinging to the tide.

Something caught Ashley's eye. An MFV—a motor fishing vessel—lay close under the town. She was painted dull gray and had obviously been requisitioned as an inshore patrol boat. Yet there was something unusual about her, something that didn't quite fit. For a moment Ashley couldn't place what it was, but then, as the trawler came into full view, he had it.

The vessel was French. It was nothing obvious. But her lines and the long canoe stern were definitely more Breton than Cornish. As the tender passed astern of her, someone came out of the deckhouse and sauntered to the rail. He was wearing plain overalls and was bareheaded. A cigarette hung from his lower lip in the Gallic manner.

Ashley had seen French fishing boats in England before—everyone had. They had been appearing regularly since the fall of France in June, three months earlier. But this was the first time he had seen one under the white ensign. He wondered if the crewman on deck had been a French fisherman and, if so, how he liked naval discipline. Not, he guessed, very much at all.

The tender came alongside a stone quay. Ashley was the first off, running up the steps two at a time and striding away across the cobblestones. Blythe was panting when he caught up with him. "Gosh, what's the hurry, old man?"

"I spied a pub, Blythe, and I didn't want it to get away." In truth he had been in a hurry to feel the land under his feet and he had run up the steps for the sheer pleasure of it. Like most people who loved the sea, he hated to spend too long on it and, after a few weeks, felt desperate for the land again.

Blythe laughed and followed Ashley up a narrow street and into a pub with a low door and thick oak beams. Ashley knew immediately that it was the sort of pub he liked—old, rather dowdy and, most important of all, unpretentious. It would be very easy to stay here all evening and drink several pints too many. Instead, he had just one pint and went out to find the nearest telephone booth.

He called his parents first, at their home in Hampshire. As always, his mother was lighthearted and gay. She considered it bad form to mention any anxieties she might have about her family, and always made a point of imparting only good or amusing news, usually about one of her many dogs. His father, now back in the Navy at a desk job after more than ten years' retirement, was more serious, and listened attentively to what his son said, limited though it was by the constraints of secrecy. When the conversation was over, Ashley put the telephone down with regret. He liked his parents very much.

Then he called the girl.

He'd met her twice, once at a party given by his sister and once when staying with an old school friend. She was good-looking in a cool English sort of way, and the sort who liked riding and hunting and going to dances. She wasn't exactly a ball of fire, he remembered, and she certainly wouldn't offer him more than a kiss on the cheek—but she might be quite fun all the same.

She was at home when he called, and in her cool voice said that yes, she would like to come out to dinner very much. She would borrow her father's car and meet him in an hour.

He walked back to the pub to find that it had filled up considerably. Blythe was at the bar, well into another drink, and Ashley made his way through the crowd toward him. He felt far less tired now; he decided he was in the mood for a party. He slapped

Blythe on the back and grinned. Blythe nodded and returned to the discussion he was having with two men, one a balding, over-weight civilian wearing the armband of the Auxiliary Fire Service, the other a silver-haired merchant navy officer. For a change, they were talking about the war.

With a sigh, Ashley settled down to listen. The AFS man was wagging his finger vehemently. "They'll invade before the end of the month, mark my words. The bombing of London and the ports—that's just to soften us up. As soon as they've knocked the RAF out of the sky, they'll be on their way!"

Ashley interrupted brightly, "Hello," and introduced himself to the two men. They shook hands.

Blythe resumed. "But the Jerries won't be able to do that. Knock the RAF out of the sky, I mean."

"But they will—they are!" the AFS man insisted. "Oh, the BBC say everything's going all right, but they just tell us what they want us to believe."

A professional pessimist, Ashley noted. He interrupted lightly, "Now, old chap, that sort of talk isn't going to win the war, is it?"

"That's as may be, but we might as well face facts!"

Ashley smiled charmingly at him. "Then what do you suggest we do to stop the Germans coming."

"Ha! Not much we can do now. It's too damn late." The AFS man tutted with contempt and took another sip from his drink.

The merchant seaman looked thoughtful and said, "I still don't understand how France went under so quickly. . . . I just don't understand even now."

The AFS man put his glass on the bar with a bang. "I'll tell you why—because the Frenchies aren't fightingmen, that's why. They ran backwards the moment they saw the first German tank."

Ashley felt the adrenaline pump into his blood. He said coolly, "That's not true."

"Well, they didn't put up much of a fight, did they?"

"Incorrect. They held Dunkirk while we got out. They fought all the way."

The AFS man was determined to press the subject, "But if they fought so hard, how did the Jerries get from Paris to Brest in five days, eh? Seems mighty strange, doesn't it?"

Blythe looked nervously toward Ashley and muttered, "Er, how about another drink . . . ?"

Ashley knew he should turn away and laugh it off, but he couldn't. After a moment's pause he said in a low voice, "You're speaking about friends of mine."

Blythe tugged at Ashley's sleeve. "How about another pub, Richard? Come on, it's just not worth it."

Ashley looked into the AFS man's belligerent piglike eyes and knew Blythe was right. With an enormous effort he closed his mouth, and putting his drink on the bar, turned to leave. At the last moment he couldn't resist a parting shot. He leaned toward the man and whispered, "When you're next fighting a fire, careful you don't get your hose up the wrong passage!" He pushed his way quickly through the press of bodies into the cold freshness of the street.

He heard Blythe come up behind him and said half to himself, "Slow strangulations for that one. I could cheerfully kill types like that."

"I agree."

"Murder by degrees."

"Yes, but it's never worth it. . . ."

Suddenly the whole thing seemed ridiculous and Ashley laughed out loud. "No, it could be the ruination of my brilliantly promising career!"

Blythe smiled with relief. "Not to mention your prospects."

Ashley could laugh now, but his future in the Navy had been a touchy point until the war. He'd blotted his copybook by answering an admiral back in something less than respectful terms. He knew Blythe had heard about it—everyone had—and the incident had given him something of a reputation in the wardroom.

Blythe said cheerfully, "How about another beer? There's the Admiral Something-or-another up the hill."

"No." Ashley suddenly felt tired again. More drinking wouldn't help. "I've other plans. I'll see you tomorrow."

Blythe winked. "Aha! Tender loving care, is it? Good luck!" With a quick wave, he walked off up the hill.

Ashley looked at the time. He still had half an hour before meeting the girl. He decided to wander down to the water, to rid himself of the last taste of the unpleasantness in the pub.

The moment he stepped back onto the quay he was glad he had come. The early evening sunlight had ripened into a warm yellowy gold, illuminating the soft purple-green Cornish hills with a mantle of vibrant color. Looking across to Flushing, its small cottages gleaming white above the water's edge, and watching the small craft catch the golden light as they swung quietly and obediently to their moorings, he had difficulty imagining losing all this to the Germans. It was unthinkable. And if, like the AFS man, one ever started to believe it, then that was the beginning of the end.

He walked idly along the length of the quay. Jutting out from the maze of houses and workshops that lined the waterfront were a number of quays and jetties with harbor craft and fishing vessels tied alongside. Against one, he could just make out the masts and upperworks of what looked like a gray MFV.

Ashley stared for a moment then, carefully gauging the distance, walked up to the main street and made his way along it until he guessed he was above the boat. At the first alley, he cut down toward the water again.

It was the right quay. The MFV lay close against the wall beside a fuel pump.

He went closer. It was the French boat all right. She was in good condition, the gray paint bright and fresh on her sides and the sails clean and neatly furled. The original fishing gear had been left intact: on the main deck were two large winches for hauling the nets and, against the bulwarks on the afterdeck, two trawl boards.

There was no one about. Ashley crouched on his heels and called down.

After a few moments a face appeared at the window of the deckhouse and watched to see if Ashley would go away. Deciding that he wasn't going to, a man emerged reluctantly onto the deck. It was the man Ashley had spotted from the tender. He was still wearing overalls and smoking. He raised his eyebrows.

Ashley smiled. "Hello. Just wondered where the boat came from originally."

There was a frown of puzzlement.

Ashley took a guess and, switching to his inadequate French, tried again.

"Ah!" The man nodded. "Concarneau!"

Ashley was pleased; he'd been right about the boat then. Concarneau was on the south coast of Brittany, and a well-known fishing harbor. He had been there once. He said so and the Frenchman nodded politely. Ashley also wanted to say how hospitable the people had been and how much he'd enjoyed it, but his French wasn't up to it. Instead he said that the town was very nice.

He would have liked to know what the boat was doing nowadays but, since the beginning of the war, one didn't ask questions like that. Instead he asked, "And where did you go to fish . . . er . . . before?"

"On the banks."

"A long way?" Ashley gestured to show what he meant.

The man shrugged. "Away four days or so."

Someone else appeared from the deckhouse, an RNVR lieutenant, dressed in uniform jacket and battered cap. "Evening. What can we do for you?"

Ashley switched back to English with relief. "Just interested to see a Concarneau boat after all this time."

"Ah. You know Concarneau?" With surprise Ashley realized the lieutenant wasn't English; there was a slight accent that was almost but not quite American.

He replied, "I've sailed around there."

"In a small boat?"

"A sloop. Smallish. Twenty-five feet overall."

"Very nice. You cruised a lot?"

"Yes, most of Normandy and Brittany."

There was a pause. The lieutenant asked, "What ship now?"

"Destroyer. A bit more solid underfoot." Ashley stood up. "Well, I must be going now." He said to the fisherman, *"Au revoir! Bonne chance!"* And, waving to the lieutenant, turned to go.

"Hey, wait a moment." The officer vanished behind the wall and, after a few seconds, appeared over the top of the ladder. "Look, er, how about coming aboard for a drink this evening?"

Ashley looked at his watch. He was late already. "Sorry, got to dash."

"Perhaps later then?"

Ashley hesitated. "Where do you come from?"

"I'm French-Canadian, from Quebec. But then you speak French too, don't you?"

Ashley threw back his head and laughed. "Exceptionally badly!"

The Canadian smiled but his eyes were serious. He asked for Ashley's name, then said, "Try and drop by later. I'd like to show you the boat."

"I'll do my best." Ashley waved again and walked off, glancing briefly over the boat as he left.

When he was halfway up the main street he stopped in his tracks. There was something wrong with that MFV.

He walked on, not quite certain what it was. It was only when he got to the hotel where he was due to meet the girl that it came to him. That boat was going to make a rotten patrol boat.

It had no guns.

The girl was beautiful, well-bred and boring. Ashley wouldn't have minded if she'd had a sense of humor, but if she had one, it was well hidden. Nor would he have minded if she'd been especially attractive. But she was too cool for that. Making love to her would be like embracing a cucumber—a distinctly one-sided experience.

Ashley decided he must be getting more particular in his old age. A few years ago he wouldn't have cared what a woman's conversation was like if she was as lovely as this one. But now he liked his women warm, attractive and—what? Funny, earthy, capable of laughter. And this one most definitely was not.

By nine the conversation was drifting aimlessly and Ashley found himself drinking too much. By ten he was bored and restless.

When she started talking about the problems of finding young men to come to the austerity dance that her father was giving for her in London, Ashley knew he had to get away. He made a show of looking at his watch and said he had to be back at his ship at eleven, which was not quite true.

The moment he'd seen her off he felt a wonderful relief. There was still a good hour before the last boat left. He sauntered down the dark main street, wondering whether to go in search of Blythe. Almost immediately he decided against it. He could drink with Blythe anytime.

186

Instead he made his way down to the water again, going carefully because of the blackout. After a while he heard the sound of lapping water and knew he must be nearing the edge of the quay. The dark outlines of a vessel showed black against the night. It was the MFV, riding high on the top of the tide.

He called across. After a moment a voice challenged him. He recognized it as the Canadian's and said, "It's Ashley. I've come to claim that drink!"

The Canadian said, "I thought you might."

Ashley climbed on board and followed the other man down the companionway. Once below, the Canadian led the way into a wardroom which must originally have been the fish hold—and quite recently, Ashley guessed; the place still reeked. Now there were two wooden bunks, a center table and an oil lamp hanging from the deckhead.

"Very nice!"

"Not bad considering this was a working boat just a few months ago." The Canadian put out his hand. "My name's Laperrine, by the way. Have a drink."

Ashley chose gin and sat down. "Your crew . . ." he began, "are they all French?"

"Only the one. The man you met. He—well, he knows his way around and was willing to sign on, so we took him. The rest are British, ex-fishermen mainly."

"And—" Ashley paused, wondering whether his question would be considered too probing. But what the hell. He asked, "Will you be patrolling this part of the coast?"

Laperrine sat down on the opposite side of the table. "Here . . . and hereabouts. Tell me, have you been in destroyers long?"

Ashley wondered what lay behind the question. He replied, "A couple of years. Before that I did a stint on torpedo boats."

"You enjoyed that?"

"Yes, very much. Fast, exciting stuff. But with war coming I thought I might not see a lot of action. So I transferred back to proper ships again."

"The top speed of this thing is six knots. Not exactly fast and exciting."

Ashley leaned forward. "But there are compensations?"

"I think so."

An infinitesimal shudder of excitement went down Ashley's

spine. "May I ask a leading question? Why don't you have any guns?"

"Ah . . . well, we do."

"But nothing mounted on deck."

"No. We keep our weapons out of sight."

The man was going to tell him more, Ashley was certain of it. He pressed, "Because—?"

Laperrine paused, as if weighing him up. "You must say nothing—and I only tell you because—well, I think you might be interested." He took a breath. "We're going to the other side, to mingle with the fishing fleets off the west coast, to . . . exchange things."

Ashley had guessed it would be something like that. He suppressed a feeling of exhilaration. Then he remembered the gray paint. "But—you can't go like this, surely."

"Oh no. She'll look just like any other Concarneau trawler by the time we've finished with her."

Ashley said quickly, "Go on."

"There's not much more to it really. We're only just setting up the operation. But we do need more people. To be exact, someone who would command another boat. You would be . . . ideal. You know the coast, you know the people and you speak French—"

"Not very well!"

"But you understand it?"

Ashley nodded as if it were entirely true, which it wasn't. He asked, "But what about the fishing fleets—surely they're kept under guard?"

"Guard boats go out with the fleets, but the Concarneau trawlers are allowed out for as much as two to three days at a time. It should be easy to slip in amongst them at night."

Yes, of course it would. Ashley could imagine it. Pretending to fish, closing with the other trawlers, passing arms, receiving information. He could see it all and the idea thrilled him.

He looked up at the Canadian. "I wouldn't mind knowing more."

Laperrine realized he had been right about Ashley. He could detect the glint of excitement in the other man's eyes. "Good. I'll tell the Department."

They had another drink then Ashley got up to leave. "By the

way, where on earth are you going to take her, to get her repainted?"

"Somewhere quiet, away from curious eyes. Our base is to be at Helford. We'll probably do it there."

The Helford River was just south of Falmouth, a quiet beautiful place, but overlooked by a couple of small villages and a number of large houses. Ashley thought: It won't be any good.

"You should go somewhere more isolated. What about the Scillies? Somewhere like New Grimsby. No one would ever see you there."

Laperrine shook Ashley's hand. "It sounds like a good idea."

It was late and Ashley had to hurry to catch the last boat back to the ship. As he walked briskly along the dark deserted streets he felt euphoric.

The whole thing was mad. Going over to the other side, masquerading as a working boat, mingling with the fleet under the noses of the Germans. It was the stuff that boys' adventure books were made of, the sort of thing he had loved to read about as a child.

That must be why the idea appealed to him so much. He had always suspected that, in some ways, he had never grown up.

He laughed out loud. What the hell did it matter?

He adored the idea; he couldn't resist it. He couldn't wait to be frightened out of his wits and exhilarated at the same time. It was what he'd been waiting for all his life.

10 David curled his body into the fetal position and thought about a field full of flowers. Flowers sent him to sleep faster than anything else. Some days he didn't need to think of anything, he just fell asleep the moment he lay down on the wooden boards. But when he was in pain it was different. It was usually his stomach which gave him trouble; sometimes the

pain was awful. But today it was his knee; heavy rain had made the quarry treacherous and he had fallen, twisting his knee and splitting open the skin. So today he needed to think of something, and it was best to think of flowers.

The sounds of the hut did not bother him. The continuous moaning and sighing, the cries of suffering, the coughing and rasping of breath did not touch him at all. His ears heard the sounds but his mind cut them out, because his mind did not want to hear them.

He lay still, concentrating on the flowers, ignoring the pain, waiting for escape into unconsciousness. Sleep was the one thing he looked forward to: it was God-given, miraculous. He waited for a long time, and then the sleep came at last, drifting in like fog out of a valley.

His mind was closed to sounds—yet he heard. He heard the sudden clatter of a stick being run along the side of the hut. Everyone heard it. Even before the door of the hut was opened men were getting off the wooden bunks and standing up, their faces impassive, their eyes staring disinterestedly at a point on the opposite wall.

Automatically David climbed down from the flat wooden shelf that was called a bunk—it was the top in a tier of three—and stood in the passage that ran the length of the hut. He felt nothing, showed nothing. He concentrated on standing upright despite the pain in his knee.

Two of the *Prominente* marched in, beating their sticks loudly against the door until all three hundred men were standing silently. There was no moaning or sighing now; the *Prominente* beat you if you made too much noise.

"You will wait!"

So they waited. David stared at the wall opposite and thought of the flowers again. The field was very large and overgrown with tall grass. But rising from the grass were tall poppies, brilliant red and moving gently in the breeze. A stronger wind came rippling across the grass, turning the color of the grass from green to yellow, and bowing the poppies' heads as if in shame . . .

David concentrated on a different picture each day. From the moment he reached the quarry in the morning until he lay down to sleep at night, his body crying for rest, he liked to develop a

190

picture, to find each small detail and fit it in place, until the composition was complete.

Otherwise he did not bother to think at all. Thinking was a great mistake. Those who thought of their past, of things they had lost, of families they were unlikely to see again: those were the ones who suffered.

David had been in Dachau almost a year. Soon after his arrival he learned that you survived only by living each moment as it came, second by second. It was important to question nothing, challenge nothing. If you desired such things as freedom, food, clean water, you simply went mad.

He also learned not to get angry. Anger was pointless. You just lived each second, each minute as it came . . .

They had taken him first to Sachsenhausen. After two days they put him on a train and transferred him to Dachau. They had been the worst, those first few days; all that came later had seemed almost bearable. On the train each car was crammed tightly with people. There was no food or water. When finally the door of the car was opened and David, blinking in the strong light, saw that some had died and were being piled at the side of the track, he began to realize that you must live without thought, without question.

The most difficult thing was understanding the system and the rules—understanding how to survive. Oddly, the SS were the easiest to deal with. They liked order, numbers that tallied and obedience. One could cope with that. On arrival there had been prisoner registration. They had waited, the two thousand Jews off the train, in a long line. They had been allowed to sit until it was their turn to stand and advance to the desk of one of the four clerks in the middle of the central compound. Their names, professions and the details of their parentage were all carefully typed on forms; they were issued a number; then they passed on to delousing and uniform issue.

Order and numbers: one could cope with that.

It was the *Prominente*'s rules that were impossible because they had none. They had been handpicked by Himmler, these *Prominente*, from jails across Germany. They were all serving long sentences, for violent crimes mostly. It was said that the majority had been here since 1933, when Himmler personally created this, his showpiece.

The *Prominente* kicked, beat, hacked . . . sometimes they pushed men off the highest point of the quarry and watched them fall to their deaths. If you worked too slowly they might shoot you—or they might drop a heavy stone on your foot, or club you, or beat you round the head. They picked people at random. You never knew who would be next. *That* was their secret: there was no order, no pattern, just uncertainty and fear. But if you were clever you learned not to care. It might be you, it might be your neighbor. Some weeks before, two men—David had not known them —had stood together at the top of the quarry, embraced briefly, and jumped to their deaths. It had been their own choice. It seemed to David that the gesture was noble, something fine and clean in the stinking cesspit of the camp.

David envied the two men their courage. It was a courage he lacked. But then he'd probably die soon anyway. If you didn't die at the quarry, dysentery or disease got you. David's bunkmate had died of typhoid the day before; that's why there'd been room on the bunk for David to curl up.

David had probably caught the disease already. The thought didn't bother him. When it came to living or dying, he didn't care either way.

The *Prominente* shouted, "Attention!"

David brought his heels together and stood straight. He estimated he could stand another five minutes at the most. That should be enough.

Two SS officers came in wearing the insignia of the Death Head battalion. One referred to a list clipped on to a board and said: "Stand forward the following: Abraham, Freymann . . ."

David stepped forward, his head hammering hard against his ribs. Perhaps . . . ?

Perhaps, dear God, this is the end.

An overwhelming regret seized him: a regret for everything that had been taken away from him—his beloved little rabbit, his home, his work. Everything he had ever cared about. *I loved it all so much.*

The other names had been read out—there were only five more of them—and now the prisoners fell into line and followed the SS men out of the hut and across the compound.

David tried to keep up, but his knee slowed him down. He

thought: So what? If he was to die anyway, what difference did it make if it was now or five minutes later against a wall outside the compound?

The thought calmed him and he stopped trying to keep up.

He was getting used to the idea of dying. His first response had been emotional, the response of a man who had something to live for. But as he limped painfully along, he could see the rational side of it. There was nothing to live for. Death would, after all, be a merciful release—his stomach trouble was getting worse and sometimes he coughed up blood. A bleeding ulcer probably. The work at the quarry had been getting more difficult: he was breathless, weak and more prone to fall. Each day the effort of pushing his body to do things it was no longer capable of doing was more agonizing.

One of the SS men turned and saw David, now ten yards behind. David thought: He'll probably club me.

But the SS man did not stride angrily toward him. Instead he waited.

David struggled on. When he came level with the soldier he braced his body for a blow. Three more steps and he was past. There was no blow. Through the corner of his eye David saw that the SS man was behind him, following slowly. Good Lord, David thought, whatever next?

They passed through the main gates and approached a side compound surrounded by a single wire fence. Three huts were inside, all quite new and in good condition—raised off the ground and fitted with windows.

David thought: Whatever reason they've brought us here for, it isn't to kill us. The place is too nice and clean.

David counted the prisoners in the group. Yes, seven in all. He recognized one: Meyer. Meyer had also been a scientist, a very important one and director of a large laboratory. Meyer looked terrible. The skin of his face and chin hung in folds, and he had the stoop of an old man. The striped uniform bagged out from his emaciated body. He was no more than fifty-five; he looked seventy.

I must look just as old, thought David. He too had lost weight so fast that the skin around his body was loose and wrinkled.

"In!" It was one of the SS men.

They filed into the hut. The inside was clean and well fitted, the wood bright and new and sweet-smelling. Along the sides were wide benches with chairs in front of them. There were also three desks, a filing cabinet, and several typewriters. An interrogation center? An office? It could be anything.

"Be seated!"

The prisoners reacted with surprise. You were not usually told to sit down. One prisoner sat on the floor. The SS sergeant snapped, "On the seats! The seats!"

When they were sitting, an officer came in, and behind him, a soldier carrying a heavy object under a cover. The object was placed on a bench.

The officer faced them, his body erect, his manner efficient. "Under the direct orders of Reichsführer-SS Himmler, this laboratory is to function forthwith! You, as prisoners of the Reich, are to serve in it to the fullest of your ability."

David was dumbfounded. They were to *work* here! It was incredible. The significance of Meyer's presence dawned on him. Another top scientist . . . it must mean *scientific* work!

The officer was saying, "You will work on projects that will be assigned to you. Your first is here." He indicated the object on the workbench. "We have obtained a device from an enemy aircraft. You are to dismantle it, examine it and analyze your findings. We must know what it does, how it does it, and the way to produce it."

David's heart lifted with hope. This was a genuine scientific project, requiring careful analysis . . . and by skilled scientists like him and Meyer. That meant they would be treated as special prisoners and not returned to the main camp.

Yet a part of him waited, listening carefully. Nobody who survived in this place ever believed what they were told. One must always wait and see. There was always a catch somewhere.

The officer continued, "Now, you are all qualified in this type of electronics, is that correct?"

Nobody was likely to admit he wasn't, David thought wryly.

"Your leader will be"—he looked at his list—"Meyer. You will work under him. You will obey him. Is that understood?"

No one dared to answer.

"You will ask Sergeant Klammer for any equipment you may

need. This project is of great importance. Herr Himmler himself is in personal control. You will work with all speed and diligence. You will produce results that will be of the highest excellence. Any questions?"

There was silence. Questions were not usually encouraged; they had got out of the habit of asking them. The officer was turning to leave when a voice said, "Yes, I have a question."

David looked around nervously. It was Meyer. He was standing, looking straight at the officer. Silly old fool, David thought; why did he have to open his mouth!

All eyes swiveled back to the officer. But there was no irritation on his face, no anger. Instead there was a slight pause and the officer said, "Yes?"

Heads turned back to Meyer. The old man said, "To work efficiently, we will need better quarters and better rations. I cannot have half my team down with disease and malnutrition." His voice was steady and surprisingly clear.

David thought: My God! You amazing old man. What a nerve.

The eyes returned to the officer. He was nodding. "Agreed."

Just like that.

Then they were left alone to make a list of their technical requirements.

They sat in a group around Meyer, searching each others' faces for confirmation of what they couldn't yet believe. One man—his name was Richter—was sobbing violently, his head down on his knees, overcome by the improbability of it all.

David was still searching for the catch, and at last he had it. When they had analyzed the device, when the work was done, suppose there were no more of these projects? What would happen then? They wouldn't be kept here. They would be taken back to the main camp, to the quarry. It would be twice as bad, having to go back.

And yet . . . the work would take several weeks, maybe months. . . . And a month in this place was a very long time indeed. Long enough to start hoping that it would last forever . . .

It didn't occur to David that there was anything wrong in wanting to work until Meyer said, "Whether or not we feel it is *right* to be involved in this project, we have no choice—"

The moral aspects hadn't entered David's mind. Here in this

camp matters of principle were irrelevant, ridiculous even. You didn't consider whether things were right or wrong: if you did you would die of outrage.

Did it bother him, that he would be aiding the Nazis against their enemies? Did it matter when Jews were fighting for their very survival? The answer came to David when his clean new uniform was issued to him, when he was able to take his first real shower in a year, when he had his first decent meal in as many months, and when he saw the sleeping quarters—clean, fresh, with individual bunks and a flushing lavatory. The answer was: you had to survive. If you refused to work, someone else would take your place. A single gesture of defiance would change nothing.

That night, as he lay on his clean, sweet-smelling bunk, he wept a little. Mainly from relief, but also from pity, both for himself and for his fragile pathetic hopes for the future, rekindled after so long. He thought of Cecile and Ellen and tried to imagine what their lives were like without him. It was more than a year since he'd seen them.

When finally he fell asleep he dreamed that he invented a magical device that would win the war for Germany. He was a hero, he was freed from the camp and given the Iron Cross with Oak Leaves. But when he looked at himself he discovered, with horror, that they had given him an SS uniform. He told them it was a mistake and tried to tear it off, but the black cloth was stuck to his skin and as he tore at it, his flesh came away in his hands . . .

He woke with a start. He thought: Is what I'm doing so bad? But no, it couldn't be, it really couldn't be. What would be bad would be to give his secret away; the small package of microfilm: *that* would be unforgivable.

The next morning, after roll call, David asked to collect something from his old hut. It was a request that would have been inconceivable two days before, but now they let him go.

When he got to the hut it was empty; the able-bodied had left for the quarry and the night's sick had been taken to the infirmary, a euphemism for the hut which housed the rank stench and hopelessness of death and disease.

When he was sure he was quite alone he went behind the door

and, using an old metal food bowl, scraped at the hard earth floor. He didn't get the right spot at first and had to search over a wider circle until, at last, his hand closed over the small package. He pushed the earth back into the hollow and stamped it down. Then, wedging the package under his arm, he walked back to the special compound. He hid the package behind the lavatory cistern in the sleeping quarters.

Then he went to work.

It was some sort of radar jamming device, that was obvious. But determining how it worked, and which type of German radar transmitter it was designed to jam, took longer. They split the device into twenty units and each took some pieces to analyze.

After two weeks they were getting somewhere. The device was aimed at the Freya early-warning system, which worked on a frequency of 125 megacycles and was capable of detecting enemy planes at a distance of seventy-five miles. David knew all about it. He should—the Freya had been developed by the Gema Company.

David could not help wondering how the British had discovered the existence of Freya and its frequency. Freya was a large unit fixed to the ground, it was not something that could be captured or examined by spies. They must have more sophisticated detection equipment than anyone had thought. But then, David realized, he was out of touch . . . *everyone* here was. It was a year since long-term research had stopped, a year since scientists had been called up or sent away to camps.

But David's thoughts went further: If the British could detect radar, then they themselves must be capable of developing it. . . . The conclusion was inescapable. He discussed it with Meyer.

The older man said briefly, "Yes, I expect they have radar by now."

"To stay ahead Germany should have continued her research, then," David said.

"In this business to stand still is to fall behind."

"But there is still some development going on?"

Meyer exclaimed, "No! As far as I can gather, we're all they have. Ironic, isn't it?"

"Surely they've kept some laboratories going?"

"Very few. And nothing of importance. I asked for detailed reports of any work that had been going on while I—in my absence. They were not able to give me anything. I tell you, we are Germany's principal electronics development laboratory now." And Meyer laughed drily. "We're cheaper this way, you see. No salaries to pay."

For the first time David began to appreciate the importance of what they were doing. He asked, "What are we going to tell them? I mean, when we give them our findings?"

Meyer said simply, "We're going to tell them what we've found. But"—he lowered his voice—"we are not going to draw their conclusions for them. Let them discover the hard way that the British have radar. I am not going to tell them. Nor are you."

David shook his head. "No, I won't tell them."

The knowledge made David feel better. It was only a small act of omission, but at least it was something positive, some small act of defiance.

"By the way, who are we reporting to? Is it really Himmler?" David asked.

"I believe so. But copies also go to other departments, including the Chief Scientist's."

"Who is—?"

Meyer looked at him in surprise. "Why, Schmidt, of course."

Nothing changes, David thought. He wished it didn't matter to him that it was Schmidt, but it did. The knowledge made his stomach twist.

After a month they handed over their second-stage results, and David was worried how much longer they could spin out their work—another two weeks, four at the most. The lab had the air of permanence about it, yet it was impossible to believe that anything was permanent in Dachau. . . .

The thought of returning to the main compound haunted him, as it haunted everyone. The seven of them had become relatively healthy. They had warmth and security. They had hope. It was terrifying to have so much.

There were several other laboratories, David discovered. One was run by the SS Health Institute, another by the Luftwaffe Research Bureau. You didn't know what was done in them: you didn't ask such things in case the answer sickened you. These

labs also seemed permanent, but you never knew about that either. . . .

David remembered that Himmler had a passion for specialized knowledge: that explained all the different labs. Before the war Himmler had organized archaeological digs, to prove some obscure theory, David couldn't remember what exactly. Something about purely Germanic races being the forerunners of the Teutonic knights. The man was crazy. That he'd reached such high rank said much about the system.

A week later, when the workload was growing lighter, the scientists grew nervous. It would be difficult to spin things out much longer. Then, like manna from heaven, another object was delivered to the laboratory. They all exchanged smiles.

Like the first device this object was to be taken apart and analyzed. With delight David and Meyer realized that it was something quite new, something they could only guess at. It would take weeks to understand properly.

They had been reprieved.

Sergeant Klammer shouted, "Assemble!"

David felt a jump of alarm. Sergeant Klammer never interrupted them when they were working. It must be something out of the ordinary.

Sergeant Klammer waited impatiently while they gathered in a group in front of him.

When he spoke, it was with such emphasis that spit flew from his mouth. "You will cease work for the time being, and tidy the laboratory. Within an hour it must look perfect. Then you will prepare answers to any questions that might be put to you concerning your work. Is that clear?"

When Klammer had gone they turned questioningly to Meyer. Meyer shrugged. "Don't ask me."

David thought: It must be Himmler. He had been to the camp before. It was his creation, and he took a personal interest in it.

When the preparations were finished they waited. They were denied permission to collect their midday meal, so they went without. Nor were they allowed to carry on any work that might make the lab untidy.

By three in the afternoon David felt faint. His stomach had got

used to having food regularly. His ulcer started to throb dully: soon the throb would grow into an angry pain.

At four they were still waiting.

Finally Klammer burst in. "Attention!"

They stood up and stared fixedly at the opposite wall. One tries to look anonymous, David thought: faceless but servile; unimportant yet valuable. You look the way they want you to look.

There were voices and the noise of feet on the steps. A group of men entered the hut. From the corner of his eye David saw the black uniforms of high-ranking SS officers.

Someone laughed loudly. David thought: They've just had a good lunch.

As they came into his field of vision, David could see that most were senior officers. He did not know their faces. Except—yes, Himmler. He was small, with close-cropped hair and a weak chin. His eyes were pale and cool behind rimless spectacles. He looked harmless, like a bank clerk.

There were others, some in civilian clothes. David saw a face he knew.

It was Schmidt.

Schmidt was hanging back in a corner, looking uncomfortable. He was regarding his surroundings, the bare walls and simple equipment, with distaste. David thought: Well might you look uncomfortable, my friend. Schmidt hadn't spotted him yet. David was waiting for the moment when he would, but Schmidt was keeping his eyes away from the prisoners' faces. David felt vaguely disappointed.

Himmler was strolling down the room, nodding as pieces of the enemy device were shown to him. Then he turned and searched for someone. His eyes fell on Schmidt and he beckoned the Chief Scientist toward him.

There was total silence.

"Herr Schmidt . . ." Himmler's voice was surprisingly soft, almost gentle. "I trust you are pleased with what we have arranged here."

Schmidt spoke in a near whisper. "Yes, it seems most satisfactory."

Himmler smiled benignly, like a kind schoolmaster. "Well, I'm

sure you will want to speak to some of the prisoners about their work. So please go ahead."

Schmidt hesitated.

Himmler made a small bow. "Yes, now, by all means. We are quite happy to wait."

Schmidt looked unhappily around him, hoping for an escape. He focused on Meyer and recognition sprang into his eyes. David thought: Of course, he knows Meyer well. Schmidt approached Meyer, and soon they were examining a cathode tube captured from a British bomber. A buzz of conversation sprang up around the room.

David was puzzled by what had transpired between Himmler and Schmidt. Perhaps Himmler was doing Schmidt a favor, and didn't want him to forget it. Perhaps Schmidt had been desperate for scientists and had been forced to ask the SS to provide them. You would think that the SS would be embarrassed to use Jews, the inferior race. But no: Himmler was obviously delighted with the laboratory. It was Schmidt who was uncomfortable here.

Schmidt was standing in front of him. "Freymann . . ."

He was looking startled and David realized it was his physical appearance which Schmidt found so surprising.

Schmidt dragged his eyes down to the bench. "And what have you been working on?"

David explained, as simply and briefly as possible. Schmidt seemed satisfied, and began to turn away. But then he paused and said, "We looked into that shortwave radar idea again, the one you kept pressing. We established once and for all that it was not possible to develop it, nor indeed wise. It would be grossly inefficient."

He was waiting for David to comment, but David stared past him and did not reply. He did not know what to say. Schmidt added irritably, "It was a waste of time and money to research it. But of course, *you* knew best, didn't you?"

David said, "Yes, it was a mistake. I see that now."

The party began to leave, their boots shuffling across the wooden floor, their voices loud and raucous. Himmler was enjoying a joke with one of his junior officers. He had obviously enjoyed his day at Dachau.

As the door closed and silence fell, David sat down wearily on

his chair. To think he had worked willingly for these people. It made him feel ashamed. It had been vanity, really; wanting to show how brilliant he was, wanting to impress. Of course, he'd talked himself into believing he'd done it for the state and was working for a great common good which touched everyone equally. He'd separated the state—the people—from the Nazis. But he'd been quite wrong. The people, the state, the Nazis were all one. You only had to see Schmidt to know that. How else could a scientist, a *thinking* man, visit this place and be untouched.

Vanity. It was leading him on even now. It was pricking him over the shortwave radar and that remark of Schmidt's. How he'd love to prove to Schmidt that he was wrong. How he'd love to show him!

Pure vanity.

Shaking his head, he got slowly to his feet and went back to work.

11   The staff car slowed to a crawl as it negotiated the wide streets of a town. The change of pace woke Doenitz up.

His staff officer, a young man called Schneider, said from the front of the car, "This is Morlaix, sir. We are approximately forty minutes from Brest."

Doenitz stared at the monotonous procession of houses and shops. All French towns looked alike to him. He closed his eyes again. He often catnapped, particularly on long journeys. It helped to clear his mind when he was working on difficult problems.

But, though he'd been over it time and time again, he could find no solution to his greatest problem: this early war with Britain.

When war was declared he'd had a meager fifty-six U-boats of

which only twenty or so were suitable for the Atlantic. Six months later he was down to a dangerously low total of thirty-two. . . .

Only this miracle, the occupation of France, had saved the German war effort.

Doenitz blessed the marvelous turn of fortune which had given him the long west coast of France and unlimited access to the Atlantic. It was everything he could have asked for. His boats no longer had to return to Germany around the north coast of Scotland and run the gauntlet of the shallow North Sea. Now they could reach their hunting grounds more safely and much more quickly. Just three months after the occupation Doenitz had transferred two flotillas to Lorient and a third here to Brest.

The car turned a corner and Doenitz glimpsed the sparkle of water in the distance. He looked at his watch. They must be nearing Brest.

Doenitz said to Schneider, "Please give me the details of the program."

There was a rustling of papers and Schneider said, "Sir. At 1230 there will be lunch in a restaurant adjacent to the dockyard. At 1430 we meet Herr Dorsch, the architect from the Todt Organization, and tour the dockyard. At 1600 we have a general review meeting with the Naval Commander, Brest. Also you will wish to meet *U-319* when it returns. The last ETA we received was 1530."

U-319 was commanded by Kapitänleutnant Fischer. Fischer was a good man. He had done especially well on this patrol. Doenitz remembered the brief radio signal received at HQ in Paris yesterday. It had reported six ships sunk. Six! And by one boat during a five-day period. It was remarkable. Yet many of the other boats were achieving great successes too. The average sinkings per U-boat per day were way up. September should be a record month, with at least fifty ships sunk.

Fischer already wore the decoration of the Iron Cross of the Knight's Cross, First Class. Doenitz would present him with the Oak Leaves this afternoon. In the U-boat arm they did not wait for boards of senior officers to approve awards; decorations were given immediately, on the dockside, when emotions were running at their highest and the men could share the recipient's moment of glory.

The car was traveling along the edge of a wide estuary. The

occasional farmhouse had given way to a string of small villas: they were coming into Brest.

Doenitz considered the rest of the day's program: the planning session with the Todt Organization man should be straightforward. It was a matter of discussing the construction of the necessary dockyard modifications. Work was already in progress. They were using Polish labor apparently, and Poles always worked hard.

The staff meeting would be the usual mixture of optimism and resignation. The staff did not bother—or maybe, Doenitz thought, they did not dare—to ask for the one thing they knew he could not provide: more boats.

Only six new U-boats were being launched this month; in August it was a disastrous two. It had been the same in May, June, and July . . . not enough even to replace losses!

The High Command always told him it was a matter of resources—what they really meant was that everything was going into Goering's precious Luftwaffe.

They were descending into the dockyard area. The car swept in through some large stone gates and approached an ugly graystone building over which flew the flag of the Third Reich and the ensign of the Kriegsmarine. On the steps of the building were the commander of the First U-boat Flotilla and his staff. An ordinary seaman was keeping a tight rein on the flotilla's mascot, a goat draped with the flotilla's insignia. Doenitz was pleased. Back in 1935 this flotilla had been the one and only U-boat flotilla, and Doenitz himself had been its commander. Doenitz remembered with pride that the men themselves had thought up the insignia and the mascot.

As soon as the greetings were completed, they went to the restaurant. The lunch was indifferent. Doenitz considered French food to be very overrated. The wine, however, was excellent, though he drank little.

He cut the lunch short and they started the tour of the dockyard early. Brest was a well-developed port, as one would expect of one of France's major naval bases, and considerable repair facilities already existed. It was a question of making modifications, Dorsch explained. The larger drydocks needed to be adapted to take two U-boats at a time; also more engineering shops and welding facilities would have to be built.

"How long will the work take?" Doenitz asked.

"Eight weeks at the most."

"Good." Once the work was done another flotilla could be moved to Brest from Kiel. Doenitz wanted as many boats as possible here, where they would be most effective.

As the party walked slowly back toward the cars the distant drone of a plane sounded high in the sky. Everyone looked up.

"One of ours."

Doenitz nodded. So it should be. Goering had promised air supremacy: he'd better deliver it. Otherwise, here in port, the U-boats would be totally vulnerable to air attack. Rumor had it that the air battle with Britain was not going so well.

He turned to the architect. "Herr Dorsch, how long would it take to create sail-in bunkers for my boats? One that would be invulnerable to air attack?"

Dorsch was taken by surprise. "Oh! Er, I would think—allowing for the fact that the roof would have to be massively thick— my goodness, yes, very thick indeed . . . er, I would say, at least six months. All the concrete . . . all the labor. How many boats would need to be protected at once?"

"Ten, twelve, more if it was possible."

"It would be . . . a massive project."

"But possible?"

"Oh yes! Most certainly!"

Doenitz was pleased. If the air battle was lost then at least his boats would be safe in port.

That left one really vulnerable point: the run across the Bay of Biscay. It was here, in the approaches to his new French bases— Brest, Lorient, La Palice and St. Nazaire—that his boats were most exposed to enemy air patrols. Rather than search the open Atlantic, it was easier for the British to wait for departing or returning boats in the Bay.

He made a mental note to ask at the staff meeting about the current state of enemy air activity. What the U-boats really needed was proper air cover. But they never got it, Goering saw to that.

Back at headquarters the flotilla commander, Korvettenkapitän Scheer, was waiting and the meeting began promptly.

The routine reports of successes, losses and mechanical breakdowns were read out. The U-boat quotient—the average tonnage

sunk per U-boat per day—was going up monthly. Everyone was pleased.

"But soon it will go up very much more," Doenitz said. He explained that, once another flotilla could be based on the French coast, they would have enough boats to reintroduce properly organized wolf-pack tactics. The wolf pack would increase kills dramatically. Doenitz also promised first-class intelligence to help locate convoys.

Then they tackled the problems. Scheer, the flotilla commander, was most concerned about air attacks. The RAF had started carrying—and dropping—depth charges. And as Doenitz had foreseen, many of the attacks were being made in the Bay of Biscay.

"But the boats manage to dive in time?" Doenitz asked.

"Yes," Scheer agreed, "but sometimes it's closer than we'd like. In bad visibility the enemy never finds us, of course. But in thin cloud they often see us first and, attacking from downwind as they do, well . . . our men neither hear them nor see them until it's almost too late. And with these depth charges . . ."

"But a good lookout solves the problem?"

"Well—yes," admitted Scheer.

"That's the answer, then, isn't it?" Doenitz said a little impatiently. "And as many boats as possible should sail at dusk to benefit from the cover of darkness. Any other suggestions?"

There was a short silence, then someone asked, "Any chance of getting the magic eye?"

A few U-boats had been fitted with a large and cumbersome radar device just before the war, but the results had been so poor that the idea of having radar in U-boats had been dropped and the sets removed. Since then all research into small sets had ceased.

Doenitz replied, "No. There will be no radar. Tests prove that sets small enough to fit into our boats would be impossible to develop." The Chief Scientist's report had been quite definite.

There was a knock at the door and a junior officer came in and saluted. "Sir, *U-319* has entered port. Estimated arrival time is 1610."

Doenitz got to his feet. "Good! Let's get down there." He always loved meeting the boats and he tried to do so as often as

possible. In the old days, when his HQ was attached to the U-boat base at Kiel, he could meet every boat at the end of every patrol. Now—well, it was impossible. His HQ was in Paris and his bases scattered around the coast of the European continent.

As he walked briskly toward the door Doenitz called to Schneider, "You have everything?"

The staff officer replied, "Yes, Admiral."

The small party arrived at the dockside. They still had ten minutes to wait. Doenitz sat on a bollard and gazed in silence across the wide expanse of Brest Harbor. He looked around only once, when the bleating of the mascot interrupted his thoughts. He saw that, in addition to the band and the official guard of honor, at least a hundred officers and men had gathered. It was always the same: everyone always made the effort to welcome a boat home. It was part of the remarkable loyalty and camaraderie that united his men. He never felt less than immensely proud of them. . . .

Though there were some he couldn't help feeling especially proud of: his two sons, one of whom was already in the U-boat service.

Someone shouted as the nose of *U-319* appeared from behind a jetty. There was loud cheering from the assembled crowd. The band struck up the *Kretschmermarch.* Doenitz felt a lump in his throat. This occasion, this moment of emotion and relief and pride, never failed to move him. His men were the best in Germany, the best in the world. They deserved to return like this, in triumph, for they were the bravest of them all. . . .

The crew lining *U-319*'s deck cheered back, waving and shouting to the crowd on the dock. They were in high spirits: obviously everything had gone well. As the submarine maneuvered alongside there was some cheerful banter between the crew and the crowd. Doenitz encouraged informality at moments like this. He reflected that, because of his presence, the comments were probably quite subdued. Fischer was in the conning tower, his face lit by a wide grin. The goat brayed loudly and everyone laughed.

When the boat was secure and the gangway rigged, the chatter of voices died away, the band stopped playing and there was a hushed silence. Everyone had guessed what was to happen. The crew stood in line along the decks. Fischer emerged through a

hatchway still in his U-boat uniform of plain blue overalls and soft white cap, and walked down the gangway. Doenitz stood waiting at the end and, as Fischer stepped onto the dock, the two men faced each other, saluted and shook hands.

The crowd waited expectantly as Doenitz said a few words. Schneider then stepped forward, a small box in his hand, and opened it. Doenitz took out the simple Iron Cross with Oak Leaves on a long ribbon, and placed it around Fischer's neck. The two men saluted again, the band struck up a tune, and a great roar went up from the crowd. Scheer presented Fischer with a bouquet of flowers and the young U-boat commander, his face a picture of pride and joy, led Doenitz and Scheer aboard his boat to present his crew to their senior officers. To complete the formalities Fischer then inspected and saluted the guard of honor.

Scheer was at Doenitz's elbow. "Sir, would you like to attend the debriefing? Or would a copy of Fischer's report be sufficient?"

"I will attend if I may."

"Of course, Admiral!"

The formal question had been asked, the reply given. But, Doenitz thought, if they hadn't asked me I would have invited myself anyway.

Fischer sat near the window, his yellow hair lit gold by the late afternoon sun. From time to time he glanced at the written log on his knee to remind himself of precise times or sequences of events. But for the most part he spoke from memory, his pale blue eyes fixed at a point high on the opposite wall, his mind back in the North Atlantic. He told first how, on their way to their designated patrol area, they had come across a small convoy, probably from the Mediterranean. They had sunk two of the ships before being chased off by a destroyer. They then continued to their patrol area.

Fischer went on: "In company with *U-253* and *U-90* we arrived at the grid reference point at 0700 on the fifteenth. We fanned out and zigzagged in twenty-mile legs, covering a corridor fifty miles wide across the expected path of the convoy. *U-90* spotted them at 1900 hours, dead ahead. She reported the sighting to us by radio. I passed on the report to Command Headquarters. I

then ordered U-253 to make her approach from the south and U-90 from the north. We ourselves would lie in wait dead ahead. At this stage it was impossible to gauge the speed of the convoy, or the pattern of its zigzag, but I ordered that there be no further communication between our boats until the action was completed to lessen the risk of detection."

Listening to Fischer, Doenitz was nostalgic for the time in 1915 when he himself had seen active service. Then he too had made reports like this: dispassionate, objective, but loaded with a multitude of things unsaid—fear, exhilaration, uncertainty. Would the convoy alter course at the last moment? Was it going faster than they had estimated? Which ship should they go for?

Fischer went on: "We dived to periscope depth and maneuvered to a position in front of the convoy and dead ahead of it. The convoy consisted of at least thirty ships, but it appeared to have a very small escort: we spotted only one frigate and three armed trawlers. Suddenly, we saw the frigate detach herself from the convoy and steam away to the south. I thought she must have spotted U-253, but later I discovered that this was not in fact the case. We never found out why she dashed off in this way. We waited, keeping an eye on both the convoy and the frigate. At 2030 we spotted the frigate coming in to make a pass across the front of the convoy. Unfortunately, this pass would bring her very near to our position. I had a feeling the convoy was about to alter course and, though I had been planning to take us a bit farther to the north, I had no choice but to dive. We stayed submerged for twelve minutes. We listened to the frigate pass then, using minimum speed, came to periscope depth again."

Fischer paused, exhilaration in his eyes. "We could hardly believe it, but when we took a look around we discovered we had come up in the middle of the convoy!"

A ghost of a smile passed Doenitz's lips. It was indeed a remarkable stroke of luck! He could imagine the amazement and the excitement in the U-boat.

"There was a large tanker coming straight into the perfect target position. All we had to do was wait! However, since it was a very dark night and the convoy was well spread out, I decided to surface. There was a good chance of remaining unseen, and I wanted a more stable firing platform. We fired two torpedoes at

the tanker. She went up straightaway. We retreated so as not to be illuminated by the burning ship. Another ship came into target position. We got her with a single torpedo. Then we saw other ships on fire: *U-253* and *U-90* were obviously busy too. At this point the frigate came sniffing around so we went down to periscope depth, but she never found us. We continued to find targets in the center of the convoy."

Fischer looked down. "We know to our certain knowledge that we sank four ships that night. We used only eight torpedoes." There was a moment's silence. No one liked the thought of ships being destroyed because men died, drowned or burned alive.

"Finally, when the convoy had passed, we surfaced. Eventually we made radio contact with *U-90* and *U-253*. They had scored four and six hits respectively. Thus we sank approximately half the convoy."

The senior officers exchanged glances of satisfaction. "And so you were not detected by the enemy at any stage?" Doenitz asked.

"No, sir! I don't think they had any *idea* of where we were. I believe that, when we're submerged, their asdic can't distinguish the noise of our engines from those of the ships in the convoy. As long as we're sufficiently close to the ships, the asdic won't pick us up."

"I agree," Doenitz said. "Again, Kapitänleutnant Fischer, my congratulations on your fine achievement. At this rate, our tiny band of boats will win the war!"

They think I am just saying that, thought Doenitz, but it is absolutely true.

The debriefing was over. Doenitz poised himself to get out of his chair.

"Sir, perhaps I did not answer quite accurately just now." It was Fischer.

Doenitz looked up sharply. "Yes?"

"We did have an engagement with the enemy, but it was much later. Just sixty miles from Brest, visibility one mile, the lookout thought he heard an aircraft engine. Fortunately he was a man with exceptionally sharp ears. I must admit I did not hear it, though I was in the conning tower. I took no chances and ordered a crash dive. We were just in time. The last man down saw a Sunderland appear to the south. It was banking sharply toward

us. When we were down we heard one bomb explode, but it was some way off. After that, nothing." Fischer shrugged. "It was a fluke. But it was lucky we had such an excellent lookout."

"Yes. It was lucky." Doenitz stood up. "And it banked only when it saw you, this plane?"

"Yes, sir."

"A fluke then." Doenitz put out his hand. "Good-bye, Fischer. And I look forward to hearing about your future patrols. May all of them be equally successful!" He leaned forward and said in an undertone that no one else could hear. "It is a long time since the old days at Kiel, isn't it?"

Fischer grinned. "Yes, sir."

"A long time . . ." Doenitz turned away and strode out of the room.

12 The apartment was in a narrow street near the Porte d'Auteuil in the *seizième*. It was small, plainly furnished, and in every way unremarkable. It was just what Vasson wanted.

It had been essential to move. He'd been in the other place six months, ever since the previous December when he'd started working for Kloffer. It had been too long.

He moved in at noon and carefully unpacked the contents of two of his three suitcases. In the bedroom was a single narrow wardrobe with just enough room for his suits. His shirts, casual trousers, pullovers and best underwear he folded carefully and placed in the drawers of a large chest in the corner. He put two mothballs in each of the drawers and another four in the wardrobe. He didn't want to get back and find all his best clothes peppered with holes.

He opened the third suitcase and checked the contents. One

inexpensive badly cut suit, three cotton shirts, three pairs of cheap casual trousers, socks, shoes, underwear—his working clothes.

He took out his wallet. Papers in the name of Lebrun, a hundred francs, and the special travel permit which he would destroy once he was over the border in Belgium. He looked again at the money: would it be enough? He couldn't think of anything he could possibly spend it on between now and the border. He had already paid six months' rent in advance and given the concierge enough money to cover the electricity and any other bills that might turn up. No, he wouldn't need any more cash; anyway the less French currency he had on him the better.

It was three-thirty. Just time to go to Sèvres, then Clichy, and back by seven.

He shut the suitcase, placed it ready by the front door and left the apartment. He shouted a word to the concierge and went into the street. His car, a six-year-old Citroën, was three minutes' walk away. It was a habit, now, to leave his car at least two streets from wherever he was living. Possessing a car was not unusual, but having enough gasoline to use it every day certainly was.

When he got to the car he went straight to the trunk and unlocked it. The large leather suitcase was still there, as he knew it would be. It amused him to think of all the people who must have walked past the car in the last few hours without having the slightest inkling of what the vehicle contained.

He closed and locked the trunk, and got into the car. Since the occupation almost a year ago the traffic in Paris had thinned down considerably; the trip to Sèvres should take fifteen minutes at the most.

In fact he reached the Porte de Sèvres in five minutes and the Rue du Vieux Moulin in twelve.

Sèvres was a suburb on the southwest outskirts of the city. Vasson had chosen it because it was quiet, genteel and, like everything else in his life nowadays, unremarkable. Rue du Vieux Moulin was a sleepy street of two-story, late nineteenth-century houses set back from the road in their own gardens. The villas, once impressive, now had the unmistakable air of decay.

Vasson drove the full length of the street to make sure that everything was quiet, parked nearby, then, taking the leather

suitcase from the trunk, set off on foot for 22, Rue du Vieux Moulin.

A few moments later he wished that, for once, he had parked outside the house; the bag was heavy.

He couldn't decide if Mme. Roche would be in. It didn't really matter either way: the old woman was incapable of a suspicious thought. You could go in with a mask over your face and blood on your hands and she wouldn't notice.

He reached the house at last and opened the gate in the low wall surrounding the austere garden, a once-neat arrangement of gravel and shrubs. In the balmy air of the warm summer day, the house was quiet and most of the shutters drawn. The old woman was probably having a nap.

Vasson walked around to the side, where some steps led down to the semibasement level. At the bottom of the steps was a door which he opened with a key. Inside was a passage with four rooms leading off it. The first, which must once have been a servant's room, was now a bed-sitter; the second was a primitive washroom with a stone sink and lavatory; the other two were storage rooms.

Vasson went into the bed-sitting room, laid the leather bag on the bed, and listened for sounds from the upper floors. Still nothing. He crossed to the wardrobe and opened the door. He kept a spare set of clothes here, as well as two sets of papers which Kloffer didn't know about. The papers, strapped to the underside of a shelf at the bottom, were still there.

He picked up the bag and started down the passage toward the storerooms. It was dark and he had to feel his way along the wall. Finally he reached a door and, opening it, fumbled for the light switch.

The room was square and windowless except for four small ventilation grilles near the ceiling. Once it must have been stacked with wine but now only a few dusty bottles lay forgotten in an old rack. The room had an earthen floor, which, because it kept the air cool, made it perfect for wine storage. The earthen floor also made the room perfect for storing articles like gold Louis and demi-barres.

Vasson locked the door and crossed the room. A wooden table straddled one corner. On it was some ancient photographic equipment: two developing trays, an enlarger and five bottles of

chemicals. Vasson had picked them up for a few francs in a pawnbroker's. Photography was what he was supposed to be doing when he locked himself in this room.

He moved the table and, taking a trowel from the leather bag, started to dig. He made a hole ten inches deep and, removing two small canvas sacks of coins and a solid bar from the bag, he carefully buried them. He spent some time flattening the earth and stamping it down with his feet before replacing the table.

That made two hundred thousand francs in gold. A tidy sum —but not enough, not enough by far.

It had taken months and months to wrest a decent wage out of Kloffer; even then it was in paper money and Vasson had been forced to go to the black market for gold. It had cost him dear. But gold it had to be; with inflation, paper money wouldn't be worth a sou in a couple of years. Then, in May, Vasson had finally persuaded Kloffer to pay him directly in gold. It didn't cost Kloffer anything—he and his friends were stealing vast quantities of the stuff—but it did save Vasson a lot of time and money.

He should have been paid in gold from the beginning, of course. It made him angry to remember that he'd had to beg, cajole and threaten to get what was, after all, only his due. He'd been shabbily treated, no doubt about that.

He replaced the trowel in the bag, closed the storeroom door and went back to the bed-sitting room. He left six months' rent money on the bed with a note saying that he wouldn't be back for some time, and left. The old woman thought he was a traveling salesman.

The house was still quiet, the old woman probably on the point of getting up. It was the perfect place for a cache. But then it was bound to be: he'd taken a lot of time and trouble to find it.

The drive to Clichy took thirty minutes. The lock-up garage still had quite a lot of stuff in it—stockings, perfume and gasoline —but there was just enough room for the car. He parked it and locked up carefully. As he walked toward the nearest boulevard he thought about the remaining stock and whether it would be a good time to sell. He couldn't make up his mind; he hadn't been following the market recently and he didn't know how prices were. What he *did* know was that new stock was almost impossible to come by; most of his old sources had dried up. Also . . . what? He'd lost interest, that was what. The market bored him: it was

too restricted and the profit too hard to come by. Besides, the big boys had moved in and begun to squeeze everyone out, just like they always did. Diversifying was the wisest thing he'd ever done.

He reached the Rue Jean Jaurès and looked for a *vélo*-taxi, but it was almost five-thirty, the rush hour, and the few that he saw were already occupied. He cursed and walked toward the nearest Métro at Porte de Clichy.

He hated the idea of taking the Métro: it was too public. Ever since the last operation, he'd had an indefinable but distinct feeling that he was no longer safe. The project had been straightforward. He had infiltrated a small escape line taking shot-down pilots from northeast France through Paris to Spain. The members of the line had been typically trusting and weak on security, but somewhere, somehow he'd disturbed something else. There was a loose end somewhere. He didn't exactly know what. . . . But he was certain, absolutely sure, someone was onto him. The word was out; it was time for him to go.

The Métro was even worse than he'd feared. He hated confined spaces and, after he changed at St.-Lazare, the train was horribly crowded. The bodies pressed close against him and he shuddered with the beginnings of panic. He changed again at Miromesnil. The train was slightly less crowded this time, but he still had to stand. After a few moments he felt a tingling in his spine. It was a feeling he never ignored. Without moving his head he looked at the reflection of the other passengers in the window. A man behind him seemed to be staring at him. Vasson studied the face desperately. Did he know him? No. He was certain he didn't. He relaxed again. It was his nerves. He was imagining things. Christ, it really was time to get away.

He got back to the apartment in Auteuil at six-fifteen. He stripped and washed the whole of his body. Washing always made him feel good. He lay on the bed, smoking thoughtfully, until six-fifty, then dressed. When the bell rang he picked up the suitcase, locked the apartment behind him, and slid the key under the concierge's door.

A car was waiting at the curb. It looked like a taxi, though Vasson knew it wasn't. Even the driver looked French. Vasson thought: Kloffer's learning at last.

Kloffer was sitting in the back, as relaxed as a fat cat. Vasson

sank onto the seat beside him. The car moved off and the German asked, "Any problems?"

"No."

Vasson waited. Kloffer was here for a reason; he wasn't seeing Vasson off out of the kindness of his heart.

Eventually Kloffer said, "This car will take you all the way to Brussels."

"I thought—"

"We decided against the train. We don't want anyone to see you leave. I think you'll agree that it's wise. . . ." Kloffer turned and looked at Vasson. "Your old apartment—we caught someone waiting outside. He had a weapon. It seems he wanted to kill you."

I knew it, Vasson thought.

Kloffer smiled. "We don't want you dead when I've promised you to Brussels. They would think me *most* inefficient!" He giggled slightly.

Vasson was wondering: Where had he gone wrong? He hated loose ends, he hated not knowing. He asked, "Who was the man? The one who was waiting for me?"

"The brother of one of the girls we arrested last week."

"Was he working on his own?"

"We don't know. He says nothing."

Vasson cursed. That meant it would be unsafe to return . . . until he knew for sure. Damn. "I must know—whether he was on his own. Also if he had a description of me, and how he knew where I was living. Everything!"

"We will do our best."

"You'd better. Otherwise—" *Otherwise I'm as good as dead.* "Otherwise I won't come back here. You understand?"

"Indeed." Kloffer looked quite happy about it. Vasson had the feeling that there was more to this Brussels trip than Kloffer was admitting to. Perhaps there was a deal. If so, Kloffer would never tell him the terms.

"Have you any more information about the Brussels operation?"

Kloffer shrugged. "Not really. But apparently there is just the one organization. They collect the airmen not only in Belgium but some in France too and send them all the way down to Spain. A long way—there must be hundreds of people involved. Yet we

haven't succeeded in stopping them. Amazing. You'd think some-one would talk!" He sniffed with irritation. "Your operation against the Paris couriers—that was excellent while it lasted. But we have evidence that all the people we removed have been replaced. No, there's only one way to get these pests, and that is from Brussels. Otherwise we'll just go on wasting our time."

"What's been tried so far?"

"I'm not sure—you must ask them. But I gather that attempts at infiltration have failed." Kloffer looked pleased.

Ah, thought Vasson, so that's it. The Brussels people had failed; Kloffer was coming to the rescue with his own man. No wonder Kloffer wasn't shedding any tears. All the more glory for him.

They were approaching the Avenue Foch. Kloffer said to the driver, "Drop me on the next corner."

Vasson said, "And the money? Are they clear about the method of payment? I want that agreed before I get there."

"Yes, yes," Kloffer said impatiently.

Gold was to be deposited in the Banque de Paris and the receipt slips sent to Brussels, Poste Restante. It was quite simple, Vasson thought, but you'd think I was asking for the moon.

The car came to a halt and Kloffer opened the door. "Good-bye. All success. I know that if anyone can do it, you can."

Praise indeed. Kloffer was getting quite pleasant in his old age.

Kloffer got out of the car and peered in through the door, his eyes sharp as a cat's. Kloffer said softly, "Oh, by the way, are you happy with your papers?"

He never usually inquired. Vasson was instantly suspicious. "Yes, why?"

"I thought you might not like the name we chose."

Vasson waited.

"Well, it's Paul Lebrun, isn't it? I thought you might not care for the Paul." Kloffer grinned briefly and was gone. The car drew rapidly away and Vasson was thrown against the seat. He stared blindly ahead, unable to breathe, a vise around his heart.

Kloffer knew his name.

God.

He felt angry, then sick with fear.

Kloffer must know that Vasson was wanted in Marseilles. . . .
Kloffer could blackmail him . . . Kloffer *was* blackmailing him?

Vasson tried to assimilate the awful fact, but it hurt, *it hurt.* And it was being vulnerable, the dreadful realization that he could be pressured—humiliated—that hurt the most.

Where had he gone wrong? How had Kloffer found out?

He didn't know, and he never would unless Kloffer chose to tell him. And Kloffer *wouldn't* choose to tell him; instead the German would let the question fester in his mind. Yes, that was Kloffer's way.

He was sure of another thing too: the timing of Kloffer's little bombshell was carefully planned. The German wanted to remind Vasson who was in control; he wanted Vasson to come back afterward, like a good boy.

Vasson shuddered. To hell with Kloffer!

But even as he thought it he knew he had lost. Kloffer had him, just *there.*

As the car sped into the gathering darkness Vasson pressed his head into the corner, his face contorted with rage and bitterness, and thought: It's all so *unfair.* Why does it always happen to me? *Why me?*

At midnight the car stopped outside a cheap hotel. Vasson had no idea where he was, except that it was somewhere in Brussels. The driver said he'd been told to take Vasson there. The hotel wasn't expecting him. At first the proprietor said he had no rooms, then he decided he had one after all, but, being his best room, it would cost a bit extra. When Vasson saw the room he realized he'd been had again—the room was dreadful: depressingly airless and none too clean. A single unshaded light hung from the ceiling. It was not his day.

For a few moments he sat on the bed and looked in despair at his surroundings. The room brought back memories of other squalid rooms: the ones in Montmartre, all shabby, all depressing; the ones in the Old Quarter, hot and claustrophobic; the bare cell at the Jesuit school, white and unspeakably barren; and—so long ago—that other room.

He undressed slowly and got into the bed. At least the sheets were clean.

Tomorrow he would spell it out to the Boches: no more cheap hotels, no more squalor. Lots of cash, lots of information, and no

interference. In one way it was irritating to have to educate them, the way he'd educated Kloffer, but at the same time he was rather looking forward to it. It was a challenge, and he would win it, the way he'd won with Kloffer.

Except that Kloffer knew his name . . .

After a long time he fell asleep.

He was in the old lady's house in Sèvres, walking along the passage, when he saw that the door to the storeroom was open and the light on. There were voices inside. He tried to get to the door but he couldn't move. He looked down and saw he had weights on his feet. Then Kloffer came out. He was carrying the gold and saying, "I knew it was here all the time! I knew! Good-bye! Good-bye!" Then Vasson's arms were grabbed from behind and he was dragged out. Kloffer called, "They're going to cut off your head, isn't that interesting?"

They put him in a cell. It was like the one at the school: bare, soulless, destroying. Father Ignatius was leaning over him. "Eternal Father, I confirm; Eternal Son, I confirm; Eternal Holy Spirit, I confirm. May the Lord forgive you, Paul, for you have sinned. Like your mother sinned."

What had his mother done? What sin could be so terrible? He heard himself ask, "What sin? What sin?" and Father Ignatius shook his head gently and said, "It is better that you do not ask, my son." "But why doesn't she come?" "She doesn't choose to, Paul, and it's better that she doesn't." "But Father Francis told me she was dead." "Well, she is in a way, Paul." "I don't understand, I don't understand!" "It is not for us to understand, my son, we must accept God's will—and with love in our hearts."

I don't understand. I never have. Why doesn't she come to me? What has she done that is so terrible? Why did she beat me? *Why does she hate me so?*

I don't understand.

German efficiency was enough to drive anyone mad, with its rigid structures, its unyielding demands and its inevitable duplications. But it did mean everything got written down.

It was all there in the files. Every operation against the escape line that operated from Brussels. There were pages and pages of facts, many of them irrelevant, but Vasson wasn't complaining,

although it took hours to sort out what was useful and what wasn't.

Generally, reports to be seen by senior officers were far too optimistic and evasive to be useful. Much better were the situation reports with limited circulation. Names, places, hypotheses, action to be taken . . .

Gradually Vasson built up a picture. The airmen got themselves to a farm or whatever, presumably having buried their parachutes and any other evidence of where they had landed. The farmer harbored them, or quickly passed them on to someone who would. As soon as it could be arranged, they were picked up by the organization proper. How were they transported? Impossible to say, but for the longer parts of the journey it was certainly by train. Several of the couriers arrested so far were young girls. Vasson could imagine them: innocent-looking, charming, pretty enough to distract if necessary. Yes, the system must work well.

The couriers were probably changed at Brussels and again at Paris and maybe a third time on the way down to the Spanish border. He wondered how careful they were: whether or not the couriers actually met and knew each other or whether they operated a cutoff system whereby the airmen were taken to a park bench by one courier and left there for ten minutes before the next came to pick them up.

He read the interrogation reports. Some of those arrested had talked, but they appeared to be small fry—collectors or minor couriers. None of them had known the names of the main couriers, those who must be in touch with the central organizers. Others hadn't talked even when they were about to die. Extraordinary how little value people put on their own lives.

The infiltration operations mounted so far had been amateurish—and that was putting it kindly. The SD had sent two of its men into the Belgian countryside dressed as Canadian airmen. They were found four days later, dead. It was no surprise to Vasson; the two men probably spoke English with a German accent and didn't know what the maple leaf meant. The line must have an interrogation center, where airmen's credentials were checked. Well, even if they hadn't they certainly would now, after that little fiasco.

Another time a Belgian-born SD agent had infiltrated the line as a courier, had sprung his trap far too soon and managed to

catch only two people. The agent had then run like hell out of Brussels and was never seen again. An amateur.

One operation had been quite successful, however. Twenty arrests were made. But Vasson couldn't find the details; the report was marked, "Refer to Luftwaffe intelligence." He must ask about that.

In the current situation report, there appeared to be only two leads. A young girl, the sister of a girl in custody, plus an older woman whose address had been found in the apartment of a minor courier. Both women had gone to ground. Nothing about this surprised Vasson: the Gestapo had probably gone straight to their homes in full view of all the neighbors and waited for them to return. Subtlety and patience were not the Germans' strong points.

He noted the names of all the suspects to date and took brief details of addresses, possible roles in the line, and probable leads. They didn't add up to much. In their usual blundering way the Germans had fouled up everything that might have been worth pursuing.

Vasson went back to Mueller's office. Mueller was his liaison man: quite senior, a colonel in the SD. For some reason Vasson didn't understand, here in Belgium escaping airmen came under the Nazi security service or Luftwaffe intelligence, and not the secret police.

Mueller was pale and fat, like a large slug. He acted as though he had indigestion; from time to time he unhappily patted his obscene stomach, which pressed relentlessly against the field-gray cloth of his uniform. "Well?" he asked impatiently. "Have you seen everything you need to see?"

"I think so." Vasson sat down, though he had not been invited to do so. Mueller would not object. Mueller, for all his arrogance and impatience, was not a problem: he was a realistic man. He wanted results and he'd made it clear he was prepared to pay for them. Vasson had forgotten his anger at being put in the seedy hotel after Mueller had agreed to all his requests.

Vasson said, "But there is one thing. An operation involving Luftwaffe intelligence. The report's not in the file."

"That was a joint operation. Extremely successful. For a week or so we operated a loop in the escape line."

"A loop?"

Mueller looked patronizingly at Vasson. "Ah? You do not know? No, why should you. We invented the idea! A loop is an extra link in the escape chain which the organizers do not realize is there and which we create to extract intelligence. We pretend we are Resistance interrogators and ask the airmen to tell us everything about their units and operations so we can check what they say with London. It works every time. During this last operation they told us everything. . . . Most useful for the Luftwaffe and most useful for us too; we got several good descriptions of the people harboring airmen. We made a number of arrests."

Twenty to be precise. But, Vasson thought, they can never use that one again, not with this line anyway.

"One more thing," Vasson said. "Is the line in direct communication with Britain? Can they actually check the airmen's identities by radio?"

"We believe not. At one time we picked up clandestine radio transmissions from this area, but no longer. . . . We must have got the operator."

"So they have no contact . . ."

"But they have backup from London; a department of the British Ministry of Defense, called MI9, sends them money regularly, and probably arms too. The British have a name for the line —they call it Meteor."

"Meteor . . ."

Mueller sat upright. "Now! We have provided you with cash, we have provided you with information; what else do you require, may I ask?"

"A work permit in the name of Paul Lebrun. My occupation should be given as engineer and the place of employment as some engineering works in, say, Lyons. Then in brackets it should say, 'On secondment duties to Wehrmacht.' "

"You want to say you're working for the Wehrmacht?"

"That's right. I'll also need a special travel permit which allows me frequent journeys between my base in Lyons and the occupied territories."

"That's all?"

"Yes."

"Now!" Mueller said disparagingly. "How exactly do you propose to bring off this amazing success that I am told you will achieve?"

"I don't know."

Mueller's face showed uncertainty: he wasn't sure if Vasson was purposely misleading him or just being difficult. "I suggest you inform me when you *do* have a plan."

"Certainly. But for a few days I want to get to know the city and feel my way around."

Mueller eyed him suspiciously. "You will not start anything without informing me, will you, Lebrun?"

"No."

As Vasson left, Mueller repeated, "And you have no plan at all?"

Vasson shrugged. "In good time. You didn't give me many leads . . ."

Mueller rose from his chair. "Please report back in two days."

Vasson hurried out, thinking: Like hell! He would report only when he was ready, and even then he wouldn't tell Mueller a damn thing about what he was doing. The Germans would only foul it up. Anyway he loved to have it all to himself; he hated to share it until the last possible moment.

His plan was the same as always: he had it all worked out. But this time it would take longer, he realized; there were so many people involved, so many contacts to make. Yes, it would take time . . . but he didn't mind; it added to the challenge and the excitement.

This one would be the best one yet, he knew it in his bones. This would be his greatest triumph.

13 Falmouth. At least it *should* be. Since the first invasion scare all the railway signs had been removed, so you had to use timetables and guesswork to decide your location. Smithe-Webb stepped off the train, sniffed the sharp, salty

Cornish air and thought how wonderfully refreshing it was after the smoke and grime of London.

It *was* Falmouth: there was a naval staff car outside the station, waiting to take him to Helford. The major settled back in his seat and admired the rolling green countryside. He only wished he could get away from London more often. But his department of MI9 was based at the War Office in Whitehall and he hardly got away at all.

In his year at MI9 he'd heard a few whispers about Helford and the naval unit there. It was a clandestine outfit, and, although he'd guessed that they went over to what was known as the Other Side, he'd heard little else. He'd had few dealings with the Navy: almost all the Allied servicemen stranded in Europe—his customers, as he called them—were airmen and soldiers.

But since MI9 had asked for the Navy's help, the DDOD(I), the head of the Navy's Irregular Operations Division, had told him a bit about the Helford operations and, what was more important, had promised to help. He had, however, suggested that the major go down to Helford and talk to someone who knew the Other Side well, someone who could advise him on the practical problems his people were likely to meet. The implication was clear: the Navy could manage their end of the operation all right, but could MI9 control *theirs*?

Smithe-Webb took the point; that was why he was here.

After half an hour the road descended steeply toward the dull glint of water visible in the distance. They passed through a picturesque village and came to the banks of a wide river. The car stopped and Smithe-Webb got out. A launch with two sailors was waiting at a jetty and, as soon as he had climbed in, it set off toward a cluster of vessels moored in the mainstream of the river. There was a large three-masted yacht which had a number of dinghies tied to it—some kind of mother ship perhaps; then, moored around it, four or five largish fishing boats. Most of them were painted regulation gray, but one had a strange combination of colors. Her superstructure and most of her topsides were gray, but her after end was bright scarlet with some kind of pattern on it. Several men were standing in a small boat, painting the scarlet with gray. The launch made a neat semicircle and approached the many-colored boat. As they drew near, Smithe-Webb could make

out the shadow of a name on the stern. It read: Marie-claire. Brest.

The launch came alongside and a sailor threw a line to someone on deck. Smithe-Webb stared in amazement. The fellow was a sight: unshaven, dirty and dressed like a fisherman. If they were playing at pirates, Smithe-Webb thought, they certainly looked the part.

Smithe-Webb put a foot up on the rubbing strake and hoisted himself over the gunwale onto the deck. He looked expectantly at the piratical figure, but after making fast the launch's painter the fellow sauntered off down the deck.

There was a voice from behind. "Good morning!"

Smithe-Webb turned and was met by a pair of penetrating blue eyes and an outstretched hand. Like the other fellow, this chap was a mess: his clothing was shabby and oil-stained, he had two days' growth of beard, and, if the major wasn't mistaken, his breath reeked of alcohol. Smithe-Webb asked uncertainly, "Er— Lieutenant Ashley?"

"Yes, I'm Ashley. But, if it doesn't seem impolite, who on earth are you?"

Richard Ashley smiled ruefully. "Sorry, didn't mean to be rude, but we've just got back and . . . we're not at our best. Come and have a cup of something. I'm not sure what we can offer you. . . ."

"Not to worry," said Smithe-Webb hastily. "Don't want to put you out or anything."

"No, no. Must find you something. This is after all a ship of His Majesty's Navy and traditions must be upheld. . . ." He laughed but Smithe-Webb noticed that the face was strained and drawn.

Smithe-Webb followed Ashley down the deck. Two men were grafting a plank of wood into a gap in the gunwale and the deckhouse was riddled with bullet holes. Ashley noticed his gaze. "We were badly strafed. One dead and two wounded. We've never been caught like that before." He led the way into the deckhouse and indicated that Smithe-Webb should take a seat. "That's the problem with going down to the Bay: it's fine once you're there, looking like any other old fishing boat, but it's a long way over there and back. We get some air cover on the way out,

but . . ." He smiled thinly. ". . . Well, it's awfully lonely on the way home. He reached down into a locker and pulled out a bottle of cognac. "Don't suppose you'd like a glass of this delicious brew?"

Smithe-Webb shook his head. "A bit early for me."

"I'll order you tea then—I think that's all we've got." He opened the door and shouted down the deck. "For myself, I'm going to have a large one of these. One of the few perks of the job. The fishermen with whom we, shall we say, *trade*, they give us this stuff. And magic it is too!"

A minute later one of the crew brought the tea, which was dark brown and very sweet and had obviously been brewing for some time. Smithe-Webb gritted his teeth and took a sip. The tea was ghastly and he grimaced. Ashley was talking to the sailor about the repair work and didn't see.

Smithe-Webb took the opportunity to size up the lieutenant. The chap was somewhere in his late twenties, though he looked older, probably because of the tiredness. He was of medium height, unremarkable features and, Smithe-Webb guessed, had a tendency to put on weight. But the blue eyes were extraordinary; you noticed them straightaway. Another unusual thing was the way the man talked. His face was immensely alive and—what was the word?—magnetic. You couldn't take your eyes off him.

The sailor was asking a couple of questions. Like the rest of the crew he was fairly unkempt and Smithe-Webb noticed he had a strong foreign accent.

When the sailor had gone the major asked, "Your crew, are they—RN?"

Ashley laughed. "Some of them! The rest could be loosely described as on loan. Free French, ex-fishermen—and very fine lads they are too."

Ashley sat down, the brandy glass at his elbow, and lit a cigarette. "I must apologize again for my rudeness. Quite honestly, I forgot you were coming. They did tell me, but you know how it is . . . !"

"Yes, I can imagine."

"In this kind of operation, you ignore half the rules—and the other half don't apply. Orders never get written down. . . . Besides which my memory is"—he laughed—"not of the best!" Smithe-Webb felt sure it was perfectly adequate.

Ashley asked, "So how can I be of help?"

Smithe-Webb said, "Right. Perhaps I'd better tell you a bit about my department first. Basically, our job is to help our chaps get out of Occupied Europe. Immediately after Dunkirk most of our customers were soldiers who got left behind after the evacuation. Quite a few made it back by getting help from the locals and making their way to neutral territory. Since then it's been mainly airmen, though we still get quite a few soldiers and even the odd sailor. Obviously it's pretty difficult for chaps to escape once the Germans have got them, but some do manage to get over the wire and our job is to try to make it easy for them once they're out. Having said that, by far the greatest number of our customers are evaders—men who've been shot down or whatever and have managed to keep *out* of German hands. We encourage the locals to look after them and get them back to us safely. Obviously I can't give you the details of how this is done . . ."

"No, of course."

"Our problem is that our present . . . er, methods . . . are under a lot of pressure, both from the Germans and from the sheer scale of the operations. The number of evading airmen is increasing and quite apart from not wanting to let our men fall into enemy hands, we *need* them. Those pilots are absolutely invaluable to the war effort. We have to get them back." Without thinking Smithe-Webb sipped at the mug of tea and immediately choked.

"Bloody awful, isn't it?" Ashley acknowledged. "But try and persuade Leading Seaman Evans to make it any other way and there'd be a mutiny. Change your mind and have a brandy?"

Smithe-Webb raised his eyebrows. "No, really." Ashley poured himself another drink and Smithe-Webb wondered if the fellow always drank like this. He brought his mind back to the matter in hand. "So . . . we're trying to open up more routes. There's an idea under consideration which would involve your outfit. At this point we're having a good look at the plan to see if it's really on or not. And that's where you come in. . . ."

"Yes, I'd heard something about it. Glad to help, of course. I've already picked up quite a few airmen. I never know when they're coming, mind, they just get bundled aboard. But there's never any problem."

"Yes, indeed. But this would be more organized, and the

numbers much greater. Also . . . we weren't thinking of the Bay
. . . rather, we were thinking of going straight across. To north
Brittany."

Ashley sat up. "Ah! I see!"

"I was hoping you might be able to tell me what would be
involved."

Ashley frowned, but was obviously excited by the idea. "Well,
of course, the whole operation would have to be organized differently. It'd be no good using these boats, for a start. MGBs would
be much better."

"Yes, that's what your department suggested."

"We're getting two, did you know that?"

The major nodded.

"They'll make a lot of difference. We can go in at night, really
fast, do the job and then be out again before anyone knows we
were there. In fact, it has already been tried once or twice."

"Oh?"

"Dropping off the odd person with his luggage, that kind of
thing. Not your department, of course?"

"No, one of the others. SOE, in all probability, sending in
agents."

"The only real problem has been to get the passengers from
the boat to the shore in one piece and not half-drowned. Even in
a fairly sheltered spot the surf can be pretty rough. But that's
being looked at . . . our chaps are trying to come up with a special
surfboat." Ashley paused. "But having said that, MGBs are definitely the answer. We could pick up ten, twenty, maybe even
thirty men in a night."

"That would be excellent. But what about the north Brittany
coast? Your CO thought it might be difficult . . . ?"

"Oh, did he? Well, let's have a look, shall we?" He called out
of the door. "Evans! Get over to *Spray* and fetch me some charts,
would you? North Brittany and English Channel." He said to
Smithe-Webb, "We carry only three charts on this boat and
they're French. Wouldn't do to be caught with a set of best Admiralty charts, would it?"

Ashley was enjoying himself, Smithe-Webb could see. The
signs of strain had gone from his face. The major found himself
liking the chap. He was a straightforward sort of person, which

228

Smithe-Webb always admired, and he had a sort of easy charm that made you warm to him. Just as long as he knew what he was doing. Smithe-Webb had the feeling he did.

"Good Lord!" exclaimed Smithe-Webb softly. There were rocks everywhere. Unless he was reading it wrong the chart showed the coast to be completely impenetrable. Even the estuaries were littered with dangers. "Good Lord!" he repeated.

"It's not as bad as it looks," Ashley said slowly. "Many of these rocks are covered except at dead low water. If one studies it carefully one can usually find a way through. Now, where roughly were you thinking of mounting your operation?"

Smithe-Webb put his finger on the coast northeast of Morlaix. "Somewhere around here if possible."

"Right, let's look at the large-scale chart." He pulled out another chart and examined it intently. "Yes, there are several spots that are possible from my point of view. But we have to find a place that's good for your people too. Have they come up with any suggestions?"

"Not yet. Communications are a bit difficult at the moment." Which meant he had no wireless operator there. Oh, that he had! It had taken long enough to persuade DDMI(P/W) that wireless operators were essential, then there'd been delays in finding volunteers and training them. After all, not everyone wanted to be a sitting duck for the Gestapo's wireless detectors.

"But you will be getting some local intelligence? On the siting of gun emplacements, and patrols and so on . . . ?"

"Oh yes, in due course."

"Right. Until then, let's assume that the main headlands are to be avoided. That would give us this cove here, and this bay. . . ." He traced the coastline more thoughtfully. "No, not this one. The cliff's absolutely sheer at this point and there's no path. . . ."

Smithe-Webb was astonished. "How on earth do you know that?"

"I tried to climb it once!"

"Good God." Smithe-Webb was impressed.

"Here . . . this cove here would be ideal." Ashley tapped the chart with his finger. "The approach is reasonably straightfor-

ward, there'd be no problem anchoring, and I can't see the Germans having guns and sentries in the bay itself. . . . Also there's decent access to the beach from the cliff, or so it would appear. I've never been there myself so I couldn't be sure."

Smithe-Webb listened in disbelief. It was too good to be true. The place was only a mile or two from Trégasnou. What a stroke of luck! But perhaps there were disadvantages he hadn't spotted. He asked, "What do my people need to look for when they recce the place? What are the problems going to be?"

"We'll only be able to operate on moonless nights so some sort of signaling arrangement will be essential—by shaded flashlight or whatever—so there really mustn't be any Germans anywhere nearby. It would be useful to know exactly how bad the surf gets too . . . you can never tell whether one spot's going to be worse than another." He thought for a moment. "Also your people will have to be prepared for some long waits on the beach; we could never give a definite time of arrival. Some nights we might not be able to turn up at all. You know— weather or engine failure or whatever. They'd have to be prepared for that . . . have contingency plans to hide all the passengers again, and so on. Oh, and we couldn't operate in high summer . . ."

"What?"

"No, I'm afraid not. The nights in midsummer just wouldn't be long enough to get us over and back in time. From Dartmouth, where the MGBs will be based, it's a hundred miles. That's well over four hours even in a fast boat. Allowing one to two hours for approach and pickup and four hours back, that's ten hours— call it twelve. We could probably operate as late as April with a bit of luck. In winter there's more bad weather, of course, but at least you can slow down and take it easy and know you have plenty of darkness to hide under."

Ashley looked up at Smithe-Webb and smiled cheerfully. "It's August now. By the time the thing is set up we'll be into autumn. So we'll have at least six months. We could get an awful lot of airmen out in that time! All it needs is reasonably good communications and some efficient organization at your end."

Smithe-Webb wished he could smile as cheerfully. Organization was the one thing he couldn't guarantee. He hadn't

mentioned that, and didn't intend to. No point in getting a sour note into the proceedings.

Richard Ashley said, "The pickup must be fast and well thought out—on both sides—otherwise . . ."

Smithe-Webb had the message loud and clear. If there was a muck-up then everyone would get caught.

". . . But I'm sure your people will be first class. The Bretons usually are."

"They're good people," Smithe-Webb agreed. He wasn't sure he could say the same for the Free French officer who was going to be organizing the line. Smithe-Webb hadn't liked the chap at all. But no point in fretting about it; they'd been forced to use him. The Free French had to be humored and that was all there was to it. But, Smithe-Webb thought sadly, it was not the same as choosing your own man, not the same at all.

But on this side of the operation he might be able to get the man he wanted. He asked Ashley, "Do you think you might be able to do the job yourself? You used to be on MGBs, didn't you? It would be tremendous from our point of view."

Ashley stroked his chin. "I was on torpedo boats actually, not gunboats. But . . . I *am* rather tempted. They say the new boats can do thirty knots. Very useful for getting out of trouble!" He smiled. "Yes, I'd love to give it a go."

He shot a glance at Smithe-Webb, and said mischievously, "We could fix it between us. If you tell the Admiralty that you need me and then I volunteer, they can't refuse, can they?" His eyes were sparkling with amusement, and Smithe-Webb had the feeling that few people refused Richard Ashley anything.

Ashley watched the launch returning toward the jetty and wondered if he should have gone into the problems in more detail.

He walked slowly along the deck. God, he felt tired. He sat on the hatch coaming and, lighting a cigarette, inhaled deeply.

He tried to think, but the tiredness was clouding his brain. Or perhaps his mind was addled by cigarettes and brandy. Just as likely.

Problems . . . there'd certainly be a few. He'd made it sound

easy and it wasn't. He should have told the major about the tricky tides and the lack of navigation aids. He should have admitted that it would be difficult to find the right place at all.

Then there was the weather: he should have spelled out the problems in more detail. Even in fairly rough conditions they might have to cancel operations; in gales they most certainly would.

Damn. He should have made the whole thing plainer.

Still . . . they should be able to get across pretty often. A lot depended on the efficiency of the organization on the other side, of course. The major had been a little evasive about that. . . .

Perhaps the escape line was brand new, or badly run or—perhaps it was a complete shambles. Yes, there was always that possibility, though he'd be surprised. The Bretons were cool, determined, closely knit people. He'd be surprised if they mucked things up.

Well, whatever the situation, he'd give it a go. It was a marvelous challenge.

Besides, he had been on the Bay run for over nine months and it was getting to him. Pretending to be a fishing boat was too much like sitting waiting to be a target at the Germans' convenience. This boat had an engine, to be sure—but it produced only six knots. As much good as a wound-up rubber band. And then there was the small problem about being captured when disguised as a French fisherman. According to the powers that be, all you had to do was to pop a Royal Navy Issue cap on your head, show your papers, and you'd be treated as a prisoner of war. Ashley wasn't so sure: he had the feeling the Germans would politely ignore the caps and line you up against a wall for target practice.

He thought back to the last trip . . . it had gone wrong from the start. They'd gone to the Scillies as usual, to their secret anchorage, and turned the boat from a gray MFV into a Concarneau trawler, complete with bright orange paint and a few fancy patterns on the transom. But as soon as they'd left, the weather had turned bad and they'd had an uncomfortable trip. When they eventually got to the Bay it had taken far too long to make contact with the fleet, and a *Raumboot* had become suspicious

and almost put a landing party aboard. Finally, on the way back, they'd been caught. Good and proper. In his mind's eye he saw it all again: everyone reaching for weapons, the low-flying plane, the bullets tearing into Jean-Pierre's body. . . . He shuddered.

Perhaps he was losing his nerve. He took out another cigarette and lit it. He looked at the hand holding the cigarette: its fingers were bright yellow with nicotine and shook slightly. Too many cigarettes. Too much booze. Definitely time for a change.

A tern called overhead, and he followed it as it soared toward the river mouth and the open sea. Anytime now it would be flying south to its winter quarters on some Atlantic island. This summer there had been thousands of terns on Scilly.

The islands: that was the one thing he would miss.

Whenever they'd sailed to the secret anchorage in the north of the islands, to paint the fishing boat, he'd been happy.

The secret anchorage lay between two islands—Tresco and Bryher—in the small inlet known as New Grimsby Harbor. He had come there before the war—when was it?—'35? Sometime then. The narrow inlet had been empty, not a fishing boat or islander's gig to be seen. He had anchored *Dancer* in the center of the basin, and rowed across to Bryher and made a camp on the shore, and walked around the island and watched the incredible surf in Hell Bay and wondered what it would be like to be shipwrecked. In the evening he had made a fire and cooked a couple of mackerel and slept under a tarpaulin in the shelter of a rock. The dawn had been still and yellow and a cormorant had dived into the cool depths of the secret harbor. Later an oystercatcher had appeared, its long yellow beak probing the stones uncovered by the falling tide. He had sat for a long time, quite motionless, not wanting anything to change, hoping it would be like that forever.

He'd been twenty-one then, fresh out of Dartmouth, and greedy for everything, preferably all at once. Strange how everyone told you there was no going back, that the simplicity of your youth could never be recaptured; strange how right they were. But one day, when the world was sane again, he'd go back. One day, when there were no gray ships of war to ruin

the quiet of that marvelous place, only *Dancer* tugging gently at her chain . . .

In the meantime he would miss the place.

He rubbed his eyes. His head ached terribly. He got wearily to his feet. He found himself reaching automatically for a cigarette and stopped in midair. He must get fit. Soon he'd be running a proper ship again, crewed by regular sailors. He was looking forward to it.

14 Julie drew the curtains over the tiny window. Peter was already fast asleep, his mouth slightly open, his breathing slow and steady. She pulled the covers up around his neck and kissed him softly on the cheek. He was such a big boy now, five and a half, and tall, oh so tall. She could hardly believe it—the time had gone so quickly. It seemed only yesterday that he was a baby.

She took a last look at him, then, picking up the flickering oil lamp, went down the steep staircase to her room. She paused and listened carefully. There was quite a wind; it was blowing around the house in long sighs. Outside, one of the cattle moved noisily against the side of the barn. Somewhere down in the village a dog was barking. Then, from almost overhead, a creaking noise. Julie stiffened but relaxed as she recognized the sound of Peter settling more comfortably in his bed.

It was a habit now, listening. And not just for Peter—that was instinctive—but for other human sounds. The sounds of people arriving with messages or sometimes even "parcels": foreign airmen with pale, frightened faces who were taken off into the night to some other more welcoming farmhouse. The comings and goings went on all the time now that autumn had come. She dreaded them; they made her horribly nervous. Yet—she

had an awful urge to *know.* It was like being punished: the sooner you were told what was in store the easier it was to cope with.

And now she heard the back door opening. Someone had come in. Her heart sank. She opened the bedroom door and went quietly through into the kitchen. Her uncle was standing in the open doorway talking quietly and urgently to someone outside in the darkness.

The clock on the mantelpiece said eight o'clock.

They must have forgotten the time. They must have! Julie hovered uncertainly, wondering whether she should interrupt.

Now the person outside was speaking. The voice was louder, less secretive: the voice of the stranger, the *leader,* as he was meant to be. He was making no attempt to be discreet; he never did. But at this time of the evening Julie could hardly believe it. The man was mad . . . or stupid! Worse, from the way he was talking, Julie had a feeling he wasn't going to stop.

The voice was saying, ". . . No, no, there is no problem there. I have Gaston from Plougat in charge. I have given him orders to bring the ten parcels from Madame Lelouche's place. It is all organized, I assure you. . . ."

Surely Jean must realize the time and how dangerous it was . . . Julie looked at the clock again. It was two minutes past eight. She could bear it no longer. She came up beside her uncle and waited for a break in the conversation. But the leader continued to speak and Julie realized that he was doing it to impress her, to show her how important he was. She bit her lip with the effort of staying silent. Eventually the man said, "Ah, madame! Good evening. I am sorry to disturb the household. . . ."

"Monsieur . . . please, the soldiers will return soon. You . . . your visits put us in danger! Wouldn't it be possible to come back later? Please!"

"Madame, our business has to be properly planned! You obviously don't understand what is involved . . . and I assure you that there is no danger."

Julie thought: This man is impossible, like a brick wall. "Monsieur, surely the planning could be less—public!"

Jean shuffled uneasily and the leader looked annoyed. Julie couldn't help feeling glad; at least she was getting through to

them. The leader said coldly, "Madame, you would do better to keep out of matters that do not concern you!"

Julie fought back a surge of anger. "Monsieur, they concern me directly—which you seem to forget at your convenience!"

Jean put a hand on Julie's shoulder and said gently, "It's all right, he's just going. Really."

"Not a moment too soon!" She strode to the stove and began to stir the soup too quickly. Immediately some of the liquid slopped over the side of the pan. There was a spitting and hissing as the soup hit the hotplate. Julie reached impatiently for a cloth and dabbed the remaining liquid off the stove. She was shaking with anger. She hated losing her temper. She knew she should try to calm down but while this dreadful man was still at the door she couldn't. A pity Tante Marie was looking after Mme. Gillet for the evening: she would have given him short shrift.

The burning soup was hissing loudly; Julie missed the sound of the front door opening and the steps crossing the front parlor. The rap on the parlor door made her jump so that she jerked at the spoon and the hot liquid spattered over her apron. She stared in horror as the door opened and the two familiar uniforms appeared. The two soldiers smiled politely at her as they always did, then looked curiously past her to where her uncle and the leader stood at the open back door.

For a moment they were all frozen, like a tableau: Julie at the stove, the soldiers and the two men at the back door. Then Jean gave the Germans a slight nod, turned his back on them and said to the man, "I'll deliver that grain in the morning, then. But I've only four kilos to spare—and I'll have to charge you a good price for it!"

The man smiled. "Fair enough. I know how it is—we must be commercial about this! Oh, and you won't forget the other matter?"

Julie realized with dismay that the leader was enjoying the scene. He was going to play it out! What conceit! And she had the feeling he was fooling no one: the two soldiers seemed distinctly suspicious. Julie clattered some plates and said rather too loudly, "The soup is ready. Please go and sit down."

The soldiers were surprised: normally Julie never spoke to them. They shuffled back into the parlor and as soon as she heard

them drawing up their chairs, she took in a tray with two bowls of soup and some bread on it. As she put the bowls on the table she heard the sound of the back door closing. The horrid man had gone. At last!

One of the soldiers started to speak to her, something about what a cold day it was. She ignored him as she usually did and he fell silent. Good. One might have to provide accommodation and two meals a day for them, but there was no law that said one had to speak to them. Julie left the room, closing the door firmly behind her.

Her uncle was standing by the stove. He made a wide expansive gesture with his hands, as if to say, What could I do?

Julie slumped into a chair and her uncle drew up another close beside her. They sat in silence until, finally, they heard the chairs being scraped back in the parlor and the front door opening and closing. The Germans had gone out for their customary drink. After a few minutes Julie spoke.

"That man . . ." She shook her head. "He is a *danger*. I know it—everyone knows it."

"Yes, but . . . Julie, please realize, we have to put up with him. He's the only contact we have, the only hope of getting all the parcels out."

"Yes, but at what cost?"

The old man sighed. "I know, I know. But you must understand that there are no less than thirty parcels waiting. If we can't make contact with the British and have boats sent over, we'll be stuck with them. The longer these parcels are here, the greater the risk for those hiding them. And there are more arriving every day! We must, we *must* keep that contact, otherwise what are we to do? Give them to the Germans, eh? Wait until our houses are bulging with British airmen and pretend they're really French. Eh?"

Julie had to acknowledge the difficulty of passing the British off as local people. Quite apart from the language difference, they *looked* so alien. "I do see the problem. But I can't understand why you should have to put up with that—that person. Surely the line could be run just with local people and perhaps one outside wireless operator. Surely!"

"Ah, but that's the problem. The only wireless operator is far

away—in Paris, I think. And this fellow, he is the only person with contact. The British sent him over. What can we do?"

"Make him be quiet for a start! Even I, a person who tries *not* to hear anything, even I know exactly who's in the organization. I could give you a list right now! And if I know, then the whole village knows, not to mention the whole of the Côtes-du-Nord!"

"But who would talk? No Breton! Never!"

Julie laughed bitterly. "I wish I had your faith in human nature!"

Then she patted her uncle's hand. He seemed so old and worried that she hated to argue with him.

The old man said softly, "We have to do something, don't we? We can't stand aside and just watch."

"I don't know. Sometimes I wonder if all these terrible risks are worthwhile. Anyway, look at me. I do nothing and *my* conscience is clear." She patted his hand again. "But I can see that you must do what you must. I don't blame you for that. Just . . . *do* try to keep it away from us, Jean, please. I worry so much about Peter. . . ."

Jean said thoughtfully, "But, Juliette, we don't hide parcels here. We agreed on that. For *your* sake, and Peter's. So there is really very little risk for you. For me—well, that doesn't matter. I'm an old man."

Julie said heavily, "Even then, they take hostages, don't they? And shoot them? Innocent women and children. Oh, the children!" She could hardly bear to think of it. There had been an incident in Morlaix, after a German had been shot. They had seized twenty women and children, lined them up and mowed them down. Julie had heard the shots from her office. She had cried with rage and uselessness.

Jean said impatiently, "That was the Communists! Stupid fools. They just kill Germans and never think of the consequences. *They're* the real dangers! I'll never help that lot of anarchists, never! And"—he wagged a finger—"I will never have another one of them in my house again. And that includes Michel—"

"I agree that their methods are—wrong. But they *are* on our side, Uncle."

"When it suits them." Jean stood up, went to the mantelpiece

and picked up his pipe, which he tapped angrily against the chimney. "They were on the German side at first, remember! Then, when the Germans invaded Russia—which anyone of any brain could have seen coming—they changed sides. Very convenient! Ha!"

He filled his pipe with a plug of tobacco and lit it in a cloud of smoke. Julie hoped he wouldn't regret it: the tobacco was his last until the beginning of the month.

The old man puffed more calmly at his pipe. "I'm sorry about Michel—but I feel strongly about the matter. I told him to his face he wasn't welcome here!"

"When?"

The old man stared at her. "But . . . didn't you know? He's back."

"What!"

"Yes, he's here. I saw him in the village today. I thought your aunt had told you? Anyway, I told him that, with regret, he was not to set foot in this house again."

Julie got to her feet. "Where is he?" She went to the table and picked up her purse. "I'm going down to the village—to see if I can find him."

The old man said, "God in heaven, why?"

"Because . . . well . . ." It was difficult to think of a reason. Finally she said, "He *is* one of the family . . . maybe he needs help."

And, she thought, because I want to see him, I want to see him very much indeed. She said, "I don't mean any disrespect, Uncle, and I understand about not having him in the house, but—"

Jean raised his hand. "Stop! Don't say any more. Talk to him if you must, but if you take my advice you won't be seen with him. And don't tell me what he's up to. I don't want to know!" He added automatically, "And be careful down the lane. I never trust those soldiers."

"I'll be careful." She blew him a kiss and, pulling on her warmest coat, hurried out into the night.

It was very dark. The wind was howling in from the sea, tearing at the hedgerows and whistling through the occasional solitary pine, bent into a tortured shape by a hundred storms.

Julie walked more quickly, her head bent low, her eyes on the dark road ahead.

Yes, she wanted to see Michel. She had been thinking about him increasingly in the last few months, hoping he'd come back. . . .

The last two years had been lonely. When Peter was small and needed her so much she hadn't minded being on her own. But since he'd been at school and often went out to play with his friends the loneliness was awful, like a terrible weight, pressing her down.

Sometimes she felt guilty at being lonely. She'd been so happy here, she'd adored the peace and tranquillity, she'd been so grateful for finding a home: in those early days she'd loved everything about it. She still did! And yet . . . the thought of staying here forever, with only Peter and Jean and Tante Marie for company, filled her with dread. She was twenty-five and the years were beginning to slip away. Twenty-five! Her chances of—why couldn't she say it?—*of finding a husband* were getting slimmer all the time. And she *did* want a husband, she knew that. Often she lay awake at night imagining what it would be like. . . . Having someone to talk to and laugh with, having someone *there.* What she wanted more than anything was to *share*—her life, Peter, everything. When she imagined being married, the lovely sensation of warmth and tenderness, she wanted it very badly.

There was no mistaking the café in the darkness: light was leaking from its blacked-out windows in a dozen places and the sound of voices and laughter floated on the air. Julie approached slowly. If Michel wasn't here, someone would probably know where he was.

She waited: there was no question of going in on her own. At last someone came out. It was an old man called Pierre, a cowherd from a nearby farm. He'd had several glasses too many. She gave him her message and directed him gently back into the café.

A few moments later the old man reappeared, nodded to her and went off into the night.

Then the door opened again and Michel was standing there.

Julie started to smile. "Michel, how lovely to . . ." But he was looking behind him. Taking her arm, he pulled her quickly away from the café.

They walked briskly, in silence. Presently they came to a barn at the edge of the village. He whispered, "In here!" Inside it was pitch dark. Julie could hear Michel tramping across a bed of straw to the far side. She put out her hands and felt her way forward. She tripped over a bale of straw, recovered, and bumped her shoulder against the side of what was probably a cart.

"All right?" His voice was close by.

"I think so." She sat down carefully and heard him sit beside her.

She asked gently, "Are you in trouble? What's the matter?"

"Mmm? No, I'm not in trouble. Well—no more than usual."

"Then, why all this?"

"I just thought it would be better if you weren't seen with me, that's all."

"Better for who?" But she knew what he meant.

"Why, better for you, of course! Your uncle doesn't want me in his house, half the village think my politics stink, the other half are prepared to argue with me over a glass of wine—but none of them would let his daughter be seen with me."

"Where have you been all this time?"

"Away."

She could tell that he didn't want to say any more. But she ventured, "You've been all right though? Safe, I mean?"

"Oh yes. Don't worry your head about me. I always look after myself."

"Michel, I must ask . . . you haven't been working with the Germans, have you? I couldn't bear that."

"Good God, no!"

He sounded outraged and Julie said quickly, "I mean, you did talk about it . . . in Morlaix. Don't you remember?"

"Ha! That was a long time ago. And I never worked with the Germans then anyway. Now? I can assure you that I kill them, blow them up and destroy them whenever I can. But the less said about that the better."

"I'm sorry. I didn't mean to . . ."

"Forget it."

Julie peered through the darkness and said wistfully, "I wish I could see your face."

He laughed. "It hasn't changed. Just older. Here, I'll have a cigarette. That'll shed some light. I've been longing for a smoke

for hours, but I'm too mean to share any of my hard-earned cigarettes with the old fools back there. They think anyone from the town has plenty to spare."

She heard him fumbling in his pockets, then there was a sudden blaze of light and he was drawing on a cigarette. She'd forgotten how deep his frown was and how narrow his mouth. She'd forgotten too how bitter was his expression. She realized she'd forgotten a lot about him. . . .

He was asking, "And how have you been?"

"All right really. We have just about enough to eat. There's no help on the farm anymore, so Jean has to keep it going by himself. Tante Marie and I help when we can. . . . And Peter does too, of course."

"Peter must be quite a young man by now."

"Yes. Five and a half."

"And he's well too?"

"Yes." She didn't elaborate. His question had been polite but automatic. She sensed he wasn't really interested.

"Are you still working in that place at Morlaix?"

She nodded in the darkness. "The same old place. Sometimes I think I'll be there when I'm sixty."

"But your papers. They've stood up all right?"

"Oh yes!" She reached out and found his wrist. "I can't tell you what a difference it's made. Knowing they're genuine has given me peace of mind. I can't thank you enough!"

She fumbled for his hand, but there was no answering squeeze, and his hand felt limp in hers. Blushing in the darkness, she withdrew. He asked, "Did you ever use that stamp and those papers you pinched?"

"No. I still don't really know why I took them. It seemed a sort of safeguard at the time."

"Well, hang onto them. They might come in useful. But for God's sake don't tell anyone about them and don't leave them lying around. Have you got them hidden?"

"Of course." Julie felt hurt: did he really think she would leave them lying around? "No one can find them. We've got two soldiers billeted on us, you know."

"What!"

His voice was very sharp and she wondered why he was so

surprised. She said quickly, "Yes, lots of people have. It's nothing unusual."

"But your uncle—he's involved with this escape line."

Julie gulped. What on earth should she say? Jean certainly wouldn't have told Michel about his involvement. How, then, did Michel know?

"Well?"

"I . . . I can't say. We don't talk about those sorts of things."

He sighed impatiently. "Come on, Julie, don't be silly! I know all about it. I heard within five minutes of coming back to the area. My people in Morlaix not only know who works the line, but they know all the operational details."

"Oh no—"

"It's common knowledge. Anyway, my comrades."

Julie's heart turned to ice. "The Germans . . ." she whispered. "Do they know?"

"I wouldn't be surprised. And what bothers me is that, when the trouble breaks, as it surely will, the finger of blame will probably be pointed at me and my friends when in fact it's that lunatic who's running your line who should be shot. He's obviously never heard of the word security. Where did they find him, eh?"

"London."

"Ah, a Free French hero then?"

"Yes."

Michel exclaimed, "The sooner you're rid of him the better."

"I know, I know. I hate the horrid little man. He's so conceited. Everyone goes along with him because he's the only link with London." She sighed deeply. "I wish they could see what madness it is."

"My advice is to keep well out of it. Don't get involved! The work is best left to men and old ones at that, then it doesn't matter so much when they get shot."

So practical—or callous, depending on how you looked at it. Julie couldn't understand how one came to think like that.

Michel stood up and the glow of the cigarette disappeared as he stubbed it against the side of the cart. A couple of sparks floated down and Julie automatically reached out to catch them before they touched the straw.

He said, "Come on! It's time we got back. We don't want Jean to think that I'm filling your head with revolution, do we?"

Julie thought: But we haven't even begun to talk. . . . Then she remembered what she'd wanted to talk about, and it didn't seem very important anymore.

She heard him move away. She got hurriedly to her feet and followed him, stumbling across the bundles of straw. When she reached the door, he was waiting. In the faint illumination of the night she could just make out his features. They were severe and hard. Julie was amazed that she could have forgotten how very serious he was and how very—unyielding.

He said, "By the way, do they tell you when a boat's coming?"

"No. I never ask—and they never tell me. Why?"

"Well, just keep out of the way tomorrow night. According to my information, there's going to be an operation then. I'm sure the information's good. No moon, you see, and the country crawling with hidden airmen longing to get home. If it isn't tomorrow night then it must be soon after. But my friends say it'll be tomorrow—and they don't usually get these things wrong."

Julie closed her eyes. Was there anything he didn't know? She said slowly, "I'll . . . take Peter away for the night. . . . Thanks for telling me."

He took her arm and guided her into the road. They walked in silence until they came to the crossroads at the center of the village. People were coming out of the café. Instinctively they drew into the darkness and followed the wall around until they were in the lane and heading up the hill toward the house.

Julie didn't want him to come any farther. She turned and whispered, "Good-bye, Michel." On an impulse she added passionately, "Don't kill Germans if you can avoid it. They'll only take hostages again. Children . . . they take children, Michel."

"Same softhearted Julie." There was a trace of scorn in his voice. He went on, "Of course we try to avoid killing Germans. But when it comes to blowing up something important, we have to do it, and that's all there is to it. Children suffer anyway, from bombing raids, starvation, lots of things. The destruction of a factory is more important than—many things. Anyway, it's nothing to how the Russian peasants are suffering . . . they're dying in their thousands!"

Julie couldn't think of a reply. He added, "Anyway, you'd do best not to think about such things. They'll happen whether you worry about them or not."

Julie felt sad and tired. She said softly, "Good-bye, Michel," and walked away.

He hurried after her and took her arm. "Julie, remember one thing—don't get involved!"

"Yes, you told me."

"But you might get into trouble without realizing it. You . . . don't know how they can drag you into these things."

Anyone would think she was a seventeen-year-old straight out of school. She pulled in her breath and said tightly, "I'll remember that."

She walked away and this time he did not follow her. Despite the steepness of the hill she moved rapidly, hitting the road with her feet, pumping her legs in steady rhythm, climbing faster and faster until she was almost home. But she didn't want to go into the house yet and she walked toward the open cliffs and the low roar of the distant surf.

For a moment she almost continued past the end of the made-up road and onto the track that led through the fields to the open heathland. Then she remembered that there were patrols along the clifftop and they shot on sight. She stopped and leaned against a low wall and wrapped her arms tightly about her.

She tried to separate her thoughts, to look at them coolly so that her anger would go away.

For one thing, it was obvious that Michel didn't care for her. He pretended to be concerned for her safety, but she couldn't help wondering why. There must be a reason. Because in every other way he was as cold as ice. The strange thing was, she didn't mind a bit now. In fact, she was rather glad because she realized she didn't care for *him* either.

There was something else too. She hated to admit it, but her pride had been hurt. She had gone to meet him, imagining he would be glad to see her—and he had treated her like a child. He had humiliated her—very subtly but very definitely.

She was angry—but not with Michel, with herself. What a fool she'd been! She'd built up a picture that bore no resemblance to the person Michel really was. She'd imagined him as a husband,

as a lover; she'd made him into what she wanted him to be. It was self-delusion. Puppy love!

It began to rain, the drops driven by the wind into a horizontal curtain of penetrating wetness. Julie pulled her coat more tightly about her and began to walk slowly back down the lane. She wasn't angry anymore, just cross and sad.

One thing: she wouldn't be so stupid again.

The most important thing in her life was Peter. He was the only one who really mattered. Tomorrow night she would take him to stay in the village, in a safe house, away from everything. Then if anything went wrong *neither* of them would get caught.

A floorboard creaked and Julie woke with a start. It had taken her an hour to get to sleep and now she was wide awake again. It was hopeless: she was as jumpy as a cat. Being in a strange bed was half the problem: Mme. Boulet's house was only a short distance down the lane, in the center of the village, but it might as well be a hundred miles away. Apart from anything else, the bed was lumpy.

She put out an arm and touched the sleeping figure beside her. That was another thing: though it was lovely to share a bed with Peter, she found it difficult to relax in case she should move in her sleep and disturb him. It was disconcerting, too, to hear the steady breathing and occasional sighs of someone sleeping beside you, even when that someone was your own child.

But what really made it impossible to sleep was knowing what was happening—out *there,* in the fields and down on the beach. Julie wondered how they got the airmen to the beach. Did they creep across the fields like shadows? Or did they walk brazenly along the roads? Whichever way, the risk was tremendous. Sometimes the Germans sent out extra patrols. . . . And then how did the boat find the right beach? Did they signal? No, surely not. . . .

She couldn't see how it could be done safely. Too many things could go wrong.

Best to try to sleep. She closed her eyes and made a conscious effort to relax her body.

Suddenly there was a faint moan. Instantly she was tense and alert again. It had sounded like someone in terrible anguish. She

listened, straining to pick up the slightest noise, but all she could hear was the roar of silence.

Then it came again, beginning as a low murmur and growing into a whine.

Julie relaxed with a groan. What a nervous idiot she was becoming! It was the wind. Only the wind! She tried to guess how strong it was now. A gale at least. The sea would be rough then, and there would be large breakers on the beach. She imagined the British boat, trying to get in toward the land. Perhaps enormous waves were breaking right over it. . . .

There was a faint tapping on the door. Julie almost jumped out of her skin. She lay rigid.

The tapping came again, soft but insistent.

She got quickly out of bed, pulled the covers up over Peter and dragged on her dressing gown. She tiptoed to the door and opened it.

Mme. Boulet was standing there, her anxious face illuminated by the candle in her hand. Immediately Julie knew something was wrong. "What is it?"

The older woman whispered, "Come down. Please. Now."

Julie tied her dressing-gown cord and, closing the door behind her, followed Mme. Boulet down the stairs. The hall was in darkness, but light was coming from the kitchen. As they approached, Julie could hear the low murmur of a man's voice.

The two women went in. M. Boulet was sitting by the stove, fully dressed, his face solemn. Another man whom Julie knew only vaguely was sitting opposite, talking urgently. When they saw the women they rose to their feet, anxiety on their faces. Julie thought: God, the Germans have found out. Everyone's been captured. Everyone's been killed!

Julie said, "What is it? Please tell me!"

The second man said quickly, "Nothing's happened! Not yet anyway. But we need your help, madame."

Julie let out a sigh of relief and sat down weakly on a chair. "Thank God . . . I thought for a moment . . ." Then she remembered what the man had said. "Help? How can I help?"

"Madame, believe me I would not ask . . . except that you are the only person. We need someone who speaks English. There is a young pilot. He is injured. We have done what we can for him

but . . . please come and talk to him. Otherwise—otherwise we are all in trouble. Please, madame."

"I don't understand . . . what do I have to do?"

"Madame, I beg of you. It isn't far. Just at Roget's farm, up near the point. You will understand when we arrive. Please, we have no time. . . ." He glanced at the clock on the mantelpiece. It was almost midnight. Julie looked at the man again and recognized him as a farmer from the next village, a nice man whose face was now deathly serious.

They were all waiting for her to speak. Julie felt the beginnings of panic. How could she possibly decide at a moment's notice? It wasn't fair!

Then she realized they must be desperate. For them to ask her something like this—and in the middle of the night—something must be very wrong. Perhaps this pilot had terrible injuries . . . perhaps he needed help . . . and he was young, the man had said. . . .

Julie said abruptly, "I'll go and get dressed," because it was easier to say that than to refuse. She hurried from the room before she changed her mind.

In the darkness of the bedroom she found some clothes and started to pull them on, wondering what she was getting herself into.

She dropped a shoe which clattered to the floor. Peter turned over and moaned quietly. Julie found the shoe and put it on. She went to the bed and put her face against the soft, gentle cheek.

She took a last look at him, murmured, "I love you," and left the room.

The staircase was in total darkness and she had to feel her way down. When she reached the kitchen the lights were out and the back door already open. A blast of cold air made her shiver. Someone helped her on with her coat and then she was outside, following the man as he led the way along the side of the house.

At the corner they met the full force of the wind. It tore at Julie's coat and blew her hair across her eyes. She pulled the coat around her and held her hair back from her face and saw that they had reached the road.

In the blackness Julie could just make out the figure of the farmer. She followed quickly before she lost him in the dark. So

they did use the roads at night. Sometimes she'd heard German trucks driving through the village at these hours. If one came along now what would they do?

The farmer's pace was relentless and when they came to the steep hill which led up to Roget's farm, Julie had to make an effort to keep up. She thought of asking him to slow down, but remembered what he'd said about there being no time. She pushed herself on, closing her mind to everything except the rhythm of her stride.

At one point she looked up and he was gone, melted into the pitch darkness ahead. But then he reappeared, standing, waiting for her. He whispered, "Nearly there," and set off again briskly. Julie made a final effort, pumping her legs, swinging her arms, and at last they arrived. The black bulk of a building loomed ahead and a low voice came out of the darkness. The farmer answered with a single word and they entered the farmhouse.

Someone took her arm and led her along a passage toward a sudden blaze of light. Julie blinked.

She found herself in what was obviously the front parlor. It was full of people. At least twenty. At first it was difficult to make out the faces, but then her eyes became accustomed to the light and she recognized several people she knew, villagers and men from outlying farms. The rest—perhaps ten or twelve of them—were strangers, all young men, all slightly out of place despite their rough working clothes.

Everyone was staring at Julie, some with a kind of horror, some with hope and relief. No one spoke. Julie had expected to see a figure on a stretcher, but there was none. Perhaps he was upstairs. . . .

A villager glanced nervously toward the far end of the room, someone else did the same . . . Julie followed their eyes. And then she saw.

One of the young men was standing by the fireplace. He had a bandage around his head and a frightened look in his eyes.

In his hand was a gun. It was pointing at the other people in the room.

Suddenly Julie understood.

She had been brought here to get the gun out of his hand.

For a long time she stood still, regarding the young man and

wondering where to start. Finally she took a step forward and smiled at him. "Hello, my name's Julie. Who are you?"

The young man stared at her, his face taut and uncertain. The gun waved slightly in his hand.

Julie thought: I must try something else. She took a breath and said brightly, "There's obviously something the matter. Would you like to tell me about it?"

The young man blinked rapidly and tried to focus his eyes.

When he spoke, it was so loudly that Julie jumped. "I know who you are! You're a spy too!" The voice was high-pitched and tense, the accent Welsh.

"A spy?" Julie laughed gently. "Goodness gracious, I'm English!" In the pause that followed she realized that this may not appear very logical and added, "I just happen to live here . . . among these good people and . . . they're trying to help you, to get you home. You do realize that, don't you?"

"No! They're not to be trusted. They're spies! I saw one with a German!"

"But . . . if they were spies they would have handed you over to the Germans long ago, wouldn't they? They wouldn't have bothered to hide you for so long if they were going to give you up." She smiled gently. "Haven't they cared for you? Haven't they bandaged your head?"

"But I saw one talking to a Kraut!"

"Maybe the German asked him something. It would have looked off if he hadn't replied, wouldn't it? We have to reply to the Germans, however much we hate it. I give you my solemn word that no one here is on the Germans' side. I am telling you the truth, believe me."

The young man clamped his lips together.

"Why don't I tell you all about myself and then you can tell me all about your family and your home. Wouldn't that be nice? Why don't we get rid of everyone else and talk, just the two of us?" She walked slowly across the room toward him. When she moved, his eyes filled with fear. But then they relaxed a little, searching her face, half-hopeful, half-uncertain. She could see that he wanted to believe in her; he was only frightened.

Finally she stood in front of him and said, "We'll tell the others to go away, shall we? And then we can talk." She signaled for the villagers to go.

People started standing up and shuffling toward the door. He shouted, "No, no! They must stay."

Everyone stopped. Julie, reaching out, touched his hand, the one holding the gun. "They only want to go down to the boat and get you people home. You want to get home too, don't you?"

"Yes, yes . . . but . . ." He closed his eyes and said wearily, "It's all so crazy."

"I know, I know. You've had a tough time, I can see that. I bet it's been terrible."

"Jesus Christ, oh God . . . !" His voice cracked and Julie felt a moment of fear.

She said quickly, "Remember your duty!"

"My duty?" The young man looked at her, puzzled, trying to understand.

"Yes. Your duty. It's quite clear. You must return to England. That is what they want you to do. And you know why? So that they can get you back home to your family. They're not going to ask you to fight again, you know . . . not after all you've done. You can go home, back to where you belong. Really." The young man's face cleared a little and Julie thought: I'm on the right track. She prompted gently, "You have a family?"

He nodded and for a moment she thought he would cry. He whispered, "Mum . . . and Dad . . . and my sister, Susan."

"And a girl? You have a girl?"

He looked at her as if his heart would break. "Yes, yes . . ." His eyes filled with tears and he bowed his head and began to sob quietly. Slowly, Julie reached forward and removed the gun from his hand. She passed it to one of the men and then, arms outstretched, took the young pilot and cradled him in her arms. He clutched at her, his head on her shoulder, his tears warm on her neck.

She thought: He's no more than a boy. And they send children like this to war . . . what madness it all is. She patted his back and said, "It's all right now. Everything's all right now."

There was activity behind her. Someone touched her arm and breathed, "We must go or it will be too late. Will you bring him? Down to the beach?"

Julie hesitated. The beach . . . No one ever went to the beach. It had barbed wire and patrols.

The young pilot clutched at her, still sobbing. She held his head

to her shoulder and patted his back again. She turned to the man waiting beside her and nodded slowly. "Yes, I'll bring him. Just tell me what to do."

Julie felt the pilot stumble behind her. She held tightly to his hand and turned her head. He had regained his balance and was tentatively stepping forward. She whispered, "Are you all right?" but the wind tore her words away. She asked again, louder.

He nodded. "Yes, I'm okay."

Julie squeezed his hand and said, "Well done. Not far now!"

She peered down the path to where the man ahead of her had been. But there was no one there, not even a shadow against the grays and blacks of the night mosaic. Julie drew in her breath and started forward again. The path was uneven and narrow, carved uncertainly into the side of the cliff and descending rapidly to the beach below. Sometimes, when a rock protruded, the path disappeared altogether and Julie had to reach down with her foot until she found it again some distance below. She went forward carefully, leaning slightly inward toward the cliff face, her left hand feeling along the safe hardness of the solid rock. She tried not to think of what lay below.

At one point she stepped on a loose stone and almost lost her footing. She was wearing the wrong kind of shoes: leather with a slight heel—horribly slippery. She should have brought canvas shoes. She also wished for the hundredth time that she'd worn a scarf: when the wind tore down the cliff it blew her hair across her face until she could hardly see.

The path seemed interminable. Behind, the pilot stumbled again; she gripped his hand more tightly.

Above the dull roar of the wind it was just possible to hear a low rumbling, like muffled thunder. As they descended it grew steadily louder. The sound of the surf. Julie's spirits rose: they must be very near the beach now.

Without warning the path fell sharply away. Julie felt down the slope with her foot, but there was nothing: no ledge, no rock, no sign of the path. She sat down, pulled the pilot down beside her and, letting go of his hand, levered herself over the edge. She began to slide downward, faster and faster. Then, just as she grabbed for a handhold, the beach came rushing up toward her. With a soft crunch, she landed on the pebbles.

She got to her feet and dusted her coat. The young pilot hadn't appeared yet. She called up, "It's all right. The beach is right here! Just slide down the way I did!"

There was no reply. For a moment she feared she was going to have to climb back up again. Then she heard his voice, almost carried away by the wind. "You sure?"

"Yes, yes. Just slide!"

A moment later a figure shot down and fell onto the pebbles beside her. Julie said, "Well done." She helped him up and, holding hands again, they started slowly down the beach.

A line of pale gray revealed the breaking surf and, to the left, a blackness, much inkier than the sky, marked the high cliffs around the cove. But where were the others? Julie stopped uncertainly and peered into the darkness.

"What's happening?" The pilot's voice sounded frightened again.

"It's all right. I'm just waiting for them to find us."

She only wished they would.

As if in answer, a shadow, darker than the rest, emerged in front of them. "Here! Follow me!" Julie, pulling the pilot behind her, followed the dark figure along the beach. They came to a finger of rock which protruded from the cliff. The rest of the group were waiting on one side of it, some of them sitting against the rock, their faces pale and indistinguishable in the gloom, others standing in groups of two or three. Julie was surprised to hear the sounds of raised voices. With dismay she realized that there was a row going on.

The pilot pulled at her hand. "What's that?"

It was a good question. But she said, "Don't worry. It doesn't mean anything. They're just having a friendly argument."

"Jesus . . . can't they shut up?"

Julie found a place against the rock and sat down with the pilot next to her. The angry voices continued. The pilot was right: it would be a good idea if they shut up. What on earth could they be arguing about? What could possibly be so important at a time like this? A man sat down wearily on the other side of her. Thinking she recognized him, she asked softly in French, "Who's that?"

The reply came back, "One of us."

Julie whispered, "Can you tell me what's happening?"

"We're waiting for the boat but . . . it may be badly delayed by the weather." He bent toward her. "In truth, I doubt it'll come at all. . . ."

Julie's heart sank. The thought of having to look after the pilot for much longer filled her with despair. She imagined having to lead him up the cliff again. That was bad enough. But then what? Would they expect her to keep the young man with her? To hide him at the house? No, it was impossible! She said to the villager, "What happens if the boat doesn't come?"

"We all go home—with our guests, I suppose."

"Do they go back to—where they were before?"

"I have no idea. You'll have to ask our leader."

There was contempt in his voice as he spoke the word leader, and Julie realized he disliked the man too. She asked, "But why's everyone arguing?"

"Because the whole thing's a mess. No one knows who's meant to be doing what. Virtually all our helpers are down here on the beach when some should still be up on the cliff. Half say the boat won't come, the other half want to wait. Our leader is telling all those who want to stay to go and all those who want to go to stay. Marvelous, isn't it?" The man spat with contempt.

The mention of the dreadful man reminded Julie of Michel's warning. It had been quite clear. He'd said that the Germans probably knew all about this. . . . If he was right and they did . . .

God.

She was terribly frightened, that was all. Yet she couldn't shake off a terrible sense of foreboding. It was partly instinct and partly a feeling that nothing could go right while this leader was in charge.

Something had changed. It was the arguing—it had stopped. Instead everyone was staring out to sea. Involuntarily Julie squeezed the pilot's hand.

There was a sudden burst of activity. Orders were passed. Three men ran down the beach. Others came along the line and told the waiting passengers to be ready to move. Julie and her pilot stood up. A tall, lanky figure detached himself from Julie's group and started moving down the beach. A dark figure ran after him and pushed him back against the rock, saying in ragged English, "Wait! When I say!"

Julie stared at the line of surf, straining her eyes to distinguish the shadows in the darkness. At first she thought she was mistaken, but then she saw it: the dark shape of a small boat coming through the surf. And then there were men jumping out, two or three of them, pulling the boat up the beach and blending with the men who had run down to meet them. Incredible. The boat had come in spite of the weather. It had not forgotten them after all.

Now four people were being led to the boat. Julie's pilot said plaintively, "Why not me? What the hell's happening?"

Julie said soothingly, "It's all right. You'll be next. I expect the boat can't take everyone at once."

The shape of the boat showed black against the whiteness of the surf and Julie realized it had been launched again. Dark figures climbed in, a curtain of water rose up as the boat met a wave, and then they were gone, vanished into the night.

Julie wondered how on earth the small boat found the large one in the darkness. She hadn't seen a single light.

It was twenty minutes before they returned. The pilot kept saying, "Christ, they're not coming back! They're not coming back!"

And Julie replied, "Of course they are. Honestly, I promise they are."

And at last the boat was back and it was time for Julie's pilot to go. She started to say good-bye but one of the villagers hissed at her, "No, you must come too. Now! Come!"

"What?" But he didn't reply and Julie, hand in hand with the pilot again, stumbled uneasily down the pebbles toward the water. As they approached the boat two men detached themselves from the waiting group and came toward them.

A man next to Julie said, "She's here, over here."

The two figures came up and a voice said, "Hello, do you speak English?"

Julie laughed nervously. "Yes."

"Look, there's this walkie-talkie we'd like to give you. I was trying to explain how it worked. Do you think you could remember a few instructions?" His voice was very English and upper class: an officer.

"I'll try." Julie made an effort to concentrate as he handed her

the walkie-talkie, a small oblong object which was surprisingly light.

The British officer spoke slowly and carefully, repeating everything twice. He spoke about frequencies, range, aerials, batteries and procedures. Eventually he said, "Do you think you've got all that?"

"Yes, I think so."

"It's always best to explain it verbally, but it is all written down as well, on the plate on the side. Look, why don't you try it? Turn it on now and then you can listen to me talking to the MGB and get the idea. Okay?"

"Yes."

The officer looked nervously around. "Must go now! Bye!"

Julie had a ridiculous urge to ask him to stay longer, but he was gone, striding toward the boat, which was already being pushed into the water. Julie searched for her pilot, but couldn't distinguish him among the people waiting around the boat. In case he could see her she raised her hand and waved good-bye.

When she reached the finger of rock she sat down and turned on the radio. There was a slight hissing and crackling then, suddenly, a voice that made her jump.

"Safely launched and on the way."

"Roger." The acknowledgment was so clear it sounded as though it had come from a few feet away. Julie waited for more. But there was nothing, just the hiss of the receiver.

A figure came up beside her and said, "Come on! Time to go! Hurry!"

She got to her feet and reached for the button to switch the radio off.

Suddenly a voice crackled, "Have run my distance but no visual yet."

"Try farther west."

"Roger."

Julie waited, mesmerized.

"Found a rock. Any ideas?"

There was a short silence. A new voice came on, stronger than the one before. "Go north, Jimmy, you forgot the tide. And look out for more rocks on the way."

"Roger."

The man at Julie's elbow whispered, "We *must* go. Come! Come!"

The radio had a strap. Julie hooked it over her shoulder and left the radio on. It couldn't do any harm while they were down on the beach blanketed by the sound of the rumbling surf.

They were almost at the path when the radio crackled again.

The strong voice said, "Got you, Jimmy. Turn east, fifty yards."

"Roger. Yes, visual now."

There was a pause, then: "Where the hell are you going, Number One?"

"Avoiding a rock, sir."

"Well, try to avoid the scenic route, won't you?"

Reluctantly Julie turned the radio off and handed it to the man who was waiting to push her up the steep slope immediately above the beach. Another villager was on the path above, ready to pull her up.

Halfway up the slope Julie almost slipped, but she managed to find a foothold and push herself until she could reach the hand of the man above. Once on the path the climb was much easier than the descent had been. It felt safer, going up, and her shoes seemed to grip the stony surface better.

As she climbed she felt ridiculously happy. The mixture of fear and elation made her want to laugh. Then she remembered the awful row on the beach and the risks they had all taken and realized it was relief that had made her light-headed.

As they reached the clifftop, she remembered too that there was still a long way to go. She didn't think about laughing again until they had crossed the heathland and reached the fields, and her uncle had emerged from the shadows and taken her arm and led her firmly back to the farmhouse. She suddenly understood why men enjoyed danger so much. She'd never felt so alive in her life!

It took her until dawn to sleep. She heard the clank of the milking pails and the sound of Tante Marie leaving to fetch Peter from Mme. Boulet's before she finally dozed off.

She kept remembering the scene on the beach and the dark silhouette of the boat against the surf. There was something warm and comforting in the memory, in the sight of the boat and the sound of the voices on the radio. The voices made her feel

nostalgic, almost homesick. It had been a long time since she'd heard an English voice.

She remembered her childhood: the school outings to the beach, the occasional walks along the Hoe, the lovely view over the sound, the chatter of her school friends.

Carefree days. She rather missed them. Then she remembered what had come after. Peter's father had had a crisp upper-class accent just like the voices of those officers on the radio. Suddenly the memories weren't warm and comforting anymore.

It was stupid to think about England.

There was no going back. There never would be.

But, even as she fell asleep, the nostalgia remained.

PART THREE

1942-
February 1943

15 Fischer's eyes began to close and, blinking rapidly, he pulled himself quickly upright. He moved to the other side of the conning tower and stared out into the murk.

Not far now. They were well into the Bay—or as it was called by his men, the Black Pit. Fortunately it was living up to its name this morning: it was a filthy day. A southwesterly gale was blowing, the sky was overcast and visibility was down to no more than a mile. Perfect cover for a submarine.

The weather was also bitterly cold, but Fischer didn't mind that either: nothing could be as cold as the place they'd come from.

The patrol had been one of the longest they'd ever been on. They'd gone almost as far as Greenland—a hundred miles short of it, to be precise. And then they'd waited. It was so cold that the boat had iced up every few hours. They'd had to half-submerge then, to get the guns underwater and melt the ice off. Not that the seawater was exactly warm, but it was just above freezing and that was all that mattered.

The wind hadn't been kind either: gale force or more almost the whole time. Conditions below had been worse than normal, and that was saying something in a Type VIIC. The accommodation had been running with water, both from the terrible condensation and from the waves that inevitably slopped down the conning-tower hatch. The men had put up with the damp and the discomfort with their usual good humor. The only time Fischer had heard rumblings of discontent was during a storm when, instead of diving to escape the pounding and rolling, he'd been forced to keep *U-319* on the surface to watch for a convoy. A lot of the crew had got sick and after six hours few except Fischer cared whether they found any targets or not.

They didn't see the convoy that day. Somehow Fischer had known they wouldn't. But he'd been ordered to watch for it, so watch he did.

It was four days later when they eventually found a target: a small convoy—only ten ships and one tanker—and well escorted by two destroyers. Fischer made contact with the other U-boats in his pack and they closed in. It was a disappointing fight: Fischer had just lined *U-319* up for the tanker when the destroyer suddenly came straight for them and they were forced to dive. The ship dropped a few depth charges and by the time Fischer had got *U-319* away and surfaced the convoy was well ahead. It took him two hours to maneuver back into position; even then he managed to fire only two torpedoes before the destroyer was onto him again. And what was worse, the torpedoes had missed—at least there had been no *sound* of an explosion. It was all very unsatisfactory.

They did manage to find another convoy and sink two small ships before they ran out of torpedoes. But two ships was a poor tally and Fischer couldn't decide whether he'd suffered from bad luck, poor intelligence or a simple lack of convoys. How did one ever know?

One thing was certain though: targets were not as easy to come by nowadays. He remembered the autumn of 1940, The Happy Time, it was called, when it was easy to sink eight, maybe even ten ships on a single patrol. Now, in January of 1942, nothing was easy.

Something always conspired against such achievements: the weather, the convoy escorts, Allied air cover, something . . .

Maybe the debriefing would shed some light. It wouldn't be long now . . .

Fischer glanced at his watch. It was almost 0800, time to get some sleep. He nodded to the second watch officer and climbed down to the attack room below.

The *Leitender*—the Chief—and two of the technicians were crouched around the periscope, which was in the raised position despite the fact they were on the surface.

"Still having trouble, Chief?"

"Yes, Herr Kaleu. Hydraulics leaking somewhere. Haven't much chance of locating the fault before we get in, I'm afraid."

There was always something. Fischer asked, "Can we raise it manually?"

"Oh, I can still give you hydraulic power, but a bit slower, that's all. I'll just have to keep topping up the oil. Don't worry, Herr Kaleu, you'll have your *Spargel.*"

Fischer laughed. *Spargel* meant asparagus; it was their nickname for the periscope. They had an abbreviation or nickname for most things—even himself. They called him Herr Kaleu, short for *Kapitänleutnant*. Emblems of authority were favorite targets: they had nicknamed the swastika *Wollhandkrabbe,* after a particularly unpleasant freshwater crab.

Fischer removed his wet-weather gear and climbed down into the control room, wondering if the periscope would ever get fixed properly. Half the repairs carried out in the dockyards never held up for very long and broke down at the worst possible moments. They had been having problems with one of the hydroplanes for three patrols now.

He made his way forward to what was politely called the commander's cabin. It was in fact nothing more than a tiny recess with a curtain across the front. Still, it was a lot better than his men got. Fischer had heard that the British submarines were quite luxurious, with one bunk to each man. Here on the Type VIIC most of the lower ranks slept where they could, in hammocks or on the floor or between the torpedoes. They were allowed hardly any possessions, just a clean set of underwear and a few odds and ends.

Fischer supposed the whole boat must stink by now, but they were all so used to the intertwined smells of lavatories, diesel and sweat that nobody noticed.

When Fischer reached his cabin he paused only to hang up his cap before lying down and closing his eyes.

He never had trouble getting to sleep and when he was dog-tired as he was now it was that much easier. And the sleep when it came was the sleep of the just: deep, untroubled and dreamless.

It seemed to Fischer he was awake a fraction of a second before the klaxon blared. By the time it was in full cry he was running. Three seconds after it sounded he was in the control room, just in time to see the first man tumbling down from the conning tower.

The diving procedure was well under way: the men were running forward to get their weight into the nose, the hydroplanes were fully angled; the boat was starting to tilt downward as she began to submerge at full speed. He looked quickly around to see if any problems were developing in the control room. None. He looked up to see if all the men were down from the tower and the hatch closed. Not yet. He tried to judge from the angle of dive exactly how long the men had before the hatch had to be shut, whether or not any remained on the wrong side.

The last man tumbled down, the hatch clanged shut.

Now they had to wait. Diving took between forty and sixty seconds. Even on a good day it was an awfully long time.

Even now only eight seconds had passed since the klaxon had sounded.

There was instant silence. The men stared across the cramped control room, their eyes locked on each others' faces.

Then for the second time that night Fischer had the strange sensation that he knew what was coming a moment before it actually happened. It seemed to him that he grabbed at a rail and tensed his body a fraction of a second before the bomb exploded.

The roar blasted his ears and jarred his senses. The boat thrashed violently, like a rat shaken by an angry dog.

Then darkness. A faint glow of light. Smoke. And the acrid smell of white-hot electrics.

Fischer yelled, "Damage control reports!"

Voices started screaming at him, "No rudder control!"

"Fire in the after ends!"

Fischer shouted, "Pressure tanks?"

"Pressure normal!"

"Pressure hull?"

"No leaks!"

There was a pause, then: "Fire in after ends extinguished, Herr Kaleu!"

"Any further damage?"

An engineer appeared from aft. "Herr Kaleu! Starboard shaft buckled. Port shaft bent."

"How bent?"

He was a young sailor, no more than nineteen. He didn't have

an answer. Then his face brightened and he said, "Well, it's still turning!"

"I want a full report from the Chief at his convenience!"

"Yes, Herr Kaleu!"

Fischer absorbed the information. No rudder, no shafts.

Christ, the bomb had blown the whole of the goddam back end off!

But the pressure hull was intact: that was the important thing. They were still diving. There was no loss of diving control. "Level off at twenty meters."

"Yes, Herr Kaleu!"

What they lacked was steering. The compass bearing was veering around. They were turning slowly to port.

"Trim?"

"Stable."

The turn wasn't too sharp then. Hope yet.

The Chief hurried into the control room. "Starboard shaft unserviceable, Herr Kaleu. Port shaft just about serviceable. But I can't give you more than—say, a knot submerged and two surfaced. Even then the engines might not like it."

It was decision time. Fischer knew immediately that there was only one decision he could make.

He turned to the first watch officer. "We'll give it fifteen minutes, Eins WO, then we'll go to periscope depth and send a signal to Brest, asking for assistance. I'll dictate the message in just a moment. In the meantime . . ." He looked around until he saw the figure of the man who'd been on watch, the second watch officer, standing in his dripping oilskins, his face sheet white. "Zwei WO, I want an incident report. Now!"

"There was no warning, Herr Kaleu. It even came from the northeast, downwind, so we didn't hear anything until it was almost on top of us. All of a sudden there it was, coming straight for us. . . ."

"This is very important," Fischer interrupted. "Are you sure it was coming straight for us?"

"Yes! No doubt about that."

Fischer nodded. "Continue."

The second officer gulped. "I could see that it was a big plane,

265

a bomber, and that it was close, awfully close. I knew that by the time we got to the guns it would be on top of us, so I ordered diving stations straightaway. . . ." He paused anxiously.

If Fischer had been there he would have ordered the men to the guns, to get in at least one burst. On the other hand there had been so little time. . . . He said quietly, "I think there was nothing we could have done either way. At least the dive has protected us from a second attack."

The young man, obviously relieved, continued, "As I closed the hatch I guess the plane was no more than, say, twenty meters away."

"Tell me, was it still overcast and the visibility low?"

"Yes, Herr Kaleu. You were there, you saw what it was like. . . ."

"Yes, yes," Fischer said impatiently. "I just wanted to know if the weather had changed suddenly . . ."

"Oh no. Just the same."

"Thank you. That's all."

The young officer left. For a while Fischer sat motionless, then he walked slowly back into the control room. A chart of the Bay of Biscay lay open on the tiny chart table. Fischer stared at it blankly.

Bad weather, overcast conditions, poor visibility . . . perfect cover for a submarine.

Like hell!

The plane must have known they were there; it must have!

He stared at the chart as if it might explain it all. But there was no simple answer, he knew that. Nothing that fit any of the known facts.

The plane had *known*! And *U-319* had been a sitting duck. Vulnerable. Unable to defend herself. It changed everything.

Fischer murmured wearily, "God in heaven!" Then, reaching for a pad and pencil, he drafted a wireless signal.

Doenitz picked up the signal and read the last few lines again. ". . . ENEMY CAME STRAIGHT IN TO ATTACK IN POOR VISIBILITY. IMPOSSIBLE THAT ENEMY HAD ADVANCE VISUAL SIGHTING. REPEAT IMPOSSIBLE. CONCLUDE ENEMY PINPOINTED US BY NONVISUAL MEANS. . . ."

Doenitz laid down the signal. This was the third time in a

month boats had reported sudden attacks, in which they had been caught unawares on the surface. He could believe that the first two boats might have had sleepy lookouts, he could believe that their commanders might have underestimated the visibility . . .

But *U-319*? Fischer? Impossible. Fischer would never conceal the facts. If Fischer said the visibility was poor, then it was.

Doenitz called through to his staff officer: "Get me Herr Schmidt at the Reich Research Directorate in Berlin."

While he waited for the call to go through, Doenitz reflected on his previous conversations with Herr Schmidt. There had been several in the last six months. On each occasion Doenitz had asked if there was any information about new British antisubmarine devices. Three times he had come right out and asked the vital question itself: Was it possible that the British planes had search radar? Schmidt had hedged the answer. His favorite expressions were "very unlikely," "improbable," and "our information suggests not." The man always promised to look into the matter again, but Doenitz had the suspicion that nobody was looking into it at all.

Well, this time there could be no doubt. Herr Schmidt would be forced to admit that the British not only possessed a search device, but that it was extremely effective. He wondered how Herr Schmidt would try to explain the phenomenon.

And however he did explain it, he had better be able to suggest a countermeasure. Otherwise . . . Doenitz sighed grimly. Otherwise the effectiveness of the fleet would be severely curtailed. Doenitz would have to order the boats to submerge as they crossed the Bay. And if the British extended their air patrols farther out into the Atlantic, then the boats would have to stay under for even longer.

That meant it would take them twice as much time to reach their patrol area: most U-boats could travel at a top speed of only seven knots submerged, compared to seventeen on the surface. Worse, somewhere along their submerged run, the boats would have to surface—for air and to recharge their batteries. Then they would be desperately vulnerable.

If too many boats were caught on the surface and lost, it would be disastrous. The U-boat arm remained desperately short of operational craft: instead of the three hundred or so he'd hoped

for, Doenitz still had only ninety, and that was after more than two years of war. And now, as if to forestall any chance of improving the situation, the winter was so severe that the Baltic ports were iced up and trials of new boats and training of new personnel had come to a complete standstill.

For Doenitz the shortage was doubly frustrating because, against his and Raeder's advice, Hitler had personally ordered much of the fleet to be redeployed. There were twenty-three boats—far too many—in the Mediterranean, where the waters were shallow and dangerous. And in the latest madness, twenty-six boats had been ordered to defend Norway against a supposed Allied invasion which, from what Doenitz heard, was very far from certain. Using U-boats as sentries was a waste of time; they could achieve much more spectacular results by squeezing the supply lines dry. But OKW—the High Command—was unconvinced. Doenitz could only advise. What more could he do?

The telephone rang. The staff officer announced Herr Schmidt and put him through. Doenitz kept the formalities to a minimum, then told Schmidt the facts. He continued, "I am having a meeting here in Paris with the Navy Technical Branch tomorrow. It is essential that you or your representative be here, Herr Schmidt. This matter is of great consequence."

The voice at the other end of the line was conciliatory. "Of course I will come myself, Herr Admiral. If I set off now I can be with you first thing in the morning. I will have one of my people with me. He will have all the available data. . . ."

Doenitz replaced the receiver, puzzled. Schmidt hadn't sounded at all surprised. Far from it. It was as if he'd been expecting the call. And his tone had been odd, too: evasive yet positive, almost as if he had a solution ready to pull out of his hat. . . .

Doenitz rubbed his forehead. The politics of dealing with section chiefs in Berlin always gave him a headache. Doubtless he would find out what Schmidt had up his sleeve when the man chose to tell him. Hopefully tomorrow.

In the meantime he must protect his boats. Even though it would slow them down considerably, he must order his boats to cross the Bay submerged.

He called for his staff officer. "Werner, take a directive to all flotillas, Operational Area West."

"As it happens, we think we can tell you exactly what it is," Schmidt said calmly. "Although we will have to make further checks, of course."

Doenitz said sharply, "Yes?"

"Well, it appears that the British bombers are being fitted with a type of radar . . ."

There was a deathly silence around the table. The technical staff stared at the Chief Scientist in horror.

Schmidt licked his lips nervously. ". . . A compact search radar."

"Are you sure of this?" Doenitz asked.

"A detection station in Normandy picked up a signal from an airborne source. It was quite definitely an intermittent signal. That means it was rotating . . . a search radar."

Doenitz said slowly, "I always understood that radar could not be made small enough to fit into an aircraft."

There was an awkward silence. Schmidt looked cross.

Doenitz sighed and asked quietly, "What about the wavelength? Is it one we understand?"

"Oh yes!" Schmidt replied immediately. "They are using a one-point-five-meter wavelength similar to our own system. It's nothing new."

"So?"

"We can manufacture a radar detector. This would pick up signals from approaching aircraft and give your vessels good warning."

"How good?"

Schmidt shrugged. "Ten, maybe fifteen miles . . ."

Ten miles . . . it was adequate—*if* Schmidt was right.

Doenitz asked, "How soon could these be manufactured?"

"It would take a lot of development. The receiver itself wouldn't be too complex . . . but the aerial—" He shook his head. "That would have to survive submergence. . . . It would take time to develop. . . ."

Doenitz leaned forward in his chair. "But we don't *have* time!"

Schmidt looked uncomfortable. "Well, perhaps a mobile aerial

might be possible. . . . But it would have to be assembled every time the U-boat surfaced and taken down again every time it dived. It wouldn't be ideal—"

"I don't care!" Doenitz interrupted. "If it works we must have it! We have absolutely no choice. I don't care if it's made out of plywood, Herr Schmidt. I want that detector in sufficient quantity, and I want it *now*!"

16

They came for David one cold February morning. There was no warning. Sergeant Klammer and a soldier simply marched in and told David to pack his belongings and be ready in five minutes. Just David, no one else.

Shocked, David asked, "Where am I going?"

Klammer shrugged; he didn't know.

When the two guards had gone David looked at Meyer in horror. The old man patted his arm and said, "Remember, they're allowing you some belongings. That's a good sign!" The faces of the other scientists were apologetic, guilty even, because they were being allowed to stay. David didn't blame them; he would have felt the same himself.

Meyer helped him pack. It didn't take long—everything fitted into a small bundle.

When the soldiers came back David turned to Meyer, wanting to say many things. But he muttered only, "Good-bye," and, unable to say more, followed Klammer quickly out of the hut into the bitter morning cold.

There was thick snow on the ground and more was falling. The path was slippery and David had to walk carefully. Suddenly he stopped in utter panic. He'd forgotten the most important thing of all! He shouted at Klammer's back, "Please! One moment!" Then, before Klammer could say anything, he hurried back to the hut.

Inside, David cried, "My medicine! I forgot my medicine!" Meyer took his arm and together they found it on the windowsill above David's bunk. David grasped the bottle and praised God. Shaking slightly, he placed it in his bundle, carefully wrapped in some overalls.

"Nothing else you've forgotten?" Meyer asked kindly.

David tried to think, but his mind was in a jumble.

Klammer arrived and barked, "Hurry!"

David whispered desperately to Meyer, "I don't think so." Then, wringing Meyer's hand once more, he stumbled out into the snow.

Klammer led the way to the main gates, where a soldier took over and marched David up the road toward the railway station. David approached it with foreboding. He hadn't seen the place since his arrival all those months before and he'd forgotten how bleak it was. The solitary station building loomed dark against the stark whiteness of the snow, and the wind was howling across the desolate expanse of sidings.

There was only one train, a train made up of cattle cars.

David's mouth went dry. He remembered the horror of the journey from Sachsenhausen, the stench, the cries, the dying people. He couldn't believe that he must go through it all over again.

He stumbled and fell in the snow. As he picked himself up, his stomach twisted in pain. He thought: I'll never survive another journey.

The soldier led the way down the train. The cattle cars stank of excrement and, it seemed to David, of human suffering too. He struggled on, his head bowed against the driving snow.

They approached the end of the train. Here there was a single carriage, painted dark gray with windows. The soldier indicated that David should get in. David's heart lifted slightly.

Inside were compartments with plain wooden seats and over-head luggage racks. The soldier pushed him into one and closed and locked the door. It was very dark, but after a while David's eyes became accustomed to the faint glimmers of light that seeped in through the drawn blinds.

He couldn't believe his luck. There must be a catch somewhere.

After a couple of hours the train started. Almost immediately the door was flung open and the compartment flooded with light.

David jumped. It was the guard, coming to tell him that he had two minutes to go to the lavatory. Later they brought him a blanket, some food—sausage and dry bread—and a cup of water.

David relaxed. He was going to be all right after all.

Slowly he stretched out on the long wooden seat and pulled the blanket over him. He tried to think, to work out where they might be taking him. He remembered too everything he was leaving behind—his work, half-completed; the safe, comforting routine of his day; the warmth of companionship. He had got very fond of his colleagues; he would miss them dreadfully.

Finally the steady rhythm of the clicking wheels lulled him into an almost dreamless sleep. Only when the train jerked to a halt did he wake. It stopped many times through the afternoon and early night, sometimes for hours at a time.

Once David woke in the night and tried to guess what time it was. Probably about three or four. He rubbed his eyes and realized he was mistaken. It must be much later: a crack of thin gray light had appeared at the edge of the blind. It was dawn. He had slept longer than he'd thought.

The train was going very slowly; the sound of the wheels had fallen to a lazy rhythmic click. There was a loud squeal of brakes. Perhaps they were approaching a station. If they were going north, they might be at Nuremberg by now, or Leipzig.

He sat up on the seat and put his eye to the crack in the blind. The blind was permanently drawn, the section of heavy black canvas fastened to the window frame with nails at three-inch intervals. But between two of the nails the fabric bagged slightly. By pulling at it with his finger and pressing his eye close to the gap, David could just see out.

He could discern several railway lines, sheds, some sidings: a largish town then, maybe even a city. The brakes squealed again and the train juddered as it slowed still further. There was a loud clattering and the carriage was suddenly jerked to one side: they were crossing onto another line. More sheds; a marshaling area. They came up alongside a stationary line of cattle cars.

Then they stopped.

With a loud clanging and shouting, soldiers were pulling back the doors of the cattle cars. Men came pouring out, jumping onto

the ground, standing blinking in the sudden light. The men were poorly dressed and foreign-looking, thin but not starving. They walked obediently across the tracks toward David's train, and after more clanging and the sound of large metal doors sliding, they boarded.

An hour later there was more shouting and from far away, at the head of the train, David could hear the locomotive panting in long deep gasps as it pulled on its heavy load. The clank of couplings sounded down the train and the carriage jerked forward. From beneath came the low rumble of the wheels on metal tracks.

David sat up and returned to the crack in the blind. The train was slipping through the sidings and crossing junctions again until he guessed they were back on the main line. A freight train appeared on the next track. David peered at the words chalked on each car, trying to read the destinations. He saw Mannheim, Frankfurt, Mannheim again. . . . Cities in the west.

Then the train was on the main line, going straighter and faster. With excitement David saw that they were approaching a station. There were platforms, station buildings, and a name. . . .

Mannheim.

Something stirred in his memory.

Of course. David remembered. This was the place he had planned to head for in his great escape from Berlin. This was the place he was going to reach without any trouble, by getting on a train and sitting quietly in a corner. He shook his head. What a child he had been!

The train passed through several small stations, but the names flashed by too fast to read them.

After a while David dozed, rocked by the motion of the train, and it was not until much later when the brakes squealed that he woke again.

A sign said Saarbrücken.

They were at the French border.

He sat for a long time, immobile, waiting. At last the train started moving again.

A small village. Name: Wendel. German name, German architecture.

Then a small town with a long name. He couldn't read the sign

because the train was going too fast. He had to stand up quickly to catch it from the corridor window.

Faulquemont.

French name. French architecture. French vehicles . . . !

Then he laughed. What a joke!

The Germans were taking him to France! They were taking him where he had wanted to go all those months ago.

He smiled for a long time. France . . . ! What a joke!

Suddenly he wasn't smiling anymore. Pain came suddenly, without warning. It came in a great stab that took the breath out of him. He bent over and, clutching his stomach, reached for the precious bottle of medicine. He swigged a mouthful and waited for the soothing liquid to quench the burning in his belly.

Trembling, he lay down, his euphoria gone, and thought disconsolately: When all is said and done, France, Germany, it makes no difference, not if I'm dying.

And I started dying a long time ago.

After that David lost track of the hours. The pain dulled his brain and the darkness confused him, and he slept most of the time. Life became a dream, a nightmare of dim awareness.

Only when the guard slid the door open with a bang did David wake up. Usually the guard placed the food hastily on the floor and left, or waited impassively while David went to the lavatory. But this time he shouted, "Out! Out! Come on!"

David tried to gather his wits. How long had he been in the train? Three days? He'd lost count. He stumbled toward the door, momentarily forgetting his bundle on the seat. He reached back, picked it up and followed the guard out of the door, bumping into the wall as he tried to find his balance.

He stepped down off the train. Sidings again. Warehouses and sheds. A large city. But very French, still very French.

The laborers were pouring out of the train too. Many of them were staggering and falling. Those who didn't get up were kicked or beaten with rifle butts, then thrown against the side of the track to where the dead and dying already lay in a pathetic pile of ragged limbs.

David tore his eyes away and followed the guard across the tracks. Suddenly there was a *Crack!* Then another: the sharp

whine of bullets. David winced but made himself keep walking. Why look back? He knew what he would see. They were killing the weak, finishing off the dying. Looking back only broke your heart.

They came to a truck. The guard indicated that David should get in the back. David had difficulty climbing up, and the guard, a boy of about twenty, helped him.

David scrambled in and the guard followed. For a while David sat quietly, then asked, "Where are we?"

The guard looked surprised at David's German. Then he snapped, "No questions!"

"Just asking."

After a short silence, the guard murmured, "Brest."

"Ah!" David exclaimed. He nodded as if he'd known all the time.

Brest: where was it? David had never been very good at geography. Brest . . . a port, surely, right on the west coast. So he'd reached the sea after all! The idea gave him pleasure.

The truck moved off. The sidings and marshaling yards gave way to warehouses and sheds, and then they were climbing a hill. David's eye was caught by the sparkle of light on water. A great natural harbor was opening out before him, a wide expanse of water that seemed to be bound by gently sloping woodland on every side.

Then the water was obscured by houses and they were skirting the edge of the city, which appeared to be built on a small plateau overlooking the harbor. As the truck turned inland, a man-made harbor appeared immediately below, with several warships at its quays. There were dry docks too. And a submarine, which was moving across the harbor, its wake a line of darker gray against the brilliant whites of the sparkling water.

The road dropped and turned, and then they were almost at water level, crossing over a small canal and rumbling through another commercial area before coming to a halt.

Almost immediately the truck started up again and David realized they had passed through the gates of a defense establishment. Most of the personnel were wearing naval uniform.

The truck stopped next to a squat brick building. The guard jumped out and indicated that David should follow.

Inside, a girl showed him up to an office and ushered him in. When David looked back he saw that the guard had gone.

A German naval officer was sitting behind a desk. He stood up, a thin, nervous-looking young man. "I am Kapitänleutnant Geissler. Please be seated."

David waited for the officer to sit before lowering himself gingerly into a chair.

"Herr Freymann, we understand you are highly qualified in radio-electrics and that you have been working for some time on the design of radio ranging devices."

David was taken aback by the "Herr." It was a long time since anyone had called him that.

The officer went on, "We have appropriated a company here in Brest to produce electronic and radio components for us. One particular piece of equipment has the highest priority. It is essential that this device is produced with all speed and in some quantity. . . ." The officer looked unhappy. "However, there have been problems . . . of a technical nature. We wish you, Herr Freymann, to supervise the technical side of the operation."

David waited for the rest.

"The device is needed to protect our U-boats from enemy attack." The officer stood and picked up a thin file from the top of a filing cabinet. "I have the technical specifications here. If you could study them immediately—then I will take you over to the manufacturing unit and you can see the organization for yourself."

David frowned. Protecting U-boats, but from what exactly? He still felt woolly-headed from the journey. As he took the file and opened it, he tried desperately to clear his brain.

There were a few pages of written specifications and a foldout plan. Both were headed: *"Project Metox. Most Secret."* David read the first page and blinked.

It was an anti-*radar* device.

He pulse quickened and his mind cleared. This meant that the British had radar, just as Meyer and he had guessed.

He looked again at the specifications. They stated the necessity for the Metox device to pick up signals at maximum possible range, up to thirty nautical miles. The absolute minimum tolerable range was six miles. That seemed very precise. . . .

David asked, "Why this six miles? What is so special about six miles?"

The officer replied, "Ah. You see, our U-boats must have plenty of warning. They need at least one minute to dive, and another thirty seconds to get below bombing depth!"

Bombing . . . ? David stared with incomprehension. Bombing. "You mean *aircraft* attack . . . ?"

"Yes, indeed!" the young man exclaimed. "These aircraft approach at over two hundred knots. We need warning of over five miles to give enough time . . ."

But David wasn't listening. The British had succeeded in putting radar in aircraft. That meant they had made it small enough. But how had they done it?

Rapidly he searched the first page of the specifications and then flipped impatiently over to the second. Where on earth was it? There! At last!

The detection device was to cover the wavelengths 1.4 to 1.8 meters.

David tried to understand.

The British radar wasn't shortwave after all. It was within a range of wavelengths Germany had been using for some time.

Nothing new at all.

David felt a mixture of relief and anxiety—relief that no one had got to the shortwave idea before him and anxiety that perhaps he had got it wrong and it wasn't possible after all.

He forced himself to read the rest of the pages, glancing at the large-scale drawing. Whoever had designed this detecting device had got the basic idea right. A simple aerial, which led to a radio receiver. When the receiver picked up a radar signal from an approaching plane it emitted a high-pitched warning. The main problem, David saw immediately, was to get the emitter to give off a strong signal whatever the range and frequency of the incoming radar waves. The receiver itself was relatively straightforward.

"What problems have you been having, then?" he asked.

The *Kapitänleutnant* breathed in with obvious annoyance. "It is difficult to be precise. Most of the devices produced so far have had small but serious defects. We don't know why. We need you to tell us, and to prevent it happening in the future."

"I see. And the technicians at this factory, are they competent?"

"Apparently so."

"And the components, where have they been manufactured?"

"Mainly in Germany, a few in France. They all appear to be up to standard, but there always seems to be something wrong with the finished sets. We need someone to make sure these faults are ironed out!"

David closed the file and stood up. "I am ready then. At your convenience."

It took only two days at Goulvent, Pescard et Cie for David to realize that the Metox project was a shambles. Some of the components weren't up to standard, the assembly line was disorganized and the French personnel were less skilled than he'd been led to expect.

The problems could be solved, no doubt about that. As always, it was a question of identifying the trouble spots and eliminating them. But he would need time—rather a long time by present standards. From the moment he arrived David had run into an unexpected difficulty: he was virtually unable to communicate.

He was a little surprised when the factory personnel failed to understand more than a few words of his French. He spoke the language badly, admittedly, but not *that* badly. Of course, it would have helped if some of the French personnel had spoken German, but they didn't and that was that. To make matters worse, the anxious young *Kapitänleutnant* kept hanging over David's shoulder, listening to his hesitant questions and glaring angrily at the French technicians when they shrugged or gave the briefest of replies.

Secretly, David was glad most of the replies were short because then at least he could understand them. Whenever one of the French started a monologue delivered at high speed and great length, he had absolutely no hope of following it, and he could almost believe it was being done on purpose, just to confuse him.

For a man who loved to communicate precisely and economically the frustration was terrible. David felt as if he were foundering in cotton wool.

The evenings only served to make him more depressed. He was escorted back to a cold bare room in some barracks within the

dockyard compound. The food, sent over from a naval canteen, was good, but David was not used to being on his own. The silence and the smallness of the room pressed in on him: for the first time in his life he could guess at the terror of solitary confinement. Before, he had always been with people, whether working, living or suffering, and he missed them.

The situation was ironic, he had to admit. Never had he been safer—never had he felt so discontented. It was, of course, because they had given him back so much. . . . He had got to expect things.

The answer was work. Work always made him happy.

He paced his room and decided on some priorities.

The first was easy: he would make a success of the project even if it killed him.

The second was not so easy: Kapitänleutnant Geissler must stop hovering over him.

And while he was about it he might as well have a third: to ask for another billet, one nearer other prisoners, somewhere with a bit of company. The request would probably be refused, but it never did any harm to ask.

He took a scrap of paper from the table and rummaged for the pencil stub which he always kept in his tiny bundle along with his other treasures: an eraser, a small slide rule and a picture post-card of Berlin; all possessions he'd been allowed to acquire while in the camp laboratory.

Taking up the pencil he wrote a work list for the next day, itemizing each action in his neat handwriting made necessarily larger by the bluntness of the pencil.

When he had finished he regarded the list critically. It was not much, but at least it made him feel that he had started.

He went to sleep immediately and woke early, his mind already busy. He jumped out of bed, examined his list, then waited impatiently to be picked up for work. When the van finally deposited him at the factory door, he went straight to his office. He got out two blueprints of the Metox device, one in German, the other in French, and, by comparing them, made a careful study of all the technical words he would need for his conversations with the French technicians.

Next came the more difficult part: the *Kapitänleutnant.*

Geissler arrived at eight sharp, as he always did. David forced

a warm smile, offered him a chair, and then, his heart in his mouth, dived straight in. "Herr Kapitänleutnant, may I ask you a great favor?"

Geissler murmured uncertainly, "Ask."

David put on a suitably serious expression. "I need to get deeply into the operation here. I need to talk to the men—at length. I also . . . have a need to do everything at my own pace. . . . In short, Herr Kapitänleutnant, I need to work on my own. Of course," he added hastily, "I will report to you regularly. Every day, if you wish! Every few hours, if you wish! But . . ."

Geissler had got to his feet and was holding up his hand, as if stopping some imaginary traffic. The officer shook his head and David's heart sank. Then Geissler said, "Say no more. I understand perfectly. If you feel you will get better results on your own, then your request is automatically granted!"

The officer clicked his heels and left. It had been so easy! David rubbed his hands.

Next, his battle with the French language. David picked up his files and left his office. He was careful to avoid the director, who was effusive and overbearing, and went in search of the chief technician, a man called Gallois. He found him in a corner of the main workshop, staring disconsolately at some components.

David mustered his best French and said, "Good morning. May I have a word with you?"

Gallois looked up and then past David's shoulder. "Ah! No lieutenant today!"

"No."

The Frenchman raised his eyebrows. "You are in charge, then?"

David wanted to say, Hardly. But he didn't know the word and settled for "No, *they* are always in charge."

"So what can I do for you?"

"Could we talk, please, about the problems on the Metox?" David spoke slowly and distinctly.

"Certainly. I am at your service."

David was rather pleased: the fellow seemed to have understood him.

On the way to the drawing office, the Frenchman suddenly asked, "You are German?"

"Yes."

There was a short silence, then: "And you work for the German Navy?"

"Work?" David laughed. "I 'work' for the people I must!"

"But—you are employed by them?"

David couldn't understand the verb. "Employed?"

"Yes. You earn money?"

"No, my friend. I am a prisoner." A look of confusion came over Gallois's face. David added, "A prisoner, just like . . ." he searched for the word for laborers, ". . . the workers I saw on the train."

Understanding came over the Frenchman's face. "Ahhh," he murmured.

The mention of the laborers reminded David. He stopped and faced Gallois. "Why are they brought here? What work do they do, all those people?"

"They are Poles. They are building the U-boat pens. Great shelters of concrete to stop bombs." He threw out his hands to demonstrate a massive explosion.

The Frenchman asked, "Why are you a prisoner?"

"I'm Jewish."

The Frenchman nodded. "I see." And walked on in silence.

When they were sitting with the plans spread out in front of them, the Frenchman said, "What happens if you cannot solve the problems? What if this Metox does not work very well?"

David snorted and indicated with his head. "Back there, I suppose, to where I came from. But don't worry. It won't happen. We will make the thing work. . . ."

They began with the problem of the aerial connection, then went on to the placing of the valves, and the suitability of the proposed amplifier.

To David's surprise they managed to cover the three main problems within an hour, in each case agreeing about the necessary action to be taken. Strangely, David's French seemed to have improved dramatically. He was elated.

David folded the large-scale drawing and beamed at the Frenchman. "A simple device, with simple problems. I knew we could sort it out!"

"Yes, one can always sort these things out. . . ." Gallois smiled ruefully.

David regarded him for a moment, then said impulsively, "Tell me, was my French so awful—when I arrived?"

"Awful?"

"Yes, you know . . . no one seemed to understand me."

"Oh, we never understand Germans very well."

"Ah." Some unsettling thoughts drifted through David's mind. "The matters we've been discussing . . . the problems with the Metox . . . why was it you were unable to solve them before . . . ?"

Gallois made a face. "The Germans, they never provide the information and equipment we need. . . . We've asked and asked. . . ."

"Yes . . . quite . . ." David thought of asking why the Germans had not responded to these demands, but something about Gallois's manner did not invite any more questions.

"Well," said David brightly. "I am sure the project will be a great success!"

"Without doubt," the Frenchman replied coolly.

David walked back to his office, his mind already going through the letters he would have to write and telephone calls he would have to make. He realized with mild surprise that his stomach hadn't been hurting at all today. In fact he hadn't felt so well in months.

It was the challenge of the work. As he thought, it was just what he needed.

17

Motor Gunboat *309* had two outstanding characteristics: she was wet and she was as explosive as a bomb.

The southwesterly Force 6 was revealing the first of her attributes: her speed was reduced to thirteen knots and she was twist-

ing and bucking like a wild horse. Every few seconds she dug her nose deep into a wave and chucked a wall of cold, very solid water back along her 110-foot length, up and over the open bridge, drenching the four men who stood there peering into the impenetrable darkness.

There was a loud thud as a particularly large wave flew up over the bows. Ashley ducked instinctively behind the reinforced glass screen. The water hit the bridge with a dull slap, showering spray in all directions. Ashley felt a rivulet of freezing water running down his back and reflected that things might be worse: an E-boat could at this minute be firing at them and igniting the perfect mixture of air and high-octane gasoline in their fuel tanks. And what a lovely bang they would make, he thought. A nice big orange *whooomph*! And the Jerries wouldn't have to worry about looking for survivors: there wouldn't be any. Instant cremation.

All things considered, he'd rather be wet.

As if reading his mind, Jones, the coxswain, shouted, "When are we getting these new boats then, sir?"

"Ah, Cox, when indeed? According to the Master Plan we already have them!"

"Yes, sir."

"But according to the grapevine, it'll be sometime at the end of the year."

Jones blew the salt water off his lips and exclaimed, "About bleedin' time too, sir. This old girl's as wet as Glasgow on a Saturday night! If I'd wanted to be a submariner, I would have bleedin' well volunteered."

"On the other hand, Jones, a diesel-powered boat could be a real bore! A dry bridge, reliable engines, nonexplosive fuel— there'd be no feeling of adventure. That first pint back in Dartmouth wouldn't taste the same at all!"

"Ha!" the coxswain retorted. "But you know, sir, I wouldn't mind about the weather, 'cept we've been having it all bleedin' winter. Not a break 'ave we 'ad, not a single one."

"No, Cox," Ashley admitted. "We can't have been saying our prayers right."

In fact, there had been breaks in the weather, but they had come during the full moon, or when *309*'s engines were out of

action, or when there was no operation planned. Whenever an operation *had* been set up it had blown Force 5 or more. Nothing unusual for winter in the English Channel, but uncomfortable, wet and—for this kind of job—dangerously slow. A delay on the outward journey meant a late arrival, a nervous wait at the pickup point, and a mad dash to get back across no-man's-land to British coastal waters before dawn.

It was already 2330 and, Ashley guessed, another two to two and a half hours to their destination. An 0200 arrival would give them only forty-five minutes—or an hour at the most—to make the pickup. It would be horribly tight. In this wind the beach party would need at least twenty minutes to reach the shore. Five minutes to sort out the passengers and get them loaded. On the way back they would have the wind behind them but it would still take, say, fifteen minutes. Horribly tight.

Worse, he had the unpleasant feeling the wind was freshening.

They'd had miserable luck all winter, one way and another. First they'd had an inexperienced navigator and, on one occasion, had waited at the wrong beach for over three hours. Then, a week or so later, the engines had started to play up. As the Chief, a Scot by the name of McFee, was always saying, "Seawater and petrol don't mix." He did his best with the three supercharged Hall Scott engines but even he couldn't make the damn things work when they weren't in the mood. Bad weather made the engines especially temperamental: "Like a woman caught in the rain," the Chief said contemptuously. A week before, they'd acted up two miles off the Brittany coast, just as they were being opened up for the journey home. The Chief had managed to coax a couple of knots out of the starboard engine, barely enough to get them out of sight of land before dawn. Eventually, water was found in the fuel system, and after it was cleared, they managed to get under way again, but not before getting a nasty fright from a patrolling E-boat.

But at least they had an experienced navigator now: that was something. All they needed was a break in the weather.

Ashley poked his head outside the screen: yes, he could swear the wind was increasing. The barometer was probably dropping through the floor. He reached for the voice pipe and called down, "Macleod! How's the barometer?"

A voice came floating up. "The jimmy's in sick bay, sir! Elliott here."

"Sick bay!" Ashley said, "Bugger!" under his breath and put his mouth to the pipe again. "On my way!"

As Ashley climbed down the exposed bridge ladder, the MGB's bows dived into a wave and he instinctively flattened himself against the side of the boat. Instead of pouring down his neck, the water merely slapped onto his back. As he made his way aft the wetness was seeping through his oilskins into his clothes. So much for oilskins.

He reached the door, yanked it open and climbed down into the relative peace of the accommodation. The sick bay was not as grand as it sounded: it was an ordinary bunk which happened to be situated next to the locker housing the medical stores. The first lieutenant was lying there, his face white and his breathing irregular. Two seamen were taking off his boots and covering him with a blanket. There was an ominous black bucket on the floor beside him.

Ashley turned to one of the seamen. "What's up?"

"Sick, sir. Chucking up and—the other, sir."

Ashley went to the side of the bunk. "Christ, Number One, couldn't you have thought of something more original? Been overdoing the champagne and smoked salmon, eh?"

"Sorry, must have been something I ate." The voice was soft with a gentle Canadian accent. "I'll be all right in a moment, I'm sure. Once I've . . ." Disbelief came over the man's face and he suddenly threw himself over the bucket. Ashley looked away; the sight of vomit always made him retch.

When Macleod had sunk back onto the bunk Ashley said, "I don't think you'll be fit for anything, Macleod. You'd best stay here."

"No! I'll be okay. Really!"

"Stay here! That's an order. We'll manage without you. Very well, in fact. You'd be surprised!" He grinned.

Macleod smiled faintly and closed his eyes. Ashley said quietly to one of the seamen, "Keep an eye on him—temperature, pulse, everything. He looks bloody awful to me."

He made his way back to the deck, thinking: Damn!

The Canadian was his best man; very keen and very able. He

must be really ill to have agreed to lie down; if he was capable of getting to his feet, he would. Ashley gritted his teeth. He'd have to find a replacement—Macleod was leader of the beach party, the only one who spoke decent French.

Apart from himself there was only one other officer on the boat: the new navigator, a man called Tusker. He was RN (Retired) and had bamboozled his way back into active service by nagging the Admiralty to death. Unlike the first navigator, Tusker was brilliant at his job. He'd got *309* through rocks and narrow channels into countless pickup points, in filthy weather and without a decent navigation aid in sight.

There was only one problem: he was forty-five and had a bad leg.

Ashley made his way forward again, tightly gripping the available handholds. The boat pitched sharply and then, trembling and shivering, heaved herself up once more, ready for the next wave.

Ashley climbed into the small space optimistically called the chart room, a wooden structure built onto the deck just in front of the bridge. Tusker was crouching over the collapsible chart table—a simple device which, when the boat pounded heavily, often lived up to its name. As usual, Tusker was making careful calculations. He never stopped, from the moment they left until the moment they got back, reworking the tides, the course, the speed and the ETA.

"How we doing, Tusker?"

"Ah, should reach Les Vaches at 0135, and drop anchor at 0200." He always used Les Vaches, a large pair of odd-shaped rocks three miles off the beach, as a navigation point. He aimed the MGB straight for them and then, as he liked to point out, when the boat almost hit them he knew exactly where they were. He'd never failed to find the rocks yet, despite the strong tides which swept at up to five knots across the MGB's track, and despite a shortage of navigation aids. All there was to confirm the dead reckoning position was an echo sounder ticking away in the corner of the chart room.

Tusker wiped some drips off the transparent plastic chart cover and pointed at the chart. "We crossed the Hurd Deep forty-five minutes ago. I hope to pick up the edge of the Plateau de Triagoz in just over an hour. That'll give us a good lead in. Unless of course we have to reduce speed still further . . . ?"

"No, we can't, whatever the weather. Otherwise we'll be too late. We're cutting it a bit fine as it is."

The two men braced themselves as *309*'s bow rose into the air and descended rapidly toward an approaching wave. There was a loud crash and the boat shuddered. Cascades of water thundered over the chart room, pouring down the windows and penetrating the cracks in the wood. Tusker methodically wiped the drips away. "Whatever the revs say, I'd be surprised if we were doing thirteen knots in this sea."

Ashley agreed. "I've allowed a bit for the sea conditions, but I daresay you're right. I still want to press on, though. Once we reach the plateau we'll start to get in the lee of the land. Things should improve then." He blew out his cheeks. "By the way, Macleod's sick, so I'll be leading the beach party. That means you'll be in charge until I get back."

Tusker's eyebrows shot up. "I say, that's a bit irregular, isn't it? I mean, why not send Talbot or Eddington to the beach. They'd do the job all right."

"No, I'd rather go myself," Ashley said crisply. He didn't want a discussion. He was perfectly well aware that a commander shouldn't leave his ship, but this was a very small ship and the circumstances unusual. "You'll want Talbot and Eddington here if there's a fight. It's more important to leave the ship properly manned. Anyway . . . after all this time I want to have a look at this beach and meet some of our Breton friends."

"As you say."

"Now, this is the form. You are to wait until 0315, at the very latest, and then you are to leave, even if we haven't returned. Is that understood?"

The other man nodded.

"And if there's any sign of trouble, the usual rules apply—get out and as quickly as possible. Just because I'm ashore, don't try to be clever and wait around. Understood?"

"Understood."

"Good!"

It was raining now, the rain drumming against the window and mingling with the salt spray in a steady deluge of running water.

Ashley murmured, "Christ! We're not going to see very much at this rate."

"No, but it may not last. We've still got an hour before we need to start worrying about visibility."

"I just wish that, for once, we'd have a bit of luck. It would make a pleasant bloody change!"

It was 0140. There was no sign of Les Vaches. Although the seas were much lower here in the shadow of the land and the boat was riding the waves more easily, the weather was still foul. Every few minutes heavy showers obliterated the few precious yards of visibility, turning the already dark night into a wall of black.

Ashley, standing at the side of the bridge, tried to resist the temptation to call down to Tusker again, but failed. He reached for the voice pipe. "Tusker! Any ideas?"

"Give it five minutes, then we'll try turning east."

"Five minutes is a hell of a long time!" Ashley knew he was sounding testy but, damn it, he was.

"Yes, five minutes should get us right up to Les Vaches," came the calm response.

"I thought we were meant to be there already!"

"Well, allowing for losing some time in those seas . . ."

"Okay! Five minutes!"

He threw the pipe back into its socket and stared into the darkness. He had four men on the bridge now, all of them searching—for anything: any sign, any indication of rocks, land, E-boats, anything. A hundred miles they'd traveled, and now they were looking for two rocks in the middle of the sea. Ridiculous!

Nothing. Not even the customary smell of the land. Ashley thought: Tusker's finally blown it.

The rain stopped. Strange new shadows flickered across the pattern of the night. Ashley screwed up his eyes. It was almost impossible to know what you were seeing, but the visibility had definitely improved, no doubt about that.

"Sir! Port bow! I think I see something!"

They all turned, an electric silence filled the bridge.

"Yes, sir." It was the coxswain's voice, steady and firm. "Just fine on the port bow, sir. A rock, I would say."

Ashley saw it. A large rock. One of two. Les Vaches.

He breathed out slowly, his body sagging as the tension eased away. He called down the pipe, "Well done, Tusker. Your rock's popped up on the port bow."

Thank goodness it had. He always had a vision of getting the boat lost and steaming onto a barely submerged rock and tearing her guts out. He tried not to think of such things, but on bad nights one couldn't help it. . . .

Tusker took some bearings and they pressed on toward the land. Because the wind was offshore and would carry the sound of their engines away from the ears of German sentries, Richard decided to risk a fast approach. Time was ticking away. It was 0150.

At two miles they reduced speed to five knots, searching for familiar landmarks feeling their way in toward the anchorage. Finally they were on station, one mile offshore in the open arm of a wide, rocky bay, lying to their grass-rope anchor. It was 0215. Only one hour at the most.

The beach lay in a cove in the western arc of the bay, its sides guarded by a myriad of small rocks. The surfboat was already in the water, the two-man crew waiting at their oars, which were muffled with heavy sacking.

Ashley jumped down and sat in the stern, a compass in his hand and the wireless on the seat beside him. At his feet was their new gadget, a hydrophone, which, when its sensor was dropped in the water, would pick up the sound of *309*'s echo sounder and guide them back to her. They would need it tonight.

The surfboat buffeted her way through the waves, the water hissing and slapping at her sides. Already the MGB was a shadow in the deeper darkness behind them.

Ashley looked at his watch. 0222.

He couldn't help thinking that for once they really were cutting it a bit fine.

The clock ticked loudly on the mantelpiece, syncopating with the gentle snores of Tante Marie, asleep in the chair on the opposite side of the hearth.

A book lay open but unread on Julie's lap as she listened to the sounds of the night. A wind was blowing, quite a strong one, rattling the windows and moaning softly around the buildings; and there was rain, coming in sudden squalls, drumming loudly on the outhouse roof, pitpatting against the glass.

She listened and almost imagined she heard the rumbling of the surf down in the cove and the scrunch of boats as they

grounded on the pebbles. Almost imagined too that she heard the sound of footsteps as the guides led the passengers past the farmhouse down to the beach . . .

Julie returned to her book. Always imagining things.

But she stared at the pages, unseeing, and thought of the waiting men and the steep path to the beach and the dark cove. She hadn't been back since that night four months ago. In one way she was sorry—she'd rather enjoyed it— but she was determined not to get involved too deeply. Her instincts still told her that it would all go wrong, that sooner or later it would end in disaster. And she couldn't bear the thought of being caught. Nothing could be worth that.

At the same time she couldn't help worrying. Especially to-night.

The night had a bad aura about it, an indefinable atmosphere of doom. She couldn't say why, or in what way. At ten she had gone to bed and tried to sleep, but her sense of despair had been so strong that she had come down to sit with Tante Marie. Of course a man would laugh at the whole idea of *feeling* these things, but for her the danger was almost tangible.

Except that now, two hours later, she wasn't quite so certain as before. Perhaps nothing was going to happen after all. It might be worth trying to go back to sleep again.

It was comfortable there by the stove. She rested her head against the chairback and closed her eyes. She'd make the effort to go to bed in a moment.

Suddenly she stiffened.

There was a slight unidentifiable sound, something that hadn't been there before . . .

Dousing the small oil lamp, she went to the door and opened it.

The wind was sighing and rustling around the farmyard, a cow shuffled restlessly in the barn, then . . . Yes, it was there! *Something* . . . Julie's blood ran cold.

But what was it! *What?*

Machines? Men?

Whatever—it was something that shouldn't be there.

She closed the door, lit a candle and took it to her room. She found warm clothes: woolen blouse, thick sweater, trousers, socks, sturdy shoes. In the kitchen she removed a waterproof

cowman's jacket from the back of the door and Jean's beret, pulling it low over her head and tucking her hair up inside the crown.

She touched Tante Marie's arm. The old woman woke with a start and exclaimed, "Where are you going? What's the matter?"

"Don't worry! I have to get out, that's all. Just to listen . . . and watch for them."

"Don't go!" Tante Marie hissed. "You don't know where the patrols are! You might stumble into one of them. Don't go, I tell you!"

Julie shook her head. "I'll be careful. . . . I just want to see that everything's all right. That's all. Don't worry." Waving briefly to the old woman, she stepped out into the night. She waited a moment to get her eyes accustomed to the darkness, then walked quietly around the side of the house to the road.

She paused and listened. Whatever that sound had been, it had gone. There was nothing now, only the rustling of the trees and the sigh of the wind.

But still, she had to go. She set off rapidly along the road, her shoes making no sound on the hard surface. After five minutes she was almost halfway up the hill that led to the open heathland. She walked steadily, her hands deep in her pockets, her mind on the necessity of reading the clifftop. Once more she would wait and listen until she knew everyone was all right.

She stopped dead. There was that sound again.

It was a low whining, far off, back toward the village.

It was like the whining she'd heard in her imagination once: the whining of trucks. *Trucks climbing.*

Up the hill toward her.

She froze, still listening, unbelieving . . .

. . . the sound of trucks climbing. *Oh God!*

Then she ran, she ran fast and straight; she ran along the dark narrow lane, up and up, on and on, until the air rasped in her throat and the heavy shoes were like lead on her feet.

She ran with grim determination, absolutely certain that she must reach the clifftop: absolutely sure that she must get there before *them.*

She ran until her lungs were bursting. *Oh God, let me get there first!*

The heathland, at last. Gorse reached up and pulled at her

clothing; the uneven ground rose and fell unexpectedly, jarring her legs, throwing her off balance. She stumbled and picked herself up again, still running.

It was dark, very dark. She tried to get her bearings. It was a long cliff and there were several paths, all leading down. Only one path was the right one. She looked ahead, trying to read the contours of the land. It all looked the same!

She tripped and fell, putting out her hands too late. Her head hit the ground and for a moment she was dazed. Then she pulled herself up and staggered forward again.

At last she saw something paler ahead. The wide expanse of the sea. Bordering it was the dark rim of the clifftop. Sobbing with relief she looked wildly right and left. Which way?

Right. Yes: right.

She ran, looking desperately for familiar landmarks.

She saw a hillock, and a hollow. . . . She was there. At the path.

She stopped, panting wildly. There was nobody. She called softly. Nobody. Perhaps the lookout was farther along the cliff.

She hesitated, then set off, down the steep path toward the rumble of the surf. This time she took the path much faster, half falling, half running, scrabbling at the loose stone hill for handholds. A rock flew up and hit her chin and her teeth closed with a sharp snap. The warm, unfamiliar taste of blood filled her mouth.

The ground fell away: she had reached the slide at the bottom. She thought of jumping, but it was at least six feet and she was too tired. Wearily, she sat down and slid. The beach rushed up, she braced her legs. They gave way under her and she landed heavily on her side.

Slowly she got to her feet. She was so tired she'd almost forgotten why she had come. She called softly. Nothing. Where were they? She thought: Oh God! Please let them be here.

The finger of rock was deserted. Down to the water then.

Suddenly, close by, a voice. Julie jumped and gave an involuntary cry. The voice repeated: "St.-Brieuc!" It must be a password and she didn't know the response.

She was shaking violently. She cried, "It's me, Julie Lescaux. I don't know the password. Please—I've come to warn you . . . ."

* * *

"We can't go now! The surfboat's already on its way!"

There was a short silence, the men huddled in a nervous group, their faces hidden in the darkness. Then everyone spoke simultaneously, one voice emerging high above the rest. Julie recognized it: it was the leader. "We must go! We must abandon the mission!" His voice was shrill, anguished.

Again, there were many voices. Julie realized with a shock that one of them was Jean's. Then there was a lone voice, a strong voice, someone who commanded, "Stop!" And there was silence again. The strong voice went on, "Those who want to go, go! The rest of us stay and get our passengers away." There were mutterings of agreement, then the leader was speaking again, his voice louder, shriller. "It's madness to stay! We must go!" The strong voice said, "Go then!" Julie realized it was the voice of the man who'd sat next to her by the rock, that first time, a man she'd later realized to be a fisherman from a small cove in the next bay: a man called Gérard.

Now Gérard came close to her, saying, "Here, Julie, the wireless! Try to make contact with them! Warn them!"

The hard oblong box was thrust into her hand. Julie grasped it. She moved unsteadily away and sat on a rock, trying to remember how the machine worked. Her body was still shaking with exhaustion and she fumbled clumsily with the knobs. She tried the on/off button, but the surf was roaring and the wind whistling so loudly that she could hear nothing. She put the receiver part to her ear: a faint crackling. Now the aerial. She pulled it up, found the transmitting button and pressed it. She called, "Hello." But there was no reply. She tried again: still nothing.

She thought: I'm doing something wrong.

Remembering that there were two different frequencies, she found a sliding switch and pushed it the other way. She called again, "Hello."

The wireless crackled and, above the rumble of the surf, a tinny voice said, "Bertie here. Please identify. Over."

She knew that she was meant to say something: a password. But it was no good, she couldn't remember it. She pressed the transmitter and said, "Beach here." Now what? Information. She said hastily, "You may be in danger. The Germans are searching the cliffs."

The wireless crackled, "Understood. But our party's arrived, hasn't it? Over."

Julie was confused until she realized she was talking to the ship, not the boat. She looked along the beach. Yes, something was happening. The men had gathered at the water's edge and a shape was showing dark against the whiteness of the breaking waves: the surfboat.

She pressed the transmitter. "They're here. We'll get them off again as soon as possible." She left her finger on the button but could think of nothing else to add.

When she let go, the man on the ship was already speaking: ". . . short message when they leave. Out."

Julie debated whether to reply, but "Out" probably meant that the man had signed off. She'd understood what he meant: they wanted to know when the surfboat left. Best not to talk again and confuse matters. She switched off the wireless and walked along the edge of the water toward the surfboat.

It was very windy: she had to lean her body forward against it. The surf was very loud, too, and it was impossible to hear anything above the thunderous roar of the surf.

As she approached the boat, the men were dragging things out of it and removing the oars from the rowlocks. She saw that one of the oars was broken. Most of the men went to one side of the boat and, with a heave, tipped it over. Water poured out and Julie realized it must have been half full.

The firm voice of Gérard was at her elbow again. "Julie! Come!" His tone was urgent, authoritative. He led her past the men to a figure who stood slightly apart from the rest.

Gérard pulled her in front of the figure and said, "Please explain that the Germans are near!"

Julie realized it was one of the British crew. She said in English, "We think the Germans are about! Searching the clifftop. They may know you're here. You must get away quickly, straightaway!"

The figure stepped closer and a strong hand gripped her arm. "Tell him, it's not just the oar that's broken—there's a hole in the boat too! We've got to find something to stuff in it, and quick!"

She translated and turned back, saying, "Yes, he understands."

The hand was still on her arm. "And tell him we can only take six passengers. It's too rough out there to risk any more."

294

Again, Julie translated. The British officer said, "Right! Let's get going!" The men were already at work: tearing a wool jacket in half to make a bung, sorting out passengers, cutting cord to whip together the two pieces of broken oar.

So little time. Julie waited anxiously, willing them to finish.

From somewhere up the beach there was an exclamation. Something about the shout made everyone stop and look up. A man was running frantically toward them, hissing, "A light . . . a signal!"

Julie looked up at the cliff and felt a thud of fear.

A dim red light, blinking through the darkness.

A warning. Blood red.

For a second there was silence, then Gérard's voice floated over the thundering surf. "The boat! We must hide the boat! In the rocks on the point. Quick!" Everyone leaped into action, hauling on the boat, dragging it along the beach.

The British officer ran up to her. "What the hell . . . ?"

"The Germans! They're coming!"

"Christ!" He shouted, "Jenkins! Turner! Pick up your weapons! Get the boat hidden, then follow these men!"

The boat was halfway up the beach now. Julie ran as fast as she could over the slippery pebbles, following the rapidly moving shadows of the men as they fled toward the rocks.

By the time she reached the point, the men had hidden the boat behind a large rock and were covering it with seaweed. As soon as the boat was camouflaged, they ran toward the jumble of rocks and boulders tumbling down from the headland above and slid quietly into the shadows of the crevices.

Panic rose in Julie's throat. Where was Jean? And Gérard? She scrambled closer to the rocks, searching desperately. Then Jean was beside her, taking her arm, guiding her.

She cried, "Oh Jean!"

"Julie, it'll be all right. All we have to do is keep quiet! Now, go in here! In here!" He pushed her into a crevice between two tall rocks. She settled herself on the stones and then realized Jean hadn't followed her. Where *was* he?

All around her there were clicking noises: the men were checking their weapons. *Where* was Jean?

Suddenly he was back, pushing another figure toward her. It

was the British officer. She hissed, "Jean! Jean! Where are you going?"

"I'll just be next door! Next rock!"

The officer had crawled in beside her and was tugging gently at the strap on her shoulder. She'd forgotten about the wireless.

"Sorry," he whispered. "But I must contact my boat. Our own set got wet."

"Of course." She felt a fool for having panicked. She passed over the wireless and listened as he clicked the switches. There was a hum and he said, "Bertie, Bertie, this is Alfie calling. Over."

Silence. Then he tried again. Still nothing. Julie felt guilty. She should have thought of calling the ship herself as she came along the beach. The wireless probably would have worked in the open. Stupid of her.

She started to say: "I'm sorry, I . . ."

But he said, "Shush!" and she bit her lip.

After another two minutes he called into the wireless again. Still nothing. She heard the click of switches and realized he was putting the set down on the ground. He said very quietly, "I think that perhaps it just isn't my day."

Then he leaned closer to her and whispered, "Sorry, I didn't mean to shut you up just then, but I thought I heard something . . ."

"That's all right."

"You've been a great help. Thank you."

Julie nodded briefly in the darkness, then turned her head to listen for sounds from the beach. She strained her ears but it was impossible to hear anything over the rumbling of the surf. Suddenly there was a scraping noise; the officer was moving forward, his figure a silhouette against the paler black of the sky, a weapon just visible in his hand.

Tentatively Julie followed until she too could see down to the impenetrable darkness of the beach.

A lot of time passed. Half an hour, maybe more. And still there was nothing.

Perhaps they were going to be safe after all.

She sensed the officer stiffen. He got up on one knee, then rose and walked forward until he was standing just clear of the rocks.

Then she heard a sound: the sound of an engine. Not a truck, not from the cliff. Something more familiar. Julie tried to place

it. It was the sound of an engine over water, like a fishing boat's but deeper, throatier . . .

She heard the Englishman say, "Christ All-bloody-mighty!" Then he turned and crawled slowly back in beside her. She thought she heard him laugh; she must have misheard. But no, there it was again: he was laughing harshly.

She whispered, "What is it?"

He said bitterly, "I think I've just missed my bloody boat!"

Ashley opened his eyes and frowned. Hanging from the ceiling above him was a model airplane made of cardboard and paper. On the walls there were a couple of bright paintings—one of a tractor, the other of a car—and two posters of Paris. A child's room. A small child at that: his feet were protruding from the end of a totally inadequate bed. It was the coldness of his toes which had awakened him.

He looked at his watch: nine-thirty. He must have been asleep for three hours.

They had waited in the rocks until five, when a lookout had come to tell them that the Germans had gone. The Bretons had had a short conference to decide who was going to take charge of the airmen, and who Ashley and his crew. He tried to understand what was being decided, but the men whispered in Breton, or, once or twice, in heavily accented French, and he couldn't make out what they were saying. Then he'd searched for the girl and asked her and she had told him that his men were to be hidden in a safe house—she wouldn't tell him where—and he in another. He asked if he couldn't be hidden with them, and she'd said no, there wasn't room. She was quite abrupt.

"Well," he said, "just tell me who to follow."

"Me. You're to be hidden in my house."

He tried to see her face in the darkness. "How very kind . . ."

"Hardly! There's nowhere else, that's all."

She was cross, he could tell, though he couldn't guess why. Best not to say any more then. He'd followed her without a word, up a steep path to the top of the cliff and across some heathland to a road. She'd started off at a cracking pace, but soon slowed and at one point she almost fell. He'd reached for her arm but, politely but firmly, she'd pulled away.

When they arrived at the back door of the house she told him

to wait outside. Within a minute she returned, leading him into a warm room, very dark: a kitchen he guessed. Again he waited while she disappeared into a back room. This time it was several minutes before she reappeared. She guided him through a door and up some narrow steep stairs to an attic—this attic.

All she'd said was "Don't make a sound and don't put your face to the window! Oh, and your clothes, they're wet, I suppose? Leave them at the top of the stairs." And then she was gone.

Two thoughts had entered his mind before he fell asleep: the first, that someone had just been asleep in this bed, it was so warm, and the second, that the cross, English-speaking lady was not very pleased to have him here, not very pleased at all.

Now, in the morning light that filtered through the one small window, he pulled his feet in out of the cold. He might as well go back to sleep: he wasn't going anywhere—certainly not without any clothes.

Suddenly he was wide awake. A door had closed in the room immediately below. Someone was climbing the stairs. He reached down to the floor and, picking up his gun, pointed it toward the top of the stairwell.

A head appeared, with dark, longish hair. The girl.

He relaxed and put the gun back on the floor.

She was carrying some bread and a mug of hot liquid, her head bent, intent on preventing the liquid from spilling. She came up to the bed and, crouching, placed the mug on the floor. The bread was more difficult: she thought of balancing it on top of the mug, but put it on the bed instead. Then she looked up at him.

He stared at her in astonishment.

He realized with a shock that he knew her.

But where on earth from? He examined her face for clues: dark eyes—tired today, with gray shadows under them—neat features, a lovely mouth and fabulous clear pale skin. Very attractive—lovely even. But *where* had he met her?

He realized he was staring: she had looked away, embarrassed, and had started to speak. ". . . We've found some clothes for you. I'll bring them up directly. It's best not to wear your other ones —they look far too Navy if you're seen. And you *must* take care not to be seen—we have soldiers billeted here."

Ashley blinked in astonishment. "What?"

"Yes, two of them. They sleep in the main part of the house, at the front. They're up at six-thirty, out by seven and back at about eight in the evening. For a meal. Then they usually go out for a drink—until about ten."

Ashley raised his eyebrows. "It's a bit close for comfort, I must say . . ."

"On the other hand," the girl said, "they wouldn't think of looking for anyone in the same house, would they? You're probably safer here than somewhere more isolated."

"Yes, I hadn't thought of that." He regarded her with new admiration.

"Just as long as you're *not* seen." She was looking at him sternly. "I'm afraid that means not going out. And no noise, either. It's vital. You do understand that, don't you?"

He sat up in bed. "I understand that very well—I understand the risk you're running. And I'm grateful, believe me."

"Fine, well, as long as you obey the rules there'll be no problems." She was so schoolmarmish that Ashley couldn't help hiding a smile. She saw his amusement and flushed.

"Right," she said tightly, getting to her feet. "I'll find you some clothes then." She brushed at her skirt with agitation.

He could see he had annoyed her. He said hurriedly, "Thank you. And I'm really most sorry for the trouble I've caused."

She hesitated, searching his face. "Don't mind me. It's been a long night and—they arrested some people."

Ashley said, "I'm so sorry."

She went on, "Three people, two local and one from—elsewhere. It could have been worse, of course. We're thankful there weren't more."

"Did these people know about the beach, about our visits . . . ?"

"Oh yes."

"So—" He didn't know how to put it. "So the Germans might extract the information from them."

"It's possible."

"Then . . . that beach might be risky. Well," he said brightly, "there must be other beaches near here! We'll arrange a pickup as soon as possible and get ourselves off your hands!"

"There's only one problem. One of the men arrested was the leader—he was the one with access to the wireless operator,

somewhere near Paris. It'll take time to set up another link, particularly if the wireless operator has to go into hiding, or gets caught. . . ."

Ashley sighed heavily. All he wanted was to get back to his boat; he hated to think of the old tub being commanded by anyone else, even if it was Jimmy Macleod. He hated too the prospect of not being able to move around, of being a virtual prisoner. He looked around the room with dismay: he didn't like the idea of being cooped up here for any length of time. What the hell was he going to do all day?

The girl had come closer. She said softly, "I'm sorry. It's going to be rotten for you, stuck up here. But I'll bring you some books —some English books. And I've got a cribbage board—" She shrugged. "If you play, of course."

He looked at her and grinned. "Under the circumstances, I'll be glad of anything, anything at all!"

She smiled back and he thought how lovely she looked when she was happy.

Then, suddenly, he had it. Where he'd seen her before. Plymouth! He'd met her in Plymouth—the girl who'd come sailing with him that day! How extraordinary!

She was turning to leave.

"Wait a minute!" he exclaimed. "D'you realize we've met before?"

Julie's heart sank. She'd known, from the moment she'd looked into his eyes, that she had met him before. It had taken her some minutes to fix the exact time and place. But she'd remembered it all: the sunny afternoon, the boat, the sail around the harbor.

And now her heart sank because she wanted it forgotten and he had remembered.

She said lightly, "Oh yes?"

"Absolutely! You came sailing with me. Around Plymouth Sound."

She inclined her head. "Oh really?"

"Yes." He looked surprised that she didn't remember. "In *Dancer*—my twenty-five-footer . . . don't you remember?" He put on a half-hurt, half-amused expression.

She nodded, as if it had just come back to her. "Oh yes. I think I remember now. It was such a long time ago . . ."

"Yes, I suppose it was." He laughed. "But what are you doing, living here?"

"My family—they live here. My uncle and aunt."

"And the child, is that yours?"

Julie hesitated. She didn't want him to know anything about Peter, nothing at all. She said abruptly, "Yes."

"How old is he—or is it a she?"

Julie went cold. Now the questions—next the mathematics. It wouldn't take him long to work it out. She thought quickly and decided it might be all right if she took a few months off. "Five. His name is Pierre. He's at school." She wasn't lying about his name: ever since the occupation she'd made sure he was known by the French version of his name.

"Well, I look forward to meeting him, if only to tell him I'm very sorry for pinching his bed. He wasn't too put out, I hope?"

"No."

"Still, it must have been rotten going into a cold bed." She saw that he was about to ask another question and, indicating the mug on the floor, she said quickly, "Your coffee's getting cold."

He exclaimed, "Oh!" and beat his hand against his head in an exaggerated gesture of stupidity. His eyes twinkling, he said, "I promise to be a better guest in the future!"

She smiled faintly and turned to go down the stairs.

He called softly, "And your husband? Is he here?"

She paused at the first stair. "No, there's no husband."

"Oh! I'm sorry. I—"

Julie immediately wished she hadn't said it. He would think she had a husband who had been killed in the fighting. But to explain further would be a mistake. Instead she murmured, "I'll go and get those clothes then."

"Thanks. And one more thing!"

"Yes."

"I'm sorry," he said apologetically, "but I've forgotten your name."

"Julie." Immediately she realized that this too had been a mistake. The less he knew about her the better, in case he was caught. She decided she was hopeless at all this intrigue.

He was smiling. "Of course. Julie. What a lovely name. I remember it now. You've probably forgotten my name too. After

all, why *should* you remember it! Anyway it's Richard. Richard Ashley."

"Yes, I remember now." She started down the stairs.

"Oh, and Julie." His voice was very soft.

A strange feeling rose in her throat. It was the way he had spoken her name: so familiar, even intimate. She swallowed. "Yes?"

"I *will* try to be good. But I'm not used to being cooped up. And not knowing what's happened to my ship doesn't help. For all I know they might have met an E-boat on the way out. . . . Look —if I get impossible or moan or gripe too much, just tell me I'm being tiresome, will you? Honestly!"

She couldn't help smiling. "Yes." She laughed. "I'll tell you."

"Thanks! And," he added solemnly, "for my part I promise to obey the rules. To the letter, ma'am." He touched his forehead in a mock salute and then smiled, just a little sheepishly, an apologetic expression on his face.

He was making fun of her, she knew. But it was impossible to take offense: he had done it so amiably. And his eyes—they were so nice and friendly. She couldn't be angry with him.

Instead she smiled at him and ran quickly down the stairs.

18

You could tell Americans anywhere, Vasson decided. They looked different in every way. Their coloring— often blue-eyed and fair-haired, rather like the Germans themselves; the height—many of them were well over six feet tall; and, most of all, the well-fed look. Somehow people who ate lots of meat looked different from those who ate bread and starch: in fact, they resembled the fat cattle they ate. They sat differently too, lounging on the train seats instead of sitting upright as the Europeans did. Some even had bright yellow nicotine stains on

their fingers: something you never got from French and Belgian cigarettes. Only because the Germans were so blind to anything but pieces of paper could these obviously alien creatures travel on the trains at all.

There were six of them, sitting in different places around the open carriage. All were airmen who'd been forced to parachute out over Belgium and been found by "friends."

They were going to Paris, where they would be transferred to a southbound train. Vasson was their courier. Eventually they would be led over the Pyrenees into Spain.

Or so they thought. Vasson viewed them with contempt: they were so naive, these people. They had no idea at all.

There was also a seventh man. The Americans thought he was Czech and a pilot in the RAF. They were almost right about the first bit—in fact, he came from the Czech-German border. But they were quite wrong about the second. The man did not work for the RAF, he worked for Vasson. And he was going to tell Vasson every detail about the escape line, every courier and safe house all the way down to Spain.

It was a lot to ask of one man, but Vasson had spent four weeks briefing him. He had also arranged for his wife and child to be placed under arrest, just in case.

One of the flyers—a young, fresh-faced boy with an awful American haircut—winked at Vasson. The boy had been a problem ever since Brussels, when Vasson had taken the group over. The boy had started chewing gum, quite oblivious to the stares of the other passengers. Then he'd started to whisper in English to his friend. Vasson had had to separate them.

Now, under Vasson's cold stare, the boy dropped his eyes and looked out of the window. There were no more winks.

They were approaching the Gare du Nord. Almost home. Vasson missed Paris very much; Brussels was dull by comparison. This was his fifth run to Paris, but he could never stay for any length of time, and this visit would be the shortest yet. After seeing Kloffer he would catch the next train back. But for once he didn't mind too much: Brussels promised a great deal of excitement over the next two days.

The train ground to a halt. The airmen got to their feet, their eyes on Vasson.

303

Vasson joined the throng of people leaving the train and strolled down the platform toward the barrier. He could feel the others following him. At the barrier two French policemen were checking papers and two *Feldgendarmen* were examining people's faces. Vasson knew they would get through all right: he'd arranged it with Kloffer.

The gendarme looked at Vasson's papers and pushed them quickly back into his hand. Yes: he'd been briefed all right.

Vasson wandered slowly into the main concourse and glanced casually behind him. All the airmen were through the barrier.

He waited until they had found him, then walked out of the station into the Rue de Dunkerque.

Only two people were at the bus stop. Vasson stood behind them. The airmen followed suit. Vasson moved closer to the Americans' leader and muttered, "I'm off now. Wait for a girl wearing a purple hat. Bye."

Vasson went through his pantomime of looking at his watch, glancing up the street for a bus and then, after shaking his head, moving away. The other Americans peered around uncertainly, wondering whether they should follow Vasson, but, seeing that their leader did not, settled down to wait.

Vasson walked back to the station, went into the booking hall and, very casually, turned back until he could watch the bus stop from the darkness of the doorway.

The next courier was meant to pick up the passengers—or parcels, as they insisted on calling them—in five minutes. In fact she arrived in eight.

It was the same girl as before: a dark, rather plain girl with a permanent frown. She was wearing the purple hat. She stood patiently behind the group until a bus, destination "République-Bastille," came along. Then she moved forward to the front of the line and got into the bus, the airmen behind her.

It was the classic cutout rendezvous. The two couriers never met and so were incapable of identifying each other. Doubtless the organizers were very proud of the method. After all, it worked very well—so long as everyone was on the same side.

As the bus drew away Vasson saw the Czech sitting in the back of the bus, staring calmly out of the window. He was going to be all right, that man. He'd deliver the goods.

But there was a backup, just in case. It was only good for the first part of the journey, but if the Czech failed it would be better than nothing. He'd asked Kloffer to provide a tail.

There hadn't been one at the bus stop, he was sure of that. Perhaps a car then. But there were no black Citroëns in sight. The only possibility was a battered old Peugeot which pulled out from the curb heading in the same direction as the bus. Perhaps that was it. If so, Kloffer was definitely improving.

The concourse was crowded, and it took Vasson some time to get across to the other side. The plain unmarked door was behind the men's lavatories, next to the railway security office. But he didn't go straight there. Instead he went into the lavatories, glancing behind him as he went. No one. He used the urinal and went out into the concourse again. This time he took a good look around. Still no one. He'd known there wouldn't be, but it was always best to make sure.

He strolled toward the unmarked door, made one last surveillance and slipped inside.

Kloffer was there, waiting.

Vasson sat down and said, "You've done as I suggested?"

"Yes, we have several tails on them. They'll be followed as far as possible."

"And the tails, they're not your usual gorillas, I trust?"

The appearance of Kloffer's men was an old bone of contention. The German said testily, "They will do their job well, don't worry."

Vasson said, "Good."

"And your man, will he do *his* job? It's a lot to ask of one man —and not one of *my* men at that."

"He's been properly briefed. As long as he can make contact all right, then nothing will go wrong."

"So!" Kloffer put his fingertips together. "That takes care of that then . . ."

"Yes." Vasson's only regret was that he wouldn't be in on all the arrests. He would have liked that.

Kloffer examined Vasson with his cold, hard eyes. "Now, the Brussels end. Are you sure you have it under control?"

"Oh yes. I'll give you the lot within three days."

"But the leader—have you identified him?"

"Finally."

"And—?"

"Tomorrow. You'll have him by tomorrow."

"After—when you've finished there—you'd better come back to Paris."

"That was what I intended."

Kloffer said deliberately, "But not for too long. And you must stay away from your old haunts. You're no use to me if you're dead." He smiled faintly. "And you would be dead—very quickly."

Vasson sighed. "You're just saying that, Kloffer, to keep me in order. I'm beginning not to believe you anymore."

"Ah . . . but there's only one way to find out. And that might be fatal for you, might it not? Besides," Kloffer went on carefully, "if you were dead you wouldn't be able to spend any of that money you're so carefully accumulating. That would be a pity, wouldn't it?"

Vasson suppressed his irritation. Kloffer thought he did it only for the money. He was a stupid man.

He decided that he couldn't be bothered to argue the point. Anyway perhaps Kloffer was right—better to be out of Paris and alive than shot in the back.

"Okay. So I don't stay in Paris. Where do I go?"

Kloffer said, "Ah! Where? Who knows? We'll see." He was obviously enjoying what he imagined to be his little moment of power. Vasson thought: Screw you.

Kloffer stood up and put on his hat. "But I promise you the job will be equally interesting and rewarding."

First the stick, then the carrot. Kloffer was so predictable.

Kloffer paused at the door. "Good-bye, and we look forward to some excellent results in Brussels."

"And I look forward to some excellent results in the money department, Kloffer."

"Don't be greedy. You earn enough."

"But am I paid what I'm worth? That's the question."

"You could be worth nothing. Remember that, Marseillais!"

Kloffer opened the door and chuckled to himself. "That's what I always call you, you know—the Marseillais!" He watched Vasson's face, then, smiling still, went out.

The door closed and Vasson clenched his fists. He took a long, deep breath to calm himself.

The bastard must have taken his thumbprint and had it sent around to every police station in the country. It was the only way he could have found out.

He hated Kloffer for knowing.

One day he'd get him. One day.

He looked at the time. There was a train for Brussels in ten minutes.

As he walked angrily across the station he thought about the Brussels job. He saw the faces of the smug intellectuals running the operation, and imagined their expressions when they realized they'd been betrayed. It was the only thing that consoled him.

The train was late arriving. Vasson decided to go straight to the Café Mirabeau for dinner. The journey had made him hungry. Also, Anne-Marie would be waiting for him, and she would tell him the news. Or rather the lack of news. Even if there had been some early arrests south of Paris, no one in Brussels could possibly have heard yet.

Anne-Marie. He'd be glad to be rid of her. She'd become a bore. When he'd first met her, she'd been rather sweet and he had enjoyed winning her over. It had taken time, of course; she'd been very cautious. She'd only just been released by Mueller and she was suspicious of everything. But he'd been patient, and in the end she had come to trust him completely, just as he knew she would. When she'd introduced him to her friends they'd given him simple jobs at first: running messages and errands, that kind of thing. At last had come the courier's job: the real test. After that he was home and dry.

Anne-Marie. The trouble had started when she'd tricked him, that terrible evening. He'd quite liked her until then. He'd even imagined what it would be like to touch her, naked, and to hold her down, tight. . . .

Then she spoiled it all. She tricked him by saying she loved him and that she just wanted to put her arms around him. *It was all her fault.* She'd flaunted herself, showing her knees, having those large breasts, smelling of sex. He'd found himself feeling her body and then she was naked and instead of staying still she *kept*

moving—putting her arms around him, trying to kiss him on the lips. It had revolted him. In the end he'd put his arm across her neck and stopped her moving until he'd finished.

After that, he could hardly bear to look at her, particularly when she stared at him with those large reproachful eyes. Why couldn't she have left him alone.

But he still had to make the effort to see her; otherwise all his work would be for nothing.

But just for one more day. That was all. He must remember that. He gritted his teeth and went into the café.

The bitch was there, sitting in a corner. She looked worried: she was probably going to be difficult.

As soon as he sat down she said, "Everything all right?"

"I think so."

"Not sure?"

"I don't know. I always think I see shadows . . . you know." It was important to sow a slight seed of doubt, just in case news of the Paris arrests reached Brussels before he'd finished the job.

She touched his hand, and it was all he could do not to snatch it away. "Are *you* all right?"

"Sure. Why shouldn't I be?"

"It was just . . . you've been so . . . withdrawn and . . . well, cold," she finished painfully.

"Oh? Well, it doesn't mean anything."

She brightened a little and he realized crossly that she had misinterpreted his words.

She said, "Oh, I'm so pleased. I thought—well, quite honestly I didn't know what to think. After . . . you know. I've been very confused."

"I've just been feeling the strain, that's all."

"But—you seemed so angry! It's been torturing me. What did I do wrong? Why were you so cross? And—why, oh *why*, Paul, did you hurt me?"

He sighed impatiently. "Did I?"

"Yes." She spoke angrily, reproachfully.

"Let's just forget it, eh? You're really blowing things up out of proportion."

She gave him an agonized look. "Oh dear, I really don't know what to think."

Vasson thought: Christ, she's going to go on and on unless I shut her up. He breathed deeply and said, "Look, dear, I'm truly sorry for what happened. I was upset, you see. I had a girl once —I've never told you this before—but . . ." He made a face as if the memory gave him terrible pain. ". . . She died. And whenever . . . well, whenever . . . I remember her I want to die too!" He looked away as if the thought were too much to bear. He couldn't help thinking what a good performance he was giving.

She said, "I had no idea . . ."

She was buying it. Good. Time to ease off the subject. "Even now, I'd rather not talk about it. All right?"

She still looked unhappy, but nodded gently.

He said quickly, "How are things here, then? Quiet?"

"Yes."

He looked pleased—he *was* pleased. Then he put on a frown. "There are a couple of things I'm a bit worried about—to do with security. I'd like to discuss them with Guy. Can you arrange a meeting?"

"But—does it have to be Guy himself?"

"Yes, it does." Of course it had to be Guy: he was the most important one of all. "And Patrice too. Any chance of our getting together tomorrow morning at about eleven?"

"I don't know . . . it's a bit unusual. They don't like too many of us to meet at once. They'll want to know *why.*"

He was so irritated with her he could shake her by the throat. Instead, he said calmly, "I'm really worried and it's important that I talk things over with them. Can't they take my word for it? I have to have that meeting."

She blinked. "All right. I'll try."

"Good." He got up to leave.

She anxiously said, "Where are you going?"

"Mmm? Oh, home, I expect."

"Don't you want to eat?"

The answer was yes but he didn't want to eat with her. It would spoil his appetite. He answered, "No, I'm going straight to bed. I'll see you in the morning. You will arrange that meeting, won't you? It's important."

He realized she still wasn't convinced. Better make sure. He put his hands on the table. "Look, after tomorrow, perhaps, we'll go

out for the day. Into the country. Would you like that? It would be nice to relax a little. I have been feeling the strain, I can see that. Shall we do that?"

Her face was a mixture of relief and uncertainty. "Yes. That would be nice."

He forced himself to smile before turning hurriedly away. Anything to keep the bitch happy. Anything to keep her quiet until after tomorrow. God! The things he had to do.

It was a spectacular morning, the light as bright and clear as glass. Though it was still winter the weather was just warm enough to sit at a pavement table without feeling the cold. Vasson turned his face to the sun and thought that he'd never felt as good as he did today.

He ordered a second pastis. Only five minutes to go. His pulse quickened and he felt a delicious sense of anticipation.

It was almost the best part, the anticipation.

Anne-Marie was the first. She walked along the pavement toward him, her head down, her expression serious. She always looked serious. Well, today she really had something to worry about! The thought amused him and he had to lower his head to hide a smile.

She saw him and, giving a slight wave, weaved her way through the tables toward him.

As she sat down he asked, "Everything fixed?"

She nodded.

He smiled brilliantly. "Excellent! Now what would you like to drink? Pernod? Coffee? Yes? Then coffee it shall be!"

She was trying to gauge his mood. She said, "You're very happy today."

"Yes! Something's happened!"

"What?"

He held up his hand. "All in good time! All in good time!"

She smiled thinly, but her eyes were serious, questioning. She was a bit wary, he decided. Nothing to worry about though.

Stupid bitch. He smiled at her. "It's such a beautiful day, isn't it?"

"Yes." She looked around nervously.

"What's the matter?"

310

"Oh, nothing. I'm just a bit jumpy. I don't know why."

Vasson eyed her sharply and wondered if she'd guessed something after all. She couldn't see Mueller and his men, of course: they were well hidden in a florist's shop across the street. And Vasson himself had given nothing away. He decided, finally, that she was just the nervous type.

Patrice, the number two in the organization, was next. He was a doctor, one of those who worked with the poor and the needy. His halo was so bright it was almost dazzling. Vasson watched him approach with satisfaction. Two down and one to go.

The doctor drew up a chair. Vasson said smoothly, "My dear fellow, a glass of something? A Pernod?"

The doctor said, "No, thank you so much. Just a coffee."

"But I want us to have a drink together!"

The doctor and Anne-Marie exchanged glances. Vasson realized he was pushing it. He said quickly, "We hardly ever see each other and it's good to drink with one's friends."

"Another time, perhaps."

At last the leader, Guy, came. Vasson spotted him while he was still some distance away on the other side of the street. The man walked casually but with infinite caution, missing nothing. A wily man—a worthy opponent.

The leader arrived at the table and, taking a last look around, sat down.

Vasson beamed at him. "Now I hope I have a customer for a drink! How about it? A pastis? A cognac?"

Guy said quietly, "No, let's have a drink after we have discussed our business. What, exactly, have you to tell us?"

A cool one, Vasson thought, a cool one. "Ah!" He raised a finger. "Good news, very good news."

"But I thought there was something worrying you?"

"*Yes,* there is that too." Vasson tried to appear suitably serious. "But to be precise it's something that should be worrying *you.*"

A nice little joke, that.

Out of the corner of his eye Vasson saw Mueller and his men coming out of the florist's shop.

A look of concern had come into Guy's eyes and he said, "What exactly is the problem? Spit it out!"

"The problem is that the Boches are onto you!"

The three of them froze, their eyes fastened on Vasson, waiting for him to go on. Vasson raised his eyebrows and shrugged mysteriously.

They exchanged glances, then stared back at Vasson, a mixture of uncertainty and cold horror growing on their faces.

Vasson looked past them to where Mueller and the men in black leather raincoats were making their way through the outer ring of tables.

The two men realized almost simultaneously. They jumped to their feet and looked desperately around them. Anne-Marie was still staring stupidly across the table.

The men saw the black leather raincoats and froze like animals gauging the wind. Vasson wondered if they would try to run for it. He hoped not: it would draw attention.

The men turned and exchanged glances, fear and terrible understanding written all over their faces. Vasson realized with satisfaction they were not going to run for it. Slowly, they sat down and stared at Vasson. The girl was sitting motionless, her mouth open.

Vasson said to the two men, "Right. Now if you just tell me where to find the courier Francine, we can be going."

There was silence.

"If you don't tell me your wives and children will be arrested within the hour."

"You bastard!" It was the girl. The dull look had gone and her eyes were blazing. "You bastard! You filthy swine! You—!" She screamed and, picking up an ashtray, raised it above her head. Before she could throw it one of Mueller's men swung at her. There was a *Crack!* as his leather-gloved hand hit her cheekbone. The ashtray fell to the ground.

Shaking with anger, Vasson leaned forward in his chair. "That'll teach you, you bitch. Next time we'll beat your face into pulp!"

Vasson took a deep breath. "Where do I find the courier Francine?"

The men were looking away, their expressions grim. Only the girl was staring at him.

They weren't going to talk. It didn't matter; he could send a false message to the courier and lure her out that way. Vasson

312

said stiffly, "Very well. If you wish to sacrifice your families . . ."

The girl let out a cry of agony, her face a picture of hate and self-loathing.

One of Mueller's men yanked her out of her seat and took her away. She screamed as she was dragged across the pavement. Vasson wished she wouldn't make so much noise; people were staring.

Vasson said to Mueller, "And the others!"

As the doctor was pulled to his feet he turned toward Vasson and said quietly, "I feel very sorry for you. May God forgive you."

Vasson said, "Screw you too!"

He finished his drink and, at a signal from him, one of Mueller's men made a show of arresting him. Vasson pretended to struggle a little, then walked quietly across the street to the parked car.

In Room 900 of the War Office, Smithe-Webb of the French Section of MI9 was waiting.

There had been no news from Meteor for three days. Meteor, the largest of the escape lines, had two wireless operators. Neither had made contact.

The major had to remind himself that this in itself meant nothing; wireless operators often had trouble getting through.

But then there was the silence from the Spanish end of the line. No airmen had come over the border for four days.

The rumors had started arriving the previous day, from other escape lines and from agents of the Special Operations Executive.

The rumors hinted at a disaster in the Meteor Line.

All Smithe-Webb could do was to hope it wasn't true—and wait.

A phone call came at four that afternoon, from the Coding and Signals Section of MI9 headquarters at Beaconsfield, just outside London. The section had received a message from Xavier, one of the Meteor wireless operators. The message was perfectly routine, asking for arms and money to be dropped in three days' time; the code used was correct; and the "touch," the operator's unique and personally identifiable Morse style, was definitely Xavier's.

But something was missing, something which made Smithe-Webb's heart sink. One of the security checks had been left out.

One of the two intentional mistakes that operators were trained to put into their messages had been omitted.

That meant only one thing. Xavier was operating under German control.

Over the next three days more and more information filtered through and Smithe-Webb's worst fears were realized.

Meteor had been devastated. Over 150 arrests had been made: men and women, some in their seventies, others no more than eighteen.

It was a disaster.

When the news broke, the Head of MI9 shielded Room 900 from the worst of the flak which rained down from the Department's enemies in high places.

But there was only one thing Smithe-Webb cared about—finding out what had happened so that it could never, ever happen again.

The next day his prayers were answered. A long signal arrived from the British Consulate in Lisbon. A man claiming to be a member of the Meteor Line had reached Portugal by means of the Pyrenees and a Spanish jail. His code name was Pierre and he had operated in Brussels. Before escaping from the city, he had heard a whisper, passed from someone who had called up to the leader, Guy, in his prison cell. The whisper was that a traitor had caused the disaster, a man who called himself Lebrun.

A traitor from within.

Smithe-Webb sighed. It was the one thing that was impossible to guard against.

All he could do was to help them prevent it happening again.

He would press for money to train agents, agents who could be sent over to start new lines, people who, above all, would be skilled in *security*. . . .

He started planning straightaway. It would be a mistake to set up another large-scale Belgium–Spain route too soon; the aftermath of the Meteor disaster would linger for a long time.

Instead he would reinforce the existing, smaller *réseaux*, particularly those well away from Meteor, perhaps on the north coast of Brittany. The recent upset there had been no more than a temporary hiccup. Most of the line was still intact. So too were the MGBs, though minus Ashley and his crew.

Yes, Brittany it must be. A new organizer, a new security system, and a much larger operation.

The line would also need a new designation. He thought for a moment, then decided to use his mother's maiden name. He would call the new *réseau* the Sheldon Line.

19

Tante Marie took a last look into the front parlor, closed the door and nodded to Julie. Julie picked up a plate of fish stew from the stove, a knife and fork from the table, and carried them quickly into her bedroom.

Julie started to climb the narrow stairs. Whispers and a small chuckle floated down from the room above. Her eyes reached floor level and she saw the two heads bent over some fascinating object on the floor.

They heard her and looked up. Richard grinned. For a moment she met his gaze and smiled back. Then she directed her eyes toward her son. Peter acknowledged her arrival with a matter-of-fact glance and said in his high-pitched monotone, "Maman, look at this. It's nearly finished!"

Julie obediently inspected the rough model ship being carved on the floor and said, "It's lovely, darling. Really super!"

Richard got to his feet and reached for the plate. "Shall I relieve you of this? It looks too good to go cold." He was still smiling, but there was something else too: an inquiring, watchful look, as if he were trying to catch her out at some game they were playing.

She looked away and said to Peter, rather too quickly, "Come on! Bedtime, young man."

"But I'm not tired."

"That's as may be, but it's still bedtime."

"Oh no! We were just going to stick the funnel on, weren't we,

Richard?" He pronounced "Richard" in the French way, softly and with no *d,* just as Julie had taught him. She was terrified that he would blurt the name out at school.

Richard put on a stern face. "It can wait until tomorrow. Go on, *jeune homme.* Do as your mother says!"

Peter made a face, then obediently got up. Julie reached down to take his hand, but he said crossly, "No, I want to walk by myself!" Julie sighed. Such an independent little beast, her son, and hardly six. She rolled her eyes at Richard, and followed Peter's stamping feet down the stairs.

She knew the bedtime stories so well that she could read them automatically while she thought of other things. Up until three weeks ago, she had thought about the shopping and the mending and Peter's clothes. But now . . . now she thought about the evening ahead.

She was fascinated by Richard's view of the world. Certain things—like politics—he found amusing; something the French would never do. He said that anything so serious which was so badly managed had to be funny. She wasn't sure she agreed with him, but the way he talked made her laugh—most things he said made her laugh. But at other times he could be very serious, and those laughing eyes became as hard as stone, and she guessed he could be very determined when he chose to be. Particularly about things he cared about, like loyalty and integrity and duty. When he talked of things like that he reminded her of an earnest schoolboy—or perhaps a knight of old: chivalrous, honest and true.

And yet—even when serious he would add almost in the same breath something so irreverent that she would gasp. At first these remarks had taken her aback and—well, shocked her. Then she'd started to find them funny and it dawned on her that he said them for that very reason: to make her laugh.

He made her talk too, about herself and what she believed in and what she cared about. She wasn't used to having long discussions. The conversations in the farmhouse kitchen were inclined to be short, almost monosyllabic. At first she had difficulty expressing herself, but gradually the words had come more easily.

"Maman, a kiss!"

She leaned down and kissed the small round cheek. "Good night, darling. I'll try not to wake you when I come to bed."

"Night-night." He was already half-asleep.

Julie hurried to the mirror. She brushed her hair a couple of times and examined herself critically. She really didn't look bad at all, she decided. She was doing her hair a new way—with a side parting—and it suited her.

She went upstairs, happy and confident.

He was sitting on the bed, finishing his meal. When he saw her he put the plate down and said, "I'm putting on weight, you know. You'll have to stop feeding me like this!"

She sat down on the floor and smiled. "Well, it's not exactly Cordon Bleu—and I wouldn't inquire about the vegetables you had in that stew. But we do our best!"

"It's wonderful!"

And Julie had the feeling he wasn't referring to the food. She said quickly, "Do you want to play crib tonight? It's about time you played an honest game and beat me!"

"Are you suggesting I cheat?" he asked.

"Yes!" Julie laughed.

He looked horrified. "How did you guess?"

"Because I win so much."

"Ah! I can't argue with that logic! I promise never to cheat again. Guide's honor." Julie smiled because he didn't mean a word of it.

He looked at her more seriously and exclaimed, "No, *don't* let's play cribbage. Let's talk instead! Come on. . . ." He settled himself more comfortably. "I want to hear the story of your life."

She felt a stab of fear. She said quickly, "No. There's nothing to tell." There was an awkward pause. She looked for something else to say. "I heard about your crew, by the way. Did I tell you? They're fine, apparently, but still very restless. Do you want another message sent over to them?"

Ashley shook his head absently. "No. It'll wait a couple of days."

He was watching her carefully. She went on quickly, "But still no news from Paris, I'm afraid. There's been a big clampdown and the wireless operators have gone to ground. We haven't managed to get a message through."

He frowned. "This Paris thing—is it connected with what happened here?"

317

"No . . . they don't think so. Our—incident—happened before the troubles there. Our problem was the leader of our group. He just talked too much and the wrong people heard. . . ."

"But—will he have talked? To the Gestapo?"

"No . . . thank goodness, there's no possibility of that."

"Why?"

"Ah . . . he died, you see. On the way to St.-Brieuc, to Gestapo headquarters."

"Oh . . . he—" Richard searched her face. "He died immediately, did he?"

Julie thought: He's quick, he understands completely. She said quietly, "Yes . . . the Germans found him dead on arrival. But then he would have died anyway—"

Julie had been relieved to hear of the leader's death. It was amazing how hard and realistic you could be when it was your child and family who were at stake.

Julie shook her head. "But none of it need have happened. If we'd had our own people running it *their* way . . ."

"For what it's worth, I'll put in a word with the powers that be when I get back." He laughed. "*If* I get back!"

Julie said gently, "I'm sorry there's no news."

He leaned forward and touched her arm. "Don't worry on my behalf. To be honest, I'm enjoying it in some ways. I've done a lot of thinking—much more than in the whole of the last few years. And I'm getting a lot of satisfaction out of making this model with your young man. Then, of course . . ." he paused and stared at her meaningfully, ". . . it's really rather nice to be locked up with you."

Julie gave him a look of amused disbelief and said, "You're just saying that!" But secretly she was pleased.

He said quietly, "You very cleverly put me off just now, when I asked you about your life. But come on, Julie, don't be such a mystery woman. Tell me . . ."

Julie said softly, "No, I'm really not ready to talk about it yet. I'm sorry." She was tempted to explain but instead she fetched the upturned packing case they used for playing cards.

He gave a small laugh. "All right. Cribbage then."

He won the first game easily and Julie said, "There, you see! When you concentrate you can beat me every time!"

He let her win the next game and the next, then Julie looked at her watch and got to her feet. "Well, work tomorrow as usual. About time I turned in." She smoothed down her skirt and looked up with a smile. "Good night, then!"

She turned to go but he stood up and touched her arm. "Julie . . ." His voice was very soft. "I wish you'd tell me . . . you know what I mean." He held her by the arms and, moving closer, kissed her on the forehead, very gently, his lips barely brushing her skin. Then, for a single moment, he put his cheek against hers and Julie thought: I'm not going to survive this. He whispered into her hair, "Julie, I want you so much . . ."

Julie pulled away and without a word made quickly for the stairs.

"Julie—"

But she was hurrying down. As soon as she reached the bedroom she pulled off her skirt and top and quickly got into bed next to Peter.

She stared into the darkness for a long time, full of longings, wretched with misery.

She wanted him too, of course she did. She wanted him with all her heart.

But there could be no question of that. He wouldn't care for her if he knew the truth. He wouldn't respect her. The humiliation would be terrible.

She closed her eyes tightly, thinking that sometimes life could be very unfair.

Richard eyed her critically. "You look terrible!"

"Thanks!" Julie managed the ghost of a smile. She was feeling much better than she had first thing that morning. She'd awakened with a thundering headache that hadn't faded until the afternoon. Now, she was just feeling tired.

She put the plate on the packing case and looked at him nervously. She hadn't seen him since the night before. She breathed deeply and said, "If you don't mind, I think I'll go straight to bed tonight. I'm tired."

He got up slowly, a frown on his face, and took her hand. "Julie, if it's anything I said last night . . . if I offended you in any way . . . I'm terribly sorry . . ."

"No! Really." She gripped his hand. "No, I'm just tired, that's all."

"Well . . . if you're sure." He paused. "You promise that I didn't upset you . . . ?"

Julie said, "Honestly," and wished he would let go of her hand. She was embarrassed.

He said softly, "If I did upset you, Julie, I assure you it was the last thing I intended."

"I know that."

Very gently he released her hand and said breezily, "Well, how about a nightcap?"

"A nightcap?" she repeated dully.

"Yes, I did a bit of bartering with your uncle. He ended up with three cigarettes and I got a bottle of wine. Rather a good deal, don't you think? Though who for, I couldn't say!" He laughed and leaned down to pick up the bottle. "Look, why don't you have a quick glass. It'll do you good! And make you sleep! Come on, keep me company! Just for a minute."

Julie knew that if she didn't go to bed now she might stay all evening. She began, "I really would, except . . ." Then she smiled faintly and said, "All right."

He grinned at her: he was pleased.

She sat on the floor and accepted a glass. He was right about the wine: it did make her feel better. After a while she felt beautifully calm and almost content again. Richard told some stupid stories about a pet goat his family had once owned and she found herself laughing. It was as if nothing had changed . . .

Except that it had.

They talked about all the usual things and he looked at her with the same eyes, alive and sparkling with fun, but . . . it was all subtly different. The words from the previous night hung in the air.

She felt deliciously drowsy; she hardly ever drank wine. She said, "I really must get some sleep now."

"Of course." He leaned forward and helped her up. "But wait! Just for a second . . ."

He went to the candle and blew it out. She heard him move across the room and the next moment a square of light appeared where he had pulled the curtain back from the window. "Come and see!"

320

She stood beside him and stared out. It was a brilliantly clear night. Stars carpeted the sky, like silver on black velvet.

He said, "I used to sit on *Dancer* and watch the night sky for hours on end."

She said, "It *is* lovely."

"It's even better when you're sitting on deck. Then you can see everything, all the constellations."

They stared in silence.

He said pensively, "After the war I'll take *Dancer* cruising again, to all the old places."

"To the Scillies?"

He turned. "How did you know that?"

"Well—you must have told me."

"Not since I've been here. I wouldn't have." He was very definite. "You know, you must have remembered that from *before*. In Plymouth." He laughed softly. "And there you were, pretending you didn't even remember *me*! You quite hurt my feelings, you know!"

"Rubbish!" Julie said firmly. "It did you good, not to be remembered. Otherwise you'd have got a big head."

"But you *did* remember me, didn't you?"

Eventually she said, "Yes, but I couldn't remember exactly where it was that I'd met you."

"Well, I knew! I enjoyed that day we spent together, and I was disappointed when you announced—right at the last moment— that you were about to go away!"

He touched her shoulder and, sitting on the bed, waited for her to sit down beside him in the darkness. He said, "Tell me. About you."

She murmured, "I'd rather not."

"But why? Do you think I won't try to understand? Whatever it is you don't want to talk about . . . can't be that bad, Julie. It can't be so bad that I wouldn't"—there was a pause—"that I wouldn't care for you anymore. You know I care, don't you?"

Julie couldn't speak.

He moved closer and took her hand. "Tell me at least . . . what happened to your husband?"

Julie stared into the darkness and thought: Whatever I say will be wrong. The past was like a terrible monster that kept rearing

up in front of her, breathing shame and guilt and eternal damnation. However much he believed he would understand, he wouldn't. He would pity and despise her.

The sky seemed even darker now, the glittering stars like lights on a tree. Taking a deep breath, she said slowly, "Peter never knew his father. And I—I haven't seen him since before Peter was born."

Richard gently squeezed her hand. "More fool him. He must be mad. So—then . . . he's not likely to show up again."

"Hardly!" She couldn't keep the bitterness out of her voice. "You see . . ." She bit her lip. "We . . ." She spoke so softly that he leaned closer to hear her. "We were never married."

For a moment he didn't speak and Julie thought that she had been right, that he wouldn't understand.

But then he put his arm around her shoulder and said, "Bad luck!"

"For me, yes!"

He said quickly, "But you mustn't think it matters anymore." He was stroking her hair, slowly, softly. "You have a lovely boy. You have nothing to be ashamed of."

"Oh yes I do!" She pulled away from him and blew noisily into her hanky. "I feel ashamed that it ever happened. . . . Except for Peter, that is. If only . . ."

"But, Julie, lots of people have affairs, and . . . well, indiscretions, without being married. Society's incredibly hypocritical about that kind of thing. They say it's forbidden—but they're doing it all the time. The secret is not to worry about it . . . about the past, I mean. It's not that important."

"It's important to *me*. I mind! And Peter will mind when he grows up and finds out. No . . . I made a terrible mistake and, one way and another, I'm going to pay for it for the rest of my life!"

He said, "But how are you going to pay for it? Nobody's going to make you pay, Julie! You'll only suffer for it if *you* let it bother you. Why should you ever *pay* for it?"

"You know what I mean," she said miserably. "People talk, people don't forgive."

"Do they know round here?"

"They've guessed."

"But they still accept you?"

"Well . . . yes."

"There you are then! What's the problem? Julie, I can assure you of one thing—it doesn't matter a damn to me!" He squeezed her hand again.

She breathed in deeply. "Well, thank you for saying so."

"It was meant." She heard him pouring another glass of wine. He handed her the glass. "Is that why you came to Brittany? To have Peter?"

"Yes, but please—don't ask any more!"

"All right." He stroked her hair. "But all I meant was, have you been here all this time? With your uncle and aunt?"

"Yes."

"Not much fun."

"At least I was welcome—which was more than I was at home."

"Ah. Your parents didn't understand?"

"Just my mother. My father's dead. We're still not speaking, my mother and me."

"After the war, though, you'll want to come back, won't you?"

"I don't know. The war . . ."

"It won't last forever."

"I suppose not."

"And then—" He paused. "You might come on *Dancer* again. For a cruise. Would you like that?"

"I'm a rotten sailor."

"I'll teach you."

"No, I mean—"

He laughed. "I know what you meant."

He put his arm around her shoulder and they sat for a long while, watching the night sky and talking quietly. Eventually he stood up. "Time you went to sleep. You still look terrible!"

She smiled faintly. "Thanks!"

He took her face in his hands and kissed her on the mouth, warmly and for a long time.

As she went down the stairs he called softly, "Julie, I'm glad you told me."

A little later, when she lay in bed beside Peter, she thought: Perhaps, given time, everything might be all right after all.

"Be careful. The door's creaky." The boy's whisper was loud in his ear.

"Right-o."

Ashley pulled the door gently, trying to lessen the squeak of the hinges. Finally the gap was large enough for him to squeeze through. He stepped out into the darkness of the farmyard.

He began to close the door behind him, but there was something in the way. It was the boy. He whispered, "Hey! What are you doing?"

"Coming with you!"

"Oh no you're not. Get back inside!" Ashley tried to push the boy back through the door, but the small body wriggled past him and shot off into the night.

Ashley swore under his breath and, closing the door, followed after him.

The boy was waiting at the gate which led into the pasture behind the house. He was jumping up and down with glee. "Beat you!"

"Look, young man, your mother will kill you if she finds out!" He thought: She'll kill me too.

Peter sighed with the exasperation of dealing with an adult. "But I often sneak out here on my own." He clambered onto the top of the gate. "Anyway she's not back from work yet. She won't know!"

"That's not the point," said Ashley reasonably. "We might get caught."

"Oh no. The soldiers never come here. Come on! Let's go up the hill. Sometimes you can see the lighthouse from there." He jumped to the ground and waited impatiently while Ashley climbed over the gate.

Then he was off again, running across the grass, a small black blur fading into the gray of the early twilight. Ashley gave up the idea of chasing after him, and strode forward, stretching the muscles of his legs, breathing the cool fresh air, drinking in the delicious moments of freedom.

How he had needed this. Being cooped up drove him mad. He knew how animals felt now, doomed to stay in cages forever. Slow death.

The only compensation was Julie, of course. He had been intrigued by her from the beginning. She had an otherworldliness, a gentle serenity that appealed to him. At the same time she was quick to laugh, and he liked that too. Damn it, he liked a lot about her.

But the revelations of the previous evening had subtly changed things. It had cost her a lot to tell him the truth, he had seen that, and he admired her for it. But it made him feel—what?—a sort of responsibility toward her, and that frightened him.

Yet he knew he cared for her. Nothing had changed that.

And nothing had changed the fact that he wanted to make love to her. Quite apart from being beautiful, she had an earthiness, a suggestion of passion, that made her extremely attractive. What was more, he was sure that she wanted him too.

He tramped on, thinking that perhaps responsibility wasn't a bad thing. After all, it had to come at some point in one's life.

"Woo-hoo." The soft cry came from a short way ahead.

Ashley climbed the last few yards to a wall at the top of the hill. There was no sign of the boy. "Come out, you rascal."

There was a giggle. Ashley followed it and, reaching over the wall, lifted the boy up and into the air. "Got you!"

Peter wriggled and tried to get free. Ashley held him high for a moment longer then let him fall into his arms. The boy dropped his head against Ashley's chest and lay there, panting slightly. Ashley hugged him and thought how much fun it would be to have a child of his own one day.

The giggling started again. Peter squirmed out of his arms and dropped to the ground. "Come on. I'll show you the rabbit warren."

They investigated the warren, although there wasn't much to see in the darkness. Then they looked for the beam of the lighthouse, but saw nothing and decided there were no convoys passing that night. Ashley stared into the darkness, trying to make out the deeper shadows of the sea and thought longingly of the MGB. Later they walked along the wall and around the other side of the hill.

It wasn't until Ashley saw the hooded headlights of a vehicle on the road that he realized they'd been gone a long time. He ran back to the top of the hill and looked down. The car had stopped outside the farmhouse.

The boy came panting up behind him. As they watched, the headlights went out.

The boy grasped Ashley's sleeve and cried, "It's the Germans! The Germans!"

"Yes. I'm afraid you're right." Ashley took the boy's hand and

led him back to the darkness of the wall. "I think we'd better wait here, don't you?"

Julie felt sick.

She looked at the clock again. Half past eight. And still no sign.

She sat absolutely still, her eyes on the wall, her hands tightly clasped in her lap. Tante Marie sat opposite, her face tortured with worry. Neither spoke: neither could begin to imagine what they would do if something dreadful had happened.

The familiar sound of scraping chairs came from the parlor. The two soldiers had finished their meal. The front door banged as they went out. Julie sprang to her feet and, going to the back door, opened it a crack. The soldiers had brought an armored car with them tonight, she had no idea why. They had parked it in the yard. Now they were getting into it and slamming the doors. She prayed that, if Richard and Peter were out there, they wouldn't choose this moment to return.

The car started with a roar and two dull beams of light sprang out and illuminated a corner of the farmyard. Then the lights were swinging away and the sound of the engine faded into the distance.

Julie took a jacket off the back of the door and hurried out into the night. When her eyes were accustomed to the darkness she started up the yard, toward the back pasture. She couldn't be sure Peter and Richard had gone this way, but it seemed likely. They certainly wouldn't have gone on the road.

She opened the gate and went into the pasture.

She let out a small gasp.

Two figures, one small, one tall, were running toward her.

Shuddering with relief, she stepped forward and scooped Peter up into her arms. Without a word she carried the child back through the yard, into the kitchen and straight to bed.

As she undressed him, Peter glanced nervously at her face. "Sorry, Mummy."

Julie narrowed her lips and said at last, "I'm going to say this once and only once. Don't ever, ever do that again. If you do, I'll hit you so hard you won't know what time of day it is. D'you understand?"

"Yes, Mummy."

She tucked him up and, without another word, turned out the light.

She went into the kitchen and, ignoring Ashley, crossed to the mantelpiece and shook a cigarette out of a packet. Her hand was trembling as she lit it.

"Julie, I'm very sorry . . . I meant to go out just for a second or two, but . . ."

Julie inhaled deeply on the cigarette. She didn't trust herself to speak yet.

"Peter followed me. Of his own accord. That's not to say I shouldn't have dragged him back. . . ." He put his hand on her shoulder. "It won't happen again."

Eventually she said stiffly, "We've done our best, you know. To make it bearable for you. I realize that going outside for a few minutes at midnight isn't as much fun as walking round the entire countryside. . . ." She made a wheeling gesture with her hand. "But it was safest. For you—and for us!" She spat out the last words, then, exhaling, shook her head. "If you knew what I'd been through in the last hour you'd . . . understand!" The unaccustomed cigarette was making her dizzy and she stubbed it out.

"I'll go back to my room." The way he said it, it might have been prison.

She realized it *was* a prison to him. She turned to say something softer, more understanding, but he was already gone.

After a moment she lit a candle and followed him. She climbed the narrow staircase and, through the banisters, saw him lying on the bed staring at the ceiling. She paused at the top and said matter-of-factly, "I know it's awful for you. But it shouldn't be long now before you can get away."

He came over to her. "I *will* go mad if I have to stay much longer. You see that, don't you?"

"And you must understand that I'll go mad if you take any more risks."

He smiled ruefully. "It's a bargain. Anything to avoid your wrath again."

She said firmly, "I was only angry because I was so worried.

"Thank you."

"Not at all." She turned quickly and went down the stairs.

*　*　*

Most of the potatoes were half-rotten. Methodically, Julie cut out the bad sections, peeled the remainder, however small, and chucked them into the pot. Nowadays you wasted nothing.

Tante Marie was tenderizing a piece of beef, beating it with a large wooden mallet until the meat was almost flat. They always had meat on Saturday evenings and, because they had their own chickens and cattle, often twice during the week as well. Most people were not so lucky.

Tante Marie put the meat into a pan on the stove, added dripping, garlic and herbs, and left it to cook.

Julie smelled the aroma and remembered that it was Sunday the next day and she could spend all day with Richard.

She realized she was staring into the pot, the potatoes forgotten. Tante Marie was watching her, a frown on her forehead. "Juliette . . . your uncle will be a little late tonight. I think—" She lowered her voice. "I think there's some news."

Julie looked up sharply. "Some news?"

"From—away. But I'm only guessing. I'm not sure. I just thought . . . I might warn you."

Julie tried to hold onto her thoughts, but they were shooting off at tangents. News. A boat? Coming soon, probably; then he would go away, she would be alone, he would be safe, she would be miserable . . .

After she had put Peter to bed she went up to see Richard and they talked and she thought: It will never be better than this. I'll never feel closer or warmer toward anyone than I do now.

Jean did not return until nine. Richard was just telling her about his sister who was married and lived in Sussex when Julie suddenly tensed. Somewhere in the house she heard a door opening.

Richard looked at her. "What is it?"

"Nothing. Just my uncle. I'll be back in a moment." She left him and hurried down the stairs. Jean was already at the bedroom door, waiting for her.

She followed him into the kitchen. He whispered, "We've heard! They're sending a boat on Wednesday. Unless the weather's bad. We'll know for sure that night—the BBC will broadcast a message."

"And the boat will take everyone—the sailors and the airmen?"

He nodded.

Julie blinked. "Wednesday night, then." She touched her uncle's arm in thanks and went back to her room. She closed the door and leaned against it for a moment. It was only four days away.

She climbed the narrow stairs, slowly, and didn't turn her head until she reached the top. The moment Richard saw her face he stood up and frowned. He said, "What is it?"

She made herself smile and said brightly, "It looks as though you're going home!"

He came toward her and grasped her arms. "When?"

"Wednesday night—unless the weather's bad."

"Good Lord above!" He laughed. "Marvelous! Marvelous!" He threw back his head and clenched his fists and grinned with delight. "Oh, marvelous!"

Julie tried to look glad, for his sake.

He took hold of her arms again. "Julie, I'll miss you."

She nodded silently.

"Wednesday—that's four days. Let's make it the best four days we've ever had! What do you say? Let's have a wonderful time! I'll take you out to the Ritz for dinner tomorrow night." He smiled wryly. "That means I'll buy another bottle of wine off your uncle and we'll eat off the packing case *together*, properly. . . . Then the next night . . ."

As he talked she watched him and thought: Only four days.

She reached out and touched his face. He stopped talking and when he saw the expression in her eyes, he leaned toward her and kissed her on the mouth, gently at first, then, when he felt her mouth moving under his, much harder. He said, "I want you, Julie."

She put her lips to his ear and whispered, "I want you too!"

She cried. Afterward.

He touched her cheek and felt the tears and said, "Julie, Julie! What is it?"

She pressed her head against his shoulder and said, "Nothing, nothing. I'm so happy, that's all."

He turned toward her and stroked her back, following her spine with his fingers until he reached the curve of her bottom. Then he pulled her against him and kissed her again, very softly, murmuring, "Julie, Julie . . . silly old thing, don't cry!"

"But it's only because . . . it was so lovely!"

"Yes!" He squeezed her against him. "It was, wasn't it?"

And then she cried again, very softly, not only because it had been so lovely but because she could see the past six years for what they really were: barren and lonely. All the routines, Peter, meals, work, going through the motions of life . . . And all that time she had only dimly imagined what it would be like to have all this.

"No more tears?"

"No." She laughed. "I promise!"

"Julie, four days is a long, long time!"

"Yes, yes!" She kissed his mouth and his cheek, then his ear and his forehead . . .

"Julie, if you go on like that—"

She pulled back, uncertain.

"No!" He laughed. "What I meant was—go on! Please don't stop!"

But she did because she didn't know the rules and she still felt a little awkward about the order of things. She wanted him to tell her, to whisper to her . . .

And then it was starting all over again and he was touching her in a special way, and she felt the beginnings of that extraordinary warmth, that quite incredible pleasure.

Later, much later, she lay in the darkness and thought that, whatever happened—even after he'd gone, she'd never feel completely alone again.

20 It was a triumph.

Output had risen to fifty units a week—and fifty working units at that. David walked slowly around the dispatch room and peered at the packing cases. Each was labeled "TESTED AND PASSED," and each label had been stamped and countersigned

with the initials of the Technician-in-Charge. It was a new idea, to have one person testing and sealing each unit before dispatch. David had introduced the system because it was one which had worked well before. He had asked for—and got—a German naval technician for the job because he'd wanted someone he could communicate with. He hadn't wanted a German for any other reason—and certainly not because he didn't trust the two Frenchmen who'd done the job before. It hadn't occurred to him not to trust them.

Another new idea had been introduced too. It was Kapitänleutnant Geissler's idea this time, though David had endorsed it and put it into operation. Each device was now the responsibility of an individual on the assembly line. If a Metox was faulty it was returned to the man concerned. If the fault was not rectified within a day, then the man was summoned for an explanation. If the fault was still not cured, the man was fired and the special exemptions on his military papers removed. Everyone knew what that meant: you could be called up for forced labor.

In the six months that David had been with the company no one had been fired. At the same time output and quality had shot up. Yes, it was a triumph. Kapitänleutnant Geissler was pleased. Presumably the Navy were also pleased. And doubtless the submarine commanders were grateful now that they had their Metox receivers to warn them of enemy planes.

A triumph. And, thought David, the worst thing I've ever done.

He paused in the doorway of the main workshop. There was a gap in the line of men working at the bench. Only yesterday a man had stood there, brave and alive. Today he was dead.

And it was David's fault. *David's.*

He had been too taken up by the challenge of the problem-solving, too intoxicated by the freedom of action to see what had been happening.

The workers had been sabotaging the Metox, from the very beginning.

There had been nothing obvious—no extra wires or smashed valves. Instead, for no apparent reason, small components had failed to function or valves had burned out. David could see now that too much current must have been forced through them or reverse polarity applied.

He should have realized, of course. It should have been obvi-

ous. But he hadn't *wanted* to see. When small suspicions had entered his mind he'd dismissed them. No one would dare to do such things, he had decided. The penalty, after all, was death.

Then David's new measures had come into operation. The subtle forms of sabotage that had been so successful were no longer effective. The men had been forced to use more open and dangerous methods. Yesterday one of them had been caught.

The penalty was death, and the man had died.

And, whichever way David looked at the event, he couldn't help feeling that it was his fault.

One of the technicians glanced up and David looked quickly away. He couldn't meet the man's eyes; he couldn't look at any of them. They thought him as bad as the rest: just another Nazi. Him! A Nazi! He turned away, full of shame.

In the passage he almost bumped into Gallois, the French chief technician. Gallois stepped aside and waited for David to pass. David almost spoke but changed his mind. It would be no use. Gallois must despise him.

David walked quickly toward the front of the building, muttering angrily to himself. He went down the front steps and out into the road in full view of the guard. He had permission to walk the short distance to his quarters under the eye of the guard. Why? Because they trusted him. And why did they trust him? Because he had shown himself to be such a good German! He laughed bitterly. What an irony.

It would have been better for everyone if he had died back there in the camp.

He walked rapidly along the road until he came to a compound surrounded by barbed wire. He walked in past the guard and along the side of a large warehouse. The warehouse served as a barracks for the East European laborers who worked on the U-boat pens. At one end of it was a long wooden hut where the guards lived. David had a cubicle to himself there. Geissler had arranged it. David had been very pleased with the cubicle, which was infinitely better than the solitary room in the naval barracks. Here, at least, he had company. He often chatted with the guards; he enjoyed talking German again. They baited him, of course, but for much of the time they overlooked his race because it was convenient to them—they sometimes needed a fourth at cards.

He, in his turn, ignored the fact that they were soldiers and beat up Poles every day.

David went into the boxlike cubicle and closed the door.

He lay down on the bed and, drawing himself into a ball, covered his eyes with his hands. He was a disgrace. A disgusting disgrace. A deeply selfish and despicable man without principles, or integrity. All those scruples he had pretended to have back in the camp laboratory. All the concern for whether he was doing the right thing. And what had he done? He had done as he was told. As time had gone on he had even been happy to obey. He had worked with all his heart and soul. What had happened to him, that he could have forgotten? Where had he lost his way?

He could see now that it had happened slowly, so slowly. His greed for security had pushed all other thoughts out of his mind. He had thought only of himself, his health, his next meal, and of the vital need to survive and preserve his life at all costs.

I have betrayed everything and everyone. My race. My Cecile. Most of all I have betrayed myself. I am not a proud man.

After a while, when the self-pity had passed, he thought about the future and suddenly an idea came to him. The moment it appeared he knew it was the answer.

He sat up and, dropping onto his knees, put his hand underneath the metal frame of the bed. He touched the familiar flat shape of the small package and, pulling it out, held it tightly in his hand.

They had traveled so far together, he and this package, that he had almost forgotten the real meaning of it. He'd tucked it away in the back of his mind as something for the future: his passport to Britain or America when the war was over, a sort of insurance policy for his old age.

But now . . .

He held it in his hand and remembered the pages of plans and specifications for the secret device.

Shortwave radar. Germany would never be able to develop it, not while her laboratories were closed and her research programs at a standstill. And if she didn't have shortwave radar she couldn't defend herself against it. Certainly the Metox would be useless against it.

It would be the perfect job of sabotage to get the plans to the

British. They should be able to develop it fairly quickly. In a single blow, David's work here would be undone.

He hugged the small package to him and said gently, "Dear God, You are looking now at a miserable worthless old man. But one who is going to try to do his best. Give me the strength to succeed. And, if You should also deign to give me positive assistance, I thank You. If not—then, dear God, I will have done my best!"

He lay down and thought: What better thing can a man do than be brave just once in his life?

David often came into work early, at about six, so that he could enjoy two hours of peace and quiet before everyone else arrived. In the early morning calm he could think more clearly than later in the day. This morning he had arrived well before six—and yet he still couldn't make up his mind what to do.

Gallois. Gallois was the obvious choice.

David couldn't be sure that he was involved in the sabotage, of course, but he must *know*. Even if he himself was not involved, he must have *guessed*.

He rose unsteadily from his chair and went next door to the drawing office, where a young trainee was standing at a high desk. "Go and ask Monsieur Gallois to come to my office, would you?"

David went back to his desk and sat down unhappily.

There were footsteps in the corridor. A bead of sweat trickled down David's forehead and he reached into his trouser pocket for a handkerchief. He mopped his brow. Gallois was already in the room, watching him. David started with surprise and, half rising, indicated a seat. "Do sit down, please."

The door was still open and David got up to close it. "Lovely weather we're having, aren't we?"

"Yes."

David sat down again. "It always makes life pleasanter, doesn't it, if the sun is shining?"

David could see the Frenchman wasn't in the least interested in the weather.

David drew breath and began again. "I—wanted to talk to you about a rather delicate matter. . . ."

The Frenchman's face was blank and uninterested. He was not going to give David any help, that was obvious.

"It's . . . well, it must seem to you that I have had every sympathy . . . every desire to make a success of this project. . . . Indeed, I did at the beginning. I saw it as a wonderful opportunity to use my skills and to—give meaning to my life again. Do you understand that?"

Gallois made a gesture which indicated, If you say so.

David leaned forward. "Please—do you see that?"

"Yes—" He shrugged. "I know you had no choice."

"But I worked hard, didn't I? For success." David looked down at his hands. "I forgot, you see. I put my own satisfaction above . . . other considerations." He looked up again. "But now—I can see I was mistaken. I should not have done what I did—so wholeheartedly. I was wrong."

Gallois was studying David's face carefully.

"The point is . . ." David went on, ". . . I want to help."

There was silence. Gallois was suspicious, and who could blame him? "Look, I am well aware of what was going on in this place when I arrived. Most of the devices were being deliberately sabotaged. But I have said nothing. So you see—despite what you may think—I *am* in sympathy with your cause."

Gallois had not moved a muscle. He sat as still as stone.

David wished the Frenchman would give him some indication of encouragement. The sphinxlike silence was—difficult. "I realize it's hard for you to say anything . . . after all, why *should* you? I can only tell you that I do wish to help . . . and that I am in a position to do so in a very definite, a very concrete way."

Gallois sat forward in his chair and cleared his throat. "Monsieur Freymann, I cannot imagine where you have obtained these strange ideas. For one thing, there has never been any sabotage at this company. It is, if I may say so, an absurd idea! And second, I really cannot be involved with any activity against—the interests of this company. I don't know why you have approached me, monsieur, but I assure you I cannot help."

He was getting to his feet. David sprang up and hurried around the desk. Gallois said, "I think it is best if we do not continue this conversation. I cannot help you, nor can anyone here. We are

335

straightforward workingmen. We keep out of trouble." He turned and reached for the doorknob.

For a moment David was frozen with indecision. Then, just as Gallois was opening the door, he grabbed the Frenchman's sleeve. "Please, you don't understand!"

Very slowly, Gallois closed the door again. "What exactly don't I understand?"

David thought miserably: I am going to have to tell him! In all this time he had never told a living soul.

As he searched for the words, acid bit into his stomach and suddenly a piercing pain hit his abdomen. The room moved in on him and he gasped for breath. He felt as if he were falling. A firm hand took hold of his arm and suddenly there was a chair under him and he was leaning forward with his head between his knees. "My tablets . . . they're on the desk there."

The bottle was thrust, open, into his hand. He took out three tablets and chewed them hard because they worked quicker that way.

Gallois's voice said from close by, "Are you all right?"

"I'll be better in a minute. In just a minute. . . . Don't go, please." He gripped the other man's arm tightly. After a while the pain eased a little and David whispered, "Don't judge me too harshly. I just ask you now, please, to listen to what I have to say. . . ." He sat up slowly, feeling very faint. "I need *your* help. . . ."

He paused to take a few deep breaths. It often eased the pain. "The thing is . . . before they made me leave my job in Germany —before the war—I stole something. A secret that could be very, very important—in the war. I am the only one who knows about it—it was my idea, you see." He stopped to look at Gallois, to see whether he had understood. He thought: Now is the moment of belief or disbelief. He pulled himself upright. "I have always wanted to get the secret to the British, so they can use it. But . . . there was never the opportunity. And then, I came here and it seemed easier to carry on and do my job. . . . You see, I was so happy just to be alive. This place seemed like heaven after . . . the camp.

"But now . . ." He shook his head. "I just cannot do nothing —like before. If you knew what the camps were like! I must do

something for *them,* and this is the one thing I can do." He looked anxiously into Gallois's face. "Tell me—do you understand what I am saying?"

Gallois's expression was guarded, worried. He sighed and whispered firmly, "Dear Monsieur Freymann, I am so sorry that you are unwell. I know you have been through a lot. I only wish there was something I could do but really, there is nothing."

"I just want to take my secret to England . . ."

"I'm sorry." The Frenchman's tone was cooler now. "There is really nothing I can do."

A terrible tiredness came over David and he slumped in his chair.

Gallois looked over his shoulder and lowered his voice. "I think it is very dangerous to talk about this. . . . Forgive me, but it really is unwise." He moved toward the door. "You're all right, are you? Do you want me to send someone along?"

David covered his face with his hands and shook his head. After the door closed he got off his chair and lay on the floor. It often helped his stomach. But nothing, he knew, would remove the dull ache in his heart.

One week later a new project was announced. Goulvent, Pescard et Cie was to build larger radar detection devices suitable for ships. The pioneering work had been done elsewhere; all that was required was to assemble components which would be sent from Germany.

For David, however, there was still a lot of work to be done, developing test programs and equipment. He worked long hours but only because he couldn't bear to go back to his room anymore. He had stopped playing cards with the guards. He had stopped talking to them—or indeed to anyone. He just wanted to be alone. Whenever there was a discussion, he cut it short. He even barked at Geissler.

He didn't bother with meals; he hated having to go to the canteen to collect them. He hated his work. He hated his life. He hated himself.

Then Geissler summoned him to his office. "It seems that they want you elsewhere, Herr Freymann." The *Kapitänleutnant* picked up a letter from his desk and examined it. "They don't

say when. . . . However"—he smiled coolly—"we need you more, so we are protesting at this proposed transfer. We have put in a request through the appropriate channels and expect to hear shortly."

Between a gap in the buildings David could just glimpse the sea, misty today, but still beautiful. He said quietly, "Where?"

"Excuse me?"

"Where do they want to send me?"

"Ah! Let me see . . . it's not a naval project, that I do know." He examined the letter again. "All I have here is a code number and prefix. Perhaps . . . wait one minute. . . ." Geissler picked up the telephone and asked for HQ. He spoke for a few seconds then replaced the receiver. "Unfortunately I cannot tell you where exactly—we do not have details—but apparently the prefix denotes an SS establishment. . . ." He added unhappily, "That is perhaps another reason why it would be best for you to stay here."

Germany. Perhaps even a camp. Back into the pit.

"Herr Freymann, I will let you know the minute I myself hear the decision. In the meantime we must proceed with the preparation for the new project. Yes?"

"Yes."

"I will do my best, Herr Freymann. I will try to persuade them to let you stay. . . ."

"Thank you." He was sincere, Geissler, but there would be nothing he could do.

The escort was waiting outside the office. David led the way down to the entrance and into the van for the short drive back to Goulvent, Pescard et Cie.

The van deposited him at the door. He went up to his office and finished his day's work. New component specifications, details of new testing equipment: work that could easily be done by someone less qualified.

That night he slept badly for the first time in months. He dreamed he was back on a bare wooden bunk, crushed between two dying men. The *Prominente* came and made them get up and go to the quarry. It was still the middle of the night. The *Prominente* thought it was very funny, to make them get up in the night. Then they started beating people. David woke up.

For a while he couldn't get back to sleep and then, when he was tired again, there was pain in his stomach. In the end he hardly slept at all.

The next morning he went to the office early and began to think how best to delegate his work load. Feverishly, he started making lists of jobs and responsibilities, grouping them under different names and departments.

There was a knock at the door. It was Gallois.

David said, "I'm glad you called in. I need to discuss this with you. It's a list of jobs that will need to be taken over by you and others when I go."

Gallois said, "You're going?"

"In all probability. Now, when this is typed, perhaps—"

"Where will they send you?"

David put down his pencil and said shortly, "I don't know. Probably back to where I came from."

"But you have done well . . . surely they are pleased?"

David rubbed his eyes. With effort he replied, "Ah, but you don't understand the way they work. There are no rules. You do badly, they send you back to a camp. You do well—the same thing happens. No rules."

Gallois hesitated. "You'll work on electronics, though. You'll have a skilled job?"

David shrugged. "Perhaps. It's not really important."

"Surely you want to work?"

"What I want isn't relevant. Anyway, I don't care. Not anymore."

Later there was a meeting about the new project. The atmosphere in the room was claustrophobic, hot and smoky. David was enormously irritated with everyone. They were so slow to grasp the basics and he had to explain the simplest things to them. Someone—a junior technician—asked yet another idiotic question. David kept himself from shouting, then said between clenched teeth, "Can't you understand *anything*? Why do you have to be so stupid? Are you *trying* to make things difficult? Really! It's impossible to deal with you people. . . ."

A second later his stomach ulcer ruptured. The pain hit him like a sledgehammer. As soon as it started he knew it was different from anything he'd felt before. He also knew that in a few more

339

seconds it would be so bad that he would have to scream. The room blurred and he felt very cold and everything began to slip away. He was grateful. It was nice to slip away.

Peace and beauty always. A hundred years at least. Whenever the burning came back to his stomach they pressed the black thing on his face and he was floating again. . . .

The sleep was gentle, like clouds, floating. . . . Flowers, there were flowers. Then whiteness again, soft and gentle. He wanted to sleep forever.

They wouldn't let him. The *Prominente* were beating him, slapping his face. Someone was shouting at him. It was a woman. She was speaking in French. "Come on! Wake up now! Come on!"

He felt the pain again and moaned, "No. No!" Why couldn't they leave him alone? He murmured, "The pain. Please, can I have something?"

A woman's voice said, "Not yet. When you're awake."

He woke up only because the pain wouldn't let him sleep. Then at last they gave him something, but it didn't help much. The days blended into one another, he slept only when he was exhausted with the pain.

Then he woke up one day and realized that for once he had slept well. The pain was much less. He let them feed him with watery milk, and his only regret was having to face the world again.

Another day he woke up and found Gallois sitting beside the bed. The Frenchman smiled. "How are you?"

David said what was expected of him. "I'm all right."

They exchanged more platitudes until David said he was tired and the Frenchman left. As David fell asleep something nagged at his memory. He should have said something to the Frenchman, something important, but he couldn't remember what . . .

The next day he remembered and groaned because it was too late and the Frenchman was no longer there.

But it wasn't too late. Gallois returned. David reached out and grasped his hands.

Gallois asked again, "How are you?"

David said, "Never mind. Please listen. I have something important to ask." He pulled himself up in the bed. "Monsieur

Gallois, when we had our conversation some weeks ago, you said you could not help me. That's as may be. But I'm sure you know of a way to get a small package to England. The information I told you about, it's all in a small package. I wanted to go with it, before. But now the information must go on its own."

Gallois started to speak but David held up his hand. "No, please don't bother with denials and so on. Whether or not you personally can find a way of getting this to its destination is irrelevant. Just come back, please, and tell me that you can get it to the right people! Please!"

Gallois said firmly, "I'll find out."

David patted his hand and fell asleep happy.

Kapitänleutnant Geissler came to see him next. "Well, are they taking good care of you? I am proud to say that we managed to bend the rules and get you in here. It's a good hospital. I trust you like it?"

Geissler paused. "What I thought you might want to know is that you are to stay with us here in Brest. It's all been decided. Of course, that's as long as you manage to retain your fitness. . . . You will, won't you, Herr Freymann?"

David nodded, dumbfounded.

"Good! Well, we look forward to seeing you back at your desk as soon as convenient. In the meantime, I wish you good health!"

David stared at the door for a long time after Geissler had gone. He was to stay . . . after all. He had been so sure, so certain that they would send him away. . . . It was most confusing. Another reprieve. Life was nothing but a series of reprieves. He didn't know what was worse: living in hope of life or in certainty of death.

The next day a nurse came in, a nurse he hadn't seen before. As she made a show of tucking in the bedclothes she started whispering to him. At first David didn't understand what she was saying. "I have a message for you. Your friends will deliver both packages. They repeat: *both* packages."

He clasped his hands together and let the understanding dawn on him. His prayers had been answered. He was to be allowed his small act of sabotage after all.

21 The bookshop windows looked blank and cold. Julie lowered her eyes and kept walking until she reached the shop door. She went straight in. A bell jangled loudly.

The proprietor was sitting behind the counter.

Julie said, "I'd like a copy of *La Grande Chance*, please."

"Is that by Maurik?"

"No, Lefarge."

The shopkeeper looked quickly around. "Follow me, I'll see if I have it in the back." He led the way through some heavy curtains into the darkness of the storeroom behind. For a moment Julie couldn't see anything, then she realized there was a figure standing before her. A voice said, "Thank you for coming."

"That's all right."

The figure came closer and Julie made out the features. It was the new man, Maurice. He had come from England with a wireless operator called Jacques.

Maurice led her toward the back of the storeroom. There was more light here. Maurice said, "The same as before, if you don't mind. There are two of them." His voice was quiet, calm and authoritative. It was like his face: trustworthy. The moment he'd started reorganizing the line Julie had known he'd be all right. He'd discarded many of the helpers and reduced their numbers to a small tight group. Most important, he was very very careful.

He indicated a door which led to a small back room. "The first's waiting in here. All right?"

"Oh yes!" It was easy now, not like the first time.

Julie walked in, sat down and faced the young man who sat at the small table. He certainly looked American, with his round face and his extraordinary haircut.

She smiled briefly. "Where do you come from?"

"I'm from Milwaukee, ma'am."

Julie regarded the airmen as if she knew precisely where Milwaukee was. "And which state is that in?"

"Wisconsin, ma'am."

Julie tried to remember where Wisconsin was. Somewhere on the Great Lakes, she thought. Midwest, anyway. She said, "That's near New York, isn't it?"

The airman laughed drily. "Don't let nobody from Wisconsin hear you say that! Chicago—that's the nearest big city. New York! Why, that's a thousand miles away."

This one was genuine, no doubt about that. But best to make sure. "You should be back in four weeks or so. Are you looking forward to that?"

The young man grinned. "You bet. Haven't seen my family for over a year."

"Let's see, it's late November now. You should be back in time for Thanksgiving then, shouldn't you?"

The airman frowned. "Why, no, ma'am. We've just had Thanksgiving. There's no way I'll get Thanksgiving with my family till next year."

"No, of course not." Julie stood up. "You wait here. They'll come and collect you in a moment."

Back in the storeroom, Julie said, "That one's all right, I'm certain."

Maurice looked pleased. "Good." He said over his shoulder, "Put that one in the cellar, Henri, and bring up the other one. Don't let them talk to each other."

This was the third time they'd asked Julie to come to the bookshop. The first time had been difficult: she hadn't known what to ask and she'd found herself going through two generations of the Americans' family histories before she struck on the idea of asking questions about Thanksgiving. Now she could do an interview in as little as five minutes.

Stool pigeons. *Mouchards.* She was pretty sure she hadn't let any through yet.

She watched Maurice as he lit a cigarette. He was about forty, stocky, and she was fairly sure he was a Belgian—but one didn't ask. After the fiasco of the previous winter no one asked anything anymore.

He ran the line with a firm hand. No unnecessary contact, no unnecessary knowledge. That's why everyone trusted him.

Maurice came up to her. "The other one's in there now. He's the one we're concerned about. He turned up near Rennes, saying he'd walked all the way from the north somewhere. That's a hell of a long walk without any help. . . . Also he seems very nervous. We checked him out with London, of course. Everything's all right there, but . . . !"

The airman jumped when Julie came into the room: he was nervous all right. He was blond, blue-eyed and pale-skinned. He looked miserable. Julie began with the usual questions: name, rank, serial number, aircraft, squadron, where stationed. These facts had already been checked, but she asked the questions again so that she could watch him and listen to his voice.

There was a strange inflection in his speech: not quite an accent, more a hint of one.

She asked, "Where are you from?"

"Omaha."

"Have your family always lived there?"

"No."

He was not very forthcoming. Julie tried again. "Where did they come from originally?"

"Europe."

"Where exactly?"

There was a silence. The boy narrowed his lips. Julie thought: Oh dear, this one's going to be difficult. On a hunch she asked, "Was it from Germany?"

The young man was looking upset. "Back to that again! You're going to be like the rest . . . !"

"What do you mean?" Julie asked softly.

"They—" He was unable to speak. Finally he said, "They—hate me! They call me a Hun! And now I suppose you're going to accuse me of being a German spy!"

"Your family *were* German?"

He nodded slowly. "But I'm an American! I'm as American as any of them! I suppose they've been telling you different?"

"No. Really. But your name—Smith?"

"My family's name was Schmidt. They went to America a long, long time ago! We changed our name—oh, fifteen years ago."

"That must have been about the time you went to school." He didn't look much more than twenty. "Where did you go to school?"

She took him through everything she could think of. School, summer camps, baseball, football, the movies he had seen, the girls he had known—not many, she guessed correctly—even the house his family lived in. She had no idea if his answers were right. She only knew that his eyes were honest and he never stopped to search for an answer and, when he spoke of home, his face lit up.

She asked him about his journey from northern France. He had walked, he said, because he felt safer that way. He thought the local people might not be friendly so he'd avoided them and stolen food as he went along. He described the places he'd been, how he'd narrowly escaped a patrol by hiding in a tree. It all sounded plausible, Julie decided. She couldn't imagine anyone making up such a long and involved story.

Finally she said, "Well, if everything goes smoothly you should be home soon—in about a month. That'll get you home at the end of December, won't it?"

He smiled and it transformed his face. "Yes! Will it really be that soon?"

That makes a change, Julie thought. Most of them complained because they weren't being airlifted back in the morning. She said, "If all goes well. But you might just miss Thanksgiving, I'm afraid."

"I don't care—just so long as I can see my folks."

Julie thought: Blast, he hasn't risen to it. I'll have to keep going.

Suddenly the young man said, "Hey! But we've just had Thanksgiving!"

"Of course!" Julie laughed. "How silly of me."

When she came out Maurice and the others were waiting expectantly. She said, "I think he's genuine. But I can't guarantee it." She hated giving them a woolly answer, but there was one awful possibility she could not rule out: his background might be everything he said it was, but he might have chosen to move back to Germany just before the war. He might be a superb liar. She said, "He certainly lived in America as a child, but whether or not he chose to stay there I cannot say. His family were German."

Maurice touched her shoulder. "Good enough. He stays with the others, then. But we keep an eye on him. Thank you for your help. It's just what we need."

Julie flushed with pleasure. "I'm sorry I couldn't be more certain—"

"No, no! Better to have doubts than pretend to be sure. Thank you again. We've kept you long enough. You should go now. Take care."

Julie put her hand on his arm. "One thing—you will call on me, won't you, for beach duty, when the boat comes?"

Maurice looked at her thoughtfully. "If you wish. It would certainly be useful to have you there. But—it means more risk, you know that?"

"Yes, I know that."

Moving away, Julie went to the thick curtain and waited behind it, listening. There was no sound. Tentatively, she pulled the curtain aside until she could see through into the shop. There were no customers: only the proprietor behind the counter.

She stepped out briskly and went around the end of the counter. Near the shop door she paused, as if looking at one of the books on the shelf, then nodding to the proprietor, went casually out into the street.

She resisted the temptation to look over her shoulder. That would never do. Instead, she looked at her watch. Her lunch hour was nearly over. She'd have to go straight back to the office. It was only five minutes away.

She walked calmly, not too fast, not too slow. She had never known it was so difficult to look natural. She decided she'd never get used to this kind of thing.

When she arrived at the office it was quiet: her boss was away for the afternoon. She finished some accounts and typed three letters, then looked at the pile of copy invoices waiting to be filed. She hated filing: it could wait.

Instead she flicked through her diary, trying to work out when the next moonless night would be. . . . That was when he would come. . . .

It was seven months since she had seen him. She'd thought about him constantly, so much so that sometimes she couldn't remember what his voice sounded like or the exact shape of his

nose. Not that those things mattered, but it did make him seem unreal and that frightened her. Sometimes she could even persuade herself that she'd never see him again.

He, his crew and the stranded airmen had finally been collected in March. The boat had come back four times after that, on routine missions. It was then that she'd expected to see him. But he hadn't been on board. Instead there had been messages, usually relayed by the leader of the beach party. *Hoping to come soon. Please be careful.*

Take care. Don't know when I'll be able to come.

In April the nights had got too short and the boats had not come anymore. The summer seemed to last forever—and not just for her but for the people hiding the growing number of airmen. Now it was autumn again and there were messages like the ones before, but no Richard.

Maybe he would never come again. But she'd go to the beach anyway, just in case.

That was why she was helping Maurice—to make sure she got to the beach. She was ashamed of her motives. Either one was committed or one wasn't. She had to make up her mind.

Immediately, she knew it was impossible. She couldn't choose between the safety of her son and seeing Richard again. She was greedy; she wanted *both.*

After. She'd make up her mind after she'd seen Richard. Yes: that was the answer.

She left the office early. There was no more work to do and, by getting the five o'clock bus, she could have an extra hour with Peter before bedtime.

She'd have to hurry. She walked rapidly, head down and arms swinging. She hated cutting things fine. She arrived at the bus stop with four minutes to spare.

She flopped into a seat, breathless and hot. Why had she hurried? Because I'm a worrier, she thought, and I'll never change now. She took the morning edition of *Ouest-France* out of her bag. There wasn't very much of it—only two pages—and it was, she guessed, heavily censored, but some news was better than none at all and, like everyone else, she read what she could.

She was aware of someone sitting down beside her as, with a

lurch, the bus set off. After so many years Julie knew the route like the back of her hand.

The person next to her shifted in his seat, and there was a voice in her ear. "You left work early!"

Julie started and then, sighing with relief, laid her hands over her heart. "Michel! You gave me a terrible fright!"

"My apologies."

The bus drew to a halt at the checkpoint that marked the beginning of the Zone Interdite, the coastal zone restricted to all but those with the necessary permit. Julie got out her papers and glanced at the permit that had appeared in Michel's hand. It was in a false name.

After the *Feldgendarmen* had inspected the papers and the bus was on its way again, Julie asked Michel, "Where have you been all this time?" How long had it been? Months.

"Morlaix. Mainly."

"But I haven't seen you around. I thought you must have gone away."

"No." It was a statement.

"Anyway—what are you doing on this bus?"

"Going your way."

She didn't ask why. With Michel, she never liked to inquire too closely. He was probably planning to blow up more Germans.

He read her and said quietly, "I'll be behaving myself, don't worry."

Julie glanced surreptitiously over her shoulder. Behind, there were two large countrywomen sitting with baskets of vegetables on their laps. In front was a girl reading a book. No one was listening.

Michel whispered, "I hear that things have got a bit more organized around Trégasnou."

Julie stiffened. How dare he! She said calmly, "What do you mean, Michel?"

"There's a new setup, isn't there? A new organization to get people out?"

"If there is, I know nothing about it."

"Of course. I must say your security's much better. Nobody's talking. That's very good."

"So how did you hear this story? If security is so good."

"Ah. Small things . . . guesswork mainly. And the silence."

"The silence?"

"Yes. No one's talking. That always means there's something going on!" He smiled at her.

Self-satisfied as ever, Julie thought. But he doesn't know as much as he pretends. That's the important thing. She said, "If there *is* something going on, *I* don't know. I keep well out of these things nowadays."

"I hope so. Whatever they may think, they're still a bunch of amateurs."

"I think not."

Michel looked at her quizzically. "You seem very definite."

"I've just formed an opinion, that's all."

"You've changed, Julie—"

She frowned. "Why do you say that?"

"You're more—self-confident."

"You're making judgments again."

"Yes. I think I'm quite good at them."

Julie sighed with exasperation. "But—you're so sure of yourself. And so intolerant of others, Michel!"

"You mean, like everyone else in your quiet neck of the woods, you think my politics stink! Well, I tell you—after the war you'll be sorry. You'll find you're living in a France run by Fascists, just like it was before the Germans came!"

Julie shook her head. "There, you see—you immediately turn everything into a political argument. All I meant was—you're very difficult to talk to!"

"Ah! But how very sure of yourself *you* have become, Julie. You're quite a different lady from the one I used to know. What *have* you been up to? I think you're busier than you'll admit. Yes, a very busy lady!"

How she hated his games. She said impatiently, "I am just the same person, Michel. Nothing's changed."

He gave her a mocking glance. "If you say so."

The bus had stopped at a village. More people got on. With a loud roar the bus started again, juddering slowly up through the gears. Like most buses in Brittany, it had seen better days.

Michel leaned closer. "All right—no more discussions. I'll tell you. I caught this bus purposely—so that I could see you."

Again, she wasn't sure what he meant. "Oh really? I didn't know you cared so much, Michel. After all, you've managed to keep away from me for at least six months!"

He looked irritated. "No . . . well, of course it's nice to see you —but actually it's about something else."

"Yes?"

He said, "Whether or not you know who's involved in . . . local activities . . . you must know someone who knows *someone.* Anyway I have an important message for them. If I give it to you, will it get to its destination?"

"But why me? Why not send it more . . . directly?"

"Directly? You're joking. There's undeclared war between your lot and mine. Or didn't you know? If your people had their way we'd never touch so much as a hair of a German's head. And that's not our idea of how to fight."

"But when you kill it means reprisals."

"I thought we weren't going to argue. . . . Anyway, you're the best contact I have. Are you going to pass this message or not?"

Julie looked him straight in the eye. "I can't promise anything, but . . ." She pretended to consider. ". . . If it's that important I'll do my best."

"I thought you might be able to."

Julie felt like strangling him.

He went on: "The message is this: there's a scientist working in a factory in Brest who wants to get to England. The man's a German Jew. He used to be in a concentration camp until they dug him out to work on some electronic gadget at this factory. In theory he's sort of a prisoner, but he's hardly guarded. It would be easy to get him out. The point is, he says he has a secret—an invention of some sort—which would be very useful to the British. He would bring all the details with him. Whether or not he *really* has a secret is another matter. . . . But they say he's very bright, so he might be of use anyway, secret or not!"

Julie tried to take it all in.

Michel thought for a moment. "And one more thing. He's not too well. He can't be shifted for another two weeks or so. They half killed him in the camp in Germany. Mind you, kinder than the way they treat most Jews. Usually they kill them straightaway. Did you know that? They're killing them all, in their thousands. Women, children, babies . . ."

Julie looked at him in horror. "You don't mean it . . . ."

"Oh yes. They're deporting French Jews right now, by the trainload. They'll never come back."

Julie stared out of the window at the clean, honest countryside thinking that it couldn't possibly be true.

"So—" Michel said. "I—do I take it the message has been received?"

"Yes. I think I've got it."

"The point is, if we get him out, will you take him off our hands?"

"I . . . I'll ask."

"Good."

The bus stopped in another village, then started again, bumping slowly along the narrow lanes. Julie wondered if Michel was holding anything back. Probably. He was a secretive man.

And this scientist—ill. How ill? It might be difficult to get him down to the beach. . . . She'd better send a message to Maurice straightaway. He would know what to do.

They were nearing Trégasnou. Michel nudged her. "If you need to contact me I'll be at my old apartment during the week and at—" He paused and frowned. "No, just at the apartment."

The bus shuddered to a halt in the center of the village. The remaining passengers began to shuffle off.

Michel said suddenly, "And another thing . . . if you ever need help—you yourself, I mean—come to me, won't you?" He was casual and offhand, as if he were asking her over for a meal, but Julie could tell that he was perfectly serious. He really was the most confusing person.

She said, "Yes . . . all right."

"Good." He got up and led the way out of the bus. Then, with a brief wave, he was gone.

Julie hurried up the hill to the farmhouse. Whatever this thing involved—even if it was as straightforward as Michel had suggested—the idea of joining forces with his friends worried her.

She sighed. At least she wouldn't have to make the decision. That would be Maurice's problem.

"They say he's not to be trusted." Maurice looked at each of them in turn.

There was silence except for the crackling of wood burning in

the stove. Someone said, "Yes, but why would he want to plant someone on us? What would be his motive?"

Jean took his pipe out of his mouth and said heavily, "Who can tell? Michel has always had extreme views. To him, anything is justified if it furthers his cause."

Julie could bear it no longer. She said to Maurice, "But he would not betray us, I'm sure of that. After all, we *are* his family."

"Family—?"

"Yes!" Julie exclaimed. "Cousins. He used to come here often. . . ."

There was silence again. Finally Maurice said, "It's what happens *before* we take delivery of this fellow that's the problem. There is no way we can be sure he's authentic. We're going to have to take *their* word for that. If they've been fooled . . . well, we'll have no defense. . . . We'll be caught at the hand-over. When you think about it, it could be the perfect setup."

Julie shook her head. "But why would they make up this story about him being ill, if he's really a Gestapo agent? It sounds unlikely . . . doesn't it?"

Maurice grunted and passed a hand over his face. "Looking on the black side, the Gestapo might need the extra time to train their agent. Who knows?"

The fisherman, Gérard, said, "But what if this scientist *is* genuine and he *does* have this secret, what then?"

Maurice slapped his hands on his knees and said, "Here's what I suggest we do. We ask for as many details about this man as possible. We try to check him out with London. You never know, they might have some information on him if he really is a top brain. We take as many precautions as possible. We risk only one person at the pickup, we blindfold this fellow, we guard him twenty-four hours a day . . ."

"So we go ahead?"

"I think we have to."

They all got up. Gérard said a quick good-night and left immediately. Maurice paused and came up to Julie. "May I speak with you one moment?"

"Of course."

He said softly, "Look, I'm concerned that you've become involved in all this when perhaps you didn't mean to. If—well, if you

should decide to change your mind, that is understood. You only have to tell me. And there'll be no recriminations."

He was asking her to choose. She thought of Peter asleep upstairs and instinctively looked upward. There was no simple answer. . . .

She said, "I'll do what I can for the moment. I'll tell Michel our decision and bring back the reply and all that. Perhaps when this scientist is delivered, perhaps then I might . . . want to be not quite so involved. . . ." She trailed off, thinking what a half-baked person she was.

"That's fine, then. But I do think we shouldn't be using your real name. We must find another for you. Would Marie-Claire suit you?"

The question took Julie by surprise. "Er—yes."

"Right, Marie-Claire you are."

A false name. Julie shivered slightly.

"Oh, and the boat. Sunday. It's coming on Sunday. You'll help bring parcels to the beach?"

Julie breathed, "Yes! That will be no problem!"

Sunday. It was three days away.

The darkness was made up of a million small dots which jumped and danced before your eyes. One moment you could see the outline of a rock against the sea, the next it had gone and there was nothing except the shimmering blackness. If you stared too long you began to see strange indistinct shapes that moved and faded and darted away. Then you had to blink and rest your eyes.

One thing at least, thought Julie, it was a perfect night for the gunboat. The sentries up on the headland wouldn't be able to see farther than the cliff edge. Also, there was hardly any wind. That meant that boat would have a fast passage. They would come, she knew it. The BBC message had said so. It had come at eight. *Benedictine is a sweet liqueur.*

Whatever happened, it would be a great relief when all the parcels were gone. There were thirty-nine of them on the beach at that very moment. It was a terrifying number, but they had been accumulating fast in the last few weeks. Many had been diverted to Spain via Bordeaux, but those who had been sent

down the line to Brittany—by train from Paris to St.-Brieuc—had all been hidden, some for as long as a month.

Julie could hear them muttering. She got up and, walking over to the voices, whispered, "Please don't talk. The sound may carry."

"But how long do we have to wait?"

"It's impossible to say. Just be patient. Please."

They were quiet and Julie returned to her place. She was sure everything would be all right. She had a feeling about it.

The only noise was the faint lapping of waves on sand.

Someone moved, probably Gérard. Then another man. Then there was a sound, an infinitesimal, soft swishing . . .

They were here.

Her heart thudded. She made herself concentrate on what had to be done. She moved along the groups of airmen and said to each, "You will see two small boats arriving soon. You must not move until you are told. Do you understand?" She crouched beside them and waited.

The surfboats seemed to take a long time. But at last they were there, first one then the other gliding in to the beach, two solid dark shapes against the paler sea. Julie waited half a minute before standing up and calling softly, "Groups One and Two?" The men—there should be fourteen in all—followed her toward the waiting boats. The surfboat crews came forward and Julie directed the two groups to different boats. The surfboat crews were already pushing their boats out and bundling their passengers in. But he wasn't there, she already knew it. Then they were gone.

Twenty minutes later the boats were back. Julie called two more groups of airmen forward. This time some of them didn't listen to her instructions and too many men peeled off in the direction of the first boat. Julie sorted them out and took the three extra men across to the second boat, which was already loaded and waiting. The three men waded into the water, rolled into the boat, and then it was gone.

One more journey, and they would be finished.

Someone was hurrying along the sand toward her. Gérard? No, too tall.

Then suddenly she knew exactly who it was.

She moved forward, laughing a little. Then he was hugging her,

so tightly she could hardly breathe. He put his cheek against hers and with a sudden shock she remembered the feel of his skin and the lovely animal scent of him. And she remembered his body, and how lovely it had felt against hers, and she murmured, "Oh, how I've missed you."

"Julie—"

He pulled away, trying to see her face in the darkness. He whispered, "There's not much time and I must know—first, are you all right?"

"Yes, yes! *I'm* all right!"

"But is it safe? I bet it isn't!"

"It's fine, now. Really! Everyone's very careful." She pushed herself up on tiptoe and put her arms around his neck and kissed him. He kissed her back, hard.

"Julie, listen—I've had an idea. It's all been okayed. I've cleared it with everyone. You and Peter must come back to England. On the gunboat."

Julie frowned in the darkness. "What—? I—"

"Look, we can fix it for the next trip. You can just disappear. No one will ever guess where you've gone. And you'll be safe, *both* of you."

"I . . . I don't know. . . . I'll have to think about it." She'd never considered going herself. But it wasn't that simple—and she couldn't explain.

He said urgently, "Please, say you'll come!"

"I don't know—I don't know! I need time!"

"There may not *be* any time . . ."

She could hear the disappointment in his voice, and understood. He must have been planning this for ages, and now she was being reluctant and ungrateful. She said, "Please—I love you with all my heart. But I must *think*. My family are here, and the others, and . . . It's all so sudden, Richard. . . . The next time you come, I'll tell you for sure, I promise. You *will* be coming again, won't you?"

"Yes. Yes. . . ."

He was still disappointed, she could tell. She pulled at his arm and sat down on the sand. He sat beside her and put his arm around her. "Julie—I thought you'd *want* to . . ."

"I do! I do!"

"Then—?"

Julie thought: He's right. I should go. I should get Peter to safety. I should be with him—I *want* to be with him. She said, "Yes . . . perhaps you're right! I'll try. I promise!"

He squeezed her arm. "Good! Good!" Then he chuckled. "I thought for a moment your affections had been stolen by a tall, dark Frenchman!"

She laughed quietly. "No, I ran after him, but he wouldn't have me!"

"He must have been mad!"

They grinned at each other in the darkness.

After a while there was the gentle sound of muffled oars and he pulled her to her feet. She suddenly realized she hadn't mustered the airmen. She said, "I'd better get the passengers," and, before he could reply, ran quickly up the beach. When she got back the boats were ready and waiting and there was no more time.

She found him by the second boat. He said, "We'll be back in a week or so. Come then, Julie! Please!"

"I'll try!"

He kissed her and ran quickly into the water to where the boat was waiting.

Then he was gone, vanished into the darkness that was the sea.

22 There was cloud at two thousand feet. Lit soft silver by the moon, it spread in a rapidly growing mantle beneath the cruising Wellington.

The pilot leaned his head against the side cockpit window and regarded the thickening cloud with satisfaction. The U-boats would think they were safely hidden under that lot.

The pilot said into his mike, "How long to turnaround, Wally?"

There was a crackle and the navigator's voice came through the earphones. "Fifteen minutes, sir."

"Right-ho."

They were flying to the limit tonight, as they always did. Eight hundred miles west-southwest into the Atlantic then a zigzag course east-southeast, across the Bay of Biscay to the French coast, then home. The pattern might yield up a U-boat or two. The only problem was the U-boats usually knew they were coming.

Life had been much simpler when the plane had first got the ASV radar more than a year before. If the conditions were right you just turned the thing on and waited for the magic words: "Radar to Skipper. Target thirteen miles to port. Angle twenty degrees." Then you flew into the darkest part of the sky and approached up-moon, so that the U-boat was beautifully silhouetted against the moon-path. By the time the U-boat spotted you it was too late for them to dive—or even fight. The pilot had got a good tally in those days: two definite hits and a probable.

Of course, the radar had been a bit temperamental and it was ineffective in rain, snow, sleet or heavy seas. But when the conditions *were* good, it could work well.

Then everything changed and the devilish U-boats kept disappearing before one's very eyes. You'd pick them up all right, but by the time you homed in on them they'd vanished. There was only one way they could do it so consistently—by countermeasure. A radar detector.

Bound to happen, of course, but still frustrating. Eventually Coastal Command worked out a counterstrategy. As soon as a target was picked up you ordered the radar scanner to be stopped and the radar aimed aft, where its waves couldn't be detected. Then you maneuvered slowly into position, asking that the radar revolve through a full circle only once every minute or so, to make sure you hadn't lost the U-boat. Only on the final run in did you leave the radar on continuously. At between one and two miles you turned on the two-million-candlepower Leigh light and, even if you didn't pick the U-boat up immediately, with a bit of luck the U-boat gunners wouldn't be able to resist the temptation of firing, thus, most obligingly, guiding you straight into your target.

357

The strategy worked fairly well, but as often as not the U-boat got wind of you before you ever got near. Real cat-and-mouse stuff. Trouble was, the mouse got away far too often.

It would be nice to gain the upper hand again.

And, with a bit of luck, they might. There was a new box of tricks on board. An experimental device. The pilot was proud of the fact that his old girl was the first in Coastal Command to be fitted with one.

H_2S, the scientists called it. Which, if he remembered his school chemistry correctly, was the chemical formula that stank of rotten eggs. Someone somewhere had a sense of humor.

A completely new type of radar, they said, which would give wonderful definition in *every* direction. Read the sea and the land like a map.

Certainly the radar operators were crazy about it. The navigator too—finding his way back to the coast was a piece of cake.

The newfangled device had been fitted only three days before, so they were continuing to use the old ASV radar as well, to be on the safe side.

The pilot looked at his watch. Two minutes to the final turn. They were deep into the Bay now, only twenty miles from the French coast. They'd run parallel to the coast as far as Brest, then head for home.

They turned. The engines droned on. An hour passed.

"Captain to Navigator. Position, Wally?"

"Fifty miles southwest of Lorient, Skipper."

Good hunting country, this. Close to both Lorient and St. Nazaire. "Captain to crew. Extra sharp lookout now—above *and* below." Fighters weren't much of a problem in the Bay, but you never knew.

The acknowledgments from the crew came back through the earphones, one by one. The pilot examined the thick cloud below. No chance of a visual. But somewhere down there was a U-boat, perhaps *several*.

Damn it, all he wanted was a stab at one. Just a stab.

The young officer watched the long nose of the submarine carve swaths of white foam through the dark sea and could hardly believe this great monster was really his. He was just twenty-six and had been an *Oberleutnant zur See* for only a year.

He wished he felt completely confident—but it was impossible. Not when he'd admired the great U-boat commanders for so long: men like Gunther Prien, who took *U-47* into Scapa Flow and sank the *Royal Oak;* or Karl Fischer, the commander with the greatest single tally of ships sunk. How could he think of himself on the same level? It was impossible.

He looked up. A thin veil of cloud was covering the moon. Some cover at least. They needed it: the air patrols were heavy nowadays. He remembered the beginning of the war, when he was a *Leutnant zur See* fresh from training. Then enemy aircraft had been rare and usually came in daylight.

Five hours had passed since they'd left St. Nazaire. They'd left late, because of engine problems, and they'd left disorganized, because of last-minute crew changes. Half the men on board had been transferred from another, crippled boat and at least ten were fresh recruits who'd completed only half their proper training. Unsatisfactory, to say the least. As soon as they were clear of the Bay he would put the men through their paces and conduct some intensive training sessions. It wouldn't make up for lack of an experienced, well-trained crew, but it would have to do.

Seven hours of darkness were left. Not enough time to clear the Bay. He stamped his feet. The winter had come early this year and it was very cold.

The junior watch officer was at his shoulder. "Radar bleep, Herr Oberleu."

The young commander nodded. It was nothing to get excited about. The radar detector bleeped and whined and whistled all the time. Often the thing drove commanders so mad that they ordered it turned off. The device seemed to hear planes everywhere.

Still, better check it. After all, he was responsible now.

He stepped across to the other side of the bridge and looked at the aerial. Introduced as a temporary measure when the British first started using radar, it had quickly been dubbed the Biscay Cross. Now, a year later, it was still being used. This one had certainly seen better days. It looked as though it had been thrown hastily down the hatch and patched together dozens of times. Nevertheless the fragile wooden structure was correctly positioned and the wires properly connected. Nothing wrong there then.

He nodded to the second watch officer and went down the hatch to the control room. The Metox technician was bent over the set, fiddling with a knob. The set emitted a piercing shriek. The technician saw the young commander and said, "Sorry, Herr Oberleu, it seems to be playing up. Shall I open it and have a look? It would mean turning it off for a while. . . ."

By habit the young officer almost referred the matter to the commander until he remembered with a slight shock that he *was* the commander. The eyes of several of the men were on him. Decision time.

He hesitated. The men's eyes hardened. He *must* decide. "No!" he said. "Don't dismantle it until we're clear of the Bay. Leave it on!"

The young commander went over to the chart table to give himself time to recover. He'd almost made a fool of himself.

He climbed purposefully back up the conning tower. The men on the bridge moved aside in deference. It was darker now, and the cloud cover was much thicker. Both the moon and the stars had disappeared. Good! He began to feel more optimistic.

"Radar bleep, Herr Oberleu."

The young commander nodded.

"Another radar bleep."

Automatically he searched the sky, but there was nothing.

There was tension on the bridge as everyone waited for another bleep. If the radar bleeps came at regular intervals, it might be an aircraft . . .

"Interference on Metox . . . permanent signal."

The young officer gripped the coaming. The cursed thing was really acting up. Useless. It was quite useless. It was said in the officers' mess that the device worked well only when the enemy were making their final run-in. That gave just enough time to alert the gunners and let them fire a few bursts on the 20mm's. Not enough time—but better than nothing at all.

"Metox functioning. No signal."

He relaxed a little.

Five minutes passed. There were no further reports from the control room.

There was no aircraft then.

The pilot was just beginning to think it wasn't going to be his night.

Then it came. "Radar to Skipper. Target twenty miles to starboard. Angle ten degrees."

The familiar excitement clutched at him. He gulped involuntarily and said, "Stop scanner. Radar aft." He switched the controls to manual and banked the aircraft to port, automatically beginning the maneuvers that would bring them into position down-moon.

"Radar to Skipper. You don't want the H$_2$S scanner off too, do you, sir?"

"Is it picking up the target?"

"Loud and clear, sir. I had nothing on the old set at all."

Of course. The range had been twenty miles: the old set had rarely managed that. He said, "Leave it on then."

They flew northwest until Radar gave the target bearing due east. Then they flew northeast until the target was bearing due south. Now the target would be in the path of any moonlight that might be filtering through the cloud. They turned for the final run-in.

So far so good. The U-boat, if it was one, hadn't dived.

"Captain to Radar. Keep it dead on the nose now."

"Roger."

"Still a good target, is it?"

"Loud and clear, sir!"

It was too good to be true. Despite the cold, the pilot's hands were sweating as they gripped the stick.

"Radar to Captain. Range four miles. Dead on the nose."

A minute and a half to go then. The pilot took her down to four hundred feet and the plane broke through the cloud base.

"Radar to Captain. Target three degrees to starboard."

The pilot made the necessary course alteration. The target was moving west: outward bound. The Liberator was down to three hundred feet.

"Radar to Captain. Target dead ahead. Range three miles."

"Roger. Captain to Navigator. Bomb doors open."

Normally they switched on the Leigh light at two miles. But with this much certainty the pilot decided to wait.

Hell, but it had better be a U-boat and not a bloody fisherman out after hours!

"Radar to Captain. Target dead ahead. Range two miles."

"Roger. Call distances at every half mile now."

"Will do."

"Captain to Navigator. I want the Leigh light on at *one* mile, and Copilot, keep shouting my height, will you? Yell if it gets too near a hundred feet."

"Right-ho, sir."

"Radar to Captain. One and a half miles, dead on the nose."

The pilot peered into the murk ahead, there was no moon-path. No sea, nothing. He was at 120 feet now. The sweat was running down his body. God, but it had better be a U-boat!

"Radar to Captain. One mile and dead on the nose!"

"Navigator to Captain. Leigh light *on*!"

The powerful beam sprang out from the starboard wing, carving a path of light far into the night.

For a moment the pilot could see nothing.

Bloody hell! Where the devil—!

Suddenly there was a yell. "There!"

And there she was.

Black. Sleek. Long.

A great big beautiful fat U-boat, a perfect target—just for them.

The pilot grunted with excitement. He knew, even before he released the depth charges, that nothing could save her. They had the beautiful black beast absolutely cold.

The young officer felt drained. He hadn't realized how tense he had been. Presumably it was something he'd get used to.

He rubbed his eyes.

There was a scream from his right. "Enemy starboard ninety!"

He spun around.

A massive light was blazing out of the sky, a great ball of white fire that dazzled the eyes. The entire submarine was covered in a bath of vicious cold light. The young officer wanted to order the light away so that they could slip back into the dark-ness. . . .

He heard the whine of approaching engines and screamed: "Fire! Fire! Fire all guns!" The guns opened up, their staccato

Rat-tat-tat tearing into the eerie silence. The tracers wove their way up toward the blinding light.

But still the light came.

He yelled, "Get the light! The light!" And then realized it was far too late for all that.

The light was so close it filled the sky. The ominous drone of the engines grew to a higher pitch.

Behind the circle of light the dark shape of the plane was visible. Large. Like a bird of prey.

And still it came inexorably nearer. The young man was filled with blind rage.

He screamed: "Fire! Fire! Fire!" as if his words would travel through the air and extinguish the terrible light.

Then the noise was a great roar, and the plane seemed to lift up and up, its black belly swooping over them. He raised his fists and cried, "No-o-oooo!"

The plane was gone. There was an instant when the engine noise was receding and the darkness was descending around the U-boat like a protective blanket—an instant when he felt a flicker of hope.

A brief moment later, he knew with awful certainty that there was no escape after all.

The boat gave a great shudder and the deck lurched under his feet.

A slow rumble grew into a thunderous boom. The shock hit his ears and buffeted his body.

The young commander realized with astonishment that the deck was falling away from his feet. He saw that the boat was rolling slowly, almost leisurely, to port.

The deck lurched again, violently, and there was another roar, much closer. The blast threw him against the side of the bridge. Water was in his eyes, in his mouth, pouring down his face. He spluttered fiercely and gasped for breath.

He suddenly thought: I must tell them.

Pulling himself up the slanting deck, he gripped the coaming and shouted, "Abandon ship!" But his voice was weak and there was too much noise. Men were running and screaming. Even if they heard, it would make no difference.

He almost shouted again, but his eye was caught by the aston-

ishing sight of the bow, just visible in the darkness. It was rising slowly but remorselessly up into the sky.

There was another explosion, this time from deep within the boat. Then another. The boat staggered, then continued her terrible climb into the sky.

Only when he saw the sea rising up toward the conning tower did he realize she wasn't climbing at all, but sliding . . . backward, deeper and deeper, backward . . .

There was frantic activity on the forward deck. Some men were trying to release the rafts, tearing at the hatch covers with their hands. The hatches would not open. A man began to scream. . . .

The young commander felt water around his legs. The sea was pouring into the conning tower. The sight made him desperately sad.

When the water reached his neck he swam for a while, thinking of his home and his parents and how much he loved and respected them, and crying because he had failed them so completely, and because he was so terribly afraid to die.

Then the waves were breaking over his head and he was swallowing water and it was incredibly cold and he knew it wouldn't be much longer.

It was twenty minutes, in fact. But he lost consciousness before he drowned and there are worse ways to die.

The streets of Berlin were dark and almost deserted. Rain and sleet were falling in a cold flurry, whipped sideways by the icy northerly wind. The roads were slippery from the long winter freeze and the staff car went slowly, the driver peering nervously through the windscreen at the unlit road ahead.

The weather had been bad for weeks. One storm after another, snow, Arctic temperatures. Doenitz reflected that even the elements were against them. Stalingrad was under siege, the Army was in retreat; at sea the U-boat crews were achieving remarkable results under terrible conditions. It seemed that the winter would go on forever.

He could do nothing about the weather.

But he could and would fight against the other problems besetting the Navy. Like complete lack of air cover and reconnaissance for his U-boats. Like lack of steel for the building program. Like

the usual continental-minded attitudes of the leadership—Hitler still had not grasped the fact that he had to win the war at sea to win the war on land. Always the same problems.

Tomorrow Doenitz would get Hitler to approve the steel allocation. And he was slowly winning on the matter of air cover too. Goering had actually been pleasant to him the last time they had met at Führer headquarters, and Hitler had pressed Doenitz rather than Goering to stay to breakfast. Promising signs.

Doenitz fingered the gold bands on his arm. How much difference power made!

He had been Commander-in-Chief of the Navy for three weeks, ever since Raeder's sudden resignation over Hitler's decision to lay up the battleships, which the leader dubbed "useless." Doenitz, on taking up his new post, had also fought the decision—and won. Since then Hitler had treated him with the greatest consideration and respect. Strange justice!

The trouble was, it might all be too late. The worst mistakes had been made and were difficult to put right.

Like the business of this radar.

Schmidt had requested an urgent meeting to discuss "a radar problem." Even Goering was going to be there. It must be something serious.

The car drew up outside the Chancellery. The meeting was in one of the smaller conference rooms. Originally it was to have been held in Goering's ostentatious Air Ministry building, but early the day before a bomb had fallen nearby and shattered all the windows. And it was Goering who'd promised that Allied bombers would never reach Berlin!

The others were already there. As Doenitz entered, everyone except Goering got to his feet. Goering was sitting at the head of the table, his massive weight wedged into a large ornate gilt chair. Doenitz carefully sat at the opposite end of the table in an equally grand chair. He noticed that Goering's eyes looked peculiar. It was said that Goering took drugs: that would account for it.

The meeting began. Schmidt was sitting on Goering's right, looking unhappy, his eyes firmly on the papers on the table in front of him. Hesitantly he started to read from what Doenitz realized was a carefully prepared statement.

After a few seconds Doenitz's hackles began to rise. Schmidt

365

was saying: ". . . The enemy aircraft was shot down near Rotterdam on the night of February twelfth, 1943. Routine examination of the wreckage by Luftwaffe personnel revealed a box which was badly damaged and covered with blood. However the box was sufficiently intact for it to be confirmed that nothing similar had ever been seen before. Superior technicians were called in but were unable to guess at the function of the box. The only clue was the words 'Experimental Six' written in pencil on the side." Schmidt turned a page and went on: "Luftwaffe headquarters ordered the box to be dismantled and brought to Berlin for closer examination. . . . The Rotterdam Apparatus, as we decided to call it, was then examined by my staff in our laboratory. However . . ." Schmidt paused and looked even more unhappy. "Two days ago, the RAF scored a direct hit on the laboratory, killing some of my staff and destroying parts of the apparatus. My staff climbed into the ruins of the laboratory and retrieved what they could. We are now trying to reconstruct the apparatus, using the parts which are left to us."

"Herr Schmidt now has the use of the best possible laboratory," Goering interrupted. "It is properly fortified so that this cannot happen again."

Schmidt looked to see if Goering had finished then returned to his notes. "With the components now in our possession it is impossible for us to reconstruct this apparatus to the point where we can make it function. We cannot therefore report on the performance, range or characteristics of the device—not unless we obtain another apparatus, more or less intact, from a crashed enemy bomber. However, it *is* possible to draw two basic conclusions: one, that it is a form of radar—a form that we have never seen before. . . ." Schmidt's voice was down almost to a whisper. He had his elbows on the table and his head in his hands, so that his face was hidden. "And two, that it works on very short wave, possibly as little as ten centimeters."

There was a long silence. Doenitz's staff eyed their commander nervously, but his mind was in the Bay of Biscay, seeing the enemy bombers hunting, tracking, killing his U-boats with their magic new eyes; and on the convoy routes, in the wastes of the North Atlantic, seeing British destroyers lying in wait, ready to pounce, without warning.

"May we understand this more completely?" Doenitz spoke

softly. "Are you saying that this radar is completely unknown to us?"

Schmidt licked his lips. "Yes."

"And—you believe it might be very effective?"

"We have no way of knowing, not yet . . ."

"And are you saying that, in the event of it becoming widely used by the British, we have no defensive measures against it?"

The Chief Scientist shifted uneasily in his chair. "We do not have any way of detecting it at present."

Doenitz leaned forward. "But *will* we?"

"It . . . would take time. We would have to understand exactly how this new apparatus worked. It is based on entirely different principles, you understand; *entirely* different!"

"Entirely different . . ." Doenitz echoed. "I see. I will not inquire as to why we ourselves have never investigated these entirely different principles!"

Goering gave Doenitz a hard stare. "May I remind you, Herr Admiral, that our radar has proved to be extremely effective in everything except this, er, field! We have led Britain, led the world, in early-warning systems. Not a British bomber nears Germany without our knowing about it!"

Doenitz said testily, "Yes, Herr Reichsmarschall, most effective when defending a landmass, but not very effective for protecting U-boats, wouldn't you agree?"

There was an awkward pause before Goering slapped the table. "Quite so! I assure you, my dear Admiral, that everything possible is being done to crack this Rotterdam problem as soon as possible." For emphasis the *Reichsmarschall* punched his right fist into the open palm of his left hand. "*First,* all companies in this field have been ordered to start research! Second, we are releasing all the necessary personnel from active service, *however* many people are needed!" He turned abruptly to Schmidt. "How many, Schmidt, five thousand? Ten thousand?"

"Impossible to say yet, Herr Reichsmarschall. But maybe as many as ten thousand. Yes."

Doenitz asked, "Why so many?"

Schmidt frowned. "We have to follow several avenues of research . . . we have to try lots of different approaches to make sure we find the right one."

My God, thought Doenitz, they haven't a clue, not a clue. He

said, "But how long will it take to develop a warning device?"

"Ah, not too long, hopefully."

"In the meantime . . . in the meantime, we are defenseless."

"Not entirely!" exclaimed Goering. "Telefunken tell me they have not entirely stopped research into other wavelengths. They might be able to produce a detector quite quickly."

"Might?"

"You will be kept fully in the picture, Herr Admiral, I assure you!"

"Yes," Doenitz said tightly. Doubtless the picture would be the same as ever—the bare minimum imparted with the maximum reluctance. "And shortwave radar itself. What would be its advantages?"

Schmidt said, "It is small . . . compact. For the rest, as I say, we cannot be sure, not until we can actually get a Rotterdam Apparatus working."

"And when could we have this radar ourselves?"

Schmidt breathed deeply. "Eighteen months . . . or two years."

Forever. Doenitz looked at Schmidt with contempt. The man had sworn that shortwave radar was impossible. The man was incompetent. Doenitz said shortly, "There is no more to be discussed, then, is there?"

Except, he thought, with the Führer, in private. Then he would make quite sure Hitler knew who was to blame for this appalling catastrophe.

While everyone else began shuffling papers, a thought stirred in the back of Doenitz's mind. "Schmidt!" he called sharply.

"Yes, Herr Grossadmiral."

"A long time ago, on the *Welle,* when you first demonstrated radar to us . . ."

"Yes, Herr Grossadmiral."

"There was a scientist of yours, someone who'd worked on radar from the beginning. He talked to me about shortwave radar. He said it was possible."

Schmidt blanched. "I—I don't remember exactly . . ."

"But I do! He was a round, jolly little man. One of *your* men, Herr Schmidt. I can have him looked up if you like. I'm sure I'll recognize the name when I see it. I remember he was quite definite, about shortwave radar. He said it could be done." Doenitz

shook his head. "I'm surprised you don't remember. You seemed quite agitated about the matter at the time."

An indefinable electricity ran around the table. There might be a fight, the staff sensed it.

"Ah . . ." Schmidt said, as if remembering for the first time. "I think I know who you must mean. A fellow called Freymann."

"Yes, that was the man."

Schmidt said quickly, "Herr Grossadmiral, we have already asked for him! Of course we have! He was an obvious first choice! Yes, indeed, he has been earmarked for the main team . . ."

"But his ideas were not worth investigating before?"

Schmidt pouted. "Why, indeed they were! But they were unworkable, quite mad! Whatever this new device may be, I'm sure it can't be anything like Freymann's ideas!"

Doenitz was unconvinced. "I see. But he *is* about to join your staff?"

"Yes, indeed! We have made a request!"

"A request?"

"Yes. Of the SS."

"Ah! He was detained?"

"He is a Jew."

"Where is he detained?"

"We have just been informed that he is working at a naval establishment—at Brest in France!"

There was a short embarrassed silence. "And a request has been made?"

"Through the appropriate channels."

Doenitz barked, "I find it surprising, Herr Schmidt, that this request was not made immediately, direct to myself. I am sure that, addressed through the highest possible channels, Freymann would be with you by now!"

Schmidt looked as if he had indigestion. "But until we realized the nature of the device we were not to know . . ."

"That this man was vital?"

Schmidt coughed. "Indeed."

"What about documents—research papers and so on. Surely something of his work remains?"

"Nothing. Apparently it was all mislaid."

"Then I hope to hear that he is with you very shortly!" Doenitz

stood up. "And I look forward to being informed that the research program is progressing with all speed. Until then, good day!"

There was a shuffling as people got to their feet. No one bothered with Heil Hitlers nowadays.

Schmidt watched Doenitz stride angrily from the room and sighed. It was a nightmare, the whole thing. But not as bad as it would be if Freymann didn't come up with the answer. When Doenitz had called Freymann "vital" he'd hit the nail on the head.

Without Freymann it would take months, years.

It pained Schmidt to admit it, but that little Jew was their only hope.

23 "You look wonderful today, madame!"

"Thank you, madame." Julie smiled broadly at the shopkeeper and, picking up her basket from the counter, went out into the road. Some of the villagers looked at her rather strangely. No woman had ever worn trousers in Trégasnou before. But then few women had ever been cowhands before. She grinned to herself. They would soon get used to it.

She'd given up her job before Christmas and it was the best thing she'd ever done. She now worked for Jean—which meant she kept going from dawn until well after dusk for her keep and no money. But it was the best salary she'd ever had; she'd never been happier. The outdoor life suited her, the physical work made her feel better than she had in years, and, best of all, she saw much more of Peter. A pity she hadn't done it ages ago.

It was the second big decision she'd taken.

The first had been even more important: she'd decided to escape to England.

At the right time. To disappear overnight would be to put her

family at risk. She would do the thing properly. First, she'd left her job. Then she'd told people she was thinking of moving away —to Rennes, or another large city. Now all that remained was to leave, quite publicly, with farewells and luggage.

She'd even set her departure date: she'd told everyone she was going in two weeks.

At the road that led to the west of the village, a front door opened and an old lady in Breton dress emerged from one of the smaller cottages, her tall white lace *coiffe* bobbing forward. She mumbled, "You're away, I hear. Thought you'd be off sooner or later!"

Julie waved and passed on. She thought: Silly old woman. But nothing could annoy her today: she was too happy. It wasn't just the thought of the actual journey and of being with Richard, it was the way everything had changed. For the first time she felt really in control of her own life. The decision to go had been hard— but once made, it was as if an enormous weight had been lifted from her shoulders.

She'd seen Richard only three times the whole winter. The weather had been atrocious. Sometimes the boat didn't come at all; sometimes it was so late there was barely time to load any passengers; at other times she guessed he'd had to stay on board because of the terrible conditions out at the anchorage. The last time she'd seen him he had urged her to leave straightaway. But there were always so many passengers waiting to go, always more than there were places for, that she couldn't.

Also Maurice and the group still needed her and that was important to her. She'd never felt really useful before and, well, she liked it. It would be disloyal to let them down and she wanted to be honorable and do what was right. By staying this extra time, until the scientist was well enough to go, she would have done enough. After that she could leave with an easy mind.

She swung around a corner into a tiny lane. She knocked firmly on the front door of a cottage and, without waiting for a reply, walked straight in.

An old man was beside the hearth.

"Good morning, monsieur!" She went past him, through a door into a back room.

Maurice was already there.

She sat down and, delving into the pocket of her trousers, handed him an envelope. He opened it and pulled out an identity card and a small box.

She said, pointing to the small box, "I brought the ink pad. All it needs is the thumbprint and the photograph, then give it back to me and I'll stamp it." She had inserted the name—a totally fictitious one—and the details of birth and parentage. Maurice had already given her the age and coloring of the new owner.

She had only two cards left after this. But Maurice knew they were precious: he wouldn't have asked her for one unless it was important.

Maurice nodded. "Right. We'll take care of the card in just a moment."

Julie was surprised. That must mean that the new owner of the card was here or very nearby. She wondered who it could be. But she didn't ask: one had learned not to.

Maurice began, "First, the scientist. What's the news?"

Julie remembered the brief talk she'd had with Michel the day before. "Everything's set for this week, but they wouldn't give me any more details."

"They wouldn't say exactly when?"

"No."

"But the scientist's out of the hospital?"

"Yes."

"And fit enough to travel?"

"So they say."

Maurice made a wry face. "I hope they're right." He thought for a moment. "We'd better aim to get him away in about ten days. I don't want him hanging about, but at the same time I do want to be sure he's everything he says he is. . . . There's still something about the whole setup that makes me uneasy. Will you help me to interrogate him? You have an instinct for it, you know."

"Thank you. Of course I'll help if I can."

"There'll be someone else too. Helping us, I mean."

"Oh?"

"Yes, a friend from Paris. He's been with us for some time now, but farther up the line."

Julie frowned. A stranger. She had a dread of strangers. "But —why has he come here?"

"He needs to lie low for a bit. He was spotted at Gare Montparnasse the other day and now the Boches are on the lookout for him. It was too dangerous."

Julie looked down unhappily. Whatever the reasons, she wished the man hadn't come.

Maurice understood her reaction. "This fellow will be useful to us, Marie-Claire. He was with Meteor. He's seen the sort of bogus airmen the Boches tried to pass down the line there. And he knew the traitor, Lebrun. He always suspected him, apparently. He's going to be very good on security."

She asked, "But how did he find us?"

"A mutual contact."

"And he's . . ." How should she put it? "He's—definitely all right?"

"I had him checked out very carefully. Our mutual friend verified him in person, face to face, in the presence of one of our couriers. Then I had him checked with London. They know him well. He'd been with Meteor for some time. And since he's been with us, he's been doing very good work, I assure you."

She smiled briefly. It must be all right. She was just worrying too much, as usual.

Maurice stood up. "You might as well meet him now. I'll call him in, shall I?" Maurice went to a back door, opened it and spoke quietly. He returned and sat down.

Slowly, almost imperceptibly, a shadow fell on the open door. Then, without a sound, a man appeared, silhouetted against the light. Julie had the strangest feeling he'd been there all the time, just behind the door, listening.

For a moment the man's face was in darkness. Then he came forward. He was looking at Julie carefully, his eyes hard and searching.

Then his lips curved into a friendly grin and his eyes warmed a little. Julie automatically smiled back and put out her hand.

Maurice said, "This is Roger. Roger, this is Marie-Claire." Roger wouldn't be his real name, of course.

They sat down. "Now," Maurice began immediately, "let's look at security procedures. As a first defense we aim for a new series of checks farther up the line. . . ." As Julie listened she stole an occasional glance at the stranger. He had a thin face with rather sallow skin and straight black hair which flopped over

his forehead in untidy straggles. He was dressed in rough clothes, but on one hand he wore a thick gold ring. His eyes were so dark they were almost black and you had the feeling they didn't miss a thing. At one point they flicked up and looked straight into Julie's eyes. She glanced hurriedly away.

". . . So, Marie-Claire, you take the Americans and the British," Maurice was saying, "and Roger, you the other nationalities. All right so far?"

Roger said, his voice low and soft, "Those already in hiding? Have they been checked?"

"Pretty well," Maurice replied.

"No so-called Czechs or Poles?"

"No, none. But—there is one odd passenger we've been asked to take. A German by nationality, no less."

Roger remained impassive. "A German?"

"Yes, but a reluctant one, apparently. A Jew who's doing forced labor for the Navy in Brest. He has some vital documents he wants to get out."

"What vital documents?" Roger asked gently.

"Ah, some scientific marvel that would be very valuable. We don't know the details."

"And he's in a Navy establishment?"

"Yes."

"Which one?"

Roger was asking a lot of questions. Perhaps that was his way, Julie thought, perhaps that was how things were done in Paris.

Maurice shrugged. "We don't know."

"And how is he to be removed?"

"That's to be arranged by some—er, friends."

Roger nodded very slowly. "It does sound rather risky. I'd certainly like to interrogate him."

"Of course. We all want to be certain about him!" Maurice sat forward in his chair. "Right, let's call it a day. Unless you have any questions . . . ?"

Julie looked at Roger. He was shaking his head. She almost spoke—she wanted to confirm the arrangements for her and Peter. But she changed her mind; it didn't seem to be the right moment anymore.

Maurice took the identity card from the table. "Here's your new identity, Roger. If we can bother you for a thumbprint . . . ?"

Roger rolled his right thumb on the pad and placed his print carefully on the card.

Maurice looked at Roger. "And the photograph?"

"Of course!" He felt in his jacket pocket and brought out a small photograph.

Maurice handed the card and photograph to Julie. She pushed them into her trouser pocket and stood up. Roger sprang to his feet and bowed slightly.

On a whim she said, "The Meteor thing . . . how did you escape?"

"A friend warned me, just before I walked into the trap."

"But the others—?"

He shook his head and sighed deeply. "Most of them gone . . ."

He looked genuinely upset and Julie felt a little guilty for having asked. She said, "Sorry—I . . ."

His eyes came up suddenly. "No—please don't worry. That's the price we have to pay sometimes, isn't it? They knew that. They knew the risks. All one can do is learn the lessons."

"Yes, of course . . ."

The distress had disappeared and now he was smiling slightly. She noticed, though, that his eyes were cold.

She muttered good-bye to Maurice and said to Roger, "I'll have your card ready in an hour."

He bowed again. "Thank you, madame."

Julie went quietly through the house and out into the lane. Her happiness had evaporated. The presence of Roger troubled her, not just because he was a stranger, but because he was something new, and new elements made her nervous.

And there was something else. What? Yes—he frightened her. It was those cold watchful eyes.

A small shiver went down her spine and, pushing her hands in her pockets, she walked quickly home.

Vasson watched her go and wondered why she had been wary.

It was probably just native suspicion. She was like the rest of them: distrustful of anything from outside. There was nothing more to it than that. After all, she had no reason to be suspicious. No, she was an earnest, well-meaning type, but definitely not too bright.

He turned to Maurice. "A good girl, that."

"Yes, the best."

Vasson sat down again. He waited for Maurice to speak: it would show the proper subservience.

Maurice said, "Right. Now, I'll try to get the rest of your new papers by Thursday, but no promises. In the meantime, lie low—"

"But I've still got my own papers—I could use them."

"No! You've been using them in Paris, haven't you? And you're known there."

"Well—yes." He had to admit it: the owner of the papers, a man called Fougères, had indeed used them in Paris before he found his way into Kloffer's dungeon. Kloffer's office had then replaced the identity photographs with Vasson's and substituted his thumbprint—and a very professional job they'd made of it too.

"Then it would be much too dangerous to use them," Maurice stated. "Just stay here until your new papers are ready."

"Of course! Whatever you say!" It didn't make any difference: he had three other identities to choose from, any one of which would do perfectly well if he needed to slip away from the village. The Gare Montparnasse scare was nonsense, of course: he'd made it up.

"When your papers are fixed, then we'll send you to Morlaix or St.-Brieuc to interview parcels as soon as they come off the train."

Morlaix was very convenient: it housed his local contact.

Vasson thought: Now for a little touch of finesse. He asked softly, "What about people *within* the *réseau*? Have they been checked recently?"

"No, but then there's hardly anyone who hasn't been with me from the beginning. Those who do join I check very carefully."

That was true enough. At the beginning Maurice had kept Vasson under close watch until his identity had been confirmed, first with London, who had okayed him straightaway—they would, of course: Fougères was a long-standing member of the Meteor Line—and then with the contact in Paris, the one who had given him the introduction to the Brittany *réseau*. The contact had, in fact, been under Kloffer's supervision for some two weeks. If Vasson remembered correctly, Kloffer had the man's

wife in the basement at the Avenue Foch. Anyway, the man had done what was required and had, in front of a witness, sworn to Vasson's identity as Paul Fougères. Vasson rather liked the name: it had an aristocratic ring to it.

Vasson walked to the window. "So what can I do until Thursday?"

"Nothing."

That suited Vasson very well. It would give him the time he needed.

But not if he was cooped up. He said with feeling, "I'll go mad if I have to stay inside all the time. All right if I stretch my legs in the evenings?"

"If you have to. But stay in the village and keep out of sight of Germans."

"Certainly. I'll be very careful." Which was true: he would conduct his reconnaissance of the village very carefully indeed.

Maurice stood up. "I'm off now. Any problems, just leave a message at the café."

After Maurice's departure, Vasson sat quite still, thinking that it was all going quite well. There were, of course, a few minor problems; but then there always were.

He lit a cigarette and drew on it deeply. First, there was the security of the line. Unfortunately it was very good. Maurice had done an excellent job. It would be impossible to slip a bogus American or Britisher through, not with that girl interviewing them. And a Czech or Pole—well, everyone knew that was how Meteor had fallen. It would be tempting fate to try the same trick again.

So—what could he get on his own? The Bretons were close people, very suspicious of strangers. It would take ten years to be trusted around here. No hope of confidences then. No way of locating the safe houses easily. Nor of identifying more than two of the couriers: Maurice had made sure of that. So what did that leave him with?

Quite a lot, in fact.

He could get the organizers, no trouble there. Maurice, the girl and the people who actually went on beach operations. And they, after all, were the real plums.

Then the Gestapo would have to do some of their own work

for a change. They would have to extract the names of the small fry. It wouldn't do them any harm—he'd been handing them things on a plate for long enough.

It wouldn't be as clean and satisfying as Meteor had been. But what the hell? After this job he would be a very rich man.

Anyway, he'd go mad if he stayed in this place too long, with its bleating sheep and the damned wind howling the place down. And the cold! He'd never been so cold in his life.

No: he'd hit them hard and quick and then he'd be off, back to Paris. And Kloffer could threaten him all he wanted: Vasson would *stay* in Paris. This time he was going home.

He went into the messy, smelly back room he'd been given. It was like a rathole: disgusting.

He picked up a bottle of wine from beside the bed and swigged at it. He could not go out until dark, but Christ! it seemed a long time away.

Suddenly he realized he'd forgotten something. Ah! Of course. There was the other matter: the scientist. What the hell was he going to do about that?

He could always do nothing, but if the Jew really was important . . .

The main problem was to find out exactly who this fellow might be. It would be no good asking Baum, his Gestapo contact at Morlaix. The fool would probably blow it straightaway by going to Brest and inquiring.

No, better to keep Baum out of it. He'd have to handle it himself.

In the meantime there was nothing to do but wait.

He swigged at the wine again, gulping the liquid down in long drafts. It was the only way to drink the stuff: it was rough as hell. Then he lay back on the bed and slept fitfully through the afternoon.

At dusk he got up. He put an old cap on his head, a canvas workingman's bag over his shoulder, and some identity papers in his pocket. Then, looking carefully out of the door, he slipped quietly into the night.

The dawn was pale and misty and very cold. Julie stepped into the yard, gulped the fresh, cold air, and watched her breath floating away in long clouds, up into the white opalescent sky.

"Maman, are we *really* going in the van?" Peter ran up to her, skipping with excitement.

"I certainly hope so! Uncle Jean got it going yesterday and it seems to be working. But we'll see."

She opened the barn door and climbed into the ancient Peugeot van. Peter hovered next to the passenger door while she turned on the ignition, took out the starting handle and, coming round to the front of the vehicle, swung energetically on the handle. After four attempts, the engine fired a couple of times; at the fifth it started.

Peter squealed with excitement and, flinging open the door, jumped in.

Julie wiped her hands on her overalls, climbed in and slowly eased in the clutch. The van lurched into the yard and bumped down the lane and through the village. Julie tried to change into second gear. There was a loud grinding noise. She double declutched and tried again. Another rasping and clattering and then the engine settled onto a lower note: they were in second gear.

Peter was laughing uncontrollably, his little face creased with delight. Julie exclaimed, "I never promised to be the world's best driver!" And then she was laughing too.

She concentrated on the road, a cross-country route to Kernibon, through narrow one-track lanes. Fortunately there was no traffic—few people had gasoline nowadays—and it wasn't necessary to stop to let anyone pass. After ten minutes a stretch of misty water came into view: the Morlaix estuary. Julie looked into the distance, across the wide river to the village where she and Peter had landed after that terrible fishing boat journey. It all seemed a long time ago now.

Julie found the right farmhouse and drove into the yard. Eventually the farmer came out and grunted at her. From his expression, he too had never seen a woman in trousers before. He waved her up to a shed then opened the van doors and slid a plank of wood up into the back. He disappeared into the shed and emerged a moment later pulling an angry squealing sow on a length of rope. He pushed and shoved the pig into the van, then closed the doors. He grunted again. Julie smiled because he sounded just like the pig. Or rather, *their* pig, as it was now. Julie politely refused the customary invitation to coffee and, waving good-bye, restarted the van.

Peter said, "Maman, couldn't we go down to the village for a minute?"

"Goodness, why?"

"I've never been there before!"

Julie was a little taken aback. Overcome with remorse, she said, "Of course, darling! Though we can't be very long, otherwise we'll be late for school."

The village was nothing much, a few cottages built around a haven formed by a small peninsula which protruded into the estuary. Half a dozen fishing boats were moored in the center of the inlet. It looked as if some had just come in: men were offloading baskets into small boats floating alongside.

Julie turned the van around and they got out. She said, "There! Even smaller than Trégasnou!"

"Yes!" Peter exclaimed. He obviously thought smallness a great recommendation. "Look at the boats! Do they go a long, long way?"

"No, darling. They're not allowed to go far." She saw that all the boats had sails furled to their masts. Because of the lack of fuel, fishing boats had to rely on the wind again, just as they had before the advent of engines.

Something caught Julie's eye. A figure had emerged from behind a stone barn on the far side of the inlet. Julie stiffened: there was something about him that was familiar. . . .

The man turned down between two cottages and disappeared. Julie frowned with disappointment.

A moment later he was back, pushing a *vélo,* which he must have collected from the alleyway. Julie stared in disbelief. The man looked just like Michel.

The man got on the *vélo* and started pedaling toward her.

Julie tried to catch a good look at his face. After a moment the man looked up into her face and wobbled.

He had recognized her too.

It *was* Michel!

But what was he doing here? Julie couldn't understand it.

He came up to her, his expression serious and unsmiling, and said sharply, "What are you doing here?"

"I might ask the same of you."

"Come on—what *are* you doing here?"

"Collecting a pig. I'm a farmhand now."

"So I see!"

Peter was becoming uneasy. Julie reached down and pulled him to her. "We were just going anyway . . ."

Opening the door of the van, she pushed Peter up into the seat.

"Julie—" Michel came up and held the door open for her. "As a favor to me—don't tell anyone you've seen me here." His face was even more severe than usual and there were deep shadows under his eyes. He looked as though he hadn't slept for days.

"All right. If that's what you want. Though . . . you're not creating trouble, are you, Michel?"

He dismissed the idea with a shake of his head. "I promise."

"In that case . . ." She picked up the starting handle, but he took it from her and, going around to the front of the van, cranked the engine into life.

When he brought the handle back, she said, "By the way, no more news about the—delivery?"

"No, nothing new. He'll be with you shortly, safe and sound."

She put the van into gear. "Good-bye then."

He nodded, his face tight and angry, and turned quickly away.

Peter said, "Mummy, why was he so cross?"

"Darling, I don't know. Really. Come on, let's get you off to school!"

But all the way there, Julie kept thinking: He's up to something. I know he is! Oh Michel, what on earth is it now?

24 It was quite a farewell. Most of the senior staff had assembled. Geissler was there, of course, and Gallois.

Geissler held out his hand. "So, Herr Freymann, I'm sorry we are to lose you after all, but I am sure that you will enjoy your new position. A great honor, a great honor!" On this occasion Geissler had not thought of questioning the order: it had come

from the High Command itself, marked "Most Urgent," and he was impressed. "I expect you will be happy to see Berlin again."

"Yes. Yes"

Geissler inclined his head slightly in the German style. "Are you sure, Herr Freymann, that you prefer to walk to your quarters?"

"Yes, thank you." David smiled in the general direction of the factory personnel. He couldn't bring himself to look at Gallois in case guilt and conspiracy should show all over his face.

He shook Geissler's hand and, grasping his briefcase tightly under his arm, walked slowly down the steps. The guard acknowledged him with a slight blink.

His heart hammering in his ears, David began the short walk down the road to the compound.

It would be any minute now. A car, probably; sweeping around the corner, opening its doors, pulling him in, roaring off. . . . David imagined the guard watching curiously, trying to work out what the car was doing, slowly realizing, pulling the rifle up to his shoulder, firing at David . . .

He felt his back itching and shivered. The urge to look around was almost overwhelming. He resisted and kept walking, slowly, to give them time.

At the access road that led down the side of the factory, he paused and looked left and right before crossing the road.

Now, surely! He reached the opposite pavement and went even more slowly. He swayed and almost lost his balance. His legs were still weak.

The compound gates were getting closer, the guards almost visible. David began to worry: it would be very risky if they waited any longer.

He leaned against the wire fence, as if resting. The road behind him was silent: no engine noises, no cars. Nothing stirred.

They weren't coming.

He moved away from the fence, and almost immediately the guard post came into sight. The four uniformed figures were disinterested and bored. He turned in through the gates, as he had a hundred times before.

They hadn't come.

David went automatically toward the hut and walked up the

corridor to his cubicle. He sat on the bed, the briefcase still under his arm.

The message had said they would come for him. But when? How? Getting him out of the compound would be impossible.

Perhaps he'd been deceived. He thought: I'm no good at this sort of thing. I don't understand.

He wasn't due to leave for Berlin until early morning, at seven. He'd wait until then, ready-dressed, just in case. In the meantime, the walk, like any physical exertion nowadays, had tired him out. He lay down.

After a while he sat up and, opening his briefcase, took out a sandwich of bread and cheese which he'd kept specially for the journey. He ate it slowly, chewing each mouthful several times.

Much later he woke and pulled himself up. He guessed it was late, probably about one or two in the morning. Something had woken him. A sound. He got unsteadily to his feet and went to the window. There was a moon, and the outlines of the buildings were just visible in the pale light. Nothing moved.

He was turning to go back to bed when the floor shuddered beneath him. He put out a hand to steady himself. A flash of light flickered against the walls of the cubicle.

A low rumble sounded from far away, the window shook, another flash of light illuminated the night sky.

An air raid. They were common enough. Only this time the Germans hadn't had time to sound the siren.

There was another flash, much closer this time. Then orange and yellow lights flickered against the buildings: an incendiary. David frowned: there was something strange about all this. What was it? Yes—he'd heard no planes. Usually you could hear the drone of the bombers as they passed overhead. There were no searchlights either.

A siren sounded close by. Inside the hut there was a deafening noise of banging doors and running feet and shouting men. A moment later the guards streamed out of the hut, running in the direction of the flickering lights.

David opened the window and stuck his head out. There was another sound now, a drumming, as if people were beating sticks against a wall. Angry people. And there were voices too, a thousand voices shouting and yelling.

It was the workers, the Poles. They were trying to break out.

David cried, "Oh no! Oh no!" and beat his fist against the wall. What *were* they trying to achieve? What did they hope to gain? It would mean death for many of them; death.

He froze. Something caught his eye: a movement to the right, in the shadow of one of the buildings. A figure, running stealthily in a crouched position.

David pulled his head back inside the window and watched, motionless. The figure paused in the darkness of the nearest building, then ran again, coming straight for David.

The figure disappeared beneath his line of sight. A few seconds later a hand appeared over the sill. A head followed. David pressed himself against the wall.

A voice. "Freymann?"

David whispered, "Yes."

"Quick! Climb out and follow me! *Quick!*"

David fumbled for his briefcase and, tucking it under his arm, approached the window. He said breathlessly, "Are you— from . . . ?"

"Shut up. No time for that. Come *now!*"

David looked at the height of the sill and said, "I can't."

The figure hissed, "You *must!*"

David pushed the briefcase through the window. It disappeared rapidly. He got his left foot up onto the sill and pushed his leg out. It was impossible to get a second leg up: the frame was too narrow. He pulled his body up and, sitting astride the sill, rested for a moment, breathing heavily.

"Come on!" The dark figure was pulling at his sleeve.

"All right! All right!" David looked down: it was a long drop, a man's height at least, and he had only one leg to land on. "You'll have to catch me, otherwise I'll fall." David levered himself out until he was hanging from the window, his right leg still in the room. He tried to pull the leg out, but some of his weight was on it and it wouldn't come.

"Have you got me?"

"Yes! Yes!"

Only one thing to do, then. Let go.

He felt himself falling, body first. A hand clutched at his arm and twisted him around. His right foot met the ground, then his

shoulder and his hip. He staggered to his feet, shaking like a leaf, and brushed himself off.

The man had hold of his arm and David found himself being pulled along. The man stopped at the end of the building and David bumped into him. Then the man was off again, running faster, his hand still grasping David's sleeve.

David ran as best he could, but he was already breathing hard. His legs were like rubber and wouldn't do what was required of them. For some reason he couldn't swing his right arm either.

They approached the perimeter fence at the eastern side of the compound. With alarm David wondered why they were going that way. There was no way out here.

Normally the fence was brilliantly lit, but now it was in darkness. They stopped at the side of a small shed and waited. The man was listening, as tense as a cat. David put his head against the wall and tried to regain his breath.

Suddenly they were off again, the fence looming up in front of them. The man pushed David to the right, then dropped to his hands and knees. There was a gaping hole in the wire. The man hissed "Down!" and David fell to his knees.

The man threw the briefcase ahead of them, then put a hand behind David and pushed. David crawled through. The man came quickly after, picked up David's case and pulled him to his feet. They were running across open ground to the dark wall of a warehouse. They stopped. David gasped for breath.

The man pulled at his sleeve. David said, "Please! Please! I can't go so fast!"

They skirted three more buildings and came to another fence. This time there was no hole. But there was a gate and the gate was open and they were through into a road.

A truck was parked in the road. The man took David around to the tailgate. It was closed. David breathed, "I can't . . . I can't . . ."

The man reached down and, grasping David's foot, heaved. David sprawled over the tailgate, unable to pull himself up. The man pushed again and David landed headfirst in the truck's load, which smelled strongly of cabbage.

"Hide yourself!"

David panted. "What?"

"Hide yourself under the vegetables!"

". . . Under?"

There was a thud as something landed beside David in the cabbages. "Your case. Good-bye."

There was silence. David took hold of the briefcase and crawled slowly over the vegetables to the far end of the truck. How did one bury oneself in a load of cabbages? Painstakingly he began to remove the cabbages one by one until he had made a hollow in them, then he lay down, his case at his side, and pulled the vegetables back over himself.

It wasn't difficult to lie still. At that moment it was all he wanted.

Five minutes passed and the truck hadn't moved. He wished they would hurry. He could hear sounds of violent activity in the compound and the docks: trucks roaring back and forth, distant shouting and an occasional rifle shot. They must be shooting at the Poles.

But why wasn't the truck moving? If they didn't get going soon, they'd never get away!

But the truck didn't move. After half an hour David realized it wasn't going to, at least not for a long time. Perhaps not until daylight. He wished they'd told him.

Eventually he fell into an uneasy sleep, waking frequently. Finally he saw a tinge of gray light through the gaps in the cabbages above his head. He drifted off again.

Suddenly there was a loud crash from immediately behind David's head. He jumped, his heart racing. Someone started whistling and the next moment there was a loud whirring and the truck's engine started up.

The whistler broke into song. "I'm dreaming of you, my love, wherever you may be . . ."

The truck stopped and started a few times. Once David heard the driver talking to someone, but then they were on their way again. The singer began to whistle once more, but softly, and the drone of the wheels fell to a steady hum.

There was silence. The truck had stopped and the engine had been turned off. David waited, tense.

The driver was whistling loudly. The cab door slammed and

footsteps came around to the back of the vehicle. The tailgate was lowered with a loud bang, and a voice called, "Hello, friend. We've arrived."

David wasn't sure what to do. He stayed still.

But the voice came again. "You're safe, friend. Time to get out."

David pushed the cabbages away from his face and tried to move, but he was very stiff. He gripped the metal side of the truck and hauled himself into a sitting position. He blinked and, looking out, saw that the truck was backed up almost to the doors of a wooden building. A man of about forty dressed in an old cap and working jacket was standing by the tailgate.

The man climbed up into the truck and walked over the vegetables toward him. "Here. I'll give you a hand."

"Thank you. That's most kind."

The man pulled David to his feet, picked up the briefcase and helped him across the uneven surface of the cabbages to the open tailgate and down onto the ground.

David now saw that the building was a barn. The man led him quickly inside and into a corner behind a pile of sacks. "You're to wait here."

"Thank you." The floor at this point was thick with straw and, gratefully, David sank down onto it.

The man had turned to leave.

David called, "Wait! Please—tell me, what was the fire last night?"

The man paused. Eventually he said, "One of the fuel dumps."

"But the Poles. Why did they try to break out?"

"They didn't."

"But the noise?"

"Noise. That's all it was."

"But—why?"

"Because they were asked to. It was a favor." The man turned again. "Best not to know any more, friend."

The barn door closed, the truck's engine started up and slowly faded away. Then there was silence. David lay down on the straw. He tried to sleep, but it was impossible, so he lay still and rested instead.

Much later there was a sound. David opened his eyes. It was a

creaking. A door opening. Someone was coming into the barn, but David's view of the door was obscured by the pile of sacks.

The person was advancing slowly up the barn. Finally, very slowly, the person came into view.

It was a man wearing a scarf over the lower part of his face. The man said gruffly, "Turn around." David turned and, almost immediately, something was placed around his eyes and tied behind his head.

The voice said, "Don't move unless I tell you." There was a rustling of straw as the man walked away, then silence.

The darkness was awful, like being in a pit. David tried to relax. They meant him no harm.

A long time passed. David's stomach ached with hunger.

Then there were footsteps. The straw rustled as someone sat or knelt beside him.

"Hello." It was the voice of a woman, rather breathless.

David cleared his throat. "Good morning."

"Are you all right?" The voice was warm, concerned.

"Yes! Very well, thank you. Very well."

"Good. We—er—heard you had been ill."

"I was. But I'm better now, thank you."

A pause. "Some others will be coming soon. To meet you. We have to ask you some questions."

David was disappointed. Questions? It sounded as if they were going to interrogate him. It had never occurred to him that they wouldn't trust him. He said halfheartedly, "Of course."

He heard paper crackling. "Here, I thought you might be hungry."

"I am, thank you." Something was placed in his hand. It was a roll. He bit into it. Cheese. He took another bite.

Julie watched him eat and felt sorry for him. He seemed so lost and bewildered. She'd be very surprised indeed if he were a German spy—he looked far too harmless. Certainly he was too frail to fight, he wouldn't be able to hurt a fly. The hands were thin and veined and when he brought the bread to his mouth they shook slightly. The face beneath the blindfold was lined and pouchy, like a dog's. She could see that he had been ill. Also, he was much older than she'd expected.

It was a pity to have to put him through an interrogation, but there was no way around it. Maurice would allow no exceptions.

She peered at her wristwatch. The others were late. But she must wait. It would be wrong to start the questions without them.

Finally, there was a creaking. The barn door opened and two people slipped in. One was the unmistakable squat figure of Maurice, the other, the taller, slimmer frame of Roger.

Julie nodded at them to show all was well and, satisfied, Maurice turned to look at the old man sitting on the bed of straw. Meanwhile Roger was approaching slowly, his eyes fixed on the corner of the sack pile. Suddenly he stopped in midstep and Julie guessed he had caught his first sight of the old man. For a moment he stared then he relaxed and leaned casually against a wooden pillar.

His eyes darted up to Julie's, and she looked hurriedly away. He was always catching her by surprise that way.

Maurice was sitting on the straw, talking to the old man in a low voice. Julie went closer and sat down beside him. ". . . Interrogation is necessary for our self-protection, do you understand? Please tell us everything. First, your name and background."

"Freymann, David Freymann. I lived most of my life just outside Berlin, in a suburb called Hennigsdorf. . . ." Out of the corner of her eye Julie saw Roger come closer and crouch silently on the straw just behind Maurice.

". . . Mainly I worked on radio-wave development. Then just before the war started, it got all difficult. Because I was Jewish, you see. I was put in a camp . . ."

"Where?" Maurice interrupted.

"Near Munich. Called Dachau. I was there some time—two, maybe three years, I don't know. Time—is difficult to judge." He spoke matter-of-factly.

"Then?"

"Then they sent me to Brest."

"Why?"

"They needed me. There are very few scientists who are experienced in radar. They had to swallow their pride."

Roger said, "Explain, please, what is radar?"

"I'll try to explain simply. It's . . . a way of using radio waves so that you can see with them, at night, in bad weather, it doesn't

matter. You can see the echo of any large metallic object—a ship, an airplane, whatever. . . . You can discover its range, and in the case of a plane its height. Nothing can hide from you. . . ."

Maurice asked, "And this is the information you're bringing with you?"

Freymann quickly shook his head. "No, radar is already known. . . ." He paused, as if debating something. Finally he said, "What I'm bringing is a refinement of it. A type which can see like a map, draw pictures almost. It will—create a great advantage."

"In what way?"

"For one thing, the Germans could not detect it as they do the existing radar. So they would have no warning of the enemy's approach. For another—it will, I believe, provide enormous detail so that for the bombers it will be like having a map of the country underneath." He cocked his head slightly. "Do you understand what I say?"

"Yes, I think so."

Freymann sat forward and felt for Maurice's arm. "Look, you cannot possibly know that what I'm telling you is the truth, can you?"

Maurice dropped his eyes. "No, you're quite right. I can't."

"Right. But do you believe I'm Jewish?"

"Well, yes."

"Now what do you suppose would make a Jew want to help the Nazis?"

"Force? Coercion?"

"True. But I'm a free man now. That leaves coercion. But I have no family for them to threaten me with. My family disowned me a long time ago!"

"I can't be sure of that."

"Ah . . . !" Freymann paused, taken aback. "Of course." He seemed so downcast that Julie had the urge to reach out to him and pat his shoulder.

"So—then, it is a simple question of whether you believe me or not." He spoke quietly and with resignation. Julie wanted to say, I believe you.

Maurice looked at Julie then Roger. "Any questions?"

Julie said, "When you talk of your family, who do you mean?"

"My wife. My daughter."

"And they've disowned you?"

"Yes. My wife was not Jewish, you see."

"But your daughter?"

"She'll have forgotten me by now—and the best thing too!" His voice almost broke. "She was pretty. And clever. She had everything before her. It was *better,* you understand. *Better.*"

Roger said sharply, "What company did you work for in Brest?"

"Goulvent, Pescard et Compagnie."

"Under what authority—what German authority?"

"The Navy. But I was on loan, so to speak, from the SS."

"And when you were working in Germany, what company then?"

"Gema. The Gema Company."

There was a short silence before Maurice got to his feet. Julie and Roger followed him across the barn until they were out of earshot.

Maurice looked at Julie. "Well?"

Julie said, "I believe him. Everything about him seems—right."

They both turned to Roger. His eyes were hooded and unreadable. Slowly, the eyes came up to Maurice's. "Yes, he's genuine."

Maurice nodded. "I agree."

Roger said, "So he goes, does he?"

"Yes."

"When?"

"Soon. The fewer who know the exact date the better. You'll be told in good time."

Roger smiled. "Of course." But he was put out, Julie could tell.

Julie touched Maurice's arm. "Can't we take the blindfold off? At least until we have to move him again."

Maurice rubbed his lip thoughtfully.

Roger interrupted. "No! It'll be much safer to leave him as he is!"

"Please. He's absolutely harmless. I'd stake my life on it."

Maurice gave his approval. "All right."

Julie ran back. The old man shrank at the sound of her steps. "It's all right," she said soothingly. "I've come to take your blindfold off."

"Thank you. How kind." She untied the handkerchief from

around his head. The old man blinked and put his hand up to his eyes. He had large, dark, sad eyes; again Julie was reminded of a mournful dog.

"I'll bring you more food later. The guard has water when you want it."

"Thank you. You really are very kind."

She touched his hand quickly then went back to the others waiting by the door.

Roger avoided her stare and put his face to the gap in the door.

"All clear?" Maurice asked.

Roger nodded and, opening the door, led the way out. As Julie stepped into the daylight, she looked up and found Roger staring at her. She almost gasped: there was rage and hatred in his eyes. For a moment she was bewildered. Why? The blindfold? Such a small incident—but what else could it be? She looked desperately at Maurice, but he had seen nothing.

God, Julie thought, the man's terrifying—and no one knows it but me.

Vasson tried to conceal his irritation. The girl had outwitted him, and he didn't like it.

It was time to get away. He said, "I'll go now. Across the fields."

Maurice looked up sharply. "But do you know the way?"

"I'll find it, don't worry. Anyway, it's time I got to know my way around. In case of trouble."

"Careful not to speak to anyone."

Vasson almost sighed with annoyance: Maurice must have told him a dozen times. "Don't worry! I won't."

"It's the accent. They'd know you were an outsider straightaway."

"But then they wouldn't tell, would they? Being good Bretons . . ." Before Maurice could answer, Vasson had gone.

He went around the barn, over a wall and into a field. He spotted a gate on the far side and began to make his way across the field toward it. Almost immediately he regretted his decision: the field had just been plowed. He pressed on, cursing under his breath as his feet slipped and stumbled over the hard, bumpy ground.

At the gate he paused and looked over his shoulder: nothing. The others were going back by the road. He looked ahead:

nothing either. Away to the right he could hear the faint sound of surf and calling gulls: the sea.

He went on, across four smaller fields until the village came into view over a slight hill. There was a farmhouse immediately ahead, on the other side of the road. He would have to cross the road and skirt the farmhouse and the village to reach the main road to Morlaix.

He approached the wall beside the road, peered over it and, climbing carefully up the rough stonework, jumped down. As he prepared to climb the opposite wall, he stopped. Someone was walking down the road toward the village.

It was the girl.

She had seen him. He waited as she approached, walking fast, her eyes down. When she was almost level with him she moved to the opposite side of the road. Then she was past, swinging on down the hill. He watched her for a moment. The trousers were ridiculous, he decided. They revealed and accentuated the movement of her bottom. She probably wore them on purpose. Bitch.

He shinned up the wall and dropped neatly over onto the other side. It was a pasture this time, with a few sheep pulling at the scant grass. The solitary farmhouse was nearby. He decided to keep close to the buildings rather than risk being seen wandering across the fields.

He came up behind the barn and peered around the corner. There was a yard and, on the opposite side, the farmhouse itself. Some iron railings with a gate separated the yard from the pasture. He would have to walk along the railings in view of the farmhouse. He waited a moment, to make sure that everything was quiet. Then, just as he was about to set off, he stopped.

Someone had entered the yard from the other end. The girl again. She was walking slowly, almost cautiously toward the farmhouse.

He ducked back behind the wall and wondered if she was looking for him.

He peered out again. She was at the back door of the farmhouse, pushing up the latch. She paused and looked around.

He pulled back before she saw him.

There was the sound of voices. Hers, and a high-pitched voice: a child's. He put his eye back to the corner.

A small boy was jumping up and down beside the girl. She took

his hand and, with one last look over her shoulder, pulled the child inside.

At last Vasson understood. The girl lived here!

She hadn't wanted him to know. He smiled to himself. The information could be useful.

He looked at his watch: only fifteen minutes to go. Not enough time to make the enormous detour which would keep him out of sight of the farmhouse.

He sauntered out from behind the wall and walked casually along the railings. He was being watched, he felt sure.

When he reached the next field, he climbed over a stile in the corner and glanced back. He was out of sight of the farmhouse.

He went diagonally across the next field, and the next, skirting the village.

Finally he gained the main Morlaix road and walked along it until he came to a small crossroads. Then he settled down to wait.

After half an hour he was still waiting. He wasn't surprised: everything in this godforsaken place was always late.

At last, the small battered bus came into view, its engine roaring. Vasson flagged it down and jumped on board.

He settled himself in a seat and decided that the day might not turn out so badly after all: there was still time to get a decent lunch off Baum. Only one thing still bothered him: the girl. She was suspicious of him. And he didn't like that, he didn't like it at all.

"Mummy, what are you staring at?"

Julie stroked Peter's head. "Nothing, darling." She moved away from the window and, going to the sink, started to peel some potatoes for the midday meal.

Jean came in through the parlor door and said, "I thought I just saw someone in the back pasture."

Julie kept her eyes down. "Oh?"

He reached onto the mantelpiece for his tobacco then remembered he didn't have any. "Yes, I'm sure I did. But . . . probably just one of the lads. Eh?"

"Probably."

It had been Roger; she had seen him.

He had been prowling around; he reminded her of a cat. She

394

thought: I don't like it anymore. The sooner Peter and I are away the better. It wouldn't be long now. The moon was on the wane: the boat would come soon.

There was a rapping on the back door. Julie jumped, but Jean just shrugged and went to open it.

There was a short exclamation then Michel strode into the room, his face like thunder.

Julie gasped, "What's the matter?"

Michel said bitterly, "*You* should be able to tell *me*!"

Julie pulled Peter up from the table. "Go to your room." The boy left, closing the door quietly behind him. Julie sat down. "Now! Explain, please!"

Michel breathed in, then began talking slowly, as if speaking to a disobedient child. "Last night, in Brest . . . the Germans were expecting us. At the fuel dumps. Three of my comrades died. Three! We were only able to fire one of the main tanks. The whole thing was a fiasco—"

"Wait!" Julie said sharply. "These fuel dumps, what have they to do with us?"

"It was a diversion, of course!"

Julie was amazed. "For the scientist? You did it especially for *him*?"

Michel dismissed the question with a wave of his arm. "Yes . . . no. Well, we were planning it anyway. But the point is, *they were waiting for us!* How did they know, Julie, *how*? My friends are asking questions! They—"

Julie stood up. "I think it would be better if you didn't go on. To start with, nobody here ever knew *when* the operation was to be—"

"But I told you!"

"You said only that it would be the end of the week. Also we had no idea you were planning a diversion of that kind. And, Michel, the old scientist *did* get away. If they'd been warned, they would hardly have let him escape!"

Michel stood up, his face hard and cruel. "But my comrades are saying, why is it that the first time we work with your lot, we get sold down the river! They are saying, we knew we should never trust them. They are saying ugly things. They are talking of revenge. What am I to say to *them*?"

Anger rose in Julie's throat. "You will tell them this! That they should look for a shark in their own ranks. Or bad planning! Or —something! Just don't use us as a scapegoat! Because it was not one of us!"

Jean tapped Michel firmly on the arm with his pipe. "Perhaps some of your own people took advantage of the opportunity, eh! Perhaps they wanted to get rid of some of their precious comrades, heh? And they wanted you to blame *us*!"

There was a long silence. Michel looked unhappily from one to the other. Eventually he said, "All right! I'll do my best to convince them! I just hope that"—he shook his head in frustration —"that what you say is true! But, for God's sake, don't blame me if—"

Julie said coolly, "If what?"

"If—emotions run high!"

She said, "I think they already have!" She went to the back door and opened it wide. "Good-bye, Michel. Please don't ever come here again."

When he had gone she sat, stunned, and thought: It's all falling apart again, just like before.

The pâté was very good but the steak was not as tender as it might have been. Vasson decided to leave the rest and pushed the plate to one side.

Baum said, "I'll send across for some of their *tarte maison,* if you like. It is really delicious."

"Yes. And some decent cheese."

"Of course!" Baum pressed the buzzer on his desk. Vasson noticed that he crooked his little finger as he did it. The man was probably a queer.

Baum smiled, his thick lips drawing back to reveal yellowing teeth. Vasson decided he would prefer to deal with Kloffer any day. Baum tapped the telephone and sighed. "The Navy—not very efficient, you know. You would think they would have come back to us by now. When did we call? Half an hour ago at least!" He picked up the piece of paper he'd written his notes on. "This —er—Freymann. If he's a Jew, I doubt he'll be of much consequence." He placed his fingers together in a neat arch. "Nevertheless, it will be rather satisfying to sweep him up into our little

net, won't it? Then we can deliver him back from whence he came." He smiled sweetly across the table. A raving queer, Vasson decided.

Baum tapped his fingertips together impatiently. "Now, where *is* Schultz? You must have your dessert! *And* your cheese!" He pressed the button again.

The door burst open and a young man, presumably Schultz, stood at attention. He looked as if he'd just seen a ghost. "Herr Oberst! The telephone, it's Paris! General Oberg!"

For a moment Baum froze, then, swallowing hard, reached for the telephone as if it were glass. He lifted the receiver carefully to his ear and said precisely, *"Ja? Ah, Herr General!"*

In the next few moments Baum said *ja* many times. Then the German jerked his head and looked at Vasson, amazement on his face.

Vasson tensed. It was something big. Concerning him. And Freymann. It must be Freymann!

After spouting a torrent of German, Baum replaced the receiver carefully in its holder, his lips quivering. Finally he said, "That was General Oberg. The head of the *entire* Gestapo in France." He paused, as if to assimilate the information, then continued, "It appears that this man—Freymann—is important to us. In fact, more than that! Vital!"

Baum's eyes were round with anxiety. "We *must* get him back, do you understand? We must not fail! It is absolutely essential!"

Vasson looked away, already calculating how he could take all the credit.

He regarded Baum for a moment and said casually, "Nothing is ever guaranteed."

Baum nearly went purple. "What do you mean by that! I thought you *had* the man!"

"Oh, I do! I do! But, when I am relying on your men to close the trap, then nothing can ever be guaranteed." Vasson stood up. "Now, it's about time we made a plan, isn't it?"

Baum agreed vehemently. "Yes! Yes! Whatever you say!"

PART FOUR

March 1943

25 Julie embraced Tante Marie very hard and said, "Thank you again. For everything."

Tante Marie sniffed and, flapping her hand with irritation, said gruffly, "Go on! Be off with you! Go on!"

Julie kissed the old woman quickly on the cheek, then, taking Peter's hand, followed Jean's dark figure out of the kitchen and across the yard. She whispered to Peter, "All right, darling?"

"Yes, Mummy, I'm fine."

Julie felt very proud of him. For the past few weeks she had been telling him the same story she told everyone else: that they were moving to Rennes. Only the previous night, when she'd heard the boat was coming, had she let him know the truth. Bless him, he'd taken it like a lamb. He even pretended to be looking forward to it, though she could see he was very nervous.

She hitched the strap of the haversack farther up her shoulder. It was light enough: she'd taken almost nothing. Peter had his own bag too, with spare clothes, a food parcel from Tante Marie and some of his favorite things: a toy truck, his colored pencils and, of course, the carved ship.

They started briskly up the road. A faint drizzle was drifting down and a film of dampness formed on Julie's face. She pulled her beret farther over her forehead and put a hand on Peter's head. He had already raised the hood of his jacket. Julie had chosen practical clothes for both of them: warm trousers and a windbreaker for him, and trousers and a cowjacket for herself.

As they climbed the long hill the dampness became a steady drizzle. The faint patter of the falling rain sounded a gentle rhythm in the stillness of the night. Julie had sudden doubts about Peter's jacket; perhaps it wouldn't be up to all this rain. She would check it later.

They reached the heathland and turned right, up a slight hill. After a while the outlines of a small building came into view. It was a shepherd's hut, made of stone with a slate roof, caved in at the far end. Jean crouched and entered. Tightly clutching Peter's hand, Julie followed.

It was dark inside, but Julie could hear the sounds of the waiting people: slight rustlings and the occasional muffled cough. She felt her way to the side of the hut and sat down in a space, pulling Peter down beside her. She put her arm around the small shoulders and hugged him. "Won't be long now!" His hand felt for hers and grasped it tightly.

Julie moved her leg and bumped it against someone else's. "Sorry."

"No, no. My fault. So sorry."

The voice was familiar. Julie whispered, "Herr Freymann?"

"Yes."

"It's me, from the barn. Are you all right? Have you been looked after?"

"Oh yes, yes. Thank you. Everyone has been most kind."

Julie thought what a nice man he was. She wondered vaguely how he'd manage the path to the beach.

Peter coughed slightly. Squeezing him against her, she settled down to wait. Her stomach was fluttering uneasily, but she forced herself to be calm. Whatever happened, she wasn't going to let herself think about all the things that could go wrong tonight.

She pressed her lips against Peter's hair and closed her eyes and tried to imagine what life would be like in England after such a long time.

There was no shelter on the clifftop. Vasson was getting wet and he didn't like it. He pulled up the collar of his jacket and crouched on his haunches.

The night was quiet: the only sound was the murmur of the sea far below and the steady splatter of the falling rain. It wasn't ideal for stalking—the air was too still—but it was good enough.

He took a look around. No sign of Baum. Thank God for that. The fool might not screw it up after all. Vasson worked out how long it would be before he could slip away and get to Baum's position. Half an hour maybe. After the passengers had gone

down to the beach. Then he could sit on Baum—physically if necessary—until the right moment.

As always, it was a matter of timing.

He took another look around. What a good lookout he had become! Maurice *would* be impressed.

Clifftop lookout was his important new job. A promotion, no less. This was the first time Maurice had trusted him with beach duty. It was most ironic.

But the rain was a nuisance. Vasson cursed: the water was soaking right through his clothes to his skin. And damn cold it was too.

Another look: still no sign of Baum. The man might stick to the plan yet.

He tried to guess what time it was. Eleven maybe. Not long before the first party would arrive.

Peering down into the darkness of the cove below, he thought what a very neat trap it made, and allowed himself a smile.

Someone entered the hut and said in accented English, "First group now."

A voice said, "Hooray!" Someone laughed nervously.

There was the sound of people moving and then the silhouette of figures against the doorway.

The old man grasped Julie's arm. "Is that us?"

"No. We go last, on our own."

A few minutes later the second group moved out. Then the voice of Gérard, the fisherman, was saying, "Ready?"

Julie stood and helped Peter to his feet, saying in his ear, "Do you want to do a wee, darling, before we go?"

"No. I'm all right, thank you." The small high-pitched voice was so faint and uncertain that Julie reached down and gave him one last hug.

Gérard led the old man out and Julie and Peter followed. It was raining more heavily now, a steady downpour.

Jean was waiting. It was time to say good-bye. Julie flung her arms around his neck and hugged him. Jean patted her back, then, pushing her gently away, took Peter up in his arms. "Take care, young man," he whispered. Then, putting Peter down, he turned abruptly and disappeared in the direction of the village.

Julie wiped her eyes and, Peter in hand, hurried off in the direction of the path. When they reached the clifftop Gérard was stepping onto the path, turning to help the old man down. As Julie waited, the dark shape of a man crouching a few feet away caught her eye. The clifftop lookout.

As she watched him he came toward her. He towered over her, his face a featureless blur. "Is that the last?"

She recognized the voice: the man Roger. "Yes."

Seeing Peter for the first time, Roger stepped in front of her and said, "Why's he here?"

"He's coming with me."

"But why?"

"We're going, both of us."

"On the boat?"

"Yes. Now—please—let us pass."

There was a pause, then a slight chuckle. "Of course." Roger put out his hand and touched Peter's cheek.

Julie pulled Peter close in behind her, moved around Roger and began to negotiate the path.

The rain had turned the path to mud. Julie went slowly because she didn't want Peter to slip and frighten himself, and because it was impossible to overtake Gérard and the scientist anyway. She could hear Gérard coaxing the old man past rocks and down the steeper slopes.

Julie slipped, grabbed for a handhold and missed. She landed on her hip. She breathed, "Damn!"

Peter's voice said anxiously, "You all right, Mummy?"

She pulled herself up and, trembling a little, laughed nervously. "I'm fine. Are you all right?"

Julie felt her way forward again, even more slowly, until at last they were near the beach. She heard Gérard saying "Just let go" and saw the old man poised on the top of the slide. Suddenly he was off, disappearing toward the paleness of the beach.

She sat down and waited for Peter to sit beside her. She whispered, "It's the slide I told you about. We'll go together, shall we?" And holding his hand, Julie pushed off. They shot down and landed safely on the sand. With relief Julie realized it was the last time she would ever have to negotiate that path.

The other two were waiting for them. Julie picked herself up

and wiped the worst of the mud off the back of Peter's jacket and trousers. Gérard moved off, with Freymann following. Julie looked at the thin, stooped figure of the scientist in his inadequate clothes, and then at Peter, his small figure huddled against the relentless rain, and thought: This is ridiculous. She caught Gérard by the arm. "What's the earliest the boat will come?"

"Half an hour, I suppose."

"Look, it's so wet and miserable, I'll take these two into the rocks over there." She indicated the far side of the cove. "It might be a bit dryer."

Gérard hesitated. "All right. I'll collect you when the time comes."

Julie turned back to the two forlorn figures and said, "If we go farther along we might find some shelter and get less wet. All right? Just follow me."

Julie led the way down to the water and along the sand. She tried to remember the layout of the rocks from the last time, all those months ago, but her memory wasn't very clear.

They came to the lower rocks and began to scramble over. Julie turned to Freymann. "Can you manage?"

"Oh yes. Don't worry about me!"

There were larger boulders now. The crevice was somewhere near here. Recognizing the dim outlines of some larger rocks, she spotted the place where she had hidden before. With Richard.

"In here!" she said triumphantly.

When the old man and the boy had disappeared into the darkness of the crevice, she followed. It had been worth coming: the rocks curved in above their heads and formed a roof with only a slight gap in between. As long as one kept away from the drips that fell steadily from the bumps and lips of the overhangs, it was relatively dry. Julie said cheerfully, "All right?"

Peter said plaintively, "I am a bit wet."

Julie felt his trousers and top, and said, "Just damp, that's all. You'll soon dry out. Think—sailors get wet all the time."

"Yes," Peter said thoughtfully. "Mummy?"

"Mmmm?"

"Does Richard get wet all the time?"

"Oh, I think so. Yes. I'm sure he does."

"That's all right then!" His voice sounded more cheerful, and Julie guessed he was beginning to enjoy his adventure.

Julie tried to see Freymann's face. "And you, Monsieur Freymann? How are you?"

Freymann's voice said, "Much better, thank you. Much better."

David sat against the rock and closed his eyes. Already he was exhausted and the night had hardly started. The worst—the boat trip—was yet to come. Still, he had traveled a long way, a long way.

He patted the bag tied around his waist. Everything in it must be wet by now. He himself was soaked through. Never mind. He mustn't complain. Not when these people were being so good and brave.

Anyway what was discomfort when one was a free man? Ha! He was amused by the idea. A free man. It sounded so grand. Although he wasn't sure he knew what real freedom was. Was it being able to do as one wished? Or was it having the opportunity for fulfillment within a rigidly structured society? He'd been thinking about it a lot recently, while he'd been hidden in the barn. He still wasn't sure what the answer was. Perhaps he was about to find out. Perhaps freedom would be a tangible state, a conscious understanding. How nice that would be.

The small boy was fidgeting. Such was the way of small boys. He leaned across and said deliberately, "Waiting's not much fun, is it?"

Silence. He could feel the boy's eyes staring at him. David thought: The boy thinks I am about to eat him.

"When I was your age I used to play a little word game to pass the time."

Still nothing.

"Would you perhaps like to give it a try?"

A pause then a cautious: "Yes, please."

"Excellent. Shall I begin then?"

Vasson lowered himself onto his belly and, holding the flashlight in his hand, pressed the button once, twice, three times before dropping his head behind a tussock of grass. There was a knot of fear in his stomach: this was where Baum and his friends might just do something stupid, like blast him out of the ground.

Come on, where the hell were they?

He wiped the rain off his face and flashed the signal again.

A small pinprick of blue light appeared through the downpour: once, twice, three times.

Vasson got cautiously to his feet and approached in a slight semicircle. The hunched silhouettes of helmeted men appeared black in the grayness. They were putting rifles to their shoulders. Vasson thought: Christ! And dropped to the ground. Then someone was striding out toward him and a foot kicked him hard in the ribs. Baum's voice said furiously, "What the hell are you doing?"

"Get those filthy rifles off me!"

Baum snorted. "Even if they had thought of shooting you, my stupid friend, they are not going to shoot me too, are they!"

Vasson got angrily to his feet. "Just keep them away from me, understand?"

Baum ignored him and said, "They're all on the beach, are they —the lot of them? We'll move in, then."

"No! We wait!"

"What!"

"Because you want the lot, don't you?"

"Yes, but—"

Vasson put his face close to the German's and spat, *"We wait."*

The MGB stole quietly in toward the coast on one muffled engine. Already Ashley could smell the strong scent of the land, an aromatic mixture of vegetable matter and earth. The weather had been foul all winter but now, finally, they'd been blessed with a clam night. The rain was a nuisance because it reduced visibility, but it was letting up and, with a bit more luck, should be gone by the time they reached the beach. Anyway, rain was better than a crystal-clear night. Once, Ashley had seen the glow of a German sentry's cigarette up on the point.

The voice of Tusker, the navigator, came floating up. "Course one-six-five degrees."

"Course one-six-five degrees," the coxswain repeated.

In a moment Tusker would start calling out the depth until, finally, at five fathoms, they would anchor.

Ashley's mouth was dry and he swallowed several times. His adrenaline was working overtime tonight. It was the thought of Julie and Peter waiting on the beach. After so long.

When she'd first told him that it would be at least a month,

probably two, before she could get away, he had been exasperated. He'd made all the necessary plans and he was surprised and a little hurt that she hadn't wanted to come straightaway. But then he'd looked at it from her point of view and begun to admire her. After all, he would have done the same. Waited and seen the job through.

The waiting had been terrible. That was because no one that he'd met in the last few months had been a patch on Julie. It had taken a long time for him to realize how much he loved her. And Peter. He loved them both, and now, at last, he would take them home.

Tusker's voice called softly, "Seven . . . seven . . . six . . ."

Ashley said, "Stop engine."

"All stopped, sir."

There was a rock close by, the water lapping against it. "Port twenty."

"Port twenty," the coxswain whispered.

The dark shape of the rock slipped past some five yards to starboard. The best anchorage was a few yards farther to the east. "Steer zero-eight-zero degrees."

". . . Six . . . five fathoms . . . five . . . five . . ."

Ashley waited another minute then gave the order to lower the anchor. There was a slight pop, then a swishing as the grass anchor-rope unwound and raced out through the stemhead fairlead.

Now that the rain had stopped, every sound was magnified by the stillness of the air. Ashley could hear the gentle hissing of the surf in the cove and the echo of the swell rumbling around partly submerged rocks.

They would have to be particularly quiet tonight: the slightest sound would carry for miles.

He waited impatiently for the men to launch the surfboats and stow the gear; then he dropped into the first boat and they were off, rowing softly toward the beach.

It had to be well past midnight. The rain had eased off and visibility had improved greatly. Julie strained her eyes for sight of a boat. But there was nothing. In the darkness of the rock cave, the word game had finished sometime ago. Peter was

asleep, his head on his bag. The old man was silent, probably sleeping too.

If you stared too hard the blackness danced before your eyes. And yet . . . Julie stiffened: there *was* something. A black blur on the water. Moving. And up on the beach dark figures were running toward the water's edge.

The boat. It must be the surfboat.

She cried out and raised her fists to the sky in a gesture of delight.

Peter woke up. "Mummy?"

"Darling, it's come! The boat's here!"

"It's really Richard? He's really here?"

"Yes, darling!" She remembered the scientist. "Monsieur? The boat. It's here!"

"Wonderful. . . . Yes!"

"Wait here, you two!" On all fours, Julie crawled out onto a flat rock. The surfboat was just riding in toward the beach. A dark mass had appeared under the cliff—the first group of passengers being gathered together. It would take five minutes to load them and twenty minutes before the boat returned. Not long. *Forever.* She desperately wanted to run along the beach that very second —but there was Peter and she couldn't leave him.

She laughed with excitement. Richard. He was there, she knew he was. He would have come himself, just to make certain. She wanted to say, I'm here, darling, of course I'm here!

The boat slid onto the beach and figures jumped out. The dark mass of the passengers started forward.

They seemed to be going very slowly. She willed them to speed up.

At the water's edge there was some more movement. She guessed the crew were floating the surfboat off again, ready for the passengers.

Behind, another black shape slowly emerged from the darkness of the sea. The second surfboat. For once it was a perfect night. Everything was going smoothly. A marvelous piece of luck. Julie couldn't help thinking that it was fate, that, after all the storms of the winter, this calm night had been arranged just for *her.*

The passengers had reached the water's edge at last. In a moment they would be on their way.

Hurry. Hurry up. This waiting is killing me. And she laughed a little, because the anticipation was so sharp and warm.

Suddenly she gasped and froze.

Light.

There was light—!

The picture in front of her jumped from negative to positive, the blacks to whites.

She blinked, disbelieving.

The surfboat and the figures around it were encircled in brilliant white.

Dear God—!

The light was coming in a long shaft from a single point out in the bay.

She uttered a small cry.

The British boat must be mad. What were they doing? *What were they doing?* She muttered, "Turn it off! Turn it *off!*"

She jumped.

There was more light. This time from the clifftop. A great cone of dazzling brilliance which swung from side to side across the cove, searching, trying to trap the running figures.

Crack! Crack! Gunfire from the clifftop. And almost immediately, a deep low *Bang!* from the bay, where yellow-tongued light flashed across the darkness.

At last she understood. It was a *German* boat out there, shining the light. Just as there were *Germans* on the clifftop.

A shot rang out, closer, much closer. Then more shots. Shouting. Men running or pausing to shoot back. Men falling.

Julie shrieked, *"No!* Please, dear God. No!"

A second great beam of light shone down from the cliffs, sweeping back and forth like the first, trapping running figures in its glare, figures which ran, then fell, figures which froze, sometimes, and raised their hands. The guns were *rat-tat-tat*ting in a continuous stream of noise, from the beach, from the clifftop, enveloping the cove. In one sweep of the light she saw men crouched behind the surfboat, guns aimed toward the clifftop.

"Mummy! Mummy!" Peter was pulling at her jacket. "Come back! Come back in! Please!"

For a moment Julie was unable to comprehend, then, slowly, she realized it was Peter calling her. Her eyes on the beach,

she pushed herself into the rock cave. "Dear God . . . dear God . . ." She buried her face in her hands and, rocking back and forth, cried with rage and despair, loudly, to shut out the terrible noise. Peter hugged her, patting her ineffectually, crying too.

On the beach the *rat-tat-tat* ting of the machine-gun fire became more sporadic.

Out to sea the low boom of the big guns had ceased and the faint roar of deep-throated engines was fading into the distance.

Suddenly, there was a deathly silence.

Julie looked up. Light was still reflecting from the beach. Sick with fear, she crawled forward on her stomach and looked down.

Soldiers were everywhere, encircling the beach, rifles at their shoulders. In the center stood a ragged forlorn group, their hands above their heads.

Gérard . . . Maurice . . . Pierre . . . many of the airmen too.

But no oilskinned figure with a cap on his head—

Inert bodies were scattered around the beach. She stared at them in horror, terrified that she would spot some clue—a fleece-lined seaboot, a duffle coat. . . .

Suddenly she realized that she couldn't see the surfboat. She grabbed at the ray of hope. He must have got away. Yes, of course —he'd got away!

Then she remembered that the British gunboat had been chased away and there was nowhere for him to escape to.

And she saw that some of the soldiers were down at the water's edge, raising their rifles to their shoulders, pointing out to sea, shouting. . . . A light was shining from the sea again, but much closer.

Her heart sank. There were heads in the water, heads swimming around a waterlogged boat—the surfboat. For a moment the swimmers seemed undecided, then one tried to dive out of sight, surfacing some distance away. But the water was too calm. They spotted him the moment he came up. The sharp cracks of shots ran out.

The lone swimmer held up a hand, as if in surrender, and began moving toward the shore. The others followed. There were four of them. They emerged slowly from the water, their arms raised.

She recognized him immediately. He walked through the other

men and stood at the front. A soldier stepped forward and searched him roughly, then pushed him forward with his rifle butt.

Richard walked quickly to the group of prisoners and made his way through them. Julie realized he was looking for somebody—*her.*

She cried very softly, "I'm here, *I'm here.*"

Shouts again. With difficulty some of the prisoners were picking up the dead and wounded. More shouts and the prisoners formed a ragged line and moved off toward the cliff path, the dead and wounded carried like sacks between them.

The last she saw of Richard was when he paused at the bottom of the path to glance over his shoulder.

Then the lights went out.

Only the weak beams of flashlights remained. She watched them weave their way slowly up the path to the clifftop. Then they too were gone and there was nothing but darkness.

She beat her hands against the hard rock until they hurt, because she couldn't *do* anything and because, *somehow,* she had the terrible feeling that it was all her fault.

A long time had passed. Through the opening in the rocks David could see a cold gray light. Dawn. How he hated it. He'd never understood how people could go into raptures over it. Dusk was more beautiful every time.

The young woman was finally asleep, poor thing. How he had felt for her. The people on the beach, they had been her friends, perhaps ever her family.

And the child: so young to understand such terrible things. What a world for a child, what a world.

But what now? The woman had been almost hysterical with grief. What if she still was? Who was to decide what they were to do? One thing was certain: David had no idea of how to get out of this place on his own.

He looked toward the patch of sky at the end of the crevice. At least it wasn't raining anymore.

He turned. The woman was awake, her eyes open and staring, a hopeless expression on her face. David recognized it: he had seen it many times before. He whispered so as not to wake the boy, "Good morning. How about some breakfast?"

She stared at him dully, her face blank. David said, "I have—let me see—" He opened his bag and rummaged inside. "Yes, cheese, *always* cheese. I think, one day I'll turn into a cheese! Then some bread. Yes, and an apple! I'm sure our young friend will like that, won't he? We'll keep it just for him."

She wasn't listening. She was looking into the distance, remembering the night. He could see that terrible thoughts were going through her head.

"Dear lady!" David said more firmly. "I think we should begin our breakfast. *Then* we think! *No* thinking until then!" He wagged a finger at her.

She slowly sat up, trying not to disturb the boy on her lap. David broke off some cheese and handed it to her with a slice of bread. She stared at the remaining food lying in the paper on his knees. He realized she was checking to see how much was left. David said, "It's all right. Plenty for me and the boy."

She ate, slowly at first then hungrily. When she had finished she started to caress the boy's hair. She was crying again.

David pursed his lips. "Well, now, let's make a plan! Let's be very practical!"

Her eyes focused and she blinked away the tears. "Yes."

"We need to decide what options are open to us. First . . ." He thought for a moment. "First, can we just walk back up the beach?" Without waiting for her to reply he said, "No. They'll have guards, won't they?"

"Up on the point. They have a post there. And they've probably got extra guards at the top of the path."

There was silence while they both thought. David ventured, "Perhaps at night . . . could we climb the cliff somewhere else?"

She shook her head. "There's no other way that I know of. The cliff here is sheer. It's impossible to reach the next cove. . . . This place is cut off."

The silence was longer this time. David thought: I wish I could think of something else, for *her* sake. For myself I don't care anymore. Enough is enough.

She gave a bitter laugh. "Not much choice, is there?"

He waved his hand from side to side. "Nonsense! We will think of something. Defeat is in the mind!"

"I suppose so, but . . ." She shook her head.

"What's your name?"

"Julie, it's short for Juliette."

"Well, Julie, there must be a way out of here. Mustn't there?"

She shrugged hopelessly. "Maybe . . ."

"For your boy's sake."

She stared at him hard, her eyes round with anger and surprise. Then she softened. "Yes. For his sake . . ." She rubbed her forehead and David noticed that her eyes had lost their lifelessness and were now alert. She said gently, "But *what*?"

He said, "There's always *diversion*."

"Diversion?"

"You know, make a noise somewhere to attract their attention. Then slip past." He formed a snaking movement with his hand. "It can work very well. I *know*!"

"Perhaps you're right. I—"

She paused and stiffened, her face suddenly sheet white. Moving the boy's head quickly off her lap, she scrambled toward the entrance. A moment later she was back, her eyes filled with fear.

"Soldiers! Coming down the path!"

David looked at their rock cave: it was no good. Far too easy to find. He grasped her arm. "Quick! We must hide!"

"Where!"

"Try to hide the boy . . . under a rock, in the sand . . ."

"Yes." The boy was already awake, dazed and frightened.

David crawled through the crevice to the far side, away from the beach. The woman followed and overtook him. She looked wildly to right and left, grabbed the boy and, scrabbling feverishly, pulled him up over a rock and out of sight.

David knew he couldn't go climbing after them. He was too slow. He might give them away. Better to stay.

But he couldn't go back into the crevice: they'd find him straightaway. He crawled around a corner and almost immediately found a much smaller gap, under the overhang of a large rock. This would do. He thought wryly: It will have to.

There was nowhere.

Julie wanted to scream. Smooth rocks. Gaps in between. Nowhere to hide! God!

And she was losing the cover of the massive boulders. The back

of her head felt as if it were ten feet square: the Germans were probably watching her even now.

Nowhere! She looked down toward the sea.

Perhaps the water . . .

Dragging Peter behind her, she crouched low and ran down a gully toward the sea.

In the water? Yes—! She hissed, "Peter, we might have to get wet!"

He nodded. She climbed onto a rock and looked around. There was a gap in the rocks beneath, where the water sucked gently back and forth with a gentle lapping noise. It didn't seem too deep and there was an overhang—

She removed her rucksack and Peter's shoulder bag and squeezed them into a narrow fissure in the rock above, where they couldn't be seen. Then she jumped. She caught her breath. The water came up to her thights. It was icy. She stumbled, found firm sand, and turned for Peter.

She reached for him and he jumped into her arms. She tried to hold him above the water but he was so heavy that he slipped through and he was up to his waist before she got a grip on him. She heard him gasp as he met the water.

Julie looked quickly around and saw an overhang where they'd be invisible from everywhere but the sea. Moving Peter onto her hip, she pushed herself under the rock and pressed her back against it. She kissed him on the cheek. "I love you."

"I love you too, Mummy." He was shivering already.

She thought: How long can we last in the water? And the tide! She'd completely forgotten about that! Perhaps it was coming up . . .

Time. It passed in fractions of moments that lasted forever. The icy water got colder. The blood too.

She held Peter closer.

She tried to guess how the time was passing. Five minutes? No, seven. Maybe eight.

A stone fell some way off. Julie gripped Peter tighter.

Another sound: someone walking over the rocks. Heavy boots. Nearer. *Much* nearer.

God!

Crunch. From just above. Just overhead.

Another crunch. Feet shuffling.

Moving away. *Away!*

Heavy boots stepping from rock to rock. Moving away!

But wait . . . *wait.* Until you're sure they've gone. It might be a trap.

She felt a great shudder go through Peter's body. She put her lips to his ear and whispered: "It's all right, darling!" He nodded but she could hear his teeth chattering. His skin was deathly cold.

But wait . . . wait.

So she waited. Twenty minutes—it felt longer. Perhaps it was thirty minutes. Peter was weighing her down, heavier and heavier. A brisk wind was blowing in from the water, scything through her clothes, making Peter's skin the temperature of ice. She whispered, "A little longer, just a little longer . . ."

With a shock she realized that the water was higher than before —quite a bit higher. It had reached her waist. The tide was coming up.

They would have to go, like it or not.

She smiled into Peter's taut pale face. "We're going now, darling."

He nodded, his jaws clamped together to stop the chattering.

She moved out and looked up. Empty sky. No Germans.

There was only one way out: up a smooth rock face. She couldn't climb it with Peter in her arms. She said, "I'll have to put you in the water. Just until I'm up. I'm sorry. . . ."

Without a word, he slid out of her arms. The water came up to his chest. He closed his eyes for a moment as the coldness hit him, then looked up at her.

"I've got to get up to that rock. Give me a heave, will you?" She waited until he had moved out from under the rock then put her foot into a notch and pulled herself up, Peter valiantly pushing from below. She paused, spread-eagled halfway up the smooth face, and took a long look around.

There was no one in sight.

She looked for another handhold. She found one away to the right and hoisted herself up the last few feet. She looked again. No one. She turned and, reaching down, took Peter's hands and pulled. She raised him a few inches but could get him no farther: she didn't have enough leverage. She lowered him back into the water. His lip quivered and silently he began to cry.

"Don't worry, darling, please!" She put her foot across onto another rock so that she was making a bridge across the gap. This time he came up, desperately slowly, until he was halfway up the rock. "Try and wedge yourself." He put out a foot to the rock opposite and locked himself against the rock face. Julie moved quickly across and, lying down on the rock again, pulled. Slowly Peter came up until he lay on the top, panting, in a pool of water.

Julie got to her feet and, taking the bags from the crack, helped Peter up. "Come on, we'll get some dry clothes on!"

She led the way cautiously up the gully. No one. Then they were on a plateau of rocks, hidden from the beach by the giant boulders. No one.

Back to the crevice then. She crept forward around a large rock and they were facing the entrance.

Her heart was thudding. Perhaps they had got the dear old man. . . . She stopped and looked inside.

"Hello, my dear!" Freymann's face peered out of the darkness at her. "They've gone. I watched them go back up the cliff. There's no one left." He smiled. "How very delighted I am to see that you are safe!"

"They've gone?"

"They've given up! They think we have vanished into thin air! We're safe!"

Julie thought: But we're not, are we? It's only a reprieve.

Darkness again, Julie chewed on the bread and knew that she had to decide.

They had shared the last of Peter's food parcel; most for Peter himself and the rest split between Julie and the scientist. At first the old man had refused to take any, but she'd insisted. For drink they'd used the brackish rainwater from pools in the rocks.

Now there was no more food and the pools were drying out. Peter had put on his one change of clothes, but they weren't very warm and he'd been cold and shivery all day. Something would have to be done. But *what*? What could one do with a small boy and a sick old man?

The thought of having to make a decision made her feel slightly hysterical. She wanted to put it off. The longer they waited the better their chances might be. . . . After a while the guards on the clifftop might go away. *Might . . .*

The decision was impossible. Julie started from the beginning again.

Freymann and she had been through the possibilities a dozen times since morning. The only thing they'd concluded was to do nothing while it was light. Darkness offered the only hope. The old man favored the diversionary tactic. He'd suggested that he should walk up the path and run to lure the guard away while Julie and Peter escaped. Julie had pointed out that David would be shot instantly and the noise could bring the other guards from the headland within seconds.

After that, Freymann was silent for a long time. Julie asked him about his life and he told her about his childhood and the happy days in Berlin. He didn't tell her very much about what happened after that and she didn't press him.

She said, "And what will you do in England?"

"Ah. Who knows? I've learned not to think ahead."

Then he'd been silent again, except to ask her to call him David.

"I'll try, monsieur." Then she laughed. "It's difficult not to call you monsieur . . . the only person of your age that I've ever called by his name is my uncle."

"How old do you think I am then!"

"Well . . . not *that* old. I—oh dear, I've offended you."

"No . . . no."

"How old *are* you?"

"Fifty-two. Or fifty-three. I'm not sure."

She was shocked. He looked well over seventy. "Yes, of course. That's what I thought . . ."

He smiled at her because she'd lied to be kind. Then he settled down to sleep again and she was left to her own thoughts.

Now it was dark and the thinking still hadn't produced a solution.

Peter gripped her arm and whispered, "Mummy! There's something. A noise!"

Julie tensed and listened. The night was very still.

There was silence. Then, suddenly, a sound: a whistle, long and low. A pause, then it came again. A man's whistle.

After a few seconds it came again, closer.

Thoughts raced through Julie's mind: friends? Germans! A clever trick?

Now the whistle was close. Panic gripped her.

A voice called softly, ". . . Juliette . . . are you there? . . . Julie . . ."

Julie froze.

". . . It's me . . . Michel."

Julie sighed audibly and scrambled up onto the rocks. "Michel . . . Michel . . . ! Here! We're here!" A moment later he emerged out of the night. Julie grasped his arms and sobbed with gratitude and relief. "Oh, bless you! Bless you!"

"Quick!" His voice was harsh and businesslike. "How many are you?"

"Just me and Peter and the old man."

"The old man?"

"Freymann. The scientist."

"Oh." He sounded cross.

"Why?"

"He'll be slow, that's all."

"He'll do his best. I know he will."

"Come on then. We've got to be quick."

Julie scrambled back into the crevice. "Come on, darlings. We're going! Don't forget anything. Have you got your bag, Peter?"

"Yes, Mummy."

Julie pulled on her haversack. "Ready?" she called.

She led the way up onto the rocks and waited while first Peter then Freymann climbed out and started down to the beach. Someone grunted: Freymann. She found him lying against a rock trying to regain his feet. "Here, let me give you a hand." She pulled him up and helped him down to the sand where Michel and Peter were waiting.

Michel said brusquely, "Right. No talking. No noise at all. And stay in line. Freymann, behind me. Then Peter. Julie, you come last." Julie saw for the first time that Michel had a machine gun slung over his shoulder.

Julie whispered, "What about the guards? On the cliff?"

"There's no guard. Not if we're quick!"

They set off briskly. Julie immediately worried that Peter and the old man wouldn't be able to keep up. But they strode out, the two of them, and in no time they had reached the bottom of the path.

But the path was a different matter. Even before they were a short way up Freymann was panting. He'd never make the top without a rest. Nor would Peter.

Freymann slowed up then stopped altogether. She heard him apologizing breathlessly to Michel. Julie leaned forward and touched Peter's cheek. After a pause, they were off again, but much more slowly. It took twenty minutes to reach the rim of the cliff. She could almost feel Michel's impatience.

Just below the clifftop Michel signaled to them to halt and crawled ahead. Then he was back and waving them forward.

Julie came up onto the clifftop just behind Peter and Freymann. Seeing Michel move rapidly off, she grabbed Peter's hand and started to run. Almost immediately she tripped over something and, glancing down, almost screamed. It was a body. Wearing a helmet. Lying inert. The guard.

She ran on, pulling Peter behind her.

David thought: I can't go on! It's not physically possible. I'll ask them to leave me behind. Then I'll make my own way.

He fell to his knees, gasping for breath. The girl stooped down beside him. "Come on! You can do it. It's not far!"

There was fire in his lungs. He tried to speak but there was no breath to spare. Instead, he shook his head.

Now the young man was back. "Get up! Quick! We've got to get to the road!"

David rasped, "Go . . . on . . . don't . . . wait!"

The young man spoke impatiently. "We can't leave you here. You'd ruin it for *us*!"

David blinked. He hadn't thought of that. He rose unsteadily and prepared to set off. Roughly, the young man thrust his shoulder under David's arm and half carried, half dragged him across the uneven ground.

They were going downhill now. David tried to take more of his own weight, but his legs were weak and, however hard he tried, he never seemed to be able to regain his breath.

Finally they came to a low wall. David disengaged himself and, determined to make an effort, climbed resolutely over. The others were already ahead of him, the young man leading the way across a field. The pace was slower now, but even so, David knew he couldn't go on much longer.

Suddenly he realized that no one was paying any attention to him. He could hide and no one would know. He wouldn't be a danger to them here.

Gradually he dropped back until the others vanished into the darkness. Then, gently, gratefully, he lay down, one hand on the ground, one hand against his aching chest.

They were skirting the village, to the north. Where was Michel taking them? To Morlaix maybe . . . but where could they hide there? At his apartment? It would be risky wherever they went.

She turned to look for David, waiting for him to loom up out of the darkness.

Michel called back, "What the hell's the matter?"

"It's David—I can't see him. We'll have to go back."

"We haven't time!"

"We can't just leave him! Here—look after Peter while I go to look." She retraced her steps.

Almost back at the wall . . . he had to be somewhere near here.

Then she saw him. Lying on the ground. She ran up. "David! David! Are you all right?"

For a moment she thought he was dead then he groaned. "Sorry . . . sorry . . . leave me here . . . leave me."

"Absolutely not! You're too important. Anyway, I need you! Where you go, I go."

"Leave me. It's no good. . . . Please."

"But the Germans will find you!"

"So?" he rasped. "All they can do is kill me."

"No. No! They'll take you back to Germany and make you work. They'll get hold of your family. Don't you see? David, make an effort, *please.*"

He didn't move and for a moment Julie thought he had given up completely. Then at last he sighed and, leaning on her, got unsteadily to his feet. Slowly, his arm over her shoulder, they set off down the hill.

They found the others and struck out across the fields toward the southwest. After a while Julie realized they must be approaching the small road that led from Trégasnou to the estuary and Kernibon. How far did Michel expect them to go? David was in a bad way, his breath coming in long shallow rasps. Peter was tired too, dragging his feet, shoulders drooping.

A hedgerow loomed up. Then a gate leading onto the road. Michel disappeared into the darkness of the hedge. She followed, then stopped in alarm. Someone else was there, waiting in the shadows. There was something familiar about the stocky figure. "Jean!"

"Quick! Into the van!"

"The van?"

Jean led her into the darkness of the tall hedge and there, parked close beside it, was the old Peugeot.

Michel was opening the back door. He took Freymann's arm. "In here. And you." He helped Peter up into the back. "Julie, you drive."

"Me?"

"Yes, unless you want to take the Sten."

For a moment she didn't understand what he meant, then she realized he was referring to the gun. It was an ugly great thing: she wouldn't have the first idea how to use it.

She grasped her uncle's arm. "Jean, thank you! Thank you!"

"Don't thank me! It was Michel."

"Take care of Tante Marie. And *please,* don't get caught!"

He said gruffly, "Off you go! Quick! There's no time to spare."

She hugged him and, climbing in through the passenger door, eased herself across into the driver's seat.

Jean was opening the gate. Michel swung on the starting handle and the old engine burst into life with an ear-splitting roar. Michel jumped into the passenger seat. "Out of the gate, turn right. Go!"

Julie threw the gear level into first and the van jumped forward. She pulled the wheel hard over and they shot out of the gate into the lane. There was no chance to wave to Jean.

It was pitch black. "I can't see anything!" she cried.

Michel reached down and flicked a switch. The lights came on but they had been well hooded: they cast only the faintest glow.

Julie peered forward, trying to maintain speed. A sharp bend reared up and she almost missed it. She pulled the wheel over and the bumper crunched into the wall with a loud bang. "Sorry."

"Keep going."

They shot through a tiny village and down a hill toward a

crossroads. Julie was on the verge of asking, Which way? when Michel said, "Straight over!"

She kept her foot down and the van shot across the intersection. Michel looked rapidly right and left, then stuck his head out of the window to look behind. He pulled his head back in and said, "Nothing."

Julie realized they were on the road to Kernibon. It was a dead-end road.

As they neared the village Michel reached over and turned off the ignition. The engine petered out and they coasted down the hill in eerie silence. "Right at the harbor!"

As they approached the bottom of the hill Julie resisted the temptation to brake too much. The van was still traveling fast as she yanked the wheel across. They shot around the corner and along the road encircling the landward side of the cove.

Finally the van slowed down and Julie pulled in toward the side. Michel jumped out, opened the rear doors and bundled the others out. Julie stepped down, trying to stop herself from shaking.

Peter ran up and took her hand, then they were following Michel along the side of the tiny harbor. Suddenly he lowered himself over the seawall and disappeared.

There was a slight clatter, some muffled movements and Michel's voice floated up. "The old man first!" Freymann eased himself gingerly over the edge and hovered for a moment, searching for a foothold, before descending.

Julie saw that there was a metal ladder and, below, a small dinghy floating on the water. She sat Peter down and, turning him face to the wall, put his hands on the rungs of the ladder. "Careful. Take it slowly."

When he was safely in the boat beside Freymann and Michel, Julie climbed down herself. She hated heights almost as much as she hated boats. Finally her foot was in the boat and, wobbling violently, she dropped into it. She landed awkwardly, bruising her shin. She clenched her teeth and stayed silent.

The boat was moving away from the wall as Michel weaved an oar from side to side over the back. Julie was amazed: she'd never realized he could do this kind of thing.

Then she remembered when she and Peter had come to collect

the sow, how they'd surprised him here at the harbor and how secretive he'd been.

They were approaching the fishing boats moored in the center of the cove. Perhaps Michel was going to hide them here, on one of the boats.

The dinghy bumped alongside the tall side of a fishing boat. Michel pushed the old man to his feet and helped him up the side. Julie went next and pulled Peter up beside her. Michel came last and tied the dinghy's rope to the fishing boat.

Julie looked around. It was a small boat, completely open and without so much as a wheelhouse. There was nowhere to hide.

She said, "Michel, we can't stay here!"

"No. But it'll take you across."

"Across?"

"To England. That's where you want to go, isn't it?"

Julie gasped in amazement. "Yes, but—in *this*?" It was much smaller than the fishing boat she and Peter had taken from Morlaix three years before. A small bit of decking at the front came halfway back to the mast, but otherwise it was entirely open. She could imagine the waves coming straight in.

Michel said, "Right. There are some waterproofs. Fresh water and so on are up in the bow. Not much, but it's all I could get hold of."

He moved along the boat to the far end and Julie followed, a feeling of hopelessness creeping over her. Michel was saying, "And here's the tiller, for steering, and here, the compass. Now, I'll light the oil lamp here, beside the compass, but keep it well masked until you're clear of the land. There *is* an engine but there's almost no fuel for it and anyway it's too noisy to use near the land so I think you'll be better off without it . . ."

"Michel! What do you mean—?"

"The sails are quite straightforward. One large and one small. If the wind comes from ahead you'll need both, otherwise you could manage with just the large one. . . ."

"Michel! What are you saying?"

He turned and said harshly, "I'm sorry, I wish I could come with you, but I can't. I *have* to stay. This is the best I can do for you, Julie—"

"No! No!" She grabbed his arm and tried to read his face in the darkness. "I *can't*, Michel! I don't know what to do!"

"I'll get the boat ready and rigged and I'll sail out with you into the bay. Then all you have to do is point north—"

"*Michel, I can't!*"

He took her by the shoulders and shook her slightly. "You *must!* It's not ideal, I'll admit, but it's a damn sight better than getting caught by the Gestapo. And *that's* the only alternative!"

Julie stared at him in disbelief. She repeated desperately, "But I don't know how to sail!"

"I told you, I'll start you in the right direction. But we must go *now*! We're losing the tide!" He ran forward to the mast and started heaving on lines. Julie grasped the side of the boat and watched him, horrified.

Peter was at her elbow. "Mummy, I can help . . . I think. Richard told me all about sailing."

Julie looked at the small pale face and automatically touched his hair. "Oh darling! I wish I . . . ." Then she remembered what the Gestapo did to children and made an effort to smile. "We'll do our best then, shall we? We'll sail to England." But even as she said it she was filled with despair.

Up by the mast Michel was pulling on a rope. Amid a great flapping and beating, a black sail rose slowly into the sky. Then Michel was leaning over the front of the boat, pulling hard on something. Suddenly he ran back, pulled another rope and dived for the tiller. Julie realized the land was moving sideways: the boat was free of its mooring. The beating noise diminished then stopped. She looked up at the sail. Its black curved shape soared up into the darkness, huge against the sky.

The mouth of the tiny harbor lay ahead. Julie winced involuntarily. The high brick jetty rushed past, an arm's length away, then they were through, slipping rapidly out into the vast blackness of the night.

Julie felt the boat move under her and grabbed at the side. It was a nightmare. She didn't understand the first thing about any of it—not the first!

Michel was calling, "Come here!"

Lurching unsteadily across the deck, she reached his side. "Now, listen very carefully. We've only got a few minutes. So *listen!* There's a flashlight just behind me, here in the bosun's box. There are the waterproofs I told you about. Here"—he placed her hand on the tiller—"is the tiller. You push it the

opposite way to the way you want to go. You'll get used to it . . ."

Julie's throat constricted.

"And now listen *very* carefully. The course . . ."

After a while Julie realized he had stopped speaking and was moving away, leaving the tiller in her hand.

"Best of luck, Julie!"

"*But—*"

He was untying something—the rope holding the dinghy—and climbing over the side.

She almost screamed.

And the next moment he was gone.

26 Vasson reached out and touched the painting. A tractor, bright red and crudely painted. Not bad, considering. Then it occurred to him—the mother had probably given the child some help with it. He imagined them sitting on the floor together, engrossed and happy in their task. The picture irritated him and he turned away.

There was a model plane hanging from the ceiling, a second picture and some posters of Paris. Angrily he yanked the cover off the bed; it was unmade, the blankets neatly folded, the calico bolster without a pillowcase.

There was a wooden chest under the eaves. He pulled it out and, raising the lid, emptied the contents over the floor. Toys, clothes, old fabrics.

Rubbish.

As he moved toward the stairs his head brushed against the model plane. He pushed it impatiently aside. The fine thread holding it to the ceiling broke and it fell to the floor, one wing bent and broken. Vasson kicked it out of his way.

He went down the narrow stairs to the room below. The

woman's room. It was clean and tidy, the bed neatly covered like the boy's.

She was expecting to be gone a long time, the bitch.

He pulled open the drawers of the dresser. The top one contained underwear, carefully folded. Scattered between the clothes were sachets which smelled of herbs. He threw everything out onto the floor.

In the next drawer were blouses, woolens—more rubbish. He dumped them onto the floor as well. Impatiently he jerked open the bottom drawer. Papers. A ration card. Some letters. An old photograph.

He leafed through the letters. They were in English and signed "Your Mother." He didn't understand English. He threw them back in the drawer. The photograph showed two people sitting on a beach. One was the girl, much younger, maybe fourteen or fifteen. She was very slim, her angular body clad in an unbecoming, old-fashioned swimming costume. She was looking straight into the camera, her eyes screwed up against the sun. Beside her was a woman, much older, rather fat, dressed in a tight frock with a floral print on it. The mother.

Vasson flipped the photograph over. There was some writing on the back: English again. It said: "Mummy and me. Cawsand. 1929."

Cawsand. It must be a place in England. The girl was not Breton at all then, but English. A worse thought—she was probably an agent, planted in France to spy. The thought made Vasson angry and uneasy. He had the unpleasant feeling that he'd been cleverly and ruthlessly deceived.

If Baum found out it would mean more flak and Vasson had had enough over the scientist. Vasson decided it would be best if Baum never heard about the girl.

He slid the photograph inside his jacket, even though it offered no clues as to where the bitch was now. And *that* was what he needed to know.

She had to be the key. She'd been with the scientist at the cliff. Now they were both missing. The girl must be hiding him.

He jumped.

A terrible cry came from the next room. Bracing himself, Vasson crossed to the door. He hesitated, half-revolted,

half-fascinated by what he might see; he opened the door and walked through into the kitchen.

Baum was leaning against the mantelpiece, examining his nails. To the left, two of his men were huddled around a chair. Vasson swallowed hard and stared, fascinated. The figure in the chair lay inert. The face was a mess, the nose a pulp of blood and bones, and the eyes reduced to slits between the purple-red swellings of cheeks and eyelids. Apart from the hair, the old woman was unrecognizable.

Vasson raised his eyebrows at Baum. Baum made a face of disgust which indicated: Nothing.

One of Baum's men put his face down to the old woman's and demanded, "Where is the girl?"

The old woman's mouth moved, as if to say something, then dropped open. With distaste Vasson saw that the gums had no teeth. She started to moan loudly.

The man standing directly in front of the chair said something to his companion in German. The other reached into his pocket and pulled out some cord. It was in two sections. They took one piece each and tied the old woman's hands to the arms of the chair, not by the wrists but across the width of her hands. Vasson moved his tongue around his mouth to remove the dryness.

The chant again. "Where is the girl?"

They each took a forefinger. Slowly, they bent the forefingers backward. The old woman cried out, a loud shriek that filled the room. She convulsed, her body arching upward, straining against the cords, and she screamed again, a long, shrill, piercing scream. Vasson put his hands over his ears. For a split second there was silence. Then there was an audible snap, quickly followed by another. Vasson stared curiously. Though the men had moved away the two fingers were still upright, at a strange angle to the hands. The old woman's head had fallen back against the chair and she groaned, a long low moan of despair.

"Where's the girl?"

The mouth dropped open again and tried to speak. Nothing happened. The old woman shook her head from side to side, first slowly then more rapidly until the movement became frenetic, like a mad animal's. Vasson felt uncomfortable and looked away.

428

The old woman's head dropped forward, and he realized she was unconscious.

Baum shifted his weight and leaned an elbow on the mantelpiece. He said something in rapid German then turned to Vasson. "We're getting nowhere." The muscles in his jaw fluttered under the unnaturally pink skin. "What's so sickening is to think that this whole business need never have happened!"

Vasson snapped, "But if your men had covered the beach properly, they would never have got away! *And*"—he stood up—"if the scientist had been properly guarded by the Navy, then he would never have escaped in the first place!"

Baum glared at Vasson and whispered, "Don't get clever with me, you little pimp!" He raised a forefinger. "And don't go spreading dirt behind my back. Just try—and I'll carve you into tiny pieces!"

Vasson backed down. "Don't get yourself in a state. We'll just have to find a way. What about the old man? The woman's husband?"

Baum rolled his eyes in exasperation. "Yes! Yes! But *where* is he now? Eh? I do not see him here, do I?" He rubbed his forehead.

Baum was right. They had nothing. Personally Vasson didn't care a damn—he was fed up with the whole job—but there was bound to be a scapegoat and he had the unpleasant feeling that Baum would try to blame the whole mess on him.

Wearily, Vasson sat down and lit a cigarette, thinking: It's all that bitch's fault; it's she who's fouled the whole thing up.

He tried to think. A year or so earlier he would have thought of something, something brilliant: some way of spiriting the girl and the scientist out of the air. Now? Now he was bored with the mechanics of it all. All he enjoyed thinking about was getting the hell out of this hole and going to Paris to reclaim his money.

Just then, there was the sound of boots crossing the front room. A soldier appeared in the doorway. He saluted and spoke to Baum in rapid German. Baum turned pink and looked apoplectic. There was a long silence, then Baum said very slowly in French, "I thought you had *caught* these people!"

Vasson shifted on his seat and said carefully, "Most of them, yes."

Baum almost choked. "Why, then, are my men being murdered?"

Vasson said sharply, "Where? Where were your men killed?"

"One man. On the clifftop."

Vasson sat up and thought: Good God, why would they want to get down to the beach again . . . ? What on earth—? Then he swore quietly. There could be only one reason. He said out loud, *"Merde!"*

Baum looked at him quickly. "What is it?"

"They were there all the time. On the beach."

"Impossible—"

"They were there."

"I don't see how—"

"Shut up!" Vasson was trying to imagine where the girl's friends would have taken her. He said, "If they've escaped from the beach that means they must have gone into hiding again, somewhere nearby . . ."

"Ha!" Baum exclaimed contemptuously. "But *where!* I tell you, there's only one way to find out. We take hostages and we shoot them tomorrow. Twenty. No! Thirty. The families of these murderers. That's the only way!"

Baum began to give orders, but Vasson knew it would take too long. *Too long.* If only he'd got the old woman's husband. It was much more likely that *he* would know. He clenched his fist and cursed under his breath.

There was a shout outside and the back door opened. A soldier came in, pulling a short, stocky man behind him. The man was sixtyish and dressed in peasant's clothes.

As soon as the man saw the bent, bloody figure in the chair he threw himself at it, crying, "Marie! Marie!"

When Vasson realized who the man was, he laughed out loud. His prayers had been answered. That's what came of being lucky.

The old man was sobbing violently. Vasson wished Baum would make him shut up.

Baum jerked his head at his men and they hauled the old man to his feet. "Please!" The old man was still sobbing. "Please, leave my wife alone! Please! She knows nothing! Nothing!"

Baum waited.

"I am giving myself up because she knows nothing. Please leave

her alone!" The old man was panting, shaking his head from side to side.

Baum said calmly, "And you know something?"

The old man's body sagged. "Yes—I will tell you what you want to know."

"Excellent." Baum smiled. "Is the girl with the scientist?"

"Yes."

"Where are they?"

"On a fishing boat."

There was a pause. The smile had vanished from Baum's face. "Where is this fishing boat?"

"At sea. But I don't know where it's going."

"You don't know where it's going."

"No, they didn't tell me."

"I see," Baum said stiffly. "You realize we will extract the information from you one way or the other."

"Yes, yes. Please, it's the truth, they didn't tell me. I suppose England, but I don't know where exactly . . ."

Vasson said, "Of course England! Where else would they go!"

The old man looked at Vasson for the first time, trying to understand who he was.

Vasson said, "The girl, she used to live there, didn't she?"

The old man nodded.

"Of course England!" Vasson snorted. "Who else was on the boat?"

"The scientist—"

"And the boy?"

The old man whispered, "Yes," and began to weep.

"No one else?"

"I don't know. I only heard about those three. That's all I know, believe me. And please, leave my wife alone. *Please!*" Sobbing bitterly, he tried to reach Tante Marie again, but they held him back.

Baum came up to Vasson. "If it's not the truth, I'll get it out of him."

"But suppose it is."

Baum clenched his teeth and said unhappily, "I will have to notify High Command and alert the coastal units. They can't have got far!"

Vasson thought: I hope you're right. He caught Baum by the sleeve. "The old man. He'll be shot, won't he?"

Baum blinked. "In the end."

"Make it soon. He's seen me."

The telephone jangled loudly. Doenitz woke up and turned on the light. He guessed it was about one. So much for catching up on some sleep.

The voice of his staff man said, "Berlin, Herr Grossadmiral. Reichsmarschall Goering calling."

There were voices on the line, then clicks. Absentmindedly Doenitz smoothed down the blanket. Finally Goering's voice said, "Ah! Admiral Doenitz?"

"Good evening, Herr Reichsmarschall."

"Herr Admiral. And how is Paris? How I envy you your little trips there. So much beauty! And so quiet, so quiet!" Quiet, Doenitz supposed, must mean there was no bombing, which was true enough.

Goering went on, "Yes, how I wish we could all take our command posts to Paris . . ." The words were slurred. Doenitz sighed under his breath: the *Reichsmarschall* was heavily drugged again.

". . . Very soon, of course, life will be quiet in Berlin," Goering continued, "but we must get this radar business under way."

Doenitz wondered where the conversation was leading to. He murmured a noncommittal "Indeed."

". . . A scientist we need has been *lost* by Himmler's idiots. We must get him back. He's at sea—"

"At sea?" Doenitz asked incredulously. Goering began a long, rambling explanation. As it proceeded, Doenitz's blood ran cold. He could see what was coming.

Goering said finally, "So a search will have to be mounted. How soon can you arrange it, dear fellow?"

"I cannot!" Doenitz retorted. "It's out of the question! It would be like looking for a needle in a haystack! Even if I had any units available, it would be a complete waste of time—"

"But I don't think you understand, Herr Admiral—the Führer himself has ordered this search. The matter is absolutely vital! You have S-boats, don't you? And your enormous fleet of U-

boats. Something can be spared, surely, for what is after all a vital matter?"

Doenitz squeezed the receiver hard. He said tightly, "I will consider what is appropriate when I receive the order direct from Führer headquarters."

"Of course, dear fellow. The order will be sent directly, I'm sure."

Goering had never called him dear fellow before. Doenitz realized this must be really important to him. If that was the case . . . Doenitz said levelly, "When—if—I receive this order, I will insist on air support. Several patrols will be needed to locate the fishing vessel. Then, and only then, *might* it be possible . . ."

The thick voice interrupted: "My dear fellow, you know that this cannot be done. The Luftwaffe's resources are fully stretched. We have to defend Germany, first and foremost. And the English Channel . . . well, I cannot spare *anything*. . . ."

Oh no, Doenitz thought, I'm not going to let you get away with it this time. "Without air support I cannot hope to find this vessel. In fact, I would almost certainly fail! I *must* have air support!"

There was a short silence. "A reconnaissance aircraft then . . ." The voice was grudging. "I'll see what's available. After all, I wish to help as much as possible. The Führer is most anxious, you see . . . most anxious. . . ." The voice became brighter. "You'll find this scientist for us, won't you, Doenitz?"

It was an impossible question. Doenitz said tightly, "I'll see what can be done."

"Good. Remember, we *need* him. Got to sort out this radar business, haven't we? Essential to get it right, essential. You do appreciate that, don't you?"

"Yes." Of course he appreciated it—how could he fail to? Two more U-boats had disappeared the day before. He added, "This scientist—why is he so vital?"

Goering laughed. "Ah! He worked on this new kind of radar, a long time ago. He understands it. He'll save us a lot of time."

A suspicion flashed into Doenitz's mind. "And his name? What's his name?"

There was a pause, then: "Um, Freymann. Yes, Freymann. A Jew—but there we are!"

Doenitz closed the conversation and replaced the receiver.

433

Freymann! So . . . he had escaped and Goering wanted him back. Or rather, it must be *Schmidt* who wanted him back. If the Chief Scientist was so anxious to have Freymann that he was prepared to put the matter to Hitler himself, then Freymann must be really vital. Schmidt must have realized that Freymann had been on the right track from the beginning. . . . Memories of a day long ago came into Doenitz's mind: the trials ship, the strange, tubby little man and the wild ideas tossed about like sparks from a firework.

Wearily, he got up and pulled his uniform jacket on over the shirt and trousers he already wore. He remembered that Freymann had been based at a naval establishment. God forbid that the Navy were responsible for letting him escape! He finished buttoning the jacket and went into the adjacent room. His staff officer jumped to his feet. Doenitz said, "I am expecting an order from Führer headquarters. Bring it to me the moment it arrives. In the meantime please tell Admiral Kohl I'm coming to the plotting room in two minutes." Protocol had to be observed. Admiral Kohl was C-in-C Gruppe West and this was his command post. Doenitz was a visitor here.

Doenitz waited one minute, then descended to the plotting room. He should wait for the Führer-Command, but there was no harm in discussing the strategy. Anyway, he knew very well that the command would come. Goering had sounded very certain.

When he entered the plotting room there was a hush, then Admiral Kohl and his staff detached themselves from their work and followed him to the vast plotting tables where an array of wooden shapes marked the positions of convoys and of each German vessel presently in the Atlantic. The black shapes representing U-boats were spread out far across the ocean, from the Mediterranean to the Caribbean, from the Cape Verde Islands to Iceland. Never before had there been so many U-boats at sea: a hundred and ten out of a total fleet of almost four hundred. The fleet was at last approaching the sort of size that Doenitz had always pressed for.

However there was not a single U-boat in the English Channel. The only vessels anywhere near were the *Schnellboote*, the fast torpedo boats with bases at Cherbourg and Guernsey.

The S-boats first then.

Admiral Kohl was waiting patiently. Doenitz said quietly, "We

are mounting a special operation. We are looking for a fishing boat which left this region, somewhere around the Morlaix River"—he took a pointer and placed it on the north Brittany coast—"sometime this evening. We do not know the exact time. The craft is heading for the English coast. Again, we do not know where exactly. But we must make every effort to find this vessel."

Doenitz could feel the officers exchanging glances behind his back. Eventually Kohl said, "There are the S-boats. They would be our best bet." He said over his shoulder, "Werner, find out how many S-boats are operational at Cherbourg and Guernsey."

Doenitz stared at the massive chart. "I wish I could tell you course and speed, but apparently this is not available either . . ."

Kohl took the hint straightaway. "I'm sure we can make an estimate. Is the fishing boat motor-powered, Herr Grossadmiral?"

"Unlikely . . . unless they have managed to steal considerable amounts of fuel. And I believe the fishing fleet is searched regularly for excess supplies. . . ." Doenitz looked questioningly at an intelligence officer who confirmed his statement. "So," Doenitz continued, "I would imagine it's using sail."

Kohl called to one of his aides. "Braun! What's the weather situation?"

There was a rustle of paper. "Channel area. . . . Yes, northeasterly, Herr Admiral. Ten knots, increasing later, possibly veering to the north."

Doenitz frowned. "Northeasterly . . . ?"

"Common in March, Herr Grossadmiral. The equinox."

"Mmm. So—what speed?"

"Four knots?"

"I agree."

Kohl went on, "Course . . . with that wind direction it would have to be west of north. The best port to make for would be Falmouth. There's nothing else west of there."

Kohl was right. The only major port on a northwesterly course was Falmouth. To the west of that was the Lizard, Land's End, then . . . he glanced farther west to the Scillies. Doenitz said, "Yes, Falmouth. So—if the boat set out, say, at eleven, it should be somewhere around here by now." He indicated a point some six

435

miles off the coast and asked Kohl, "How long before it gets out of S-boat patrol range, would you think?"

"We don't usually operate S-boats beyond forty miles from the coast at this point . . . enemy air patrols have been very heavy. . . ."

"Forty miles. . . . But the escaper will be thirty to forty miles off by sunrise. The S-boats won't be much use to us!"

Kohl blew out his cheeks. "The Luftwaffe . . . I suppose there is no hope of an air patrol?"

Doenitz kept his eyes on the table. "We have been promised air reconnaissance."

No one spoke. They had been promised air support countless times before. It rarely turned up. And when it did the planes usually had very limited range.

"But even if we do receive air support, that will not be enough," Doenitz said grimly. "We will have to deploy additional units. . . ."

Doenitz waited for Kohl to suggest the only solution, but he did not. Eventually Doenitz said, "We'll have to send a U-boat."

Kohl sighed deeply and asked quietly, "Is it really that vital, Herr Grossadmiral?"

Doenitz nodded. "Yes, I'm afraid it is."

There were no brass bands anymore, no garlands either. Nowadays the boats arrived and left as quietly as possible, sliding in and out of their dark, dank pens like snakes from a hole. Nor did the men laugh anymore: many of the old guard was gone, long buried in their tomb-ships. The fresh recruits had never learned to laugh: they were too frightened.

Except for Fischer's men. Fischer's men thought their commander was as close to God as anyone could get because he had kept them alive so long and because they believed that, after all this time, he would keep them alive forever.

It was one of the reasons Fischer couldn't sleep, even when he was desperately tired. No one could sleep with that kind of responsibility.

He felt tired now, and the patrol had only just begun.

They were heading southwest from Brest, beginning a long loop out toward the North Atlantic. *U-319* was traveling on the

surface in company with two other submarines. The idea was that, in a group of three, the boats had a reasonable chance of fighting their way out of an air attack. In the event, Fischer doubted that all three boats would actually escape a concerted attack—more like two. If that. The air patrols were efficient, heavy, and, if anything, getting worse.

According to the chart in front of him, they were only sixty miles out. It should have been more but they'd left late: *U-64* had been delayed with engine trouble. That meant they wouldn't be clear of the Bay by dawn . . .

The Bay. The Black Pit. Ever wider, ever deeper. Like everything else it got more difficult to face, more difficult to cross. The Happy Time was long gone.

Not that the kills weren't high—far from it. But Fischer sensed a desperation that hadn't been there before: the satisfaction, the excitement had gone.

"Herr Kaleu, Flotilla HQ are signaling."

Fischer hurried over to the wireless area. The operator was typing a long signal into the Enigma cipher machine, his assistant copying down the deciphered letters as they appeared. Fischer peered over their shoulders and his heart quickened. It was a personal signal from Doenitz. Fischer was pleased. Just like the old days!

He began to read the body of the message and a small frown appeared on his face. When the staccato sound of the Morse ceased and the operator had typed in the last of the signal Fischer reached forward and picked up the sheet carrying the completed message. He read it again slowly, from the top.

It began in Doenitz's usual informal way: DOENITZ HERE. GOOD TO SPEAK TO YOU AGAIN, FISCHER. IT'S BEEN A LONG TIME.

Then came details of a special operation. *Imperative,* Doenitz called it. *U-319* to abandon her patrol and proceed with all speed to search the following area—map references were given—to intercept a fishing boat believed to be at H17 P15—another map reference—at 0100 hours, and thought to be proceeding at four knots under sail on approximate course 330. Possible destination H24 P23. Occupants of boat to be captured but not harmed.

It was repeated that the orders were urgent and immediate. After acknowledgment *U-319* was to maintain radio silence

except in emergency. Doenitz signed off: IF ANYONE CAN DO IT, YOU CAN.

Fischer tried to work out what it all meant. But however he looked at it, the whole thing was incredible.

He went to the chart table to check the map references, but he'd already worked out the rough position. The middle of the English Channel.

If anyone but Doenitz had asked him he would have requested more information. But Doenitz had guessed all that—which was why he'd asked Fischer personally. IF ANYONE CAN DO IT, YOU CAN. Fischer thought: I hope you're right.

Fischer went back to the wireless operator and dictated a reply: U-319 WILL PROCEED IMMEDIATELY. I WILL TRY MY BEST.

Back at the chart table he pulled out the large-scale chart of the English Channel and checked the map references again. Triton, the U-boat cipher, was of course secure and the Enigma machine itself invulnerable, but where vital information on the positions of German vessels was concerned, the references were an additional safeguard.

Fischer thought again: Incredible. What a hell of a job!

The search area lay between thirty and forty miles south-southeast of the southernmost point of the English mainland—the headland known as the Lizard.

Fischer drew a line between the last estimated position of the —he almost called it "target" then corrected himself—of the *prey*, and the given destination, the port of Falmouth, which lay to the northeast of the Lizard. Where the line intersected the search area he drew a cross.

He said to the navigating officer hovering at his shoulder, "A course, please, to *there.*"

The navigator bent over the chart. Fischer said to his first officer, "Eins WO, a signal please to *U-64* and *U-402*. Tell them we have new orders and are leaving them directly."

He returned to the chart. "How far to the search point?"

"One hundred and ten miles exactly."

Fischer calculated how long it would take to cover the distance. On the surface, flat out at seventeen knots, seven hours. He looked at his watch: 0130. Dawn was at 0700 roughly. Not enough time. At dawn he'd have to submerge and he'd still be sixteen

miles short of the search point. Still, he'd be in the right area and it wouldn't take long to complete the distance, even at the paltry seven knots they did under the surface. So, on target at about 0930.

Not bad. If this fishing craft was really doing four knots then he should be there well ahead of it. Even if it was doing six knots, he'd still be all right.

"Drop clear astern of *U-64* and then turn to starboard onto course—?"

"Zero-zero-eight degrees, Herr Kaleu, until abeam of Ushant."

"Course zero-zero-eight." The order was repeated by the first officer and coxswain.

Fischer looked around for the Chief. He was standing in the after section of the control room. "Chief, I'm going to need everything. Seventeen knots if you can manage it."

The Chief tried to frown, but Fischer could tell that he was pleased. He liked a challenge. "Right, Herr Kaleu. I'll see what I can do." He disappeared in the direction of the engine room.

"Let me know when we're on course, Eins WO."

After a few minutes the confirmation came. Fischer gave the order for full speed ahead.

The order was repeated through the control room. The whine of the diesels rose to a steady din and the vibrations ran through the boat.

It was a long time since Fischer had taken a U-boat into the Channel—a long time since anyone had. The British controlled it too effectively. He wondered what he'd find there—the lot probably: air patrols, motor torpedo boats, minesweepers . . .

Too much, far too much. There was only one point in *U-319*'s favor: the British wouldn't be expecting a U-boat in the waters where submarines had been proved so vulnerable. They wouldn't believe anyone could be so stupid.

It wasn't much of an advantage. But it was all he had.

From the outside the building looks solid and impenetrable—but not enormous. Certainly not large enough to house the operational headquarters of the British Admiralty. That is because most of the building is underground, a warren of subterranean

rooms protected from bombing by concrete walls and roofs several feet thick. Not surprisingly, the building is called the Citadel. It lies in the heart of London, next to the main Admiralty buildings, to which it is connected by underground passages. Deep within it are two large adjoining chambers that resemble billiard rooms. Both contain tables about nine feet square on which are enormous charts overhung by brilliant lights which shine day and night. In the first room is the Main Plot, where all surface movements—both Allied and enemy—are plotted, as well as relevant air activity. Next door is the Submarine Tracking Room. Its sole purpose is to track enemy submarine movements in the Atlantic.

And, despite German beliefs to the contrary, it does it remarkably well.

On this occasion the night watchkeeper was busy. Although the main interpretation of the data was carried out by the day staff, a lot of information came in during the night and it was his responsibility to decide if there was anything requiring immediate attention, and to generally sort things out for analysis in the morning.

His staff of three had five sources of information: sightings, aircraft radar fixes, radio direction finding, Special Intelligence, and tracking using a combination of all available facts. Radio direction finding was very efficient as long as the U-boat transmitted for long enough. Then the various stations around the country could take cross-bearings on the signal and obtain a fix. But it was the euphemistically named Special Intelligence that really nailed the U-boats. Also known as Ultra, the information came from Bletchley Park, the Government Code and Cipher School. No one outside Bletchley Park really knew how the German codes had been cracked, but cracked they had been, though it usually took a day or more to decipher the signals. Once, some months earlier, the Germans had changed their codes and there had been a hiatus while the ciphers were broken, but after a while the information had come filtering through again.

Sometimes the deciphered signals arrived in a matter of hours. Then the ex-lawyer who headed the department acted quickly, passing information to the naval and air commands and directing convoys from the path of the waiting wolf packs—when the politicians allowed. Sometimes they did *not* allow, fearful that the Germans would awake to the fact that their codes had been broken.

More often than not it was twenty-four hours before the information came through, a time when the Head of Department had to make decisions based on calculated guesses as to what the U-boats might be doing. It was amazing how often the Head's hunches proved correct. He was an astonishing man.

For the third time in an hour the watchkeeper leafed through the deciphered Ultra signals that had come in at 0200. Nothing out of the ordinary. Routine signals from headquarters. Brief acknowledgments from the U-boats. He had checked the U-boats' call signs against those known to be at sea. They all tallied.

A teleprincess—one of the girls from the telex and communications room—came in and put a telex from Bletchley Park in front of him: a decoded message sent to U-boat headquarters by an escort vessel. At 2300 the escort had reported dropping three U-boats at T3, the buoy which marked the end of the swept channel leading out of Brest. The U-boats concerned were *U-64*, *U-402* and *U-319*.

The watchkeeper got up and, taking three tokens, marked them with the U-boats' numbers. He calculated the approximate distance the U-boats would have traveled since 2300 and placed the tokens on the plot, some fifty miles west of Brest.

U-319. He knew that number. Even before he looked it up on the list he remembered that it was Fischer's boat. Yes, there she was: *U-319*. Commander: Karl Fischer. Flotilla: Ninth. Base: Brest.

Fischer was well known. A very successful skipper, a German hero. He'd been around a long time.

The watchkeeper only wished he knew where the devil was heading for. Sometimes one didn't find out until too late. Sometimes one never found out at all.

He returned to his desk. Almost immediately the telephone rang. It was Bletchley Park. He listened carefully, asked a couple of questions, and replaced the receiver. He stood up and stared thoughtfully at the plot!

U-boat headquarters had sent an unusually long message on the Atlantic U-boat frequency. The message had just been intercepted and wouldn't be decoded for some hours, but it had had an urgent priority prefix. That was sufficiently unusual for Bletchley to call him.

Something was up then. Perhaps German intelligence had

discovered the position of a convoy, perhaps a new strategy was being implemented. . . .

The watchkeeper stared at the plot as if it could tell him the answer. But there was only one thing that could do that—the decode.

And that, as always, took time.

27

NxW. North by west . . . where on earth was it! It had *disappeared* again.

Julie tried to read the letters on the dimly lit compass card. The boat lurched and she put up a hand to brace herself against the post that held the compass.

Come *on*! Which way? Which way?

Think. The compass was showing *W*—west. North was to the right. Therefore she wanted the card to swing—which way? She almost shouted with frustration: it was impossible to work out.

Frantically, she pulled the tiller toward her and watched the card. It hesitated then swung slowly toward north.

She breathed a sigh of relief, then made herself concentrate again. NxW. North by west.

NxW for one hour. Don't forget. NxW—north by west.

The problem was the compass. It wouldn't stay still. It kept swaying from side to side. And it moved in the opposite direction from the one you expected. The tiller did too!

NxW for one hour then you'll be safe.

Then you'll be safe. . . . So there must be dangers either side— rocks, shoals, islands. . . . She remembered on placid summer days seeing the rocks in the estuary and, farther out, black towers marking hidden plateaus.

She gulped and gritted her teeth. However hard she tried it was absolutely impossible to keep straight on NxW. The best she

could do was to keep NxW in the center of the swing. Even then, if she took her eyes away for a moment, it seemed to dive away.

She jerked the tiller toward her. The card swung the wrong way. She shoved the tiller away and the *N* shot around toward the front of the compass. Too far! She yanked at the tiller again until NxW hovered for a moment on the marker before swinging inexorably away. She shouted out loud, "Damn you!"

She closed her eyes tightly for a moment and made an effort to clear her mind.

She opened her eyes, breathed deeply, and concentrated again. At last the compass evened out somewhere around NxW. She remembered something Richard had said, about boats having a feel to them, a balance . . . there was none that she could sense, none at all!

A sound floated back, a whimper. . . . She peered toward the middle of the boat. "Peter? Peter! Are you all right, darling?"

"Mummy!" The voice was tearful. "I'm awfully cold!"

"Yes, I know. But—" Could she leave the tiller and get to him? No—it was too risky, even for a moment. She shouted, "Try to get under the deck at the front. And—look in your bag—"

"What?" His voice was faint, plaintive.

The course had veered again; Julie jerked at the tiller. "Your bag, darling, look inside it. There's another sweater somewhere!"

"What?"

Julie gripped the tiller and tried not to scream. She shouted angrily, "Just do as I say and don't argue!"

There was a silence, then: "I've got it."

Julie calmed herself down. She said steadily, "Take off your jacket and put on the sweater, then crawl up— No! Put the jacket back on *first, then* crawl up to the front. It'll be warmer there. Tell me when you get there."

"All right."

For an instant Julie wondered what had happened to the old man: he was very quiet. She thought of calling to him but decided against it. Later. She had too much to think about now.

The boat moved suddenly and Julie reached for the post again, her heart lurching with fear. The waves—they were a little larger, she was sure of it. She shivered violently and looked quickly down

at the compass. The boat was miles off course. She thought: This is hopeless, *hopeless*! I can't *possibly* manage on my own! God, why did Michel think I could!

If only there was someone else!

Richard . . . best of all, *Richard*—why couldn't *he* be here? He would know exactly what to do. He must have been through lots of experiences like this. The thought encouraged her. She tried to recall other things he had told her about sailing, things that might help. . . . But she could remember nothing: he'd talked about compasses and courses but he'd never explained how you actually held a course, far less how you managed the sails.

Peter's small voice floated back on the wind. "Mummy, I'm here!" In the front, presumably.

Julie shouted, "Try to go to sleep now, darling."

"All right."

She looked down at the compass. Good Lord: it actually read NxW.

The night was so dark it was impossible to see anything clearly. The sky was slightly less black than the sea—but that was all. Julie stared ahead, trying to make out shapes. But there was no distance, no perspective and after a while the blackness seemed to rear up in front of her like a wall.

The compass read NW. She pulled the tiller toward her. NNW. Then, a sudden swing to N. She pushed the tiller away again. NxW—at last. *Stay there!*

She glanced up again, and shivered. It was eerie, the darkness. It made her feel utterly remote, like being on a hilltop, quite alone. And then there was the silence. Though it was broken by the whisper of the wind and the swishing of the water and the occasional slap of a wave on the boat's side, it was unnerving too.

She shivered again and couldn't stop. With faint surprise she realized she was terribly cold. No time to get more clothes on. Later. Later.

NxW for an hour—then you'll be safe.

How much time had passed? She had no idea. It felt like hours. It was far too dark to read her watch. She put her wrist down to the compass and, leaning forward, tried to see the hands by the reflection of the compass light. The thing was a stupid woman's watch: it had a tiny face without numbers. Useless! She put her

face closer. At last she thought she saw the hands. Midnight—?

An hour gone!

The compass had sheered violently off. She pulled on the tiller. Damn! Wrong way! Why did the blasted thing have to work *backward*!

There: NxW. She put her wrist to the compass again and, steadying the boat, thrust her face down to the flickering light. It took half a minute to be sure, but yes: it was almost midnight. She'd wait another ten minutes to be on the safe side. Perhaps even more, to be absolutely sure.

She felt the beginnings of relief. Over the first hurdle. Something anyway, to have got this far.

Half-smiling, half-miserable, she thought: Richard would be proud of me!

Then she remembered where he was and despair settled on her like a lead weight.

Don't . . . don't think . . .

Mechanically she glanced at the compass.

It wasn't there.

Her heart went to her mouth. She gulped. It had gone. The light had gone! There wasn't a flicker.

She said out loud, "No! Dear God!" And, clamping her hand over her mouth, thought: What on earth do I do *now*!

Relight the oil? But she had no match.

Think. What had Michel said? He'd mentioned something . . . a flashlight. Yes! Where? In a box. That was it, he'd said it was in a box. She knelt down, one hand still on the tiller, and felt around. Nothing. The other side, then. Floorboards . . . a rope . . . farther behind. . . .

Her hand came to an upright wooden surface. She felt up to a top lip and a lid. It was a box, full of things: rough ropes, a square metal box, then—a round metal object. She cried out in triumph. Standing up again, she found the switch and a narrow beam of yellow light illuminated the darkness, half blinding her. Fumbling, she switched it off. Far too bright.

She reached into the box again and scrabbled around until she found a piece of cloth. Putting it over the flashlight, she turned the switch on, being careful to keep the beam pointing downward. That was much better: the beam was reduced to a dull pool

of light. She shone it at the compass. Not bad! Only NNW! She pulled the tiller toward her and the card swung back toward NxW. She giggled slightly.

She switched off the flashlight. Mustn't waste the batteries.

She let her body sag. The boat heeled slightly and she stepped back to regain her balance. The back of her knees came up against something hard and, feeling with her hand, she realized it was a seat. Of course: a seat for the helmsman. She sank onto it and wedged her foot up against the compass post. It was much more comfortable.

She wondered if the full hour and a quarter had passed. Probably not: best to wait.

She tried to concentrate on the steering, to keep on course without having to shine the light too much. Sometimes it worked, sometimes not. Most of the time she just stared forward, trying not to see the darkness rearing up in front of her.

Finally she shone the flashlight on her watch. Twenty past twelve. She clenched her fists and, looking up, said, "Thank you, God!" She almost shouted the news to Peter, but decided not to: he was probably asleep by now.

What next? *Then anything between north-northwest and northeast* . . . or was it northwest and northeast?

She couldn't remember.

No, he'd definitely said between NNW and NE.

Julie felt into the box for some rope and, resting the tiller against her knee, unwound a coil. Her fingers were dreadfully stiff from the cold and from gripping the tiller so tight. Eventually she managed to tie a loop onto the tiller. She went to the side of the boat and felt along it for an anchor point. She found one on the top of the rail: a wooden thing with a point sticking out either end. She'd seen them used for tying up ropes before. She took the rope and wound it several times around the wooden thing, which had a name she couldn't remember.

Next she took the other end of the rope to the other side of the boat and tied it to another wooden anchor point. She shone the flashlight on the compass and watched. NNW moving toward NW. She slackened one side of the rope and tightened the other, to move the tiller slightly across. The course held steady on NW. She loosened the right-hand rope a little more. The course came

446

up to NNW and she tightened it again. The course was holding. More or less.

Taking the flashlight she quickly made her way along the left side of the boat toward the front. She knelt down under the small expanse of decking. There was Peter, curled in a ball, sleeping peacefully. She felt his cheek: warm enough, but not as warm as she'd like.

She shone the light forward and saw, right in the point of the bows, some dark material folded under a lobster pot. She crawled forward and pulled the material out. It was a sack. Under it was another. She went on pulling until she had four. She crawled back and put two over Peter.

Now the old man. He must be on the right-hand side somewhere. She was still blinded from using the flashlight and waited until her eyes readjusted to the darkness. Then she saw him: a dark shape huddled under the steep side of the boat. She went over and knelt by him.

He was very still. She asked tentatively, "Are you all right?"

Silence. Julie reached out and touched his arm.

There was a slight moan. She thought: Thank goodness, at least he's alive! "Are you all right?" she repeated.

"Eh? Oh . . ." The old man's voice was low, rough. "Oh . . . yes, yes . . . I'm all right." He tried to laugh. "I'm just not as young as I used to be, that's all!"

"I'm so sorry, I didn't mean to wake you."

"No, no dear girl. Please don't apologize. I only wish I could help you. I'm of no use at all, I'm afraid. Perhaps later . . ." His voice was breathless.

"You just stay there and rest. Don't worry about me. I can manage! Here—" She put the two sacks over him. "Are you comfortable, or would you like to go up to the front? It's a bit more sheltered there."

"Thank you so much. I'm all right here."

There was a loud slap: a wave against the side. Julie said sharply, "I must go now—back to the steering. . . . Just shout if you need me."

And then she was gone. David pulled the sacks more tightly around his legs and wished he didn't feel so ill. He closed his eyes,

his head against the side of the boat. Immediately, he became disoriented and his head began to swim. The boat was rocking gently from side to side. If it went on rocking, he thought grimly, he would be sick.

He burped slightly, a pang of acid stabbing his stomach. So he was to suffer that too! His stomach chose its moments very well.

He closed his eyes and tentatively let his head fall to one side. He decided he would be more comfortable lying down. Taking the bag from around his waist, he felt in it and found his tablets. He took one and, putting the bag on the deck, lay down with his head on it. Yes: that was better. He didn't feel so sick, lying down. He might even be able to sleep.

He would feel better later. Then he would give Julie a hand.

Julie untied the tiller and brought the boat back on course. Almost immediately she sighed with annoyance: she'd forgotten to get a sweater. But perhaps it wasn't necessary; it didn't seem quite so cold as before. . . . Then she remembered that awful time on the fishing boat; and something Richard had said, about cold being the greatest danger of all, much more dangerous than the waves themselves. She retied the tiller and set off toward the bow.

Her bag was beside Peter, right up under the deck. She supposed Michel had put it there in case it rained. She undid the strap and poked around until she found the thick wool sweater. She took off the cowjacket, pulled the sweater on and put the cowjacket back over the top. She felt warmer already. There was a scarf in the bag too; she took it out and tied it around her head.

Peter was sleeping peacefully. She went straight back to the tiller. When she shone the flashlight on the compass she almost laughed: the course had settled on NxW. She decided to let the boat sail by itself; the course was a good one and much steadier than anything she could achieve.

She sat on the helmsman's seat and tried to think. How far was it across the Channel? She had no idea. How long would it take to get across? She had no idea of that either!

Brilliant.

Try again. The Channel must be at least a hundred miles wide —perhaps even two hundred. Say a hundred and fifty. How fast were they going? Goodness only knew!—perhaps fifteen miles an hour. No: on second thought, that was quite a rate. What was

walking speed? Five miles an hour, four? A bit faster than that, say six then.

Six miles an hour. A hundred and fifty miles. Mental arithmetic: always one of her worst subjects at school. Sixes into one hundred and fifty. . . .

Eventually she got there: twenty-five. Of course. Six twenty-fives made a hundred and fifty.

Twenty-five hours then, call it twenty-four.

Immediately she became depressed.

It was a dreadfully long time. A whole day out in the middle of the sea, a day when they would be exposed like a goldfish in a bowl. There were bound to be German patrols . . . aircraft . . .

If they survived the day then there'd be most of the next night, a night when the land would be getting closer and closer, rushing toward them. How on earth would she know where it was, the land? And how would she know when the boat was about to crash into it?

I can't do this, she thought, I just can't do it!

Silently she cried, the tears hot on her cheeks. It was all such a mess. Everyone at the village caught and dead or more probably tortured. Richard a prisoner. And here—Peter and the old man relying on *her*, probably the most incompetent person in the world!

Angrily, she wiped the tears away. Whatever happened, crying wouldn't do any good.

Later, she realized a long time must have passed—several hours at least. Apart from checking the compass from time to time she stared ahead into the darkness, her mind half on what had happened at the beach, half on the nightmare she was living through now. One event seemed to lead on from the other, in a horrible dreamlike way.

For a while she dozed, perched uneasily on the seat, images drifting in and out of her mind, the beach and the boat blending into a terrible fantasy of water and blazing lights and anger and suffering. The Germans were taking everyone away . . . Jean, Tante Marie and Peter, *even Peter*—

Suddenly she was awake.

She looked blindly around, wondering what had awakened her. The boat was still sailing along, the water hissing and gurgling past the hull. But the sky was different. It was clearer now: there

were stars, thousands of them, carpeting the sky so that the sail stood out black against them. But there was something else and she couldn't place it. She shone the light at the compass. NW— northwest. The course had changed a little. But was that it? No—

Then she had it. The wind, it was much fresher. She felt it cold against her face, pulling at her scarf. A muted fluttering sound came from above, like a thousand birds beating their wings. Now and then there was the creaking of wood against wood.

Yes, there was more wind. The movements of the boat were much quicker than before and, instead of rocking gently from side to side, the craft was tilted stiffly at a slight angle, its nose going down and up, down and up, like a rocking horse.

The bow hit a wave with a *Crump!* and Julie realized that it was this sound which had awakened her. A fine spray floated back on the air and drifted onto her face. Shaking slightly, she shone the light at the compass again. Still northwest, but tending to veer off toward the west. Not good enough. She untied the tiller and moved it until the compass read nearer to north.

Immediately the fluttering sound changed to a flapping and there was a fierce rattling as something close to Julie's head started to shake angrily.

She yanked the tiller back the other way. The flapping stopped, but when she looked at the compass the course was back west of northwest. Michel had specifically said she must steer between north-northwest and northeast. She was definitely *outside* that.

What should she do? She could leave the boat on this course —but that *must* be wrong. The sails, then, she should stop them flapping. But how?

She tried bringing the boat back onto a northerly course once more, but the flapping started again, louder than ever. "Damn!" She quickly pulled the tiller the other way. The flapping stopped. She breathed out sharply.

She stayed at the tiller steering northwest for a long time, frozen with indecision. She should do something to the sails—she knew *that* much—but what? And if she didn't—God, she'd probably miss England altogether.

Impossible.

Because there was nothing else to do, she held the northwesterly course, thinking all the time: I'm failing! Miserably failing!

450

Perhaps if she held on, perhaps the wind would change. . . .

A long time passed. Dimly she realized that she could see the side of the boat stretching away from her. When she looked again the bow itself was there, a faint black smudged against gray. Then the sea itself, waves like the ripples on an iced cake, but gray and murky. To the right, a thin line of pale white light appeared, stretching across the horizon from side to side; with a slight shock, Julie realized it *was* the horizon. The white light filtered gradually up into the sky, turning a delicate crystal yellow, the color of pale primrose. One by one the stars disappeared until the sky became a clear unbroken dome over her head.

Dawn.

Instinctively, Julie looked behind, but it was still too dark to see anything. She looked again a few minutes later. It was difficult to tell: the gray area between the sea and the sky was too indistinct.

Half an hour later the southern horizon was visible, a gray line behind the boat. There was no land in sight. They were clear of the coast, then. That was something at least.

But when she looked at the vast expanse of water around her, stretching out barren and cold in every direction, she didn't feel so glad. It looked enormous.

In the front Peter's figure was clearly visible, curled up under the sacks. He was sleeping soundly. So was the old man, over on the right-hand side of the boat. Good. There was no point in everyone being tired.

The compass was visible now in the gray light. Still northwest. Still the *wrong* course.

She stayed frozen at the tiller a moment longer, then made herself stand up. *Time to get going.*

She said out loud, "Right!" Gritting her teeth, she tied up the tiller and eyed the ropes that were coiled or fastened at various points around the boat. There were two sails. The first, a big one, almost square, was fastened to the mast on its front edge, to a long wooden pole on its lower edge and to another, shorter pole high up on its top edge. The fourth, back edge wasn't fastened to anything. Up in front of the mast, there was another, smaller sail, triangular and attached to a sharp piece of wood that stuck out in front of the boat. She remembered: the piece of wood was called a bowsprit.

The big sail first. There was one rope which seemed to make the sail go in or out. The rope wound back and forth between wooden pulleys. She wasn't sure why—to make things easier perhaps.

The rope was tied off around a wooden anchor thing—was it called a *fastener*? Tentatively she reached forward and untied the rope. Her heart hammering against her chest, she very slowly began to take off the last turn.

Suddenly there was a great jerk and the rope almost flew out of her hands. She cried out and, holding on grimly, tried to get a second turn of rope back onto the anchor-fastener. As she moved her hands the rope jerked out, pulling her knuckle sharply against the hard wood of the fastener. She gasped in pain and let go.

The rope whistled out from the coil, snaking up angrily toward the sail. The next moment there was a thunderous noise: the racket of beating canvas and rattling pulleys. The sail had gone mad, beating itself about in a frenzy, gyrating back and forth until the whole boat vibrated.

Julie stared, aghast.

What now?

She put her hands over her ears to black out the dreadful noise.

There was still some rope left in the coil; it hadn't all run out. Shaking like a leaf, she reached down, picked up the rope and cautiously pulled in on it.

"Mummy!"

Peter was standing beside her, rubbing his eyes and looking curiously up at the sail. "Mummy, shouldn't we pull it in?"

She said wearily, "Yes, Peter, we should."

"I'll help you, then!" He was shouting to make himself heard over the thrashing of the sail.

"Don't you dare touch it!" Julie screamed. "Just—leave it!"

There was no reply, and she saw that he was looking at her hurt and shamefaced. She sighed. "Sorry, I'm just tired, sweetheart, that's all. I'll be all right in a moment." She wiped her eyes on her sleeve and said ruefully, "The trouble is, I don't know *how* to get the sail in."

"You put the rope under the cleat."

"The cleat?"

"Yes." Peter pointed at the wooden anchor-fastener thing.

452

"That's what it's called—a cleat. Richard told me. And I know you put ropes round it to take the strain. That's what he said. . . ." He trailed off.

She almost kissed him. "Let's have a go then, darling!"

She picked up the rope and, with Peter tugging ineffectually behind, began to pull. Soon the rope was jerking in her hands. She bent down and slid the rope under the lower arm of the cleat. Alternately she pulled and rested, letting the cleat take the strain of the rope. The clattering of the sail lessened slightly.

Then she had the idea of standing on the other side of the deck, so that the rope was doubled back from the cleat. It was a great improvement: the rope was less inclined to jerk out of her hands.

The pull on the rope became much stronger and, though she put her full weight against it, she couldn't get it in any farther. She rested for a moment, panting.

Suddenly the noise from the sail became worse. Julie, bewildered, realized the rope had gone almost limp in her hand. She pulled wildly, gathering in great lengths of it, and quickly tied the rope off around the cleat.

She looked up at the sail: it was almost tight in!

Elated, she looked at the compass. North by west—or thereabouts! And the sail full: a miracle.

How it had happened she didn't know. Then she noticed that the tiller had become untied. Perhaps that had something to do with it.

She went forward and hunted for the rope that controlled the other, smaller sail at the front. She found it and, eyeing the sail with trepidation, undid the rope. It didn't have nearly so much pull on it and she was able to haul it in quite easily.

Returning to the tiller she undid the lines that tied it and said gaily to Peter, "I'll make a sailor yet!"

The child smiled back and, coming to her side, put his hand in hers. "Mummy, I'm hungry. Is there any breakfast?"

Julie's heart sank. Breakfast. She'd never thought of breakfast. Had Michel said anything about food? Water, yes, he'd definitely mentioned that. But food? No.

How did one tell a six-year-old that there was nothing to eat? She said softly, "There isn't any breakfast, darling. Sorry." She took a deep breath. "We're going to have to go without until we get to England." She squeezed his hand.

"Without—anything?" The voice was subdued.

Julie forced herself to sound brisk and matter-of-fact. "Without anything. We finished all the food when we were on the beach, remember?"

"Perhaps there's some on the boat . . ."

It was very unlikely. "Perhaps. Why don't you go and have a look, eh?"

He nodded brightly and, dropping to his knees, started rooting around in the large box where Julie had found the flashlight.

It would, at least, keep him busy for a while.

A movement caught her eye: the old man was leaning over the side of the boat, his head down, as if staring at the water. For a moment Julie couldn't think what he was doing then she heard a faint retching sound and looked quickly away.

She'd quite forgotten about being sick. Extraordinary. She couldn't understand why it hadn't happened to *her*.

There was a *Crump!* from the front and a thin veil of spray came flying back into her face. More wind: definitely more wind. The tiller felt different in her hand: it was moving of its own accord and she had to push harder to get the boat back on course. The boat was going faster too, haring along like the wind. Perhaps her calculations had been wrong; perhaps they'd get to England before nightfall. The idea of more wind made her nervous but it might be a blessing after all.

There was a whoop from the front. Julie tensed. Peter's face appeared around the mast, waving madly. What on earth was he so excited about?

He emerged, holding a bag, and weaved his way back down the boat. He dumped the bag at her feet in triumph. "Food!" he yelped.

Julie blinked. "Food?"

"Yes, tins, Mummy! Cans of fish and beef and potatoes and *petits pois* and . . ."

She stared in astonishment as Peter opened the bag to reveal the cans, about ten of them, a little rusty but obviously quite usable. The whole thing was odd enough—Michel having this boat—but the food. . . . A thought came to Julie and she suddenly understood everything.

This boat was for *Michel's* escape. He'd planned it all—bought the boat, prepared it, put the food on board, even worked out the

course for England. He'd planned it all—and then given the boat to her.

Crump! Spray flew into Julie's eyes and spattered against her jacket. "Take the bag back to the front, Peter, so it doesn't get wet. And you stay there too and have something to eat."

"But it's awfully bumpy up there. Can't I stay here?" He was whining. Tiredness.

"Well . . . all right! We'll eat here together. See if you can find an opener or a knife or something."

He disappeared into the box behind her and rummaged around. "Nothing here, Mummy, only this." Dispiritedly, he held up a metal spike.

"Try the front, then."

"The bow, you mean. That's its *proper* name."

Julie made an effort not to clip his ear. "Don't argue with me!" she shouted. "Just go and look."

He wandered off down the deck. Instantly Julie regretted her anger: she was tired and hungry too.

The bow rose then dipped violently. There was more spray, heavier this time and icy cold: she could feel it seeping through her trousers. The wind seemed colder too; she shivered despite the extra sweater.

Peter came back along the deck, his hair dripping with water. "Oh darling, you're all wet!"

"There was a big wave!" His lower lip trembled and he started to cry.

"Come on, let's get some food inside you!"

"There's no opener!" He was crying in earnest now, his face creased in despair.

One thing after another. Julie took a deep breath and said calmly, "Let's use the spike then. That'll have to do."

Pushing her back against the tiller to hold it steady, she reached into the bag for a can and, holding it against her leg, tried to puncture it with the spike. On the third attempt the spike slid off and dug into her thigh. Hopeless.

God, she felt tired.

She put her hand into the bag to see if there was an easier can, perhaps a flat sardine-type with its own opener. She felt around and came out with a long metallic object—a can opener. She clapped her hand to her forehead and shook her head. It

was, of course, where any intelligent person would have put it.

She opened a can of meat and one of sardines. "When you've eaten, go and see if Monsieur Freymann wants anything, will you, Peter?" He nodded, his mouth full of meat. Julie looked to the rail, but David wasn't there anymore. He was lying on the deck again. His face was sheet white; he wouldn't want anything to eat. A drink, maybe . . .

Where was that water Michel had talked about? Heaven only knew.

She stuffed a sardine into her mouth and was surprised to find how hungry she was. She ate ravenously, then opened a can of potatoes and ate most of that too before passing it to Peter.

Crump! The water was flying over the bow more frequently now. Did it matter, all this water? She remembered how wet it had been on that large fishing boat when she and Peter had tried to escape before, yet the crew hadn't been worried.

Peter got a face full of water and she made him go to the uphill side of the deck, where there seemed to be less spray. She moved across to the same side and took the tiller in her other hand.

Only then did she realize just how much the boat was tilting to one side. The deck was at a considerable slant and the mast was leaning at a distinct angle. Each gust of wind made the tilt worse. What was there to stop the boat going right over?

She had a sudden memory of another time . . . with Richard all those years ago. The boat had tilted then, quite far. She remembered clinging to the side, terrified. But *he* hadn't been concerned, not in the slightest. She whispered, "Oh Richard, why the hell aren't you here!"

There was a *whoosh* and a swishing sound. Water was racing along the downhill side of the deck. *Where had it come from?* Immediately Julie thought: We're sinking!

She clutched at Peter. "Oh God, darling!"

"It's all right, Mummy, it'll go out through the scuppers."

Julie stared at him in amazement. "The scuppers?"

"Yes. Richard told me. When we were carving the model. They're holes in the sides, down there. For letting water out."

". . . For letting water out . . ."

She watched, fascinated, as the water gurgled away through the small slits. A moment later the boat tipped again and the water

came back, only to gurgle harmlessly away as before. "What else did Richard tell you?"

The little face went blank. Julie realized it was the wrong way to ask. She tried again. "Did he talk about what to do in strong winds?"

"Ummm, well, I know what you do in *gales.*"

Julie gripped his shoulder. "Yes, darling!"

"You shorten sail!"

"Yes . . . and?"

"You reef! That's what you do!"

"Reef. . . . That's what he told you?"

"Yes."

Julie had no idea what that meant. And Peter was still thinking, she could tell by his face. Eventually he said, very slowly, "You let the sail down a bit, then you tie up the loose bit with all those ropes hanging from the sail there. Richard drew me a picture."

"I see."

She couldn't imagine how it was actually done, but at least she might have a vague idea if worse came to the worst. But when did a strong wind became a gale? How did you *know* when to reef?

Her head was aching violently: she couldn't think. Damn it. One thing at a time. Gales might never happen!

She settled back on the helmsman's seat and forced herself to stop worrying. After all, things could be a lot worse.

At that moment David Freymann cried out in agony and from far away in the eastern sky came the low hum of an approaching plane.

28 The wind was coming from the northeast and freshening.

Fischer, at the chart table, was more certain than ever that the prey couldn't be heading for Plymouth—the course

would put him hard on the wind. Too uncomfortable and too slow.

No: Falmouth it had to be.

But the speed estimate would have to be revised. Even a small boat would be doing more than four knots in this wind. Five, maybe more.

Fischer marked off two points along the prey's course line. The first point marked the prey's position if he was doing a steady six knots; the second, his position at four knots. These, then, marked the limits of speed probability. The gap between the two positions was twenty nautical miles.

Now, if this fellow strayed from his course, which way would he go? To the west almost certainly, because of the freshening wind. Fischer marked off a second course line ten degrees to the west of the first. The result was a long thin box approximately a hundred square miles.

A hundred square miles . . . one hell of a lot of sea . . .

It would be impossible to search it all. No, the best thing would be to patrol back and forth across the probable track and wait for the prey to come to them. A waiting game.

The soonest that the prey could possibly be here was . . . right now. Unlikely, though, because he wouldn't have been doing six knots the whole time. At the other extreme, the latest he'd arrive was in five hours' time, at 1500 hours.

A waiting game.

In the meantime, there was little danger of meeting enemy surface units here: *U-319* was in the unofficial no-man's-land between Britain and France. But nearer Britain there would be a lot of shipping—minesweepers, coastal convoys—and maybe even some minefields. The chart showed one mined area just to the north. But Fischer was skeptical: in all likelihood the intelligence was not only out of date but not too accurate in the first place.

And overhead there was no such thing as a no-man's-land. The air was anybody's. Except that, around here, it was mainly British, which was one of the reasons U-boats no longer operated in the Channel.

A young seaman was manning the search periscope, circling slowly. Fischer watched him for a moment, his mind on what

would happen if they did manage to find this fishing boat. To capture the occupants they'd have to surface. The operation would take a good fifteen to twenty minutes—if they were lucky. It was an awfully long time to be on the surface in broad daylight.

Hell! What an operation!

The periscope stopped circling. The young seaman yelled, "Aircraft bearing zero-four-five! Range—four to five miles!"

Fischer pushed the young man aside and took a look. A Catalina or something like it. Definitely one of the enemy's. Closing.

"Down periscope! Alter course forty-five degrees to star-board!"

Fifteen minutes: he'd wait fifteen minutes before he took another look.

After five minutes he said again, "Alter course forty-five degrees to starboard." The order was echoed twice.

They waited, as they'd waited so many times before, the crew automatically falling into Silent Routine, though no ship was tracking them. The only sound was the quiet hum of the electric motors.

After a long while Fischer looked at his watch and barked, "Up periscope."

The periscope hissed up and, quickly lowering the folding handles, Fischer put his eye to the lens and made a quick circle: nothing. Then a slower one: nothing. The plane had gone.

It had been on a routine reconnaissance patrol, Fischer decided. It was unlikely it had seen them.

"Resume course. Resume patrol routine."

The men relaxed and started to move around again. Fischer made another circle of the horizon. No fishing boat in sight. But the sea was definitely rougher. From one point of view that was a good thing: it meant there was less chance of the periscope being seen. On the other hand it would be more difficult to spot the prey . . . if they ever got anywhere near it.

"Wireless signal, Herr Kaleu."

With the resumption of Patrol Routine the rod aerial—also periscopic—had gone up. Fischer went over to the wireless operator and watched him tap the signal into the Enigma machine. Fischer picked up the decoded message, said, "Strict-

ly *no* acknowledgment!" and strode over to the chart table.

He was jubilant: the target had been spotted! By one of their own reconnaissance planes—which meant the position wouldn't be terribly accurate, aerial fixes never were—but it was a darn sight better than nothing.

He measured the coordinates off the side and top of the chart and penciled in a cross. There! Seen *there* at 0930 hours!

Slow. Going much slower than he'd thought. Almost at the lower edge of the box he'd drawn—and to the west, *well* to the west! Where could they be making for?

And the slow speed, that was a surprise too. They had averaged only four knots. Perhaps the fishing boat had set out later than first thought, perhaps that first position was wrong. . . . All supposition.

The point was, he must get *U-319* farther to the west, into the prey's path. . . .

And then?

Then he'd wait. Nothing had changed. It was still a waiting game.

In the Submarine Tracking Room the Head sifted slowly through the information that had come in during the night, measuring it against the probable speed and track of the various boats and trying to calculate where wolf packs might be forming.

The job was getting increasingly difficult. The problem was one of scale. Never had there been so many U-boats—four hundred in existence, two hundred and fifty operational and probably well over a hundred actually at sea. It was almost impossible to keep track of them all, though he and his staff did their very best. Especially *now*.

He remembered the morning meeting and the appalling statistics—twenty-one ships lost from just two convoys. The Vice-Chief of Staff had said, "We have reached a crisis in the battle of the Atlantic." The crisis was simple—if the U-boats weren't driven off, the convoys couldn't get through.

No one needed to be told the consequences of that.

To fight the menace there was to be a new strategy. Ultra information was to be used to the full and convoys always diverted out of the path of waiting wolf packs; all convoys were to get full support group protection; and, finally, production of the

new H_2S radar, which trials had proved to be so successful, was to be rapidly accelerated and units fitted to all bombers of Coastal Command.

It was make or break. The last-ditch stand.

Doenitz knew that too.

Over the years the Head had learned to understand the way Doenitz's mind worked. The U-boats' tactics reflected Doenitz's thinking, his favorite strategies, his master plan. A year before, when air patrols and radar had made things too difficult for the U-boats in the North Atlantic, the Grand Admiral had transferred the larger ones to the South Atlantic. And the Head had foreseen it, just as he had foreseen that Doenitz would then send them to the American coast. It's what the Head would have done himself.

Now Doenitz had put everything back into the North Atlantic.

This was Doenitz's last-ditch stand too.

The Head reexamined the log entries made by the night watch, and the decodes.

Mainly routine. No specific evidence of a new wolf pack forming. The only unusual thing was the long message sent at 0115 hours and prefixed urgent.

A signal on the U-boat frequency—possibly an acknowledgment—had been sent ten minutes later. The signal was too short for the DF people to get a good fix on its sender, but a rough estimate had put the U-boat in the Bay of Biscay.

Just one acknowledgment . . . a single U-boat involved then. Curious. A change of orders perhaps? A new destination?

What he needed were the Ultra decodes.

An hour later he had them in an enormous pile.

Short messages, lots of them: acknowledgments, damage reports, notification of successful attacks (too many of them, always too many of them) . . . these he passed to his staff for routine processing.

He picked up the long signal and read the message with growing astonishment. Good Lord, what on earth did it all mean? A fishing boat, occupants to be captured but not harmed. Extraordinary.

He went to a side table. On it was a large chart marked with grid references. At the beginning of the war, the Germans had made no attempt to disguise their grid references, and once a German chart had been obtained for the Tracking Room, it was a simple

matter to read the references off. But now the references were disguised by a code which was changed every month and sometimes took quite a while to crack. At the moment they were still guessing. The code had only just been changed.

Grid references. The signal had dozens of the blasted things . . .

Some were familiar and did, he knew, lie somewhere in the Bay. Others were unfamiliar. . . . H17 P15, for example. The Head knew the prefixes *H* and *P*, but he'd never seen them with those numbers and in that combination. Deduction—this boat was being sent somewhere different. Not into the Atlantic, or to Greenland or Iceland.

Chasing a fishing boat . . . Biscay coast? Possibly. But the grid references didn't look right, certainly nothing like those used by U-boats when, after Allied air attacks, they sometimes had to call for assistance.

The north French coast then?

No U-boats had been into the Channel for a long time. Too dangerous and too few convoys to make it worthwhile.

He studied the signal again. The fishing boat was believed to be heading for another place with the same prefixes and fairly similar coordinates. It would be easy to assume that the second place was a port or refuge—but it could just as easily be a point miles out to sea, a rendezvous. . . .

The Head called to one of his assistants and asked her to check whether any of the various clandestine organizations knew anything about a meeting with a fishing boat.

Back to the coordinates. Assuming the first of each pair of coordinates was the latitude, then the second position was at a higher latitude, assuming again that the code followed the normal practice and the numbers got higher the farther from the equator you went . . .

An awful lot of assumptions.

But if the assumptions *were* right, then the second place was to the north of the first.

The fishing boat could conceivably be going north from somewhere like Bordeaux. . . . But no, the coordinates would have been familiar. Also he felt instinctively that it didn't quite fit. They'd never send a U-boat if the fisherman was making a run for another part of Occupied France, or for neutral Spain, they'd send a coastal patrol boat or, even better, an E-boat.

That was it! Of course!
They had sent a U-boat.
Not anything else.
Why?

The mission was important, of course, as Doenitz had stressed. But there must be more to it than that. This fishing boat had to be going somewhere where *other* craft couldn't go. Like toward enemy territory. Or *past* enemy territory, where Allied air patrols were likely to be heavy. Yes, *yes.*

The English Channel.

It had to be.

But where *exactly*? East Channel? No. However vital the operation was, Doenitz would never send one of his boats on a suicide mission. It was so shallow in the east Channel the U-boat wouldn't stand a chance.

So west Channel. Why not?

The Head went to the plot and, picking up *U-319*'s token, which the night staff had placed outside Brest, moved it to the middle of the English Channel to the south of Plymouth.

Then, pulling his ear thoughtfully, he lifted the telephone.

He might be wildly wrong and be sending Coastal Command off on a wild goose chase. But he had another one of his feelings about this one.

It was Doenitz's postscript. IF ANYONE CAN DO IT, YOU CAN.

There could be only one reason Doenitz had said that. Because he was asking his man to do the impossible. He was asking him to go into the jaws of the lion.

29 Julie slapped his face.
Awful, but it had to be done.
He stirred slightly. "Monsieur Freymann! David! David! Wake up!"

He was almost unconscious. In desperation she put her mouth to his ear and shouted, "You've got to move!"

There was a *Crump!* from the bow and, after a moment's pause, heavy spray came flying over the deck. Julie ducked too late and the water trickled down her neck. The old man was getting soaked too: that's why he had to be moved.

His eyes flickered open. The cold water must have roused him. "You've got to move. To the front, over *there.*" Julie indicated the bow. "Otherwise you'll get soaked!"

Taking his arm, Julie pushed him into a sitting position and began to pull him along the deck. At first she could feel him helping, shuffling sideways on his behind, but then he sagged and his weight fell against her leg, his face white and contorted with pain.

She crouched down and, her arm around his shoulders, waited awhile. The boat hit another wave and the inevitable deluge of heavy, cold spray rained down over them.

Julie blew the water off her lips and, standing up again, tried to drag the old man, but he was terribly heavy and she couldn't keep her balance on the unsteady deck. Panting, she knelt and shouted desperately, "Please *try,* David. Please *try.*"

Julie started pulling and felt him helping again. This time they reached the shelter of the small decked area under the bow. The motion of the boat was much more violent up here but at least it was dry.

"Just a bit farther, then you'll be comfortable!"

The old man made a final effort and, at last, Julie settled him against some coils of rope. He lay back and closed his eyes. She covered him with sacking and placed a rolled-up section of tarpaulin under his head.

She looked at him fondly and, very gently, stroked his head. "Sorry I had to slap you." But he didn't hear: he was unconscious again. She examined his face anxiously. It was deathly white, with an almost green tinge to it, and his breath was coming in short, shallow pants through a gaping mouth.

The pills: the old man had mentioned pills. She should try to get some more down him. He'd thrown the last lot up.

In his bag, she found a small bottle half full of white tablets. It had to be them: there were no others. The bottle had no label

and no instructions. She guessed at two tablets and shook them into her hand.

Water. She'd need water.

Up by the lobster pot in the box, she found a large rope-clad bottle full of clear liquid. She opened it and dipped a finger in. Water. But no mug or cup.

She placed the tablets on the old man's tongue; then, raising his head slightly, she put the bottle to his lips and tried to tip it up. It was too heavy. She wedged her body against the side of the boat and, resting the old man's head against her chest, used both hands on the bottle. Water poured everywhere. Some went into the old man's mouth. He spluttered and coughed, but the pills seemed to have disappeared. It was something at least.

A moment later the old man groaned and, clutching his stomach, turned his head to one side and threw up over Julie's leg.

Julie stared in revulsion and realized with unhappy certainty that unless she moved away the same thing would happen to her too. The uncomfortable feeling in her stomach was rising fast toward her throat. She got up and, lurching toward the rail, swallowed hard and gulped at the fresh salt air.

When she felt better, she looked at David again. He seemed peaceful enough. She couldn't face going back to him, not just yet. The smell . . .

Holding tight to the rail, she made her way cautiously along the tilting deck to the tiller. Peter was curled up against the side of the boat on the uphill side, at the back, where it was dry. He was asleep, a slight frown on his face.

The course on the compass had changed a little—slightly more westerly than before. Julie altered the tiller lines and the course improved slightly, but she could already hear a slight fluttering from the sails. They'd start flapping if she moved the tiller any farther. The sails would need adjusting again. It would have to wait: with a bit of luck it might not be necessary and, anyway, she couldn't face it at the moment.

She searched the sky. No sign of that plane. It was quite extraordinary: it had seen them, she was certain. It *must* have. It had changed its course and flown almost directly overhead. Yet it hadn't come down to shoot at them, or even to look more closely.

Julie had taken Peter and dived under the bow and waited for

the *rat-tat-tat* of bullets. But the sound had never come. Instead the plane had stayed high, the hum faint, and then the sound had faded slowly away into the distance.

There was no sense in worrying about it. The point was, the plane hadn't come back.

Time: almost noon. Her eyes were aching and her head felt as if it were banded with iron. She would have to sleep sometime. But at the moment she felt oddly light-headed and awake and in need of *doing* something—that if she kept busy everything would turn out all right.

Chores: she would get the chores done. Just like at home.

The compass light. It had to be repaired. She thought: But I don't have the first idea *how*.

She drew a deep breath. No harm in looking anyway.

To the side of the compass, mounted on the brass base, was a small flap fastened by a finger bolt. It undid easily. Inside there was a wick. She touched it: dry. No fuel, then. Her heart lifted. The problem might be quite simple after all.

A filler cap: there had to be one. She peered into the small opening, then drew away sharply because the odor made her queasy. A moment for fresh air, then she took another look. Nothing.

Anxiously she searched all the way around the brass compass mount. There it was at last, on the forward side! A small brass cap which, when unscrewed, smelled of kerosene. She put a finger in. It came out dry.

All it needed was fuel. *All!*

She went to the box where she had found the flashlight. The fuel had to be in there.

It wasn't.

She made her way up to the bow, choosing her moment between waves and flying spray. David seemed to be sleeping peacefully. She put a hand on his brow. He was warmer than before but his color was still terrible. She wished there was something she could do for him.

Crouching, she went up into the point of the bow. Another rope-clad container. She opened it excitedly. More water.

She searched carefully under the lobster pots, ropes and the single tarpaulin. Nothing.

466

Where else?

She made her way back toward the tiller. Halfway along the deck, in the center, was a raised section built up from the deck in a large square. It had a sort of lid on it. The way into the hold, presumably, where the fish were usually stored.

The fastenings around the lid were stiff. She tried to prize one open and tore a fingernail. She bit off the nail and tried again. She needed leverage. The spike. The one that Peter had found in the box.

It was still there. She brought it back to the hatch cover and, putting it under the clip, levered outward. The clip sprang open. Triumph.

The other clips gave way more easily. The cover itself was heavy, but, standing on the uphill side, she managed to lift it slightly, then, using the slant of the boat, to slide it downhill.

She looked over the edge of the opening into the hold. Much of it was dark, but immediately below her there was a large square brilliantly illuminated by the open hatch.

Julie stared in disbelief, but that was no mistake.

The hold was full of running water. Spray pattered onto Julie's back, but she didn't notice; she was mesmerized by the water flowing in a great torrent through the boat. After a moment she realized the water was streaming first one way then the other as the boat seesawed across the waves. At its fastest the water made a great rushing noise; then, as the boat reached the crest of a wave, it slowed down and paused before beginning its frantic return journey.

There was tons of it.

Julie wondered how long it had been there—and how fast it was coming in.

"Mummy!"

Peter was standing by the rail, well aft, out of the spray. "Mummy!" he called again. He was looking unhappy. Julie got to her feet. The bow hit a wave and spray flew back over the deck and into the hold. She should cover the hold again—but there was so much water in it already that a bit more would make no difference.

When she got to Peter he held out his arms and she hugged him. "Mummy, I need to go to . . . I want to do a poo."

Julie sighed. "Of course, sweetheart."

"But where, Mummy?"

She hadn't thought of that. Up till now it had just been a question of standing him near the scuppers. A bucket: that would have to do. Knowing Peter, there wasn't much time.

"Wait here."

She looked in the large wooden box beside the tiller and up in the bow. There *had* to be a bucket somewhere.

No bucket. But there was a square tin box full of fishing tackle. She threw out the tackle and, grasping the tin box, ducked out from under the decking.

"Please . . . please . . ." It was David. He was looking at her with pleading eyes.

Why did everything have to happen at once? Julie crouched down and touched his arm. "Can you wait a minute? I've got to get back to Peter . . . !"

Without pausing for an answer, she hurried down the deck. Just in time by the look on Peter's face. Without ceremony, she pulled down his trousers and sat him on the tin box.

"Ouch!"

"I can't help it! It's the best I could find!" She supported the child's weight, so he wouldn't have to sit on the sharp edges.

"Mummy, what about paper?"

"Wait here." The boy grabbed for the helmsman's seat as she let go of him.

Her brain was seizing up, she could feel it. She made an effort to think. Paper. On a boat? Never! It'd be soaked in a moment. What then? A rag—yes, a rag.

In the bow was an oily black rag. It would have to do.

David was grasping her arm. "Please, must talk . . . it's very important . . . *please.*"

"Yes! Yes! In a minute." She was beginning to whine. "Sorry . . . I really *will* be back—but I've got to take this to my son."

As she made her way aft for what seemed like the twentieth time, Julie thought: It's just a matter of keeping going, that's all.

David made an effort to keep his eyes open. Mustn't let go. *Not yet.*

He had to tell her, had to get it to her . . .

Before he couldn't anymore.

468

He felt so weak. The pain was eating into him, gnawing at his body. He wanted to escape, to drift away so that there'd never be any pain again.

But first he *must* talk to the girl. And *then* he'd close his eyes and slip away. And there'd be no more pain, just peace.

But not yet. Mustn't let go. . . . Not yet.

When Julie got back David was asleep. Whatever he'd wanted to say could wait. She'd talk to him as soon as he woke up.

In the meantime . . .

She searched the deck carefully. There had to be a way of getting the water out. "Manning the pumps," that's the term they used in the stories she'd read. But was this boat big enough to have a pump? And if so, what would it look like?

There was nothing on deck that looked remotely like a pump. Nothing for it then . . .

Taking the flashlight, she lowered herself over the edge of the gaping hold and into the darkness. She stepped into swirling water up to her calves. Immediately, she wished she'd left her shoes on deck. Too late now.

The beam from the flashlight revealed an empty shell. Julie stooped and shone the light right up into the bow. Nothing: just the timber frame and, halfway down, the mast coming through from the deck above. Behind, nothing either.

Crouching, she climbed forward. The water was surging around something heaped on the floor—the anchor chain.

No sign of any kerosene. No sign of a pump.

The boat lurched and she grabbed for the mast. Nausea rose in her throat. She knew she must get out, and fast!

As she let go of the mast something cold touched her hand. *Must get up on deck.* . . . Swallowing fast, she shone the light back on the mast to where her hand had been. A pipe. It ran parallel to the mast, down into the bottom of the boat, where it was lost in the murky water. She gulped hard. Where the spar disappeared through the deck, it ran horizontally for a short distance until it stopped at a large metal object suspended from the deckhead.

I'm going to be sick.

She rushed for the open hatch and hoisted herself quickly over the coaming onto the deck.

She fell against the downhill rail and heaved miserably for

several minutes before staggering back to the helmsman's seat. Resting her head against the compass, she waited for the faintness to pass. It would be so easy to sleep now, to let go.

After a few minutes she stood up and, still shaky, made herself go forward to the mast. She looked to one side of it to where the metal thing must be just under the deck, and there, set into the planking, was a short thick metal post. She'd thought it was some kind of bollard, but now she could see it was mechanical: it had a socket thing, and bits that obviously moved.

Spray shot through the air and struck her coldly on the cheek. She dropped to her hands and knees and looked more closely at the mechanical post. The socket was designed to take some sort of handle that could move it back and forth.

A handle. She was getting tired of looking for things. . . .

She glanced around halfheartedly and, right beside her, attached by a clip to the mast, was a long straight piece of pipe iron. A handle.

It fitted the socket.

She pulled the cover across the open hatch so that no more water could get in from above, and, sitting on the edge of the hatch, started to pump. At first the handle went back and forth quite easily, then it became stiffer and she realized it was only now beginning to draw up water. She settled into a rhythm and wondered how long it would take to empty the hold.

The pump was situated in what was probably the wettest part of the deck, where the spray was at its thickest. Water dribbled down her neck and into her clothing, which clung damp and sticky to her skin. But the action of the pumping was at least keeping her warm. She gave a small snort of amusement—you could make anything sound good if you tried.

After half an hour or so, she lifted the hatch cover and shone the flashlight down. Still tons of water. She'd half expected it. She settled back into the pumping, trying to clear her brain of everything but the necessity to pump. But her mind kept wandering: thoughts of home, and Jean, and Tante Marie, and *him.*

She made herself sing, and enjoyed it until she ran out of songs.

Her back began to ache. She rested, but it was a mistake: her back ached twice as much when she started pumping again.

After a while her hands blistered and she had to stop because

470

of the pain. Wearily she lifted the corner of the hatch cover and peered down. The water had almost gone. She nodded with satisfaction. Wrapping her hands in rags she pumped again, more quickly, desperately, until at long last there was a sucking noise and the pump was dry.

She put the handle back in its clip on the mast and slowly, shakily, made her way to the tiller seat.

The course read northwest. *Too far west.* She rested her head against the glass bowl and closed her eyes.

"Mummy . . ." A small hand was placed on her arm. "Mummy, are you all right?"

"Yes, darling, I feel fine." It was about the last thing she felt.

"I opened another tin. I thought you might be hungry after all your pumping."

She put her arms around his small waist and her head against his chest and said in a tight voice, "Thank you."

A faint cry sounded from the bow. It was David. His hand was raised as if to wave. She'd forgotten about him. Wearily, she got to her feet and began the long wet journey down the deck.

She was coming back at last!

David willed her to complete her uncertain passage along the heaving deck. She paused halfway and for a moment he feared she'd changed her mind, but after waiting for a break between waves and ensuing spray, she came on.

As soon as she dropped to her knees beside him, he grasped her hand. It was very hot. He was surprised because she looked so cold: her hair clung damply to her forehead and hung in long wet strands around her shoulders. Her face was very pale, apart from two bright patches of color that burned on her cheeks, and her eyes were red and swollen, with dark smudges underneath.

"My dear, you must rest . . . sometime."

She squeezed his hand. "Don't worry about me. I'm fit and healthy. It's you who must take care. Would you like some water? You must be desperate for some by now."

She reached for the large glass bottle and, removing the stopper, held it to his lips. He drank greedily.

As she replaced the stopper he opened the bag he wore around his waist and, reaching in, took out a small package.

He grasped her hand and, concentrating hard on the words, said, "You remember . . . in the field. When you came back for me. I want to thank you."

"Don't be silly. Of course I came back for you. I couldn't leave you, could I?"

"At the time . . ." He coughed and breathed deeply. ". . . I wanted to give up. But I'm glad I didn't. You see . . ." He waited for a spasm of pain to pass.

"Are you all right?"

"Yes, yes . . ." As soon as he could, he went on. "You were right . . . about them making me work. They would have got hold of my Cecile. . . . They would have threatened things. This way, I'm *protecting* her. Just like I promised."

She almost spoke, but he interrupted. "This package. It's got everything . . . about my ideas. The drawings. The specifications. Please, you must take care of it. In case anything happens to me—"

"It won't!"

He shook his head irritably. "You will promise," he went on slowly, "that you'll take care of it . . . and hand it to the right people. It must be the right people. . . . Do you understand?"

She regarded the package and weighed it thoughtfully in her hand. Then, coming to a decision she pushed the package down inside her jersey and buried it somewhere in her underwear.

David relaxed. He was free at last. The weight was off his shoulders. Now he could *really* sleep. "You're a good girl."

She leaned forward and kissed him gently on the cheek. Stroking his forehead, she asked, "What about taking some of your pills?"

"Pain's not so bad now . . . anyway . . . make me sick. Better not." It was a lie about the pain, it was as bad as ever, but he didn't want to bother her.

She was regarding him thoughtfully. "You know, I should thank you too. For snapping me out of it when we were hiding on the beach. If you hadn't—I would probably have stayed in a daze. . . . I only wish I hadn't got you into *this* mess."

She didn't understand at all. She thought she was failing.

David said desperately, "No . . . no, you're *trying*. And that's worth *everything*! *Everything*! You must realize that *trying* is the most important thing of all . . ."

472

She looked unconvinced. "If you say so. Now rest. Please." She kissed his cheek again.

"Remember," he murmured. "Trying is the most important thing."

"Yes!" She gave a small laugh and, touching his hand, got to her feet and set off toward the stern.

David lay back, his mind at rest. Now, at last, he could sleep in peace.

Her body was seizing up like her mind. As she moved back along the deck she felt her whole body complaining. Her neck was almost unmovable and every time she turned her head a sharp pain shot through her temples.

Peter's face lit up at the sight of her. "Mummy, here! You still haven't had any lunch. I've kept some for you!"

She sat beside him, under the bulwark, and tried to eat.

"Mummy, are you going to be better now?"

"I expect so. I'm . . . just tired, that's all."

"Why don't you sleep and then I can keep watch?"

"No, Peter, it—" Then she thought: Why not? The boat was sailing itself. Peter would probably keep a better lookout than she would. Yes: why not?

It was an awful responsibility for a six-year-old. But it would be night in a few hours. She'd have to be awake then and, without sleep—well, she'd never do it.

She said carefully, "Will you promise to wake me the *moment* you see anything?"

The small head nodded.

"Or the moment the weather changes . . . black clouds or more spray . . . or rain . . . ?"

"Yes, Mummy."

"Or if you see a ship or . . . anything floating, or a plane. . . . You'd wake me then too, wouldn't you?"

"I promise, Mummy. Don't worry. I'll keep a really sharp lookout!" He smiled excitedly and pulled himself up onto the helmsman's seat.

Julie stood up and took a long look. The sky was still clear, but there was a slight haze around the horizon. The sea appeared as vast as ever—and as impossible to cross.

A sharp lookout. . . . She lay down on the deck with her head

on her arm and wondered if Peter had learned the phrase from Richard.

Richard. He must have been through this sort of thing countless times. The thought gave her comfort. Then she saw him in another setting—in a prison cell, hungry, cold, raging to be free. Hastily she tried to shut the picture out of her mind before worse things appeared.

When she finally drifted into an uneasy doze, a series of disconnected thoughts rampaged around her brain and several times made her wake with a start. After a while her brain began to slow down. Only one thought remained. Something she should have done. What was it? As she drifted off into a deep sleep, she remembered at last. The course. It was still wrong. She hadn't reset the course.

30

A needle in a haystack.
And yet, and yet . . .

With his finger Fischer traced the fishing boat's course from Morlaix to the position the plane had reported, then followed the penciled line on, in a straight projection. His finger arrived at a point midway between the Scillies and Land's End. It was the fifth time he'd checked the projection, but the result was always the same.

He still couldn't understand it. Where was the boat making for? Why go all the way around Land's End and then be faced with a long trek up the north coast of Cornwall, against the wind? The alternatives were—what? Wales or Ireland. Wales—again why bother? Ireland then. Now that *was* a possibility, particularly if the occupants of the fishing boat were seeking the safety of a neutral country. When one thought about it, the whole affair did smack of politics . . . Fischer decided that it was the most likely destination.

However there was still one thing that didn't make sense.

If the fishing boat was holding her course, why the devil hadn't they seen her yet?

U-319 was zigzagging four miles to either side of the prey's projected track. The visibility was still good. Using the search periscope they should be able to spot even a small boat at four miles. She must have masts and sails that would be clearly visible against the skyline.

Even allowing for the worst: for *U-319* speeding away from the approaching prey on the wrong leg of the zigzag, and for the fishing boat being as much as four miles off course, they should still see her on the return leg because of their superior speed and because each leg of the zigzag took them very slightly forward along the fishing boat's track.

They should have seen her, but they hadn't.

Fischer sighed deeply and chucked the pencil down onto the chart.

The control room was quiet except for the gentle hum of the electric motors. The men were at their positions, engrossed in their jobs. The man at the periscope was swiveling slowly, his eyes fixed to the lens.

Fischer wondered how long it had been since he had slept properly and decided that it must have been over thirty hours ago. He should try to snatch some rest now but he knew he wouldn't be able to. Not while the hunt was on.

Once darkness fell—once they'd missed the boat for certain—then he'd sleep. During the night there was nothing they could do; they had no way of finding a small boat under cover of darkness. All he could do would be to maneuver *U-319* into a position ahead of the fishing boat and lie in wait for it at dawn. By then the margin for error would be enormous—the prey might have changed course a dozen times.

A needle in a haystack . . .

Men were moving around the control room, changing places, whispering in muted voices. The watch change. Sixteen hundred hours.

He was tempted to go to the periscope and take a look, but decided against it. A man from the new watch was just settling in. When the fellow finished his first track in about fifteen minutes, perhaps then he'd look for himself. It was partly superstition:

Fischer had the feeling that, if he restrained himself, the fishing boat was more likely to turn up. Ridiculous, of course . . .

Fischer wandered aft, toward the engine rooms. The Chief spotted him and, wiping his hands on an oily rag, made his way between the massive diesels to meet his commander.

Suddenly there was a muffled exclamation, the sound of voices from the direction of the control room. Fischer froze for a moment then, turning quickly, retraced his steps. No Klaxon—not an aircraft. What then?

Eins WO—the first officer—was at the periscope. ". . . Bearing two-eight-zero!"

Fischer strode up and tapped him on the shoulder. The first officer stood aside. "A small craft, Herr Kaleu!" Fischer put his eyes to the lens.

For a moment he could see nothing, just seas, larger than before. He checked the bearing—280 degrees—and waited. A wave rose in front of the horizon then fell again.

There!

Fischer felt the adrenaline leap into his veins.

"Raise attack periscope!"

There was a hiss of hydraulics as the much larger attack periscope rose from the bowels of the boat. The search periscope had a wide field of vision, covering large areas of the sky as well as the sea, but had limited powers of magnification; the attack periscope, on the other hand, had a small field of vision but much greater magnification. Fischer pulled down the handles and, swinging the periscope around, put his eyes to it.

Greatly magnified waves obscured the horizon. He waited. They fell away.

There she was!

A small boat. Under sail.

The silhouette was unmistakable, even from this distance. He guessed the range to be over four miles. He could see almost nothing of the hull. It was hidden among the waves—but the mainsail showed black and distinct, a tiny curved shape against the brilliant yellow of the western sky.

The boat was sailing north.

He allowed himself a moment of satisfaction, then let his natural caution take charge. It might be a British fishing boat . . . but

unlikely in mid-Channel. It might be another escaped French fishing boat—equally unlikely. The coincidences of time and position were too great.

It *had* to be the prey.

Next—how to capture it. He'd have to approach submerged, then surface at the last minute. That way the occupants wouldn't have time to think about fighting. He wanted to avoid fighting, not only because he'd been told to bring back the occupants unharmed, but because the operation had to be completed in the shortest possible time, to avoid being caught on the surface.

He hated the idea of surfacing in broad daylight, particularly here. But it would have to be done.

Automatically he began to swing the periscope around, walking with it in a circle, sweeping the narrow band either side of the horizon. No ships and with this periscope he couldn't see much of the sky.

It was time to close in. "Alter course to—"

He broke off. Something was wrong: he identified it. The stupid man on the search periscope wasn't swiveling it around, wasn't searching! Fischer felt a surge of anger.

"*Sweep!* Sweep the sky!"

The man, obviously shaken, rapidly spun the periscope.

Fischer clenched his fists. Fool! That was the way to get caught. An aircraft could spot the wake of the two periscopes at a hell of a distance. But Fischer knew the sailor at the periscope: normally he was a good man. He decided to let the matter pass.

Now, the order to alter course.

A sharp cry, half shout, half scream, rent the air.

"*Enemy aircraft!*"

In reflex Fischer shouted, "*Down periscopes!*"

The two shafts began to hiss downward.

"*Take her down! Alter course forty-five degrees to starboard!*"

The order was repeated.

Fischer had no idea whether the plane had been close, whether it was even making a bombing run, but he wasn't going to take any chances. He strode to the chart and looked at the depth of the water here. He barked, "Take her down to thirty meters!"

After what seemed a long, long time but really was only a couple of seconds, the submarine reacted to the reangled hydro-

planes and her nose tilted downward. Slowly, peacefully, the boat slipped farther and farther into the depths.

Everyone tensed and reached for a handhold, waiting for the shock of the depth charges.

The silence lasted a long time.

The voice of the coxswain sounded calmly through the stillness. "Depth fifteen meters . . . eighteen meters . . . twenty meters . . ."

"Alter course another forty-five degrees to starboard."

"Altering course forty-five degrees starboard, Herr Kaleu."

At last it came. "Depth thirty meters."

Fischer exhaled. The men shifted their weight and exchanged glances. No depth charges. They were safe.

"You!" Fischer barked at the sailor who'd been manning the search periscope.

The man approached, ashen white.

"Bearing and range of enemy plane?"

The man gulped. He was shaking like a leaf.

"Bearing and range of enemy plane!"

The man's mouth was gaping slightly. Fischer raised his hand and quite deliberately slapped the sailor's face. The man fell back in surprise. For a moment Fischer thought he was going to cry.

Fischer repeated more quietly, "Bearing and range of enemy plane."

The man's eyes cleared. "Behind us, Herr Kaleu," he began breathlessly. "No—slightly to starboard. Bearing about . . . I . . . I'm not sure." He was shaking again.

Fischer said sharply, "But a British plane?"

"Oh yes . . . a Catalina, I think."

"Was he closing on us?"

"Yes! Oh yes! Straight for us, it was coming straight for us."

"Diving on us?"

"Head on! About half a mile away. No—less. Less!"

Fischer said briskly, "Stand down and pull yourself together!"

Fischer went to the chart table, a wave of depression pressing in on him.

They might have been seen. It changed everything.

The enemy might send more aircraft, perhaps patrol boats. . . .

They'd be hunted down.

Unless . . . unless they stayed submerged and slipped away. But the orders had been clear: he had no alternative but to close in and try to accomplish the task.

Damn! So near and yet so far.

He thought of the fishing boat sailing on, oblivious to everything, a victim ready for the taking, yet maddeningly beyond his reach.

He dared not surface now. He wasn't even sure if he dared go to periscope depth.

He'd take a look in half an hour, he decided. The plane might have given up by then. Even if it hadn't, he'd have to risk it, otherwise he'd lose the prey.

He passed the time bent over the chart, calculating and recalculating the course and speed necessary to stay on the fishing boat's tail. As before, the fishing boat remained slightly to the west of its projected track. Maybe the wind was backing. He redrew its course line and calculated the maneuvers necessary to get the U-boat onto the new track.

At the end of an hour he checked with Sonar: there were no propeller noises. He gave the order to go to periscope depth. There was the muted hiss of blowing tanks.

". . . Twenty-five meters . . . twenty . . . fifteen . . ." Then they were leveling off. Finally came the words: "Periscope depth!"

Fischer pulled up the search periscope and, his heart in his mouth, put his eyes to the lens.

She was a long way away, in the country somewhere, lying in a barn, which accounted for the hard floor. Nearby was some soft straw, but she couldn't move her limbs to get across to it. Her body was like stone, heavy and lifeless. For some reason the barn was very noisy: a whistling and swishing and roaring was reverberating around its bare wooden walls. It was moving too, the barn, the floor tilting strangely. . . . Now something was shaking her. An animal—large, like a cow—was butting its head against her arm. The creature was getting more agitated. . . .

"Mummy! Mummy! Wake up!"

Julie opened her eyes. Instantly she closed them: the light was blinding. Reality began to seep through into her consciousness: the awful awareness that a real nightmare was lying in wait for

her, ready to pounce when she woke. She grasped at the image of the barn and tried to push her mind back to it, back to the soft straw . . .

"Mummy, *please* wake up! There's a plane!"

Julie opened her eyes again and screwed them up against the light. A plane . . . Rubbing her face with her hand, she sat up. A sharp stabbing pain shot into her temples. Grasping the rail she pulled herself to her feet and the headache settled into a rhythm of dull throbbing blows that made her slightly sick.

"Plane . . . ? Where . . . ?" Her eyes refused to focus properly.

"There!" Peter pointed away to the right. *"There!"*

Julie stared for several seconds before she saw it, a tiny black speck flying low just above the horizon. It was moving toward the north, rising now, gaining height. It seemed to hover for a moment; it was turning. It took a long curve away until it was hardly visible, then headed toward them, getting larger again. For a moment Julie thought it was coming straight at them, but then the dot was banking and dropping down again, retracing its path along the far horizon, toward the south. It repeated the maneuver, going back and forth along its path several times.

The boat lurched and Julie clung to the rail to stop herself from falling. Peter grasped at her jacket.

"I'm hungry . . . I want to go to sleep . . ."

The small face was pale and tired and frightened. He had done very well, considering. Julie tried to sound, if not cheerful, then reassuring. "Of course. Let's open a can or two. Then you curl up down here."

She bent to search in the food bag and felt sick again. The boat was moving more jerkily now, its seesaws more violent. She fed Peter quickly and settled him at the back of the boat under the high wooden side, out of the wind and spray.

She rubbed her aching temples and searched for the plane again. It had gone. Maybe it had been German anyway.

It had clouded over. High up there was a solid ceiling of white; lower, there were angry black clouds scudding across the sky. The sea was gray and forbidding, the waves marching relentlessly toward the boat, their crests breaking with an audible hiss. Their onward procession was mesmerizing, almost hypnotic.

She dragged her eyes away. *Must think* . . . David . . . She made

her way slowly along the deck, bumping sharply against the mast. The old man seemed all right. He was fairly warm and breathing normally. She lifted his head and put the water bottle to his lips. The motion of the boat was much worse up in the bows and it was difficult to get any water into his mouth, but finally David indicated that he'd had enough and fell back against the rope.

The sickness was rising again. She hurried back to the tiller, shivering as water from the side of the boat splattered against her legs and seeped through her trousers.

Course? WNW: west-northwest. Still off course—too far to the west. She frowned, then grasped at an idea—perhaps it was a *good* thing. By heading too far west she'd probably miss the land altogether. Then she wouldn't have to worry about hitting it during the night. Once it was light again, *then* she could head the boat back toward the land.

It would solve a lot of problems.

Yes. She'd let the boat go where it wanted. Then—no land, no fighting with the sails, no worries. She became a little more cheerful.

She looked at her watch. Five-thirty. God, was that all? She'd slept only for a couple of hours. No wonder she felt so terrible. Still without any sleep at all she might have felt even worse.

She shivered again. So cold . . . and the headache, still hammering away . . .

She sat on the helmsman's seat, watching the bow rise and fall against the pattern of the waves. It stopped her feeling sick. After a while she dozed, waking only when the boat lurched and threatened to slide her off her seat. She came to with a jerk and stared forward again, concentrating on the gray smudge of the horizon, which seemed increasingly distant.

She should take a good look around and search for ships, but she couldn't be bothered.

She thought: I don't care anymore, I really don't. I just want this to *end* . . . to get somewhere, *anywhere* . . .

Later she dozed again and woke with a jump when spray pattered against her face. The spray had never come this far back before.

Disoriented, she realized the boat was tilting farther over, the downhill side of the deck awash with running water. The bow

was digging deeper into the waves, pushing up solid sheets of sea which, caught by the wind, flew diagonally back over the boat and fell on the deck in heavy cascades before running away to the scuppers on the lower side. As the boat met each wave it gave a great shudder, pausing for a second to throw off the weight of the water before picking itself up and leaping forward to meet the next onslaught. The mast was leaning at a sharp angle, and the big sail bellied out, taut and strained except for the back edge, which vibrated violently. The boat rolled and almost dipped its rail in the rushing water. Julie held her breath. The boat came back a little and the water receded.

The boat rolled again, then again. Julie watched with terrible fascination as the rail came ever closer to the rushing water. She thought: What's to stop us rolling right over? Perhaps she needed to do this reefing business, perhaps that would slow the boat down. . . .

Miserably, she regarded the enormous bulging sail and knew that she wouldn't even know where to start. It was impossible to do anything while the boat was careering along like a mad thing.

The scene frightened her. After a while she realized what made it so terrifying.

The world was getting grayer, the outlines less distinct, the dark colors blacker.

The horizon was a blur, a featureless gray blending into the gray of the sea and the sky. The shape of the bows was beginning to fade.

Julie thought: I *might* have done something, I really *might*.

But not in the dark, not *ever* in the dark.

As night fell and the grays faded into blackness, fear gripped her even tighter until it held her firmly, mindlessly, on her seat by the tiller.

Two hundred miles out in the Atlantic the Liberator swept high over the darkening sea, searching.

The patrol had been going on for four hours now, with another three to go. The plane was flying one leg of a gentle zigzag designed to take it over the likely path of U-boats heading north to their hunting grounds.

Then, suddenly, the wireless operator received a signal.

A few minutes later the plane abandoned her search pattern and, banking steeply, headed east toward the position given in the signal—the last known location of the U-boat—which was thirty miles south-southeast of Land's End.

Later, after the pilot had done some thinking and the navigator some calculations, the course was changed to take the plane toward the English coast.

The U-boat must have been submerged all day, the pilot reckoned, which meant her speed would have been no more than seven knots. If, as he'd been told, she was heading north, then he would intercept her near the coast.

Where on the coast was another matter. The U-boat was shadowing a small fishing boat, apparently, but its destination was unknown. Falmouth? Ireland? Could be anywhere.

The pilot decided to make a single sweep along the coast at a distance of five miles off. The channel between the Scillies and Land's End must be covered, also the Lizard, and the approaches to Falmouth. He wouldn't have time for much more, not with the freshening headwind.

Only one thing was certain. At some point during the night the U-boat would have to surface, to get air and recharge her batteries. And for quite a long time, at that.

There was just a chance they might catch her. . . .

But where should they start from? How far west might the U-boat have gone?

He said to the navigator, "Course to the Scillies, please. We're going to begin there and work our way eastwards."

They lie at the end of the world, the Isles of Scilly: far beyond the land, a nest of rocks and islets cut off from the mainstream of British life. On a chart they are mere pinpricks situated twenty-one nautical miles west-southwest of Land's End: a cluster of small dots on the wide immensity of the sea—the last fragment of land for three thousand miles. Being so remote and isolated, they remain, for the most part, unnoticed.

But sailors know and mark them well.

Sailing inward, toward the major European ports, ships must find their way into the beckoning but treacherous arms of the English Channel, between the rugged north coast of Brittany on

the one hand, and the Scillies, harbinger of the English mainland, on the other. For many vessels this will be their first landfall for thousands of miles. Even in good conditions navigation can be the most uncertain of sciences, but after long periods of bad weather, or in fog or storm, the chances of error increase dramatically. When the weather is thick the navigator can do little but make his calculations, check the distances run—and then resort to hope, optimism and prayer.

He has reason to pray. The Scillies lie in wait for the unwary —eager to ensnare and reluctant to release.

The islands are unusually low—barely 160 feet at their highest point—and therefore difficult to see from any real distance. In bad weather you can find yourself very close, even hear the surf on the rocks, before you realize you are on top of them.

Ships are led to their doom by the wind, which, for a greater part of the time, blows from the west, pushing ships speedily homeward, hastening the ship on her way, so that sailors have reason to be grateful to it. That is, unless the navigator is mistaken in his calculations. Then the wind blows the ship toward the crouching islands and the low teeth of the hidden reefs. A jagged gray mass of rocks is suddenly spotted close ahead, someone hears the thunder of surf on the ledges and the ship tries to turn, too late. All too late. Escape is impossible. The wind drives the vessel farther and farther onto the rocks, until she pounds heavily, and the teeth bite through, and the guts are torn out of her, and she is gone.

There are so many wrecks around the islands that even the inhabitants cannot count them. Hardly a year goes by without one, two—or in a bad year maybe a dozen—vessels meeting a lonely end on one of the outlying rocks.

The men who live here have a realistic, practical attitude toward shipwrecks. The Lord taketh away, the Lord giveth. . . . There is money in salvage; sometimes there are rich pickings to be found on the long white beaches. Who would not take advantage of that which is given?

But they save the people first. Bravely, sometimes in gale-force winds, they set out in their open gigs and row to the dying ship to save whomever they can.

Five islands are inhabited, four of them forming a circle around

a shallow sound which was itself part of the land more than two thousand years ago. Most of the people live on St. Mary's, the largest of the islands, which is just three miles wide. Across the sound to the north lie Bryher and Tresco, separated by an inlet which is the secret harbor of New Grimsby, where boats may hide.

Each of these islands has two distinct sides to it, like a coin. There is the windward side, bare and treeless, raked by the remorseless wind and salt spray, where only heather, hardy gorse and a few stalwart flowers grow in the peaty soil. However, over the slight hills, in the lee of the land and screened from the wind by tall hedges of pittosporum, veronica and tamarisk, there is a surprising fertility, with an abundance of early spring flowers, grain crops and grazing for domestic animals.

The fifth and smallest inhabited island, St. Agnes, which lies to the southwest of St. Mary's, is similar to the others—and yet somehow different. Located outside the circle formed by the other four, it is surrounded by deep water. Its western shore, craggy and strewn with massive red and silver granite boulders, marks what ancient men believed to be the end of the world.

Or very nearly . . . because the land has not ended—not quite. Though few would call it land.

Strewn over the sea to the southwest for a distance of four nautical miles are numerous islets, rocks and half-hidden ledges. Some say that there are fifty islets around the main islands, some say a hundred. Many of them are here, to the southwest. No one has tried to count the rocks.

Some of the larger ones support colonies of seabirds—puffins, shearwaters, petrels and gulls. Others are colored gray-green with lichen and coarse vegetation.

But many are quite bare. Washed by a hundred thousand Atlantic storms, the silver granite is unvisited, save for the seals who lie resting in the clefts before diving back into the restless rolling waves.

The most westerly of the rocks are so low that only the leaping, cascading surf reveals their position. In storms the angry white curtains of spray shoot high, high into the air—a terrible warning if you should be lucky enough to see it. The local people call these rocks ledges, though reefs might be a better name. They have ripped many a hull apart. Some vessels sank immediately; others

pounded slowly and painfully to death, spilling cargo and people into the water for several days.

Once, a long time ago, the Royal Navy lost fifteen ships of the line on the Western Rocks—the pride of the British fleet. Two thousand men drowned. In the late nineteenth century, during the height of the steamship era, a crack passenger ship died an agonized death on the Retarrier Ledges with the loss of three hundred lives.

The carnage had to be stopped. It was decided to build a lighthouse. They chose the Bishop Rock, the last rock before the Atlantic, the final jagged point before the safe depths of the open sea. It is a small rock, only a few yards square. But there was no other choice: there was nothing bigger.

They made three attempts. The first time the sea swept the structure away before the light was even lit. The second time the structure stayed up, but, pounded by winter storms, started to shake itself to death. Finally they built a third one around the second because it was easier that way—though nothing achieved in that wild, windswept desolation could ever be called easy. It took years of superhuman effort to build the third mighty tower —but it stayed up.

Now it stands proud and tall above the sea, unmoved even by the waves that sweep over its 160-foot height—the tallest light-house in Britain. And the loneliest.

To navigators the light is a godsend; in good conditions its powerful beam is visible eighteen nautical miles away. Even in poor conditions you are likely to see it before you are too close. In fog the loud blare of its foghorn will warn you away from the rocks. Sailors love the light: they have taken to asking how far out from the Bishop they have sailed, or how far back to the Bishop it might be, or how long it will take to reach the Bishop. To the sailor the Bishop means home.

The light is a godsend . . . when it's lit.

Tonight, like most nights during World War II, it is not.

Only when a convoy is passing does the light flash twice every fifteen seconds, and then dimly.

Tonight, like most nights, there is no convoy. The light is unlit, the revolving lens still.

The Western Rocks lie in total darkness, just as they used to before men dared to build the light.

31

Damn! Damn!
He'd missed her.

He still couldn't understand it. Had he misjudged the distance? Or, while *U-319* was down deep, hiding from the plane, had the little boat changed course?

Whatever had gone wrong, when they'd returned to periscope depth there'd been no fishing boat in sight. Fischer had ordered All Ahead—full speed—toward the northwest, thinking the prey had passed them.

But nothing. *Nothing.*

He had stayed at the periscope himself, sweeping the horizon until the waves danced in front of his eyes.

Then darkness had fallen.

It was infuriating. Fischer went back to the chart and recalculated the fishing boat's course. This time he allowed for a slightly more westerly drift, laid off the effects of the tide—also running to the west for the next few hours—and projected the line forward.

It led straight to the Isles of Scilly.

He should have considered that possibility before. It seemed a curious destination—but, on second thought, a very clever one. No one would ever think of it.

Whoever was in this little boat had brains and nerve, he had to give them that.

But it wouldn't make any difference: he'd still chase them, up to the very rocks if necessary.

There was one problem though—one major chance of failure. The little boat would reach the islands before dawn and if the skipper knew the islands well he might try to enter during darkness and slip out of Fischer's reach. If, on the other hand, he

didn't know the islands, he would *have* to hold off till dawn or run a high risk of wrecking his boat.

Fischer was willing to gamble that the skipper was a stranger to the islands.

He'd catch him at dawn, then, trying to creep in. But he'd have to get in close, to be sure.

He asked the young navigator to find the largest possible chart of the islands. Even before he saw it he knew it wouldn't be very detailed—but it would have to do.

In the meantime he had another problem. He would have to surface to charge his batteries and compress some air for diving purposes. He had no choice. The power to the electric motors was already running low.

He called the Chief and together they calculated the minimum charging time they would need.

Six hours.

Full daylight at 0700. They'd have to get onto the surface by 0030 at the latest.

Six hours. A long time.

Then he had an idea.

It wouldn't eradicate the danger entirely, but it would reduce it considerably. It was risky: very. But it was the only way.

The navigator brought the chart, the best he had. It covered the area from the Scillies to Falmouth. "There's also the pilot book, Herr Kaleu. I could make a larger sketch chart from that."

"Very well."

"Any particular features that you want me to look out for?"

Fischer stood back from the chart. "Yes—rocks . . . or rather a lack of them. We need an area near the islands which is safe from rocks, yet close enough to make us *look* like a rock. . . . You see, we have to find somewhere to hide."

The water came out of the darkness, flying across the deck in great sheets, drenching everything. Despite the waterproofs, Julie was soaked through. Her eyes were sore, her eyelids sticky as if covered with glue, and her lips were swollen and tender from the salt. She didn't bother to duck when she felt the bow hit a wave. She didn't care anymore.

She was hand-steering now, the tiller jerking and bucking in

her hand. Since the wind had come up, the boat wouldn't sail by itself. . . . Not that she knew which way the boat was heading half the time. The compass was unreadable. She'd completely forgotten about the oil for the compass light. It was too late now. From time to time, when she remembered, she shone the flashlight on the compass, but its beam was getting dimmer and the course was difficult to read. God only knew where they were heading. It didn't seem important anymore.

Her eyes drooped, her head fell forward. She awoke with a jerk. God, her head ached. . . .

She wondered if Peter was all right. And David. She hadn't heard either of them for hours. She should go and see, but she didn't. It was so much easier to stay here . . . not to move, to let her mind drift. . . .

She vaguely realized that the tiredness and the cold had paralyzed her brain and frozen her willpower. It was weak and shameful to give in to it, she knew, but she was incapable of moving, of acting, of *doing.* . . . She was in a sort of trance, half believing that if she stayed still and ignored things, the nightmare might somehow go away. She thought: It's *safer* to stay here— and, oh God, *easier* too—and I've got to steer, haven't I? And, if Peter and David needed me, they would have shouted, wouldn't they? And I'm so tired, I can't do any more . . .

Time seemed to spread out before her like a fan, wider and wider . . . until suddenly the fan closed and there was no time anymore. She was confused. . . . She couldn't even remember how long she'd been at sea. One night? Four?

Once she saw grass growing out of the water. . . . Another time she saw lights, sparkling. . . .

Now, once again, she dozed.

And then she was wide awake.

A noise. She could hear it, loud and distinct, above the persistent wail of the wind.

A *tearing* noise . . .

A second later there was a loud flogging.

The sails?—Or the mast . . . !

She stood up, feeling the first touches of panic. What to do? Christ, what to do?

"Mummy!" Peter was almost screaming.

"It's all right. Just sit tight!" Julie shouted.

The piece of rope was still fastened around the tiller. She took a loose end and tied it to the cleat on the uphill side of the boat. Then she made her way carefully across the deck and tied the other end to the lower cleat.

The flogging and rattling were deafening. Julie pocketed the flashlight and made her way forward along the uphill side of the deck. She lunged for the mast and found it. It was vibrating and shaking violently—but it was upright. Something at least.

An avalanche of spray poured down on her. She blew the water off her lips and wiped her eyes with her sleeve. She reached for the flashlight and shone it upward at the sail.

Or what remained of it. There was a tear right across the middle, from one side to the other. The tattered remnants of canvas were beating themselves to death, shaking the wooden spars like a dog shaking a rabbit.

They would have to come down: the sail, the long wooden pole at the bottom of the sail, the shorter pole at the top. The ends of the two poles were both held by ropes, ropes that must end here, at the bottom of the mast.

But which ones? A dozen ropes were tied to cleats on a wooden frame at the base of the mast.

Trial and error was the only way. She undid one rope and gently let the last turn slip off the cleat. Nothing: there was no tension on the rope. She tried the next. Ah! A lot of tension here. She searched the sail for signs of something coming down . . . nothing. Without knowing why, she shone the flashlight forward. The little sail—it was half down! Blast!

She hoisted it up again as best she could and tried another rope. At last: the outer end of the lower pole was moving downward. Right: mark that one and look for the ropes controlling the shorter, higher pole.

She found one finally and let it down until the outer end was almost in the water. Now the other inner end, the one joined to the mast. Triumphantly, she found that one too and lowered it.

The two poles were lying almost parallel to each other, just a few feet above the water, but swung well out from the boat. Somehow, she would have to get them in.

She went back and hauled in on the rope near the tiller, the one

she'd used to adjust the sail. There was much less pressure on it now and, to her surprise, the lower pole came in quite easily. She lowered it carefully onto the deck. Panting hard, she regarded the upper pole. She couldn't see any way of getting it in: in the dim yellow beam of the flashlight she could see no rope leading from its end toward the boat.

The boat lurched and the pole suddenly swung inward, lunging over the deck.

She waited for it to happen again. It swung in once, but not so far and she couldn't reach it. At last it swung right over, almost knocking her off her feet. She threw an arm around it and held on for dear life. The boat rolled back, jerking her against the boat's side. She held on grimly and looked for something to tie around the pole. She felt around, and her hand touched a rope which was fastened to the pole. She grasped it and held tight. The boat lurched and the pole tried to swing out again, dragging her toward the rail. She gripped the rope tighter, until it ground into her flesh. Then the boat rolled back and the pole swung in again. She stepped quickly backward and, fumbling around the base of the mast, felt for a cleat. The pole started to pull outward, but she got one turn of the rope onto the the cleat; waited, then got two more turns.

She went to the other side of the mast and, finding the right rope again, lowered the pole onto the deck.

Triumph! As she leaned panting against the mast, she smiled to herself in the darkness. She'd actually succeeded!

She said aloud, "Well done."

She unfastened the rope which held up the little sail in front and tightened it a bit more, then rubbed her hands. What next? She had the ridiculous feeling she could do anything now. Getting the big sail down had been only half as difficult as it had looked. Everything else would be easy!

First—David . . . She went forward and shone the dim yellow beam of the flashlight into the area under the deck. David was awake and bewildered, his eyes large and staring. He seemed to be in constant pain. "Sorry . . . not helping . . ." he whispered.

"Don't be silly. Just rest!" As she put the water bottle to his lips she noticed in the beam of the flashlight a dark stain on his sleeve. Vomit . . . and—she stared, horrified—blood. "Are you all right?"

"I'm . . . all right."

But he wasn't, she could see that. She shook her head miserably. "I shouldn't have let you come!"

"No! No!" He gripped her arm. "I'm glad, very glad. . . . I always wanted to get to England. Are we almost there?"

Julie blinked. "I don't know."

He closed his eyes. Julie watched him anxiously for a moment, then pulled the sacking up around his chin and made her way back to the stern.

Peter next. He was crouching in the corner of the deck, sobbing quietly. She hugged him and whispered to him until, at last, she managed to calm him. She adjusted his jacket so that it better protected his head from the spray, then went to the tiller to check the compass.

Northwest—or thereabouts. Not bad! Not bad at all!

But something had changed. It took her a moment to identify it. The boat was riding the waves much better now. There was less water coming over and the deck was not tipping so far. The tiller wasn't jerking about so much either, and the lines seemed to be holding the boat on course again. Yet the wind hadn't diminished. She realized dimly that the loss of the sail had made things easier. A blessing in disguise! She felt almost euphoric.

But the jobs now, the jobs! Pumping: that was essential. But before that, something she had been meaning to do for hours. She had noticed two life preservers on either side of the tiller, attached to the back of the boat. She found one, unhitched it and slipped it over Peter's head. She took the other one forward, to David and, waking him gently, made him put it on. There wasn't a third.

Then she went to the pump and, after inserting the handle, began to pump methodically, singing loudly as she rocked back and forward. Now and then she almost laughed. In the strangest way, she was ridiculously happy.

It took well over an hour this time. The sweat poured off her, and she felt hot and clammy inside her wet clothing. Her back ached, but she ignored it, working herself harder and harder.

Once she paused and thought: I've discovered the secret of all this—perhaps it's the secret of everything! Never give in! Richard wouldn't have. He would have enjoyed the challenge . . . Maurice too . . . yes, the secret is . . . *never give in*!

492

When she could barely pump anymore, the handle went slack in her hand, the pipe sucking on empty air.

She staggered back to the stern and flopped onto the helmsman's seat.

She made an effort to concentrate. There was one more thing . . . what David had asked . . . about arriving. . . . *When?*

She had no idea. What had she worked out before? Twenty-four hours . . . that meant they should arrive *now*! God—!

But wait. They had been going much more slowly since the big sail was down. That would make a difference.

Also, they'd been west of their course for most of the time. She corrected herself: no, *all* the time . . . which meant they would miss the land altogether. They *must*, otherwise—

She had a nasty thought that had been in the back of her mind for some time. Perhaps Michel had given her a course to a *safe* part of the coast. Perhaps, by steering outside it, she was even now leading them straight for a dangerous part of the land. . . .

She could think of only one thing to do. Steer even farther west. To be absolutely sure.

Yes! *West*-northwest. That would be the safe thing to do!

Until dawn at least. Then she would turn the boat east again. . . .

She decided to hand-steer. But before she settled down, she reached into the oddments box and found another length of thin rope. She went to Peter and, kissing him, tied one end around his waist and the other around her own.

It was probably the wrong thing to do. If anything happened she would drag him down. . . .

But whatever happened she wanted to be with him. She couldn't bear to think of him floating away from her. She murmured: "Where you go, I go." Then she untied the tiller and put the boat onto its new course.

"What you got, Radar?"

"The Scillies, bright and shining, Skipper!"

"Range?"

"Bishop Rock ten miles, bearing zero-three-zero."

"And how's the picture?"

"Good. There's a strong breeze blowing, about twenty-five

knots, but I'm not getting too much clutter. The waves can't be that big, probably because the wind's offshore."

"Right-ho. Taff?"

"Yes, Skipper?"

"When we get within five miles of Bishop Rock give me a course to a point five miles south of the Lizard, then we'll take another leg in towards Falmouth."

"Roger, Skipper."

"And Radar, shout when you see anything, however small."

"Always do, Skipper."

The pilot looked down into the blackness and wondered what the submarine was doing. Racing for home? Creeping between the Scillies and Land's End? Hiding near the shore?

There might just be time for more than one run. If so, he'd try another farther south, then perhaps a sweep to the north of the islands. He'd decide nearer the time.

The intercom crackled.

"Radar to Skipper. Contact ten miles to starboard, angle twenty degrees."

The pilot licked his lips. "Where is it in relation to the islands?"

"Five miles south of St. Mary's. But it's a really small target, Skipper. I mean, it doesn't *look* like a U-boat. Though I can't be sure."

"Keep an eye on it. Taff?"

"Yes, Skipper."

"Give us a course to the target."

"Roger."

"Wireless?"

"Yes, Skipper."

"Have we been notified of any friends at sea in this area?"

"No, sir. No convoys. No MTBs or MGBs."

"Radar, could it be a mine?"

"Don't think so, sir. And we don't usually pick up anything that low in the water."

"But it's definitely a target?"

"Oh yes. No doubt about that."

If it had been the old radar the pilot might have doubted him, but it wasn't, it was the H_2S and he believed him.

"Wireless to Skipper."

"Go ahead."

"We *were* notified that the U-boat was meant to be pursuing a small craft, sir. Maybe this is the small craft—?"

That was exactly what the pilot had been thinking. If so, then where was the U-boat?

The navigator's voice came over the earphones. "Taff to Skipper, course for target zero-five-five degrees, range ten miles."

The pilot switched to manual and took the plane onto her new course, reducing height at the same time.

He exchanged glances with Reid, the copilot, and said into the mike, "Might as well go and have a look."

"Definitely!"

But the pilot had a feeling about this one—a bad feeling. Something told him it wasn't a U-boat.

"Range five miles, Skipper."

"Right-ho." As the pilot took the plane down to seven hundred feet he felt the familiar exhilaration, the thrill of the chase.

"Radar to Skipper. Look . . . I may be nuts, but . . ."

"Out with it!"

"I've got a moving rock. Just to the south of St. Agnes. Quite close in. . . . But it's *moving*, sir."

The pilot stared unseeing into the night, his mind racing.

It couldn't be! But even as the pilot thought it, he knew it could . . . just possibly . . .

He said into the mike, "Size of contact?"

There was a slight pause. "Larger than the first, though still small. Not a ship at any rate. *Could* be a U-boat!"

Jesus Christ! *Yes!*

The bastard was hiding.

"Taff, guide me into this second contact. Reid, keep me above the rocks. How high are they, Navigator?"

"Navigator to Skipper. If we make a run from the southeast to the northwest, there's nothing above seventy-five feet."

"Right! Guide me in!"

He would go straight in. Straight in and light her up at one mile.

Then—*Bam!*

It was the U-boat, he *felt* it was the U-boat. And trying to hide, the bastard!

But there was no hiding place, not for U-boats. Not anymore.

*　*　*

The sea was sluicing over the long, narrow bows, creating great swaths of phosphorescence which ran off in rivers of sparkling silver to the dark water beneath.

Normally Fischer would have worried about the phosphorescence, but *U-319* was moving slowly so there was almost no wake to give them away. Besides, it was quite choppy and the luminescent path cut by the submarine would be indistinguishable from the multitude of breaking crests, flashing white and silver against the dark background of the night.

The northeast wind was cold. Fischer pulled his scarf tighter around his neck and, moving over the hatch, shouted, "Position."

A voice came floating faintly up. "Half a mile south of St. Agnes Island."

He hoped the navigator was right. After so long without a proper fix—visual or star—it was impossible to be positive. The navigator had got what he believed to be good bearings on radio beacons issuing from the French coast. Nevertheless Fischer had told the lookouts to keep a sharp watch for white water, just to be on the safe side. . . .

These islands were the very devil. Lots of rocks and islets scattered around, especially here to the southwest. And the rocks rising steeply from the sea floor so that depth soundings could give no warning.

The only warning they'd *ever* get would be white, breaking water. . . .

They'd been up on top for an hour now, making tight circles in the area between a mile and half a mile to the south of St. Agnes. Five hours to go. A hell of a lot of time. . . . Fischer hated being on the surface in a place like this. But to enemy radar, *U-319* would hopefully be just a tiny speck, another rock in the chaos of white blips that marked the Scillies.

He paced a small bridge; then, on a whim, decided to go below to have another quick look at the chart. There was nothing to see up here anyway.

He half slid, half climbed down the ladder and, still in his wet-weather gear, went to the chart area. Just before dawn, at about six, he would take *U-319* to the entrance to St. Mary's Sound and wait for the prey. The little boat would have to go in

that way: it seemed to be the only entrance into the islands—or at least the only *safe* entrance.

Then he'd grab the occupants—and quick. Once he was spotted all hell would break loose. He'd have five minutes—ten at the most. But there was no other way.

There was a muffled shout. Fischer tensed.

Then a cry. Fischer's blood ran cold.

The Klaxon shrieked through the silence, whooping obscenely. "Dive! Dive! Dive!"

Fischer thought: *Oh God, no!*

There was a burst of noise.

Men were running forward to the bow to get the nose down; the watch were pouring down the tower from the bridge; the rest were busy in the control room, spinning stopcocks, handling levers, shouting as they completed each maneuver. There was a loud hissing noise as the main vents were opened, and Fischer stared at the depth meter, waiting—*willing* it to go down . . .

Christ! He remembered they were doing only four knots. At that speed it would take forever. *Christ.*

Everything was happening with infinite slowness.

Fifteen seconds gone . . .

The last man fell down the tower and the hatch clanged shut.

The depth meter was beginning to show something—*at last.* But the water would barely be washing around the conning tower. . . . Come on. *Come on.*

One meter. So slow!

Twenty seconds gone.

Fischer looked over the coxswain's shoulder. The stick was fully forward, the hydroplanes at maximum pitch, angling the nose down—but slowly, so slowly . . .

God, one could go mad in such a moment . . .

Thirty seconds gone.

They should have been down by now.

Depth—four meters. Conning tower covered . . . not deep enough!

She was going faster now. Eight meters. Almost at periscope depth . . .

Forty seconds gone . . .

Perhaps they'd manage it after all.

Then time stood still. And *U-319* took off.

Its port side shot up, up, up, twisting sideways and upward by the bow. Fischer felt a momentary surprise as the floor rose against his feet. The control room spun rapidly around and he was falling.

Then came the noise, a vast long echoing boom that stunned the ears and reverberated in the brain.

There were shouts . . . dull noises that dimly penetrated ringing ears . . . men lying on the floor, reaching out . . .

Panting, Fischer pulled himself up. He tried to shout. But nothing came out. He tried again: "Damage reports!"

The messages came back, slowly at first.

"Flooding in fore ends. Watertight door closed!"

"Flooding in accommodation!"

The bow was settling down from its strange upward tilt, settling down—and falling.

He shouted, "Blow forward tanks." If he didn't get more buoyancy into her, she'd sink like a stone.

"Depth twenty meters!"

Fischer gulped: she was falling too fast!

"Forward tanks blown!"

"Blow aft tanks!" It was risky, but even if they came up stern first it was better than falling this fast.

Men were pouring aft now, out of the accommodation. As the last man came through, the watertight door was bolted shut.

"Accommodation flooding rapidly, Herr Kaleu. We couldn't stop it."

Fischer's eyes fastened on the depth gauge. It was falling steadily.

"Aft tanks blown!"

Thirty meters . . . thirty-three . . . still falling.

And they had blown all the main ballast tanks.

The nose was tilting farther and farther down. . . .

Fischer raced for the chart. How deep—?

Sixty-eight meters.

Christ, they were going to hit the bottom *hard.*

Forty meters . . . Fischer tried to think: What else? What else?

He looked at the men who had crowded in from the forward sections and yelled, "All of you to the after ends!"

498

The frightened faces were blank and stunned, but they obeyed, grabbing handholds to start the uphill climb to the after sections.

But the nose was tilting farther and farther down . . .

Depth: fifty meters and accelerating.

"Brace yourselves!"

Men flattened themselves against bulkheads or crouched against partitions. Then there was silence.

Those who could see the depth gauge watched it, their eyes round with horror.

Fifty-five meters . . . sixty . . .

She hit at sixty-one. The impact pushed in the first fifteen feet of the bow, opening up the already damaged forward compartment and completing the flooding process.

Fischer was aware of the breath being knocked out of his body, of his head meeting hard metal.

Then there was quiet, except for the hiss of leaking pressure pipes and the moans of men in pain.

U-319 was on the bottom.

Fischer pulled himself up against a partition. The floor was steeply tilted: the submarine was at an angle of about forty-five degrees, her stern high above the sea floor.

She was still moving though: twisting over, slowly and gently onto her port side.

Fischer brushed at the warm blood running into his eyes. There was something wrong, something *else* . . .

He peered around the partition. Ahead was the bulkhead that separated the control room from the accommodation. The water-tight door was still closed and locked tight. But to one side of it water was hissing out in a fan from the bulkhead itself. Fischer stumbled down the slope of the deck and fell against the bulkhead. He put his fingers to the metal. The water was spraying out from a wide fracture which ran from the deckhead almost to the floor.

He looked at it for a long time, then turned.

The men were watching him, their faces blank, patient, passive. Someone appeared from aft. "Flooding in the engine room, Herr Kaleu. We're trying to patch it up now."

They couldn't save her. They'd try, of course, but Fischer knew

it would be no good. Neither could they escape; no one had ever made a free ascent from this depth and lived.

Fischer stared back at them. For the moment there was nothing he could say.

He would think of something later, something appropriate, to prepare them for the end.

But all he could think of now was that they had put their faith in him and they had been wrong.

There is nothing I can do for you, my friends.

It might take them a day to die, maybe more, depending on how long the air lasted.

Then he looked down at the gathering water and thought: No, it'll be quicker than that. We're going to drown first.

He shook his head and smiled at his brave uncomplaining men with affection.

He wanted to say: I never was a god. Why did you ever think I was?

But they already knew he wasn't. They could see it in his face and, one by one, they looked away.

Julie wished it wasn't so dark.

She wasn't worried about the sailing now—the boat seemed to be dancing along quite happily—but she did wish she could see.

Still . . . there was only this night to survive, and then, sometime in the morning, land would come into sight—or a plane—help of some kind at any rate. She could almost imagine it now—the massive overwhelming *relief.* And the peace.

A picture floated in front of her eyes, as real as if she had seen it herself: a small cottage, standing alone on a hilltop, with a wonderful view of the distant sea pale and sparkling in the sunshine. The cottage was whitewashed and surrounded by a small garden with borders of softly colored flowers. Sitting in the garden were two people: she was one of them. The other was Richard. They had been there some time, living in the small cottage. They were very happy.

Extraordinary how clear it all was. She tried to hold onto it but the other pictures flashed into her mind: a small terraced house —her mother's—a clifftop, her uncle and aunt walking on it, a dance at Plymouth. . . . Then everything got jumbled and people were laughing at her, and it was some kind of nightmare, and they

were pointing at her. . . . Then she was drifting away, out to sea, in a strange boat without a tiller. . . .

She woke up. Reality. She checked the course and took a look around. In the darkness by the stern, she could just make out the dark shape of Peter's body curled up in the corner.

Then she heard it.

A faint noise, so indistinct that at first she thought she was mistaken.

Wide awake now, she had heard it again. A faint—something. . . .

A whispering? No, more of a swishing. . . .

She gulped and stood up.

Where was it coming from?

She looked around wildly. The sound seemed to be all around her. Or was it ahead?

It faded, then died away. Perhaps she was imagining it. . . .

No! There it was, like muffled thunder, a soft boom which rolled, then fell away. . . .

She stood still, gripped by fear.

Again, a low rumble. Closer. *Closer.*

She clamped her hand to her mouth.

Then she saw it and almost screamed. A flicker which grew into a long smudge of glimmering whiteness.

It was water—white water, leaping, moving, rising, falling back, a great line that stretched across the sea in front of her.

She yanked the tiller toward her. Pulling, pulling until it would go no farther.

"Turn! Turn! *Please* . . ." She pulled on the tiller until her hands hurt.

The boat turned on a wave and lurched over, throwing her sideways against the side.

She grasped the rail and turned back to look.

White water . . . rising, thundering up against black walls, falling back . . .

She cried out, *"Oh God!"* And watched the terrible water, mesmerized.

Then she remembered. The tiller: she had let it go. She reached for it, found it, took hold . . . and realized she had lost all sense of direction.

The white water was to her right now. Turn still more: she must

turn still more. Away, away, back to the open sea . . . Whimpering slightly, she pulled on the tiller. The white water was almost behind her . . . *behind* her . . . yes, yes—behind her. . . . For a moment the white water seemed to be dragging her back, then it was fading, turning gray again . . .

She collapsed, shaking and weak, onto the seat, murmuring, "Oh, oh . . ."

Something made her look up—a sound; a dull roar; falling water.

Somebody screamed. She dimly realized it was herself. Ahead of the boat was a wall of brilliant silver and white, cascading downward and backward, rushing toward them. Then a wave rose, higher and higher, and the little boat was rushing forward, hurtling headlong toward a black mass climbing into the sky, blacker than the night.

She grabbed for the tiller and pulled desperately, but the wild forward motion of the boat was inexorable. The black mass loomed higher and larger, rushing forward to meet the boat.

She screamed again and turned to reach for Peter. A second later the breath was pushed from her body and she was flying headlong. *Peter! Peter!* She was twisting in the air; turning; then landing on something brutal and hard.

She screamed, *"Peter!"*

Some way below her she saw the dim outline of the back of the boat, where Peter had been, but so dark that she couldn't see *inside.*

"Peter!"

Water came roaring toward her in a great deluge, flooding over the boat. She grabbed at something and, closing her eyes, held on tight. The water came thundering over her head, filling her eyes and ears and trying to drag her away. She held on until her arms were breaking. Something jerked at her waist, pulling at her body.

The water subsided, sucking back in a great gasp, as if taking another breath.

She panted for air and tried to move toward the stern, toward Peter, but the rope was tight around her waist, dragging her to the side.

"God, let me go! Let me go!"

She pulled on the rope, tried to yank it off, tried to tear it off, grappling wildly at the knot. Then she remembered—the rope! *The rope was Peter!* She screamed, *"P-e-t-e-r!"* and slid down the deck in the direction of the rope. Nothing. She groped around. She touched something soft and reached for it just as the next wave came thundering over the deck, knocking her sideways, roaring into her mouth. She groped—grabbed—found—clung— pulled him in to her body. . . .

She clung to him. She held him as the water carried them forward, bumping, crashing them along, forward. . . .

Something hit her head with a great bang. She swallowed water. Then they were up against something hard, and now the other way, now they were being dragged back, back, back.

And she clung to him. And in that fraction of a moment she would have died for him, *wanted* to die for him, the child of her body. She would have held the water back with her bare hands and clawed at the rock with her fists and killed any man or anything that stood in her way. . . .

But now the water was carrying them forward again, faster this time and angrier, a great crested wave that carried them up, up, racing forward to hurl itself on the unyielding granite, forward onto the mighty rock.

The deck had disappeared from under her. Instead there was only the water, spinning her around, trying to drag her down. She swallowed water, tried to breathe, choked, gasped for breath, found some precious air, gulped water, felt the sea close over her head . . . flung out an arm and tried to fight her way up. . . .

Still the wave raced forward.

And still she clung to him.

Then they were falling, falling in the great cataract of water. Julie braced herself. In that instant of time she saw a vast panorama before her: a split second which covered all the happiness and joy of her life.

Something hit the back of her body with a sickening impact, hit her so hard that her chin met her chest and her breath was exploded from her lungs. Then the water was clawing at her, dragging her over rough, sharp things . . .

Everything began to slip away . . . she was drifting gently . . . the world was purple . . . white . . . black.

In a moment of lucidity she was aware of a terrible pain in her side. One last time she murmured the child's name.

Then she was slipping away . . . into a cloud where a soft gentle wave enveloped her, soothing her aching head, removing all pain, making everything right again . . .

David thought: How strange that I should die here, in the sea.

The boat lurched again, slipping farther down, wood scraping loudly and unhappily against granite.

The rushing waves came higher into the raised bow, grabbing at David's legs.

David thought: I'll be ready for you when you come.

He'd already said his last prayers and made his peace with God. Now he concentrated on the small house in Germany, as it used to be, in the days when they had been so happy.

He started from the time Cecile was very small. He remembered her pudgy little arms reaching out to touch his nose, he remembered the three of them in the park . . .

A wave washed up to his chest and covered his head with spray.

Was that the one God had intended for him?

No. When he could hold on no more, *that* would be the one.

He had reached Cecile's school days when the wave finally came. It was larger than the rest. It washed into the bow with a thunderous roar and as it receded his hands were torn from the boat and he was traveling with the water . . .

Free at last. In a way.

He made himself go limp and waited, suspended by the life preserver. Water filled his mouth and nose and he choked and spluttered and fought for breath. He was disappointed. He'd thought death would be easy, just a matter of closing your eyes and waiting.

But the fight for breath became more difficult. He had no strength left. He was ebbing away.

For one brief moment the soft air touched his face, then a wave hissed over him and filled his mouth and he knew he wouldn't struggle anymore.

The life preserver slipped up over his shoulders and he was floating downward, drifting gently. In the last few moments panic gripped him, but he calmed himself by remembering that he was a lucky man: his troubles were finally over.

32 Joe Treleaven sniffed the air. It was cold for March and cold for the islands. The low dormer window was opaque with condensation. Puffing a little, he pulled a heavy oiled sweater over his head and, leaning down, rubbed the wetness from the glass.

It was almost sunrise. The dawn light was clear and hard as a diamond, the sky a yellow dome above the blackness of the sea. It would stay cold all day, Joe decided.

Easterlies, they were the only winds which could bring this kind of cold to St. Agnes. He shook his head and stomped down the cottage stairs into the kitchen.

He shook down the ashes in the stove, opened the vent and poured more coal into the top. He picked up the kettle and, opening the latch, went into the yard. He paused, as he always did, and looked toward the Western Rocks. The wind of the previous night had dropped and the air was still. It might be a good fishing day. Perhaps he'd take the boat and go lining for scad. But then perhaps he wouldn't; perhaps he'd go weed-gathering for pig feed instead.

He filled the kettle from the water barrel and, returning to the kitchen, put it on the stove. He made himself a breakfast of porridge and tea, then pulled on his jacket to go and feed the animals. As he approached, the pigs snorted in wild agitation. He gave them their usual mixture of vegetables and kelp and threw the chickens a handful of grain.

The sun was up now, turning the tall tamarisk hedges a vibrant green. Beyond the fields, over the rugged shoreline, the faraway lines of jagged rocks shone a dull pink-gold in a sea of palest yellow.

There was a distant buzzing sound in the sky. Joe screwed up

his eyes and spotted the glint of a plane far away above the needlelike Bishop, heading south.

After it had gone he gazed a little longer, but more casually, eyeing the weather and getting the feel of the day. He decided he would go weed-gathering instead of fishing, though he wouldn't enjoy it half as much.

He began to turn away, but something made him pause and look back. He stared at the distant rocks for a long time; then, slowly, thoughtfully, he walked back into the cottage and closed the door behind him.

He cleared the breakfast things from the table and piled them in the washing-up bowl. Then he went into the front room to the mantelpiece. The telescope was an old one which his family had come by many years before—probably from a wreck, though no one would admit it.

He took the telescope up the stairs to the bedroom. The small window hadn't been opened all winter and was warped with damp, but it finally yielded. He extended the telescope, rested it on the sill and peered through it until he was satisfied. Then he closed the window, compressed the telescope and went down to the kitchen again. From the back of the door he took a long oilskin coat, a sou'wester and a toweling scarf, and placed them on the table. He removed his stout farmer's boots and pulled on a pair of long seaman's boots. Picking up the oilskins, he left the cottage and made his way up the lane toward Lower Town, one of the four settlements on St. Agnes.

When he reached the handful of dwellings he went straight to a cottage near the beach and knocked on the door. A man appeared. "Mornin', Jeremiah," Joe said.

"Mornin', Joe." The man eyed the oilskins.

"There's somethin' out on the rocks."

The man nodded and without further comment disappeared inside. After a while he returned with oilskins of his own, and together the two men made their way to the beach. A heavy boat was sitting at the top of a long concrete slipway, two pairs of oars lying across the thwarts.

Without a word the two men threw their oilskins into the boat and dragged her down the slipway. Once she was afloat they gave a last push, hopped effortlessly in, fitted the oars into the row-locks and pulled away.

From the cove they crossed the expanse of Smith Sound and passed between the low rocks of the Hellweathers out into the open sea. From here it was two miles to the main group of the Western Rocks.

They rowed silently, each man intent on the slow, steady swing of his stroke. There was a swell running, the last remains of the waves whipped up by the gale the night before. But the surface itself was unruffled by wind and the sharp bow of the boat cut cleanly through the glasslike water.

Joe sat on the forward thwart, the better position for piloting. He had noted the thrust of the tide as they passed through Hellweathers Neck and every now and then he glanced over his shoulder to get his bearings on the rocks ahead. They came abreast of Melledgan and the Muncoy Ledges to the south. After another fifteen minutes, Joe saw the profile of Gorregan and the Rags out of the corner of his eye. Not so far now.

He paused in his stroke and took a good look at the rocks ahead. The other man paused also. "Where d'ye reckon, Joe?"

Joe pursed his lips. "I reckon Rosevean. Well, let's start there at any rate."

The two men had searched the rocks many times. Once, before the war, they had found the wreckage of a small boat and, on one of the higher rocks, the body of a man. He was on his knees, his hands clasped together as if in prayer, his body crouched, his head pointing toward the mighty Bishop Lighthouse as if in hope of rescue. When they got to him he was cold and stiff as a board and it had been the devil's own job to straighten him out.

Joe feathered an oar to turn the boat to port and head her between the Rags and Rosevear. As Rosevear came up abeam he slowed the pace and examined the rocky surface of the islet with a critical eye. Nothing there. Only gulls, the occasional tuft of scurvy grass and the jagged patterns of the rocks themselves.

The boat passed on, going due south now. They came to a scattering of small rocks; then, finally, the islet of Rosevean, a little taller than its sister, Rosevear, but smaller and utterly barren.

As they approached the islet they stopped rowing and let the boat drift under her own momentum. The only sound was the rumbling and swishing of the sea as the swell rose up the sides

of the rock and rushed and tumbled in among the cracks and crevices, only to recede again, the water falling away from the granite walls in tumbling cascades.

The other man was pointing. Joe followed the direction of his finger. Something was lying in the white froth at the base of the rock face. It looked like wood.

The boat drifted on. They came abreast of the islet. There were more fragments in the water here. Again, they looked like wood.

The two men scanned the uneven surface of the rock but Joe saw it first. A great blob of darkness against the pallor of the rock.

They came closer and realized that it was a ragged triangle of reddish-black material, caught on a spur of rock some fifteen feet above the sea. It looked to Joe like canvas.

Joe began to row the boat around in a circle away from the islet. Still the men stared at the rock.

There was something else: a touch of bright scarlet. This, too, was quite high up, half-hidden behind a knoll. Joe pointed to it, and as they rowed, more of the object came into view. It was familiar, something both men had seen before: the brightly painted transom of a small boat.

"Better take a look."

They rowed back toward the rock, to a ledge they knew well: a ledge a man could jump onto.

"I'll go," Joe volunteered.

"Right-ho."

Joe shipped his oars; and as the other man brought the boat in toward the rock, he stood up. He waited while the swell took the boat down; then, as the boat rose again, he placed a foot on the thwart and, in the moment that the boat hovered at the top of the wave, he stepped across onto the ledge.

From here a gully led to the top. There was only one point which was difficult to climb, but Joe knew the handholds.

When he reached the top he clambered across the rock to the side where he'd seen the blaze of scarlet. It was wood all right and, as he had thought, part of a boat. By the brightness of the paint, a fishing boat. By the gay designs, a French one.

He moved over to where the triangle of reddish black was spread across the rock. Yes: part of a sail. It was still attached to

508

the gaff, and the gaff was suspended by a halyard which had caught itself around the spur of rock.

But there was more.

Trapped by fingers of rock or marooned in rock pools and tiny plateaus were all kinds of jetsam: rope, more pieces of tattered canvas, fragments of black-painted wood—even a life preserver.

The small boat had been smashed into a thousand pieces.

He climbed on, as close to the edge as he dared, peering down among the gullies and crevices.

He reached the northern side of the island and turned back. There was nothing worth risking his neck for.

Then he realized that he'd missed something: a black, sacklike object draped over a small outcrop. There was something else underneath it.

He went nearer until he could look directly down. He stared for a long moment, then murmured, "Poor devils."

He clambered back to the other side of the islet until he could see the rowing boat. He whistled and indicated to the other man that he should row the boat around to the east side.

Joe clambered back to the point directly above the sacklike object. With his face to the rock, he climbed carefully and slowly downward, pausing frequently to get his bearings. Yes, at least one body and perhaps another.

The last few feet were almost vertical rock. He found a foothold and jumped. He waited for the boat to appear around the corner and waved until he was sure that Jeremiah had seen him. Then he went over to the bodies.

He knelt. One was a woman, her body arched around a finger of a rock, as if a wave had tried to pull her back into the sea and the rock had prevented it.

Beside her was a child of about six or seven, his face white, his eyes closed.

The two were roped together.

Joe put his hand on the woman's forehead. Cold. He put his hand against her neck and felt for the artery. Nothing.

Then a flutter. A glimmer.

He moved quickly. He straightened the woman's body and laid her on her back. There was a nasty wound on her head.

He rubbed her hands vigorously then patted her cheeks. He felt her neck again. The fluttering was still very faint.

Something made him look up. He started with surprise.

The child's eyes were open, staring blankly.

Joe took his hand. It was icy cold. The child was almost frozen to death. Joe rubbed his hands, roughly, almost angrily, then patted the white cheeks.

The child blinked.

"Now then, young fella, ye're goin' to be all right, you hear? I'm just goin' to get yer something warm. Right?"

The child stared. Joe turned and shouted to Jeremiah, who threw a rope up. A few minutes later Joe had hoisted up the oilskins and an old piece of canvas they kept in the boat. He took off his own sweater and placed it over the child with an oilskin on top. Then he put the canvas and Jeremiah's oilskin over the woman.

He shouted down to Jeremiah, "We'll need four more men, another boat, more warm clothes—oh, and a plank of wood to get them down on, Jeremiah."

As the other man rowed off in the direction of St. Agnes, Joe knelt beside the woman and went through his rubbing and patting treatment again. Warmth and blood flow, that was what she needed. There was no response, but he kept going. It was probably the bump on the head that was doing the damage.

Then he returned to the child. This time the boy watched him as he approached.

"Hello, young lad."

Fear came into the child's eyes. His lips moved but he couldn't speak, his teeth were chattering so much.

"Don't worry, we'll soon 'ave yer warm!"

Finally the child said, "Mummy—!" And tried to move nearer the woman.

Joe restrained him gently. "She'll be all right, don' yer worry!"

"Mummy—!" He was sobbing now.

Quickly Joe said, "Look 'ere, who else was with yer? On the boat—? Can yer tell me?"

The child was crying, rivers of tears falling from his cheeks, his face contorted with despair. "M-M-ummy—! P-p-lease let me g-go to M-M-Mummy—!"

510

Joe didn't know what to do. He'd never had dealings with children. He didn't know they could be so strong-minded. "Look 'ere, she's not too well. She's best left on 'er own, take my word for it!" He put a friendly but firm hand on the child. He didn't want the lad throwing himself around the place.

The child was sheet white now. "G-go away! Go away, you horrible man! L-leave us alone!"

Joe was taken aback. That was strong talk. He retreated a little and said uncertainly, "Well . . . you won't touch 'er 'ead, will yer?"

"No-no!"

"Right, well . . ."

The child got to his knees and, crawling across to the woman, put his arm around her waist and pushed his head against her side. He murmured to her as if she were awake.

Joe shook his head. What a thing. He covered the boy with the clothing, and, when the child was calmer, asked him again, "Was there no one else with yer, lad?"

This time the child turned his head and nodded slightly.

"Yes? 'Ow many?"

The boy looked away and Joe thought he wasn't going to answer. Finally the child said, "D-David. D-David."

"David, was it?"

The child closed his eyes and pushed closer to his mother.

"Was it just 'im?"

The child said something. Joe put his head closer. "What did you say?"

"Just him," the child whispered.

Joe patted his arm reassuringly. He should say something but it was difficult to think what. Eventually he mumbled, "Well, don' yer worry. We'll find 'im. We'll find 'im. One way or the other."

And they did. Four days later. When his body, bloated with gases, floated to the surface again.

PART FIVE

May 1943– June 1945

33 The car came to a halt, the road blocked by fallen debris. A row of tall buildings had been almost totally destroyed. The ruins were smoldering in the dawn light, the heavy smoke in strange contrast to the pink blossom on the one surviving cherry tree.

Doenitz said, "I'll walk from here."

The driver leaped from his seat and opened the rear door. Doenitz stepped out and briskly picked his way around the piles of stone and mortar, his staff officer on his heels. The Hotel-am-Steinplatz was just around the corner. Doenitz noted that the hotel was still standing: one of the few buildings in central Berlin that still was.

He strode into the hotel and down to the basement. But instead of going straight to the tracking room as usual, he went to his office and closed the door behind him.

He needed time to think.

It was the day of decision.

He picked up the sheet of statistics on his desk. It was now May 23. In the first twenty-one days of the month the U-boat arm had sunk 200,000 tons of Allied shipping—a lot less than in any of the previous three months, but still a commendable total, considering—

He brought his eyes down to the paragraph marked "U-boat Losses."

Thirty-one boats in just twenty-one days.

It was an unprecedented rate.

It was a disaster.

Boats had been lost everywhere—while hunting in the open Atlantic, off Iceland and, as ever, on passage across the Bay of Biscay.

Nowhere was safe anymore.

Thirty-one . . .

He gritted his teeth and tried not to imagine how it had been for the men. . . . And, in particular, for one of them, the special one so close to his heart. . . .

With effort he turned his thoughts back to the problem. No one could tell him exactly what system or secret the Allies had hit upon. No one had offered a countermeasure. Maybe the British had spies in the Kriegsmarine itself, maybe they had broken the German ciphers, maybe . . .

Maybe that Rotterdam device which Schmidt and his scientists were still trying to rebuild held the key to it all. . . .

Doenitz had the feeling it did.

But nobody could tell him one way or the other. Not with certainty.

Meanwhile his men died.

The men had a name for what was happening. They called it the Thunderbolt. This month of May was becoming known as the Month of the Thunderbolt.

He looked up at the safe neutral walls of his underground office. Head of the German Navy and powerless to protect his men. He had done his best but it had not been enough.

He was left with only one possible decision and he must make it now.

He must withdraw all his wolf packs from the North Atlantic.

He had been brooding on it all night; now he was certain. He couldn't go on sending his men to their deaths. Nothing could be worth that.

The consequences of the withdrawal would be grave. It would give the Allies the freedom to plan their invasion of Europe. It would also give them the means of achieving it. Once their convoys could get through from North America unimpeded, they would quickly stockpile weapons and supplies. Then there would be no stopping them.

He had told Hitler this, he had explained it all. Doenitz wasn't sure whether the Führer had understood the implications fully, but Hitler had been sufficiently worried to summon Goering and ask for a progress report on the Rotterdam device. Goering had brushed the matter aside, as he usually did, saying that radar probably wasn't at the root of the trouble anyway. . . .

In the meantime he must withdraw the wolf packs.

Doenitz picked up the telephone. "A meeting of senior staff in five minutes, Henker." The staff officer acknowledged the order. Doenitz asked, "What else must be attended to this morning?"

"Special meeting with Herr Scheer at eleven to discuss the shortfall in the U-boat program, Herr Grossadmiral. Then some general correspondence. Oh, and some bereavement letters."

"How many?"

"Five, Herr Grossadmiral."

"Right." He replaced the receiver.

Bereavement letters. Doenitz was in the habit of personally writing to the families of missing U-boat commanders, even though his present rank did not demand it. He'd always done it in the past, and he liked to continue the practice.

Five. He'd already written ten this week.

He must also write another letter. To his wife. He'd written to her when the news of his son's loss had first come through. Somehow it hadn't been too bad then. But time was making it worse, not better, and it was becoming increasingly difficult to find the right words.

He covered his face with his hands. Previously he had always managed to avoid thinking about his sons. He had been careful to close them out of his mind so as to show no favoritism. One could not let emotion cloud one's judgment; one could not ask about a particular U-boat just because it carried one's own flesh.

Now—now he wished he'd thought about them more often. He wished he'd *seen* them more frequently.

Now one was lost.

He must write to his wife again. It would be impossible to find the right words.

He sat upright and breathed in sharply. In a sense, all the crews were his sons. He must do his best to prevent any more of them from dying.

There was a knock at the door. Doenitz reached hastily into his pocket and, taking out a handkerchief, rubbed his eyes where some dust seemed to have got into them. The staff officer appeared in the doorway. "The meeting is assembled, Herr Grossadmiral."

Doenitz got to his feet and, straightening his tunic, marched from the room.

* * *

"It's here in Paris, the job."

"I thought Paris was too dangerous for me."

Kloffer shrugged. "You worry too much. Time has passed. People forget."

Vasson thought: They never forget.

They were sitting in the back of Kloffer's Citroën, parked in a side street near the Étoile. Vasson viewed the scene with annoyance. There was an atmosphere to the city which hadn't been there before. The people were more optimistic, more defiant. The sullen desperation had gone.

"Yes," Kloffer went on, "it's the students again. Communists, agitators. . . . Usual stuff—"

"Look, before we talk about this," Vasson interrupted firmly, "there's the matter of payment. I haven't had the second payment for the Brittany job."

Kloffer's eyes gleamed angrily. "You never give up, do you? You never learn! The job was a mess, remember? And you were the one who messed it up. I strongly advise you not to mention the money again. Otherwise—even *I* will lose patience!"

Vasson was so angry that he couldn't speak for a moment. Eventually he said deliberately, "I've told you before, it was nothing to do with me. It was that disgusting queer, Baum. *He* made the mistakes!"

"So you say, Vasson, but in Berlin it's *your* name that's got the mud all over it. Nothing will change that."

Vasson clenched his teeth. He hated Kloffer using his real name. He said with difficulty, "So am I to understand that I will never be paid?"

"That's correct." Kloffer spoke matter-of-factly, but there was an edge of impatience in his voice.

Vasson said stiffly, "I see." It was the one thing he couldn't forgive. Not being paid.

Kloffer gave a small sigh of relief. "Good. Now, where were we?"

"One more thing," Vasson interrupted. "Am I to be paid for *this* job?"

There was an infinitesimal pause. "Of course."

He was hiding something, Vasson could tell. "What are the terms?"

518

"The best available, given the circumstances."

Vasson's pulse quickened. The bastard was going to try and screw him. "Tell me."

"No more gold. There's none available."

Vasson said nothing.

"Also this is going to be a simple job for you. It shouldn't take more than a week. The payment will be a single payment of five thousand. On completion."

It was chicken feed. Vasson let his rage rise and subside again. "Tell me," he said carefully, "is it that I'm worth less than before . . . or that you now regard me as expendable?"

Kloffer considered for a moment. "Your price has gone down. That's all there is to it."

"I see."

"You'd be blind *not* to see, Marseillais. You have to realize that things have changed. You're not as—well, we don't need you so much as before. We've got other methods. And other people—people as good or better than you."

It was a lie about the other people, Vasson knew it. There wasn't anyone better. As for the other methods—they were cruder, that was all. And less effective.

There was a silence.

Kloffer glanced at him. "Shall we get on, then?" He waited a moment, then began listing information and instructions.

Vasson pretended to listen, but his mind was already elsewhere, planning his moves, working out times and, most important of all, calculating how best to cover himself so that Kloffer would never find out the truth.

When Kloffer had finished, Vasson asked casually, "Fougères. Is he dead?"

Kloffer said irritably, "Fougères? Who's he?"

"The Meteor Line. Based here. I used his identity in Brittany."

"Ah. . . ." He thought for a moment. "Dead. Yes, I'm almost certain."

"And the other man. The one who swore to my identity?"

"Yes, yes! Dead too! Why do you worry about such matters?"

"I just like things neat and tidy, that's all."

"You mean, you're frightened!" Kloffer looked amused.

"Not at all."

519

"But you should be."

"I thought you said it wasn't dangerous for me in Paris."

"It's dangerous for you everywhere." Kloffer removed a piece of fluff from his sleeve. "But don't worry, we'll protect you."

It was a lie. Vasson knew they would never protect him.

"All right? Are you clear about the job? Any questions?"

Vasson shook his head. "No questions."

"Well, well. Quite a change . . ." Suspicion flashed into Kloffer's eyes. "You're not planning anything stupid, are you?"

"What?"

"Running for it."

Vasson snorted with amusement. "No, Kloffer. As you always tell me, there's nowhere to hide."

"Yes, and don't you forget it, Paul Vasson."

Vasson thought, Good-bye, you bastard. May you rot in hell.

As soon as he reached the apartment near the Porte d'Auteuil he set feverishly to work.

He took the three suitcases down from the top of the wardrobe and left them open, two on the bed and the third, which was shabbier, on the floor.

From the wardrobe and the chest of drawers he removed his best clothes and packed them hurriedly in one of the better cases. The cheaper working clothes which he'd used in Paris he placed in the second. The oldest clothes and the ones he'd worn in Brittany he threw into the third.

Then he pulled out a drawer and, turning it over, tore off a small flat package which was stuck to the underside. Inside were two sets of identity papers. He took one set, which he'd never used before, and slid them into his wallet. The second set, which were in the name of Fougères, he placed in an ashtray. With a shaking hand he put a match to them. When they were burning nicely he added the set he'd been using since his return to Paris, and watched them as they curled in the flames. When both sets were burned he tipped the ash into an empty cigarette packet and threw it into the wastebasket.

He closed all the suitcases and, picking up two of them, carried them down to the ground floor, where he left them just inside the street door. He returned and, taking a last look around, picked

up the third case and closed the apartment door behind him. By the time he reached the ground floor, he was slightly out of breath. He knocked on the concierge's door.

When she appeared he said, "I'm going. Urgent business. I won't be back. Are we up to date?"

The old woman shrugged. "I suppose so!" Which meant they were up to date and he didn't owe her anything.

"Here. Take this." He handed her the third suitcase. "It's full of clothes I don't need. For a worthy cause."

Picking up the two remaining cases, he walked around the corner and across two streets until he came to the car.

He put the cases in the trunk, got in and sat for a moment until he was calmer.

He started the car and took the familiar road to Sèvres and 22, Rue du Vieux Moulin.

He drove slowly past the house to make his customary check, then turned around and drove past again, just to be on the safe side. He parked two streets away and, leaving the cases in the trunk, walked briskly back to the house.

The villa was deathly quiet, shrouded by its air of slow decay. Vasson hurried up the drive, his footsteps sounding loud on the loose gravel. He ran the last few feet on tiptoe, then paused at the basement door and listened.

Nothing.

He let himself in and went to the bed-sitting room. From the underside of the shelf he took one of the two sets of papers that Kloffer didn't know about and slid them in his pocket. This particular set was incomplete: no photographs, no thumbprints, only a name. The name belonged to a boy who'd been born and brought up in the French West Indies but had died just before the war, shortly after coming to France to work. The authorities didn't know he was dead. The identity was a marvelous one: it had taken a lot of research to find it.

He went along the passage to the storeroom and, moving the table, dug down until he found the waterproof bag. It contained the only cash he had: sixty thousand francs. He put it in his inside pocket. The money would keep him for a year if necessary.

There was another bag lying at the bottom of the hole. He pulled it out and, opening it, looked at the contents thoughtfully.

It was an Enfield Number 2 revolver, which he'd obtained from one of the members of the Meteor Line. With it were twelve bullets.

He'd never used the gun—or *any* gun for that matter. But he knew he could if he had to. Should he take it now? A picture of Kloffer flashed into his mind and, without another thought, he loaded the revolver and thrust it into his pocket with the spare bullets.

He smoothed back the earth and, leaving some money and a note for the old lady, locked up and left.

Next, the car. He drove to the river and parked on the embankment. He waited a moment, thinking hard. How long would it take Kloffer to realize? A day? Two days? Maybe even longer.

Or was the German already suspicious?

He got out, locked the door, removed the cases from the trunk and threw the keys in the river.

He carried the cases to the side of the main boulevard and waited. Standing anonymously by the road was soothing and he didn't mind having to wait. Finally, after half an hour, an empty *vélo*-taxi came along and he hailed it.

The *vélo* took him across the city to the Gare d'Orléans, where he deposited his case in the checkroom.

Afterward he found a public telephone and, referring to a slip of paper in his wallet, lifted the receiver and asked for a number. He gripped the receiver more tightly and held his breath. He might be lucky.

Someone answered. It was the person he wanted. He spoke haltingly. A time and place were agreed.

Vasson replaced the receiver, his hand damp with sweat.

He had a quick pastis at the station bar, then walked to the Métro and took a train east. After changing trains he got off at the Place Gambetta and started walking through some of the unfashionable areas of the *vingtième*.

He went to several rooming houses before finding the right one. It was the right one because the concierge was drunk and didn't bother to take him up to the room herself. She didn't even look at his face.

At one point he thought he was wrong and she was going to be nosy after all. When he came downstairs, she asked him what

he did for a living. He replied, "Doorman," and she was satisfied.

"Just don't want anyone who's going to be trouble, that's all!"

"No trouble."

He paid for the room and left quickly.

Four hours until the meeting.

He went and had a meal. He ate very little but drank a great deal, a bottle of wine and several glasses of rough cognac. He wanted to be very very drunk by ten.

At half past nine he paid for the meal and went in search of a *vélo*-taxi. The taxi driver dropped him near the Porte de Pantin.

The cool night air cleared his head a little. He swore quietly. He should have had more to drink. He wasn't drunk enough by far.

He followed the directions he'd been given. Past the cattle market, down to the canal, turn left and the warehouse was a few yards along on the left.

The area around the canal was very dark, but eventually he found the warehouse. He didn't know whether he was glad.

The other person hadn't arrived.

He paced back and forth feeling very light-headed.

He tried to think what he might have forgotten or left undone. Was there anything that would lead Kloffer to him?

He shook his head. No, he'd forgotten nothing. Kloffer would never find him, not in a million years.

Kloffer thought he was being so clever, planning to feed him to the wolves.

But not anymore.

Not after tonight and *this*. The thought of what was to come made Vasson's stomach turn and he closed his eyes.

There was a sound. Vasson jumped. A man stepped forward from the shadows. He was large, his head almost square on his massive shoulders. In the faint moonlight Vasson could just make out his features. His face was puffy and his nose broken: he looked like a former boxer, which was exactly what he was.

"*Salut.*"

Vasson stared, mesmerized. "*Salut.*"

"You're sure about this?"

Vasson gave a high-pitched laugh. "Of course!"

"What exactly do you want?"

"What are you offering?" The question was so ludicrous that Vasson giggled softly.

"How different do you want to look?"

Vasson made an expansive gesture. "Completely."

"The money?"

"Here." Vasson reached in his pocket and threw some notes on the ground. "One thing—!"

"Yes."

"I don't want to feel any pain!"

"All right." The man stepped forward. Fear leaped into Vasson's throat and his knees began to buckle.

He made a conscious effort to close his eyes, thinking: Dear God, please let it be quick and not too painful.

He needn't have worried on either count.

A fraction of a second later the boxer's right fist smashed into his face.

After the first shock Vasson never felt a thing.

The big man put everything into his first blow. Backed by 210 pounds of solid muscle, his fist sank deep into Vasson's left cheek and shattered the bone. The force sent Vasson flying backward against the side of the building. As he fell to the ground his head hit a stone and he lost consciousness.

The big man finished the job in his own time. He sat Vasson up and smashed the nose a couple of times, just to make sure it was broken properly. He smashed the right cheekbone to match the left. Then he paused for a few minutes while he examined the results. He decided a smaller jaw might improve things, so he broke that too.

The eyes were difficult, of course. Not much one could do to make them look different. But he tried his best, cutting the eyebrows deeply in a couple of places and thickening up the bones underneath.

Finally he was satisfied that he couldn't do any more without risking internal bleeding. He left Vasson lying on his side so that he wouldn't inhale his own blood.

When he arrived at the nightclub where he worked he phoned a priest he knew and, disguising his voice, told him there was a seriously injured man down by the canal who couldn't, for political reasons, go to a hospital.

524

It wasn't kindness. He just didn't want the customer to bleed to death by mistake. He'd never killed anyone in his life.

He promptly forgot all about the incident. Which was a mistake.

Vasson never forgave him for calling the priest.

Three weeks later the big man was found dead in an alley, a neat nine-millimeter bullet hole in his back.

34 St. Mary's post office was crowded, the people waiting patiently in a long line. The woman behind the counter seemed slower than ever. Finally Julie stepped forward. "Good afternoon. Do you have anything for me?"

"Name?"

The woman always asked her that. You'd think she'd know by now. Julie suppressed her irritation and said calmly, "Lescaux. Madame Lescaux." It was the way the major from M19 had addressed her in the first letter.

The woman searched the rack but Julie knew, even before she turned around, that there would be no letter.

"Sorry, Mrs. er—Lascoo."

"Thank you." She squeezed past the waiting people out into the main street, pausing to take a deep breath of the fresh May air.

Every day it was the same: no letter. More doubts. Less hope. Every day it was more of an effort to be cheerful, to cope with life.

Some days it didn't seem worth bothering at all.

A voice said, "Afternoon!" It was one of the men who ran ferries between St. Mary's and the outlying islands.

Julie forced a smile.

The man shuffled his feet and asked kindly, "Boy all right, is 'e then?"

"Yes, thank you. He's fine."

"Amazin' 'ow they get over those things, these young people."

"Yes." Except, Julie thought, that he'll never get over it. He had seemed all right after the sinking, even when she'd told him about David. But later, when the letter had arrived and she'd told him about Jean and the others, he'd changed. He'd become quieter, more troubled, not the Peter she used to know.

"You be stayin' with us awhile?"

She hesitated. "Er—yes, I think so."

"Well, you always be welcome 'ere." The boatman looked down, embarrassed.

"Thank you."

"Bye for now, then!"

"Bye. And thank you again."

She turned away with relief. The islanders had all been very kind, and they must think her ungrateful, the way she kept to herself and avoided their company. But she hated making conversation, particularly about the war. She just wanted to be left alone.

She walked briskly up the hill until she came to a place high above Hugh Town. She sat on the ground, her hands clasped around her knees, and looked out at the view. She often came here in the afternoons when she was waiting for Peter to come out of school. The scene was wonderful: you could see St. Mary's Pool below and, away to the west, the glittering rock-strewn wastes that led to the open sea. In the north lay the Mediterranean-blue waters of St. Mary's Road and the vivid green, yellow-fringed island of Tresco and, beyond, the starker, less brilliant Bryher.

There were rumors about these northern islands. It was said that fishing boats painted in French colors sometimes appeared from the open sea, crossed the sound and disappeared between Tresco and Bryher toward New Grimsby Harbor. The craft were known locally as "the mystery boats."

Richard. He'd hinted at secret operations in the islands. It would be just the sort of thing he'd have been involved with.

She thought of him all the time, where he might be—in some hidden, secret place perhaps. Or in a POW camp—it *was* just possible—or, when she was really depressed, she pictured him dead.

She thought of Jean too. And Maurice. And the others.

She tried not to imagine what they had been through before they died.

But the thing that really hurt, now, was the suspicion that they —and she—had been forgotten.

Why, otherwise, had she had no more news?

She took the letter from her bag for the hundredth time. She hated the very sight of it: so efficient, so emotionless, so British:

Dear Mme. Lescaux . . .

Thank you for letting me talk to you for so long. . . . most useful . . . help prevent the loss of others. . . . However I regret to inform you that news has now reached me from the other side. . . . Your uncle, Jean Cornou, died in Rennes prison during the first week of April. So too did the agent known as Maurice, and at least ten others. Of your aunt I fear we have no news at present. If I receive any I will, of course, let you know. . . . Deep regrets. . . . You also enquired about Lieutenant Ashley. He has been posted missing. There is no record of his having entered a POW camp, or of his being held by the German Security Forces. Indeed, there is no information about him at all. Enquiries have been instigated through the normal channels. . . . Again, so sorry. . . . If there is any news I will, of course, let you know. Some good news, however. The special parcel you delivered to me has been passed straight to the appropriate department and is receiving their immediate attention.

It was signed A. E. Smithe-Webb (Major).

She folded the letter and put it back in its envelope. She got up and paced along a narrow path that led to an old fort on the hill.

He'd said he would let her know . . . that had been four weeks ago. Since then, nothing. The silence was driving her mad. She couldn't believe there was no news at all. *Something* must have filtered through from the other side. If not about Tante Marie, then about the survivors of the *réseau.*

And about the traitor.

It must have been a traitor. It *had* to have been.

And she knew who that traitor was.

There was no proof, of course, but she *knew.*

The cool, calm major hadn't believed her. He had listened patiently but he had been doubting, politely but firmly *doubting.* He had pointed out that "Roger"—whose real name was Paul Fougères—had been vouched for and checked. Maurice had even had him personally identified. Perhaps, the major had suggested quietly, it had been someone else?

The hill steepened, but Julie kept her pace until she reached the ramparts of the old fort. She sat and lifted her face to the warm sun. The islands were quite lovely now. Most of the heathland was covered in carpets of blooms—pink, yellow, white; flowers called sea pink, thrift, hottentot fig . . .

But no amount of loveliness could make things right again.

From the top of the hill it was possible to see some of the islands to the southwest. The tip of St. Agnes and the beginnings of the Western Rocks. Hard to believe that they were the same rocks . . .

David was dead. They'd buried him in the quiet, shaded churchyard at Port Hellick on the southern side of St. Mary's, next to the dead from other shipwrecks of long ago. Every two days or so she walked there, picking a bunch of wild flowers from the hedgerows to place on his grave.

There was only one consolation for his death. His package had been delivered.

Quarter to four. Time to go and meet Peter.

At the school she waited outside the gate with the other mothers. At four sharp a door opened and the children poured out, skipping and running and making a lot of noise. Julie spotted Peter, slightly apart from the crowd, walking quietly. Her heart went out to him. He looked so lonely.

When he saw her he gave a small wave and quickened his pace. She leaned down to kiss him. "How was it, then?"

"All right."

They began to walk slowly down toward the town. "What did you do today?"

"Oh, spelling. And arithmetic . . ."

"Do you hate it terribly?"

"No," he said matter-of-factly. "It's all right."

They walked on in silence.

Julie glanced down at him. He was frowning slightly. "What is it, Peter?"

"Nothing."

But she could see he was disturbed. "Come on. Much better to tell me."

There was a long pause, then he murmured, "I had a bad dream."

"Why didn't you tell me about it before? What was it about?"

He bent his head and she knew he wasn't going to reply.

They were almost into the town, only a few yards from the lodgings. Julie didn't want to go into the boardinghouse while they were talking like this.

"Let's go and watch the water." She led him across the road and down an alleyway to the sea. They sat on the harbor wall and Julie asked again, "What was the dream about, Peter?"

Eventually he whispered, "Uncle Jean. And Tante Marie."

"And it was a bad dream?"

"There was—" The high voice faltered. "—The Germans took them away."

Julie stared out across the harbor. She often had dreams like that herself.

Peter asked, "Is that where Tante Marie is, Mummy, with the Germans?"

She replied quietly, "I don't know. I wish I did."

He was silent again, picking at the stone wall with his fingers.

Julie said impulsively, "Peter, suppose I went to London, do you think you could manage on your own for a few days? Mrs. Eldon would look after you."

He froze. "Mummy, don't go away. Please!"

She took his hand. "It would only be for a few days. Promise. I—I'm going to try to find out about Tante Marie." She added, "And maybe Richard too. If there's any news. I won't be long."

He looked crestfallen.

She added brightly, "And I tell you what, since you've finished *Swallows and Amazons*, I'll see if I can borrow another Arthur Ransome before I go in the morning. How about that?"

There was the faintest smile.

"But for now, how about helping me to send a telegram?"

Julie jumped to her feet and, holding Peter's hand, made her

529

way back to the post office. For the first time in a month, she felt almost cheerful.

Smithe-Webb looked at his watch and wondered when she'd arrive. The telegram hadn't been very specific.

She arrived in fact just ten minutes later.

As soon as Julie was announced, Smithe-Webb and his assistant, Forbes, went straight down to the main entrance.

She was waiting by the door, a slim, nervous figure pacing back and forth over the stone floor. She was wearing a dress that was shabby and rather too large for her. Refugee issue, Smithe-Webb decided. It made her look particularly vulnerable.

"Mrs. Lescaux?"

Julie spun around, as tense as a cat. Immediately Smithe-Webb noticed the wound on her head, which, though almost healed, was still conspicuous.

He put out his hand. She shook it, her enormous dark eyes searching his face. He said straightaway, "No news, I'm afraid."

She sagged visibly.

Smithe-Webb said quickly, "Look, there's a flat we use not far from here. Shall we go there and talk?"

He led her by the elbow toward the door while Forbes went ahead and hailed a cab. During the ride she didn't speak. Smithe-Webb asked politely, "How's the head? All healed up now?" She didn't answer and he didn't bother to try again.

The flat was on the fourth floor of a mansion block in Victoria. Forbes unlocked the door and said cheerfully, "What about some coffee, then?"

Smithe-Webb led the way into the sitting room. "Do sit down. *Will* you have some coffee?"

"Thank you."

She looked so thin and pale that he asked, "How about something to eat?"

"Oh. Well, if you have anything . . ."

As he'd thought—she'd had no breakfast. He told Forbes to dig up a sandwich and said to her, "Won't be a moment." He took out his pipe and tobacco pouch and began the solemn ritual of lighting up. Through the clouds of smoke he took a good look at her.

She was in a bad way, obviously very depressed. When she smiled she was probably good-looking—she had lovely eyes, a clear skin and a wide sensuous mouth. But at the moment her face was grim.

Her eyes darted up to him. "No news at all?"

"Sorry. We've put out a request about your aunt but with no one on the spot, it takes time."

"Yes, I understand." She looked at him again. "And Richard Ashley?"

Smithe-Webb examined his pipe. "I have to admit that . . . the lack of news is worrying. He still hasn't been registered as a POW."

"The Gestapo have him then."

"It's by no means certain. All sorts of things could have happened—"

"Yes—"

She was very pale, sitting motionless on the edge of her chair. Forbes came in with a plate of food and a mug of steaming liquid and put them on a side table.

She didn't move.

"You must eat!" Smithe-Webb got up and put the plate on her lap.

Mechanically, she picked up the sandwich and took a bite. The taste seemed to revive her and she began to chew. She said, "Major?"

"Yes, Mrs. Lescaux?"

Her eyes were suddenly hard and bright. "What about Roger —the man called Paul Fougères? Have you had any more news of him?"

"Apparently he was executed in Paris quite recently."

She looked startled. "You're sure?"

"Not absolutely. . . . It's hard to be definite."

She was shaking her head slowly from side to side.

"You still think it was him?" asked the major.

"Oh yes!"

Smithe-Webb raised his eyebrows and didn't reply.

"I *know* it was. As soon as you have contact with Brittany again, you'll hear it from there too, I'm sure! They'll know by now! They always find out."

Smithe-Webb cleared his throat. "I—er have heard from Rennes, through another organization—"

She sat up.

"Apparently no one has heard anything definite."

"*Nothing?*"

"There's no certainty it was a traitor."

She stared at him, thunderstruck. "But it *must* have been. Can't you find out more? Someone *must* know."

The doorbell rang, and Forbes went to answer it. "Look, I've invited a chap from the Scientific Intelligence Service who'd like to ask you a few more questions."

"About the package?"

"I expect so."

The man from SIS was round and balding with pebble glasses —just what you'd expect.

He pumped the girl's hand warmly and sat down in a chair beside her. "I'm a sort of intelligence officer—but on the scientific side," he began. "I hope you don't mind if I ask you some questions."

"Please go ahead."

The SIS man adjusted his glasses. "When Freymann told you about the—er—device, what else did he tell you? Did he say *how* he got hold of the plans, for instance?"

She thought for a moment. "As I told the major before, they were David's own plans. He'd been working on them. As I understood it, they were *his* alone."

"But did he say if anyone *else* knew about them?"

"He gave the *impression* that no one else knew. But I couldn't be sure."

"Did he mention destroying duplicate plans or anything like that?"

She shook her head. "I don't remember. The major—and the other people I talked to before—they asked me all these questions. And I'm afraid I still don't remember."

The SIS man nodded sympathetically. "It was just that you'd had a big bump on the head then, and we thought that now you were fully recovered a few things might have come back to you."

"No. Sorry. Is it really vital?"

"Yes. Very."

She thought for a moment. "I suppose you want to know if the Germans have got hold of the idea?"

"Yes, that's just what we'd like to know!"

"David's idea was a good one then?"

"Indeed."

"Oh, I'm so glad!" She smiled, the first time Smithe-Webb had ever seen her do so. It transformed her face.

She asked, "It'll be really useful then—to Britain? To the war effort?"

The SIS man licked his lips nervously and looked at Smithe-Webb, as if for assistance. "Well . . . er. In a way, yes."

Smithe-Webb thought: My God, he's made a hash of it, bloody fool.

The girl was staring at the SIS man, confusion on her face. "What do you mean—*in a way*?" She looked questioningly at Smithe-Webb, then back to the SIS man. "Can't you use it after all? I thought you said—"

"Please forgive me," the SIS man said unhappily. "Of *course* we can use it—"

"You're not telling me the truth!"

Smithe-Webb breathed in deeply and said, "What he hasn't actually mentioned, Mrs. Lescaux, is that—we already have this type of radar." He hurried on, "Now that doesn't mean that what you did was any the less important. You stopped the Germans from getting hold of Freymann and the secret, and that *was really vital.*"

A look of blank incomprehension was on her face.

He added quickly, "You see, it was vital that Freymann be brought out of France. Otherwise the Germans could have tortured the information out of him. They could have held his family prisoner and *made* him work for them!"

She murmured something. Smithe-Webb missed it and hesitated. She said again, "So it was all for nothing. All for nothing."

"No. Mrs. Lescaux. Really—" Exasperated, he turned to the scientist. "You tell her, old chap."

"What Major Smithe-Webb says is absolutely right. The Germans don't have the radar and that gives us a tremendous edge. . . . Do you see?"

"But there were other ways, weren't there?" she cried bitterly.

"Like destroying his plans so they'd never be found, like hiding him and stopping him from being caught. Instead . . . he died, trying so hard—!" She put a hand over her face.

The SIS man was on his feet looking perplexed and mildly alarmed. Smithe-Webb said, "Better go, old chap."

After the man had left, Smithe-Webb pulled up a chair and patted Julie's arm. "Now look, what Freymann did really *was* important. You do believe that, don't you?"

She took a large breath and raised her head. Eventually she said wearily, "Yes, I believe you. It was just that . . . I was so hoping that David's invention would be *useful.* In a positive way. I wanted it for him— I—I wanted him to have the *glory.*"

"I understand that. But what he did was very brave, you know. And very positive. I mean, he whisked the information away from under the Germans' noses, didn't he? They'll kick themselves when they find out."

Forbes brought in some fresh coffee and she sat drinking quietly. Smithe-Webb could see that she was thinking hard.

Suddenly she put down her cup and looked directly at Smithe-Webb. "Send me back. I want to go back."

Here it was, Smithe-Webb thought. She was bound to ask. He sighed deeply. "Mrs. Lescaux, it would be most unwise. Think about it. You'll be on the Gestapo's list of most wanted people. They'll have your photograph, your description. You couldn't go anywhere *near* north Brittany. Besides, what could you achieve there? Think about it. What could you *do?*"

"What could I do!" she exclaimed. "I'd find the others! And regroup the line! And—"

"Find the traitor—?"

She hesitated, then she said firmly, "If I could. Yes."

"Well, with all due respect, I really don't think it would be wise for you to go looking for him on your own. As for regrouping the line . . . well, I'm afraid we wouldn't want that. We wouldn't want to inflict the risk on the same village again. In fact—well, I shouldn't tell you this, but we've already got plans to operate from another part of the coast. So you see, there really wouldn't be a job for you to do. If there *had* been, you would have been the first person on our list. Really."

"So you won't send me."

"No."

"I could do special training. Wireless, guns—"

"No."

"But I could work in another district. Away from Trégasnou. Away from north Brittany altogether!"

Smithe-Webb shook his head firmly. "No, Mrs. Lescaux. You don't understand. Anyone who's been compromised—agents, members of the Resistance, it doesn't matter *who*—does *not* go back. It's an absolute rule. It's too dangerous for *others* . . ."

She whispered tightly, "I see."

She got up and walked to the window and looked out for a long time.

Eventually she turned and said rather crossly, "Don't think I've given up. I'll keep trying, you know. The Free French might send me."

"I can only tell you that no one goes to France without the approval of my superiors. And I'm sorry to say that they won't give it."

Her shoulders sagged. Smithe-Webb felt rather sorry for her, but it was for the best. She had to accept the situation.

"All right," she said quietly. "All right. But will you promise me one thing? Will you promise to get me back the moment it's possible, the moment the Germans have gone?"

He stood up and shook his head. "Well—it's jolly difficult to promise something like that. Well . . . all I can say is that I'll do my best. But I can guess how it'll be after an invasion. They'll be ferrying tons of equipment across the Channel, there won't be any room for passengers . . ."

"I'll get across *somehow*. Just promise you'll get me some papers —or whatever I need. *Please*."

She was standing close to him, looking up at him with those beautiful dark eyes. Suddenly she smiled a little. The effect was quite lovely and rather touching. Smithe-Webb softened. She *had* been very brave and MI9 *did* owe her a debt. He thought: What the hell. "All right. I'll do my best. But no promises!"

She gripped his hands. "Thank you!"

"You may have to wait a long time," he added gently.

"Yes, I know that. . . ." She nodded slowly. "A year? People are saying we'll invade in a year."

"It may well be longer."

She sat down. "I'll wait, then. For as long as I have to."

35 It was September. The *next* year.
A whole sixteen months later.

The Eighth Corps of Patton's Third Army had come and gone, sweeping the Germans before them, chasing them into the fortified west coast cities of Brest, St. Nazaire and Lorient, where they rallied to fight again . . .

Behind them the Breton countryside seemed untouched except for an occasional overturned Jeep, a few cratered roads. The fields themselves were gold with late crops and the rippling corn was largely undamaged by so much as a tire track.

In the towns it was different. The marks of war were all too evident, in the ruins of the occasional house flattened by a shell; on the facades of the buildings riddled with bullet holes; in the empty shops, almost devoid of goods; and in the general air of decay. The townspeople were different too: thinner, harder and solemn with the knowledge that their troubles were far from over. It would be a long time before they'd have money in their pockets again.

And in the wake of the Germans' departure came the reopening of old wounds—public mourning for those who had been deported, tortured, killed . . . for the hostages, the innocents, the children . . . for the loss of pride and the deep humiliation of four years of occupation.

Among some of the people there was resentment too at the new occupation. At the small groups of cocky well-fed American troops who replaced the Germans at sentry duty and on street corners and in cafés. So brash, so *alien*, so lacking in understanding, these young men, none of them realizing that all the French people wanted was to be left alone.

Left alone to their own lives and their own wars—

There were recriminations, often bitter. Against those who had

done nothing . . . against those who had helped, supported, *collaborated* . . . and not only against those who were *known* to have collaborated, but against those who *might* or *could* have collaborated . . . It was a time of innuendo, suggestion, rumor. . . . It was a time to settle old scores. Men pointed fingers at their enemies and rivals, innocent or guilty. A few were ostracized: girls who'd been seen with Germans had their hair cut off; dead men appeared in alleys, summarily executed by their peers.

Of course, most rejoiced at the new freedom; most welcomed the new era with optimism. But for many the liberation brought fresh uncertainty, renewed bitterness and, in some, a hunger for revenge.

Amazingly the old bus was still running, though because of the fuel shortage, it went only twice a day.

As it progressed slowly through the country lanes, the shudderings and roarings were as bad as ever and, from the way the vehicle juddered and rabbit-hopped, one of the gears must have given up altogether.

Julie was rather glad. She didn't want anything to have changed. She sat by the window in a seat she'd occupied dozens of times before on the endless journeys to Morlaix and back. It made her feel at home.

As the bus ground up the slight hill toward Trégasnou, she looked at the familiar countryside and felt a sense of unreality. Perhaps because she'd been dreaming about this moment for so long.

The bus stopped. Julie picked up her case and climbed out. The village seemed untouched, the small gray cottages snuggling together as cozily and firmly as ever.

There was no one about, not even nosy old Mme. Grès, who knew everyone's comings and goings. Julie strolled over to the café and paused at the door. She'd never been inside before. The interior was dark and at first she couldn't see. Then, as she put down her case, she made out the *patron* standing behind the counter, staring at her.

There was a moment's silence, then recognition spread over his face. "Madame!" he said expansively. "Welcome! Welcome!"

Julie looked around her. How extraordinary: the place wasn't frightening at all. Two men were drinking coffee at a table in the

corner, otherwise the place was empty. She walked up to the bar and placed her hands on the counter.

"Madame—welcome, welcome!" the *patron* was repeating. "Please! A little something—a glass of Pernod. Sadly we have no cognac . . ."

Julie said quietly, "No, I won't. Thank you all the same."

The *patron* waited expectantly.

Julie began, "Monsieur, my aunt . . . where is she, do you know?"

His face clouded and he said carefully, "Yes, madame. She's at Madame Boulet's. . . ." He trailed off and looked away.

"How is she?"

The *patron* shook his head. "She—er . . . she's—" He dropped his voice and whispered confidentially. "She's not of this world anymore, if you understand me. But she's being well looked after, I assure you. Madame Boulet has nursed her like a saint, like a saint!"

It was just as the War Office had informed her. Over a year ago, in a letter. She asked, "But does she know people? Does she recognize them?"

The *patron* pursed his lips. "I believe . . . I believe not *usually*, no. But I'm sure she'd recognize *you*!" He was only saying it to please her, Julie could tell.

"What about—the old group?" She saw that he knew exactly what she meant and went on, "Is there anyone left? I want to . . . get in touch."

"Ah." He raised his eyebrows and said mournfully, "Few are left, madame. Most were taken, oh, more than a year ago now—"

"Yes, I know that," she interrupted. "But is there anyone still here?"

He thought for a moment. "There's old Rannou . . . up the hill. . . . He ran a safe house. . . . Then there's Doctor Le Page in Plouagat . . . lots of Americans stayed there. . . . But"—he shrugged—"that's about it really."

Julie couldn't remember meeting either of the people he mentioned. That was because Maurice's security had been so good. "But what about the group in the village?"

"No," he whispered. "No . . . all gone. A sad day, that was . . . a sad day. . . ."

538

"Did you ever hear what happened to the British crew, from the gunboat?"

"No. . . . we never heard. We thought they must have been taken to Rennes with the others. No one ever saw them again."

She nodded. Nothing new, then.

Rennes. Everything seemed to have happened in Rennes. The Gestapo had killed Jean and Maurice and the others there. They might have taken Richard there. It would be the best place to start.

"Thank you," she murmured. "I'd better go see my aunt now. Oh—" There was something else. "The farm. What's happened to my uncle's farm?"

"The neighbors—they're looking after the animals and doing the harvesting. But the house . . . that's empty, madame."

"Yes." She imagined the house, damp, deserted and cold. She moved away from the bar. "Well, I'll go and visit my aunt now."

"Of course." The *patron* came out from behind the bar. "It must be a long time since you last saw her. A long time since you went away."

"Eighteen months," which was, Julie thought bitterly, far, far too long.

She said, "Good-bye then. And thank you."

She walked toward the door and picked up her case. Footsteps sounded on the bare wooden floor behind her and she was aware of the *patron* at her elbow. He took hold of her arm and gripped it tightly.

She looked up with surprise.

He was wildly excited, his eyes dancing.

"Yes—?" she asked.

"I quite forgot to tell you! Good news! Good news!"

She frowned. "Yes!"

"The traitor! The traitor!"

Her heart leaped. "Yes! *Yes*—!"

"They've got him!"

Her mouth dropped open. She stared, dumbfounded. "Got him . . . ?"

"Yes, they charged him in Rennes a week ago. He was in Paris, about to make a run for it. Huh! But they were on his trail all right. No trouble! They brought him back to Rennes and now

he'll pay the price!" He made a guillotine motion with his hand. "Ha! He'll pay all right!"

Julie made the effort to speak. "Who? *Who?*"

"Ah!" The *patron* was smiling and formed his lips to speak. Then quite suddenly his face froze and he put his hand to his mouth. "Madame, I quite forgot . . . oh dear God, I'm so sorry. Please, madame, prepare yourself for a shock—!"

She put her face up to his and shouted, *"Who?"*

"It's . . . Michel, madame. The Communist. Michel Le Goff. Your cousin."

Neither of the massive doors would budge. The top hinge of the right-hand door had broken, so that the door had fallen and wedged itself firmly against the other one.

The count gave a last ineffectual pull, then stood back, panting hard and feeling his age, which was seventy-two. In the old days the coachmen and grooms would have sprung forward to open the doors. In the old days a hinge would never have been allowed to fall into disrepair.

It was hopeless. These doors hadn't been opened since the beginning of the war: they obviously weren't going to open now. The count decided to give up and enter the coach house by the side door.

He made his way slowly around the wall of the coach house, which, with the stables and gardeners' cottages, was screened from the château by a long hedge, once carefully trimmed but now grown wild. Through a gap in the hedge the count noticed that another section of drainpipe had broken loose from a wall of the main house. Too bad. Like everything else it would have to wait. Repairs took money and money was the one thing he didn't have.

As he opened the side door to the coach house he wondered, not for the first time, where all the money had gone.

Stepping into the darkness, he fumbled in his pocket and lit a match. He would need an oil lamp. He went back to the château and searched the dusty, empty rooms until he found one. It took him another twenty minutes to get the lamp clean and the wick trimmed.

Back at the coach house he lit the lamp, turned up the wick and

peered into the darkness. The giant tarpaulin, once green but now gray with dust, sat humped over the massive object in the center of the floor.

It was a long time since the count had been in here. He'd rather forgotten about the coach house and its contents. He eyed the tarpaulin thoughtfully. Better get it off and start dusting and polishing straightaway. Before the war he'd never dusted or polished anything in his life but, since the staff had gone, he'd got used to all sorts of things, even cooking and washing-up.

He put down the lamp, then tugged at the tarpaulin. It was snagged somewhere. He went around the other side, freed a corner rope and pulled again. The tarpaulin slid smoothly to the floor.

The count stood back. Not bad, not bad at all. Better than he'd dared to hope.

The car gleamed magically in the flicker of the dim lamplight, its paint a deep, almost black ruby-red, which glowed warmly in the drab darkness of the coach house. The great sweep of its body reached from the rear wall almost to the doors.

It was a soft-top D8/120 Delage. His last great indulgence before the war. He'd bought it in '37, the same year he'd set up Elfie, the glorious Elfie, in an apartment in the Avenue Foch.

He sighed. Perhaps he *had* been just a little extravagant.

He found a piece of rag and began to dust the fenders and hood. When he'd finished, he eyed the car critically. The chrome-work could do with a good cleaning. There was a shelf littered with jars and cans and he searched through them for some chrome polish. Once the chrome was brightened up, he decided, the car would look very good indeed. He might even ask a bit more for it. The chap had sounded very keen: perhaps he might go as high as seventy thousand.

He wet his lips. That kind of money would tide him over nicely.

From outside came a loud hissing noise and the crunching of wheels on gravel.

The count hastily wiped his hands and went out the side door into the drive.

It was the taxi from the village, wheezing and snorting like a wild animal. Like many vehicles, it had been converted to run on gas extracted from a charcoal furnace strapped to one side. A

well-dressed young man had stepped out and was speaking to the driver.

At the sound of the count's footsteps the young man turned.

The count's gaze faltered for a moment. What an extraordinary face! It looked as if it had been horribly injured at some time: the nose had obviously been broken and the cheek and jaw bones were lopsided, giving the man's whole countenance a curiously crooked look. Thick white scars ran through the dark eyebrows and a longer, more livid scar ran down the length of one cheek.

The count stretched out a hand and smiled. "How d'you do? Monsieur Lelouche, I presume?"

"Yes." The young man hesitated, then shook the proffered hand briefly. He said immediately, "Where is the car?"

"In here." The count indicated the coach house. "Unfortunately I have not been able to get the doors open. No help, you understand. Would you care to come round the side for the moment?"

The young man said coldly, "No, let's open the doors." He beckoned to the taxi driver and together they lifted the right-hand door and swung it open. The count pulled open the other door which moved quite easily.

The car glinted brightly in the morning light, its color now revealed as a rich gleaming wine-red.

The sunlight also revealed that the count's rag had missed some patches of dust and that he had been right about wanting to clean the chromework, which looked decidedly dull. The count wished he'd started work on the car the day before.

"When was she built?"

"1937. That was when I bought her. Brand new. Hardly been used."

"How long's she been sitting in here?"

"Since the war." That didn't sound too good and the count added hastily, "She's been looked after, though. Always checked regularly, polished and so on. . . ." A lie, but then one had to embroider a little.

"And the body's by Letourneur and Marchand?"

"Oh yes, only the best."

The young man walked around the car, his eyes gleaming thoughtfully, his fingers running gently over the sleek lines. "Is it in running order?"

"It *should* be . . ."

The young man raised his eyebrows. The count had a feeling that the fellow hadn't believed a word of what he'd said. The old man's confidence began to wane: perhaps the visitor wouldn't offer such a good price as he'd thought.

The young man opened the driver's door and leaned inside to release the hand brake. The young man closed the door, went around to the front of the car and the next moment the Delage was rolling out into the sunshine.

The visitor paused for breath and remarked, "The battery's flat, I suppose?"

"Er . . . I don't know."

The young man got into the car, found the crank handle and passed it to the taxi driver, who took it to the front and started winding. Nothing happened, not even a rumble.

After fifteen minutes the young man put his head out of the window and said to the taxi driver, "Can you fetch a mechanic from the town?"

The driver nodded, and the taxi went hissing and snorting down the drive.

Lelouche came over to the count. "Shall we talk about price? Assuming the engine *does* work . . . eventually." He sounded very doubtful.

"A good idea!" The count did some quick mental arithmetic and decided that, in view of the dead engine, he'd settle for sixty thousand. He'd paid a hundred and twenty for it seven years ago. Since then prices had doubled, more or less. So in real terms he'd be getting about a quarter of what he'd paid for it. That seemed fair enough.

The two men walked slowly along the drive, toward the front of the château. The young man was considering. He said suddenly, "I'll give you twenty. Twenty thousand."

The blood drained from the count's face. He could hardly believe his ears. He said weakly, "Twenty—? But it's worth at least—*at least* fifty!"

"I don't think so." The eyes were very certain, very calm.

The count averted his gaze and said bravely, "I won't accept a sou less than forty-five!"

The young man stopped. "That's a pity. A great pity." There was contempt in the hard black eyes. The count shuffled uneasily.

"I don't think you'll find many buyers around at the moment, even at a reasonable price. And certainly none at that—unrealistic —price. There's no market for cars at the moment. None at all."

He was right. The count knew he was right. It was infuriating.

Lelouche regarded the crumbling facade of the château with apparent uninterest. "If you want a sale you'll have to be a little more realistic."

The count sighed. "Very well. But twenty thousand is *ridiculous*, monsieur. Out of the question! What's your best offer?"

Lelouche shook his head. "Twenty-five. And that's being very generous. It isn't worth any more. And that's my final offer."

The count swallowed hard. It was ludicrous, insulting! And yet without the money . . . It didn't bear thinking about. He couldn't go on living here in penury and squalor. He wanted to get back to Paris, to his friends, to the comfort of a smart apartment. . . . He was too old to change now.

He'd advertised for two months in *Auto* and this had been the only inquiry.

He shook his head. "Forty. Forty, monsieur. Not a sou less."

The young man's eyes were hard now, like bullets. "I said my final offer was twenty-five. I meant it." He turned on his heel and strode away.

The count watched in dismay as the young man walked to the coach house and leaned against the wall. The old man's heart sank. He was beaten and he knew it.

He waited a few minutes, then walked over to Lelouche with as much dignity as he could muster. "Thirty-five."

The young man sighed heavily. "I said twenty-five."

"All right! *All right!*" The count could have wept. What a waste! His lovely car, worth nothing. Nothing! Tears of humiliation and anger pricked his eyes and he sniffed loudly. He made an effort to pull himself together. Because he was an aristocrat and breeding was everything, he forced himself to smile and say, "Well, monsieur, you drive a hard bargain, I must say!"

"Do I?" The young man shrugged slightly.

For some minutes the count found it difficult to speak. He kept thinking of what one used to be able to buy with a hundred thousand francs—and how little one could get for twenty-five nowadays.

Lelouche was walking around the car again. He stopped and,

manipulating some clips, released the soft top and folded it back. He got into the car and sat at the wheel.

The count wandered over and leaned unhappily against the door. After a while the count found the silence embarrassing and, more out of politeness than interest, asked, "You'll find enough petrol to run it, will you?"

The young man's lips narrowed. "Yes, I've been saving my coupons."

The count nodded. Out of a lifetime's habit of making conversation he went on, "There's so little of everything nowadays. Food. Necessities . . . It's been a long four years. Did you have a hard war, monsieur?"

The young man dropped his eyes. "As hard as any."

"You were in the fighting?"

A slight hesitation, as if not wanting to boast, then: "Yes."

"I thought so! By your face . . . If you'll excuse my saying so."

There was a silence.

Despite the difficulty of the conversation, the count persevered. He wanted to show that he could rise above such petty considerations as resentment and hurt pride. "Which service were you in?"

Again the slight pause. "Air Force. I joined the British."

"Ah."

At that moment the taxi reappeared around the corner. The count was relieved.

It took an hour for the mechanic to clean the plugs and the points, change the oil and adjust the timing. Fortunately no actual parts were in need of replacement.

The mechanic closed the hood, wiped his hands and, with some ceremony, cranked the handle. The Delage started first time, the engine purring smoothly like a large, well-fed cat.

There hadn't been much wrong with her. The count felt sick.

The young man approached him and, without a word, counted twenty-five thousand francs off a roll that contained at least fifty.

The count took the money. "We'll need a bill of sale . . ."

"I have one." Lelouche took a document out of his pocket and, laying it on the car hood, wrote on it. Then he said, "Sign here."

The count looked at the document. It was a proper bill of sale. The young man's name, Lelouche, and an address in Paris were already entered, and he had apparently just added the car's details, the count's name and address and the date. The young man

was holding out a pen. The count took it and said, "I'll need a copy of the details."

The young man's eyes dropped. He looked cross. Eventually he said, "All right." And he tore a piece of paper out of a notebook, wrote down the details of the sale and gave them to the count.

"I'll get the car's papers," the count said. He went into the château, found the *Carnet de Route* and handed it over.

The young man walked back to the car, got in and drove off.

It was only after the low throb of the exhaust had faded around the bend in the drive that the count realized that neither the taxi driver nor the mechanic had been paid.

Clenching his teeth, the told man took the roll of bills from his pocket and counted out some money.

As soon as he was out of sight of the château, Vasson let out a great laugh of delight.

She was a beauty! Fantastic!

In need of some attention, of course. But not anything that a good mechanic, a little money and a bit of elbow grease couldn't cure.

He took the car carefully out onto the main road and concentrated on getting the feel of her. The steering was heavier than he was used to and the pedals stiffer. But it was only a question of familiarity. He pushed her gently up through the gears. Once in high he eased off the throttle and listened to the engine for signs of trouble. But she was going as sweetly as a bird. After a while he put his foot down and heard the engine note change from a steady purr to a more urgent roar. The car surged forward.

The speedometer crept up; the wind pulled at his hair and buffeted his cheeks. The tall poplars lining the road swished by, faster and faster. The long straight road stretched out ahead, empty of traffic, seductive, luring him onward.

He kept his foot down. The speedometer on the walnut dashboard read eighty . . . ninety . . . a hundred kilometers an hour.

He held his breath. His heart was almost bursting with joy and excitement. . . .

Then he lost his nerve and slowed down.

He was trembling. He laughed to himself, and shook his head.

It had been worth all the effort. And all the waiting. He'd never been so happy in his life.

Then the slowness seemed tame. He wanted the intoxication —the exhilaration—of the speed again. He pressed gently on the accelerator and felt a wave of delicious physical pleasure. . . .

Yes! This was better than anything, *anything* . . . !

He had to slow down for the villages, but on the straightaway he let her fly. . . . On and on, with no end to it.

The suburbs of Paris came too soon.

He felt a vague disappointment until he saw how people stared at the car. Then he enjoyed himself again, pretending that he hadn't noticed their glances, looking as if he'd owned the car all his life.

Oh yes! It had been worth all the waiting.

And the price—that made it even better. What a bargain it had been. Vasson couldn't believe his luck. The stupid old count was typical of his class. Useless with money. His type didn't deserve to have it in the first place.

Eventually Vasson slowed the Delage down and guided it carefully through a narrow archway, into a cobblestone yard and up to some garage doors. He jumped out, opened the doors and drove the car carefully in.

He turned off the engine and sat for a moment in the silence, reluctant to leave the soft luxury of the leather seat. When he did get out it was to touch the long lines of the hood, to admire the four external exhausts which led out of the right-hand side of the engine casing and into the fender, and to feel the fine, elegant sweep of the rear, which seemed to go on forever.

Eventually he stepped out into the courtyard and closed and locked the doors. He hated to go, but it wouldn't be for long. He'd be coming back the next day with a mechanic, to get the generator and battery problems sorted out.

Automatically he glanced around to see if anyone was watching him, but the dirty windows overlooking the courtyard were blank and anonymous. He'd been careless, he decided, driving through the Paris streets with the top down. In time it wouldn't matter who saw him but this was just a bit too soon after the occupation to be affluent. . . . Rather, he corrected himself, to be *seen* to be affluent.

Once he'd got the club going it would be different.

He walked the short distance to his apartment, the fourth he'd rented that year. It was as dingy and cheap as the others. Soon

he'd have decent quarters. But not quite yet. Again, it would be too soon.

But then, as he'd discovered with the car, the waiting would make it all the better.

He changed out of his best clothes and put on something cheaper and more casual.

Then he went out again.

It was a long journey to the *dix-huitième* by Métro; he had to change trains twice. As soon as he came out into the daylight and saw Pigalle and the familiar streets leading up to Montmartre, he felt at home.

He walked a short way up a side street until he came to an almost derelict building. There were many buildings in Paris like this at the moment, their leases unsold, their owners vanished, their occupants bankrupt. It was a perfect time to make a good deal.

Vasson had bought a forty-year lease on this property for almost nothing—but then he'd paid in gold, and gold was worth more to a seller than any amount of paper money.

He ran down the steps to the basement, found the door open and went in. The builders were there, tearing out the partition walls of what had once been a series of storerooms.

Vasson wandered around, exchanging a few words with the workmen. He wanted to establish friendly terms with them so that they'd push harder and finish the job on time and, more importantly, on budget.

He'd worked the figures out very carefully. He should get his money back within eighteen months.

He stood to one side and examined the scene. Already one could get an idea of how large the room would be. Just right. There'd be a bar in the far corner, a small dance floor and plenty of small tables. Then, the special touch . . . a girl, dancing all by herself, high up in a golden cage. Gold! He liked the irony of it.

That was what he was going to call the bar.

The Golden Cage.

An English name. Very smart. The sign would be gold on black. He'd helped to design it himself.

He smiled. It was happening at last. And what made it so satisfying was that he'd earned it all himself. Every single penny.

36 The police station was busy. People strode across the hall from one anonymous door to another, or from the main door to a sergeant sitting stoically at the front desk, and then back again. The waiting area was crowded, all the seats long taken. No one looked at Julie. She sat very still, staring at the opposite wall.

She'd been there for several hours, waiting at first, then giving her statement, and then waiting again. She would probably have to wait for most of the day, but she didn't mind; she would stay for as long as necessary.

It was almost midday. Her stomach was rumbling. She ignored it for as long as possible, then took a piece of bread out of her pocket and chewed on it. It would have to last until the evening: she could afford only one meal a day. She'd managed to save very little from the small pension the War Office had arranged for her, and most of that had gone on the train and ferry fare.

The sergeant at the desk was eyeing her with an expression of patience worn thin. He sighed heavily and beckoned. She put the bread back in her pocket and walked over.

"The commissaire's still tied up, madame. And probably will be all day. Look, we *have* the details. Every single word is in your statement. The matter will be looked into by the appropriate department—"

"But I still want to see the commissaire—"

"He won't see you, madame! He's too busy."

"Then I'll wait until he *is* able to see me. Thank you."

The sergeant shook his head and rolled his eyes.

As she returned to her seat, she felt the sergeant's despairing gaze drilling into her back. She knew what he must think of her, but the statement she had given wasn't enough. She had to be *sure*.

She tried to sleep, but it was difficult: the chair was narrow and uncomfortable. Finally she managed to doze, dreaming strange disturbing dreams which blended in with the sounds in the hall so that she couldn't tell what was real anymore.

Then she sat and thought about Peter and how he was getting on without her. Later, she dozed again. The hours were interminable.

When she next looked at her watch it was nine in the evening. It had been a long day. To get to Rennes by nine that morning she had left Mme. Boulet's before dawn. Now she had missed the last bus back to Morlaix.

A door opened. Laughter came drifting through. That's all they were probably doing, Julie thought angrily, telling jokes!

She strode over to the desk. The sergeant looked up wearily. She said, "Please—ask again! Please!"

The sergeant made a face. "They already know you're here. There's no point. Anyway"—he looked at a clock—"the commissaire's hardly likely to see you now. He's had a long day."

"But he's still here?"

The sergeant had been caught out and he didn't like it. He pressed his lips firmly together. Julie said, "I'll wait then," and went back toward the chair. She looked for other vacant chairs to pull together for a couch, but there were none. On an impulse she lay down on the floor, put her handbag under her head and closed her eyes. It was much more comfortable.

There was a hush. People paused in the hall. Someone was approaching. "Madame, get up, please." It was the sergeant's voice.

She didn't reply.

"Madame, do you want me to move you by force?"

She opened her eyes and said, "No. But I must stay. I'm sorry." Beyond the sergeant's legs she saw people staring and quickly closed her eyes again.

There was a pause, then the footsteps receded. Julie breathed deeply. She was beginning to regret her impulse. They'd probably throw her out.

After a while the footsteps returned. "Madame, get up. Now, please."

"No." She could hardly believe she had said it.

He growled, "Come with me. *Please.*"

She held her breath.

The sergeant dropped his voice. "To see the commissaire, madame. That's what you wanted, isn't it?"

Julie opened her eyes. He meant it. She got to her feet, triumphant. The sergeant was already walking toward one of the doors. She followed him hurriedly, her eyes on the floor to avoid the curious gazes of the onlookers.

She was shown straight into an office marked COMMISSAIRE DE POLICE. Behind the desk sat a dark man in shirt sleeves, a cigarette in his mouth, a plump belly protruding toward the desk. For several moments he viewed Julie through heavy-lidded eyes. Eventually he indicated that she should sit down. Then he said, "Well, madame, I hear that you've been disrupting the entire police station. May I ask why?"

"I had to see you."

"Yes?"

"It's about Michel Le Goff!"

The commissaire raised an eyebrow. "What about him?"

"He's innocent. He was on our side. I can swear to that!"

"Indeed?" The tone was sardonic.

Julie paused, slightly nonplussed. She pressed on: "He's not guilty of the crimes he's charged with. He must be freed!"

"Ah." He glanced down at some papers on his desk. "And this is the evidence you are presenting?"

She peered over the desk. "Is that—?"

"Your statement."

So he had seen it after all. She had been certain it would be ignored or forgotten. She murmured, "Yes. That's my evidence."

"Would you like to go over it again? Now?"

She could hardly believe her luck. "Yes!" She took a deep breath. "I was a member of the *réseau* led by the agent known as Maurice, at Trégasnou. I interrogated the parcels—the airmen, I mean. And . . . I did beach duty . . . and all kinds of jobs. I was with the group for over a year. . . ."

The commissaire said solemnly, "You were very patriotic, madame. And very courageous."

Julie blinked at the unexpected compliment. "Anyway, Michel Le Goff helped us. A lot. He got a very important scientist out of

551

a factory in Brest and delivered him to us and then, when everything went wrong and the Boches closed in, he helped us to
escape—"

"Helped who exactly?"

"Me. And my son. And this scientist from the factory . . ."

"No one else."

"Well—no. The others had already been caught."

"Go on."

Julie stared at him. "That was it. I mean, he was on our side.
His actions prove it. . . . He gave us his boat, he risked his life
. . . I know him. I don't believe he betrayed us!"

The commissaire said gently, "Why not?"

"I'm sorry?"

"Why couldn't he have betrayed you? Or rather, the others?"

Julie thought hard. "Because—because he saved us."

"He saved *you,* madame." The slightly mocking tone was back
in his voice. "Tell me, what was your relationship with Michel Le
Goff?"

"He was—*is*—my cousin. A distant cousin by marriage, in fact.
But that means nothing. Half the people in the village are
related."

"Nothing more?"

Julie felt herself blushing. "Certainly not! Whatever you're
implying, it wasn't like that! Not at all!"

The commissaire looked at her dispassionately. "If you say so,
madame."

There was a knowing look on his face. Julie glared back at him,
hating herself for blushing, hating him for not believing her.

She made an effort and said calmly, "My evidence will go before the examining magistrate, won't it?"

"Yes. But there is a great weight of evidence against Le Goff.
He will go to trial, I can assure you."

"What evidence?"

"People—reliable people—heard him swear to get his revenge
on your *réseau.* Apparently he believed that they were responsible
for his comrades getting caught in Brest—on that evening, when
the scientist was being removed from the factory."

Julie frowned. He knew it all.

"Also, he was seen in the company of informers from time to
time. Believe me, he was trouble. Always."

Julie said quickly, "But what about the others—in my *réseau*? There were plenty of others who might have betrayed us. Have you looked into them? Have you *interrogated* them?"

"Madame, the Germans left only six weeks ago. We've had very little time. We have dozens of people coming in every day. You saw them out there! All of them have so-called information. Most of it's sour grapes and make-believe! There are hundreds of cases under investigation. . . ."

He raised a finger. "However, we *have* done some work on this particular case and we *have* followed up the obvious leads. Many of your *réseau* died, as we know. Here in Rennes. Others, we can tell from the Gestapo records, were sent to Germany." He threw out his hands in an expansive gesture. "Whether they are still alive or not we do not know. We *cannot* know until Germany is defeated."

"What about Fougères?" she demanded.

"Ah! The man you accuse." He said with emphasis, "He died, madame. In Fresnes. Well over a year ago. We have confirmation from Paris."

Julie stared in disbelief. "There was no doubt it was him?"

Without a word the commissaire got up and went into an adjacent office. A few minutes later he came back with a file and flicked through it. "Fougères was seen by two other prisoners before he died. They were positive it was him."

"When? When did the prisoners see him?"

The commissaire looked at the file. "In approximately April last year."

It was about the time Jean and the others had died. It seemed to fit. . . . "But why was he taken to Paris when none of the others were?"

"I cannot say at this stage." He started to shuffle the papers on his desk. The interview was clearly over. "I'm sorry, madame. Now if you'll excuse me, I have a lot of work to do."

She stood up. "But, but—there's more. I must know if you have information about the British crew! The men off the boat, the ones who were captured at the same time—"

"British—?" He sucked in his breath and shook his head. "No. Foreign sailors would have been prisoners of war, and we don't deal with them. You should try the Americans. They might know."

"But the crew were brought *here,* to Rennes. To the *prison.*"

"Sorry. Any record of foreign prisoners would be in the hands of the Americans. Really, you must go and see them."

"I have." And there had been nothing, no trace. It was as if Richard and his men had vanished.

"Ah." The commissaire tapped his fingers on the desk. "I really must get on now. If you please, madame!"

"At least let me see my cousin!"

The policeman stood up. "Quite impossible. At least not without permission from the examining magistrate. Applications take days and even then I doubt you'd be allowed to see him. People charged with treason don't get visitors! Good-bye, madame."

She lingered, reluctant to leave.

The policeman was getting impatient. "I'll have you shown to the main hall." He called to someone in the next office, then sat down and studied the papers on his desk.

Julie said quickly, "Monsieur . . . will you be interrogating him again?"

"What—?" He looked up vacantly. "Probably, yes."

"Couldn't you face him with *me*? With someone from the group he is supposed to have betrayed? Wouldn't that be useful?"

The commissaire was way ahead of her. He shook his head. "Madame, really—"

"But it might help your interrogation considerably!"

He looked at her quizzically. "In what way?"

"He might talk freely."

"You read too much fiction!"

"But you have nothing to lose! *Please.*"

"Madame, I just cannot—!"

But she nearly had him, she knew it. She leaned over the desk and said passionately, "He'll answer questions from me, I *know* he will!"

The commissaire regarded his hands, then shot a glance at her. He sighed and shook his head unhappily. "You win. Be here at eight tomorrow morning."

Julie clasped her hands together.

"But remember this! It's only because you were in the Resistance. No other reason! And whatever you do, don't tell anyone I let you see him. All right?"

"I promise!"

Julie closed the door behind her, pleased to have achieved something at last.

Then she remembered it was a very small victory and there was still a long way to go.

The prison was large and somber and forbidding, its high walls dotted with small barred windows from which escape was clearly impossible.

Inside it was worse. Dark and terrible, rank with the smell of humanity and suffering and untold horrors; yet hauntingly silent, as if empty of inhabitants.

A warder led the way down a series of long gloomy passages whose walls threw off a palpable cold. Julie shivered involuntarily.

"Not so good, eh?" remarked the commissaire. "They haven't done much to it since the Germans left. But then most of the new inhabitants are collaborators and black marketeers . . . so—" He shrugged.

They came to a door. The warder unlocked it. The commissaire said, "Wait here until you're called," and disappeared.

Julie leaned against the wall in despair. Her mind was full of terrible visions, of Jean and Maurice and Gérard and Jacques and the others.

Here.

The Gestapo had brought them *here.* She wanted to know nothing—no details. Not where their cells had been, or the place where they'd been tortured, or the courtyard where they'd been taken to die.

The door was opening. "Come in!"

Hesitating slightly, she stepped inside. The room was large and almost bare, and dimly lit by a single barred window. There was a table in the center. Michel was sitting on the far side of it.

He looked up, startled. She thought: They didn't tell him I was here.

She smiled faintly. "*Salut,* Michel."

He stared at her, confusion and amazement on his face.

The commissaire said abruptly, "Madame, can you identify this man?"

"Yes, he is Michel Le Goff."

"And do you affirm that he arranged the escape of the scientist, Freymann, from the factory of Goulvent, Pescard et Compagnie in Brest?"

Julie sharpened her wits. She hadn't realized it was going to be like this. She looked at Michel for help, but he was still staring at her. As she brought her eyes back to the commissaire's, Julie noticed that there was a young man in the corner, taking notes on a shorthand pad. She would have to be careful.

She replied slowly, "He was the contact—between his group and ours. I don't know if he actually arranged the escape."

"But as contact man, he knew certain facts about your group? The mode of operation, the people involved?"

Julie said firmly, "No! He knew nothing. Maurice was very careful!"

"Your leader?"

"Yes."

"But perhaps you told Le Goff certain things—?"

"What things do you mean?"

"Things about the group."

"No!"

"Consider very carefully . . . I will ask you again. Perhaps Le Goff discovered certain facts about your group. Perhaps you mentioned certain things without realizing—?"

"No!" Julie said angrily. "He knew nothing!"

"Then how did he know where to find you when you were hiding on the beach? How did he know *which* beach to go to?"

She hesitated. This was becoming a nightmare. "It . . . must have been through my uncle. Jean must have asked Michel for help and then told him where to find us."

There was a pause. Julie looked to Michel for confirmation, but she had the feeling he wasn't really listening.

The commissaire asked, "After he'd collected you from the beach, he took you to a fishing boat that he kept hidden in Kernibon?"

"Yes."

"And you escaped on it?"

"Yes."

"Did he say why he had a fishing boat?"

Julie blinked. "No. I supposed it was to escape if the Boches got onto him."

556

"But suddenly he felt no need of it and gave it to you. I wonder why he should do that?"

"Because—we were in desperate need. The Gestapo were looking for us . . . they would have killed us. He gave it to us because he was *kind*. He wanted to help."

"Indeed . . . or perhaps because he had just done the Boches a favor and felt safe. So safe he wouldn't be needing the boat anymore and could afford to be generous to his—friend?"

Julie felt herself turning scarlet. She wanted to step up to the commissaire and slap his big, fat face. Instead she said quietly, "That is not true. None of it is! He wasn't the traitor! I've told you who was—it was the man Fougères."

The commissaire ignored her remark. "Is there any more evidence that you can offer?"

She said quietly, "No."

"That will be all, thank you."

Julie caught hold of the commissaire's arm. "Please," she whispered, "can I have a few words with him in private?"

The policeman's eyes were cold. "No, madame."

"Not in private, then. With *them* present." She indicated the warder and the man with the pad.

The commissaire was considering. Eventually he said grudgingly, "All right! But no more than five minutes." He turned abruptly and the warder let him out of the door.

Quickly, Julie sat down at the table. "How are you?"

Michel shook his head. "You shouldn't have come."

"But why not?"

"Because . . ." He shrugged. "It won't do any good!"

"No! Don't say that! We'll—"

He interrupted, "How's Tante Marie?"

Julie shook her head. "Not—well. She hardly knew me."

"And Peter?"

"He's fine. I left him in the Scillies. But, Michel, we haven't much time. Please tell me how I can help you!"

"The boat. It got you to England all right then?"

"Not quite," Julie said unhappily. "It was wrecked. It was my fault."

"You did well to get there at all."

Time was slipping away. She said urgently, "What *can* I do to help you?"

"Help me? I think no one can. They're out to get me, and they will. One way or another." He smiled but there was a hint of false bravado in it.

"But there must be evidence! Michel, who really did it, do you know?"

He laughed. "You ask *me*?" He shook his head. "How should I know? All I can say is it wasn't one of mine."

She gripped his hand. "I believe it was a man called Fougères. A stranger on the line. He came from Paris and was supposed to have survived the Meteor collapse. But I always distrusted him!"

"And what's happened to him, does anyone know?"

She withdrew her hand. "They *say* he's dead. But—"

He gave a small shrug as if he'd expected it.

Julie said crossly, "You've given up hope!"

"I'm a realist, that's all."

She sighed deeply. "Michel, what can I do for you when you won't give me any help!"

"Don't concern yourself, Julie. My friends are doing what they can. They're asking around . . ."

"Have they found out anything?"

"I'm not sure."

"How do I find these friends?"

For a moment she thought he wasn't going to answer, then he said, "In Paris, a bar called Chez Alphonse. Ask for Pierre."

She nodded. "I'll do everything I can. Everything!"

There was a pause. He asked, "Have you any money?"

Her face fell. "Not much."

"If you can get into my apartment you'll find some hidden under the bottom plate inside the oven. Just pry it up. All right?"

She nodded. "I'll return any I don't need."

He gave a bitter laugh. "It's not important." A strange look flashed into his eyes—a look of fear and despair. It sent a chill through Julie's heart.

The warder said, "Time up!" and moved toward the door.

Hurriedly, she touched his hand. "I've never really thanked you for what you did. The boat . . . and getting us from the beach . . ." She shook her head. "You should have kept the boat and got away. . . ."

"No, you needed it more." He stood up and pushed the chair

into the table. He smiled and his grave, lined face looked a little less severe. "Take care!"

"I'll do everything I can—"

"Sure."

He then turned quickly and walked to a door on the opposite side of the room. Though she waited an instant, he never looked back.

37 It was almost as if there had never been a war. The city lay pale and gleaming under the late September sun, its long boulevards and elegant buildings apparently unscarred by bombs and bullets. Julie was faintly surprised: it was so different from the devastation of London.

When one looked closer, however, one could see signs of the long occupation: years of deprivation and neglect had left buildings in urgent need of repair; the streets were littered and uncleaned; and walls were daubed with slogans or, in some cases, with rough white crosses where people had died.

Nevertheless, the atmosphere was festive. Even the shabbiest buildings were draped with bright flags—many of them homemade. More than a month after the city's liberation the bright colors of the Stars and Stripes and the Union Jack still hung from dozens of balconies. But, brighter, taller, prouder than these was the Tricolores, flying high above the rooftops of a hundred buildings, a symbol of many things, but to most Parisians a symbol, above all, of freedom.

Julie found a room at a small hotel in the *treizième,* then went in search of the place called Chez Alphonse. It wasn't listed in the telephone directory, but a shopkeeper knew it and gave her directions. It was a small bar, narrow and dim, its walls yellow with nicotine. When she asked for Pierre, the bartender told her Pierre

might not be in for days, but it should be possible to send him a message. Julie composed a short note on the back of an envelope and left it with the bartender. He told her there was no point in coming back until much later, at about nine.

It was only five. Julie went to a *brasserie* and ordered a meal. It was difficult to make rabbit stew last four hours, but she managed it, by ordering coffee afterward, then water and then coffee again. The bread coupon she'd proffered entitled her to a full three-course meal, but she wanted to economize. She had money—she'd taken Michel's from the hiding place in the oven and there had been quite a bit—but she didn't want to squander it, not only because it might have to last a long while but because it was Michel's.

To pass the time Julie watched the people in the street. The Parisian women were incredibly well dressed, though how they managed it when materials were so short amazed her. They made Julie feel inadequate and inelegant; her frumpy, secondhand suit was dowdy by comparison. She tried hard not to mind but failed.

At last it was almost nine and Julie headed back toward the bar. The streets were busy. Everyone seemed to be out for a stroll, talking in groups or wandering in and out of cafés.

Chez Alphonse was crowded and noisy, the atmosphere thick with smoke. The barman was busy, and it was some minutes before she managed to catch his eye. He nodded to a man at the far end of the bar who stood up and came over to Julie.

He smiled and said, "I'm Pierre." He was about forty, fair and boyish and jolly-looking: not at all the way Julie had imagined a hard-core Communist to look. He took her elbow and said above the noise, "Come. We can't talk here. Let's go for a stroll."

As they began to walk slowly up the street, Pierre said, "So! They're still trying to hang everything on Michel, are they?"

"I'm afraid so."

"He always made enemies, Michel. Always attracted trouble, even in the old days."

"The old days?"

"At university. I was his tutor."

Julie looked sideways at him. She asked, "Have you found out anything? That might help Michel?"

He shook his head. "Nothing. I've asked around—my friends in the police and so on. But no rumors, nothing. Mind you, the

authorities have their hands full at the moment, sorting out the black marketeers from the collaborators, and the collaborators from the informers." He snorted. "Most of the real villains will get clean away, of course. They'll have covered themselves well and in a little while they'll pop up as magistrates and bankers and swear they were never Fascists."

They came into a wide boulevard full of light and activity and crowded cafés.

Julie said, "The traitor, the man I'm looking for, he came from Paris. At least I'm fairly sure he did. *Someone* must have known him . . . or seen him. His name was Fougères."

"The name means nothing. He probably used a hundred different names. Do you have a photograph?"

Julie shook her head. She wished she had. But when she had prepared the identity cards she was always careful not to keep any spare photographs. It was maddening when she thought about it now.

"Never mind. Let's go and see what we can find." He quickened his pace.

"Find? Where are we going?"

"I'm not promising *anything*, but there's someone you should see. Someone who might know something."

Julie ran a little to keep up. "Who?"

Pierre gave a short laugh. "Ah . . . well, you see, we like to help the police out. In our own small way."

Julie was confused.

"We've caught ourselves someone. Someone who might otherwise have avoided the full force of justice."

Julie tensed. "Who?"

"An informer."

"And he might have known—"

Pierre said firmly, "Not necessarily. But he knew the Gestapo well enough. He worked for them for at least two years. He might have heard something about your man, you never know. Anyway, let's go and see."

Julie tried to absorb the full meaning of what Pierre had said. This informer—would he have known about other informers? Would they have met? It seemed very unlikely. And would they have had the same contacts? Again, it seemed unlikely. She decided not to raise her hopes too high.

She found the idea of the captured informer disturbing; she couldn't help wondering what they would do with him afterward. She wanted to ask more questions, but in the glow of the occasional light Pierre's face looked stern and unboyish and she decided against it.

They walked in silence for ten minutes, into a darker quieter area with few cafés or restaurants. Julie had no idea where they were. Eventually they came to a tall, red-brick apartment building.

Pierre guided her into a narrow alleyway at the side and then to some steps which led down to a cellar. The alley was dark, filthy and oppressive. Julie hung back.

Pierre turned. "It's all right. Just follow me."

He went down the steps and knocked softly on a door at the bottom. After a long pause, the door opened slightly. Pierre put his head to the crack, murmured a few words, and the door swung open.

Julie entered, half-frightened of what she might see.

It was a bare cellar, cold and damp, its floor scattered with rubbish. A blinding electric light hanging on a wire from the ceiling cast a pool of white over the center of the room, leaving the walls in deep shadow.

Immediately under the light was a chair. A man was sitting on it. He was bound to the chair by a rope which had been passed several times around his chest, pinning his arms to his sides. The front of his shirt was covered with blood which seemed to have come from his face, though it was impossible to be sure because his head was lying forward on his chest.

Pierre strode across and, grasping the man's hair, raised his head. Julie gasped. The face was a mess, the nose bloody and the eyes blackened.

She stared hard for several moments.

Then she exhaled.

She had never seen the man before in her life.

She kept looking, just to be sure. But there was no doubt of it.

"You don't recognize him?" Pierre asked.

"No."

Pierre let the head fall again. "No reason why you should."

There were two other men in the room, the one who had

opened the door and another who came up to Pierre and said under his breath, "I think we've got the lot. Shall we—?"

Then they were whispering and Julie couldn't hear any more. Eventually the conversation finished and Pierre came back to her. The man in the chair jerked his head up and moaned. Julie held her breath. Then he slumped forward again.

She asked, "What exactly did he do?"

"He was a little sneak, a telltale. . . . He shopped people to the Gestapo. For money. Not much money, either! That's because he enjoyed doing it!" He shouted, "Didn't you, you, *con*? Eh!"

The figure in the chair whimpered and rocked his head from side to side.

"But he doesn't enjoy it so much now." Pierre snorted. "His national socialist principles didn't last very long. In fact, he's prepared to swear to anything just at the moment."

The figure began to wail, a continuous whine that rose and fell like a dog howling in the night.

Pierre regarded the sight with distaste. "Four of my comrades died because of him."

"I'm sorry."

"It's always the spineless little shits who do the damage. Look at him! He's terrified!"

Julie shook her head. "Our traitor wasn't like that. He was clever . . . hard . . . and cunning. Not like that."

"Ah. Well, let's find out what this creature knows."

Pierre went up to the chair and pulled up the man's head again. "Your masters sent someone to Brittany. Do you know who? *Do you know who?*"

The man shook his head from side to side, his eyes were wide with fear. "No . . . no . . . Brittany . . . no!"

Julie stared, repelled by the bloody face.

Pierre was getting impatient. He waved to one of the other men. "Encourage him, Charles, will you?"

"No, please!" Julie exclaimed.

Pierre paused in surprise.

Finally he shrugged. "All right. If you wish." He said to the figure in the chair, "The lady is kind. She doesn't want you to suffer. Tell her what she needs to know, eh? Otherwise we'll go

back to the other way. Tell her! Who else did your masters use? Who was sent to Brittany? *Eh?*"

The wild eyes swiveled around and fastened on Julie's face. The mouth opened and closed, like a fish's. Eventually the man whined to Julie, "They're—going—to—kill me!"

Julie looked to Pierre for help. He said roughly, *"Tell the lady what she wants to know."*

"I know n-nothing! *Nothing!* I was innocent! The Gestapo blackmailed me. They forced me into it. Save me! *Please! Please!*"

She said quietly, "If you could tell me what you know . . . I'd be grateful."

The man gulped. ". . . I heard very little. They were *very* careful. They forced me to tell them things, then they made me go away. *Really.*" He was sobbing.

The sight was pathetic, cruel. Julie forced herself to remember that this man was a murderer, just like Fougères. She pressed, "But gossip . . . rumors . . . there must have been *something.*"

"I can't think . . . I can't think!"

Pierre said roughly, "Who was in charge of informers?"

"Kloffer."

"And did Kloffer ever talk about his—agents?"

"No! Kloffer was too grand for me. I never talked to Kloffer! I wasn't important enough! I wasn't one of their informers. I only dealt with stockings, perfume—I was never an informer. Never!"

Pierre said to Julie, "He's lying," and made a sudden movement toward the chair. The man jerked back his head in terror.

"Who *did* you deal with then?" Pierre demanded.

"There was a sergeant—and a junior officer. *Not* important people. They never told me *anything.*"

"Try harder."

"Oh please, *please!*" He was whining again. Suddenly he stopped. After a long pause, he gulped and said, "The sergeant . . . he was in charge of false papers. I never had any, of course! I was only a black marketeer. I wasn't important enough. But . . . others did."

Pierre urged, "Others?"

"No names were ever mentioned. Never. But—once or twice I heard things. F-from the sergeant mainly. He'd talk about successes. Things they'd found out, groups they'd smashed, th-that

sort of thing. There was one man, a t-top man, someone who w-worked for them all the time . . ."

Julie held her breath. "*Yes—?*"

". . . The tip of one of his fingers was m-missing! So the sergeant said. . . ."

The man desperately searched Julie's face for a sign that he had said the right thing. She looked at Pierre and shook her head.

Pierre said coldly, "No good, *con.*" He began to move away. "That's it then."

"*No-o-o! Please, I beg you.*" Then he began talking so fast that Julie missed the first few words. ". . . And there was another. Someone they gave false papers to all the time. He was important, I knew. He'd started as a dealer, like me. Then he became an informer. The sergeant talked about him a couple of times. I never heard a name, never a *name.* But they called him the Marseillais. Or the Man from Marseilles. Something like that."

A Marseillais. Julie tried to recall Fougères's accent. It had been educated, without, as far as she could tell, any regional accent. Not very likely, then.

She asked, nevertheless, "Did this sergeant ever say what this Marseillais had done exactly? What sort of jobs?"

The prisoner's head fell to one side and she thought he was going to faint. "Infiltration. His s-speciality. Very s-successful . . ." The puffed eyes reopened. "*Réseaux* . . . he got inside an escape line . . . for airmen . . ."

Julie stiffened and put her face up to the prisoner's. "Which line?" She took him by the shoulder and shook him. "Which line?"

"I don't know."

"Was it Meteor? Was it? Or ours in Brittany?"

"I don't know . . ." The man's voice trailed off. He had fainted.

Julie stood for a while, watching him.

Pierre took her aside. "It's not much."

"No." It was almost nothing. She asked, "What about this Kloffer? Was he captured?"

Pierre shook his head. "No! The Gestapo were the first people to disappear. He'll be holed up in Germany by now, planning his excuses."

Julie looked back at the man in the chair. "What about him?"

Pierre murmured, "We'll decide later."

He went to the door. "Here, I'll see you back." As she stepped

out into the cool night air a howl rose behind her. Julie clenched her fists and walked quickly up the steps toward the street.

Pierre caught up with her and they walked in silence for a while. Eventually he asked, "What will you do now?"

"I don't know."

"Will you go back to Brittany?"

"There doesn't seem much point. Fougères wouldn't have gone back there."

"So you'll stay in Paris?"

She sighed heavily. "I suppose so."

"Then keep in touch. I might hear something. The police might come across your man, you never know. He probably shopped a lot of other people too. It's bound to catch up with him sooner or later. I'll leave messages at Chez Alphonse from time to time. Okay?"

"Yes."

"And I'll ask about this Marseillais. Perhaps if he really *was* important he might be your man."

She stopped and looked at him. "The one back there. Couldn't you give him to the police?"

Pierre's face was sad and cold. "What would *you* do if he had killed *your* friends?"

Julie looked away.

When they came to a street which Julie recognized, she said, "I can find my own way from here."

They said brief good-byes and separated. Julie walked back to the hotel, deeply depressed. She went straight to bed and lay awake most of the night, thinking.

The next day she returned to Chez Alphonse. There was no message.

She returned every evening for a week, after long days spent at police stations, military headquarters and obscure departments of the new French government.

Nothing. No information on the Marseillais. No information on someone who might, at one time or another, have called himself Fougères.

The other branches of the Resistance could not help either. Fougères? No, he had been one of their own. He had never betrayed anyone. Had someone impersonated him then? They didn't know. Fougères had disappeared when the Gestapo made

it too hot for him in Paris. He'd phoned a friend and said he was going to Brittany. Description—yes, tall and dark, that was Fougères. He was long dead now, taken from Fresnes and shot at Mont Valérien.

But they would make more inquiries. No traitor would stay alive and unavenged while they still lived. If she ever heard a whisper about the true identity of the Brittany traitor, she had only to contact them—

On the eighth day there was a message at Chez Alphonse. It said: "No trace of anyone known as the Marseillais. Nothing on any other informers. Sorry. Pierre."

That night in bed she spent a long time thinking about the number of infiltrators the Gestapo might have used on a regular basis—was it a few? Or a dozen?

And what made one of those infiltrators really successful, so successful that he stood out from the rest?

By the morning she thought she knew, and she made her decision.

The woman was leaning over him, her face leering and cruel. He laughed, loud and triumphant. He tried to move but she held him in a viselike grip. He couldn't *believe* how strong she was.

He tried to call out. But however hard he tried his lips wouldn't move.

He made a superhuman effort to get free.

His limbs were heavy and useless. They wouldn't move either!

She was killing him now, slowly but surely. Covering his face, squeezing his neck . . . He gasped for air, cried for breath . . . *sucked* for the precious air . . .

But she squeezed tighter.

He was panicking now. The blood was roaring and singing in his head.

He was *desperate* for air. . . .

Death rushed up to him, nearer and nearer. He *sensed* it coming. . . .

And all he could think was: It's not *fair*.

Then she was laughing again, the sound fading and swirling in the distance. Everything was fading . . .

With a terrible shock he realized he had slipped over the edge of a precipice and was falling down and down . . .

Oh Christ! I'm so frightened. Maman, help!

Maman!

He woke up sweating and murmured, *"Merde!"*

He looked up at the ceiling and tried to calm himself.

What a stupid thing. He hadn't had a dream like that for a long time. Why should it come back now?

There must be a reason.

He rolled over and, taking a cigarette from a packet lying on the floor, lit it thoughtfully.

No, there was no reason for the dream.

It usually came when things were going badly. But nothing was going badly at the moment. In fact, everything was going very well. . . .

Perhaps he'd overlooked something. Quickly he went over everything in his mind: the club, the permits, the financial calculations, the details—always the details.

He'd forgotten nothing.

Still, that dream bothered him. He hated its power over him.

Angrily he stubbed out his cigarette.

He closed his eyes and tried to think of all the good things that were happening, like the car and the new suit he had bought. Yes, there were *lots* of good things.

The dream meant nothing.

No one would ever find him.

He was safe.

The dream belonged to the past. And the past was locked safely away.

38 The Man from Marseilles.

Julie looked at the people milling around the station and thought: But they're all from Marseilles!

She picked up her case and walked out of the station into the

street. Though it was barely nine, the sun was blazing out of an empty sky. She hadn't realized it would be so warm in October. Her woolen suit felt too hot.

She was standing in a wide boulevard, busy with cars and an occasional horse-drawn vehicle. She was struck immediately by the noise—the honking of the horns and the loud conversations —and by the color: the people seemed brighter, more exotic. It was partly their clothes and partly the different races—Arab, Senegalese and Asian.

She looked around blankly. She wasn't sure where to start.

She crossed the boulevard and began to wander down what seemed to be a main street. After a while she paused. This sort of wandering would do no good; she had to do something positive.

The police first, then. She stopped and asked a shopkeeper for directions to the nearest police station.

It was not far—five minutes away—but it was the wrong police station. She needed the Police Judiciaire—the criminal investigation branch.

It was a long walk and her case was heavy. She stopped and removed her jacket. She should have done it before: her blouse was damp with sweat.

It took half an hour to find a sufficiently senior officer and explain what she wanted.

Then they laughed at her as she had known they would. Not rudely or unkindly, but politely, with a shake of the head.

"A man called the Marseillais? Madame, have you any idea how many characters are called by that name?"

But they did let her look at the rogues' gallery. There were vast numbers of wanted men and ex-convicts. After three hours one face began to look much like another and Julie lost heart. Why should she find him there anyway? He probably had no criminal record. Nevertheless, before she left, she arranged to come back the next day, just in case.

She ate a late lunch in a pavement café then, taking a slip of paper from her purse, made a telephone call. The number belonged to a friend of the Paris Resistance: a man called Alain.

The number rang. A woman's voice replied.

"I want to speak to Alain, please."

"You mean Doctor Hubert? I'm afraid he is at the hospital at present. Please try later."

Julie rang off. They hadn't told her he was a doctor. She decided to try again in the evening.

In the meantime she had the rest of the afternoon to spare. When the waiter brought coffee, she said, "I'm a stranger to the city. Can you tell me where I am? In relation to the center?"

"La Canebière is about five minutes away. Down there." He pointed with his hand.

"And that's the center?"

"It's the main street."

"And where would I find a reasonably priced hotel? I mean— a cheap one?"

The waiter shrugged. "All kinds of places. But nearer the harbor is probably your best bet."

"Where's that, please?"

"Turn right at La Canebière. It's at the far end."

She found La Canebière immediately, a wide street full of shops and restaurants. It looked a long way to the harbor and she boarded a bus. After five minutes she glimpsed the water, got off and walked the last few yards, over the road ringing the harbor, to the quayside.

The harbor lay before her, its waters pale and tranquil, crowded with fishing boats and trading ships. To the left the city rose in an orderly jumble of multicolored buildings to a magnificent church, the famous Notre-Dame-de-la-Garde which Julie had seen in photographs.

To the right there was a quay. . . . She frowned.

Then there was nothing. For quite a long way.

It looked like a giant demolition site.

Julie picked up her case and walked over, trying to imagine what could have happened to the place.

She climbed what had once been a narrow street of houses. Now there was little more than a mass of masonry, splintered wood and an occasional door or window lying crushed and forlorn on its side. The place was disconcerting, like a graveyard. Here and there were makeshift stalls and shops constructed out of the ruins, where traders—Arabs, mostly—were sitting waiting

for business. There were shanties too, with smoke coming from their roofs and washing hanging outside.

At the top of the street was a junction with a larger road. On the opposite side were buildings again, more people, and order.

She took a last look at the extraordinary wasteland and crossed the street to the normality of the other side.

She was hot and very tired. The first hotel she came to was run-down and dirty, the second had a girl standing provocatively on the doorstep, and the third looked dark and uninviting. She decided on the third because she couldn't face going any farther; her arm was at breaking point. She should have left her case at the station.

The room they gave her was clean and tidy and perfectly adequate. She lay down and rested her aching feet until six, when she went in search of a phone.

The doctor still wasn't in. Would she like to leave a message?

Julie hesitated, instinctively reticent. Then she remembered that the war in France was over and there was no more need for secrecy. She said, "Tell him a friend from the Resistance called." She left her name and the number of the hotel.

The next morning there was a message. Dr. Hubert would come to the hotel at twelve.

She spent the morning with the Police Judiciaire, looking at more pages of photographs. Still nothing. She wondered if she'd recognize him even if she saw him.

She got back to the hotel breathless and fifteen minutes late. An elderly man who had been sitting in a chair beside the reception desk rose to his feet with some difficulty.

She asked in surprise, "Doctor Hubert?"

He bowed slightly. He was at least sixty, probably more, and was painfully thin, with a marked stoop. He was leaning heavily on a stick.

She said hurriedly, "I'm sorry I'm late."

"Not at all," he said softly. "It is a pleasure to meet anyone— who is a friend." He blinked at her over his spectacles. "Are you here on a visit? Or—?"

"I need some help."

"Ah. In that case, perhaps you would care for some lunch?"

They found a *brasserie* a few streets away and ordered what

seemed to Julie to be an extravagant meal of *soupe de poisson,* veal —when had she last had veal?—and wine.

As they talked, Julie decided that Alain Hubert was a remarkable man. Gentle and self-effacing, he seemed an unlikely resistance hero. Perhaps that was why he'd never been caught.

When the food arrived, Julie ate heartily; she'd almost forgotten what good food tasted like.

"So this person might have come from Marseilles?" the doctor asked.

"Might, yes. It's not much to go on, is it?"

"Well, who can say? Someone might recognize his description, you never know."

"The police didn't."

"If he's not known to them, the only thing I can suggest is the *milieu.*"

She blinked in surprise.

"Most of the crime in Marseilles is highly controlled. There's an organization which runs almost everything—black market, prostitution and, of course, drugs. They know a lot more about what goes on in this city than the police do."

He was describing a world that Julie didn't understand at all.

"How do I find them?"

"Ahh, that I don't know." He looked at her over his glasses, his eyes twinkling. "I don't move in those circles actually."

She grinned. "No, of course not."

"It would have been easier in the old days, before they demolished the Old Quarter, the *bas-quartier.* It was the center of all that."

"What happened to it? Why was it torn down?"

"The Germans decided it was undesirable and had it flattened. The real reason, I think, was that they couldn't control what went on inside."

They finished their coffee and the doctor insisted on paying for lunch. "It's my pleasure. Forgive me, but I have to go now."

"Of course."

He swiveled in his chair and reached for his stick. Julie got up to help him. He said, "There is just one thing. . . . There's an old friend of mine, a chap who's been in a little trouble from time to time. He might know how to contact the right people. . . ."

"I thought you said you didn't mix with that sort of people." Julie laughed.

"Ah, well, one's not so choosy about one's friends in prison."

"In prison?"

He got slowly and painfully to his feet, falling slightly against the table as he did so. She held his arm until he had regained his balance. "This leg . . . slow to mend . . . an infernal nuisance. . . . Yes, prison. We were lucky, he and I. . . . We were lucky. . . ."

So the mild manner had not deceived the Gestapo after all. It explained his frailty and the broken, badly mended leg.

He was holding out his hand. "It was a great pleasure, madame. I'll make inquiries of my friend. I'll telephone. Good-bye." He made his way slowly down the street.

Six hours later there was a message. It read simply: "Try Henri's Bar off the Rue Caisserie. Good luck."

She had no trouble in finding Henri's Bar: the hotel proprietor directed her straight to it. The place was narrow-fronted and dark. She hesitated, then drew a deep breath and marched straight in.

The interior was dimly lit and, seeing a vacant table beside the door, she sank quickly into a chair. Immediately she changed her mind. She might as well go the whole hog. Getting up, she perched on a stool at the bar.

The place was, she imagined, typical. Dark polished wood, yellow paint and the odor of a thousand cigarettes. But there were exotic smells too, of spices and herbs and strange unfamiliar scents. A handful of regular customers sat at the bar, well into café-cognac, pastis and wine and cassis.

Behind the counter was a young man, busy serving customers, and an older, plumper man, carefully adjusting the rows of bottles that lined the back of the bar. The older man was surreptitiously watching her in a mirror. She guessed he was the proprietor.

The young man came by and she ordered coffee. As he went to get it she saw two oranges behind the bar and immediately wished she'd ordered orange pressée. Oranges were virtually unobtainable in England.

The coffee was put in front of her. A moment later the proprietor drifted past.

"Excuse me—" Julie asked quickly.

The proprietor continued on as if he hadn't heard her, took his time putting a bottle on a shelf, then slowly returned. He said without looking at her, "Yes."

"I want information."

"Oh yes?" He gave her a hard look. "What kind of information?"

"I'm looking for someone. Someone who might have lived around here, or visited the Old Quarter. . . ."

"His name?"

This was where it got difficult. But there was no way around it. She said, "That's the problem . . . I don't know it. All I know is that he was called the Marseillais."

The proprietor looked at her from under his eyebrows. "The Marseillais?" He nodded slowly as if humoring an idiot. "The Marseillais? Madame, can you imagine how many people are called that in the world? Eh? Every *mac* in Marseilles! And whenever a Marseillais goes away, guess what people call him! Why yes, they call him a Marseillais, that's what!"

Julie nodded. "I realize it sounds ridiculous but—he must have been known here. Before he went away. Known . . . in bars, around the place. . . . He was the kind of person who might have been involved in—*le milieu.*"

"So—? Half the population of this place is involved in *something*!" He was glaring at her, hostile now.

Before Julie could say any more, he moved away and served another customer.

Five minutes later he returned, hurrying past on the far side of the bar. She leaned over the counter and said, "Please, another word—?"

He hesitated for a moment, poised to walk away.

"Look . . . can you give me the name of someone who could help me? This man—the one I'm looking for, he's wanted by—" She almost said the police, but realized it might count against her. "By the Resistance. He was a traitor. He's responsible for people's deaths."

She had him now: he was moving closer, his eyes curious. The

574

rest of the bar was silent too, and five pairs of eyes watched her intently.

Julie said, "He worked for the Gestapo. He has to be found to save an innocent man. And—for other reasons."

The proprietor stared at her thoughtfully. "Ahh. Well . . . that's different. But—it won't exactly be easy." He asked skeptically, "What do you know about him? Did he have an accent? Did he speak like a Provençal? Like *me*?"

"No."

"Mmm. An educated type, maybe?"

"Yes, very likely. I know it's not much to go on, but I could give you a description. And then—perhaps you could ask around? Perhaps you know someone—?"

He nodded. "I'll ask the boys." He used the slang word *malfrats* —good-for-nothings. Taking a pencil stub and an old till receipt, he painstakingly wrote down the details she gave him: dark hair, thin, about thirty, medium height, gold ring, no accent. It wasn't much. She made him add: clever, probably well educated, dislikes women.

"I'll do what I can, but—" He shrugged. "I can't promise anything."

She pressed him, "How long before you might get news—?"

"Who knows? Two hours? Two days? You come back from time to time, then I'll tell you how long it'll take!"

Three days later Julie thought: I'm wasting my time.

The proprietor—Henri—was earnest and well-meaning, but she began to wonder if he had all the contacts he'd hinted at. He didn't seem to be getting anywhere at all.

But then, she thought unhappily, perhaps there wasn't anywhere to get to. There was no proof—not even a shred of a suggestion—that the Marseillais and Fougères were one and the same man.

And yet Fougères had been so very *good* at deceit and treachery that he *must* have been important to the Boches. She couldn't believe he was just a casual informer.

Yet she had to face the possibility that the two men weren't the same. If so, where did that leave her? There were no more leads to follow.

That was really why she had come to Marseilles—because it *was* the only lead.

After an aimless walk around the harbor she went back to the bar, utterly dispirited. It would be the third time she'd looked in that morning, and Henri's shrugs and "Don't worry" and "Be patient" were getting on her nerves.

But when she went in, something was different. Henri was smiling slyly, his eyes gleaming. He ducked under the flap and, coming out from behind the bar, beckoned her to one side. "Someone wants to see you. He's been away, that's why there's been a delay. He'll meet you this afternoon."

"Who?"

"Ahh," he whispered conspiratorially, "he's what you might call the *Patron*—with a capital *P,* you understand. You're very lucky. He's interested in your story. And if anyone can help—*he* can!"

"Where do I find him?"

"No problem, just be here at three. It's all arranged!"

She was there at two-thirty. She drank coffee nervously and, though she'd hardly ever smoked in her life, accepted two cigarettes from Henri.

By three her eyes were fastened to the door. By ten past, she was looking desperately at Henri. He said, "Don't worry. We keep *marseillais* time here. Nice and slow."

At a quarter past, a long black car drew up outside. Henri led her to the door. "Good luck!"

The driver was standing beside the car. He had a broken nose, large shoulders and a surly expression. He looked just like a criminal. It suddenly dawned on Julie that he probably *was* a criminal. As she approached he slid into the car.

Henri ushered Julie into the back, and the car eased gently through the narrow streets until they reached a wide boulevard. Then they accelerated past the harbor, across several junctions and onto the hill topped by the magnificent church. The back of the driver's head didn't invite conversation.

After five minutes or so, the driver braked and turned into a street full of small shops. They stopped, and Julie guessed she was meant to get out.

As she opened the door the driver murmured, "In there," and

indicated with his finger. It was a restaurant. The driver added something in slang that she didn't understand. Then he translated. "The waiter," he explained, "ask the waiter."

She crossed the pavement and pushed open the door. It was very dark inside. She paused, trying to get her bearings.

Someone appeared from the shadows. "Come this way."

She followed the man to the back of the room and saw the figures of four men dimly visible at a table. As she approached one of them rose to his feet. The conversation at the table petered out.

Julie shook the man's hand and sat in the chair he offered her. As her eyes got accustomed to the dim light, she took a good look at him. He was well dressed in a conventional but slightly flashy way. His suit was obviously expensive, and there was a gold chain visible across the waistcoat and another around his wrist. Several rings glinted dully on his fingers. As he sat back in his seat she caught the whiff of liberally applied cologne. His face was pleasant, his eyes twinkling under a high forehead and receding hairline.

He inquired, "Would you like some wine? Or a coffee?"

"Nothing, thank you."

He said, "My friend Henri tells me you're looking for someone." He had a strong *provençal* accent, but the voice was soft and soothing.

"Yes. Someone who came from here. Probably a long time ago."

He sipped some wine. "Tell me about him."

"Everything?"

"As much as you know."

She told him about Brittany and the escape line and the betrayal and how Michel had been accused; and she told him about the man from Paris, the outsider with the narrow face, the lanky hair, the dark almost black eyes and the sallow skin. She finished, "And he was cruel, that's what I remember most."

"And his manner?"

"Cold. Always—watchful. And underhand. Devious."

"And—how did he speak?"

"He had no accent," she admitted, "not that one could catch anyway. Certainly nothing like—" She hesitated.

"Like mine?"

Julie nodded.

"And you said something about women. About him not liking women."

"No . . . he hated them, I would say. And he was frightened of them—well, wary, anyway."

The *Patron* sipped more wine. "No facial scars or anything like that?"

"No."

There was the sound of the restaurant door opening and closing. The *Patron* looked around. "Ah, here we are!"

A man put an envelope into the *Patron*'s hand. He opened it and shook out the contents. "Some pictures for you to look at. Just a few ideas." He placed them in a pile on the table and turned to one of the others. "Throw some light on the scene, will you, Isso?"

A lamp was switched on and, blinking, Julie picked up the first photograph. It was a snapshot of a family group. There were five people: a middle-aged couple and three young men, presumably their sons. The faces were blurred but she knew immediately that none of them was Fougères. She put the picture back on the table.

The second was in fact two photographs: a front and side view of an unsmiling man with frightened eyes. The pictures looked like the shots she'd seen at the Police Judiciaire. She didn't recognize the face.

She picked up the third picture and as she did so, she caught sight of the one now visible on top of the pile. It was of a formal group, a dozen or so young men standing stiffly in a garden with, at either side, four black-robed men: priests. The picture was blurred and indistinct and had been taken in strong sunlight, so that the participants were frowning against the glare. But there was something—*familiar.*

With a trembling hand, she reached for it. Very slowly.

But even before she picked it up she knew.

It was him.

It was him.

She looked closely. Very young, perhaps only fourteen, but the hair, the narrow face . . . *him.* It was a moment before she could speak. Then she whispered, "This one. This is the one."

The *Patron* took the photograph gently from her hand. "You're sure?"

"Yes. Positive."

He shook his head and murmured, "So! I knew the bastard would turn up again somewhere! Scum always do."

"What's his name?" she demanded.

The *Patron* stared thoughtfully at the photograph. "His name? Vasson. Paul Vasson."

She said it over to herself. "And what was he? Where did he come from?"

"He was the illegitimate son of a whore—a junkie whore at that. The authorities found him starving in a cupboard when he was about eight and handed him over to the Jesuits. The priests did what they could. They educated him well—Vasson was always a clever bastard." He paused. "Later he became a small-time pimp with ambitions. He wanted to make the big time. He had expensive tastes . . ."

"And?"

"He disappeared in 'thirty-five. No one's seen him since. Not that we haven't been looking." He laughed bitterly. "We would love to find him, believe me!"

She was gripped with excitement. "But now we've got him, haven't we!"

He regarded her patiently. "Got him? Listen, people have been looking for him for years. . . . The police—*they* would like to find him. Me—*I've* had the word out for a long time now." He shook his head. "Nothing. Someone once said they'd seen him in Toulon. But we never found him there. Another time someone saw him in Paris . . . but never a real lead."

He held up the photograph. "Then I got hold of this. In about 'forty, it was. One of my men showed it round. Thought I'd got the swine then. He'd been seen all right, in Paris, the *dix-huitième*. Working in clubs, that kind of thing. Thought I'd got him. I put the word out. But he's a cunning bastard. . . ."

"What happened?"

"He disappeared again. Vanished. Never a trace."

Julie was crestfallen. "Oh . . . I see."

He shrugged. "He'll still be in a big city somewhere—Paris probably. With his tastes he wouldn't be caught dead in a provincial town. But apart from that . . ."

Julie sighed. "Well . . . at least I know who he is, that Vasson was Fougères. That should be enough to free my cousin."

"You don't seem very happy . . ."

She frowned and looked at her hands. "I can't bear to think of Vasson not being caught."

"Well . . ." He shrugged. "You never know. The police might still get him. . . ."

"But suppose they don't?"

There was a silence.

"Where will you go now?" he asked.

She considered. "To Rennes first to free my cousin, then—Paris." She had made up her mind. "Yes. Paris."

He watched her for a moment. "And what are you going to do there?"

"See if I can help the police, identify him if necessary . . ."

"You will look for him?"

She didn't know what to say. She wasn't sure what she was going to do. Eventually she murmured, "If I have to."

"He's a dangerous man—a lunatic!" He leaned forward and shook his head. "Please, be very, very careful! Look—if you're really determined then you'll need help. What about money?"

"I've got enough for the moment."

"If you need more, just phone this number in Paris." He wrote it on one of the restaurant's cards. "I'll tell them you're coming. They'll be able to help in other ways, too."

"Other ways?"

"Manpower . . . that kind of thing." The *Patron* tapped her hand. "Look, if you *should* happen to find him, keep clear. Just let my people know straightaway—they'll be *neater* than the *flics*, you understand. Whatever you do, don't approach him yourself. He'll kill you as soon as look at you. Just let my people know—they'll deal with him."

She had no doubt they would. "Thanks for your help. May I take the photograph?"

"I'd like it back when you've finished with it." She put it carefully in her bag along with the telephone number. He got up and helped her to her feet.

As they walked to the door she asked, "What did he do? When he was in Marseilles, I mean?"

The *Patron* opened the door and the sounds of the street flooded in. He said quietly, "He bought me three years inside, that's what he did."

"Oh!" She didn't know what to say.

"And . . ." His face clouded. "He killed a woman." There was a pause. *"My woman."*

Julie stared, aghast. She stammered, "I'm sorry. . . ."

He shrugged and said briskly, "Now remember, if you *do* come across the bastard, whatever you do don't go anywhere near him. Just call that number and mention my name."

She stretched out her hand. "I don't know your name."

"Jojo. Just say Jojo sent you."

There was a midnight train to Paris. Julie packed her case, paid the outstanding money on the room and, with plenty of time to spare, went to the bar to say good-bye to Henri.

He welcomed her effusively and pressed a cognac on her. She rather liked it. She liked it even more a few moments later when the alcohol sent a warm glow around her body. Suddenly she felt tremendously optimistic.

She knew so much more about him, his name and his background. And most important of all, she had the photograph. What a bit of luck that was! Somebody somewhere must have seen him. Somebody somewhere would know where he was. It would just be a question of looking hard enough and for long enough in the right places. . . .

The telephone at the end of the bar rang. Henri answered it, put it down on the counter and came over to her. He indicated with his head. "Telephone."

She went to the end of the bar and lifted the receiver cautiously. "Yes?"

"Madame? It's me." She recognized the *Patron*'s voice. "I remembered something. . . ."

Julie gripped the receiver. "Yes?"

"It's not very much, but it might help— You remember I said he had expensive tastes? Well, he always longed for a fancy car. He was quite mad about it. Always had pictures of it in his room, even in his wallet. . . . A Delage. He wanted a Delage. Nothing else would do. You know the car I mean?"

Julie tried to hide her disappointment. "I know."

"Well, it's not much. . . . But he really was crazy about that car."

"Thank you for telling me."

"Good luck."

Julie replaced the receiver. A car . . . a Delage . . .

She shook her head. A long time had passed. Vasson had probably forgotten he had ever wanted a Delage—dreams didn't last. At sixteen she herself had wanted—what was it?—a fur coat. She never thought of having one now.

No, the car wouldn't lead her to Vasson.

But the photograph would. That was the key.

39

"Are there any further charges against Le Goff?" The examining magistrate peered at the commissaire.

"Not at the present time."

"I order, then, that Le Goff be released forthwith." The magistrate stood up and walked out. Julie got to her feet and stared blankly at the high, ornate chair where the magistrate had been sitting. She should feel triumphant, or at least relieved. Instead she felt dissatisfied, almost cheated.

The commissaire was waiting for her in the aisle. "You were very certain in your identification of Vasson," he said. "I wish all witnesses were as definite."

They walked out to the front steps of the law courts.

"You are a very determined woman, madame."

"And what's wrong with that?" Julie demanded.

"Nothing—please don't misunderstand me."

"When will Michel be released?"

"Within the hour. One of my men can take you over there, if you like."

"That won't be necessary, thank you."

The commissaire looked surprised. "You're not going to see him?"

She shook her head briefly.

"I thought—"

"You thought wrong, monsieur. I told you that before."

"Ah. I stand corrected."

As they reached the pavement, the commissaire said, "We believe Vasson was involved in other crimes, that he may have betrayed the Meteor Line."

Julie looked at him sharply. "He was Lebrun?"

"Possibly. But it is difficult to find anyone who might identify him. They all died or got sent to Germany." He added, "Where can I contact you—in case we have news?"

"England. I gave my address to your inspector. I'm going to Paris today, then on from there." It was almost the truth. "But —*will* there be any news?"

"In due course. His description will be everywhere by now. And his photograph. We'll find him."

"But it's been two weeks."

The commissaire threw up his hands. "Two weeks. That's nothing! He could be anywhere, hiding under an assumed name. . . . It will take time."

"Yes." She stared thoughtfully at the sky, then said abruptly, "Good-bye, then, monsieur."

"Good-bye, madame."

The commissaire watched her slim figure walking briskly away and thought how deceptive appearances were. She might look soft and gentle, but she was like steel inside.

Julie sat in the train and read the letter again. It was from Peter, in his best rounded handwriting. He was very well, he said. He went to tea every day with John (his best friend) and on Saturday they had been fishing all day (this last part was underlined). He was glad about Michel. He sent her lots of love.

She put the letter away. He sounded happy enough. Julie had been in France almost a month now. It was a long time to leave a child. But he was eight, quite old enough to look after himself.

She got out her purse and counted the money in it. Five hundred francs or thereabouts. A hundred of her own and four hun-

dred which she had taken out of Michel's money. She had put the remainder of Michel's money in an envelope with a letter and left it with his concierge. In the letter she had explained how the money had been spent, wished him well and excused herself for not seeing him on his release.

She hadn't seen him either during the two weeks the police had been unraveling the Fougères identity. Instead she had gone to Trégasnou and arranged for the sale of the farm to provide money for the proper care of Tante Marie.

It was the end of her life at Trégasnou. Perhaps of her life in Brittany too. Her debt to Michel had been repaid; she didn't want the embarrassment of his gratitude.

Five hundred francs . . .

She already had her train ticket back to England, so the cash should last three weeks. No, that was optimistic for Paris. Perhaps only two.

Two weeks, then. She would give herself two weeks.

She became a good walker. For eight days she walked all day— and a lot of the night too. She tried a hundred places—cafés, restaurants, shops—in half a dozen different areas.

No one had ever seen Vasson.

After the cafés, restaurants and shops she drew in her breath and tried the clubs. It took a lot to walk into a club, a woman alone, and ask for information. Sometimes she had to wait, standing conspicuously in a corner, while someone was fetched. Then people stared, wondering what a woman like her was doing in such a place. Even though she wore the darker and plainer of her two staid suits, she had to learn how to be unobtrusive and to turn down all kinds of propositions, some blunt and exotic. Once, a man actually stuffed a thousand francs into the neck of her blouse and started pulling her toward the door.

She hated everything about the clubs, the darkness, the stink of tobacco, the leering men. To keep sane, she forced herself to see the light side of it. It was there—if you looked hard enough.

But time was slipping away. Twelve days had passed, and no Vasson. It was as if he'd never been to Paris. . . .

The clubs didn't open until nine-thirty or ten, so she spent the earlier part of the evening inquiring in restaurants and cafés.

Then, once the doors of the clubs opened, she went in quickly, anxious to be away before too many customers arrived.

She completed the narrow streets of Montmartre and started on the area around Pigalle.

One evening she managed three clubs before eleven. She came to a fourth and, without bothering to examine the name on the neon light, went straight down the red-lit stairs. It was better going straight in—there wasn't so much time to hesitate.

No one was at the desk so, without slowing down, she walked across to the bar, where a barman was polishing glasses. She pulled out the photograph, which she had masked with black paper to hide the other figures, and thrust it across the counter.

The barman looked at it, then asked, "So who's looking for him?" That was what they always asked. That, or "In trouble, is he?"

She replied, "I'm looking for him. It's a personal matter." It was the answer she always gave. It usually brought a knowing smile and a comment about all poor devils being on the run from some woman or another, and she wasn't going to give him a hard time when she found him, was she?

This time the barman said, "You're looking for him, eh?" He eyed her thoughtfully. "It doesn't seem very likely."

Julie looked at him in surprise. "Why not?"

"You don't seem the sort to have mixed with him."

Julie tensed. "You know him?"

The barman took another look at the picture. "Used to. Used to work here, the bastard."

"When? When was he here?"

"Ohhh. Must have been before the war. Yes, just before . . ."

"And since then?"

"He was around for a while afterward. Started dealing in specialties. You know, stockings, cigarettes, that kind of thing . . ."

"Then?"

The barman shrugged. "Don't know. He wasn't seen again."

"You've heard nothing since?"

"Nothing. Not that I've asked, you understand. And he wouldn't exactly be welcome in this place. He half killed the boss." He rolled his eyes.

"What did he call himself then?"

"Ah . . ." The barman frowned. "Can't remember exactly . . . wait a minute. . . . Biolet. That was it. Biolet."

Yet another name. Julie asked, "Where did he live, do you know?"

"No. Never knew. Never cared."

Julie racked her brain for more questions. "Did he have money in those days?"

The barman laughed. "Money! Never. Always broke. Tried to get into the big time, but never made it. A real loser. Too clever-clever, see. No one around here liked that, not one bit."

And that was it. He knew nothing more.

Two days later Julie found another person who thought he recognized the photograph. A café proprietor up a steep hill above Pigalle. But he too hadn't seen Biolet for a long time. After some thought he remembered that the last occasion must have been '39 or '40—before the occupation. He too mentioned that Biolet had always been broke.

After that—nothing.

She had been in Paris fifteen days.

Wearily she went back to her cheap, cheerless hotel in the *treizième* and fell onto the bed, exhausted.

Clubs, cafés . . . Montmartre, Pigalle . . . He'd been there all right *before* the war.

But after—? Nothing.

Perhaps he had gone away. To another large city.

Another area. Another name. Another job.

Would he even *need* a job? The Germans must have paid him well; he was their most important informer. Yes, he *must* have money, and for the first time in his life!

She opened her eyes wide.

Of course. *That* was the difference. He had *money*.

The big time at last. All the things he'd ever dreamed about. She tried to imagine him with money . . . dressing well, wearing gold jewelry. Indulging expensive tastes.

All the things he'd ever dreamed about. She remembered the last-minute phone call from the *Patron*. Perhaps there had been something in it after all. It was worth a try—

Just one more day. She'd give it one more day.

* * *

Julie trudged along the Champs-Élysées, looking for the right number. Most of the buildings didn't seem to have any numbers, but at last she spotted some small figures high above a doorway; there was still quite a way to go. She eyed a passing bus longingly. It would be quicker and easier by bus, but it would cost money and she was running dangerously short.

She was down to her last fifty francs and her train ticket home. In Paris fifty francs would last two days, maybe three if she cut down on her food.

She walked on, watching the numbers. There was a smart shop selling handbags, a cinema. . . . It must be the next one.

The shop front was clearly visible now. She stopped and stared.

It was empty. Most of the windows were boarded up. Only one window still had glass in it and that was whitewashed on the inside.

She went up to the window, found a tiny gap in the whitewash and peered through. There was a large empty showroom, littered with rubbish and a few posters of cars.

She stepped back and looked up. The sign, made of letters fastened onto a marble fascia, had fallen off. But the shadow of the letters remained. The name of the agents. Then, in smaller letters: DELAGE.

She went around to the side. A door, firmly closed.

Dead end. She'd got this address from a garage. Obviously their information was out-of-date.

She should try another Delage dealer—if there was one.

She tramped along until she found a post office. She looked up Delage in the telephone directory. Not listed.

Next idea.

None. She felt weak and tired and decided to go back to the hotel to rest. It was a real indulgence: she'd never allowed herself that luxury before. She saw a bus stop and, weakening, caught a bus in the direction of the *treizième*. She began to plan what she'd do when she got there: she'd go mad and buy cheese, fruit *and* bread and take them back to the hotel and eat the lot.

She had to change buses twice. At the second change she was overcome by guilt at her extravagance and decided to walk the last mile or so.

On the way she looked up and saw a garage. Without hesitating she walked straight in. A mechanic was working on a car.

She asked, "Where would I buy a Delage if I wanted one?"

"A new one, impossible. They haven't been making them recently, or hadn't you noticed?" he said with heavy irony. "A secondhand one . . ." He shrugged. "Wherever you could find one. There must be plenty about if you have the money."

She thought: A real help. "What about servicing one, then. Where would I go?"

"Juno's Garage. They're the only ones who work on them nowadays." He gave her an address. It was on the other side of the city, near the Bois de Boulogne, back the way she'd come.

She hesitated, thinking of the cheese, fruit and bread, and the nice soft bed, then marched firmly back toward the bus stop.

Juno's was a large garage full of smart cars in various stages of repair. There was a sporty racing-type car, a limousine and a long, sleek open-top—all magnificently expensive.

A fierce-looking woman was perched inside a glass booth, guarding the working area. She raised a sliding window and asked sharply, "Yes?"

"I'm looking for a Delage," Julie asked.

"What do you mean *looking*?"

"I want to find someone who might have bought one recently."

The woman inspected Julie from top to bottom and raised her eyebrows. "We don't buy and sell."

"I just wondered if you knew of any Delages for sale—or recently sold, in the last few years."

"We're not record keepers." The woman slammed the window shut.

Julie went past her into the garage. The woman spotted her and, pushing up the window again, started yelling. Julie walked briskly on.

She found a mechanic who was working on a long silver touring car. She said, "Hello."

He turned around and smiled appreciatively. "H-e-l-l-o!"

She admired the car. "Lovely. I didn't know people could still afford things like this."

"Not many can! This one's been locked away all through the war. Now we're trying to get it going again. Anyway—what can I do for you?"

"I want to find someone who owns a Delage."

The mechanic made an extravagant gesture. "For you, I'd buy one myself!"

Julie smiled. "If I wanted to buy a Delage where would I look? A secondhand one, I mean."

"You want to *buy* one!" He regarded her even more admiringly, wiping his hands on a dirty rag.

"No, not me exactly," Julie said hastily. "In fact I want to trace someone who *may* have bought one. In the last few years."

"You ask a lot. . . . My goodness, it would be difficult to know where to begin! And there aren't many about nowadays. Most of them are still off the road. . . ." He looked over Julie's shoulder and made a face. "Ooops!" The fierce-looking woman was waddling aggressively in their direction.

Julie said hurriedly, "Any ideas?"

"What about the police? They have a register of all owners."

"No—this person wouldn't be using his own name, you see."

The mechanic laughed. "More and more mysterious!" The fierce woman panted up to them, prepared for a speech. The mechanic quickly took Julie's arm and led her toward the main doors. "There *is* something called the Delage Society. Or there *used* to be anyway. I've got the address somewhere. Would that be of any use?"

"Yes, please. Anything."

He opened the door of the glass booth and riffled through some papers on a shelf. He came out with a slim magazine in his hand. "Here. They used to send out these things every few months. The address of the editor will be in there somewhere."

The fierce woman had followed them and was standing a few feet away, hands on her hips, eyes blazing.

"Better get back to work. Good luck!" The mechanic grinned at her, his expression full of many meanings, all of them nice.

Julie smiled back. He had cheered her up.

A few yards along the street she opened the magazine. On the first inside page there was the name of the publisher and farther down, the editor, with an address in Paris.

The address was on the other side of the city.

Julie sighed and looked for a bus.

It was an apartment building. There were two long rows of bells with names on them. Some of the names were very faded and

Julie had trouble reading them, but she finally found the editor's name and pressed his bell.

There was a buzz. She pressed against the street door and it opened. The apartment was on the fourth floor. When she arrived, breathless, at the head of the stairs, a man was standing on the landing, waiting.

The editor of *La Société des Propriétaires de Delage* was about sixty. He wore shabby clothes and smelled strongly of garlic and old vegetables. He welcomed her warmly. "I don't get many visitors. Please come in. Come in!"

The apartment was none too clean and rather shabby, like its owner.

The editor bounced around like a small boy, offering her a seat and a cup of coffee. Then he sat absolutely still, listening to what she had to say.

He nodded slowly and promised to help all he could. But there was a problem. "We had to cease publishing at the beginning of the war," he explained. "And even before the war, only about half the owners belonged. . . . As for finding out what's happened to the cars since then—new owners and so on . . . it would be *difficult.*"

"This person *might* have been an owner before the war. It's just possible . . ."

He shot out of his seat like a jack-in-the-box. "Say no more!" He disappeared into another room and a few minutes later returned in triumph with a dusty box full of yellowing papers. He pulled out the papers and looked at her expectantly. "Name?"

"Vasson. Or Fougères. Or Biolet." Even as she said them Julie realized the man she was looking for wouldn't now be using any of those names. This would never lead anywhere.

After half an hour of riffling through the papers, the editor was satisfied that no one with any of those names had ever been members of his club. "I'm sorry," he said.

"What about buying a secondhand Delage?" Julie asked. "How would one find one?"

"Ahhh!" The editor rolled his eyes earnestly toward the ceiling as if that could give him the answer. "Mmmm. A newspaper. Yes, through a newspaper! That's about all that's been published, you see. Though there is *Auto*—I believe that's kept going after a

fashion. Here, I'll give you the address." He scampered into the other room and came back with a piece of paper.

Julie said wearily, "Thank you. You've been most helpful." At the door she asked, "Did you have a Delage yourself once?"

"Me!" He laughed heartily, throwing back his head in a great guffaw. "Goodness gracious no! I could never have afforded even a twentieth of one. I was only an enthusiast! I just loved being *near* the lovely things, you understand. The most beautiful cars ever made. . . ."

The *Auto* office was only a twenty-minute walk away. Although it was late—almost five—and the place likely to be closing, she decided to try anyway.

In the end it was farther than she thought. By the time she found the right doorway she was so tired she could hardly climb the four flights of stairs. No energy: she hadn't eaten since breakfast.

She arrived, shaking slightly, in front of a half-glazed door inscribed with the word AUTO in scratched gold letters.

She knocked and someone called, "Enter."

The office was a single room with a large desk on which a lanky man of about thirty was sitting, speaking into a telephone. He waved her into a seat and continued his conversation, which mainly consisted of sighs and tuts and expressions of despondency.

Julie flopped down and, seeing a copy of *Auto* on a side table, she picked it up and leafed through. Most of the magazine was made up of articles and photographs of racing cars, but at the back there were six pages of advertisements.

Julie scanned them quickly. There was a Delage for sale . . . and a second and third. She looked for the date at the top of the page and felt a pang of disappointment. March 1938. Years ago.

The telephone receiver was banged down into its cradle and the lanky young man said, "How can I help you?" He was, he explained, the editor, subeditor, secretary and sole reporter of *Auto* magazine. "We've had to cut down a bit. We haven't been able to publish very often. No paper, you see! No money! Nothing much to report—no new cars, hardly any races. . . . But you never know, we might be able to manage three edi-

tions this year." He added morosely, "Better than nothing, I suppose."

She asked to see some of the recent editions. "Oh, *those*!" he said heavily. "They're *awful*. I was only allowed four pages and an edition of five thousand. Hardly worth printing!" He looked up. "When you say recent, how recent?"

"Since the beginning of the war."

The editions for the last several years contained a surprising number of advertisements. The editor commented sadly, "Everyone's trying to sell cars they can't afford to run." He pointed out the racing and sports types, the Bugattis, Maseratis and Mercedes. Then there were the plush tourers, Delahayes, Bentleys—and Delages. Julie saw with relief that there weren't too many Delages advertised. She started making a list. With only three editions per year, the total number of Delages advertised, when she added them up, was only twenty-four. Some of those were duplicates of previous advertisements and when those were eliminated she ended up with sixteen.

Some Delages had been advertised under box numbers. "May I have the names and addresses of the sellers?" Julie asked.

"I'm not meant to . . ." the editor sighed. "But . . . seeing as the whole world's gone mad and I don't much care . . ." He pulled a number of files out of a cabinet and threw them on the desk. "Here! They're all in there somewhere."

And they were—scribbled in almost illegible pencil or in heavy black ink with the words half-smudged. After forty minutes she had them all. "Thank you. If I need to look at some more back copies, may I come and see you again?"

"Why not?" he exclaimed desperately. "I'll still be sitting here, most likely. No events to cover, no new cars. . . . God, yes! Why not! Come and cheer me up!"

It was only when Julie got back to her room and was eating great mouthfuls of bread and cheese—the fruit had been too expensive —that she inspected the list carefully.

Her heart sank. The Delage owners were spread all over the country, some as far away as Nice. Contacting them would be impossible: letters would take too long and telephone calls would be too difficult and expensive.

There were telegrams, of course. But sixteen . . . They would cost more, much more, than she could afford.

She lay back on the bed and, shaking off her shoes, examined a blister on her heel. The entire thing was hopeless. Why *should* Vasson have bought a car at all? Perhaps he'd hidden all his money and was lying low. Perhaps he'd squandered it years ago. . . .

The big time . . .

What did it mean to him now?

She should go home. She barely had enough money to feed herself on the train. Her shoes were worn out. She should give up.

But then she remembered the hard black eyes and the *coldness* of him, and she muttered, *"Merde."*

One more day. Just one more day.

She sat up and, reaching for her bag, searched in the zip compartment. The card was there, where she'd put it all those weeks ago.

Jojo had offered help. Well, she wasn't too shy to ask now. To use the language of the street, she needed the necessary. And the necessary was money.

The count heard the sound of crunching gravel on the drive and hid. He was quite an expert at hiding now; creditors and angry tradespeople arrived almost daily.

There were footsteps. The front bell jangling. The count peered through a crack in a shutter and saw a bicycle. It looked vaguely familiar. Of course—he had it now. It was the postman's.

Why would the postman be here in the afternoon? It must be bad news—a summons for a bad debt or something like that.

He chuckled. Only six more days and the château would be stripped of all its remaining valuables. Then he would disappear to Paris and they could send all the summonses they wanted.

The count watched the postman come into view, mount his bicycle and ride off down the drive. As soon as everything was quiet he hopped silently down the stairs to the main hall. An envelope had been slipped underneath the front door.

A little nervously, the count strode over, grabbed the envelope and tore it open.

"Good Lord!" he exclaimed.

It was a telegram. It read: INTERESTED IN BUYING DELAGE. IS YOURS STILL AVAILABLE?

It was signed LESCAUX, followed by a post office box number in Paris.

At the bottom the post office had stamped: ANSWER PREPAID.

The count said: "Damn! Damn and blast!" He'd known it! That deal had been a disaster. People were lining up to buy the car, and he'd thrown it away. God, what a waste!

"Damn!" he repeated and stomped off in the direction of the cellars to see if he could find a last bottle of claret.

He considered whether to reply. He decided against it. He didn't see the point. He'd sold the damned car, hadn't he?

Another telegram came four days later. It read: IF CAR SOLD, STILL INTERESTED. URGENTLY NEED INFORMATION. PLEASE USE PRE-PAID REPLY. LESCAUX.

The count took more interest. Whatever this was about, he could smell money. He slipped down to the village and sent a reply, saying that he'd sold the car recently and adding that he'd be in residence for only two more days.

The following day there was the sound of an approaching car on the drive. The count took cover on the first floor. Through the shutters he saw the village taxi draw up. Out of it stepped a girl. Even from this distance he could see that she was a good-looker.

He straightened his tie, walked down the stairs and flung open the front door.

The girl said, "I sent the telegram."

"Come in! Come in!" He gestured toward the main salon, which was the only room still with any furniture in it. He offered her a Louis XV chair and apologized for the rickety legs. When they were seated, he smiled at her charmingly. "And to what do I owe this singular pleasure?"

"*Auto* magazine. I've been contacting everyone who's advertised a Delage for sale in the last few years. You advertised, so here I am."

The count smiled again, though he had the feeling his charm was wasted on this serious young lady. "But why come to me when I've already sold my car?"

"*Because* you've sold it. Your car was one of the few that did sell."

The count hesitated. "Ah. Not many have sold, then?"

"No. Apparently there's no market for them."

The count tried to feel mollified about his deal with the scar-faced young man, but he couldn't believe he hadn't been cheated.

"Please continue," said the count. "Why are you looking for a car that's already sold?"

"I want to contact someone, someone who may well have bought one."

The count's curiosity was pricked. "You mean a *particular* person?"

"Yes."

"Someone you wish to trace?"

"Precisely."

What a businesslike young woman this was. Normally the count didn't like that in a woman, but in this case it would be an advantage. When they got to the nub of the matter—the money—she would be easy to deal with.

"So—you wish to have details of the person who purchased my car."

"Please. Perhaps I could show you a photograph, to see if you recognize him. . . ." She dug into her handbag and passed him a small, indistinct photograph. It showed a young man, no more than twenty, with a thin face and dark lanky hair.

The count swore under his breath. This wasn't the man. And if it wasn't the man then there couldn't be any financial negotiations. How annoying!

The count pretended to muse. "Mmmmm. It's hard to tell. This is a young man. . . . The person I sold to was older, definitely older. . . ."

"In his thirties?"

"Mmm. Maybe. Maybe."

The girl leaned forward anxiously. "What about the eyes? Do they look familiar?"

"Maybe. Maybe." The count pretended to examine the face, then focused more sharply. Yes, now she mentioned it, there *was* something familiar about them. Good Lord. Maybe it *was* him after all! He said, "Yes, it definitely *could* be him. But the man I sold the car to was heavily scarred. His face was terrible, quite *unpleasant* to look at. He'd obviously been horribly injured in some way. What he looked like before . . . well, it's difficult to be

sure." Which was true enough and it should keep her sufficiently interested to come up with the money, which was the important thing.

The girl's eyes were blazing with excitement. "Heavily scarred . . . ?" She paused, deep in thought, then asked, "But medium height, dark-haired and thin?"

"Yes."

"And his manner? Was it—?"

"Hard. Unfriendly. Not a very nice fellow at all."

The girl's face was triumphant and full of hope. "It just might be him!" she breathed.

"You're obviously very keen to make contact."

"Oh yes!" she exclaimed. "You *do* have an address, don't you? And a name?"

So she didn't even know his name. Better and better. "Will— *might*—this information be of value?" the count began.

For the first time she faltered. "—Of value?"

The count lowered his voice. "Will this information be of material value to anyone?"

She was confused now. "If you mean, will it be of financial value, the answer's no."

"I meant, rather, of sufficient value to someone to enable them to . . . you know . . . recompense me for my trouble and the inconvenience of searching for the right papers."

Her expression had hardened. "The person concerned has very limited means, very limited indeed. This is a matter of honor, of justice, not—money!"

The count was unimpressed. Honor, justice, it was no matter: the price was what counted. He'd learned his lesson from the scar-faced young man. When the market was all in your favor you named your price.

"I see," said the count soothingly. "In that case I'm sure a very small fee will be sufficient. Shall we say four thousand?"

"Four *thousand*!" she gasped. "Out of the question. I don't have a tenth of that!"

The count made tutting noises. "What a pity! There we are then." He started to his feet.

She had turned quite pale, an expression of desperation on her face. She opened and closed her mouth a couple of times then whispered, "One!"

596

"Three and a half!"

They settled on three. The girl looked as though she'd been hit over the head. When she turned her back to take the money out of her purse, the count guessed her pocketbook was rather full. He immediately regretted having let her beat him down. Why was it he always got cheated by people with lots of money?

He left her in the salon while he went to find the bill of sale. He copied the name and address of the young man on some blank paper, then put the bill of sale in his pocket. He took the piece of paper to the girl. "There we are!"

She looked at the name and address as if she could devour it. "Lelouche . . ."

He asked, "Could I have your address—just in case I remember something . . . ?"

She reached into her handbag and pulled out a scrap of paper and scribbled on it.

The count placed the paper carefully in his wallet. "Did you keep your taxi?" he inquired.

"It's coming back in a few minutes."

It couldn't be better. The count said gallantly, "I'll go and see if it's on its way. Sometimes the fellow forgets."

"That's not necessary."

"No, I insist!"

Quickly he pulled on a coat, took his wallet and, leaving her pacing the hall, hurried down the drive.

He met the taxi a short distance away on the main road. He flagged it down, told the driver that the visiting lady had already left, and asked to be taken to the station in her place.

A Paris train came almost immediately. As the count got in he calculated that it would be a good two hours before the girl realized what had happened, walked to the station and found a train.

Two hours should give him plenty of time.

With a final lurch the cage rose to the ceiling. One of the workmen, balancing on a plank supported by scaffolding, guided the hook at the top of the cage into the massive eye which protruded from the ceiling.

"What I'd like to know," one of the workmen mumbled, "is how the girl's gonna get *in* there."

"Rope ladder."

At the sound of Vasson's voice the workmen fell back. Vasson stepped forward and eyed the cage critically. With the correct lighting it should look all right, he decided. The only disappointing thing was the height of the cage. He'd wanted it farther away, more inaccessible. But the ceiling couldn't be raised any more, so this was it.

There was silence, the man waiting expectantly. Eventually Vasson said, "Yes, that's fine." He could almost hear the sigh of relief; this was one of the few jobs he hadn't asked them to redo in some way.

But it had been worth it. The group of storerooms had been completely transformed. There was now one large room, which, because of the lighting, looked pleasingly intimate. Around the sides were booths with seating for between two and six people, while in the center were a dozen small tables. At one side was a stage with room for a performer and an upright piano, drums and bass. On the other side of the room was a bar.

The color scheme was black, beige and gold. To soften the effect there were exotic plants everywhere, between the booths, hanging from the ceiling, around the light fittings. No one had ever used plants before.

Vasson had overspent his budget, but already everyone was talking about the place. At the opening the cage would be covered with a drape, then, accompanied by appropriate music, it was going to be unveiled to reveal a girl painted with gold. Her skin, that was. Apart from a G-string she'd be wearing nothing else at all. It would be a sensation.

He hurried through the club into his office, a small room at the rear. A thousand things still remained to be done before the opening, and there was only one day left.

Half an hour later there was a tap on the door.

"Yes," Vasson barked impatiently.

The new barman poked his nose into the room. "Someone to see you."

"Who?"

"Wouldn't say. But something important."

Vasson sighed. "Very well."

A minute later the barman showed someone in. Vasson looked up and stiffened.

It was the stupid old boy—the count.

Vasson swore to himself. He should never have put this address on the bill of sale; he had known it was a mistake when he did it. He said quietly, "Whatever you want, forget it."

The count sat down in a brand-new chair. "But I bring you good news."

Vasson said quickly, "I don't think so." And, standing up, called for the barman.

"I wouldn't be hasty if I were you. I bring you news from the past."

Vasson suddenly felt very cold. Slowly, he sat down again. "The past?"

"Yes. It's information which I think you will be very happy to have." The count grinned like a cat.

Vasson's mouth felt dry. He licked his lips. "Well? Go on."

The count said triumphantly, "Someone's looking for you! Someone who knew you some time ago."

Fear clutched at Vasson's heart, but he kept his face impassive. He asked quietly, "This person found me through the car?"

"Yes. Knew you'd bought it. Must have seen you at the wheel perhaps?"

"Perhaps. And who is this person?"

"Ahhh. That's the question, isn't it?"

The old bastard wanted money then. Vasson considered the alternatives. He could beat the information out of him, or . . .

"I don't think the information will be worth enough to pay for."

"No?" inquired the count sweetly. "But on the other hand, maybe it will."

Vasson picked at his fingers. "If I *was* interested, then what would you be able to tell me?"

"Name. Address."

"How do I know the name and address would be real?"

"No assurances. But I think they would be."

"Is it just the one person?"

The count considered. "I think I can say it's probably only the one."

"Did the person say he'd seen me in the car?"

"Ahh. Really I feel unable to answer. . . ." The count looked supercilious, like a complacent schoolmaster.

Sickening old sybarite. Vasson observed him with distaste. But the choices were limited. He *had* to know. "I'll offer you five hundred."

The count shook his head and laughed. "Really! Really! Five thousand would be a little nearer, don't you think?"

It was more than the club would take in on a good night. "You're out of your mind!"

But he wasn't and Vasson knew it. Eventually they settled on four thousand.

Vasson handed over the cash and, his heart hammering, asked with difficulty, "The information?"

"A girl. Named Lescaux. Dark hair. Mid- to late twenties. Her address is Hôtel Hortense. It's a cheap place in the *treizième*. She came to see me today. She had an old photograph of you. I didn't recognize you at first—the face was unmarked—but then I saw a similarity in the eyes and realized it must be you after all." He paused, watching Vasson's reaction.

"What . . . what led her to you?"

"The advertisement."

"So she never saw me at all . . . in the car?"

"She didn't say."

Vasson stood up stiffly and murmured, "Get out and don't let me ever see your face in here again."

The count needed no second invitation and disappeared rapidly from the office.

Vasson thought carefully for five minutes, then, taking his coat from the peg, slipped out the back door into the night.

40 The address was somewhere near Pigalle. The street, when Julie found it, looked familiar and she remembered that she'd been here a week or so before. It was narrow and very dark, except for the occasional blaze of light from a small

bistro. She went slowly, keeping close to the side and pausing to look for the indistinct, sometimes invisible street numbers on the shop fronts and doorframes.

She stopped in a doorway, her heart beating in her ears. The one she wanted was just two away now. Next door was a shop, closed and shuttered. Then, beyond, a dull gold pool of light spilling out of a doorway onto the pavement.

That must be it. The sign hanging over the door wasn't illuminated, but she could just make out some sort of painting on it. Above, there was a name. She wasn't sure, but it looked like The Golden Cage. A club then? How strange. She could have sworn the place hadn't been there before.

She drew a deep breath and, crossing the street walked past on the opposite side. Without being too obvious, she took a good look. It was definitely a club. But not, apparently, open for business. The door was open but there was a plank straddling the entrance and, just inside, some kind of notice on a board.

She continued walking, resisting the temptation to look over her shoulder. She reached a deep doorway and slipped quickly inside. She peered back along the street.

Nothing. No one had seen her. She relaxed a little.

What next? It would be madness to go in, in case Vasson was there. So she must wait; wait and watch.

Assuming this *was* the right address.

The count's behavior had been so extraordinary she still didn't know what to make of it. At first, when he didn't return, she'd given him the benefit of the doubt, but after trudging wearily into the railway station at the end of a long walk from the château she had found the taxi driver waiting there. Slowly, the truth had come out. The count had done it on purpose. But *why*? What could have made him want to run away like that? Perhaps he was Vasson's friend and partner. Or perhaps she'd got this far only to be tricked and sent on a wild goose chase. This club might have nothing to do with Vasson at all.

She moved to a corner of the doorway where she could watch the club while keeping in shadow. The street was getting busier as the evening trade picked up. A man came into the doorway to proposition her. Julie got rid of him quickly enough—he was as nervous as a cat—but she knew she'd got away lightly. Next time

it might not be so easy. She remembered she still had a lot of money on her—over two thousand from the money the *Patron*'s friends had given her. She wished now she'd left it at the hotel.

Someone was coming out of the club—a man dressed in baggy clothes with a beret on his head. Another man also appeared, this one carrying a workman's bag, and the two of them walked off in the direction of Pigalle.

Workmen. That would explain why the club wasn't open.

After that no one came in or out for several hours. The time passed slowly. She was ravenously hungry; for once she'd forgotten to put any bread in her pockets.

By ten-thirty she was numb with cold. Then, just before eleven, four or five people emerged from the club. She peered forward, trying to see their faces in the darkness.

Workmen again: most wore old clothes and carried tool bags. Another man appeared, well dressed and smoother-looking than the others. He moved the plank, turned off the lights, closed the front door and locked up. He was very tall, with thick, bushy fair hair.

None of them was Vasson.

The men walked off. The club looked deserted; clearly it was closed for the night.

She should go back to the hotel and get some sleep. There was no point in staying here.

She hesitated, then decided to take a quick look. It wouldn't take a minute and it couldn't possibly do any harm. She stepped out of the doorway and, looking quickly from left to right, crossed the street and walked up to the front of the club. She peered up at the sign. Yes: The Golden Cage. Below, pasted on the door, was a notice. The club was opening on November 14. She realized with a slight shock that the fourteenth was the following night.

What a stroke of luck! If Vasson had any connection with the place, he was bound to be there. She could stand in the shadows until he arrived. But would she recognize him at a distance? From the count's description he was terribly scarred.

The street was darker now, full of deep shadows. Apart from the faint drone of traffic the only sound was the distant beat of music. She started to walk. Suddenly her hackles rose and she shivered slightly. She walked faster, an uncomfortable feeling in

her spine, until she was safely into the brightness of Place Pigalle.

As she took the Métro across the city, an idea came into her head. She should get one of the *Patron*'s friends to take her to the opening. Yes! That would be perfect. She could easily imagine arriving with all the other guests, looking into the scarred face, knowing immediately it was him, seeing the shock on his face. . . .

In the next moment she knew it would never work. It would be madness to let Vasson see her.

No, the best thing would be to identify him from a position of safety, somewhere close enough but not too close. Then once she was certain that it *was* Vasson she would tell the *Patron*'s friends. Yes, or the Resistance. Either group would kill him straightaway.

The police would be too kind—or would they? Perhaps it would be better to let him sweat through a long trial and the fruitless pleas for clemency before he was taken out and shot in cold blood. That way he would have more time to think about what he had done.

It was a fifteen-minute walk from the Métro to the hotel. Tonight it seemed longer because she was dog-tired, but finally the dreary facade came into view. The Hôtel Hortense was extremely modest, which was why she'd chosen it, so modest, in fact, that there was no night porter. The front door was locked at eleven, after which the guests were expected to let themselves in using a key for which they had to put down a generous deposit.

Julie fumbled in her bag and swore quietly. The key wasn't in the bottom, or in the side compartment. She looked nervously up and down the dark deserted street. Eventually she found the key wedged inside the pages of her pocket diary. She unlocked the door and went in, closing the door gratefully behind her.

The lobby was lit by a single white light, which cast a cold inhospitable glare over the floor and left the rest of the hall in shadow. Julie walked across to the stairs and started to climb. She had taken a room on the fourth, topmost floor because it was cheaper there. In the center of the staircase was an ancient elevator in an open mesh shaft, but like most elevators in Paris at the moment it was usually out of order. She didn't even bother to try it anymore.

The building was quiet. The only sound was the slight creaking

of the boards under her feet. The hotel had very few guests—at least Julie hardly ever saw anybody.

At the first landing, she paused. There was a sound, coming from the lobby. A gentle rattling. She realized that someone was trying the street door.

She went on, a little faster now, up toward the second floor.

From below there came a faint clang. Someone had closed the elevator door. Julie reached the second landing and hurried on. Suddenly the elevator machinery burst into action with a loud whine. Julie jumped. The wires started humming. The elevator was coming up.

She reached the third floor and looked down the central well. The elevator was rising steadily toward her, but the top was closed and it was impossible to see inside. Panting slightly, she hurried across the top landing to her door. She opened her bag and started to look for the room key.

The elevator mechanism whirred louder and louder. The key was nowhere to be found; Julie shook her bag impatiently.

There was a loud *Clunk!* and silence. The elevator had stopped. There was a click as the gate was opened.

Julie thrust her hand into the outside compartment of her bag and at last her fingers closed over the large metal key tag. She raised the key to the lock but her hand was trembling so badly that she couldn't get it in.

A soft footstep fell on the thin carpet behind her.

She whirled around.

It was the tallest, blackest man she'd ever seen. Julie put her hand to her chest and laughed nervously. "Oh, good evening! You startled me!"

The man was in French Army uniform. He was grinning from ear to ear, revealing an enormous row of white teeth which were in startling contrast to the blackness of his skin. The soldier bowed low and straightened up again, swaying slightly. Julie realized he was drunk.

He said in a low booming voice, "Mademoiselle, my sincere apologies!"

Julie nodded politely and quickly let herself into her room. As she closed the door, she saw he was still standing there, beaming happily. Drunk, but quite harmless, she decided. She turned on the light and locked and bolted the door.

The room was simple: a bed, a rug on the floor, a chest of drawers and a narrow wardrobe. But it was clean and, most important, no one in the hotel took any notice of her.

She threw herself onto the bed and stayed there for a moment because it was so lovely to lie down. Reluctantly, she got up and, opening the double windows, reached out to close the shutters. The window was a dormer, set into the roof behind a parapet. You couldn't see the street from there, but you could see an enormous amount of sky. It was very clear tonight and, above the faint glow of the city, a thousand stars were shining.

It had been a long time since she had seen a night sky.

For several moments she stood and watched and remembered Brittany a long time ago.

The night was cold. She fastened the shutters and closed the windows.

Slicing some cheese onto a piece of stale bread, she ate ravenously. Then, gritting her teeth against the cold, she undressed as quickly as possible and pulled on her nightdress.

She didn't bother to wash, but hopped straight into bed, shivering violently. She spread her dressing gown over the thin blankets, pulled her coat off the chair and spread that over as well.

She wriggled down into the bed and curled up, wondering whether she'd ever feel warm again.

It was a bit of luck, the black soldier coming along like that. Vasson even helped him to find his key.

Vasson waited for the elevator to disappear, then slipped quickly behind the reception desk and looked for the registration book. It wasn't there. He looked around. Immediately behind the desk was a door which probably led to an office. The registration book should be in there. He tried the door; it was locked. He cursed softly.

Something caught his eye and he let out a small hiss of triumph. To the right of the door there was a notice board covered with yellowing fire regulations and taxi numbers—and a fresh white piece of paper with a list of rooms and, where appropriate, names. There weren't many guests—just six or so—and it took him only a second to find the name he wanted.

Lescaux. Room 25.

He took a swift look around the lobby, then tiptoed quickly

across to the stairs. He ran lightly up to the first floor, checked the room numbers, and continued up the building.

As he approached the fourth floor he slowed down and listened.

Silence.

He climbed the last few steps and paused again. Softly, he padded across the landing until he could see the numbers on the doors.

Room 25 was in the left-hand corner, at the front of the building. Vasson crept up to the door. Someone was moving about inside. There was a click, as if a window was being closed.

He looked around the landing. On the opposite side were several other bedrooms, then a door marked *"Salle de Bain"* and another marked "W.C." Beyond was a plain painted metal door. He ran across and tried it, but it was locked. He looked up. Above was a sign: SORTIE DE SECOURS. Beside it was a key hanging on a nail.

He took the key and tried it in the lock. At first it wouldn't move but then he pulled on the handle and the key turned easily. He opened the door and put his head out. He looked both ways; then, satisfied, pulled his head back in and closed the door without locking it.

He walked lightly across to the bathroom, which was open, and went in. He flicked on the light, locked the door and turned the light off. Then he sat down on the floor to wait.

He fingered the gun in his pocket and decided against it. Far too noisy. No, it would have to be done quietly—the other way.

Damn the woman. She'd been trouble all along.

What really upset him was that she'd found out about the car. But how? He couldn't imagine and it was driving him mad. He'd never told anyone about it, he was certain, at least not for years and years. . . .

Was she alone? Had she told anyone else? He'd have to risk it. If he didn't deal with her, he'd be a dead man anyway.

Damn her.

He leaned his head against the bath and, looking unseeing at the night sky, waited impatiently for the minutes to pass.

She couldn't sleep. Every time she started to drift off she woke with a start and began to go through the day's events all over

again. In addition, she needed to go to the lavatory. She should have gone before, of course, but the bed had been too inviting. Now the trip couldn't be put off any longer. Irritated, she got out of bed and pulled on her dressing gown.

She unlocked the door, walked quickly across the landing and went into the WC.

When she came out, she went toward the bathroom to wash. She tried the door but it wouldn't budge. She glanced up at the fanlight; there was no light showing through. She tried again, pushing hard against the door, but it was firmly locked. She stood still for a moment, then gave up and went back to her room, locking the door behind her.

She threw her dressing gown back over the covers and dived into the still-warm bed. This time she was determined to get to sleep. She closed her eyes and concentrated on relaxing each part of her body, limb by limb.

Eventually she dozed off, but then she thought of Richard and was immediately awake again. She often thought of him, but tonight the memories were particularly vivid. It was that lovely night sky. She could almost see the little attic room. She missed him terribly.

She relaxed her body again and tried counting sheep.

Bump!

She was wide awake instantly.

A sound. *Something nearby.*

She stayed perfectly still, listening to the roar of the silence.

Perhaps the sound had come from the street. . . .

She stiffened.

A sound. This time a faint scratching. *Close.*

She sat upright, her heart hammering, and strained to locate the origin of the noise.

At first she couldn't hear anything, then it came again, a soft, barely audible scratching. An animal? She tried to see, but with the shutters closed the room was very dark; the only light came from a faint gap under the door.

Slowly, she pulled on her dressing gown and tied the cord. Then she swung her legs out of bed and, careful to make no noise, stood up. She listened again.

The scratching had stopped.

She felt her way across the room until she reached the door. She put her ear against it. Nothing. Automatically, she checked the key and the bolt to make sure the door was secure. She put her hand up to the light switch, then changed her mind and moved slowly back to the center of the room. She stood absolutely still, straining her ears.

This time the scratching, when it came, was louder.

Now she placed the sound. It was coming from near the window. She crept forward and, stooping down, listened again. A mouse, probably . . .

The sound was muffled now, and soft. She crept right up to the window and waited, completely still.

Nothing.

There was silence again. It lasted so long that she almost gave up.

Click!

Julie started and looked up. There was a sudden movement. A rectangle of light appeared in the window where the shutter had been.

Julie screamed.

The head and shoulders of a man were silhouetted against the light.

She staggered back against the bed.

The silhouette vanished. Julie stared in horror at the place where the man had been, the image of the crouching figure engraved in her mind. It was *him*, it had to be! *It was him.*

She couldn't move, she couldn't tear her eyes away from the window. *Was he still there?* She pressed the back of her knees against the bed and reached for the bedpost.

Silence again.

She tried to gather her wits, but all she could think was: It's *him*! It's *him*!

The silence stretched on.

Suddenly, another movement.

She stifled a scream.

An arm. At the window. It had something in its hand.

She cried, *"No!"* and scrabbled around looking for something —*anything.* Desperately she lunged at the chest and pulled out a

drawer. Raising it above her head, she ran to the window and rammed it against the frame.

She shouted, *"No-o-o!"* and pushed the drawer harder and harder against the window.

For a while she stayed there, her head against the drawer, murmuring "God!" over and over again.

Then she moved her head away from the drawer and listened.

Not a sound.

She raised her head and looked. The arm had vanished.

She was frozen with indecision. He must have gone—*or had he?* For a moment she could have sworn he was still there, waiting under the windowsill, poised to raise his head like some ghastly jack-in-the-box. . . . The next minute, she was sure he wasn't there at all.

But if he wasn't there, *where had he gone?*

She knew one thing: *she had to get away!* With an enormous effort of will, she dodged to one side of the window and, shaking violently, put the drawer down on top of the chest. Then, with her eyes fastened on the window, she slipped off her dressing gown. She reached for her coat and pulled it on over her nightdress. She fumbled with two buttons and gave up on the rest.

Shoes . . . where were her *shoes?*

She felt around with her feet and touched one. She bent down and pulled it on. Crouching lower, she put a hand under the bed. Nothing. She almost cried out. She reached again and found the second shoe. Panicking, she grabbed it and pulled it hastily on.

All the time she watched the window. Nothing.

Slowly she stood upright and moved sideways toward the door. Quietly she slid back the bolt and turned the key in the lock. She listened carefully. Silence.

She gripped the handle, turned it and opened the door a crack. A beam of light darted in from the landing. She paused, suddenly full of doubt. Slowly she put her eye to the crack.

She could see the WC and the bathroom opposite, then the elevator and, to the right, the head of the stairs.

The landing—what she could see of it—was empty.

It was now or never.

She flung open the door, ran out and stopped dead.

A scream stuck in her throat.

He was standing against the wall at the top of the stairs, crouching slightly, poised like a cat.

She stared, horror-struck. The face was livid and ugly, the angry scars red against the pallor of his skin.

But it was Vasson all right. She recognized the eyes. Hard. Dark. Glittering in the dim light. Watching her carefully.

For a moment they were both still, watching one another.

Then he moved.

She cried out and went rapidly backward, past the door of her room, along the landing. She looked wildly over her shoulder. *Where was the black soldier?*

She drew a deep breath and tried to shout. Vasson was coming faster now. A wall came up against her back. She screamed at last.

Vasson lunged forward. She dodged sideways but he caught her hair and pulled her head with a snap. She cried out in pain. He clamped his hand over her mouth, digging his fingers into her cheek. She kicked and pushed at him with her arms. But his other hand closed firmly around the back of her neck.

She lashed out again with her feet and felt her shoes fly off. She tried to claw at his face but he was keeping her at arm's length, gripping her head tightly between his hands.

He started to drag her across the floor. She struggled, throwing herself desperately from side to side, trying to tear the hand away from her face.

God, where was the black soldier! Surely he'd heard!

Vasson was pulling her faster now. She tried to dig her heels into the thin carpet, but he yanked her off balance and her feet went out from under her. Her legs cartwheeled as she tried to regain her grip.

He gave a final heave, something hard bumped against her side and then everything was dark. *They were in her room.*

She heard the door close and struggled harder. She kicked viciously in all directions and heard him inhale sharply as her foot met his shin. Her next shot hit the bedpost and jarred her leg.

She aimed for his shin again but suddenly her head was being jerked sideways, fast. There was a moment of dizziness, then a sickening thud as her skull hit something solid. She saw stars and stopped struggling.

Still dazed, she needed a moment to realize what was happen-

ing. He had pushed her onto the bed and had moved his hand away from her mouth. She tried gathering her strength to scream, but froze. . . . *There was something tight on her throat. His hands* . . . around her neck. *Getting tighter.*

Cold terror gripped her. Then she really started to fight.

She tore at his hands, digging her nails deep into the skin. She kicked with her feet, great wheeling kicks that circled the air. She felt him shift his body over hers, to stop the kicking. She pulled up her knees in a quick movement. She clipped him in the groin, not very hard, but he retreated a little. She arched her back and wriggled sideways onto the floor. His hands loosened slightly as he followed her, then he gripped her throat again, much tighter.

She couldn't breathe. She tore at his hands. His hands were the only thing that mattered. *His hands.* Then she remembered she *must kick too.* She thrashed her body from side to side, striking out with her feet. She felt something in her stomach—something heavy, squashing her—*a knee.*

She couldn't breathe.

Air. She must have *air.*

Kick! Kick! A loud *crash!* And a muffled exclamation.

The hands around her neck loosened. She opened her eyes and, twisting her body, scrabbled away like a crab. She threw herself at the window and wrestled with the latch. He was almost on her.

She ducked and screamed, really loudly. She screamed until he grabbed her firmly by the throat again. This time he squeezed very tightly straightaway.

This was it. She couldn't struggle anymore.

Breath, no breath. *G-o-d. Agony.*

Her ears were roaring and singing, her head felt as if it would burst . . .

G-o-d. I'm going to die . . .

Blackness.

Then a vague perception.

Awareness.

I don't understand.

A voice, a movement, the weight lifting off her body. The hands leaving her throat. She drew in great gulps of air, enormous, greedy gasps of air, and felt the coolness shoot into her lungs.

She opened her eyes, bewildered, dazed. There was light, a yellow light from the door. *Someone else. A voice.* A deep voice . . .

Everything faded for a second. She made an enormous effort to understand. A large shape was filling the doorway. A voice. *The black soldier.* "Hey . . . hey," he was saying. "What's happening, little lady?"

Julie blinked and sat up. Giddiness hit her.

Vasson was crouched, watching the soldier like a hawk.

Julie's head cleared. She looked from Vasson to the figure in the doorway. Realization came. *This was her only chance.* She rose uncertainly to her feet, her head splitting with pain, and staggered toward the door. Vasson sprang up and grabbed her arm.

Julie shouted at the soldier, "Help me! *Help me!*"

The soldier swayed forward a little. Vasson dropped Julie's arm. The soldier said, "Hey! Hey! Let us all cool down now." She dimly realized he was still very drunk.

She stumbled to the doorway and tried to squeeze past him. He swayed toward her and she caught the whiff of drink. He grasped her hand. "Now, why don't we all relax, hey? What's the problem, little lady?"

She cried, *"Please! He's trying to kill me! Please let me get away. Please."*

"Now, now . . . Why don't we all relax, hey?" He leered at her, his large face inches from hers.

She darted under his arm and staggered across the landing and down the stairs. She tried to run, two steps at a time, but tripped and fell against the banister. She took them singly then, her limbs shaking, her lungs gasping, *begging* for breath.

Faster, she had to go *faster.*

Third floor—

Above her she heard voices raised in argument, then silence. Her leg gave way under her. She lurched to one side, grabbed the banister, and pushed herself forward.

Second floor—

She ran on, her legs wobbling, half listening for other sounds. All she could hear was the beating of her heart and the rasping of her lungs.

First floor. Just one more. As she raced across the landing and launched herself down the last flight of stairs something caught her eye and she glanced hastily upward.

Legs. Running legs, beyond the wire mesh of the elevator shaft. Above, but coming fast.

She gave a small cry and hurtled on. She jumped the last step into the lobby. The front door beckoned. She ran for it and stopped dead.

No! He'd get her in the street.

Looking wildly about, she darted past the desk and down a dark passage. On one side, she knew, was the dining room. *Not in there! Nowhere to hide.*

On the other side was the kitchen. *Kitchens had back doors.* Still running, she looked back over her shoulder. No one in sight. She pushed at the kitchen door. It was a swing door and opened easily. She fell in and, panting wildly, spun around to grip the door and close it slowly so it wouldn't swing back the other way. The door had a circular window in it. She peered through. Nothing.

The kitchen was dark, but there was a large window along one side and by its pale light she could just make out the interior of the room. A large table was in the center.

She shuffled around it. *There must be a door.* She reached the far corner. A door. She opened it. Cupboard. She closed it again.

God. He'd be here any moment. . . .

She felt her way forward. A recess here . . . behind it—a passageway! She stumbled along it, the flagstones cold under her bare feet. Yes! A door!

She tried the door. It was locked. She found a key in the lock, turned it and tried again. Still locked. She gulped. *God, please let it open.*

Desperately, she felt the surface of the door with her hand. There must be a bolt. There was one at the bottom. She exhaled in triumph. It slid back quite easily. She tried the door again.

It still wouldn't move.

She imagined Vasson creeping along the passage toward the kitchen door.

She felt the door again and guessed there must be another bolt right at the top, out of her reach. She felt around for something to stand on. There was an object standing on the floor. A large fire extinguisher. She put her bare foot on it and, balancing precariously, reached up.

Her hand fell straight onto the top bolt and she tugged at it

quickly. It wouldn't budge. She made another effort and tugged harder. At last it shifted, but slowly, the noise rasping loudly in the stillness. At the same time her foot slipped and she landed heavily on the flagstones. The fire extinguisher clattered over, rolling noisily along the passage.

She wanted to scream.

She held her breath and shivered violently. The extinguisher stopped its roll and there was a terrible silence.

At the front door Vasson froze, his fingers on the handle.

It had sounded like something falling, a vague clattering. From the back of the hotel somewhere.

He listened for a moment, but apart from the panting of his own breath, there was silence.

He decided to check the street anyway. If she'd gone that way he'd still be able to see her.

He threw open the door and darted out. Nothing. No running figure, no moving shadows. Just to be sure, he sprinted to the other side of the street and looked wildly up and down. But she wasn't there.

The hotel, then.

He ran softly back across the street and into the lobby, closing the door quietly behind him.

There were several doors off the lobby and two passages. Starting on the left he began trying the doors methodically, one by one.

She tried the door. This time it opened.

She closed it again and leaned against it, trembling.

Silence.

Where was he? When he came for her what would she do? Run? *God, he'd catch her just like that!*

She thought for a moment, then made herself creep back toward the kitchen and peer in. The room was empty and quite still. She looked toward the far door. Its round window, faintly lit by the distant lobby light, stared back at her, blank and expressionless.

She forced herself to go right into the kitchen. She crept toward the table and felt along its length. There *must* be a drawer! There wasn't.

614

He was getting nearer, she felt it. . . .

I can't stand this!

Along one wall was a cabinet. Lots of drawers here. Hurrying now, she tried one. Papers, all papers . . . the next drawer, *better* . . . spoons, large ones . . . forks . . . *but no knives.* She fumbled with the last drawer.

At last! . . . Knives, neither large nor sharp, but *knives.* She picked one up and, looking hastily over her shoulder, started for the back passageway. Something caught her eye. The stove. Something *behind.* She stopped.

Knives, lots of them. Long kitchen knives . . .

She threw the small knife aside and picked up a long one. She touched it: very sharp.

She looked over her shoulder and, darting down the passageway, fell against the door. She thought for a moment and deliberately turned the key in the lock—he might come at her from the *outside.*

Then she waited, her fingers around the key. *Ready.*

She leaned her head against the door and breathed deeply. Her neck was hurting horribly and her head was stabbing with pain. Worse, her legs were like jelly. She wouldn't be able to run. . . .

She bit her lip. *Must hold on.*

The silence crept on endlessly.

She couldn't believe how long it was—

She wanted to fling open the door and *run.* But no. He might be outside. . . . Better to *wait.*

She jumped.

The sound of a truck echoed from the distant street.

That was all. . . .

She rested her head on the door again.

She stiffened. Was there another sound?

Dear God! Her heart missed a beat.

Her fingers tightened over the key. She stared up the passageway into the kitchen, peering into the darkness, *listening.* . . .

A faint sound.

From the kitchen.

Her heart leaped into her mouth. Hastily, she turned the key, then the handle and started to pull the door open.

Something caught her eye. *A dark shadow was racing across the kitchen.*

She leaped out of the door. She ran, bicycling her legs, pumping her arms, pushing her bare feet painfully against the rough surface. The nightdress flapped around her legs—it was *tight, too tight,* she couldn't stride out—

She was in an alleyway, very dark. It seemed to have no end—

She heard the thud of feet behind her.

She gasped and raced on, faster and faster.

The footsteps were closer.

The alley—*where did it go?*

She stumbled and almost fell. She righted herself and tried to accelerate again.

She could hear his panting now. G-o-d.

Light, a glimmering of light.

She raced for it, came to a corner, swerved around.

The street. Some way ahead. The ground was rougher now. She cried out. A terrible pain in her foot! Something sharp was in her foot! She tried to run on, but something was sticking *into* her foot!

She hobbled desperately.

He was coming up behind her. *Close!*

She wanted to keep running, to run until her heart burst, to run *forever.*

She let out an animal cry and spun around. She whirled around and faced him. She braced herself, the blood screaming in her ears.

He was still running. He was trying to bring himself up short but his momentum was too great. He was cannoning into her.

She screamed, "No!" And in the split second before he hit her she gripped the handle of the knife in both hands and, with a loud grunt, thrust it forward.

His body hit hers with a thud, carrying her backward. She fought to keep her balance but reeled back under his weight and fell. His body came down on top of her with enormous force, crushing the breath out of her.

His hand was on her neck and she felt blind terror.

Then his hand fell away and, by the light of the streetlamp, she saw his mouth open in a ghastly grimace. With a roar, he rolled off her and onto his back. He clutched his belly and, raising his head, stared in blank amazement at the blood seeping out from

beneath his hands. He fell back, pain and disbelief on his twisted scarred face.

Julie got unsteadily to her feet, the knife still in her hand.

Sobbing quietly, she walked backward.

Sharpness stung her foot. She cried out and, dropping the knife, reached down. Glass. She got hold of it and pulled.

A movement.

She jumped.

He was getting up.

He had one hand on the ground, levering himself up, the other on his belly.

She growled, "No-o—!"

The knife! *Dear God, where was the knife?*

He was on his feet now, swaying slightly, his eyes daggerlike.

She caught a gleam. The knife. At her feet.

He moved forward.

She grabbed for the knife. He was still coming. Her fingers gripped the handle and she held the knife out in front of her. *Keep away from me, keep away!*

He paused, wary this time, maintaining his distance, arms out, ready to spring.

He began circling, panting slightly. Occasionally he put a hand to the wound in his stomach.

She thought: I didn't hurt you enough, *not enough.*

One hand went to his pocket. Then something was in his hand, reflecting dully in the streetlight. A gun.

There was a faint roaring from the street: a truck. The sound grew louder until it filled the alleyway.

Vasson's eyes flicked away, toward the street, and then down to the gun. He was fiddling with the mechanism, trying to make it work.

Now. It's now or never. Dear God—

Gathering all her strength, she lunged forward. She saw his eyes dart up, his hands rise in defense—

She raised the knife high above her shoulder and with a long gasp plunged it forward and *down,* hard, *hard* at his chest.

Was it in? Had she hurt him at all? She kept straining to push the handle farther in, sobbing, "Keep *away, keep away. Leave me alone. A-l-o-n-e!*"

At last she realized the knife was rigid, fixed in the man's body. She let go and fell back.

Vasson looked at the knife in amazement. It was sticking out of his chest. Pain shot through him, worse than anything he had ever imagined.

He couldn't believe it. She'd stabbed him again. *Hard. He couldn't believe it.*

He gasped for breath. There was a soft gurgling noise. His lungs drew in liquid.

Very slowly, he slid down, first to his knees, then onto his side. Wet, black blood trickled from his chest to the ground.

He lay still, hoping that the terrible pain would go away, the bleeding stop. . . .

He felt very heavy, his limbs like lead. He was choking.

What did I do? Dear God, what did I do? It's not fair, it's not fair.

His lungs expanded but found only blood. He panicked, gasping for breath. He felt as if he were drowning.

At last the realization came—this horror would be the last, this final prison the smallest, darkest room of all . . .

He wanted to cry out but the darkness was already closing in.

Why did you abandon me? Why?

Why are you abandoning me now?

I don't understand.

She watched as blood trickled out of his mouth. Suddenly he gasped. The eyes rolled once, then were still, glazed and unblinking.

She stood, sobbing quietly, horrified lest he move again.

She shook her head slowly from side to side, moaning, "No-o," over and over. There was the sound of a car in the distant street. She blinked and, looking hastily around her, hobbled into the darkness of the alley. Her foot was in agony. There was still glass in it. She pulled, and a fragment came away. The foot was bleeding heavily; she was leaving a trail of blood. She tried to tear the bottom off her nightdress and make a bandage, but the material was too tough. She found a handkerchief in her coat pocket and tied that around the foot.

Hopping and hobbling, she went back down the alley toward the hotel.

The door was still open. She closed and bolted it and hopped through the kitchen to the lobby. It was empty. She climbed the stairs as fast as she could, walking on the heel of her injured foot, and reached the top landing. She found her shoes lying where she'd kicked them and picked them up. The door of her room was open. She went in, switched on the light, and locked the door.

For a moment she stood perfectly still with her eyes closed; then methodically, she started to do what had to be done. She took off her coat and nightdress, which were both bloody, and wrapped them neatly in a bundle. Then she put on her dressing gown and picked up some street clothes. She went across to the bathroom and, trembling wildly, stripped completely and washed herself all over. She dressed and went back to her room.

The trembling had become a violent shaking. She ignored it and, taking out her writing pad, picked up a pen and began to write. At first she couldn't hold her hand still, but she gripped the pen tighter and forced herself to concentrate. She printed carefully, in plain block capitals. The first attempt wasn't right and she tore it up and started again. Finally she was satisfied. The message was simple, but it would do the job.

It read:

PAUL VASSON. ALIAS LEBRUN, ALIAS FOUGERES, ALIAS THE MAN FROM MARSEILLES. TRAITOR, COLLABORATOR, MURDERER. BETRAYER OF METEOR AND TREGASNOU RESEAUX.
    JUSTICE!

She read it several times.

The wording shouldn't lead the police to her. It could have been someone from Meteor, *anyone* in the Resistance.

It was two-thirty. Before she lost her nerve, she went quickly down the stairs to the kitchen, unlocked the back door and, after looking carefully up and down the alley, limped along to the corner. The distant street was deserted. The body was still there, lying heavy and inert like a sack of coal. Averting her gaze from the staring eyes, she put the piece of paper beside it and weighted it down with a small stone.

She forced herself to look. Swallowing hard, she leaned down

and gripped the knife handle protruding from Vasson's chest. She closed her eyes and pulled with all her might.

The knife shot out and she staggered slightly.

She looked over her shoulder and scurried back into the darkness, around the corner and along the alley to the hotel.

She closed and locked the door, checked that she hadn't dripped blood onto the floor from her foot, and crept into the kitchen. Carefully, she washed the knife, dried it and returned it to the rack where she'd found it. Then she climbed quickly back to the fourth floor.

As she reached for her doorknob she heard loud snoring from the next room. The black soldier. It had to be. She listened to the steady rise and fall of the snores and felt a wave of despair. The black soldier could give her away.

She went into her room and locked the door behind her, then turned off the light and lay down on the bed, fully clothed.

As she stared at the dark ceiling, she suddenly realized that the black soldier would probably remember nothing of what had happened, nothing at all.

That left the bloodstained clothes—they would have to be disposed of. She would throw them in the river, weighted down with a stone.

Then there was the hotel register. Yet the body was some distance away. There was no reason why they should look here.

Even if they did, who was Juliette Lescaux?

No! She was safe.

She closed her eyes.

Who was Juliette Lescaux? She didn't know anymore.

She had been someone, a long time ago.

The shivering started again, first gently then so violently that her teeth rattled.

She pulled the bedclothes up and, curling into a ball, closed her eyes tightly against the terror of the darkness, desperate for the oblivion of the sleep she knew would never come.

EPILOGUE

Summer. Nineteen forty-five.

There had been dancing and flag-waving on VE Day, cheering and hymn-singing on VJ Day, but for sheer uninhibited happiness there was nothing to beat the homecomings.

All over Britain there were joyous reunions, first in the privacy of homes and then outside in the streets and village lanes. People wept and laughed and hugged and shook hands, and realized that life would never be as sharp or intense again and weren't sure whether they were sorry or glad that the war was over.

For those not welcoming sons, husbands and fathers it was still a good time because the festivities took their minds off the austerity and bleakness that seemed to have become a permanent part of British life.

In the main street of Hugh Town, St. Mary's, a banner reading WELCOME HOME was strung between two houses. The day before, no less than five men had returned: three soldiers, a sailor and a merchant seaman. It had been a day of great rejoicing.

Peter looked out of the window and giggled. "Mummy, there's a soldier kissing Tommy Blair's sister!"

Julie came in from the other room and went to a mirror on the wall. She patted her hair, put on some lipstick and viewed herself critically. Older, of course. There were tiny lines at the corners of her eyes and the sides of her mouth. Less young in other ways too. The look in her eyes, mainly. She frowned and turned away.

Peter was still giggling. "That soldier's hugging another girl!" He turned to see if she had heard. He gasped, "Hey. Mummy, you *do* look smart!"

"Not really," she said briskly. "It's just my old suit remade, that's all. Now, are you ready? Have you combed your hair?"

Peter came closer and peered at her blouse. "You've got Tante Marie's brooch on!"

"Yes, it seems a pity not to wear it." Tante Marie had died at Christmas—a welcome release under the circumstances.

"And Mummy!" He was jumping up and down now. "That smell! Have you put on *perfume*?"

"Shush!" Julie said impatiently. "We should go soon. Are you ready?"

"Mmm." Peter shuffled off in search of something. A moment later he wandered back and asked, "D'you think he'll be different? You know . . ."

"What do you mean?"

"Will he *look* different?"

"Good Lord, how should I know? Now hurry up and comb your hair. It looks terrible."

The letter from Major Smithe-Webb at the War Office had been waiting for her when she returned from France in November. It was brief and factual. Notification had been received from the Red Cross that Lt. Richard Ashley was being held in a POW camp near Stuttgart in Germany.

She couldn't believe it. Alive! She had been bracing herself for bad news for so long that the letter took her entirely by surprise.

Alive! Her first reaction was joy and relief. For *him*. Because he had always been so full of life and optimism and burning energy it seemed only right that he *should* be alive. Because by staying alive he had cheated Vasson and that was a victory.

She was happy for herself too—at first. Then she had doubts. In Brittany, in the old days, everything had seemed so simple, a matter of right or wrong, and black or white. She had loved him with all her heart. She still did. And yet . . .

Nothing would ever be straightforward again. The events in France weighed heavily on her mind. She dreamed terrible dreams not only of Jean and Tante Marie and Maurice, but of blackness and running feet and blood. . . . She often woke in the night, crying out. At those moments she felt unbearably lonely.

Life with someone like Richard would offer love and security. Perhaps even peace of mind if . . .

If everything was the same. If he still loved her. If they both hadn't changed too much.

You couldn't stop people changing, she decided. It just happened. It was a long time since Brittany—two years. For him two years in a camp. Now he was back home. With his family, his own people, the old way of life.

"Mummy, I'm ready. Come on!"

She led the way out of the house and along the street toward the harbor, her face solemn and pale.

Peter bounded along at her side. "Will we go and have tea later, at the hotel, like we do on birthdays?"

"I don't know what we'll be doing yet."

"But I thought . . ."

"Quiet!" she snapped. A moment later she sighed. "Sorry. I didn't get to bed till late." She'd been finishing a dress for someone. It was her trade, now, remaking clothes into new styles.

They walked in silence for a while.

"Mummy, you *are* glad he's back, aren't you?"

"Of course, darling! I'm—delighted." And terrified, she thought, because in a way I'd rather remember everything—*him* —as it used to be.

They turned onto the mole that formed one arm of the shallow bay and walked past the interisland boats waiting at the steps, toward the end, where the steamer docked.

Halfway along she paused. "Let's wait here."

"But the ship stops up there!"

"I know, but—I'd rather we waited here."

She wanted to avoid the group of people who were gathering at the ship's berth.

The *Scillonian* was late. She wandered slowly along the quay, back in the direction of the town. It was a balmy day, the breeze no more than a faint stir, and the light was that strange translucent white peculiar to the islands. It was so very peaceful here, which was why she had grown to love it.

"Mummy! There it is!"

She spun around. A trail of smoke showed above the high wall of the mole. A few minutes later the bow of the *Scillonian* appeared, and the steamer began to maneuver slowly into her berth.

She walked back to Peter and took his hand.

After a while the lines were secured and the gangway lowered. People started to come off in ones and twos. A couple of sol-

diers walked jauntily down the gangway, waving to some people on the quay.

Then Peter was pointing. "There! There he is! Look!"

She spotted him immediately. He was wearing his naval uniform and carrying a bag. He seemed taller than she remembered. As he came down the gangway he paused for a moment and she knew he was searching the knot of waiting people. He reached the quay and, looking around again, made his way clear of the onlookers.

She waved. He saw them then and, waving back, started toward them.

Julie didn't move. The boy tugged at her hand. "Come on, Mummy!"

"You go."

The boy ran forward, a little shyly, and she heard him shout, "Hello!"

Ashley stopped and, smiling, said, "Hello, young man! How are you?" He reached out and tousled Peter's hair. "You're a sight for sore eyes, I must say."

He looked up to where Julie stood and came toward her.

"And you too."

She smiled. He embraced her, gently, then bent and kissed her cheek and held her at arm's length, looking into her face. She stared up at him and was surprised. There were so many things she'd forgotten about him. . . .

She said quickly, "How marvelous that you're safe."

"And you!" He was going to say more but changed his mind. She realized he was nervous too.

He tucked her arm in his and they began to walk slowly along the quay toward the town, Peter hopping up and down beside them.

She asked quickly, "Will you be able to stay awhile?"

"Several days, at least. Then I must go back and see my family. Did you get my letters?"

"Yes. Thank you for writing. It was—lovely to hear so soon."

"You . . . you look just the same," he said.

"Do I?" It wasn't true, but she smiled anyway.

She glanced up at him and noticed how thin he was and how pale his face. His eyes were the same, warm and caring, but she

sensed a reserve behind them that hadn't been there before.

It was just as she'd thought. He'd changed.

A woman Julie knew slightly passed by and smiled. It was a knowing smile directed first at Julie then at Richard. It happened twice more and Julie quickly suggested they go and have some tea.

They chose the hotel on the harbor. Peter thought it was the best place in the world because it had scones and a sweet mixture that resembled jam. No cream, though; that was still unheard of.

Because of the boy, they talked lightly about school and homecomings and how difficult it was to find eggs and fruit and chocolate. Food, they decided, was not what it used to be.

Richard said, "But it's a darn sight better than I've been used to, I can tell you."

"Didn't you get anything to eat in the camp?" Peter asked. "Was it awful?"

But Julie interrupted, "Not now, Peter. Richard won't want to talk about that now."

"Some other time, Peter." He looked away and Julie saw that he was frowning.

Later they separated, he to take a room in the hotel, she to put on her best dress and brush her hair and dab a little more perfume behind her ears.

"Can't I come too?" Peter asked hopefully.

"No, another time. You can come to dinner another time, but not tonight." She'd arranged for him to go next door to Mrs. Trehearn's for the evening.

He accepted defeat gracefully and went off to find out what Mrs. Trehearn was cooking for supper.

Julie was ready early and sat by the window to wait. Her stomach was fluttering. Excitement. Richard still had that power over her. Yet in many ways he was a stranger. And she was a stranger to him. . . .

Finally he arrived. He was handsome in his formal dark uniform. And attractive. Very. She decided she was pleased about that.

They walked slowly to the hotel and talked about the Scillies and the sort of war the islands had had.

Richard stopped and pointed to the far side of St. Mary's

Sound. "In the early days we used to take Concarneau trawlers there, to New Grimsby, and repaint them in their proper colors."

"Yes, I know. Everyone guessed what was happening."

He laughed. "I should have known. There isn't much you locals don't know."

They walked on a little way. "It all seems a long time ago, doesn't it?" he said.

"Yes."

The dinner was execrable, but then everyone was used to that. However it was made more palatable by a bottle of wine which the hotel proprietor had been keeping for a celebration. It was a celebration, wasn't it? Julie said that yes it was.

"Not a touch on your uncle's stuff."

"No."

He smiled briefly and looked at her over his glass and she knew he was remembering the evenings in the attic room.

There was a silence. Eventually he said, "Smithe-Webb told me everything, about what happened to the others. I never saw them, you know, after we were taken from the beach. Only my crew, and even then we got split up. I'm very very sorry. And I'm sorry about your aunt."

"It was a blessing. She wasn't well . . ."

"But this traitor . . . Smithe-Webb told me you'd identified him and proved that someone else was innocent—your cousin, wasn't it? That was wonderful, Julie, a great achievement!"

She murmured, "Thank you."

"But how on earth did you do it? How did you find out who he really was?"

She hesitated. "It's a long story. . . . But it was the Resistance and other people—friends—who really found out who he was. Not me."

"The major thinks you're something of a heroine all the same." He smiled warmly at her. "But I knew that anyway."

She dropped her eyes.

He went on, "This fellow Vasson . . . I gather the Resistance executed him. That's something. It won't bring the others back and it sure as hell won't make up for my two lost years. But I bet they made him go through it before they finished him off!"

"Yes, I suppose so. . . ." She opened her mouth to say more,

but couldn't. She wanted to tell him, to share the dreadful weight of it. . . . But what would he think? How would he look at her once he knew she was capable of such a thing?

Better not to tell, much better.

Perhaps one day . . . perhaps never.

Instead she asked him about the camp. Haltingly and a little unwillingly, he sketched out the story. With relief she realized that there were whole areas of his life that he too didn't want to talk about.

Finally he said, "It drove me mad, being locked up. There were thousands in the same boat, of course. But even now I can't talk about it without . . ." He shook his head.

She reached over and gripped his hand. "Then don't!" He looked up in surprise.

She said, "Let's talk about something else! Something. . . *nice*!"

He laughed. "What a marvelous idea." Julie noticed that the reserve had gone from his eyes.

They started to talk of less serious things and she felt more at ease. She even found herself laughing, something she hadn't done for a long time. She'd forgotten how funny he was, how warm and vital. She began to remember other things, forgotten words, small incidents. . . .

She thought: Perhaps he hasn't changed so much after all.

They talked a little about the future, though not too much and not too deeply. He had lots of plans. She realized that, for Richard, the future was everything. She was glad, *thankful*—he made her feel optimistic again.

After a while he paused and asked, "Do you remember the holiday we were going to have?"

"You mean . . ."

"Here, in the Scillies. On *Dancer.*"

"Yes, of course I remember. Perfectly."

"Well? Would you like that?"

She smiled slowly. "Very much. I'd like that very much indeed."

Later, when the wine was finished and the meal cleared away, she watched him and thought: There's something else I'd like very much too.

You.

In that respect nothing had changed at all.

And why not now, tonight?

Yes. Life was too short.

Yes, she would stay with him tonight, whatever . . .

Then, in time, maybe everything would be all right. Maybe there would be love and security, and a new life. Perhaps the nightmares might eventually go away. . . .

At least she'd be happy while she found out.

She smiled at him across the table.

"I'd love some fresh air. Shall we walk along the beach for a while, before we go home?"

POSTSCRIPT

By the outbreak of war, Germany had developed several successful early-warning radar systems to guard herself against air attack. These systems were large and land-based and worked on medium to long waves. Thus convinced of Germany's security, Goering ordered a halt to all long-term research. The many Jewish scientists and technicians involved in the work were sent to concentration camps.

Later, when it was realized that the British possessed radar, there was panic and the armed services, industry and finally even the concentration camps were combed for technicians.

An electronics research laboratory was set up by the SS in Dachau. Eventually over a hundred skilled prisoners were employed on dismantling captured enemy equipment.

Right up till the moment in August 1943 when the captured Rotterdam device (the British H$_2$S shortwave radar) was finally pieced together and made to function (it revealed a perfect "picture" of Berlin) the German experts were convinced that shortwave radar was both impossible and impractical.

14 May 1943, Führer conference minutes.
Admiral Doenitz's report:

> We are at present facing the greatest crisis in submarine warfare, since the enemy is for the first time making fighting impossible and causing us heavy losses, by means of new location devices.

Admiral Doenitz, *Memoirs.* January to March 1943, *Collapse of the U-boat War.*

Radar, and particularly radar location by aircraft, had to all practical purposes robbed the U-boats of the power to fight on the surface. Wolf-pack operations against convoys in the North Atlantic, the main theater of operations . . . were no longer possible.

. . . I accordingly withdrew the boats from the North Atlantic.

We had lost the Battle of the Atlantic. . . .

Many, many brave men and women risked their lives to help Allied servicemen escape from Occupied Europe. Occasionally, an airman shot down over Belgium would find himself back with his squadron in England in just two to three days. The record was nine *hours*. Usually it took a little longer. . . .

There were numerous escape lines operating through Belgium and France, most of them functioning on arms and money sent by MI9 in London.

One of the most successful lines was Comet, which ran from Belgium through Paris to the Pyrenees and Spain.

In 1943 the Brussels end of the line was hit hard by the Gestapo, and over a hundred people were arrested, many dying by firing squad or in the horrors of the concentration camps.

For a while the Paris branch of Comet continued to function until that too was hit by a terrible blow. This time the traitor was identified. He was a new courier by the name of Jean Masson. It was an assumed name—as were all the names he used in his long and terrible career.

His real name was Jacques Desoubrie.

Later Desoubrie penetrated another escape line, farther to the west. As a result of this treachery seventy British and sixty American "parcels" were caught and sent to Buchenwald concentration camp.

There is evidence that, on the orders of his masters, the Gestapo, Desoubrie penetrated at least two other lines. . . .

The French Resistance was at its strongest in Brittany.

However, early attempts to establish an escape line through Brittany met with difficulties, mainly organizational. Later in the

war properly trained agents were sent in, and the Shelburne Line was born. Motor gunboats, crewed with great bravery and daring by officers and men of the Royal Navy, made regular runs from Dartmouth across the Channel to rock-strewn beaches on the Brittany coast, right under the noses of the Germans. Knowing that coast as I do, I can only marvel at the incredible feats of navigation they performed.

The Shelburne Line was very successful; it transported 307 servicemen and agents to England in a single year.

When the Germans came sniffing around, the gunboats sometimes had to depart in a hurry. On more than one occasion, some members of the gunboats' crews *did* get left on the beach.

The traitor Desoubrie continued his career of betrayal and treachery until the end of the war.

Then his luck ran out. He was, in fact, brought to justice and executed in Lille.

But it might have been different. . . .

ABOUT THE AUTHOR

Clare Francis is no stranger to success. Although still in her mid-thirties, she has achieved eminence in enough fields to cover several lifetimes. Born in Surrey, England, at thirteen she was accepted at the Royal Ballet School. At seventeen, she entered London University where she received her degree in analytical and descriptive economics. Following a career in marketing for a multinational corporation and as product manager for a food company, she decided she should travel "before it was too late," thereby embarking on the sailing feats that have made her world-famous. She has twice sailed the Atlantic alone, establishing a new women's speed record on one of the crossings. With her husband, from whom she is now separated, and a crew of eleven, she completed the Round the World Race of 27,000 miles, finishing in the top third. Her exploits have been the subject of three television films and two previous books, and she was host for the major television series *The Commanding Sea,* which also became a book. She now lives in London with her son, Thomas. *Night Sky* is her first novel and she is already at work on a second.

N

E N G L

Plymouth

Falmouth

Dartmouth

Helford River

Lands
End

Lizard

English Cf

North

Atlantic

Ocean

• Morlaix

Brest

B R I T T A

Concarneau

Lorient

B a y   o f   B i s c a y